VAJRASAMĀDHI SŪTRA: WŎNHYO'S EXPOSITION

VAJRASAMĀDHI-SŪTRA

Wŏnhyo's Exposition

Translated with an Introduction by

ROBERT E. BUSWELL JR.

MOTILAL BANARSIDASS PUBLISHERS
PRIVATE LIMITED • DELHI

First Indian Edition: Delhi, 2011
First published by the University of Hawai'i Press under the title **Cultivating Original Enlightenment: Wŏnhyo's Exposition of the Vajrasamādhi-Sūtra**
Reprinted with permission

ISBN: 978-81-208-3500-9

MOTILAL BANARSIDASS
41 U.A., Bungalow Road, Jawahar Nagar, Delhi 110 007
8 Mahalaxmi Chamber, 22 Bhulabhai Desai Road, Mumbai 400 026
203 Royapettah High Road, Mylapore, Chennai 600 004
236, 9th Main III Block, Jayanagar, Bangalore 560 011
Sanas Plaza, 1302 Baji Rao Road, Pune 411 002
8 Camac Street, Kolkata 700 017
Ashok Rajpath, Patna 800 004
Chowk, Varanasi 221 001

Printed in India

By Jainendra Prakash Jain at Shri Jainendra Press,
A-45 Naraina, Phase-I, New Delhi 110 028
and Published by Narendra Prakash Jain for
Motilal Banarsidass Publishers Private Limited,
Bungalow Road, Delhi 110 007

Contents

Preface

Wŏnhyo's *Exposition of the Vajrasamādhi-Sūtra (Kŭmgang sammaegyŏng non)* is one of the finest examples of a scriptural commentary ever written in the East Asian Buddhist tradition. The *Exposition* is the longest of Wŏnhyo's extant works and is widely regarded as his masterpiece. His commentary is especially important for understanding the crucial role that the notion of the inherence of enlightenment played in the development of East Asian Buddhist thought and the ways in which this notion influenced Buddhist meditative practice. In this book, I try to make the case that the *Exposition* is equally important simply as commentary. Commentary as a genre is one of the most complex and prolix in all of Buddhist literature and is certainly the most difficult to translate intelligibly and accessibly into another language. Since this book is one of the first attempts to translate the complete text of an indigenous East Asian Buddhist sūtra commentary into English, I have deliberately chosen to err on the side of literalness in order to convey the substance and flavor of the text. In order to help guide the reader through the labyrinth of interlocking sections that make up Wŏnhyo's *Exposition,* I superimpose an outline schema over my translation of Wŏnhyo's text. This device may help patient readers to uncover the many rewards that accompany careful study of Wŏnhyo's work.

I first read sections of Wŏnhyo's *Exposition of the Vajrasamādhi-Sūtra* informally together with Lewis Lancaster and Mark Blum in the early 1980s and read the entire commentary carefully in the late 1980s, while I was working on my book *The Formation of Ch'an Ideology in China and Korea.* In addition to its other aims, that book provided a study and translation of the *Vajrasamādhi-sūtra,* the scripture that is the basis of Wŏnhyo's *Exposition.* I drew heavily on Wŏnhyo's interpretations in preparing my rendering of the *Vajrasamādhi-sūtra,* but at that point I did not have the inclination to take on the task of translating all of Wŏnhyo's commentary. The initiation of the Collected Works of Wonhyo series finally gave me the impetus I needed to return to the commentary and undertake a complete, annotated translation. Approximately one-fifth of Wŏnhyo's commentary consists of verbatim extracts from the text of the *Vajrasamādhi-sūtra,* and I am grateful to Princeton University Press for its permission to reproduce that material in this volume. My earlier translation of the sūtra was to a large extent guided by Wŏnhyo's readings, so

I have had to make only relatively minor revisions of my earlier sūtra translation in this rendering, in order better to ensure that all passages fully conform to Wŏnhyo's interpretation. In order that this book may stand on its own as a self-contained study, I have also freely adapted, where appropriate, relevant material on Wŏnhyo and his *Exposition* that appeared previously in my *Ch'an Ideology* book and in other related articles. Portions of my translation of the synoptic introduction to Wŏnhyo's commentary appeared previously in *Sourcebook of Korean Civilization*, volume 1: *From Early Times to the Sixteenth Century* (New York: Columbia University Press, 1993), but they have been substantially revised and annotated here.

I am grateful to the two prepublication reviewers, Charles Muller and Yong-pyo Kim, for their careful reading of the manuscript and their many valuable suggestions. I also benefited at crucial points in my research from stimulating conversations with Alexander Mayer and Jörg Plassen, both of whose obsession with East Asian Buddhist commentarial literature surpasses even my own. My discussions with Professor Plassen on the *Kŭmgang sammaegyŏng non* and Wŏnhyo's exegetical style give me all the more reason to anticipate the publication of his ongoing research on Wŏnhyo. I would also like to thank several of our present and former students at UCLA who graciously helped me over the years with many of the myriad details involved in preparing a manuscript of this size: James Benn, William Chu, George Keyworth, Seunghak Koh, Richard McBride, Mark Nathan, Mihwa Park, Pori Park, Patrick Uhlmann, Sherin Wing, and Harumi Ziegler. Funding for research assistantships was provided by grants offered by the Research Committee of the UCLA Academic Senate and the Medieval and Renaissance Studies Center, and I benefited as well from support offered by UCLA's Center for Buddhist Studies, Center for Korean Studies, and Department of Asian Languages and Cultures. Last but certainly not least, I would never have been able to devote myself to this project without the generous support offered by the International Association for Wŏnhyo Studies and its founder, Sung-bae Park. The assistance of all these agencies is gratefully acknowledged.

I have benefited time and again from the pioneering work of Korean colleagues who have studied and translated this complex commentary. My own initial pass at the text was informed by the pioneering Korean translations of the *Exposition* by Ki-yong Rhi (Yi Kiyŏng) and Kim Talchin. More recently the field has benefited from a new Korean translation by Ŭn Chŏnghŭi and Song Chinhyŏng, which marks a major leap forward in our understanding of the *Exposition*. Ŭn and Song have produced an extremely careful translation into true vernacular Korean, with copious explanatory notes and extensive annotation. Unfortunately for me, I was already well into my translation when their book appeared, but I was still able to refer to it in the course of finalizing my rendering. Of course, any errors of omission or commission that may remain are my own responsibility.

Finally, I would like to express my deepest gratitude to Yi Kiyŏng (Kiyong Rhi) and Ko Ikchin (Ik-Jin Koh), professors emeritus at Dongguk University, who were profound inspirations to me both personally and professionally. Professor Rhi was the first scholar to translate the complete *Kŭmgang sammaegyŏng non* into modern vernacular Korean, and my English rendering has benefited greatly from his pioneering work. Professor Koh's soteriological interpretation of the commentary has stood the test of time and shaped my own understanding of Wŏnhyo's text. Both men were always generous with their time, even when I was a fledgling monk and novice scholar in Korea, and their counsel was of great help to me almost three decades ago in shaping my future research interests. The tragedy of their loss is tempered only by the delight of seeing their sons emerge as consummate scholars in their own right.

A NOTE ON THE FRONTIS: A portrait of Wŏnhyo painted in 1993 by the monk Sŏkchŏng *Sŭnim* (b. 1924), a Korean Intangible Cultural Asset. On a visit to Kozanji in Japan, Sŏkchŏng *Sŭnim* was able to view the thirteenth-centry Japanese scroll *Kegon engi emaki* (Illustrated Scroll of the Miraculous Origins of the Flower Garland School), which illustrates the story of Wŏnhyo writing his *Exposition of the Vajrasamādhi-Sūtra.* Sŏkchŏng *Sŭnim* based his portrait of Wŏnhyo on that Japanese rendering of the eminent Silla monk. Sŏkchŏng *Sŭnim* is currently the master at Ch'ilbo Monastery in Seoul and is renowned in Korea for preserving the arts of *tanch'ŏng* temple decoration and Buddhist painting. This portrait is in the collection of Wŏnhyosa, located on Mudŭng Mountain on the outskirts of Kwangju, which was founded in the sixth century, putatively reconstructed by Wŏnhyo between 661–668, and forever afterward associated with his name. I am grateful to Mr. Daehyun Shin for photographing this portrait and providing information on its composition.

Abbreviations and Conventions

HPC	*Han'guk Pulgyo chŏnsŏ*
IBK	*Indogaku Bukkyōgaku kenkyū*
j.	*juan* (roll) [Chinese]
k.	*kwŏn* (roll) [Korean]
KSGN	*Kŭmgang sammaegyŏng non* (referencing the *HPC* edition, as embedded here)
Liebenthal	Walter Liebenthal, "Notes on the 'Vajrasamādhi' "
Mizuno	Mizuno Kōgen, "Bodaidaruma no *Ninyūshigyō setsu* to *Kongōzammaikyō*"
PGHP	*Pulgyo hakpo*
SGYS	*Samguk yusa*
T	*Taishō shinshū daizōkyō*
VS	*Vajrasamādhi-sūtra* (referencing the edition in *Taishō* 273, vol. 9)
XZJ	*Xuzangjing*
Yuancheng	*Jin'gang sanmei jing zhujie*
Zhuzhen	*Jin'gang sanmei jing tongzong chi*
ZZ	*Zoku zōkyō*

Citations from the *Kŭmgang sammaegyŏng non* as well as all of Wŏnhyo's other works are taken from the editions in the *Han'guk Pulgyo chŏnsŏ* (Complete Works of Korean Buddhism) and are generally listed in the following fashion: *HPC,* followed by *HPC* volume number, page, register (a, b, or c), and line number(s). For example, *Yijang ŭi, HPC* 1.805c9. The *HPC* edition of the *Kŭmgang sammaegyŏng non* is cited by page, register, and line number(s). For ease in consulting the Korean text of the *Kŭmgang sammaegyŏng non,* I have bracketed page and column references to the *HPC* into the body of the translation, in bold: for example, **[605b].** In both my annotation and Wŏnhyo's own cross-references to his commentary, I have cited references to the *Exposition* according to the page number in the *HPC* edition and have placed the reference in parentheses, together with the page number: for example, (p. 665b). Citations to the *Vajrasamādhi-sūtra* itself are to the recension embedded in Wŏnhyo's *Kŭmgang sammaegyŏng non* and are cited by the *HPC* page numbers, which are bracketed in the translation (e.g., *KSGN,* p. 631a).

Citations from the *Taishō* canon are listed in the following fashion: title, transliterated according to the language of provenance (with Sanskrit title, if relevant, in parentheses) and roll number; *T[aishō]; Taishō* serial number; *Taishō* volume number; page, register (a, b, or c), line number(s). For example, *Dafangguang fo huayan jing (Avataṃsaka-sūtra)* 23, *T* 278:9.542c27-543a1. Citations to the *Xuzangjing* (Supplement to the Tripiṭaka) are to the Hong Kong reprint edition of the *Dai-Nihon zokuzōkyō* (Xianggang Jingyin Xuzangjing Weiyuanhui, eds.). All citations from Pāli texts are to the Pali Text Society editions.

Transliterations of Asian languages follow the systems commonly used in the scholarly community: McCune-Reischauer for Korean, Pinyin for Chinese, revised Hepburn for Japanese. I have adopted many of the modifications and enhancements of McCune-Reischauer romanization proposed in Robert Austerlitz et al., "Report of the Workshop Conference on Korean Romanization," but not the suggestion to abandon the separation between final *-n* and initial *-g*.

Buddhist terminology that appears in *Webster's Third New International Dictionary* I regard as English and leave unitalicized: this includes such technical terms as dhāraṇī, dhyāna, skandha, and tathāgatagarbha. For a convenient listing of a hundred such words, see Roger Jackson, "Terms of Sanskrit and Pali Origin Acceptable as English Words." I have, however, expanded the list to include compounds formed from accepted words, for example, vajrasamādhi and tathāgatadhyāna.

I transliterate the indigenous technical terminology of East Asian Buddhism according to the Korean pronunciation of the literary Chinese, followed by the Chinese, where relevant: for example, *pon'gak/benjue*. Standard, pan-Buddhistic terms (e.g., *kleśa, saṃyojana*) are typically cited only in Sanskrit.

In rendering Buddhist technical terms, where the literary Chinese is a translation, I translate; where it is a transcription, I transcribe. Thus, whenever a term is italicized (e.g., *kṣāntipāramitā*), the literary Chinese (viz. Sino-Korean) has itself been a transcription. In some cases this results in such hybrid forms as *amala*-consciousness (for *amalavijñāna* or "immaculate consciousness"). The only exception is technical terminology that has now entered the English language (e.g., skandha); such terms are typically translated, not transcribed, in literary Chinese.

PART I

Study

I. Contemplative Practice in the *Exposition of the Vajrasamādhi-Sūtra*

The original enlightenment of each and every sentient being is constantly enlightening all sentient beings . . . , prompting them all to regain their original enlightenment.

—Vajrasamādhi-sūtra, chapter 4

East Asian Buddhism is founded on the assurance that the prospect of enlightenment is something innate to the mind itself and inherently accessible to all living creatures. This doctrine of "original enlightenment," along with its related teaching of the "womb (or embryo) of buddhahood," is basic to most of the indigenous schools of East Asian Buddhism and holds pride of place within the Korean tradition as well. Given, however, the delusion we persistently face in ourselves and the evil we see surrounding us every day, it is obvious that the fact of *being* enlightened does not mean that we have necessarily learned to *act* enlightened. How, then, can enlightenment be turned from a tantalizing prospect into a palpable reality that manifests itself in all our activities? How, in other words, can we recover the enlightenment that is said to be innate in our minds and make it a tangible force in our daily lives? These are the crucial questions that the eminent Silla exegete Wŏnhyo (617–686) seeks to address in his *Kŭmgang sammaegyŏng non,* which I translate here as the *Exposition of the Vajrasamādhi-Sūtra* (or *Book of Adamantine Absorption*).[1]

Wŏnhyo is the vaunt-courier of Korean Buddhist scholasticism and arguably the most important monk ever produced within that tradition. Koreans primarily know Wŏnhyo in his various roles as mystic, thaumaturge, iconoclast, and proselytist, and more recently even as touchstone of national-unification ideology. But above all else, Wŏnhyo was a commentator, whose religious insights are expressed almost exclusively through scriptural exegesis. In his *Exposition of the Vajrasamādhi-Sūtra,* Wŏnhyo brings to bear all the tools acquired through a lifetime of scholarship to the explication of a scripture that has a startling, even unique, connection to the Korean Buddhist tradition. I will explore Wŏnhyo's associations with the *Vajrasamādhi-sūtra* in the section on the writing of the *Exposition,* but for now let it suffice to say that it is Wŏnhyo who first saw outlined in this sūtra a way of *cultivating* original enlightenment systematically.

Wŏnhyo explored the issue of original enlightenment and its recovery elsewhere in his writings, but never in such detailed and thorough a manner as we find in his *Exposition of the Vajrasamādhi-Sūtra.* As one of the last—if not *the* last—of his writings, the commentary presents Wŏnhyo's views on enlightenment and practice in their most sustained and mature form. In earlier writings, such as his influential commentary and autocommentary on the *Awakening of Faith (Kisillon hoebon),*[2] Wŏnhyo follows that treatise in describing the one mind as having two distinct, but complementary, aspects: an absolute, "true-thusness," aspect; and a conventional, "production-and-extinction," aspect. Through this treatment, Wŏnhyo could demonstrate that the mind was simultaneously deluded and yet enlightened, explaining how it was that sentient beings could be "originally" enlightened and yet still have to progress through a process of "acquiring" enlightenment. In this *Exposition,* however, Wŏnhyo instead explores the applications in practice of original-enlightenment thought. Specifically, Wŏnhyo examines here original enlightenment's soteriological role: that is, the way in which the enlightenment that is foundational to the mind actively motivates ordinary, deluded sentient beings to aspire to become enlightened buddhas. In Wŏnhyo's presentation, the notion of original enlightenment is transformed from an abstract concept into a practical tool of meditative training. Wŏnhyo's analysis discerns in the *Vajrasamādhi-sūtra* a map of six sequential types of meditative practice, which culminate in the "contemplation practice that has but a single taste." In Wŏnhyo's account of this process of contemplation practice, the ordinary affective consciousnesses are transformed into an "immaculate consciousness," wherein both enlightenment and delusion are rendered ineluctable and all phenomena are perceived to have but the "single taste" of liberation. In his *Exposition,* therefore, Wŏnhyo fuses his ontological outlook with his view toward practice, synthesizing around the "contemplation practice that has but a single taste" the various religious and intellectual currents then prominent in Silla Buddhism. For all these reasons, the *Exposition of the Vajrasamādhi-Sūtra* has long been viewed within the Korean Buddhist tradition as one of Wŏnhyo's masterworks, if not in fact his magnum opus.

The Role of the Tathāgatagarbha in Salvation

Key to Wŏnhyo's discussion of the *Vajrasamādhi-sūtra* is the notion of tathāgatagarbha *(yŏraejang/rulaizang),* the womb, or embryo, of buddhahood, a concept closely allied to that of "original enlightenment" *(bon'gak/ benjue).* In the *Exposition,* Wŏnhyo places his discussion of Tathāgatagarbha thought within an exegetical framework derived from his contemporary Yogācāra (Consciousness-Only, or Mere-Representation) scholiasts on the Chinese mainland.

The notion of tathāgatagarbha can be reduced to a simple premise: that deluded, ordinary beings possess in their very makeup the capacity to achieve the apparently rarefied state of enlightenment. This possibility remains forever potent because Tathāgatagarbha thought denies the reality of ignorance itself, positing instead that the mind is intrinsically luminous but dulled by adventitious defilements.[3] Since defilements remain forever extrinsic to the mind's true, enlightened nature, the individual has actually never been deluded at all; that presumption of ignorance is nothing more than a mistaken belief produced by unsystematic attention *(ayoniśomanaskāra)*. Enlightenment therefore involves nothing more than relinquishing one's misperception that one is ignorant and accepting the reality of one's true, enlightened state.[4] When the deluded sentient being finally realizes enlightenment, one finds that one's ordinary state of mind is nothing more than the original enlightenment that has always been present.

In his exegesis of chapter 2 of the *Vajrasamādhi-sūtra,* Wŏnhyo offers an extensive discussion and detailed analysis of differing approaches to describing the tathāgatagarbha. The first is a threefold schema, which Wŏnhyo draws from both the *Anūnatvāpurṇatvanirdeśa* (Neither Increase Nor Decrease Sūtra) (*KSGN,* p. 615b) and especially the *Foxing lun* (Buddha-Nature Treatise), a śāstra attributed to the renowned Indian scholiast Vasubandhu (fl. ca. mid-fourth–mid-fifth centuries C.E.) but probably composed in China by the Indian translator Paramārtha (499–569). The latter text offers the more familiar treatment of tathāgatagarbha as the container, the contained, and that which is cloaked and concealed (*KSGN,* p. 615b). Wŏnhyo follows with a discussion of the twofold schema of the "void" and "nonvoid" tathāgatagarbha, taken from the *Śrīmālādevīsiṃhanāda-sūtra* (Lion's Roar of Queen Śrīmālā) (*KSGN,* p. 616b). At the end of the discussion, he clarifies the interconnections between the two schemata.

Wŏnhyo viewed the *Vajrasamādhi-sūtra* as providing a way to fuse more passive descriptions of the tathāgatagarbha, as something obscured by discriminative thought, with explicit interpretations of it as an active agent in salvation. The tathāgatagarbha, as Wŏnhyo sees it described in the *Vajrasamādhi,* is not merely a benign force, submissively acquiescing to the vagaries of defilements and discrimination; it instead secrets itself away inside ignorance and taints so as to beckon the benighted, ordinary person toward enlightenment.

The most precise description of the *Vajrasamādhi*'s interpretation of tathāgatagarbha appears not in the eponymous seventh chapter, but instead in chapter 2, "The Practice of Nonproduction": "The tathāgatagarbha is that characteristic of discriminative awareness, subject to production and extinction, which conceals the principle *(i/li)* so that it is not made manifest. . . . Its nature is calm and motionless" (*KSGN,* pp. 616c–617a).[5]

This terse yet cogent definition alludes to one of the major aspects of tathāgatagarbha: that of "concealment" *(saṃdhi/abhisaṃdhi; unbok/yinfu)*. Concealment has two distinct dimensions: first, the tathāgatagarbha is an active agent of liberation, secreting itself away within the minds of sentient beings so as to motivate them soteriologically; and second, tathāgatagarbha in its more passive sense is concealed, and thus obscured, by the defilements. It is the passive denotation that is most commonly seen in Tathāgatagarbha literature, from the earliest stratum onward.[6] Wŏnhyo's interpretation in the *Vajrasamādhi,* however, brings out the active dimension: tathāgatagarbha is not merely a hapless object hidden away behind the veils of adventitious defilements but is instead an active potency that conceals the "principle" (=dharmakāya, the true body of reality). As the concealer, tathāgatagarbha thus works at revealing that principle to the adept through the process of "acquiring" his or her enlightenment. Wŏnhyo's treatment accentuates this more dynamic interpretation of concealment:

> "That characteristic of discriminative awareness, subject to production and extinction" refers in fact to the void tathāgatagarbha. Even while elucidating in this passage the aspect of the agent of concealment, however, it does not say that this alone is the tathāgatagarbha. The statement "the tathāgatagarbha is that . . . which conceals the principle so that it is not made manifest" refers to the nonvoid tathāgatagarbha, which means tathāgatagarbha from the standpoint of the aspect of the object of concealment. The words "its nature is calm and motionless" elucidates the fact that, although the nature of this storehouse is concealed, it is unaltered. (*KSGN,* p. 617a)

Wŏnhyo's interpretation of the *Vajrasamādhi-sūtra* also clarifies the soteriological function of tathāgatagarbha and especially its relationship to two different interpretations of enlightenment: as something innate, or "original" *(pon'gak/benjue);* and as something that has to be actualized over time through practice, that is, temporal or "acquired" *(sigak/shijue).* The notions of "original" and "acquired" enlightenments are seminal to the *Awakening of Faith (Dasheng qixin lun),* and Wŏnhyo often resorts to them to describe the process of salvation. Both terms will play important roles in Wŏnhyo's exegesis of the *Vajrasamādhi-sūtra* as well.

In Wŏnhyo's view, the principles of original and acquired enlightenment derive from an assertion made in the *Awakening of Faith* that the one mind can be bifurcated for heuristic purposes into two aspects: the true-thusness *(chinyŏ/zhenru)* and production-and-extinction *(saengmyŏl/shengmie)* aspects, corresponding respectively to absolute *(paramārtha)* and conventional *(saṃvṛti)* truths, or the unconditioned *(asaṃskṛta)* and conditioned *(saṃskṛta)* realms. Thusness *(tathatā)* is in turn also twofold: empty of either self-nature or defilements, but also full of the myriads of wholesome qualities that contribute to enlightenment.[7] This characterization of the absolute aspect of mind as being both empty and full is a clear indication that true thusness is construed as being the equivalent of the tathāgatagarbha; indeed, a similar distinction between empty and full is also known in Indian Tathāgatagarbha scriptures.[8] This same equation of thusness and tathāgatagarbha is also drawn in the main Indian treatise on Tathāgatagarbha thought, the *Ratnagotravibhāga,* where tainted thusness *(samalā tathatā)* is tathāgatagarbha while untainted thusness *(nirmalā tathatā)* is the realization of the dharmakāya.[9]

In addition to being simply thus, however, the one mind is also said to be subject to "production and extinction," one of the ways in which the East Asians translated the Indian term "saṃsāra," the ordinary realm of existence that is subject to continual birth and death. This conventional aspect is the *ālayavijñāna,* or "storehouse consciousness," an eighth level of consciousness in the Yogācāra system, which served to "store" the seeds *(bīja)* and proclivities *(vāsanā)* produced by past actions until the conditions were ripe for them to sprout as karmic retribution. The *Awakening of Faith* defines the *ālayavijñāna* as "the intersection *(hwahap/hehe)* of that which is not subject to production and extinction [the absolute] with that which is subject to production and extinction [the phenomenal, in such a way that] they are neither one nor different."[10] But because the *Awakening of Faith* states explicitly that "the production-and-extinction aspect of mind [= *ālayavijñāna*] exists on the basis of the tathāgatagarbha,"[11] conventional states of mind always retain the potential to be transformed into the absolute mind of true thusness. This transformation takes place through a process of acquiring enlightenment—that is, religious cultivation. At the completion of this soteriological process, however, one realizes that the enlightenment one has acquired through practice is in fact identical to the enlightened dharmakāya that has always been innate—what the text terms "original enlightenment." The difference between these two types of enlightenment is but a matter of perception: the innate luminosity and purity of the tathāgatagarbha and dharmakāya are seen as "original," or intrinsic, by the saints but as something that must be "acquired" by the ordinary person. Once enlightenment was recovered, these two aspects of mind were seen to be merged in the one mind. As the *Awakening of Faith* says, "The mind, though pure in its self-nature from the beginning (= true-thusness aspect, or tathāgatagarbha), is accompanied by ignorance (= production-and-extinction aspect, or *ālayavijñāna*)."[12]

Wŏnhyo regarded the *Vajrasamādhi-sūtra* as the scriptural source of both the one-mind/two-aspects hermeneutic and the two types of enlightenment outlined in the *Awakening of Faith,* even though we now know that the *Vajrasamādhi-sūtra* was written some hundred years after the *Awakening of Faith.* But to Wŏnhyo, who was unaware of this chronology, this scenario would have been eminently plausible, since śāstras like the *Awakening of Faith* were considered to be the elaboration of ideas originally preached by the Buddha in the sūtras. Wŏnhyo located the source of this one-mind/two-aspects hermeneutic in the following passage in chapter 2 of the *Vajrasamādhi:* "The nature of the mind of sentient beings is originally void and calm. The essence of the mind that is void and calm is free from materiality and characteristics" (*KSGN,* p. 612a). In his exegesis of this passage, Wŏnhyo interprets "void and calm" as the one mind, "the mind of sentient beings" as the production-and-extinction aspect, and "free from form and characteristics" as the true-thusness aspect. But because the production-and-extinction aspect is that through which the true-thusness aspect is revealed, the *Vajrasamādhi* says that "the nature of the mind of sentient beings is originally void and calm." However, Wŏnhyo clarifies, "the essences of those two aspects are nondual and they therefore are both nothing more than this dharma of the one mind" (*KSGN*, p. 612b). This "dharma of the one mind," which is the "original tathāgatagarbha," is then said to be "calm and motionless" (*KSGN*, p. 614c)—characteristics identical to those attributed to the vajrasamādhi, the special absorption after which the sūtra is named.[13] Wŏnhyo ultimately sees the sūtra culminating in a thoroughgoing fusion of all Buddhist practice in the tathāgatagarbha,[14] illustrating that he considered Tathāgatagarbha thought to be the very core of the text: "The myriads of spiritual practices are perfected, and one accesses the fountainhead of the tathāgatagarbha, which has but a single taste. . . . The sixth chapter, 'Tathāgatagarbha,' exhaustively incorporates all of these approaches and reveals that they are all of a single taste" (*KSGN*, pp. 608c–609a).

Wŏnhyo similarly found in chapter 4 of the *Vajrasamādhi* the scriptural basis for the *Awakening of Faith*'s crucial twofold gnoseology of "original enlightenment" and "acquired enlightenment": **"The original enlightenment of each and every sentient being is constantly enlightening all sentient beings . . . prompting them all to regain their original enlightenment. They become enlightened to the fact that all the affective consciousnesses are** void, calm, and unproduced" (*KSGN*, p. 630c).[15]

In Wŏnhyo's interpretation,

> The text here offers a thorough elucidation of the two types of enlightenment: original and acquired. **"The original enlightenment of each and every sentient being"** is the aspect of original enlightenment. **"They become enlightened to the fact that all the affective consciousnesses are void, calm, and unproduced"** is the aspect of acquired enlightenment. This [juxtaposition of phrases] elucidates the fact that acquired enlightenment is in fact identical to original enlightenment.[16] (*KSGN*, p. 631a)

It is also interesting to note that Wŏnhyo has managed to find reference to acquired enlightenment in the *Vajrasamādhi*, even though the term, while perhaps implicit in the above passage, is never explicitly mentioned anywhere. (When a text served their purposes, East Asian exegetes, like exegetes in all scholarly traditions, display an uncanny ability to find what they needed, no matter how vague the reference.)

Based on the interpretations offered in the *Vajrasamādi-sūtra* and the *Awakening of Faith*, Wŏnhyo views the original and acquired enlightenments as nondual. As a passage in chapter 4 of the sūtra states: "When one is enlightened to the fact that thoughts are unproduced, one's mind becomes calm and serene. That is the inspiration of original enlightenment. That inspiration is motionless" (*KSGN,* p. 636c). Wŏnhyo tells us in his exegesis:

> "That is the inspiration of original enlightenment" expresses comprehension of the meaning that there is no distinction between acquired enlightenment and original enlightenment.[17] As a treatise *[Awakening of Faith]* states:
>
> > If a person gains no-thought, he then comes to know the characteristics of mind—production, maturation, decay, and extinction—because these are equivalent to no-thought. Nevertheless, in actuality, there are no such differences in acquired enlightenment because the four characteristics exist simultaneously and are not independently established; they are originally impartial and are identical to the one enlightenment.[18]
>
> Nota Bene: "In actuality, there are no such differences in acquired enlightenment": this explicates the passage in this sūtra "that is the inspiration of original enlightenment." "These four characteristics exist simultaneously and are not independently established; they are originally impartial": this explicates the passage in this sūtra "that inspiration is motionless." (*KSGN,* p. 637a)

Earlier in the *Vajrasamādhi,* the scripture had explained how "unmediated contemplation" enabled the meditator to leave behind the subject-object distinction: "It enables all those sentient beings to leave behind mind and self, for both mind and self are originally void and calm. If they attain voidness of mind, then that mind will not illusorily project anything. Free from all illusory projections, they will then attain nonproduction *(anutpatti)*" (*KSGN,* p. 611b). Wŏnhyo explicates this process of achieving nonproduction in terms of the original and acquired enlightenments. The first part of the passage, "if they attain voidness of mind, then that mind will not illusorily project anything," refers to original enlightenment.

> When one penetrates to the fact that mind and self are originally void, one straightaway gains the void and calm mind of original enlightenment. This void and calm mind originally leaves behind the clinging subject; and because it leaves behind the clinging subject, it is originally free from illusory projections. As the sūtra says, "If they attain voidness of mind, then that mind will not illusorily project anything." "Not illusorily project anything" means that there is no deception or falsity. (*KSGN,* 611c)

Acquired enlightenment is described in the passage "free from illusory projections, they will then attain nonproduction."

> When one gains this void and calm mind of original enlightenment, the discriminations created by the clinging subject are no longer able to arise, and regardless of the state of mind produced, there will be no illusory projections. As the sūtra says, "Free from all illusory projections, they will then attain nonproduction." In this wise, they acquire the mind of nonproduction and tally with that principle which is originally void, calm, and free from projections. (*KSGN,* 611c)

The *Vajrasamādhi*'s analysis of tathāgatagarbha also recalls a distinction the *Awakening of Faith* makes between the calm, unchanging essence of the mind *(ch'e/ti)* and its active, adaptable function *(yong/yong)*. In chapter 7 of the *Vajrasamādhi,* the tathāgatagarbha is equated with the "original edge of reality" *(bhūtakoṭi; pon silche/ben shiji)* that is beyond all distinctions—the equivalent of original enlightenment, or the essence. But tathāgatagarbha is also the active functioning of that original enlightenment—the "inspirational power of that fundamental faculty"—which induces the adept to access his or her inherent enlightenment. The tathāgatagarbha is thus both the "original edge of reality" that is beyond cultivation (=essence) as well as the specific types of wisdom and mystical talents that are the byproducts of enlightenment (=function). In its description of this sequence, however, the *Vajrasamādhi* notes that "accessing the tathāgatagarbha has no access point; it is like a sprout that matures into a fruit" (*KSGN,* p. 661a).[19] This caveat ensures that the student will not mistakenly presume that the realization of the immanence of enlightenment is a conditioned process that unfolds gradually. Rather, acquiring enlightenment is as ineffable as original enlightenment: both are nondual, in the same way that essence and function are ultimately unitary. Hence, original and acquired enlightenments are both subsumed in the tathāgatagarbha, as the consummation of practice reveals only the "one taste that is unascertainable" (*KSGN,* p. 609b).

Wŏnhyo's Analysis of "Immaculate Consciousness" and the Innate Purity of Mind

A concept in the *Vajrasamādhi* closely related to tathāgatagarbha is that of a ninth mode of consciousness beyond the eight ordinarily posited by the Yogācāra school of Mahāyāna. This is the so-called immaculate consciousness, or *amalavijñāna,* which may originally have been posited in China by Paramārtha, an important Indian translator of many seminal works on Yogācāra, Tathāgatagarbha, and Abhidharma philosophy. In his own writings, Paramārtha condemned the Yogācāra school's eighth "storehouse" consciousness, or *ālayavijñāna,* as being fundamentally impure, positing instead that only a ninth mode of consciousness—which he termed the *amalavijñāna,* or "immaculate consciousness"—was pure.[20] Conceptually, *amalavijñāna* also provides a means of synthesizing different philosophical filiations within the broader Mahāyāna Buddhist tradition: as "immaculate," *amalavijñāna* emulates the tathāgatagarbha's emphasis on the innate purity of the mind; but as a form of "consciousness," it could be placed within the Yogācāra school's compartmentalization of the mind. The use of *amalavijñāna* to synthesize variant tendencies in Mahāyāna philosophy is particularly prominent in the *Vajrasamādhi,* a characteristic to which Wŏnhyo, and all later commentators to the sūtra, have drawn attention. Indeed, the commentators saw in the synthetic focus of the text a ready means of resolving the perceived differences between the tathāgatagarbha and the *ālayavijñāna.*

The *Vajrasamādhi* displays some ambivalence as to the respective nature of the *ālaya* (storehouse) and *amala* (immaculate) vijñānas. In chapter 4, the *Vajrasamādhi* portrays all the consciousnesses, up through and including the eighth, as being defiled. These are called "affective consciousnesses," which must be "constantly transmuted so that they will access the *amala.*" Whatever special status other texts might accord the *ālayavijñāna* as the ground of existence, the *Vajrasamādhi* nevertheless relegates it to the same level as the delusory consciousnesses: it is subject to discrimination and thus inextricably bound up with the mundane world of the senses: "Each and every one of the eight consciousnesses is generated with the sense-realms as condition" (*KSGN,* p. 631a).

Elsewhere, however, the *Vajrasamādhi* is rather less clear-cut concerning the *ālayavijñāna*'s defiled nature. In chapter 5, for example, the eighth and ninth consciousnesses are treated in almost identical terms, both becoming "limpid" and "pure" once the mind is freed from its dichotomizing tendencies *(punbyŏl/fenbie; vikalpa).* After the contaminants *(āsrava)* from the *ālayavijñāna* are stemmed, all discrimination will vanish, and the bodhisattva will realize the voidness of dharmas. Through such nondiscriminative wisdom *(mubunbyŏl chi/wufenbie zhi; nirvikalpajñāna),* taints are abandoned and the bodhisattva realizes original enlightenment, which, as we will see, is the *amalavijñāna.* Because the *ālayavijñāna* is then no longer swayed by sensory experiences, the sixth and seventh consciousnesses, which process those perceptions and interpret them in terms of self, will never arise again either.[21]

Wŏnhyo's exegesis treats the penultimate eighth consciousness (the *ālayavijñāna*) as the basis of the contaminants and equates the ninth consciousness (the *amalavijñāna*) with the original enlightenment, drawing upon a tautology that Wŏnhyo derives from the *Vajrasamādhi* itself.[22] Looking back at the ambiguous passages in the *Vajrasamādhi* in the light of Wŏnhyo's treatment, we see that Wŏnhyo treats the *amalavijñāna* cum original enlightenment as the force that renders enlightenment accessible. As chapter 4 says, "The original enlightenment of each and every sentient being is constantly enlightening all sentient beings . . . prompting them all to regain their original enlightenment" (*KSGN,* p. 630c). Wŏnhyo also notes in his *Kisillon pyŏlgi* (Autocommentary to the *Awakening of Faith*), "Because of the influence of original enlightenment, [the deluded mind] comes to have a modicum of enlightened function *(kagyong/jueyong).*"[23] The *amalavijñāna* as original enlightenment is therefore constantly acting on sentient beings, exerting a beneficial influence that ultimately will prompt those beings to rediscover their inherent enlightenment. This treatment of *amalavijñāna* as the catalyst of enlightenment corresponds to the active interpretation of the tathāgatagarbha followed elsewhere in the *Vajrasamādhi.*

The soteriological implications of *amalavijñāna* are brought out more fully in a passage in chapter 6 of the *Vajrasamādhi,* where the sūtra incorporates the theory of *amalāvijñāna* into his comprehensive mārga schema: "**True thusness has voidness as its nature. As its nature is void, its knowledge is empyreal, incinerating all the fetters. In an equipoised and balanced manner, the three stages of virtual enlightenment and the three bodies of sublime enlightenment radiate brilliantly in the ninth consciousness so that there are no shadows**" (*KSGN,* p. 656c). The treatment of the *amalavijñāna* here in terms of virtual enlightenment *(tŭnggak/dengjue)* and sublime enlightenments *(myogak/miaojue)* is closely allied to that found in another Chinese apocryphon, the *Pusa yingluo benye jing* (Book of the Original Actions That Adorn the Bodhisattva).[24] The *Vajrasamādhi-sūtra,* like that indigenous sūtra, attempts to synthesize the variant mārga schemata presented in translated Buddhist texts into a comprehensive regimen, which culminates in the two levels of enlightenment, virtual and sublime, which the *Yingluo jing* calls the Immaculate Stage *(Mugu chi/Wugou di)* and the Sublime-Training Stage *(Myohak/Miaoxue).*[25] By treating *amalavijñāna* in terms of specific soteriological stages, the *Vajrasamādhi* raises the discussion of that mode of consciousness beyond mere psychological abstraction to concrete religious praxis.

Wŏnhyo's exegesis of this passage brings out the relevant associations between these two final stages of the mārga and the *ālaya* and *amala* vijñānas, helping to clarify in the process the relationship between those two models of consciousness:

> The previous stage of virtual enlightenment is still involved with birth and death and has not yet uncovered the fountainhead of the mind; for this reason, it is located among the eight consciousnesses. But upon reaching sublime enlightenment, one forever leaves behind birth and death and fully returns to the fountainhead of the one mind of original enlightenment. Hence, he accesses the radiant purity of the ninth consciousness. . . . But returning now to the fountainhead of the mind, one experiences their original substance, and, consequently, all the characteristics of those shadows vanish.[26] (*KSGN,* p. 657a)

The correlation the *Vajrasamādhi* makes between the *amalavijñāna* and the path shows that the idea of an immaculate form of consciousness was not merely an abstract psychological concept but a concrete soteriological tool: it was the motivating force that rendered ordinary people capable of enlightenment. Like the tathāgatagarbha, *amalavijñāna* was not primarily intended to explain why a person mistakenly believes himself to be deluded (i.e., to function as the origin of ignorance) or to serve as the ground of existence (i.e., to play an ontological role)—two of the ways in which East Asian exegetes had employed the *ālayavijñāna* concept. Instead, once the *amalavijñāna* was "acquired," the student would learn that it has always been present, subtly influencing the individual—that is, it was "original enlightenment." Wŏnhyo's exegesis explicitly draws out the soteriological implications of this ninth mode of consciousness.

But the *Vajrasamādhi* does not stop at merely demonstrating the soteriological import of *amalavijñāna* or explaining how it relates to stages on the path. Wŏnhyo's interpretation draws out its pragmatic utility, by relating *amalavijñāna* to a specific meditative technique that will bring about its re-cognition. This is the practice of no-thought *(munyŏm/wunian)*, which is described as the "benefit" or "inspiration" *(i/li)*—that is, the practical application or functioning—of original enlightenment cum *amalavijñāna.*

> "How can one prompt those sentient beings not to give rise to a single thought?"
>
> The Buddha replied: "One should prompt those sentient beings to sit with their minds and spirits calm, abiding in the adamantine stage. Once thoughts are tranquilized so that nothing is generated, the mind will be constant, calm, and serene. This is what is meant by the absence of even a single thought."
>
> Muju Bodhisattva said: "This is inconceivable! When one is enlightened to the fact that thoughts are unproduced, one's mind becomes calm and serene. That is the inspiration of original enlightenment." (*KSGN,* p. 636b–c)

Wŏnhyo finds implications in the *Vajrasamādhi*'s treatment of amalavijñāna and tathāgatagarbha that go beyond the scholastic controversies summarized earlier concerning the nature of consciousness. As Wŏnhyo interprets the sūtra, the enlightenment that is immanent in the mundane world—the foundation of East Asian Buddhist doctrine—could actually be viewed as a practical catalyst to religious training. This is the implication Wŏnhyo discovers embedded in the *Vajrasamādhi-sūtra,* in the so-called six stages of contemplation practice that culminate in the "contemplation practice that has but a single taste" *(ilmi kwanhaeng/yiwei guanxing).*

Cultivating Original Enlightenment and the "Contemplation Practice That Has But a Single Taste"

As we have seen, Wŏnhyo's *Exposition of the Vajrasamādhi-Sūtra* employs many of the same sources he used when writing his commentary and autocommentary to the *Awakening of Faith;* and like that earlier treatise—as indeed in so much of his writing—his *Exposition* draws from the analysis of the one mind and its two aspects. Where Wŏnhyo goes beyond his earlier commentary to the *Awakening of Faith* is in his attempt to construct through his exegesis of the *Vajrasamādhi-sūtra* a comprehensive system of meditative practice, focusing on six divisions of contemplation practice that lead to the experience of the "contemplation practice that has but a single taste." This "single taste" is an ancient metaphor used in Buddhist texts to describe the overriding soteriological import of the Buddhist teachings. One widely quoted locus classicus for the term appears in the Pāli *Cullavagga:* "As the vast ocean, oh monks, is suffused with a single taste, the taste of salt, so too, monks, is my Dharma and Vinaya suffused with but a single taste, the taste of liberation."[27] In Wŏnhyo's interpretation, the various stages of contemplation through which enlightenment is acquired culminate in a realization that they all have the same one taste of enlightenment. As Wŏnhyo presents the *Vajrasamādhi-sūtra,* therefore, it prescribes a practical way of actually cultivating original enlightenment, rather than just passively acquiescing to it.

In Wŏnhyo's explication of the sūtra, the *Vajrasamādhi* outlines six specific divisions of contemplation practice, which finally culminate in this "single-taste" contemplation. In his exegesis of the *Vajrasamādhi* (pp. 608c ff.), Wŏnhyo interprets chapter 1 of the sūtra, "Prologue," as surveying the basic qualities of the adamantine absorption (vajrasamādhi), the eponymous concentration after which the text is named. There, the vajrasamādhi is said to be a unique variety of absorption accessed by the Buddha himself, in which all doubts are resolved and all things subsumed into the one, all-encompassing buddha-vehicle. Chapters 2 through 7 of the scripture provide the progressive outline of six divisions of contemplation practice that are best suited to adepts training during the Semblance Age of the dharma (Pratirūpaka), when Buddhism was presumed to be in its initial stages of degeneration. The first division, "Rejecting All Characteristics of Sense-Objects to Reveal the Signless Contemplation" (which corresponds to chapter 2 of the sūtra), explains the technique of signless contemplation, which frees the meditator from the tendency to assume that both person and dharmas are ultimately real. The second division, "Extinguishing the Mind Subject to Production in Order to Explain The Practice of Nonproduction" (viz. chapter 3), describes a type of practice in which one trains to become completely unattached even to the fruits of meditation, thus allowing the mind to achieve perfect calm. The third division, "The Inspiration of Original Enlightenment" (viz. chapter 4), explains how the practitioner may thence continue on to benefit all sentient beings through relying on the powers inherent in the innate enlightenment of one's mind. The fourth division, "Abandoning The Spurious to Access Reality" (viz. chapter 5), describes the transition from illusory perception to true reality. The fifth division, "Sanctified Practices Emerge from the Voidness of The True Nature" (viz. chapter 6), explains that all spiritual practices derive from the innate voidness of the true nature. This contemplative process culminates in the sixth division, "Immeasurable Dharmas Access The Tathāgatagarbha" (viz. chapter 7), which reveals that all the approaches to practice discussed previously culminate in accessing the tathāgatagarbha—the realization of the original enlightenment that is inherent in all beings. The concluding chapter 8, "Dhāraṇī," removes any lingering doubts on the part of the audience as to the message of the sūtra and transmits the scripture to posterity.[28] For Wŏnhyo, then, the *Vajrasamādhi-sūtra* provides the foundation for a practical soteriology of original enlightenment by shifting the *Awakening of Faith*'s accounts of mind and enlightenment from ontology into the realm of actual practice.

Wŏnhyo summarizes his approach to the text succinctly in the preface to his *Exposition,* where he clarifies the progressive relationship that pertains between the different chapters of the scripture.

> These practices that are unproduced arcanely intuit signlessness *(ānimitta).* The signless dharmas correspondingly become the original inspiration. Since this inspiration is the original inspiration and yet is unascertainable *(anupalabdhi),* it does not waver from the edge of reality *(bhūtakoṭi).* Since this edge is the edge of reality and yet is devoid of any nature of its own, that authentic edge is also void. All the buddhas, the tathāgatas, repose therein and all the bodhisattvas accordingly access it; thus, reference is made to accessing the tathāgatagarbha. These are the main ideas of each of the six chapters [of the main body of this scripture].
>
> In the approach to contemplation [outlined in this scripture], six practices are established, from the initial resolute faith *(adhimukti)* through virtual enlightenment *(tŭnggak).* When the six practices are completed, the ninth consciousness in turn appears. The manifestation of this immaculate consciousness *(amalavijñāna)* is the pure dharma-realm *(dharmadhātu);* [its manifestation] then transmutes the remaining eight consciousnesses into the four wisdoms. Once these five dharmas are perfected, one is then furnished with the three bodies *(trikāya).* In this wise, cause and fruition are not separate from phenomenal objects and wisdom. Since phenomenal objects and wisdom are nondual, there is only this one taste. Thus, the contemplation practice that has but a single taste is considered to be the theme of this sūtra. (KSGN, p. 604c)

As further substantiation for this interpretation, in his opening comments to the second prologue section of the *Vajrasamādhi,* Wŏnhyo gives four different hermeneutical schemata through which to examine the sūtra, which culminate in "the fountainhead of the tathāgatagarbha, which has but a single taste" (KSGN, p. 608c).[29]

> The beginningless churning of all deceptive conceptions typically results from nothing more than the affliction of discrimination, which derives from clinging to signs *(lakṣaṇa)*. Now, wishing to reverse this churning in order to return to the fountainhead, one must initially subvert all these signs. For this reason, [the sūtra] first clarifies the contemplation of the signless dharma.
>
> Even though all these signs may have been subverted, however, if one actualizes the mind that performs that contemplation, then that contemplating mind will continue to be produced and one will not experience original enlightenment. Consequently, one must annihilate all productions of mind. Therefore, the second [approach of contemplation practice] elucidates the practice of nonproduction.
>
> Once one's practice has stopped producing anything, one then experiences original enlightenment. Drawing from this [experience], one transforms living things and prompts them to gain the original inspiration. Hence, this third [approach] clarifies the aspect of the inspiration of original enlightenment.
>
> If, while relying on original enlightenment, one inspires sentient beings, then those sentient beings will be able to leave behind deception and to access reality. Therefore, the fourth [approach] clarifies the access to the edge of reality.
>
> Internal practice is signless and unproduced. External proselytism is the original inspiration's access to reality. In this wise, the two types of benefit [of oneself and others] are replete with myriad spiritual practices, which all derive from the true nature and conform to true voidness. Consequently, the fifth [approach] clarifies the voidness of the true nature.
>
> Relying on this true nature, the myriads of spiritual practices are perfected and one accesses the fountainhead of the tathāgatagarbha, which has but a single taste. Therefore, the sixth [approach] elucidates the tathāgatagarbha.
>
> Since one has returned to the fountainhead of the mind, one then has nothing more that needs to be done. As there is nothing more to do, there is nothing that has been left undone. Hence, it is said that these six approaches [of contemplation practice] therewith subsume all the Mahāyāna. (*KSGN*, pp. 608c–609a)

In Wŏnhyo's *Exposition*, then, each chapter of the *Vajrasamādhi-sūtra* is interpreted as describing one aspect of the path of cultivating original enlightenment and accessing the tathāgatagarbha, which "subsumes all of these approaches and reveals that they are all of a single taste" (*KSGN*, p. 609a). Hence, by correlating this "contemplation practice that has but a single taste" with the tathāgatagarbha, Wŏnhyo fuses his ontological outlook with his view of soteriology. Wŏnhyo's *Exposition* vividly demonstrates how original enlightenment "inspires" all of Buddhist contemplation practice, from the initial turning away from sensory objects in signlessness until everything in existence comes to be seen as coextensive with enlightenment itself.

II. The Writing of the *Exposition*

The *Vajrasamādhi-sūtra*, or *Book of Adamantine Absorption*,[30] the root text of Wŏnhyo's *Exposition*, is a scripture that was of seminal importance for Wŏnhyo and the Silla Buddhist tradition. Wŏnhyo occupies a crucial role in the traditional legend of the discovery of the sūtra. Wŏnhyo's time-honored associations with the text are indicated by the fact that the tale of the sūtra's recovery figures prominently in the earliest extant account of Wŏnhyo's life, which appears in the *Song Gaoseng zhuan* (The Song Biography of Eminent Monks), compiled between 982 and 988 by the Chinese monk Zanning (919–1001).[31] Let me relate here just the portions relevant to the recovery of this sūtra and the writing of the *Exposition*. It is a good story.

Wŏnhyo's Associations with the *Vajrasamādhi-sūtra*

Zanning's account of Wŏnhyo's life leading up to writing his *Exposition of the Vajrasamādhi-Sūtra* begins with a controversy among Wŏnhyo's peers concerning his participation in an *Inwang kyŏng* (Ch. *Renwang jing; Book of Benevolent Kings*) convocation, a sūtra-recitation ceremony that was periodically convened during the Silla and Koryŏ dynasties to enhance the fortunes of the kingdom. Over the opposition of elders in the order, the Silla king orders that Wŏnhyo be allowed to join the convocation. Sometime later, the queen is stricken by a mysterious illness, which shamans say can be cured only if medicine is brought from overseas. The king immediately dispatches an envoy to Tang China to fetch the requisite medicine. But while still en route across the sea, an old man suddenly appears from out of the waves and leads the envoy down to the Dragon King's palace deep beneath the ocean, where he has a personal audience with that ophidian monarch. The Dragon King informs the envoy that the illness of the Silla queen had merely been a pretext to ensure that a long-lost sūtra, the *Vajrasamādhi-sūtra*, would be reintroduced to the world. The Dragon King commands that, upon the envoy's return to Silla, the random folios of the sūtra be collated by the siddha Taean (d.u.) and commented upon by Wŏnhyo. In order to ensure the scripture's safe return to Silla, the pages are wrapped in waxed paper and hidden inside the envoy's thigh.

After being escorted back to the surface of the sea, the envoy returns to court and informs the king of the events that had transpired. The king summons Taean, but since the siddha refuses to "cross the threshold" of the palace, the king instead sends the folios to Taean at his residence. Once he has finished collating the materials, Taean sends the sūtra directly to Wŏnhyo, who is residing at his birthplace of Sangju, outside the Silla capital of Kyongju. Wŏnhyo orders the messenger to prepare an oxcart for him and sets his writing table between the ox's two horns. (We are told that this placement symbolizes the *Vajrasamādhi-sūtra*'s reference to the two enlightenments of original and acquired.) Wŏnhyo writes his commentary, complete in five rolls, while riding on the cart. The king then schedules a convocation at Hwangnyongsa (Yellow Dragon Monastery), where Wŏnhyo is to lecture on his commentary. Just before the convocation, however, a "menial lackey" of Wŏnhyo's opponents in the order steals the newly written exegesis. The king delays the lecture for three days so Wŏnhyo can rewrite an "abbreviated" version of the commentary, in three rolls, which he expounds to universal acclaim. Zanning tells us in conclusion that both the "expanded" and "abbreviated" versions of the commentary "are in circulation in their native land. The abbreviated version was transmitted to China. Later, a Trepiṭaka [specialist in the canon], who was a sūtra-translator *(pŏn'gyŏng samjang/fanjing sanzang)*,[32] finally changed [the title from a 'commentary' *(so/shu)*] to an 'exposition' *(non/lun)*."[33]

Debates about the Sūtra's Authorship

Wŏnhyo's apparently close involvement in the publication and dissemination of the *Vajrasamādhi-sūtra,* which Zanning relates in his biography, is decidedly peculiar since the sūtra had traditionally been considered by East Asian Buddhism to be a fourth-century translation of an originally Indian or Serindian work. To the Chinese, however, this scripture had been lost since at least 602. It was presumed to have returned to circulation during the early eighth century, after a century-long hiatus. In contrast to this traditional view, I sought in a previous book *(The Formation of Ch'an Ideology in China and Korea)* to show instead that the *Vajrasamādhi-sūtra* actually was composed in Korea around 680 to 685 and that this new scripture had nothing to do with the long-lost fourth-century translation but was instead a completely new, indigenous sūtra. I also proposed that the author might have been a person called "Pŏmnang," a putative early Korean adept of Sŏn (Ch. Chan; Jpn. Zen), who wrote the sūtra to convey certain soteriological ideas emerging within the nascent Sŏn/Chan movement of the time. I also sought to demonstrate that its "appearance" in Silla Korea was closely associated with Wŏnhyo's religious career.[34]

My argument about the pedigree of the scripture has received much attention within the scholarly community, and my thesis about the Korean provenance of the sūtra remains uncontroverted. Much controversy remains, however, regarding the authorship of the text. Writing for a Korean scholarly audience in 1988, Kim Yongt'ae, the doyen of contemporary Korean Buddhist studies, drew from much of the same body of hagiographical, catalogue, and textual evidence I had developed in my 1985 dissertation and 1989 book to confirm my hypothesis that the *Vajrasamādhi-sūtra* was written in Korea. In his survey of potential authors for the scripture, he suggests that, in addition to the obvious candidates Taean and Wŏnhyo, Wŏnhyo's mentor Hyegong (d.u.) should also be included among the possible candidates.[35] Hyegong seems to have been one of the most influential monks in Wŏnhyo's coterie, and both Hyegong and Wŏnhyo were known to have been adepts of unhindered practice *(muaehaeng/wuaixing)*, traveling around the countryside singing and dancing in the streets. We also know that Wŏnhyo consulted regularly with Hyegong in the course of his writing: as Hyegong's biography tells us, "Whenever [Wŏn]hyo wrote a commentary to a sūtra, he would always visit the master to inquire about his doubts."[36] But apart from this terse notice that Wŏnhyo respected Hyegong's understanding of Buddhist doctrine, there is no evidence of any sort linking Hyegong to the *Vajrasamādhi-sūtra.*

Other scholars have returned to Taean as an obvious candidate for the authorship of the *Vajrasamādhi-sūtra;* he is, after all, the person Zanning specifically names as having first received the sūtra and "collated" the folios—that is, he redacted the text. For example, the eminent Japanese scholar of Zen Yanagida Seizan, who has been extremely gracious and supportive in his evaluation of my argument about the provenance of the sūtra, has suggested that Taean might have compiled the *Vajrasamādhi-sūtra* by extracting the sūtra from Wŏnhyo's *Exposition.*[37] Han T'aesik also reiterates the *Song Gaoseng zhuan*'s statement that it was Taean who composed the *Vajrasamādhi-sūtra* and then asked Wŏnhyo to write a commentary to the sūtra.[38] As the *Song Gaoseng zhuan* legend indicates, Taean, the mysterious collator of the *Vajrasamādhi-sūtra,* is strongly implicated in the "rediscovery" of the sūtra. Apart from his mention in this tale, however, Taean is utterly unknown and fits better the realm of myth than of history.

Other colleagues have suggested to me privately after reading my book that the associations between Wŏnhyo and the *Vajrasamādhi-sūtra* seem so fortuitous that Wŏnhyo himself deserves a second look as a possible author. I had remarked in my *Ch'an Ideology* book about the "possibility that Wŏnhyo may have written the *Vajrasamādhi* to further his own syncretic vision, while incorporating unwittingly fragments of originally Ch'an materials that somehow had made their way to Korea."[39] While I could not rule out definitively the prospect that Wŏnhyo himself authored the text, after surveying the internal textual evidence in the sūtra itself, I was confident that "as enticing as the prospect may seem, Wŏnhyo is not our man."[40] If Wŏnhyo had authored the sūtra, we would also expect to see at least some signs that the scripture had been composed along with its commentary (as when an exegete writes a commentary and autocommentary simultaneously); but I see no definitive evidence of this tendency anywhere in the two texts. The prospect that Wŏnhyo authored the sūtra remains tantalizing but ultimately out of reach.

Most recently, Ishii Kōsei carefully analyzed the "Accessing the Edge of Reality" chapter (chapter 5) of the *Vajrasamādhi-sūtra* and surmised that the sūtra was directed at advanced lay practitioners of Buddhism, who were neither renunciants nor householders and who were dedicated to Tathāgatagarbha thought, well versed in a wide range of Mahāyāna sūtras, and engaged in "guarding the one" meditation. He therefore doubts that the sūtra was composed as a means of transmitting surreptitiously the teachings of Chan, as I had hypothesized. However, he takes no final stand on the authorship issue, except to downplay the chances that the sūtra was composed by a Chan adept like Pŏmnang.[41] Careful readers of my book would, however, have realized that I too admitted that the putative connections between "Pŏmnang" and the historical Chan and Sŏn schools were so tenuous that "any identity we might thus claim between Pŏmnang and the author of the *Vajrasamādhi* is, finally, speculative." As I concluded in *Ch'an Ideology*, we may never be able to prove definitively who composed the *Vajrasamādhi-sūtra*, but "in the absence of any definitive evidence to the contrary, the author may be called 'Pŏmnang,' provided, of course, that one understands by this name not the paleographic Pŏmnang but instead a historical shell with the requisite background to compose the *Vajrasamādhi*. While perhaps not the completely satisfying conclusion one might like to this story, more than anyone else it is Pŏmnang who deserves the prize of authorship."[42] Given the present state of the evidence, I believe this is still the most defensible conclusion.

The *Exposition of the Vajrasamādhi-Sūtra* as Wŏnhyo's Last Major Work

The *Exposition of the Vajrasamādhi-Sūtra* is one of the few works of Wŏnhyo's that I believe we may place chronologically with some degree of confidence.[43] Drawing on both textual and hagiographic evidence, a strong case can be made that Wŏnhyo's *Exposition* is in fact his last major work, composed just a few years before his death in 686. The *Exposition*, like virtually all of Wŏnhyo's works, bears no composition date. The only treatise by Wŏnhyo that I know to carry a date is his *P'an piryang non* (On Inference), whose postface states that it was completed at Haengmyŏngsa, in the second year, cyclical *sinmi*, of the Xianheng era of the Chinese Tang dynasty, seventh month, sixteenth day (August 25, 671).[44] We ordinarily might expect that internal textual evidence would give us the best hope of establishing a chronology of his works, but this turns out to be a chimera since Wŏnhyo's style is fairly uniform throughout most of his exegetical works, and his citations of scriptures provide few definitive indications of the relative order of his oeuvre.[45] There is, however, one source of external evidence that gives us some crucial hints about the relative chronology of Wŏnhyo's writing: the later hagiography of Wŏnhyo, "Wŏnhyo pulgi"

(Wŏnhyo, the Unbridled), that appears in the Korean historical miscellany *Samguk yusa* (Memorabilia of the Three Kingdoms), compiled sometime during the thirteenth century by the Buddhist monk Iryŏn (1206–1289).[46] While postdating Wŏnhyo's life by several centuries, Iryŏn's account provides an invaluable retrospective view of the principal stages of Wŏnhyo's scholastic vocation and where the *Exposition* should be placed in Wŏnhyo's oeuvre. Let me draw from this hagiography to outline why I believe the *Exposition* to be Wŏnhyo's last major work.

Iryŏn's biography of Wŏnhyo, like many of those found in the *Samguk yusa,* begins in stereotypical fashion, following earlier Chinese models of the various *Biographies of Eminent Monks,* but supplements its account with a variety of ancillary materials, including local legend and lesser-known stories in *hyangjŏn*s (local biographies). In Wŏnhyo's case, this penchant is especially apparent, perhaps because Iryŏn hailed from Wŏnhyo's own native area and would have been familiar with regional tales concerning the eminent Silla sage.[47]

In the last major section of his hagiography of Wŏnhyo, Iryŏn seems to restart his narrative with what looks to be an explicit attempt to outline the major periods in Wŏnhyo's life, placing the writing of the *Exposition* at a period just before his death. This chronological reiteration opens with (1) Wŏnhyo's birth and early years, followed by (2) an exegetical period that culminates in the composition of his *Chinyŏk Hwaŏmgyŏng so* (Commentary to the Jin Translation of the *Avataṃsaka-sūtra*).[48] Wŏnhyo then stops writing and (3) embarks on his eccentric career as a wandering proselytist, which (4) he abandons to return to scholarship one last time in order to write his *Exposition of the Vajrasamādhi-Sūtra.* Iryŏn's rough chronology concludes with (5) an account of Wŏnhyo's death and funeral. Iryŏn, as is known from other sections of his work, was quite concerned with chronological fidelity and often tried to sort out contradicting dates.[49] I believe this concern with offering a relative chronology of Wŏnhyo's life may be Iryŏn's reason for backtracking at the end of the biography in order to include this recapitulation of the eminent Silla monk's career.

Including the period of Wŏnhyo's early vocation and study when traditional sources tell us he made one or two aborted attempts to travel to China (which Iryŏn covers later in his biography of Wŏnhyo's colleague Ŭisang [625–702]), Iryŏn divides Wŏnhyo's life into six distinct stages. Let me list them here, with provisional dates:

1. Birth and adolescence (617–631)
2. Ordination and early vocation (ca. 632–661)
   a. Attempted China trip(s) (ca. 650–661)
3. Textual exegete (ca. 662–676)
   a. Birth of his son, Sŏl Ch'ong (ca. 662)
   b. *Hwaŏmgyŏng so* as final composition before retirement (ca. 676)

4. Proselytist among the people (ca. 677–680)
5. Return to scholarly exegesis (ca. 680) [viz. to write the *Exposition*]
6. Death and funeral (686).[50]

For our purposes here, let me focus only on the chronology of Wŏnhyo's exegetical and proselytizing periods, and how these relate to his possible decision to return one last time to scholarship to write his *Exposition of the Vajrasamādhi-Sūtra*.[51]

The continuity in both style and content apparent in most of Wŏnhyo's exegetical works suggests that they may have been written in close succession. While this is not to claim that all of the hundred or so works in some two hundred rolls attributed to Wŏnhyo are authentic, Wŏnhyo's authorship of most of the twenty-some extant compositions has not been questioned (with one notable exception, the *Yu simallak to*).[52] Since Wŏnhyo, we are told, was so determined to travel to China (ultimately unsuccessfully) to enhance his knowledge of Buddhist scholarship, it seems reasonable to presume that he would not have felt himself competent to write most of these commentaries until after his attempted pilgrimage.[53] I therefore presume that many of his writings probably postdate his return from his aborted attempt(s) to travel to the mainland.

Political events on the peninsula at the time provide some further information that may help us to sort out the dates of his exegetical period as well as to clarify when Wŏnhyo might have left on his subsequent proselytizing mission among the people. Even after the fall of Koguryŏ in 668, peace still did not reign on the Korean peninsula. In 667–676, Silla itself was invaded by the combined armies of Tang soldiers and Paekche mercenaries, which would have made extensive travel difficult, if not impossible. Hence, if Wŏnhyo actually did go on tour to "sing and dance his way through a thousand villages and a myriad hamlets,"[54] as Iryŏn states in his biography, this proselytizing excursion toward the end of his career probably could not have commenced until after the withdrawal of Tang Chinese forces in 676. If so, Wŏnhyo would have had approximately fifteen years, from 661 to 676, to complete most of his commentaries. The one confirmed date we have for one of Wŏnhyo's works, the 671 date of the *P'an piryang non,* converges nicely with the chronological scheme I propose here.

Although our present state of knowledge does not allow us to ascertain much about the respective composition dates of most of Wŏnhyo's works, there are some indications that the *Samguk yusa* biography is attempting to provide some chronological clarification for two of his most influential works: his *Hwaŏmgyŏng so* and his *Exposition of the Vajrasamādhi-Sūtra.* I believe Iryŏn's conclusion is that the *Hwaŏmgyŏng so* was the last work Wŏnhyo wrote before his departure to proselytize among the people; an extraordinary series of events later prompted him to return one final time to major scholarship before his death in 686 to write the *Exposition,* his commentary to the newly recovered *Vajrasamādhi-sūtra.* Most scholars have presumed that Wŏnhyo wrote his *Exposition* around 665, and later, as the final event in his life, Wŏnhyo then started his *Hwaŏmgyŏng so* but dropped it unfinished and went off to proselytize.[55] But my reading of the *Samguk yusa* account suggests instead that Iryŏn was attempting to place Wŏnhyo's retirement before the writing of the *Exposition.* According to Iryŏn's chronology, Wŏnhyo seems to have voluntarily abandoned his scholarly activities even before completing his *Hwaŏmgyŏng so,* perhaps intended to be his magnum opus given the importance of the *Avataṃsaka-sūtra* at that time in both Silla and Chinese Buddhism.[56] It is also intriguing that Wŏnhyo stopped his commentary at the "Transference Chapter" *(huixiang pin)* of the *Avataṃsaka-sūtra,* the chapter in that seminal scripture that deals with how a bodhisattva transfers to all other creatures the merit he has accumulated over eons of religious cultivation. It is intriguing to speculate that reading this chapter might have inspired Wŏnhyo to "lay down his brush" and go off among the people to proselytize. In any case, the clear implication I draw from this account is that Wŏnhyo had judged his exegetical and scholarly career to be at a close; he had nothing more to say as exegete and was content to go "on the road" among the people. Although no date is known for his *Hwaŏmgyŏng so,* if Wŏnhyo had ten years as a proselytist before his death, we may provisionally assume that Wŏnhyo's work on the commentary was completed sometime around 676, after which he retired to a life of disseminating the dharma among the people of Silla Korea. Although this missionary period was apparently devoted primarily to delivering popular sermons and didactic teachings, he may well have composed some of his songs and short tracts dealing with Buddhist faith and moral discipline during this time, as Sung Bae Park has suggested.[57] The little evidence we have, then, suggests that Wŏnhyo's main exegetical efforts preceded his proselytizing stage.

After perhaps a decade spent traveling among the people spreading the name of the Buddha, another event intervened that took Wŏnhyo away from his missionary vocation and compelled him to return to the mainstream of Silla scholastic life: the "appearance" of the *Vajrasamādhi-sūtra.* Wŏnhyo was obviously fascinated by the text, enough to convince him to suspend his travels and return to scholarly writing, apparently for this one last time—and purportedly to write two separate versions (as Zanning's biographical account states above), a claim I will discuss in the following section. My surmise that Wŏnhyo's *Exposition* is his last major work, composed just a few years before his death in 686, is supported by the fact that the *Vajrasamādhi-sūtra* is neither quoted nor cited in any of Wŏnhyo's other compositions, even though his *Exposition* quotes extensively from the full range of texts he had consulted in his earlier writings.[58] Given a scripture as important to Wŏnhyo as was the *Vajrasamādhi-sūtra,* it is hard to imagine that he would not at least have referred to it in one of his earlier works if the text had been available to him. It is therefore safe to date the *Exposition* to a time after the completion of the major part of Wŏnhyo's oeuvre and, from the hagiographical accounts, to sometime between the composition of his *Hwaŏmgyŏng so* around 676 and his death ten years later.[59]

The Two Alleged Versions of Wŏnhyo's *Exposition*

But a thorny issue is raised in traditional accounts of the writing of the *Exposition* that deserves further investigation: Zanning's claim in Wŏnhyo's oldest extant biography that he actually wrote two versions of his *Kŭmgang sammaegyŏng non,* one an "abbreviated," the other an "expanded" exegesis.[60] Both versions of the *Exposition* were said to have circulated in Korea, while only the "abbreviated" version was known to the Chinese. Is there any bibliographical evidence—indeed, evidence of any kind, apart from Zanning's statement—that two separate versions of the *Exposition* ever existed?

As the concluding portion of the *Song Gaoseng zhuan* biography of Wŏnhyo states, the first version of Wŏnhyo's exegesis of the *Vajrasamādhi* was written in five rolls *(kwŏn/juan)*. However, because "menial lackeys" of Wŏnhyo's opponents within the order stole that commentary, Wŏnhyo was forced to write in three short days a second "abbreviated commentary" *(yakso/lüeshu)*. This latter commentary, in three rolls, was so highly regarded by the Chinese that it came to be designated as an "exposition" *(non/lun),* not a mere "commentary" *(so/shu),* thereby placing the composition on a par with treatises (*vyākhyā* or śāstra) written by Indian bodhisattva-exegetes. Despite his assertions that Wŏnhyo thus wrote two separate commentaries to the *Vajrasamādhi-sūtra,* Zanning never indicates in his narrative that the earlier "expanded" commentary was either recovered or rewritten. Obviously, there was a gap in his information concerning the currency of these texts that Zanning was not able to fill. His concluding remarks that both the "expanded" and the "abbreviated" commentaries were still extant in Korea—although only the "abbreviated" version had circulated in China—seems hardly satisfactory and leaves us with more questions than it resolves. For instance, if the original "expanded" commentary were still in circulation in Korea, why is there no record that it was ever recovered from the thieves who stole it or that it was recomposed by Wŏnhyo? And why was the "expanded" commentary still not available in China fully three centuries later?

There is also a brief reference to the composition of the *Exposition* in the *Samguk yusa*'s biography of Wŏnhyo. Iryŏn does not corroborate the statement of his Chinese predecessor that there were two separate commentaries. Iryŏn's only comment is that "owing to the inducement of the Dragon of the Sea, he received a royal command while on the road and wrote the *[Kŭmgang] sammaegyŏng so.*"[61] Iryŏn's laconism concerning the writing of the *Exposition* suggests that he had no knowledge of there being either two independent versions of the commentary, as Zanning had presumed, or any controversy about possible differences in the number of rolls in the recension that was available to him.

Zanning's claim that there was an original "expanded" commentary in circulation anywhere in East Asia is, as we shall see, dubious at best and most probably wrong. It is bibliographical information from later Korean and Japanese catalogues of Buddhist texts that provides vital clues for resolving the question.

Ŭich'ŏn (1055–1101) in his 1090 catalogue of East Asian Buddhist works, *Sinp'yŏn chejong kyojang ch'ongnok* (New Compilation of a Comprehensive Catalogue of the Doctrinal Repositories of All the Schools), cites only one listing for Wŏnhyo's *Kŭmgang sammaegyŏng non,* "in six [alt. three] rolls." In his interlinear note to this entry, he cites in rather curious fashion Zanning's account concerning the writing of the commentary: "the *Monks' Biographies* [Zanning's *Song Gaoseng zhuan*] states: '[Wŏnhyo] wrote a commentary *(so)* in five *kwŏn*. Later, a Trepiṭaka, a translator of sūtras, changed the [title] to an exposition *(non)*.' "[62] The mistake Ŭich'ŏn has made in this account is to have combined Zanning's reference to two separate commentaries—the expanded commentary in five rolls, the abbreviated exposition in three—into one: he assumes the five-roll *so* to be identical to the three-roll *non* he includes in his listing of extant works. Since the number of rolls *(juan/kwŏn)* in which an East Asian text was divided was arbitrary, it was quite common for one text to be divided into varying numbers of rolls. From his reference, it is clear that Ŭich'ŏn knew of only one commentary on the *Vajrasamādhi-sūtra* by Wŏnhyo, but circulating in two different divisions—one in six, the other in three rolls. Both of these versions were, however, identical in content. But Ŭich'ŏn was not aware of a separate text in five rolls and apparently assumed that Zanning's reference to an earlier *so* must refer to the same six- or three-roll *non* that he cited in his catalogue entry—hence, his misreading of the *Song Gaoseng zhuan* entry.

Ŭich'ŏn was one of the first cataloguers in East Asia to recognize indigenous Buddhist writings as being of equivalent stature to the translated treatises of the imported Indian tradition. He saw it as his personal mission to compile a collection of East Asian Buddhist literature so that those native works would be preserved for later generations. With this end in mind, Ŭich'ŏn sent agents throughout East Asia in search of rare editions and finally compiled his catalogue of these texts, which lists 1,010 titles in 4,740 *kwŏn.* He subsequently arranged to have these texts carved as a xylographic *Supplement (Sokchang)* to the first Koryŏ Buddhist canon.[63] If the five-roll "expanded commentary" to which Zanning referred was in fact extant anywhere in East Asia at that time, the chance that it would have escaped Ŭich'ŏn's agents seems remote. Hence, by the eleventh century at least, we can be sure that the "expanded commentary" was nowhere to be found in East Asia—and least of all in Korea, where its existence would have been most plausible, especially given Zanning's late-tenth-century assertion that it was still in circulation on the peninsula.

Evidence from Nara period Japanese manuscript repositories places the presumed existence of this five-roll commentary in even more jeopardy. Ishida Mosaku in his listings of Nara Buddhist manuscripts (which, for convenience's sake, I shall refer to as *Nara shakyō*) includes three copies of Wŏnhyo's *Kŭmgang sammaegyŏng non: Nara shakyō* numbers 2152, 2153, and 2154, which were copied in Nara in, respectively, 743, n.d., and 763.[64] Although there is some variation in the titles, each is in three rolls, and they seem to correspond to the work cited by Ŭich'ŏn in his catalogue—the extant recension of the *Exposition*. Although the Nara manuscripts were copied only a few decades after Wŏnhyo's death in 686, when a work that might later have been lost might still have been in circulation, we have no record of any five-roll "expanded commentary" ever having been copied. A 914 Japanese catalogue of Flower Garland and Logic works, *Kegonshū shosho byō immyōroku* (*T* 2177), by Enchō (fl. 914), lists only the three-roll *non*, lending further support to the premise that a five-roll *so* never circulated in Japan.

The extant bibliographical information on *Vajrasamādhi-sūtra* commentaries available in the East Asian catalogues is tabulated in Table 1. The only evidence apart from the *Song Gaoseng zhuan* for the existence of a five-roll commentary to the *Vajrasamādhi* is the notice in *Tōiki dentō mokuroku* (Catalogue of the Transmission of the Lamp [of the Teachings] throughout the East) (*T* 2183), a Japanese catalogue compiled in 1094 by Eichō (1014–1095). Eichō refers to Wŏnhyo's three-roll *Exposition*, as have all previous cataloguers. However, along with these otherwise-unidentified works dealing with the *Vajrasamādhi*—which we may presume were Japanese compositions, as they do not appear in any other catalogue—Eichō lists an anonymous *ronso* (expository commentary) to the *Vajrasamādhi*, in five rolls. While this notice immediately conjures up images of a long-lost "expanded" commentary preserved in hidden Japanese manuscript caches, I think it is a mirage. The Chinese, as the biographer Zanning and all Chinese bibliographical cataloguers attest, never saw a five-roll commentary. The Japanese of the eighth and tenth centuries similarly knew only of the three-roll exposition that is still extant today. Even the Koreans accepted only the authenticity of this three-roll recension, to the point that their principal cataloguer, Ŭich'ŏn, read Zanning's reference to two commentaries in such a way that it could only refer to one. I am convinced that Eichō never knew personally of a five-roll commentary and, drawing upon Zanning's entry in the *Song Gaoseng zhuan*, included this entry in his catalogue merely for the sake of completeness. All these factors lead inexorably to the conclusion that there was never a five-roll "expanded" commentary in circulation anywhere in East Asia. Despite Zanning's assertions, it was probably never written at all.

But why would this tale that Wŏnhyo wrote two versions of his commentary have been told? First, Wŏnhyo's own closing verse to his *Exposition* notes that he had "commented briefly" (*yak kisul*) on the sūtra (*KSGN*, p. 677b), perhaps suggesting to some readers that a more extensive version was in circulation. In addition, the style of the *Kŭmgang sammaegyŏng non* may have

TABLE 1

Listings of *Vajrasamādhi-sūtra* Commentaries in East Asian Catalogues

Catalogue	Compiler	Date	Citation (*Kŭmgang sammae-/Kongō sammai-*)	Kwŏn Number/Comments
Nara shakyō #2152		743	*kyōron*	3/rolls 2 and 3 only copied; anonymous
Nara shakyō #2153		n.d.	*ron*	3/by Wŏnhyo
Nara shakyō #2154		763	*ronso*	3/by Wŏnhyo
Nara shakyō #2154 (?)		743	*rongi*	3/anonymous; authorship uncertain
Kengonshū shosho byō immyōroku (*T* 2177)	Enchō	914	*ron*	3/p.1133a14; by Wŏnhyo
Sinp'yŏn chejong kyojang ch'ongnok (*T* 2184)	Uich'ŏn	1090	*kyŏngnon*	3 (alt. 6)/p. 1171b10; by Wŏnhyo
Tōiki dentō mokuroku (*T* 2183)	Eichō	1094	*kyōron*	3/p.1152a26; by Wŏnhyo
(?)			*kyōronso*	5/p.1152a27; anonymous
(?)			*kyōgi*	1/p.1152a28; anonymous
(?)			*kyō shiki*	3/p.1152a29; anonymous
(?)			*kyō shiji*	1/p.1152b1; anonymous

contributed to suspicions that there had at one time been a longer version extant. At points in the *Exposition,* Wŏnhyo abbreviates his treatment, referring the reader to another of his works, his *Yijang ŭi* (The Doctrine of the Two Hindrances)—which Wŏnhyo here always calls the *Yijang chang* (Essay on the Two Hindrances)—for fuller explication.[65] That fact that there is such cross-referencing in the exegesis indicates that the *Exposition* postdates at least some of Wŏnhyo's other works. Finally, in a few spots the commentary seems to provide little more than the basic structure of his argument, without the detailed references one usually finds elsewhere in the *Exposition.*

But this story of the theft and rewriting of Wŏnhyo's *Expositon* is perhaps most significant at the level of myth—that is, as a statement of Wŏnhyo's scholarly impeccability—and reflects the folkloric quality of the *Song Gaoseng zhuan* hagiography. The forced rewrite of a sacred book is a common topos in pan-Buddhistic folklore and is used both to attest to the perfect consistency of an author as well as to test his mettle and understanding. We find the same topos used, for example, in the hagiography of the renowned Theravāda exegete Buddhaghosa (ca. fifth century C.E.). According to Sinhalese Buddhist tradition, Buddhaghosa's magnum opus, the *Visuddhimagga* (Path of Purification), was twice stolen by the King of the Gods, Sakka (Skt. Śakro Devānām Indraḥ), as a test of Buddhaghosa's scholarship. By checking the final draft against the two purloined versions, Sakka was able to verify Buddhaghosa's complete consistency as an author and, by extension, the unimpeachability of Sinhalese religious writings.[66] Though the thief in our story hardly has the prestige of a Sakka, his pilfering of the *Exposition* presents a similar type of test for Wŏnhyo. Here, however, the tale attests to Wŏnhyo's perseverance in the face of persecution and his determination to ensure that the message of the *Vajrasamādhi-sūtra* not be lost. Wŏnhyo's ability to reproduce his work accurately—and rewrite his commentary over a short three-day period—might also suggest the purity of the textual transmission of the Korean Buddhist tradition. Hence, Zanning's claim that Wŏnhyo wrote two independent commentaries to the *Vajrasamādhi* is significant primarily as folklore, not textual history.

Close inspection of East Asian bibliographical catalogues therefore reveals that there were never two separate recensions of Wŏnhyo's *Kŭmgang sammaegyŏng non* in circulation either in Korea or anywhere else in East Asia.[67] Ultimately, if Wŏnhyo ever had composed an "expanded commentary" on the *Vajrasamādhi-sūtra,* it vanished forever with the "menial lackey" who is said to have stolen the text right after its completion. Therefore, we may with confidence presume that the only version of Wŏnhyo's *Exposition* that ever circulated is the one extant today, which I translate in full in Part 2 of this book.

III. The *Exposition* as Commentary

The *Exposition of the Vajrasamādhi-Sūtra* is Wŏnhyo's longest, and arguably greatest, commentary. Looking at the paucity of works written in Silla Korea before his time, it is no exaggeration to say that it was Wŏnhyo who created the scholastic tradition of Silla Buddhism.[68] The vast majority of Wŏnhyo's works are explicitly commentaries, and even those that are not are still strongly exegetical in character. The East Asian tradition itself also treats Wŏnhyo primarily as a commentator, as seen, for example, in the *Song Gaoseng zhuan*'s listing of Wŏnhyo in its "doctrinal exegetes" *(yijie)* section, together with a number of other Korean scholiasts who played important roles in the development of the learned schools of Sinitic Buddhism.[69] In my view, his role as a commentator constitutes Wŏnhyo's major contribution to East Asian Buddhism.

To call Wŏnhyo a commentator is neither to deny the many other roles he played in his full and varied life nor to disparage other aspects of his religious career; rather, it simply acknowledges that the primary vehicle through which Wŏnhyo conveyed his philosophical and spiritual insights was scriptural exegesis. In this proclivity, Wŏnhyo emulates intellectuals writing within most traditional civilizations, where much of spiritual and religious understanding was conveyed through exegetical writing. "Commentaries and commentarial modes of thinking," John Henderson remarks, "dominated the intellectual history of most premodern civilizations, a fact often obscured by . . . modern scholars' denigration of the works of mere exegetes and annotators. Until the seventeenth century in Europe, and even later in China, India, and the Near East, thought, especially within high intellectual traditions, was primarily exegetical in character and expression."[70] This traditional esteem for commentary is frequently obscured in contemporary treatments of religion, which valorize meditative experience over religious exegesis, or which misguidedly presume that things old and primary (viz. scriptures) are somehow superior to the new and derivative (viz. commentaries).[71]

The *Exposition of the Vajrasamādhi-Sūtra* is the longest work in Wŏnhyo's oeuvre. In this treatise, Wŏnhyo applies his mature exegetical skills to the explication of a sūtra that has profound associations with Wŏnhyo personally and the Korean Buddhist tradition as a whole. Below I will examine the structure and style of Wŏnhyo's *Exposition* as a quintessential example of the East Asian commentarial form. Despite the obvious care with which Wŏnhyo works his way through this sūtra, his commentary is not solely intended as an exegesis of the meaning of each term or passage in a text. Rather, his exegesis, like all Buddhist commentary, also seeks to demonstrate, first, how each section, part, and division of the scripture resonates with the rest of the sections, parts, and divisions of the text; and second, how this one text reticulates within the entire fabric of the Buddhist scriptural teachings. Scholars often mine commentaries for their detailed coverage of the specific meaning of scriptural terms and passages, but in their form and structure, commentaries are much more importantly the "metalanguage" of the text, which presents the commentator's larger vision of the scripture and its place in the Buddhist doctrinal edifice. The mission Wŏnhyo sets for himself in this commentary is large indeed: he attempts nothing less than to demonstrate that the entirety of Mahāyāna Buddhism is revealed in this single sūtra. Indeed, the act of writing commentary may itself be a core form of Buddhist practice—the commentator's own virtuoso performance, or reenactment, of the insights he finds presented in the scripture.[72] Indeed, in his virtuosity at manipulating the commentarial form, Wŏnhyo can be deemed not simply a paragon of Korean scholarly achievement but someone who was emblematic of the highest achievements of the Sinitic Buddhist tradition as a whole.

The Buddhist Commentarial Genre

Commentary is the principal genre through which Buddhist beliefs and insights have been conveyed throughout history. Commentary has a long pedigree within Buddhism, which in all probability can be traced back to the inception of the religion itself. There are enough instances in Indian Buddhist literature of a commentarial explanation in one textual tradition being the canonical reading in another, and vice versa, to "suggest that the commentarial and canonical traditions which underly *[sic]* them are equally old, and the material upon which they are based must pre-date the separation of the sects. It seems probable that some of this material, since it is accepted as canonical by some sects, must go back to the earliest days of Buddhism, perhaps to the time of the Buddha himself."[73] Some of the works attributed to the Buddha himself are explicitly exegetical in character, such as the Pāli *Mahāpadesa-suttanta* (Great Exegesis), which provides the Buddha's analysis of the standards of religious authority. Other Indian sūtras are nascent exegeses of the Buddha's terse sayings or enigmatic verses given by his senior disciples. One example is the *Mahākaccāna-Bhaddekaratta-sutta* (The Ideal Lover of Solitude Scripture, Spoken by Mahākatyāyana), which offers the Buddha's verse interpretation *(uddesa)* of the significance of solitude, followed by Mahākatyāyana's extensive analysis *(vibhaṅga)* of the meaning of the verses.[74] A similar structure is found in much of chapter 7 of the *Vajrasamādhi-sūtra* itself, where the verse explanations of the Buddha are elaborated upon by the interlocutor, Pŏmhaeng. Certain of these early Indian commentaries, such as the Theravāda *Mahānidessa* (Great Exposition), a third-century C.E. commentary on the fourth and fifth books of the *Sutta-nipāta* (Collection of Sūtras), were thought to be so ancient that they were considered to be canonical in their own right.

Buddhist exegesis probably began simply enough by explaining one word in terms of another. Even dialogues attributed to the Buddha himself commonly use synonyms as a way of helping his audience understand his teachings.[75] From this start, early scholiasts within the Buddhist Order began to provide either common synonyms or more elaborate explication of terms in their exegeses of passages in the Buddhist texts.[76] Wŏnhyo's commentary is indeed filled with such use of synonyms to explain his material, such as when he glosses "spell" as "supplication" (*KSGN,* p. 656b).

A second way in which explanations of terms are often given in Indian Buddhist texts is etymologizing *(nirukti,* or *nirvacana),* an exegetical tool developed within Sanskrit literature that was adopted by Buddhist commentators. This technique involves the use of "folk etymologies," that is, etymological analogies that relate words that are phonologically similar but semantically unrelated. In analyzing the title *bhagavat* (lord), for example, the commentators might explain that the lord is he who has blessings *(bhagī),* is fortunate *(bhāgyavā),* has gone to the end of being *(bhav-anta-go),* and so forth, drawing on a series of unrelated words to convey a range of possible connotations for the root term. Such etymologizing appears in even the earliest stratum of Buddhist canonical materials and is taken up frequently in all subsequent Buddhist commentarial literature.[77] This propensity for etymologizing often develops into what in Sanskrit is called *śleṣa,* or multiple explanations of a term, which generally involves a lengthy series of folk etymologies offering various attributes, characteristics, or epithets. These multiple etymologies were often used in religious litany rather than for purely philological purposes.[78]

As in much of Indian commentarial writing, the disciplines of linguistics, poetics, and logic came to provide much of the methodologies and styles of argumentation that were used in Buddhist commentaries. Although the terminology differs, typically a sūtra would be commented upon by an expository *upadeśa* (clarification) or *bhāṣya* (explanation) or subject to a more intricate gloss called either a *vyākhyā* or a *ṭīkā*.[79] Broadly speaking, Indian Mahāyāna sūtra commentaries tend to be more expository in form, drawing out the implications and significance of the text in question but without necessarily dwelling extensively on specific terms, lines, and passages in the text. Vasubandhu's (fl. ca. mid-fourth to mid-fifth centuries) commentary on the *Vajracchedikā* (Diamond Sūtra), for example, is divided into seven topics that deal with the training of the bodhisattva as outlined in the *Diamond Sūtra,* the achievement of realization, and how the sūtra gets its title; but the treatment of each topic for the most part stands independently, and the commentary makes no attempt to gloss even major passages in the sūtra, let alone most individual terms.[80]

In East Asian Buddhism as well, there were different designations for various types of commentarial writings, many of which are reflected in Wŏnhyo's oeuvre. Generally, exegeses involving detailed glosses of a scripture were termed *so/shu,* "commentary," and had only semicanonical status. (It was in fact the Korean cataloguer Ŭich'ŏn, in the eleventh century, who first insisted that such indigenous East Asian compositions could be so profound in their own right that they too deserved to be included in the canon.) More expository treatments of the thought presented in a scripture were called *chongyo/zongyao,* literally "thematic (or doctrinal) essentials," that is, exegetical summaries. The term *non/lun,* "exposition," was generally reserved by the East Asians for independent treatises (śāstra) attributed to the eminent Indian Mahāyāna exegetes whom the East Asians designated "bodhisattvas"; translated from Sanskrit, such texts were accorded canonical status on a par with scriptures attributed to the Buddha himself. Hence, as I have discussed above, conferring the designation *non* on Wŏnhyo's exegesis of the *Vajrasamādhi,* as Zanning's biography of Wŏnhyo mentions, would have been the equivalent of placing Wŏnhyo on a par with the bodhisattva-exegetes in the heartland of Buddhism—a mark of the high esteem in which this commentary was held in East Asian Buddhism.

Indian Buddhists made periodic attempts to outline the principles that should govern commentarial writing. The Theravāda *Nettippakaraṇa* and *Peṭakopadeśa* (both from perhaps the first century C.E.) develop in tandem an elaborate hermeneutical theory based on two broad rubrics: "interpretation as to sense" *(byañjana;* Skt. *vyañjana)* and "interpretation as to meaning" *(attha;* Skt. *artha).*[81] In the Mahāyāna śāstra literature, one of the few explicit statements outlining the process of commentarial exegesis appears in Haribhadra's *Abhisamayālaṁkārāloka-prajñāpāramitāvyākhyā* (The Ornament of Realization):

> Those who relate the meaning of sūtras,
> Must state their purpose *(prayojana)*, their concise meaning *(piṇḍārtha)*,
> The meaning of the words *(padārtha)*, their sectional divisions *(anusaṃdhi)*,
> And the contradictions [raised by opponents], with their rebuttals *(codyaparihāra)*.[82]

The implications of this process for both commentarial structure and interpretative theory are drawn out in their most systematic and sustained fashion in the *Vyākhyāyukti* (Science of Exegesis, or, more literally, Exegetical Propriety), by the renowned Indian scholiast Vasubandhu. This text, still little studied by Buddhologists, "is a treatise on the art of proper *(yukti)* commentary *(vyākhyā)*, providing not only practical examples of how one is to go about the process of 'explaining the *sūtras*,' but also elucidating certain theoretical concerns that arise in the process of determining what constitutes (both structurally and ideologically) a proper commentary."[83] In the third chapter of the *Vyākhyāyukti*, Vasubandhu explains four distinct aspects of "the meaning of the words" *(padārtha)*: synonyms *(paryāya)*, definition *(lakṣaṇa)*, etymology *(nirukti)*, and its subdivisions (*prabheda;* perhaps implying subsidiary meanings, or connotations, in this context). Although the *Vyākhyāyukti* was never translated into Chinese (it is now available only in a Tibetan rendering), similar forms are typical of East Asian Buddhist exegesis as well, including Wŏnhyo's *Exposition.*

East Asian Exegetical Forms

Wŏnhyo's *Exposition of the Vajrasamādhi-Sūtra* is a masterpiece of the traditional style of exegesis employed within the East Asian Buddhist tradition. Like virtually all Korean Buddhist materials in the premodern era, Wŏnhyo's works are written in the peculiar Buddhist argot of literary Chinese, whose terse logographic form challenges the resources of even the most talented English translator.

There is probably no religious literature that is so deceptively simple, yet in fact so utterly prolix, as is the commentarial literature of East Asian Buddhism, including that of Korea. Commentarial literature may seem relatively straightforward to the first-time reader. Typically the commentator will include a brief introduction outlining the significance of the scripture that is the object of exegesis and the broad structure of the commentary. This introduction will be followed by passages of the scripture, including the exegete's comments, which will often involve a detailed line-by-line, even word-by-word, analysis of the text. But this simple style masks what is often an immensely complex hermeneutical structure that is superimposed over the commentarial sections. A reader (and, indeed, a translator) must retain control of this massive interpretative schema if the thread of argument running through the commentary is to be intelligible. Wŏnhyo's commentaries are typical of this East Asian commentarial style. The first three sections of this *Exposition* are essentially introductory, lasting a little over three pages in the Korean *Han'guk Pulgyo chŏnsŏ* (Collected Works of Korean Buddhism) edition—barely 4 percent of the commentary—while the final section goes on for some seventy pages.

Wŏnhyo's commentarial style is a thoroughgoing fusion of imported Indian commentarial practice and indigenous Sinitic scholarly exegesis, primarily based on Confucian models. As a genre, East Asian Buddhist commentary owes much to both traditions. Stylistically, many of the features discussed previously regarding Indian Buddhist exegesis hold for East Asian commentaries as well. In their structure and overall approach, East Asian Buddhist commentaries also parallel closely the exegetical tradition of Confucianism that began during the Han dynasty,[84] in which

> commentary makes the claim that every word, every sentence, every paragraph of the canonical text is profoundly significant, deserving of the most genuine and thorough reflection. . . . Commentary acts as a response to the text of the classic. Commentary, in its response, aims to bring out the meaning of the classic. In bringing out its meaning, commentary fixes the range of meanings that the classic can have. And these properties together attest to perhaps the fundamental assumption of commentary: that the base-text, the classic, speaks with authority and insight and consequently is worthy of such interpretive engagement.[85]

Within Confucianism, interlinear commentary, which may have derived from oral exegesis, emerged as a means of bridging the linguistic and cultural gulf the Han dynasty Chinese felt from the ancient Zhou dynasty, when the books that came to be recognized as the classics were written. The commentary's close attention to every nuance of the classics served to render those texts accessible to contemporary readers but at the same time also transformed them into religious and cultural icons.

The translation of Buddhist texts from Sanskrit, Middle Indic, and Central Asian languages presented similarly momentous challenges of understanding to the Chinese, challenges that were far more difficult to tackle than those that confronted Zhou and Han period Chinese. Rarely were Chinese translations from Indic languages readily accessible to their target audience. More often than not, they were grammatically awkward, semantically ambiguous, filled with obscure concepts and inscrutable terminology, and peppered by bizarre transliterations, in which Chinese logographs were used solely for their phonological value in rendering foreign loan words into Chinese. Even such a renowned translator as Xuanzang (d. 664), whose works are widely respected for their scholarly accuracy, used such a peculiar argot of Chinese (much worse in fact than the "Buddhist Hybrid English" found in modern English translations) that his translations were rarely read. Compounding the problem were the large number of indigenous, or "apocryphal" texts—sūtras composed outside the Indian cultural sphere but following the narrative structure of Indian or Central Asian scriptures—that circulated as authentic scripture.[86] We now know that many of the seminal texts of the East Asian tradition were not translated Indian sūtras at all but instead were indigenous scriptures composed on the model of authentic Indian texts. The *Vajrasamādhi-sūtra,* the root text of Wŏnhyo's *Exposition,* is just such a scripture. One strategy such scriptures took in order to increase the odds of being accepted as authentic was to mimic as closely as possible the style of translated scripture. Thus, despite their Sinitic provenance, such texts are often no more transparent to the reader than are translations of imported materials. In such conditions, commentaries play a crucial role in mediating the gulf that separates the archaic (or putatively archaic) sacred text from the contemporary reader. This role would be even more important for an intellectual tradition, like that of the Silla kingdom, that was just beginning to crystallize around Buddhism. It is no wonder, then, that among the first acts Wŏnhyo would take as the architect of the Silla Buddhist exegetical tradition would be to write commentaries on the most important of the Sinitic Buddhist texts then making their way into Silla Korea.

Chinese Buddhist scholars from virtually the inception of their tradition began to develop their own strategies for approaching the mass of new scriptural material making its way into China and into Chinese. Dao'an (312–385), an important vaunt-courier in the nascent Sinitic scholarly tradition, is claimed to have developed an exegetical schema through which to analyze a sūtra's narrative structure. This schema is the so-called three divisions of scriptural exegesis *(sanfen kejing),* which posits the following major sections common to all scriptures: (1) the prefatory setting *(xufen; nidāna),* which specifies the time and place where the sūtra was delivered, and lists the audience in attendance; (2) the main body *(zhengzongfen),* which relates the doctrines and practices that are the subject of the discourse; and (3) the dissemination section *(liutongfen; parīndanā),* which describes the confidence and insight the scripture inspires in its audience.[87]

The Chinese Tiantai school attributes to Zhiyi (538–597) a list of five general hermeneutical issues that should be addressed before beginning the in-depth exegesis of any sūtra. These are termed the "five categories of profound meanings" *(wuzhong xuanyi):*

1. explicating the meaning of the title *(shiming)*
2. analyzing its fundamental intent *(bianben)*

3. clarifying its principal themes or doctrines *(mingzong)*
4. expounding its "function" or impact on people *(lunyong)*
5. classifying the sūtra *(panjiao),* that is, delineating its place within the entire corpus of sūtras expounded by the Buddha.[88]

Wŏnhyo substantially follows both of these exegetical schemata in his treatment of the *Vajrasamādhi-sūtra.* The first three parts of his *Exposition* correspond in large measure with the prefatory issues that the Tiantai school insists should be addressed before beginning the main commentary. Part 1 of Wŏnhyo's commentary, "A Statement of Its Main Idea" *(sul taeŭi),* describes the main purport of the sūtra in classic interlocking parallel style often used in East Asian mystical writings;[89] it corresponds to the second of Tiantai's five categories. Part 2, "An Analysis of the Themes of the Scripture" *(p'yŏn kyŏngjong),* highlights the contemplation practice that has but a single taste, the essential point of the sūtra in Wŏnhyo's analysis, and ten different ways to approach the exegesis of the scripture as whole; it corresponds to the third of Tiantai's five categories. Part 3, "An Explication of the Title" *(sŏk chemok),* mentions the three different titles given to the scripture and gives an extensive etymological treatment of the meaning of the main title, *Vajrasamādhi;* it corresponds to the first of Tiantai's five categories. As I mentioned before, these three introductory sections of the text constitute barely 4 percent of the *Exposition.* The Tiantai school's fourth and fifth categories—the text's impact and classification—do not receive a separate designation in Wŏnhyo's exegesis but are discussed at various points in the main body, Part 4. "An Exegesis of the Text."

Part 4 of Wŏnhyo's *Exposition,* which is his detailed "segmenting and explicating" of the text itself, follows closely Dao'an's three divisions of scriptural exegesis. In this last major part of the *Exposition,* which constitutes almost 96 percent of the whole commentary, Wŏnhyo's section 1 is the prologue, which corresponds to Dao'an's section on the prefatory setting; section 2 is the main body, and covers all except the last chapter of the text; and the epilogue corresponds to the dissemination section. The only discrepancy is that Wŏnhyo differentiates a separate section 3 in his treatment, which is the last "Dhāraṇī" chapter of the *Vajrasamādhi.* Thus, in its overall format, Wŏnhyo's *Exposition* is deeply beholden to commentarial schemata developed within the East Asian Buddhist tradition.[90]

Given the immense gulfs in religious and cultural understanding that needed to be bridged, it is no surprise how complex and prolix East Asian Buddhist commentary becomes. Sinitic Buddhist exegetes learned to gloss most every term of significance in the text. Wŏnhyo's *Exposition* is as long as it is because he takes such pains to gloss virtually all crucial passages and important terms appearing in the scripture. Let me take as but one example Wŏnhyo's exegesis of a single sentence in chapter 3 of the scripture: **"The prajñā that produces nothing does not abide anywhere and is not absent any-**

where" (p. 628c). Wŏnhyo glosses virtually every term of consequence in his exegesis:

> "**Anywhere**" means in all loci, whether absolute or conventional, active or still, and so forth. "**Does not abide**" means that it is unascertainable in any of these [loci]. "**Not absent**" means that there is nothing it does not ascertain in any of these [loci]. The reason this is the case is because, in all these loci, it is not so and yet not not-so. (p. 629a)

In this encounter between sūtra and commentator, the scripture may set the agenda, but the commentary controls the discussion; the relationship between the two is utterly symbiotic and interdependent. As Wŏnhyo's biography tells us, in the case of the *Vajrasamādhi,* in fact, the history of the scripture's "rediscovery" in Silla is so intertwined with Wŏnhyo's summons to write its exegesis that we can almost presume that there would have been no scripture if there had been no commentary.

Exegetical Mappings

But there is another level of complexity to East Asian Buddhist commentaries that makes them even more impenetrable to the reader: traditional commentators typically superimpose over the text of the scripture itself a hermeneutical superstructure, called a "segmental analysis" *(kepan),* that seeks to tie each section of the scripture into a coherent interpretive whole. This coherency is established not only by highlighting patterns apparent in the text, but also by explaining away any obvious inconsistencies or lacunae.[91] A commentator's hermeneutical strategy can sometimes be so heavy-handed that it sometimes seems almost to bludgeon the text into submission to his overall vision, at times seemingly even displacing the scripture itself.

Even a casual perusal of Wŏnhyo's *Exposition* will reveal how complex this hermeneutical superstructure can become in East Asian commentaries. The exegete is constantly placing markers along the way to help orient the reader as to where he or she is in the commentary by demonstrating how each specific passage connects to the entirety of the text—but, in most cases, with nary a reference to such words as "section," "part," "division," or the like. In Wŏnhyo's opening exegesis to chapter 7 of the sūtra, for example (p. 659b), he tells us that this chapter is the sixth division of the Sequential Elucidation of Contemplation Practice, which is the principal theme of the scripture in Wŏnhyo's treatment. That chapter, he tells us, is divided into two [sections], of which the first [section] is in two [subsections], the first [subsection] in four [parts], the first [part] in two [subparts], and so on, seemingly ad infinitum. In the *Exposition,* the sections, parts, divisions, segments, and so forth, that Wŏnhyo outlines eventually lead down to some twelve levels of subheading, until even a small portion of text becomes thoroughly enmeshed in the broader interpretation that Wŏnhyo establishes for the sūtra. By embedding sections within parts, divisions, and segments, as if the commentary were an elaborate set of nested boxes, Buddhist commentaries epitomize the ubiquitous tendency toward categorization that is common to all scholastic traditions.[92]

It is a daunting task indeed for a reader to make his or her way through such a thicket of interpretation, and the East Asians have long struggled with how best to render this elaborate hermeneutical superstructure in a way that will be accessible to the reader. One of the most common traditional devices was to create a "segmentation of the text" *(kwamun),* an elaborate schematic diagram of the divisions of the commentary, essentially mapping out the text so that the narrative is rendered in visual space. This sort of hermeneutical device serves almost as a form of "scriptural cartography,"[93] which is an entirely legitimate, and time-honored, strategy in the East Asian commentarial tradition. Charts can serve as useful tools for visualizing the intricate structure of the commentary. (One can almost imagine the author of a commentary creating such a chart for himself to help him keep track of where he is in his own exegesis; unfortunately, no examples of such "autocartographies" have ever surfaced.) Alexander Mayer has suggested to the contrary that the use of charts most probably derives from a homiletic context, in which charts served as visual guides used during oral interpretations of sūtras.[94] One can only marvel at the massive scriptural cartographies that the contemporary scholars Satō Shigeki, Ŭn Chŏnghŭi, and Song Chinhyŏn have constructed for Wŏnhyo's *Exposition.*[95] These diagrams can themselves become so colossal in size that they become as daunting to peruse as the narrative itself. I do not intend in any way to disparage these attempts to map out the *Exposition,* which after all follow an entirely legitimate and time-honored strategy in East Asia. But because cartographies are documents that stand separate from the commentary itself, I find them less effective in *reading* the commentary, especially in translation. When actually reading the commentary, we need instead some way of superimposing the hermeneutical structure over the text of the commentary itself, so that readers can see at a glance where they are in the multiple levels of exegesis. Alexander Mayer has devised a novel set of symbols to indicate the different levels of heading within the exegesis, but following his system requires learning his elaborate codes.[96] I have taken a rather different tack in this translation, using an admittedly prosaic outline format to keep track of the exegesis, and arbitrarily supplying designations for the different portions of the text: titling them sections, subsections, parts, divisions, and so forth. (See Table 2 below for my schema; and for a comprehensive schematic outline of all the sections of the *Exposition,* see the Appendix.)

This style of exegesis actually has a long pedigree in Western Buddhist Studies, where outline format has been frequently applied in translations.[97] To ensure that Wŏnhyo's own statement of his hermeneutical structure is

TABLE 2
Outline and Internal Subheading Designations for Wŏnhyo's *Exposition of the Vajrasamādhi-Sūtra*

PART ONE: A STATEMENT OF ITS MAIN IDEA
PART TWO: AN ANALYSIS OF THE THEMES OF THE SŪTRA
PART THREE: AN EXPLANATION OF THE TITLE
PART FOUR: AN EXEGESIS OF THE TEXT
- Section One: Prologue
- Section Two: Main Body
  - First Division of Contemplation Practice: Rejecting All Characteristics of Sense-Objects in Order to Reveal the Signless Contemplation
  - Second Division of Contemplation Practice: Extinguishing the Mind Subject to Production in Order to Explain the Practice of Nonproduction
  - Third Division of Contemplation Practice: The Inspiration of Original Enlightenment
  - Fourth Division of Contemplation Practice: Abandoning the Spurious to Access Reality
  - Fifth Division of Contemplation Practice: Sanctified Practices Emerge from the Voidness of the True Nature
  - Sixth Division of Contemplation Practice: Immeasurable Dharmas Access the Tathāgatagarbha
- Section Three (A): Dhāraṇī (Codes) and Section Three (B): Dissemination

Internal Subheadings [outline and designation as used in translation]:

1. I [section]
2. I.A [subsection]
3. I.A.1 [part]
4. I.A.1.a [subpart]
5. I.A.1.a.i [division]
6. I.A.1.a.i.a [subdivision]
7. I.A.1.a.i.a.1 [segment]
8. I.A.1.a.i.a.1.a [subsegment]
9. I.A.1.a.i.a.1.a.i [portion]
10. I.A.1.a.i.a.1.a.i.a [subportion]
11. I.A.1.a.i.a.1.a.i.a.1 [level]
12. I.A.1.a.i.a.1.a.i.a.1.a [sublevel]

not obscured when reading the English version, I have been careful always to place my outline structure in brackets in the translation so that the reader will know this is my interpolation, not Wŏnhyo's. What such an outline format lacks in elegance, I hope it gains in utility.

The Political Role of Exegesis

As the ultimate arbiter of canonicity in Sinitic Buddhist countries, the state inevitably came to insert itself into the relationship between sūtra and commentary. As I have discussed above, one of the roles of a commentary was to circumscribe the range of possible meanings of a text, to filter out possible extraneous messages and to focus the reader on issues that the commentator—and, by extension, his benefactors—believed to be most worthy of attention.[98] In East Asia, where the state officially sanctioned a text by such mechanisms as including the scripture on the list of "canonical" materials, such circumscription of meaning often meant trying to ensure that the reader understood the text the way the state wanted it understood. Throughout the tale surrounding the appearance of the *Vajrasamādhi-sūtra* in Silla Korea, the state was closely involved in the recovery, editing, interpretation, and dissemination of the scripture. In the *Song Gaoseng zhuan* hagiography of Wŏnhyo's life, we are told that the envoy of the Silla court abandoned his quest to consult with Tang medical experts and returned straight home to Silla with a text—the *Vajrasamādhi*—conferred directly to the Silla Koreans by the Dragon King himself. The royal court ordered the reclusive Taean to place the uncollated folios of the sūtra in their proper order and to redact the text. Finally, the court commanded that Wŏnhyo write a commentary to the newly restored scripture and give a series of public lectures derived from that commentary at Hwangnyongsa. It is also no surprise that the very first act that would accompany the appearance in Silla of a new Buddhist scripture would be the writing of a commentary upon it. Sponsoring the editing and publication of a scripture newly "escorted" to Korea and ensuring that it was disseminated accompanied by a complete commentary by the foremost Silla Buddhist exegete, Wŏnhyo—all these acts would confirm that Silla could participate as an equal in the wider pan-Asiatic Buddhist tradition. Having such a definitive commentary written virtually simultaneously with the *Vajrasamādhi*'s "appearance" would also invest the sūtra with an imprimatur of authenticity, a matter of no small concern for a text that turned up under extraordinary, and potentially dubious, circumstances. The very act of commenting upon the terms, passages, sections, and chapters of the scripture invests the root text with meaning and significance. Such exegesis seeks to offer a definitive interpretation of its meaning, which stabilizes the understanding of this new text for the audience. In addition, having such an eminent scholiast as Wŏnhyo engage with the scripture, and in such a public forum, tells the potential audience that the scripture is worthy of attention.

Given the state patronage behind this endeavor, we might expect that the attention the commentator would bring to the text would inevitably reflect the interests of his royal sponsors. Such an act would demonstrate Silla's participation in the wider pan-Asiatic Buddhist exegetical tradition and confirm that its cultural achievements deserved to be considered the equals of their counterparts elsewhere in East Asia. Since the discovery of the *Vajrasamādhi,* the scripture was intimately entwined with the issue of Silla's "cultural self-sufficiency" vis-à-vis China.[99] Buddhist scholiasts, like their Confucian counterparts, were part of the cultural elite in premodern East Asia, and writing commentaries served as a sort of "cultural insignia."[100] The writing of commentaries demanded such a high level of general literacy, doctrinal training, intellectual achievement, and cultural familiarity that it would immediately validate the insights of indigenous Silla culture as being on a par with the meccas of Buddhism in China and India. It is not surprising, then, that as soon as Silla ideology began to coalesce around Buddhism, Silla Buddhist monks like Wŏnhyo would have begun to write commentary. To Wŏnhyo's patrons, then, because respected, literate Buddhists composed commentaries on scriptures, composing commentaries would help make Silla a respected, literate Buddhist country.[101]

This concern with demonstrating Silla's ability to participate in the broader Sinitic tradition of Buddhism must certainly account for the court's active interest in having the newly discovered *Vajrasamādhi* collated and annotated. During Wŏnhyo's lifetime, Silla had embarked on a rapid "Buddhicization" of the empire, especially as a means of unifying the recently conquered territories of the old Koguryŏ and Paekche kingdoms. Silla was the last of the three main kingdoms of ancient Korea to form and, in turn, the last to adopt Sinitic culture, including Buddhism. Its isolated geographical position in the far southeast of the Korean peninsula kept Silla from becoming part of the formal tributary system that governed relations between the Chinese empire and its peripheral regions until the middle of the sixth century. Silla thus did not receive any direct transmission of Buddhism from the Chinese court until 549, almost two centuries after Koguryŏ and Paekche. But Buddhism seems to have been filtering into Silla from Koguryŏ at the local level by the middle of the fifth century, in tandem with important political changes occurring in the kingdom. During that period, Silla was evolving from a tribal confederation into a hereditary monarchy. This process culminated in the creation of a Sinicized state during the reign of King Pŏphŭng (his name means "Flourishing of the Dharma," r. 514–539), who put in place a centralized bureaucracy modeled after Chinese political institutions.

But a unifying ideology was crucial to the successful completion of this process of state formation and, especially, to justify the concentration of power in the monarchy. Some texts of Mahāyāna Buddhism, such as the *Renwang jing* (Book of Benevolent Kings), which figured in the story of the recovery of the *Vajrasamādhi*, and the *Suvarṇaprabhāsottama-sūtra* (*Jin'guangming jing*; Simile of Golden Light Sūtra), provided ideological justification for allegiance to the king, helping to loosen persistent tribal and clan ties. Such political exigencies may have contributed to the decision of the Silla king Pŏphŭng to force the aristocracy to recognize Buddhism as the official state religion. Though the nobility resisted the move, they were eventually won over, according to legend, by the martyrdom of one of their fellow vassals, the grand secretary Ich'adon (d.u.), in 529. Subsequent kings lent vigorous support to the adopted religion, constructing monasteries, sponsoring Buddhist ceremonies, and even becoming monks themselves. Pŏphŭng's successor, Chinhŭng ("Flourishing of Truth," r. 540–575), brought the aristocracy into this politico-religious nexus by forming the *hwarang* (lit. "flower boys"), a military and religious organization of noble youths trained according to Buddhist principles, charging it with responsibility for the moral and military protection of the nation.[102]

The doctrinal teachings that came to be supported in Silla were those that helped to justify at an ideological level a centralized bureaucracy reporting to an autocratic monarch. It was Hwaŏm thinkers, and especially Wŏnhyo's close friend Ŭisang (625–702), who reaped the benefits of such political interests. Hwaŏm's doctrine of "consummate interfusion" *(wŏnyung/yuanrong)*—where, as Ŭisang says, "in one is all and in the many is one; one is all and the many are one"—was well suited to such a system of statecraft.[103] In return for its ideological sanction of the Silla monarchy, Hwaŏm received munificent official support and established a nexus of state-sponsored monasteries throughout the realm. The first of these Hwaŏm monasteries, Pusŏksa, was built in 676, right around the time Wŏnhyo wrote his *Exposition.* Many strands reminiscent of Hwaŏm doctrinal positions are found in the *Vajrasamādhi-sūtra,* which may account at least in part for the court's interest in having Wŏnhyo explicate the text immediately upon its appearance in Silla.

Now fully committed to Buddhism, the Silla state and the Buddhist religion became intricately intertwined, the state supplying generous material donations and extensive political support to the religion, the religion interceding with the powerful deities and bodhisattvas of Buddhism on behalf of the state and its welfare. The drive for peninsular unification only intensified the coalescence of thought and religious practice in Silla around Buddhism. It should come as no surprise, then, that in the years bracketing the 669 unification of the Korean peninsula under the Silla banner, there was a massive efflorescence of Buddhist scholastic studies in Korea, with Wŏnhyo at their very center and commentarial literature as the emblematic genre.

Wŏnhyo's Hermeneutical Strategy of Analysis and Synthesis

In his lengthier works, including most of his commentaries *(so)* and "thematic essentials" *(chongyo),* Wŏnhyo often employs a nascent hermeneutical approach to explicate the text, an approach that was first explained by Pak Chonghong: explications based on "analysis" (*kae;* lit. "to open up" [for analysis]) and "synthesis" (*hap;* lit. "to combine together" [in a synthesis]), which reveal the text's "themes and essentials" *(chongyo).*[104] In analytical mode, Wŏnhyo seeks to unpack for the reader the vast array of teachings and doctrines appearing in a text as a way of illustrating the diversity and originality of Buddhist doctrinal teachings. In synthetic mode, Wŏnhyo seeks to explain how the variant ideas described in a text can actually be viewed as complementing one another. Both of these hermeneutical devices applied together then yield a description of the principal topic and insight of the text: its "themes and essentials."

Wŏnhyo's two largest commentaries both adopt this hermeneutical tool in their interpretive approach. As Wŏnhyo notes in his *Taesŭng kisillon so* (Commentary to the *Awakening of Faith*): "If [the meaning of this treatise] is 'opened up' for analysis *(kae),* then it has as its themes *(chong)* immeasurable, limitless meanings. If these are 'combined together' as a synthesis *(hap),* then it has as its essentials *(yo)* the two aspects and the one mind."[105] In his *Exposition of the Vajrasamādhi-Sūtra,* Wŏnhyo similarly explains: "The themes and essentials *(chongyo)* of this scripture involve both analysis *(kae)* and synthesis *(hap).* Discussed from a synthetic standpoint, the contemplation practice that has but a single taste is its essential. Explained from an analytic standpoint, the ten approaches to dharma *(dharmaparyāya)* are its theme. . . . [But] even opening them up analytically does not add to the one; even bringing them together synthetically does not take away from the ten. Neither increase nor decrease *(anūnatvāpūrantva)* is the [sūtra's] theme and essential" (*KSGN,* p. 604c). Wŏnhyo's hermeneutical approach, then, typically starts with a broad, general perspective on the scripture, gleaned by applying both analytical and synthetic perspectives, culminating in a description of the scripture's essential theme. Only after orienting the reader to the broader themes of the scripture does Wŏnhyo then go on to begin his detailed explication section by section.

The Grand Synthesis of Commentary

Creating a coherent and systematic text out of the often-haphazard format of Mahāyāna sūtras requires considerable exegetical aplomb, if not in fact a total leap of faith. Mahāyāna scriptures, like the sūtra genre as a whole, have a tendency to anthologize. D. T. Suzuki's characterization of the *Laṅkāvatāra-sūtra,* a distant relative of the *Vajrasamādhi,* is apposite in reading our scripture: "The whole *Laṅkāvatāra* is just a collection of notes unsystematically strung together, and, frankly speaking, it is a useless task to attempt to divide them into sections, or chapters *(parivarta),* under some specific titles. Some commentators have tried to create a system in the *Laṅkāvatāra* by making each paragraph somewhat connected in meaning with the preceding as well as the succeeding one, but one can at once detect that there is something quite constrained or far-fetched about the attempt."[106] There are some continuities of interest in the *Vajrasamādhi* that attracted the attention of Wŏnhyo and later commentators. It is also true that the major orientation of the scripture is soteriological, given its stress on the concepts of samādhi, tathāgatagarbha, and original and acquired enlightenment. Rather than the systematic "synthesis" that Wŏnhyo perceives, however, an eclectic "amalgam" or "mélange" may be a more accurate portrayal. In its need for commentarial explanation to bring some order to its message, then, the *Vajrasamādhi-sūtra* is in the very best of company.

Let me explore how a traditional commentator like Wŏnhyo proceeds to create a methodical exposition out of the *Vajrasamādhi*'s rather haphazard presentation. Wŏnhyo first finds obvious evidence of the *Vajrasamādhi*'s grand synthesis of Mahāyāna doctrine in the alternate titles given to the scripture in its epilogue (see *KSGN*, p. 675c): "Since there is nothing it does not refute, [this sūtra] is titled *Vajrasamādhi* [Adamantine Absorption]. Since there is nothing it does not establish, it is titled *Mahāyānasaṃgraha-sūtra* [Compendium of Mahāyāna]. Since there are no concepts or themes that are not subsumed within these two aspects, it is also titled *Anantanirdeśasiddhānta* [Source of Immeasurable Doctrines]" (*KSGN*, p. 604b). The opening portions of Wŏnhyo's "Exegesis of the Text" (*KSGN*, pp. 608c–609b) are an elaborate account of how all the chapters of the scripture work together to present a comprehensive picture of contemplation practice and how, in turn, "these six approaches [of contemplation practice] therewith subsume all the Mahāyāna" (*KSGN*, p. 609b), as I have discussed previously. Wŏnhyo subsequently offers an alternate interpretation of how these six chapters assimilate all of Mahāyāna by showing that they all culminate in the "single taste" of liberation. He then offers various groupings of the six chapters into three parts or two divisions, or again as having but "one taste that is unascertainable," demonstrating that a systematic approach to contemplation is outlined in the sūtra. Ultimately, "there are none of the characteristics of the Mahāyāna dharma that [this sūtra] does not subsume and none of its doctrines that have immeasurable meanings to which it does not gain access" (*KSGN*, p. 604c). Through his commentary, then, Wŏnhyo manages not only to tame the sometimes unruly structure of the sūtra, but also to connect the scripture's implicit message to the entirety of Mahāyāna Buddhism. Each chapter, passage, and ultimately line in the *Vajrasamādhi* is thus shown to have a consistent message that is projected systematically throughout the text—and this message is rendered perfectly compatible with the larger canonical tradition.[107]

By validating the message of a specific sūtra as being consistent with the canonical "word of the Buddha" *(Buddhavacana)*, the commentary thus serves as well to confirm the impeccability of the Buddhist scriptural transmission as a whole—and really of the entirety of the Buddhadharma. This concern with the consistency of the canon is a rather peculiar feature of the East Asian Mahāyāna tradition that has few analogues within Indian Mahāyāna. In discussions on the issue of scriptural authenticity, there seems, in fact, to be evidence *via silentio* that Indian Mahāyānists specifically sought to deny the validity of arguments that appealed to the testimony of history because they knew they would lose such an argument.[108] In their treatments of this matter, they instead made recourse to a more elastic definition of scriptural authenticity in which the "word of the Buddha" need not simply be the actual words spoken by Śākyamuni himself but could instead mean anything based on the dharma that was "well spoken" *(subhāṣita)*. "Well spoken" meant that a statement (a) was significant *(arthopasaṃhita)*, not nonsense; (b) was based on dharma, or reality *(dharmopasaṃhita)*, not illusion; (c) destroys defilements *(kleśahāpaka)*, rather than causing their increase; and (d) illuminates the benefits of nirvāṇa, rather than increasing the faults of saṃsāra.[109] By rejecting the role that the testimony of history could play in determining scriptural authenticity, the Mahāyānists were ipso facto demonstrating their apparent awareness of their own deficiencies regarding history: since they were never going to win the historical argument, they simply deny the validity of history altogether in favor of the doctrinal or philosophical principle that their scriptures are authentic because they conform to "reality" or "the nature of things" *(dharmatā)*.[110] In this wise, Indian Mahāyānists were able to counter Śrāvakayāna attacks on the authenticity of their scriptures and to advocate a more open definition of a Buddhist canon, which required neither consistency nor comprehensiveness.[111]

East Asian Buddhists of the premodern era were not as obsessed as are modern scholars with the historical realities of Buddhist scriptural development, nor did they display much awareness of the living pluralism of the different cultural manifestations of their religion. For the East Asians, Buddhism did not develop historically over centuries, in diverse geographical regions of Asia, before making its way to East Asia, where it blended with indigenous beliefs and practices to form the uniquely "Sinitic" strand of the religion. This interpretation is a peculiarly modern scholarly construct, which has no foundation in traditional views about the religion.[112] East Asians of the premodern age instead viewed Buddhism as a universal religion pristine and pure in its thought, its practice, and its realization. The hermeneutical strategies employed by Wŏnhyo and his East Asian colleagues, including both their adaptation of indigenous commentarial forms and their development of doctrinal taxonomies *(pan'gyo/panjiao)*,[113] sought to demonstrate how the plethora of competing Buddhist texts composing the canon—each claiming to be pristinely Buddhist but seeming at times to be almost diametrically opposed to one another[114]—were all actually part of a coherent strategy within the religion, as if all of Buddhism's variations were in fact cut from whole cloth. Buddhist commentators saw themselves as active participants in this universal transmission of the Buddhadharma going back both spatially to the Buddhist homeland in India and temporally to the time of the Buddha himself. The very act of writing commentary therefore validated the continued vitality of the Buddhist textual transmission, making the insights of the Buddha himself come alive in the present. It is my challenge here as a translator to ensure, in the same way, that Wŏnhyo's insights come alive to contemporary readers in the West. You will be the judge of my efforts, as you read through the translation of Wŏnhyo's *Exposition of the Vajrasamādhi-Sūtra* that follows in Part 2 of this book.

PART 2

Wŏnhyo's *Exposition of the Vajrasamādhi-Sūtra*: An Annotated Translation

Exposition of the *Vajrasmādhi-Sūtra*
(Kŭmgang Sammaegyŏng Non)

By
WŎNHYO,
A Śramaṇa from the Kingdom of Silla

ROLL ONE

There is, in brief, a four-part structure to the explication of this sūtra:

First [Part One]: A statement of its main idea;
Next [Part Two]: An analysis of the themes of the sūtra;
[Part] Three: An explanation of the title;
[Part] Four: An exegesis of the meaning of the text.

Part One: A Statement of Its Main Idea

Now, the fountainhead of the one mind *(ekacitta)*, which is distinct from existence *(bhava)* and nonexistence *(abhava)*, is independently pure. The sea of the three voidnesses *(trayaḥ śūnyatāḥ)*,[1] which subsumes absolute *(paramārtha)* and conventional *(saṃvṛti)*, is profoundly calm. Profoundly calm, it subsumes dualities and yet is not unitary. Independently pure, it is far from the extremes and yet is not located at the middle. Because it is not located at the middle and yet is far from the extremes, dharmas that are nonexistent do not linger in nonexistence and characteristics *(lakṣaṇa)* that are not-nonexistent do not linger in existence. Because it is not unitary and yet subsumes dualities, those phenomena that are not absolute need not be conventional and those principles that are not conventional need not be absolute. Because it subsumes dualities and yet is not unitary, there are none of its absolute or conventional qualities that are not established and none of its tainted or pure characteristics that are not furnished therein. Because it is far from the extremes and yet is not located at the middle, there are none of the existent or nonexistent dharmas that are inactive and none of its affirmative or negative *(sibi)* concepts with which it is not equipped. Accordingly, though refuting nothing, there is nothing not refuted and, though establishing nothing, there is nothing not established. This alone can be called the ultimate principle that is free from principles and the great suchness that is not-such. This is said to be the main idea of this sūtra.[2]

Thanks to this great suchness that is not-such, the words preached [in this sūtra] sublimely accord with the middle of the circle *(hwanjung)* [of the heavens].[3] Due to its ultimate principle that is free from principles, its referents that have to be interpreted leap outside the square [of the earth]. Since there is nothing it does not refute, [this sūtra] is titled *Vajrasamādhi* [Adamantine Absorption]. Since there is nothing it does not establish, it is titled *Mahāyānasaṃgraha-sūtra* [Compendium of Mahāyāna]. Since there are no concepts or themes that are not subsumed within these two aspects, it is also titled *Anantanirdeśasiddhānta* [Source of Immeasurable Doctrines].[4] Now, only one of these titles has been adopted to place at the head [of the sūtra] **[604c]** and, accordingly, it is titled the *Vajrasamādhi-sūtra.*

Part Two: An Analysis of the Themes of the Sūtra

The themes and essentials of this scripture involve both analysis *(kae)* and a synthesis *(hap)*.[5] Discussed from a synthetic standpoint [I], the contemplation practice that has but a single taste is its essential.[6] Explained from an analytic standpoint [II], the ten approaches to dharma *(dharmaparyāya)* are its theme.

[I. Synthesis:] "Contemplation practice:" "Contemplation" involves a spatial dimension,[7] which pervades both transcendent experience [lit. phenomenal objects] and wisdom; "practice" involves a temporal perspective, which extends to both cause and fruition. "Fruition" means that the five dharmas[8] are consummately complete; "cause" means the six practices are fully mastered.[9] "Wisdom" refers to the two enlightenments: original and acquired. "Transcendent experience" refers to the disappearance in tandem of both absolute and conventional. These disappear in tandem and yet neither is extinguished; these two are both enlightenment and yet both are unproduced *(anutpāda)*. These practices that are unproduced arcanely intuit signlessness *(ānimitta)*. The signless dharmas correspondingly become the original inspiration. Since this inspiration is the original inspiration and yet is unascertainable *(anupalabdhi)*, it does not waver from the edge of reality *(bhūtakoṭi)*. Since this edge is the edge of reality and yet is devoid of any nature of its own, that authentic edge is also void. All the buddhas, the tathāgatas, repose therein and all the bodhisattvas accordingly access it; thus, reference is made to accessing the tathāgatagarbha. These are the main ideas of each of the six chapters [of the main body of this scripture].[10]

In the approach to contemplation [outlined in this scripture], six practices are established, from the initial resolute faith *(adhimukti)* through virtual enlightenment *(tŭnggak)*. When the six practices are completed, the ninth consciousness in turn appears. The manifestation of this immaculate consciousness *(amalavijñāna)* is the pure dharma-realm *(dharmadhātu)*; [its manifestation] then transmutes the remaining eight consciousnesses into the four wisdoms.[11] Once these five dharmas are perfected, one is then furnished with the three bodies *(trikāya)*.[12] In this wise, cause and fruition are not separate from phenomenal objects and wisdom. Since phenomenal objects and wisdom are nondual, there is only this one taste. Thus, the contemplation practice that has but a single taste is considered to be the theme of this sūtra. For this reason, there are none of the characteristics of the Mahāyāna dharma that [this sūtra] does not subsume and none of its doctrines that have immeasurable meanings to which it does not gain access. Wouldn't this mean that its titles are not frivolously given?

The synthetic treatment of the contemplation that has but a single [taste] has been stated succinctly as above.

[II. Analytical standpoint:] From an analytical standpoint, the themes [of this scripture] can be explained via ten approaches—that is to say, from an approach based on monads **[605a]** up through an approach based on decads.

What is the approach based on monads? Within the one mind, one thought stirs, and, by conforming to the one reality, one cultivates the one practice, gains access to the one vehicle, abides in the one path, makes use of the one enlightenment,[13] and awakens to the one taste.

What is the approach based on dyads? Not lingering on either of the two shores [of saṃsāra or nirvāṇa], one therewith releases the two assemblies [of ordinary people *(pṛthagjana)* and disciples (śrāvaka)]. Not grasping at the two kinds of selfhood,[14] one therewith leaves behind the two extremes.[15] Penetrating to the twofold voidness [of person and dharmas], one does not fall into the two vehicles [of śrāvakas and pratyekabuddhas]. Fusing together the two truths [absolute and conventional], one does not turn back from the two accesses.[16]

The approach based on triads means that, taking refuge oneself with the three buddhas,[17] one receives the three moral codes,[18] conforms to the three great truths,[19] and gains the three liberations,[20] the three levels of virtual enlightenment,[21] and the three bodies of sublime enlightenment *(myogak)*.[22] One accesses the three groups of voidness[23] and annihilates the minds associated with the three states of existence.[24]

The approach based on tetrads means that one cultivates the four right efforts *(catvāri prahāṇāni)*[25] and accesses the four bases of supranormal powers *(catvāra ṛddhipādāḥ)*.[26] [Through] the power of the four great conditions,[27] the four postures[28] are constantly sharpened. One transcends the four absorptions *(catvāri dhyānāni)*[29] and leaves far behind the four types of denigration.[30] The four wisdoms flow out from the stage of the four vast [wisdoms].[31]

The approach based on pentads means that, with the production of the five skandhas,[32] one comes to be endowed with fifty evils.[33] For this reason, by planting the five moral faculties *(pañcendriyāṇi)*,[34] one develops the five powers *(pañcabalāni)*,[35] immerses oneself in the sea of the five voidnesses,[36] topples the five ranked levels,[37] gains the purity of the five dharmas,[38] ferries across the beings in the five destinies,[39] and so on.

What are the approaches based on hextads, heptads, octads, enneads, and so forth? Perfecting the cultivation of the six perfections *(ṣaṭ parmitāḥ)*,[40] one forever abandons the six sense faculties *(ṣaḍāyatanāni)*.[41] Practicing the seven aspects of enlightenment *(saptabodhyaṅgāni)*,[42] one annihilates the sevenfold object matrix.[43] "Its sea of the eight consciousness is limpid and the flow of its ninth consciousness is pure."[44] From the ten faiths[45] up to and through the ten bhūmis,[46] the hundreds of practices are completely accomplished and the myriads of meritorious qualities are consummately fulfilled. In this wise, all of these approaches are the themes of this sūtra. They all appear in the text of the sūtra and will be explained at the appropriate passage in the text.

Nevertheless, these latter nine approaches are all included in the approach based on monads, and the approach based on monads contains all nine; none is distinct from the contemplation of the single [taste]. Therefore, even opening them up analytically does not add to the one [taste]; even bringing them together synthetically does not take away from the ten. Neither increase nor decrease *(anūnatvāpūrantva)* is the [sūtra's] theme and essential.

Part Three: An Explication of the Title

This sūtra has three different titles: one, *Mahāyānasaṃgraha-sūtra* (Compendium of Mahāyāna); two, *Vajrasamādhi;* three, **[605b]** *Anantanirdeśasiddhānta* (Source of Immeasurable Doctrines). The first and last titles will be explained in the next part [4].[47] Here, however, I will first explain the middle title, because only this name appears at the head of the text. This [compound vajrasamādhi] has two [elements to explain]:

initially [I], an explication of *vajra;*
subsequently [II], an explication of samādhi.

The first [section on *vajra*] is also in two [subsections]:

initially [I.A], the connotations [of the word *vajra*];
subsequently [I.B], an analysis [of the compound vajrasamādhi].

[I.A. Connotations of the word *vajra*:][48] The word *vajra* is a term that is used metaphorically: solidity is its essence; "to string together" is its quality. Vajrasamādhi also should be understood to have these two [aspects]: the edge of reality is its essence; its efficacy is to string together. "The edge of reality is its essence" means that it realizes the principle and probes the fountainhead [of the mind]. As a later passage says, "**[It] realizes the meditative absorption [that knows] the true reality of dharmas**" (*KSGN*, p. 608b).[49] "Its efficacy is to string together" has these two senses: first, it shatters all doubts; second, it strings together all concentrations. "It shatters all doubts" means that it provides explanations that resolve doubts. As a later passage says, "**[It] is certain to excise doubts and regrets**" (p. 608b).[50] "It strings together all concentrations" means that this concentration can catalyze the functioning of all other samādhis in the same way that stringing together precious gems can make them functional [as jewelry, etc.]. As the *Dapin jing* (Multitudinous Chapters Sūtra; viz. *Pañcaviṃśatisāhasrikāprajñāpāramitā-sūtra, Perfection of Wisdom in Twenty-Five Thousand Lines*) says, "Why is it called vajrasamādhi? [Because] by abiding in this samādhi, one can shatter all samādhis."[51] Its commentary says in explanation,

> "Vajrasamādhi": Just as there is nothing that adamant *(vajra)* cannot bore through, so too is it with this samādhi: among all dharmas, there are none that it does not penetrate. It can catalyze the functioning of all other samādhis in the same way that only *vajra* can bore through amber, cornelian, and beryl.[52]

Nota Bene: This sūtra says, "... shatter all samādhis." "Shatter" means "string together," as in the commentary, where it says "string together" in explanation of the sūtra's [use of the word] "shatter." [The vajrasamādhi] penetrates to the fact that all samādhis are devoid of own-nature and frees those samādhis from any sense of being ends in themselves. This is because [the vajrasamādhi] is free from impediments *(apratighātitā)* and thus is autonomous *(aiśvarya)*. The meaning of the title should be understood in this manner.

Next [I.B], the analysis [of the compound vajrasamādhi] has two [parts].

Initially [I.B.1], an examination of samādhi and prajñā.

Question: Vajraprajñā and vajrasamādhi are both called *vajra;* what is the distinction between them?[53] Explanation: [1] the former is prajñā; the latter is samādhi. **[605c]** This is the distinction. [2] Moreover, vajraprajñā conflates cause and fruition; vajrasamādhi is positioned at the fruition-ground *(vipākabhūmi)*.[54] [3] Moreover, *vajra* as prajñā has three different aspects: [a] its substance is firm; [b] its functioning is efficacious; [c] its appearance is both wide in girth and sharp at its edge. *Vajra* as samādhi is concerned only with [the two aspects of] firmness and efficaciousness. These are the distinctions.

Next [I.B.2], we distinguish [three] related concentrations: (1) vajrasamādhi [adamantine absorption], (2) *vajracakrasamādhi* [adamantine-wheel concentration], (3) *vajropamasamādhi* [adamant-like concentration]. The *Multitudinous Chapters Sūtra [Pañcaviṃśatisāhasrikāprajñāpāramitā-sūtra]* says, "What is *vajracakrasamādhi?* Abiding in this samādhi, one is able to keep hold of all classes of samādhi. What is *vajropamasamādhi?* Poised in this samādhi, one can string together all dharmas without seeing that any such stringing together has occurred."[55] Its commentary explains:

> Question: How is it that these three types of samādhi are all called vajra[samādhis]? Response: The first is called vajra[samādhi]; the middle is called *vajracakra[samādhi];* the last is called *vajropama-[samādhi]. "Vajropamasamādhi,"* the Buddha said, "can string together all dharmas without perceiving that any such stringing together has occurred."[56] Vajrasamādhi can penetrate all samādhis. *Vajracakrasamādhi* can enable its holder to take charge of all samādhis. These are the meanings as they have been expressed personally by all the buddhas.

That commentator explains:

> *Vajropamasamādhi.* This [samādhi] can destroy all defilements *(kleśa)* and fetters *(saṃyojana)* without anything remaining. It is just like Śakro Devāṇām Indraḥ, who annihilated the armies of the asuras while grasping a *vajra* [thunderbolt] in his hand.[57] Similarly, this [samādhi] is the final thought-moment *(citta)* of the [unenlightened] trainee *(śaikṣa).*[58] Following that thought-moment, he next gains one of three kinds of bodhi:[59] either śrāvaka or pratyekabuddha [bodhi] or the supreme bodhi of the buddhas.[60]
>
> "Vajrasamādhi." This [samādhi] can shatter all dharmas[61] and [thereby allow students] to access the nirvāṇa that is without remainder *(anupadiśeṣanirvāṇa),* where they will never again be subject to rebirth. It is just like real *vajra,* which can shatter all mountains, obliterating them completely without remainder.
>
> *Vajracakra[samādhi].* This [samādhi] can vanquish all the buddhadharmas,[62] without any obstructions or impediments.[63]

Explanation: In this passage, "vanquish all the buddhadharmas" is like the army-"wheel" *(cakraratna)*[64] of a cakravartin [wheel-turning emperor], **[606a]** which can conquer all kings until there are none who have not been vanquished. For this reason *[vajracakrasamādhi]* is different from the two previous types of vajra[samādhis].

How do the two previous types [viz. *vajropamasamādhi* and vajrasamādhi] differ from one another? There are five differences.

1. The difference in their analogies. *Vajropama[samādhi]* vanquishes the

armies [of the asuras], while vajra[samādhi] obliterates the mountains [of fetters].[65]

2. The difference in the dharmas [they counteract]. The former *[vajropamasamādhi]* shatters defilements; the latter [vajrasamādhi] shatters all dharmas.[66]
3. The difference in their statuses. The former *[vajropamasamādhi]* is positioned at the training stage *(śaikṣamārga);* the latter [vajrasamādhi] is positioned at the stage of adepts *(aśaikṣamārga).*
4. The difference in their names. The former type is called "adamant-like" *(yŏ kumgang; vajropama)*[67] samādhi, while elsewhere it is named "diamond-simile" *(kŭmgang yu; vajropama)*[68] samādhi. The latter is called simply vajrasamādhi; it does not require [any such suffix as] "like" or "simile." The reason for [this difference in the names is] to elucidate the fact that there is a distinction between the concentrations [associated with] the causal ground [viz. *vajropamasamādhi*] and the fruition ground [viz. vajrasamādhi]. Cause involves efficacy *(ābhoga);* fruition does not involve efficacy *(anābhoga).* [This sequence is expressed in the phrase] "Reducing it and reducing it again, one therewith reaches the unconditioned."[69] *Vajropamasamādhi* has only slight resemblance [to vajrasamādhi]:[70] it merely shatters defilements; it does not shatter all other dharmas. The *vajra* [in vajrasamādhi] suggests that its efficacy is identical to that of adamant: that is, there are no material things that it is unable to bore into and shatter. You should know that the functioning of this [vajra]samādhi is just the same, for there are no dharmas that it does not shatter.
5. The differences in their instruction. There is a vajrasamādhi [which is the equivalent of *vajropamasamādhi*] positioned on the *śaikṣamārga,* as is discussed in the *[Jin'gang sanmei benxing qingjing] buzeng bujian jing* [Neither Increase Nor Decrease Sūtra],[71] as well as a vajrasamādhi located on the *aśaikṣamārga,* which is explained here in this sūtra. Now, in this sūtra, the samādhi that the Buddha accesses shatters all dharmas so that they all become unascertainable *(anupalabdhi).* For this reason, it is called vajrasamādhi. In the six kinds of analysis [of nominal compounds in Sanskrit grammar, the first type of vajrasamādhi mentioned above] is analyzed as a *karmadhārayasamāsa* [appositional determinative compound]. Those names that include a simile [such as *vajropamasamādhi*] are analyzed as an *avyayībhāvasamāsa* [indeclinable compound]. As far as the title of the sūtra is concerned [i.e., the second type of vajrasamādhi mentioned above], it should be analyzed as a *tatpuruṣasamāsa* [dependent compound], because "samādhi" is the primary [element, and *vajra* is the dependent element].[72]

Next, the second [section, II], the explication of the term samādhi, is in two [subsections]:

initially [II.A], the explication [of the meaning of samādhi]; subsequently [II.B], an overview [of different types of concentrations].

[II.A, explication of the meaning of samādhi:] An ancient master said, "There [in India], it is called 'samādhi'; here [in China], it is called 'correct consideration.' "[73] The following passages will be given in explanation of this statement. **[606b]**

It is said that, when one is absorbed in a state of concentration, there is meticulous and correct consideration and examination of the sense-spheres; hence, it is called "correct consideration." As the *Yogācāra[bhūmi-śāstra]* says, " 'Samādhi' means that there is meticulous investigation and one-pointedness of mind *(cittaikāgratā)* with regard to the sense-spheres."[74]

Question: Concentration necessitates tranquillity *(praśabdhi)*, and tranquillity entails one-pointedness; so how can you say that meticulous examination occurs? The functioning of investigation necessitates thought and imagination *(vitarkavicāra)*; so how can you say that concentration involves investigation?

Answer: If you claim that guarding one-pointedness is what is meant by concentration, then abiding in lethargy and torpor *(styānamiddha)* would perforce be concentration. If correct investigation entails thought and imagination, then investigation conducted via perverted wisdom *(kuprajñā)* must not involve thought and imagination. You should know that investigation is of two types: if it refers to [a faculty that] involves both perverse and correct mental and verbal discrimination *(vikalpa)*, then it entails both thought and imagination, and thus is just discrimination. But if correct investigation refers to [a faculty that] meticulously perceives the sense-spheres, then it is in fact the functioning of concentration and does not entail thought or imagination. Concentration, [in contrast,] subsumes both discrimination and nondiscrimination; hence, it meticulously analyzes that thought and imagination.

Furthermore, one-pointedness is also of two types. If a person is one-pointed while being lethargic, deluded, dull, and dark, and one is not able to investigate meticulously, then this is simply lethargy and torpor. But if one is one-pointed while being neither torporific nor distracted, and one investigates meticulously, then this is called concentration. For this reason, investigation differs from lethargy and torpor. Hence, you should know that one should not judge the difference between concentration and distraction based on the distinction between one-pointedness and fluctuation of thought. Why is this? Because, although quick-witted eloquence [of a bodhisattva in deep samādhi] might involve rapid fluctuations of thought, it would still be concentration; although a dull mind might settle for long periods on one object, this would still be distraction. Now, this vajrasamādhi is said to entail correct investigation because it is free from being either correct or incorrect and involves neither consideration nor nonconsideration.

It is instead to be differentiated from discrimination and perverted thoughts, but it is also not the same as empty space or aphasia *(acittaka)*. Therefore, "correct consideration" is the name that we reluctantly apply to it. The term "samādhi" can be explicated briefly in this manner.

Next [II.B], an overview of different [types of concentration] has two [parts]:

initially [II.B.1], **[606c]** distinguishing the different designations [of concentration];
subsequently [II.B.2], an overview of their general categories.

[II.B.1, distinguishing the different designations of concentration:[75]] The names for concentration are not all the same. There are, in brief, eight types.

1. *Samāhita*. This is translated as "equanimous control" *(tŭngin)*. It is called "equanimous" because it leaves far behind the extremes of lethargy *(styāna)* and restlessness *(auddhatya)*. It is called "control" because it controls the activation of all the meritorious qualities, such as the spiritual powers *(abhijñā)*, and so forth. Alternatively, equanimous control derives from the absence of remorse *(kaukṛtya)*, from bliss *(ānanda)*, and from ease *(sukha)*; for this reason, it is called "equanimous control." This is why it is different from the concentrations of the desire realm *(kāmāvacara)*.[76]
2. Samādhi. This [is translated as] "equanimous retention" *(tŭngji)*. The meanings of "equanimous" are the same as explained above. It is called "equanimous retention" because it can regulate the mind and keep it from becoming frenzied or distracted. Alternatively, it is called "equanimous retention" because it balances concentration (samādhi) and wisdom (prajñā) and keeps them conjoined.[77] The antiquated transcription *samaje* (samādhi) is also "equanimous retention."
3. *Samāpatti*. This is translated as "equanimous arrival" *(tŭngji)*. Since one is able to arrive at an exalted stage through equanimous retention, this is called "equanimous arrival."[78]
4. Dhyāna. This is translated as "tranquil thought" *(chŏngnyŏ)* because it cogitates calmly or, alternatively, because it tranquilizes distracted thoughts. The antiquated transcriptions *sŏnna* or *chiana* [Prakrit: *jhāna*] are simply dialectical variants and are the equivalent of "tranquil thought."[79]
5. *Samatha*. This is translated as "stopping" *(chi)*. Because it makes the mind "stop" on an object, it is called "stopping."[80]
6. One-pointedness of mind *(sim ilgyŏngsŏng; cittaikāgratā)*. It is called "one-pointedness of mind" because its nature is to make the mind stay focused exclusively on one object. The antiquated translation "one mind" *(ilsim; ekacittaka)* was an abbreviation of this.

7. Concentration (*chŏng;* translating samādhi or dhyāna). It is called "concentration" because it meticulously "concentrates" on an object.
8. Correct consideration *(chŏngsa; samyagupanidhyāna).* This meaning has been explained above (p. 606b).

Some teachers advocate that the transcriptions *sammae* (samādhi) and *sammaje* (samādhi) are merely "equanimous retention" (samādhi); they are not different terms. This explanation is incorrect. Why is this? Among the ten kinds of concentration found in the *Golden Drum Sūtra* [viz. *Suvarṇa-prabhāsottama-sūtra*], those belonging to the first three bhūmis are called *sammaje,* while those of the latter seven bhūmis are called *sammae.* If it were the case that both these terms were identical to "equanimous retention," then what would be the point of giving them different names and explaining differently the former and latter sets?[81]

What other evidence is there for assuming that these two transcriptions are different? **[607a]** If the differences were caused by dialectical variations, then both names would not have been in use in a single locale [where this scripture was composed]. If the former and the latter [transcriptions] are simply different equivalencies for the same term [i.e., samādhi], then a single text should not contain both these terms. It is like *sammaje* and *sammaji,* which are simply different transcriptions for the same term [samādhi] and are distinguished because they appear in earlier and later strata of texts; hence, it should be patently obvious that they are the same. But when the transcription *sammae* appears in the same text together with *sammaje,* what justification is there for assuming that they are identical? For this reason, you should know [that the transcriptions *sammaje* and *sammae* should be distinguished] according to the explanation above.

The second [part, II.B.2], an overview of the general categories [of concentration], can be grouped into four general categories.[82]

1. Concentration and equanimous retention. These two terms have the widest import. They include [dharmas] both associated with and dissociated from the outflows *(āsravānāsravadharmāḥ)* as well as the three realms of existence *(traidhātuka)* and are present in distracted states of mind *(vikṣipta-citta)* associated with the desire-realm.[83] This is because samādhi, also called concentration, is included among the five constituents of the mental concomitants of restricted range *(viniyatāś caitasikā dharmāḥ),* which is the [second] of the six divisions of mental concomitants *(caitta).*[84]
2. One-pointedness of mind and samādhi *(sammae).* These two terms are of the next widest import. Although they are pervasive throughout the desire-realm, they are not invariably subsumed by all distracted states of mind. This is because the one-pointedness of mind implicit in either the *pratyutpannasamādhi* [constantly walking samādhi][85] or the nine types of mental abidings *(cittasthiti)* associated with the desire-

realm *(kāmapratisaṃyukta)*[86] is also included in the preparatory mental states *(prayogacitta)* of the desire-realm.[87]

3. *Samāhita* and tranquil thought. These two terms are of narrower import because they are not included among the mental states associated with the desire-realm and because they are nurtured only by tranquillity *(praśabdhi)*.[88]
4. *Samāpatti* and *śamatha*. These two are of the narrowest import and are only distinguishable in the state of concentration itself. This is because *śamatha* does not include the one-pointedness of mind that is associated with the four types of wise practice *(sajong hyehaeng)*;[89] and *samāpatti* is not included among the three samādhis—of voidness *(śūnyatā)*, signlessness *(ānimitta)*, and wishlessness *(apraṇihita)*.[90]

The range of import of these eight terms may be narrated roughly in this manner.

Part Three, An Explication of the Title, is completed.

Part Four: An Exegesis of the Text

VAJRASAMĀDHI-SŪTRA, CHAPTER ONE: PROLOGUE

From here onward is
Part Four: **An Exegesis of the Text and an Explication of Its Meaning**
It is in three sections:

Section One [607b] is the prologue.
Section Two includes the six chapters including and following chapter 2 [viz. chapters 2 through 7]; this is the main body, [the sequential elucidation of contemplation practice].
Section Three (A) is the "Dhāraṇī [Codes]" chapter. The two pages of additional text [in the epilogue] starting with the words "At that time the Tathāgata addressed the congregation, saying" (p. 675a) are the dissemination **Section Three (B).**[91]

Section One: Prologue

The prologue section includes two types of prologues:

[I] generic [prologue];
[II] specific [prologue].

Thus have I heard at one time.[92] The Buddha was dwelling in the great city of King's House (Rājagṛha), on Mount Gṛdhrakūṭa [Vulture Peak],

> together with a great assembly of ten thousand bhikṣus [ordained mendicants], all of whom had attained the arhat path. Their names were Śāriputra, Mahāmaudgalyāyana, Subhūti—there were many arhats such as these. Furthermore, there were two thousand bodhisattva-*mahāsattvas* [adepts intent on enlightenment]. Their names were Haet'al [Liberation; Skt. Vimukti] Bodhisattva, Simwang [Mind King; Skt. Cittarāja] Bodhisattva, Muju [Nonabiding; Skt. Apratiṣṭhita] Bodhisattva, and other bodhisattvas like these. Furthermore, there were eighty thousand elders *(gṛhapati)*. Their names were Elder Pŏmhaeng [Chastity; Skt. Brahmacarya], Elder Taebŏmhaeng [Great Chastity; Mahābrahmacarya], Elder Jyotiṣka [Kor. Suje; Luminary], and other elders like these.[93] Furthermore, there were six hundred million devas, dragons, yakṣas [demons], *gandharvas* [demigod musicians], asuras [titans], *garuḍas* [mythical birds], *kiṅnaras* [half horses/half men], *mahorāgas* [great snakes], humans, and nonhumans *(amanuṣya)*.

In this generic prologue [I], there are six components. The first three clarify that [the sūtra] was conveyed through the personal transmission [of the buddha himself]; the latter three authenticate the instructions of the Great Master. The first three aspects are (1) "thus," (2) "have I heard," (3) "at one time." What are the latter three aspects? They are (1) the instructor [the Buddha], (2) the place and setting [Mount Gṛdhrakūṭa near Rājagṛha], (3) the congregation of followers.[94] The congregation of followers includes these four types: (1) the śrāvaka congregation, (2) the bodhisattva congregation, (3) the congregation of elders [viz. the laity], (4) the congregation of various classes of beings. The details regarding each of these [groups] are as commonly explained.

> At that time, the Lord, surrounded by the great congregation, preached a Mahāyāna sūtra on behalf of all the great congregation, titled *Ilmi chinsil musang musaeng kyŏlchŏng* **[607c]** *silche pon'gangnihaeng* [Practice of the Single Taste, Truth, Signless, Nonproduction, the Decisive Edge of Reality, and the Inspiration of Original Enlightenment]. If one hears this sūtra or retains even one four-line verse of it, that person will then access the stage of the Buddha's knowledge; one will be able to proselyte sentient beings with appropriate expedients and become the great spiritual mentor *(kalyāṇamitra)* of all living things.

From here onward is the second [section, II], the specific prologue. It is in four subsections:

one [II.A], the subsection on the setting [lit. inspiring awe];
two [II.B], the subsection on preaching the sūtra;

three [II.C], the subsection on accessing samādhi;
four [II.D] the subsection on reiterative verses.

The setting subsection [II.A] is as in the sūtra passage "**at that time, the Lord, surrounded by the great congregation.**"

The preaching the sūtra subsection [II.B] starts with the sūtra passage "**preached a Mahāyāna sūtra on behalf of all the great congregation.**" The narrative structure of this sūtra is like that found in the prologue to the *Lotus Sūtra.* As that text states, "At that time, the World Honored One, surrounded by the fourfold congregation, preached a Mahāyāna sūtra titled *The Immeasurable Doctrines.*"[95] In the treatise on that [sūtra],[96] this *[Immeasurable Doctrines] Sūtra*'s name is classified as an alternative title for the *Lotus Sūtra.* The notion here is that [the *Immeasurable Doctrines Sūtra*] was preached earlier and therefore it is named in the prologue section [of the *Lotus Sūtra*]. Now, looking at the narrative structure of this *[Vajrasamādhi-]sūtra,* [these two subsections, II.A and II.B] are the words of this sūtra editor's *(kyongga)* prologue, and we therefore acknowledge that there must have been a separate sūtra preached extensively beforehand. After preaching [that prefatory sūtra, the Buddha then] accessed samādhi, and only after emerging from this samādhi did he then preach the *Vajrasamādhi-sūtra.* After preaching the overall theme of this sūtra, he then explained the title of the sūtra. We thus should understand that this title *Ilmi chinsil* [Practice of the Single Taste, Truth . . .] is the title of the *vaipulyasūtra* [expanded scripture] preached earlier. In this wise, although the principal intent of these two sūtras may be the same, their style is different. The text preached beforehand [the *Single Taste Sūtra*] extensively expounds on approaches to dharma that are intended to benefit that current [audience], while the text preached later [the *Vajrasamādhi-sūtra*] concisely incorporates all these approaches to dharma in order to benefit those in the dharma-ending age. Therefore, the extensive preaching [of the *Single Taste Sūtra*] was done first in order to outline the rationale for this sūtra.

In this subsection on preaching the sūtra **[608a]**, the text is in two [parts]:

initially [II.B.1], a prologue that gives the sūtra's title;
subsequently [II.B.2], praise for the sūtra's efficaciousness.

From "**If one hears**" onward is this second part.

> **After the Buddha had preached this sūtra, he folded his legs into full-lotus position and entered into the adamantine absorption *(vajrasamādhi)*, with his body and mind immovable.**

This is the third subsection [II.C], on accessing samādhi. Initially accessing samādhi before proceeding to preach a sūtra elucidates the fact that only those who have experienced quiescence and quietude will be able to awaken to, and preach, the dharma. Furthermore, it elucidates that the silence of the sages and saints is not mutually exclusive of the sages' and saints' preaching of the dharma, which is performed in conformity with the times.

> At that time there was a bhikṣu named Agada in the congregation, who arose from his seat, joined his palms together, and genuflected in foreign fashion [*hogwe;* with his right knee on the ground]. Wishing to proclaim[97] the meaning of this [sūtra that had just been preached], he recited gāthās:

This is the fourth subsection [II.D], the reiterative verses. In order to elucidate the fact that the principal intent of the *Single Taste Sūtra,* which was preached beforehand, and [the *Vajrasamādhi*], which was preached subsequently, are not discrepant, he therefore versified this preceding expanded sūtra in concise gāthās; through this technique, he was subsequently able to expound that sūtra concisely. The passage is in two [parts]:

initially [II.D.1], a prologue;
subsequently [II.D.2], verses.

The sūtra editor's prologue thus culminates in these concluding verses.

[II.D.1: Prologue:] The name Agada means either "expeller" or "eliminator." It is the name of an herb.[98] Because it can completely cure any kind of illness, it is therefore called "expeller." This bodhisattva is also just the same: he is named after this herb because he can cure all the illnesses—the defilements—of sentient beings.

In the eight stanzas of these verses [II.D.2], there are two subparts:

first [II.D.2.a], the initial seven stanzas [II.D.2.a.i, ii] that versify the preaching of the sūtra;
last [II.D.2.b], one stanza that versifies the access to samādhi.

This first [subpart] is also in two [divisions]:

three quatrains [II.D.2.a.i] that are a succinct clarification;
four verses [II.D.2.a.ii] that are specific elucidations.

1. **That Lord who is filled with great friendliness,**
2. **His wisdom penetrates without obstruction.**
3. **Intending to ferry across sentient beings on a vast scale,**
4. **He has explained the meaning of the one truth,**
5. **All this was accomplished via the path that has a single taste,**

6. Never by means of the Hīnayāna.
7. The meaning, "taste," and place of his sermon,
8. All leave the unreal far behind,
9. They access the stage of wisdom of all the buddhas, **[608b]**
10. That decisive and true edge of reality *(bhūtakoṭi)*.
11. All the audience has transcended the world,
12. There is no one who has not achieved liberation.

These three quatrains that provide a succinct clarification [II.D.2.a.i] involve four notions:

one, the first two lines [ll. 1, 2] praise the efficaciousness of the preacher;
two, one quatrain [ll. 3–6] praises the teachings that are the describer;
three, one quatrain [ll. 7–10] praises the doctrines that are the described.
four, two lines [ll. 11, 12] praise the superlative benefit of these teachings.

In the second [stanza], "the meaning of the one truth" refers to the one mind. Based on the dharma of the one mind, there are two types of approaches. The support for both these approaches is just this one reality; therefore it is called "one truth." "The path that has but a single taste" means that there is only one vehicle. The remainder of the passage is obvious.

13. All the innumerable bodhisattvas,
14. Each ferry across all sentient beings.
15. For the sake of the congregation, they question extensively and profoundly.
16. Learning of the dharmas' characteristic of calm extinction,
17. They access that place of certitude [of attaining enlightenment; *(samyaktva)niyāmāvakrānti*].

From this point onward [II.D.2.a.ii] are specific praises of the questions and the responses. [In this first subdivision, II.D.2.a.ii.a], these five lines [ll. 13–17] praise the breadth and depth of the questions, for they can prompt one to know calm extinction and to access the edge of reality.

18. The Tathāgata, through his knowledge (jñāna) and expedients *(upāya)*,
19. Speaks so that [all beings] will be sure to access reality,
20. All this is in accordance with the one vehicle,
21. There are no extraneous tastes.
22. In the same way that, soaked by a single rain,
23. The multitudes of plants all grow verdantly.
24. [So too], according to their natures, which are each discrete,
25. Soaked by the dharma that has a single taste,
26. All things achieve complete fulfillment,

27. Just as if, soaked by a single rain,
28. All their bodhi sprouts were matured.[99]

This is the second [subdivision, II.D.2.a.ii], praising the superlative inspiration behind the Buddha's response, which is in three [segments], the instruction, simile, and correlation. You should know that these are, in order, four lines [ll. 18–21, viz. the instruction]; two lines [ll. 22, 23, viz. the simile]; and five lines [ll. 24–38, viz. the correlation].

29. Accessing the adamantine taste,
30. He realizes the meditative absorption [that knows] the true reality of dharmas.
31. He is certain to excise doubts and regrets,
32. And to perfect the seal of the one dharma.

This is the second [subpart, II.D.2.b], versifying the access to samādhi. The first half [ll. 29, 30] is a direct versification of the preceding accessing of samādhi. The second half [ll. 31, 32] is, by contrast, a versification of the start of the subsequent dharma preaching. The teaching that is preached subsequently has two **[608c]** superlative abilities: one, "**to excise doubts and regrets**," in the same way that adamant is able to destroy anything; and, two, "**to perfect the seal**" of the one vehicle, in the same way that adamant can never be pulverized. The two lines of this latter half [ll. 31, 32] elucidate these two aspects.

The text of **Section [One], Prologue**, is finished.

Section Two: Main Body, the Sequential Elucidation of Contemplation Practice

The broad outline of the main body [of the *Vajrasamādhi-sūtra*] is in two major [sections]. [Section 2], its first six chapters [chapters 2 through 7 of the sūtra], provides specific elucidations of aspects of contemplation practice. [Section 3], the final "Codes" chapter, completely resolves all remaining doubts.

There are six divisions to section [2] on the Sequential Elucidation [of Contemplation Practice]:

One [First Division]: The "Signless Dharma" chapter clarifies the signless contemplation.

Two [Second Division]: The "Practice of Nonproduction" chapter elucidates the practice of nonproduction.

Three [Third Division]: The "Inspiration[100] of Original Enlightenment" chapter draws on the original [enlightenment] to inspire all things.

Four [Fourth Division]: The "Accessing the Edge of Reality" chapter proceeds from illusion to access reality.

Five [Fifth Division]: The "Voidness of the True Nature" chapter demonstrates that all practices derive from the voidness of the true nature.
Six [Sixth Division]: The "Tathāgatagarbha" chapter elucidates the infinite approaches through which to access the tathāgatagarbha.

All six approaches to contemplation practice are in this wise thoroughly covered. This is possible because the beginningless churning of all deceptive conceptions typically results from nothing more than the affliction of discrimination, which derives from clinging to signs *(lakṣaṇa)*. Now, wishing to reverse this churning in order to return to the fountainhead, one must initially subvert all these signs. For this reason, [the sūtra] first clarifies the contemplation of the signless dharma.

Even though all these signs may have been subverted, however, if one actualizes the mind that performs that contemplation, then that contemplating mind will continue to be produced, and one will not experience original enlightenment. Consequently, one must annihilate all productions of mind. Therefore, the second [approach of contemplation practice] elucidates the practice of nonproduction.

Once one's practice has stopped producing anything, one then experiences original enlightenment. Drawing from this [experience], one transforms living things and prompts them to gain the original inspiration. Hence, this third [approach] clarifies the aspect of the inspiration of original enlightenment.

If, while relying on original enlightenment, one inspires sentient beings, then those sentient beings will be able to leave behind deception and to access reality. Therefore, the fourth [approach] clarifies the access to the edge of reality.

Internal practice is signless and unproduced. External proselytism is the original inspiration's access to reality. In this wise, the two types of benefit [of oneself and others] are replete with myriad spiritual practices, which all derive from the true nature and conform to true voidness. Consequently, the fifth [approach] clarifies the voidness of the true nature.

Relying on this true nature, the myriads of spiritual practices are perfected and one accesses the fountainhead of the tathāgatagarbha, which has but a single taste. Therefore, the sixth [approach] elucidates the tathāgatagarbha.

Since one has returned to the fountainhead of the mind, **[609a]** one then has nothing more that needs to be done. As there is nothing more to do, there is nothing that has been left undone. Hence, it is said that these six approaches [of contemplation practice] therewith subsume all the Mahāyāna.

Furthermore, there is also an alternative interpretation of these six chapters. The first chapter reveals the dharma that is contemplated, dharma referring here to the essence of the tathāgatagarbha of the one mind. The second chapter clarifies the practices that are the agents of contemplation, practices referring here to the nondiscriminative contemplations [that develop during] the six [stages of] practice. The third chapter, the "Inspiration of Original Enlightenment," elucidates the production-and-extinction aspect of the one mind. The fourth chapter, "Accessing the Edge of Reality," elucidates the true-thusness aspect of the one mind. The fifth chapter, "Voidness of the True Nature," negates both absolute and conventional without subverting the two truths. The sixth chapter, "Tathāgatagarbha," subsumes all of these approaches and reveals that they are all of a single taste.

Through these two alternatives, we completely cover the notion that these six approaches subsume all aspects of the Mahāyāna.

Alternatively, these six chapters may be grouped into three approaches. The first two chapters cover the beginning and the end of contemplation. The next two chapters [treat] the fundamentals and derivatives of proselytism. The final two chapters subsume both these causes so that fruition [viz. enlightenment] is achieved. Furthermore, the first two chapters negate signs and return to the origin. The middle two chapters give rise to practices from out of this origin. The final two chapters elucidate both this return and this arising. Accordingly, these two threefold [hermeneutical divisions] completely subsume all the Mahāyāna.

Alternatively, these six chapters may be grouped into only two approaches. The demise of both signs and production are the "Inspiration of Original Enlightenment"; the edge of reality and true voidness are the "Tathāgatagarbha." Furthermore, the preceding approach [from "Signless Dharma" to "Inspiration of Original Enlightenment"] neutralizes falsity and elucidates the cause; the subsequent approach [from "Accessing the Edge of Reality" to "Tathāgatagarbha"] elucidates truth and perfects the fruition. In this wise, both these twofold approaches also completely subsume all the Mahāyāna.

Alternatively, these six chapters involve but a single taste. Why is this? Signs and production are devoid of nature. Original enlightenment is devoid of origin. The edge of reality leaves behind all edges. The true nature is also void. So how is it that one gains the nature of the tathāgatagarbha? As it says below in the "Tathāgatagarbha" chapter: "These consciousnesses are perpetually calm and extinct; but that calm extinction is also calm and extinct" (p. 664c). The "Codes" chapter states: "The seventh [consciousness] and the five [sensory consciousnesses] are not produced. The eighth and sixth [consciousnesses] are calm and extinct. The characteristic of the ninth [consciousness] is to be void and nonexistent" (p. 670b). In this wise, the one taste that is unascertainable **[609b]** is in fact the essential point of this sūtra's theme. Since there is nothing to obtain, there is nothing that is not obtained. Therefore, as there are no approaches that are not opened [through this scripture], it offers a theme that has immeasurable aspects. Although there may be only this single taste, since it can be opened up into six approaches, I explicate it based on a sixfold exegetical division of the text.

First Division of Contemplation Practice: Rejecting All Characteristics of Sense-Objects to Reveal the Signless Contemplation

First, I will explain the meaning of the title of this chapter. "Signless" means the signless contemplation, which subverts all signs. Next, the term "dharma" means the dharma that is the topic of contemplation, which is the dharma of the one mind. The signless contemplation refers initially to this aspect of its being the first division of the six divisions [of contemplation practice]. The dharma that is the topic of contemplation refers subsequently to the dharma that is contemplated within the first of these six approaches. Now, this first chapter elucidates both these two aspects and is therefore titled "The Signless Dharma Chapter."

VAJRASAMĀDHI-SŪTRA, CHAPTER TWO: THE SIGNLESS DHARMA

> Emerging from his samādhi, the Lord then spoke these words.

The exegetical structure of the text of this chapter is in three sections:

First [I], the section on his emerging from samādhi;
Next [II], the section on his starting to speak;
Finally [III], the section on [the congregation's] gaining benefit.

The first and last sections are the preface [and epilogue] of the sūtra editor *(kyŏngga)*. The second section is the actual words of the Buddha himself.

In the initial section [I] are elucidated three types of perfection.

One [I.A] is the perfection of the time for preaching the dharma, as in the sūtra's reference to "then."

Two [I.B] is the perfection of the preacher of the dharma, as in the sūtra's "the Lord." He who masters the five penetrations *(t'ongdal)*[101] is honored by the world because he is able to explain, in accordance with their meaning, the most profound of dharmas.

Three [I.C] is the perfection of his autonomy, as in the sūtra's "emerging from his samādhi, . . . [he] spoke these words." When the Tathāgata accesses samādhi, there is nothing that can alarm or startle him, for he has gained autonomy in both abiding in and emerging from samādhi.

> "The stage of wisdom of all the buddhas accesses the real characteristic of dharmas because of the nature of certitude."

From here onward is the second section [II], his actual starting to speak, which is in two [subsections]:

one [II.A], an extended prose narration;
two [II.B], reiterative verses.

This initial [subsection, II.A], on the extended prose narration, is also in two parts:

one [II.A.1], a concise overview;
two [II.A.2], an extensive explanation.

In this part on the concise overview [II.A.1], **[609c]** "overview" has two aspects:

initially [II.A.1.a], an overview of the signless contemplation;
subsequently [II.A.1.b], an overview of the dharma that is contemplated.

In the signless contemplation [subpart, II.A.1.a], there are two passages:

initially [II.A.1.a.i], an overview of the fact that the Tathāgata himself accesses the signless contemplation;
subsequently [II.A.1.a.ii], an overview of the fact that he prompts others to access the signless contemplation.

[II.A.1.a.i] The words "himself accesses" refer to the sūtra's passage "**The stage of wisdom of all the buddhas accesses the real characteristic of dharmas because of the nature of certitude.**" "**The stage of wisdom of all the buddhas**" means, as above, the wisdom that is associated with accessing the vajrasamādhi, for it exerts control over all meritorious dharmas. "**Accesses the real characteristic of dharmas**" means that this wisdom of the buddhas subverts all characteristics because it penetrates to the real characteristic of all the dharmas. "**Nature of certitude**" *(kyŏlch'ŏngsŏng; *niyatatā)* is the real characteristic of dharmas, which is not produced by the buddhas: whether buddhas appear or not, its nature is itself just so. The next word, "**because,**" means that the significance of the preceding phrase ["**accesses the real characteristic of dharmas**"] is perfected via this **nature of certitude**, for if it were not a certitude, then it would not be the real characteristic. Furthermore, taking the prior phrase together as a unit clarifies the significance of the passage that follows [i.e., by parsing the passage as **Because the stage of wisdom of all the buddhas accesses the real characteristic of dharmas, the nature of certitude, therefore . . .**] because the tathāgatas themselves access the real characteristic of dharmas and are therefore able to prompt others to gain the inspiration of signlessness.

"[The buddhas'] expedients *(upāya)* and superpowers *(abhijñā)*[102] are all the inspiration [lit. benefit] of signlessness *(alakṣaṇatva)*."

This is the second passage [II.A.1.a.ii], which prompts other to access [the signless contemplation]. The term "**expedients**" refers to the expedients of the eight events [in a buddha's life], that is, from his descent from Tuṣita Heaven up through his access to nirvāṇa.[103] The term "**superpowers**" refers to the six superpowers, which proselytize sentient beings through the three means [lit. wheels, viz. of body, speech, and mind]. "**Are all the inspiration of signlessness**": in this wise, the eight expedients and six superpowers all arise from [the buddhas'] own access of the real characteristic, and they are able to prompt others to gain the inspiration of signlessness.

The overview of the signless contemplation [subpart, II.A.1.a,] is complete as above.

"The explicit meaning *(nitārtha)* of the one enlightenment is difficult to comprehend and difficult to access. It is not something that is known or cognized by any adherents of the two vehicles [of śrāvakas and pratyekabuddhas]; it may only be known by the buddhas and bodhisattvas."

From this point on is the second [subpart, II.A.1.b], an overview of the dharma that is contemplated, which also includes two passages:

one [II.A.1.b.i], **[610a]** an explicit overview of the profundity of the dharma that is contemplated;
two [II.A.1.b.ii], explaining this profound dharma to others.

[II.a.1.b.i] "**The explicit meaning of the one enlightenment**" means such concepts as the one mind, original enlightenment, and tathāgatagarbha, because there are no other dharmas that are more profound than these. "**Difficult to comprehend**" means that this concept is extremely profound and "**is not something that is known or cognized by any adherents of the two vehicles.**" "**Difficult to access**" means that its essence is extremely profound and can only be accessed by the buddhas and bodhisattvas. Since he uses this latter passage to explicate the previous passage, if we want to elucidate the real characteristic of dharma that is accessed by the buddhas' wisdom, as in the overview presented in the previous part, it then refers directly to these dharmas of the one mind, original enlightenment, and tathāgatagarbha. As the *Laṅkāvatāra-sūtra* [Scripture on the Entry into Laṅka) says, " 'Calm extinction' means the one mind. 'One mind' means the tathāgatagarbha."[104] Now in this passage "**the real characteristic of dharmas**" is the aspect of calm extinction and "**the explicit meaning of the one enlightenment**" is the aspect of one mind and tathāgatagarbha. As the *Fahua lun* [Treatise on the Lotus Sūtra] says, "All the buddhas, the tathāgatas, are able to know that dharma's ultimately real characteristic."[105] The term "**real characteristic**" refers to the immutability of the essence of the dharma-body of the tathāgatagarbha. Now this scripture's reference to "**one enlightenment**" means that all dharmas are only this one mind and all sentient beings are but this one original enlightenment. Because of these qualities, it is called "**one enlightenment.**" In the disquisition that follows, further analysis will be offered.

> **"All [the tathāgatas] explain the single taste to those sentient beings who are capable of deliverance."**

This [passage, II.A.1.b.ii] clarifies that all [the tathāgatas] speak the profound dharma to others. "**Those sentient beings who are capable of deliverance**" means that there are none of the sentient beings proselytized by the tathāgatas who do not flow forth from the one mind. "**All explain the single taste**" means that there are none of the doctrinal teachings spoken by the tathāgatas that are not intended to prompt access to the taste of the one enlightenment. [This passage] seeks to clarify that the original one enlightenment of all sentient beings just flows forth from out of their ignorance and in accordance with their fantasies. None of those beings will fail to return to the fountainhead of the one mind through the tathāgatas' clarifications concerning the single taste; and when they return to the fountainhead of the mind, they will all be unascertainable. Hence it is said that the single taste is in fact **[610b]** the one vehicle.

The initial [part, II.A.1] on the concise overview, is completed as above.

> **At that time, Haet'al Bodhisattva arose from his seat, joined his palms together, genuflected in foreign fashion, and addressed the Buddha:**

From here onward is the second [part, II.A.2] on the extensive explanation. It is in two [subparts]:

initially [II.A.2.a], a request;
subsequently [II.A.2.b], an explanation.

The request is in two [divisions]:

initially [II.A.2.a.i], a prologue involving personal etiquette;
subsequently [II.A.2.a.ii], clarification in the form of an address.

The prologue [II.A.2.a.i] includes two passages. The first [passage, II.A.2.a.i.a] refers to both the time and the speaker. "**Haet'al Bodhisattva**" prompts all sentient beings to gain liberation *(haet'al)* together; he serves as the interlocutor who brings up the dharma that is to be explained. The second [passage, II.A.2.a.i.b] is the prologue involving personal etiquette, as in the sūtra passage "**arose from his seat,**" and so forth.

> **"Lord! After the Buddha's demise, the right dharma *(saddharma)* will vanish from the world and the semblance dharma *(pratirūpakadharma)* will linger on in the world.[106] During the final age of the dharma *(saddharmavipralopa)*, sentient beings [who are tainted by] the five turbidities *(kaṣāya)*[107] will perform all types of evil actions and will transmigrate among the three realms of existence without respite."**

From here onward is the second [division, II.A.2.a.ii], a request in the form of an address, which is in two [subdivisions]:

initially [II.A.2.a.ii.a], he alludes to the era;
subsequently [II.A.2.a.ii.b], he requests that [the Buddha] speak to them.

In this first [subdivision, II.A.2.a.ii.a], the statement "**the semblance dharma *(pratirūpakadharma)* will linger on in the world. During the final age of the dharma**" refers to the fact that the initial sūtra [the *Single Taste Sūtra*] offered an extended explanation that was intended to benefit the right-dharma age, while this sūtra [the *Vajrasamādhi*] is intended to proselytize those in this era of the semblance dharma. This is because [the buddhas] establish teachings that differ according to the genuineness or frivolousness of the age.

> **"I beg that the Buddha, out of his friendliness and compassion, will proclaim the single taste that is decisive and true to those later generations of sentient beings and prompt those sentient beings equally to achieve liberation together."**

This is the second [subdivision, II.a.2.a.ii.b], a request that [the Buddha] address them. "**Will proclaim the single taste**" is a request to explain the taste of the explicit meaning of the one enlightenment. "**Decisive and true**" is a request to explain the contemplation that accesses the real characteristic of dharmas. "**Prompt those sentient beings equally to achieve liberation together**" means to prompt those sentient beings in the semblance-dharma and final-dharma [ages] equally to achieve the final liberation that has but a single taste.

Based on this statement, the teaching involves four alternatives:

One, the direct **[610c]** proselytization of the right-dharma age, together with inspiring those in future times; this refers to the prior sūtra and so on.
Two, the direct proselytization of the semblance-dharma age, together with inspiring those in past times; this refers to this sūtra.

Three, proselytizing all those in both past and future; this refers to all other sūtras.
Four, [teachings] that do not inspire those in either past or future; this excludes all the teachings listed above.

> The Buddha said, "Oh son of good family! You have asked me the causes surrounding my appearance in the world. I wanted to proselytize sentient beings and to prompt those sentient beings to obtain the fruition [of enlightenment] that transcends the world. This one great matter is inconceivable, because it involves great friendliness and great compassion.
>
> "If I were not to respond [to your questions], then I would fall into niggardliness [for hoarding the dharma I have learned]. You should all listen attentively and carefully, and I will proclaim [the answers] for you."

From here onward is the Buddha's proclamation to them [II.A.2.b], which is in two [divisions]:

one [II.A.2.b.i], praising the question [II.A.2.b.i.a], and consenting to preach [II.A.2.b.i.b];
two [II.A.2.b.ii], his proclamation in response to the request.

In his praise of the question [II.A.2.b.i.a], the words "**the causes surrounding my appearance in the world**" refer to accessing the contemplation of the real characteristic [of dharmas]. "**The fruition that transcends the world**" refers to the liberation that has but a single taste. "**This one great matter**" means "supreme" and "identical." It is "**inconceivable**" because it leaves behind words and eradicates thoughts. As the *Saddharmapuṇḍarīka-sūtra [Lotus Sūtra]* says, "All the buddhas, the world-honored ones, appear in this world solely because of this one great matter."[108] A commentator's [viz. Vasubandhu] exegesis states:

> "This one great matter" involves four discrete denotations. What are the four?
>
> First is the meaning of "supreme," for apart from the buddhas' knowledge of omniscience alone there is no other [similarly supreme] matter. As the *[Lotus]* sūtra says, "They wish to put on display the buddhas' knowledge and insight in order to purify sentient beings' knowledge; this is why they appear in the world." "The buddhas' knowledge and insight" means that the tathāgatas could realize [that truth] through the knowledge that accords with reality because they know its truth.
>
> Second is the denotation of "identical," for the dharmakāyas of all the śrāvakas, pratyekabuddhas, and buddhas are identical. As the sūtra says, "They wish to demonstrate to sentient beings the

> buddhas' knowledge and insight; this is why they appear in the world." "The dharmakāyas . . . are identical" means that the dharmakāya and the buddha-nature are not different.
>
> Third **[611a]** is the denotation of "nescient," for all the śrāvakas, pratyekabuddhas, and so forth, do not know that reality. "Not know that reality" means that they do not know that ultimately there is but one buddha-vehicle. As the sūtra says, "They seek to help sentient beings awaken to the buddhas' knowledge and insight; this is why they appear in the world."
>
> Fourth is [the denotation of] prompting them to realize the stage of nonretrogression, for they demonstrate that they wish to confer on [sentient beings] their immeasurable wisdom and deeds. As the sūtra says, "Because they seek to help sentient beings to access the buddhas' knowledge and insight, they therefore appear in the world."[109]

Now in this excerpt "this one great matter" has four specific denotations. The first is the denotation of "supreme"; as the passage above states, "**Because the stage of wisdom of all the buddhas accesses . . . the real characteristic of dharmas.**" Second is the denotation of "identical," as in the sūtra's line "**the explicit aspect of the one enlightenment is difficult to comprehend and difficult to access.**" Third is the denotation of "nescient," because it is not something that is known or cognized by any of the adherents of the two vehicles. Fourth is the denotation of "prompting them to realization," as in the line "**all [the tathāgatas] explain the single taste to those who are capable of deliverance.**"

[The subdivision on] praising the question [II.A.2.b.i.a] is now complete.

Next, [the subdivision on] consenting to preach [II.A.2.b.i.b] is also in two passages. The initial passage [**If I were not to respond (to your questions] . . .**] reveals that it would be, to the contrary, a mistake not to preach. The subsequent passage [**You should all listen attentively and carefully . . .**] means that he consents to preach if they listen appropriately and in conformity with proper etiquette.

> **"Oh son of good family! When you proselytize sentient beings, do not conceive that proselytism occurs; do not conceive that proselytism does not occur. Such proselytism is great indeed!"**

From here onward is the explicit proclamation [division, II.A.2.b.ii], his proclamation in response to the request, which is in two [subdivisions]:

initially [II.A.2.b.ii.a], a clarification regarding the signless contemplation, which is an extensive clarification of the inspiration of signlessness;

subsequently [II.A.2.b.ii.b], an elucidation of the mind of one enlightenment, which offers an extensive explanation of the preceding aspect of one enlightenment.

The [subdivision] on signless contemplation is also in two segments:

one [II.A.2.b.ii.a.i], an explicit explanation of the characteristics of this contemplation practice;
two [II.A.2.b.ii.a.2], a series of dialogues that resolves all doubts and objections.

The initial [segment] is also in two [subsegments]:

initially [II.A.2.b.ii.a.i.a], the expedient contemplation,
subsequently [II.A.2.b.ii.a.i.b], a clarification of the unmediated contemplation.

In this expedient contemplation [subsegment, II.A.2.b.ii.a.i.a], there are four passages: the first passage [**when you proselytize sentient beings**] describes the proselytist, the last passage [**such proselytism is great indeed**] praises the greatness of this proselytization, and the middle two passages [**do not conceive that proselytism occurs . . . does not occur**] are an explicit clarification of the characteristics of contemplation. "**You should not conceive that proselytism occurs**": When you first cultivate contemplation, **[611b]** you annihilate all characteristics, extinguishing any conception of this illusory characteristic of proselytism. "**Do not conceive that proselytism does not occur**": Since you have subverted all characteristics of proselytism, you next must neutralize the characteristic of voidness as well as have no conception about a voidness that is free from proselytism. Why is this? Since sentient beings originally are deluded to the fact that the mind is separate from characteristics, they instead cling to all characteristics. Because their thoughts are agitated, thereby producing states of mind, they first must subvert all characteristics and extinguish the mind that clings to characteristics. Although, furthermore, they may have already subverted the characteristics of existence, which are illusory projections, they still cling to that nature of voidness, which is free from projections. Because they cling to this nature of voidness, they give rise to conceptions regarding this voidness. Therefore, they also must neutralize this nature of voidness, which is free from proselytism. At that time, they do not generate any thoughts that cling to voidness and cannot help but be in concord with the middle way that is free from dualistic extremes and thus "**access the real characteristic of dharmas,**" which is the same as that of all the buddhas. Because they proselytize in this wise, their proselytism is great indeed!

Question: On what stages does this expedient contemplation occur?

Answer: If it is cultivated through faith, it occurs [on the stage of] the ten faiths. An analogous contemplation occurs during the thirty states of mind [preceding the bodhisattva's entry onto the ten bhūmis (grounds), viz. the ten abidings, ten practices, and ten transferences]. If we explain its pristine practice, it involves the four wholesome faculties *(nirvedhabhāgīya-kuśalamūla)*.[110] This is because it is an antecedent expedient for bringing about access to the first [Pramuditā-]bhūmi.

Question: Elsewhere it is said there are three contemplations that are free of own-nature [viz. the no-own-nature of signs, production, and ultimate truth]. Why does it only say here that there are two negative types [signlessness and nonproduction]?

Answer: Signlessness and nonproduction can be combined into a single type because the sign and the production that are abandoned both involve existence. Furthermore, these two types of contemplation both involve thought and imagination *(vitarka-vicāra)*. But once you have dispelled the notion of no-own-nature, then, because thought and imagination no longer occur, it is valid either to distinguish them from one another *(kae)* or to treat them together *(hap)*.

This ends the discussion on expedients [II.A.2.b.ii.a.i.a]. Next we elucidate the unmediated contemplation [II.A.2.b.ii.a.i.b].

> **"It enables all those sentient beings to leave behind mind and self, for both mind and self are originally void and calm. If they attain voidness of mind, then that mind will not illusorily project anything. Free from all illusory projections, they will then attain nonproduction *(anutpatti)*. The mind that does not produce anything derives from such nonprojection."**

This [subsegment, II.A.2.b.ii.a.i.b,] clarifies the unmediated contemplation's nondual characteristics because it leaves behind the duality of both the clinging subject and the objects of clinging.

Leaving behind the objects of clinging means leaving behind all the characteristics of both persons and dharmas. This is of two varieties: one, leaving behind through dispelling; two, leaving behind through annihilation. **[611c]** "Leaving behind through dispelling" means that the characteristics to which one clung initially are now extinguished and removed. As this sūtra says, "**It enables all those sentient beings to leave behind mind and self.**" "Leaving behind through annihilation" means that the characteristics to which one clung initially are originally void. As the sūtra says, "**for both mind and self are originally void and calm.**" As for the terms "**mind and self**": the person is called "**self**"; dharmas are called "**mind,**" because the mind is the chief that supports all dharmas. When one penetrates to the fact that all persons and dharmas are originally void, the characteristics to which one had grasped previously do not then arise. Therefore these two types of "**leav[ing] behind**" are simultaneously perfected. This ends the discussion on leaving behind the object of clinging.

What is meant by leaving behind the clinging subject? This means that one leaves behind all the discriminations created by the clinging subject. This is also of two types: one, the "original leaving behind"; two, the "acquired leaving behind."

The term "original leaving behind" means that, when one penetrates to the fact that mind and self are originally void, one straightaway gains the void and calm mind of original enlightenment. This void and calm mind originally leaves behind the clinging subject; and because it leaves behind the clinging subject, it is originally free from illusory projections. As the sūtra says, "**If they attain voidness of mind, then that mind will not illusorily project anything.**" "**Not illusorily project anything**" means that there is no deception or falsity. The term "acquired leaving behind" means that, when one gains this void and calm mind of original enlightenment, the discriminations created by the clinging subject are no longer able to arise, and regardless of the state of mind produced, there will be no illusory projections. As the sūtra says, "**Free from all illusory projections, they will then attain nonproduction.**" In this wise, they acquire the mind of nonproduction and tally with that principle which is originally void, calm, and free from projections. Therefore, it says, "**The mind that does not produce anything derives from such nonprojection.**" Because provisionally it may be called a mental object, we can say that it "**derives.**"

Acquiring this "leaving behind the clinging subject" is the aspect of acquired enlightenment. Originally leaving behind this mind of voidness is the aspect of original enlightenment. Even thought their aspects may be twofold, they are unified in the one enlightenment because they both leave behind subject and object, new and old. As an explanation in a treatise [the *Awakening of Faith*] says, "Hence, acquired enlightenment is identical to original enlightenment."[111] You should know that this enlightenment ultimately leaves behind such characteristics as production and extinction, beginning and end; while temporally, from the first bhūmi up to the buddha bhūmi, it merely involves such distinctions as "partial" and "complete." **[612a]** As the "Benfen" section of the *Daśabhūmikasūtropadeśa* [Treatise on the *Ten Bhūmis Sūtra*] says, "In their own essences, voidness and existence are originally nondual and unannihilated."[112] An extensive explanation follows there. Furthermore, this one enlightenment includes both the aspects of acquired and original [enlightenments]: because it involves the aspect of original enlightenment being made fully manifest, it is valid to say that it involves authentic cultivation; and because it involves the aspect of being perfected through the cultivation of acquired enlightenment, it is also valid to suggest that it is cultivated anew. But if one grasps prejudicially to either one, it will involve neither one of these [aspects].

Now we will set aside these two treatises and return to an exegesis of our original sūtra text.

The extensive clarification of the signless contemplation [II.B.2.b.ii.a] is completed as above.

> Haet'al Bodhisattva addressed the Buddha: "Lord! The nature of the mind of sentient beings is originally void and calm. The essence of that mind which is void and calm is free from materiality *(rūpa)* and characteristics *(lakṣaṇa)*. How are we to cultivate and train so that we may obtain that mind which is originally void? I entreat the Buddha to proclaim this for us, out of his friendliness and compassion."

From this point onward is the second [segment, II.A.2.b.ii.a.2], a series of dialogues that resolve doubts. Four exchanges [II.A.2.b.ii.a.2.a–d] resolve sequentially some specific doubts.

In the first [exchange, II.A.2.b.ii.a.2.a], the question [II.A.2.b.ii.a.2.a.I] has two intents. One, the mind-nature of sentient beings may originally be void and calm, but active thought has been flowing out from it since time immemorial; how, then, will we gain the original mind through methodical cultivation? Two, the essence of the void and calm mind may be free from materiality and characteristics, but sentient beings innately cling incessantly to the characteristics of existence; how, then, will we gain the mind of voidness by training in nonexistence? Therefore, it says, "**How are we to cultivate and train so that we may obtain that mind which is originally void?**"

Question: The mind of sentient beings discussed herein must be the mind of the six affective consciousnesses, which is subject to production and extinction. How will it ever come to know the original enlightenment of the one mind?

Answer: As the *Awakening of Faith Treatise* says, "There is a dharma that can give rise to the faculty of Mahāyāna faith: . . . it is called the mind of the sentient being. . . . Based on the dharma of the one mind, there are two types of approaches."[113] An extensive explanation follows there. Moreover, as a scripture *[Laṅkāvatāra-sūtra; Scripture on the Entry into Laṅka]* states, " 'Calm extinction' is called 'the one mind.' "[114] Now, our passage here states, "**The essence of that mind which is void and calm is free from materiality and characteristics.**" Though there may be some inconsistencies in the terminology employed, the intent [of the three scriptural passages] is essentially the same. "**Free from materiality**" means that it is free from such aspects of materiality as color *(varṇarūpa)*, appearance *(saṃsthānarūpa)*, and so forth. "**Free from characteristics**" means that it is free from **[612b]** such characteristics as production and extinction. This passage elucidates the true-thusness aspect of the mind. The preceding term "the mind of sentient beings" refers instead to the production-and-extinction aspect of the mind. But because the true-thusness aspect is made manifest through the production-and-extinction aspect, it therefore says "**the nature [of the mind of sentient beings] is originally void and calm.**" Nevertheless, the essences of these two aspects are nondual, and they therefore are nothing more than this dharma of the one mind.

> The Buddha replied: "Bodhisattva! All the characteristics of the mind originally have no origin and originally have no original locus; they are void and calm, producing nothing. If the mind produces nothing, it then accesses void calmness.[115] At that ground of the mind *(cittabhūmi)*, where all is void and calm, one then attains voidness of mind. Oh son of good family! The signless mind is free from both mind and self. It is the same with all the characteristics of dharmas."

This answer [II.A.2.b.ii.a.2.a.II] has two [subportions]:

the explicit answer [II.A.2.b.ii.a.2.a.II.A];
the answer that resolves [a doubt, II.A.2.b.ii.a.2.a.II.B].

In the explicit answer [subportion, II.A.2.b.ii.a.2.a.II.A], the term "bodhisattva" refers to Haet'al Bodhisattva, as it also does in the passages below. "All the characteristics of mind": since there is a distinction made between the ratiocinative mind of the eight consciousnesses and the formations *(saṃskāra)* and characteristics that are associated with mind, whether they be formations or characteristics, all remain subject to the four characteristics [of production, subsistence, decay, and extinction]. "Originally have no origin and originally have no original locus": all the characteristics of mind have seeds *(bīja)* as their origin, but if you seek the original seed, it can never be found. This is because, at the very moment that [a seed] appears in the present, it has already become past. If it existed at the present moment, then [that seed] would be identical to its fruition and there would be no difference between its beginning and its end, as if [seed and fruit] were both the two horns of a single ox. But if [that seed] has already become past, then it could not serve as an efficient cause *(kāraṇahetu)*;[116] and because it has no essential nature, it would be [illusory] like a rabbit's horns. The logic here is patently obvious. For this reason, it says that it "originally ha[s] no origin." Moreover, the arising of the mind that is subject to production and extinction is necessarily dependent on this original locus, for if this original locus did not exist, [that mind] could not be produced. The term "original locus" refers to the simultaneous faculties [viz. the internal sense bases that are the supports for the production of mind and mental activities]. Since the five sense faculties are all material dharmas, whether or not they are operative, they are all unascertainable. The remaining three types of supports are all immaterial dharmas, so whether or not it is the proper time for their appearance, they are all **[612c]** unascertainable.[117] Therefore, it says, "originally have no original locus." This means that, since time immemorial, they have had no original locus. Since they have no original seeds, they also have no original locus. You should know that the characteristics of mind are originally unproduced; therefore, it says, **"they are void and calm, producing nothing."**

When in this wise you examine the notion that nothing is produced, then the mind that performs this examination also has nothing that it produces. At that time, **"it then accesses"** the original **"void calmness."** The void calmness it accesses is the one mind and everything on which it is dependent is called its **"ground."** Therefore it says, **"It then accesses void calmness. At that ground of the mind *(cittabhūmi)*, where all is void and calm. . . . "** Although all sentient beings originally evolve by clinging constantly to the characteristics of existence, if they nevertheless rely on this approach and aspire to this sort of examination, they then will be able to gain the mind that is originally void. Therefore, it says, **"One then attains voidness of mind."** There may be some inconsistencies in the terms "the mind is void" and "voidness of mind," but both of these just refer to the aspect of the original enlightenment of the one mind. The explicit answer to the question is completed above.

From here onward is the answer that resolves [a doubt, II.A.2.b.ii.a.2.a.II. B]. **"The signless mind"** refers to the essence of the one mind. **"Is free from both mind and self"**: this resolves the issues raised in the previous discussion: in the void and calm mind that is free from production and characteristics, both the characteristics of mind and self are left behind. **"It is the same with all the characteristics of dharmas"**: this once again resolves an issue regarding the void calmness: it leaves behind not merely these two characteristics of mind and self, but also all remaining characteristics—the compounded and uncompounded, and so forth . . . up to the superior *(uttara)* and the supreme *(anuttara)*—for in this signless mind, there is nothing that is not left behind.

> **Haet'al Bodhisattva addressed the Buddha: "Lord! If sentient beings have a conception of self or a conception of mind, what dharma will awaken those sentient beings and prompt them to leave behind such bonds *(bandhana)*?"**

From this point onward is the second exchange [II.A.2.b.ii.a.2.b]. The previous exchange briefly clarified an approach that would subvert [misconceptions about] the characteristics of existence. Now, this exchange specifically elucidates an approach that involves leaving behind two kinds of bonds. It also refers specifically to two kinds of illness, in order to engage in an inquiry about their remedy.

[In the question, II.A.2.b.ii.a.2.b.I], the term **"conception of self"** is the illness of grasping at personality; the term **"conception of mind"** is the illness of grasping at dharmas. As for the term **[613a] "such bonds"**: if we treat each of them separately, grasping at personality is the coarser bond and grasping at dharmas is the subtler bond. Discussing them generically, these two types of grasping both involve a coarser and a subtler bond. Moreover, the fact that these two types of grasping involve both types of bonds means that they involve the bond through association [with the mind] *([citta]saṃprayuktabandhana)* and the bond through sense objects *(ālambanabandhana)*. In the *Yijang chang* [Essay on the Two Hindrances], this idea has already been fully explained.[118]

In the answer [II.A.2.b.ii.a.2.b.II], there are two [subportions]:

initially [II.A.2.b.ii.a.2.b.II.A], a treatment for the grasping at personality;
subsequently [II.A.2.b.ii.a.2.b.II.B], a treatment for the grasping at dharmas [and the view that validates the existence of the mind].

In the [subportion] on the treatment for the grasping at personality, there is

initially [II.A.2.b.ii.a.2.b.II.A.1], a generic [treatment];
subsequently [II.A.2.b.ii.a.2.b.II.A.2], a specific [treatment].

> The Buddha replied: "Oh son of good family! If there is someone who retains a conception of self, he should be encouraged to contemplate the twelvefold chain of causal conditioning *(pratītyasamutpāda)*."

This is the generic treatment [II.A.2.b.ii.a.2.b.II.A.1], which involves contemplating the twelve limbs [of conditioned production]. In brief, it involves two approaches.

One [II.A.2.b.ii.a.2.b.II.A.1.a] is the contemplation of conditioned production as uncreated *(akriyā)*, which cures the attachment to a creator *(kartṛ)*; as it is said, "Because of the existence of this matter, that matter comes into existence."
Two [II.A.2.b.ii.a.2.b.II.A.1.b] is the contemplation of conditioned production as impermanent, which cures the attachment to permanence; as it says, "Because this matter is produced, that matter comes to be produced."

Ever since we became attached to the notion of an existing self, these two [the notions of a creator and of permanence] have served as the roots [of our existence]; but once we remove these roots, all the branches will accordingly vanish.

> "The twelvefold chain of causal conditioning originally derives from cause and fruition. The production of cause and fruition is stimulated by the operation of the mind. But the mind does not exist, much less the body.
>
> "If there is a person who conceives of a self, he should be encouraged to abandon his view [that the self] exists. If there is a person who

conceives that there is no self, he should be encouraged to abandon his view [that the self] does not exist."

This is the specific treatment [II.A.2.b.ii.a.2.b.II.A.2]. The specific treatment is bifurcated into

one, [II.A.2.b.ii.a.2.b.II.A.2.a], the treatment through the comparison particle "**much less**";
two [II.A.2.b.ii.a.2.b.II.A.2.b], the treatment through a follow-up statement.

In the treatment [for the grasping at personality] through the comparison particle "**much less**" [II.A.2.b.ii.a.2.b.II.A.2.a], the line "**originally derives from cause and fruition**" means that the specific derives from the general. Speaking generally, there is only cause and fruition. "Cause" includes two links [viz. ignorance and karmic formations, leading from the past to the present time periods] or three links [craving, grasping, and becoming, leading from the present to future]. "Fruition" includes five links [consciousness, name and form, six sense-fields, contact, and sensation, leading from past to present] and two links [birth, and old age and death, leading from the present to the future]. Furthermore, "cause" includes ten links [viz. ignorance, karmic formations, consciousness, name and form, six sense-fields, contact, sensation, craving, grasping, and becoming, leading from past to present], and "fruition" includes two links [birth, and old age and death, leading from present to future]. Therefore the source from which all these [links] derive is just cause and fruition. "**The production of cause and fruition is stimulated by the operation of the mind**": the arising of cause and fruition has the mental activities as its source, because the mind serves as the operative cause *(kāraṇahetu)* and the mind also receives the fruition. "**But the mind does not exist, much less the body**": Based on the explanations provided above about the rationale governing investigation, **[613b]** if even the mind is unascertainable, then how **much less** so is the existence of the corporeal body that is created by the mind! And if the body and mind do not exist, then how **much less** so could there exist a self? Furthermore, since the mind does not exist, cause and fruition also are void. And if even cause and fruition are void, how **much less** chance is there that a self exists? Furthermore, because cause and fruition are void, the twelve limbs are void; so how **much less** chance is there that a creator, a recipient, and so forth, exist? As a scripture *[Dazhidu lun]* says, "The bodhisattva contemplates that the twelvefold [chain of] causal conditioning is inexhaustible, like empty space."[119] This is what is meant here. This ends the discussion on subverting [the grasping at personality] through the comparison particle "**much less.**"

What is the treatment through a follow-up statement [II.A.2.b.ii.a.2.b.II.A.2.b]? It is the statement "**If there is a person who conceives of a self, he should** be encouraged to abandon his view [that the self] exists." Examining the previous subversion through the comparison "much less" extinguishes the attachment to [the notion of] an existing self. "If there is a person who conceives that there is no self, he should be encouraged to abandon his view [that the self] does not exist": this follow-up statement brings an end to the illness that the self does not exist. Why is this? Although the previous subversion of the attachment to self cures the illness of the non-Buddhists [who posit a permanent self], clinging to the notion of nonself remains. Since one has become trapped by the illness of two-vehicle adherents, one now must attend to subverting the attachment to the view of nonexistence. If even the self originally does not exist, how much less is this the case for the nonexistence of an existing self?

Thus we have finished the two contemplations, the generic and the specific, which subvert the attachment to self.

> "If a person conceives that the mind can be produced, he should be encouraged to abandon [his view that] the nature [of the mind] is subject to extinction. If a person conceives that the mind can be extinguished, he should be encouraged to abandon [his view that] the nature [of the mind] is subject to production.[120] Once these views about the nature are extinguished, he will immediately approach the edge of reality."

From here onward is the second treatment [II.A.2.b.ii.a.2.b.II.B], treating [the grasping at dharmas and] views involving actualization of the mind *(chonsim)*. This is bifurcated into

an explicit treatment [II.A.2.b.ii.a.2.b.II.B.1];
a reinterpretation [II.A.2.b.ii.a.2.b.II.B.2].

[Explicit treatment, II.A.2.b.ii.a.2.b.II.B.1:] Two-vehicle adherents grasp at dharmas and actualize the mind; they postulate the existence of a mind that is subject to production and extinction and thus impermanent. Therefore one subverts production and extinction and thereby extinguishes this view that actualizes mind. If actualization of the mind occurs and develops into an illness, it will then subvert that previous quality of extinction, because it is principally through the support of the extinction of that [matter] that production is actualized in the present. If one perceives that extinction occurs later and one is attached to the existence of the mind in the present, then even though the mind may not be extinguished, it will still [be illusory], like a rabbit's horn. "He should be encouraged to abandon [his view that] the nature [of the mind] is subject to production": this means that it is illogical for there to be extinction without production. "Once these views about the nature are extinguished, he will immediately approach the edge of reality": once he subverts his perception of this quality of extinction, he perforce **[613c]** will not cling to production; once he subverts his perception of this quality of production, he perforce will not cling to extinction. This is because, if one does not cling to either production or extinction, there will perforce be no actualization of the mind.

> "Why is this? Originally, production is not extinguished; it is not[121] extinction and not production. Both are nonextinct and unproduced, unproduced and nonextinct. It is also just the same with the characteristics of all dharmas."

This is the reinterpretation [II.A.2.b.ii.a.2.b.II.B.2]. Why is it that seeing the production of the mind causes the extinction of the extinction-nature and seeing the extinction of the mind causes the extinction of the production-nature? This is his reason for asking "Why is this?" which leads to a further response to this question. "Originally, production is not extinguished": if one seeks the mind that was produced previously, it can never be found; and if it can never be found, what dharma is it that is extinguished? In this wise, one who does not actualize the mind's quality of extinction in the past cannot posit that the mind is produced in the present. Therefore, it says, "Both are nonextinct and unproduced." This explicates the reason behind the statement "he should be encouraged to abandon [his view that] the nature [of the mind] is subject to extinction."

Next it says "unproduced and nonextinct." This explains that if extinction has not occurred in the past, production will not be possible in the present. In the same way, if the mind has no quality of production in the present, one cannot posit the mind's [future] extinction. Therefore, it says "unproduced and nonextinct." This explicates the reason behind the statement "he should be encouraged to abandon [his view that] the nature [of the mind] is subject to production." Just as mental dharmas are neither extinguished nor produced, so too should all other dharmas be viewed in the same way. Therefore, it says, "It is also just the same with the characteristics of all dharmas."

Question: If you had presumed that the mind was produced but have now correctly subverted this [notion of] production, then why must you also subvert [the notion of] that mind's extinction in the past?

Answer: Since it is apparent that production is occurring in the present, it is not easy to subvert [the notion of] existence. But since the previous state of mind has already passed, it is not difficult to understand [the notion of] voidness. Therefore, by first subverting what is easy, one then neutralizes what it difficult. Based on this sequence, you subvert now the quality of production and then, through this, you neutralize later the clinging to extinction. This is called the ingenious therapy of the Medicine King [Buddha; Bhaiṣajyaguru].

> Haet'al Bodhisattva addressed the Buddha: "Lord! What view is extinguished when a sentient being perceives that a dharma is produced?"[122]

From here onward is the third exchange [II.A.2.b.ii.a.2.c]. Following the previous exchange, which clarified the illness of the view involving the objects of extinction, we now have this exchange, which elucidates the medicine for the view involving the agent of extinction. **[614a]** Furthermore, the previous [exchange] subverts views involving the two extremes of production and extinction, while the present [exchange] subverts views concerning the two limits of existence and nonexistence.

Now, regarding the intent behind this question, he is asking, "When a meditator who is in accord with the intent of the Buddha's teachings observes that a dharma is produced, what view will this cause to be extinguished? And by extinguishing what view would one ask about the intent of the Buddha's teachings?" Now in order to allude to one extreme [viz. that of production], he must also elucidate how extinction is to be contemplated.

> The Buddha replied, "Bodhisattva. When a sentient being perceives that a dharma is produced, this causes the extinction of the view of nonexistence. When he sees the extinction of dharmas, this causes the extinction of the view of existence. Once these views are extinguished, the true nonexistence of dharmas is achieved and he accesses certitude, where [the attainment of the state of] nonproduction is certain."

"When [a sentient being] perceives that a dharma is produced": when one observes in unmediated fashion the causally conditioned production of conventional dharmas—at that time, one can leave behind the view that clings to voidness. Therefore, it says, "this causes the extinction of the view of nonexistence." "When he sees the extinction of dharmas": when one observes in unmediated fashion the original extinction of conventional dharmas—at that time, one can remain far removed from the view that clings to existence. Therefore, it says, "this causes the extinction of the view of existence." In this passage, if one were to ask why he uses the words "causes the extinction," it is because the Buddha's teachings enable a meditator to experience extinction. The intent here is directly to clarify that, when those who are cultivating contemplation practice observe the production of dharmas, they just stay far removed from the view of nonexistence, without validating production; and when they contemplate calm extinction, they merely stay far removed from the view of existence, without clinging to extinction. This is the case because how would they validate production, if production were originally calm and extinct? and how would they cling to extinction, if extinction occurs as a response to production? As a gāthā will state below (see p. 658c):

> Objects that are produced by causes and conditions,
> Those objects are extinguished, not produced.
> Extinguish all objects subject to production and extinction,
> And those objects will be produced, not extinguished.

For this reason, one is able to remain far removed from the two extremes [of existence and nonexistence] without grasping at the middle. This would be the same for one who leaves behind nonexistence but clings to existence or who subverts existence but clings to voidness—these would involve deceptive voidness, not true nonexistence. Now, although one leaves behind existence, one does not validate voidness; and, in this wise, one then gains the true nonexistence of all dharmas. Therefore, it says, "the true nonexistence of dharmas is achieved." The meaning of "certitude" is as was explained previously (p. 609c). When one gains true voidness, one observes that the mind is unproduced, because one remains far removed from all existent and nonexistent states of mind. Therefore, it says, "nonproduction is certain." **[614b]**

> Haet'al Bodhisattva addressed the Buddha: "Lord! If a sentient being were encouraged to linger in the state of nonproduction, would that mean it was [the achievement of the acquiescence to] the nonproduction [of dharmas; *anutpattika-(dharmakṣānti)*]?"

From here onward is the fourth exchange [II.A.2.b.ii.a.2.d; this passage is the question portion, II.A.2.b.ii.a.2.d.I]. The previous [exchange] clarified the fact that authentic contemplation remains far removed from the characteristics of both extremes; the present one elucidates the false understanding that does not avoid lingering in production. Assume there is a person with meager learning who is cultivating contemplation practice and who discriminates based on concepts and words. He observes the nonproduction of dharmas and becomes absorbed in distraction. While lingering in this state of nonproduction, he presumes in this wise that this really is nonproduction. But later, when he withdraws from his absorption, he develops utmost conceit *(abhimāna)* and assumes that he has already achieved the acquiescence to the nonproduction of dharmas *(anutpattikadharmakṣānti)*. In order to treat this sort of illness, he brings up the illness and asks, "[If a sentient being were encouraged] to linger in the state of nonproduction, would that mean it was nonproduction?"

> The Buddha replied, "Were one to linger in nonproduction, that would actually be producing something. Why is this? Only when one does not linger in nonproduction is it really nonproduction."

The answer [II.A.2.b.ii.a.2.d.II] is bifurcated into

a brief reply [II.A.2.b.ii.a.2.d.II.A];
a detailed reiteration [II.A.2.b.ii.a.2.d.II.B].

This is the brief reply, which involves two passages. The first passage clarifies appropriately that production involves lingering in the state of nonproduction because it entails the production of the discriminative mind. The second passage, to the contrary, explicates nonproduction: if the mind does not linger in the state of nonproduction and remains far removed from all discrimination, this will then entail the acquiescence to the nonproduction [of dharmas]. Therefore, one should know that, where lingering occurs, it will not involve the acquiescence to nonproduction—such is a contrary explication. This ends the text of the brief reply.

> **"Bodhisattva! If one produces nonproduction, production and extinction would therewith be produced. When production and extinction are both extinguished, production inherently would not be produced and the mind would be constantly void and calm; and that which is void and calm is nonabiding. Only the mind that does not abide anywhere is then really unproduced."**

This is the detailed reiteration [II.A.2.b.ii.a.2.d.II.B], which is bifurcated between

initially [II.A.2.b.ii.a.2.d.II.B.1], details on the aspect of production;
subsequently [II.A.2.b.ii.a.2.d.II.B.2], details on the aspect of nonproduction.

If the mind lingers somewhere and thereby produces objects that are [inherently] unproduced, there then would occur the production of objects that are subject to production and extinction; therefore, it says, "**If one produces nonproduction, production and extinction would therewith be produced.**" Although the production of objects may be extinguished, [614c] by continuing to cling to the notion that extinction means nonexistence, the mind that serves as the clinging subject will be produced with regard to nonexistence as extinction, thereby validating both production and extinction. How can that be "**nonproduction**"? In this wise, these two passages detail the [description of] production above.

Authentic "acquiescence to nonproduction" is not the same as this. Externally, it does not validate that extinction which is the object of clinging; internally, it does not produce that production which is the clinging subject. For this reason, it says, "**Production and extinction are both extinguished.**" However, the statement "**both extinguished**" does not mean to imply that they both return to nonproduction. One may seek original production, but it will never be produced; and since it will never be produced, how would it ever be able to return to nonproduction? At such a time one realizes the original void calmness; therefore, it says, "**Production inherently would not be produced and the mind would be constantly void and calm.**" In this wise, in void calmness subject and object are both in equilibrium and there is no mind, the agent of lingering, that lingers in any state of voidness. Therefore, it says, "**That which**

is void and calm is nonabiding." In this wise, this then comes to be named the "acquiescence to the nonproduction of dharmas." Therefore, it says, "**[Only the mind that does not abide anywhere] is then really unproduced.**"

The disquisition on the contemplation of nonproduction [*sic;* signless contemplation][123] is finished as above.

> **Haet'al Bodhisattva addressed the Buddha: "If the mind does not abide anywhere, then what need is there for religious practice? Is there then still training left to complete *(śaikṣa)* or is no further training necessary *(aśaikṣa)*?"**

From this point on is the extensive explanation of the aspect of the one enlightenment [II.A.2.b.ii.b]. It involves eight exchanges [II.A.2.b.ii.b.1–8], bifurcated into two major sections. The first two exchanges [II.A.2.b.ii.b.1–2] are an explicit and extensive treatment of the aspect of the tathāgatagarbha of one enlightenment. The six subsequent exchanges [II.A.2.b.ii.b.3–8] resolve all the remaining doubts and objections by elaborating on the initial discussion.

Now the question in this initial [exchange, II.A.2.b.ii.b.1.a] asks about the mind that does not abide anywhere. If there "**is still training left to complete,**" then it is certainly not the case that it is nonabiding. If "**no further training is necessary,**" then it would not entail any further contemplation practice. Furthermore, if there "**is still training left to complete,**" then there should still be states of mind that are to be produced. But if "**no further training is necessary,**" then [nonabiding] would be a frivolous principle.

> **The Buddha replied, "Bodhisattva! The mind that is unproduced—that mind has neither egress nor access. It is the original tathāgatagarbha, whose nature is calm and motionless."**

In the [answer subsegment (II.A.2.b.ii.b.1.b)], there is

initially [II.A.2.b.ii.b.1.b.I], an elucidation of the rationale; and
subsequently [II.A.2.b.ii.b.1.b.II], an explicit answer to the question.

[II.A.2.b.ii.b.1.b.I] To elucidate the rationale **[615a]** means that when one achieves the state of nonabiding, the mind is unproduced. That mind is constantly calm and extinct, so there is never any egress from contemplation. It penetrates to the original nonarising, but it is also not something that has ever been accessed. Therefore, it says, "**That mind has neither egress nor access.**" Since contemplating the mind in this wise involves neither egress nor access, it is in fact the mind of the tathāgatagarbha of original enlightenment. This [line] explains that the acquired enlightenment is identical to the original enlightenment. Since the mind that is unproduced is the original [enlightenment tathāgata-]garbha, its nature is originally calm and never again springs into action. How then would there ever be any further access or egress, activity or rest? These words reiterate its aspect of being free from egress or access.

> **"It is not subject to further training nor free from further training. When there is neither training nor nontraining—that then is the state where no further training is necessary. 'Training' means to ensure that there is no need for either training or not training."**

This is the explicit answer to the implication of the question [II.A.2.b.ii.b.1.b.II], which is bifurcated into

initially [II.A.2.b.ii.b.1.b.II.A], rejection;
subsequently [II.A.2.b.ii.b.1.b.II.B], assent.

[II.A.2.b.ii.b.1.b.II.A, Rejection:] Since it is not accessed temporally, "**it is not subject to further training**"; and since it ultimately is not egressed, "**it is not . . . free from further training.**" Furthermore, since there is no mind that is the agent of abiding, therefore "**it is not subject to further training**"; and since there is also no mind that does not abide anywhere, therefore "**it is not . . . free from further training.**" Here, he rejects both [positions]; thus, this passage is a rejection of these propositions.

[II.A.2.b.ii.b.1.b.II.A, Assent:] "**When there is neither training nor nontraining—that then is the state where no further training is necessary**": where there is no separate object of training, there is also then no subject of training. Because of this aspect, he accepts [the reality of] this state where no further training is necessary. Based on this aspect that there is nothing further in which he needs to train, he assents to this state where no further training is necessary. "**'Training' means to ensure that there is no need for either training or not training**": although this is not a contemplation that involves any abiding, it is not free from the training in nonabiding. Because of this aspect, he consents to [the reality of] the state that is subject to further training. And since there is a state subject to further training, there are objects of training in the lower bhūmis. Based on this aspect that one is not free from further training, he consents to this state where further training is necessary. This is a noncommittal [lit. autonomous] response, in which he accepts both alternatives.

> **Haet'al Bodhisattva addressed the Buddha: "How is it that the nature of the tathāgatagarbha is calm and motionless?"**

From here onward is the second exchange [II.A.2.b.ii.b.2]. The previous [exchange] clarified that the acquired enlightenment is no different from the nature of the tathāgatagarbha of original enlightenment. **[615b]** Now, [this exchange] directly elucidates the fact that the nature of the tathāgatagarbha is a concealed storehouse *(garbha),* which is motionless. In this [exchange, the Buddha] briefly clarifies the aspect of tathāgatagarbha.

There are approaches [to explaining the concept of] tathāgatagarbha based on a twofold account [II.A.2.b.ii.b.2.b] and a threefold account [II.A.2.b.ii.b.2.a] [*sic;* the coverage is reversed in the exegesis that follows].

Regarding the threefold account [II.A.2.b.ii.b.2.a], as the *Anūnatvāpurṇatvanirdeśa* [Neither Increase Nor Decrease Sūtra] says:

> In the realm of sentient beings, we explain that there are three types of dharmas that are all true, real, and such, and that are neither different nor discrepant. What are these three dharmas?
> 1. Those pure dharmas whose essences are associated with the original limit of the tathāgatagarbha. Those dharmas accord with reality, are neither false nor spurious, and are neither separated nor cut off [from the original limit of reality]; they involve knowledge and are inconceivable dharmas. Ever since there has been this beginningless, original limit, there have been these essences of dharmas that are associated with purity.
> 2. Those impure dharmas that involve the bondage of defilements, whose essences are dissociated from the original limit of the tathāgatagarbha. Those impure dharmas that involve the bondage of defilements are separated, cut off, and dissociated from the original limit. They can only be eradicated by the tathāgatas' bodhi-knowledge.
> 3. Those existent dharmas that, throughout the future, are impartial, uniform, and consistent with the tathāgatagarbha. This means that, as the foundation of all dharmas, they are furnished with all dharmas, they are endowed with all dharmas, and they are neither separated nor cut off from mundane dharmas.[124]

Nota Bene: This [passage] elucidates an approach based on three types of tathāgatagarbha. What are the three? (1) The tathāgatagarbha as the container. When it abides in its own nature, it is able to contain at the fruition-ground the meritorious qualities of the tathāgatas. The tathāgata as container is called the tathāgatagarbha. (2) The tathāgatagarbha as the contained. This means that impure dharmas, which involve the bondage of defilements, all exist within the knowledge of the tathāgatas; they are what are perceived and grasped by the tathāgatas. The objects perceived by the tathāgatas are called the tathāgatagarbha. (3) The tathāgatagarbha that is cloaked and concealed. This refers to the tathāgata as dharmakāya, which is concealed by defilements. Since the tathāgatas choose to cloak themselves, it is called the tathāgatagarbha. The Trepiṭaka [Master of the Canon] Paramārtha has explained it in the above fashion.[125]

Analyzing this passage, the line "Those existent [dharmas] that, throughout the future, are impartial, uniform, and consistent" means that the essence of the one mind pervades all three limits [of past, present, and future]. **[615c]** But because he has already elucidated the original limit in the previous two approaches, in this approach he explains the future limit. Furthermore, wishing to elucidate the meaning of tathāgata [lit. thus-come], the phrase "throughout the future, are impartial, uniform, and consistent" is the meaning of "thus" *(tatha)* and the words "existent [dharmas]" is the meaning of "come" *(āgata)*. As the *Foxing lun* (Buddha-Nature Treatise) states:

> This true thusness is both the thusness that exists within what is not thusness as well as the thusness that exists within what is not non-thusness. The thusness of the two-vehicle adherents is the thusness that exists within what is not thusness, but not the thusness that exists within what is not non-thusness. Why is this the case? Two-vehicle adherents are swayed by their contemplation of what is actually spurious and false, and presume that the characteristics of impermanence, and so forth, are true thusness. Their contemplation of the spurious and false exists only at [the stage of] cause, not at the fruition-ground. Therefore, this thusness is subject both to maturation and decay. The thusness of bodhisattvas leaves behind the spurious and false, and perceives thusness from the standpoint of the true nature. Therefore, it does not distinguish whether it is the causal or fruition-ground and it is subject only to maturation, not decay.[126]

An extensive explanation is provided there. Therefore we know that the line "throughout the future, are impartial, constant" is an explicit elucidation of the meaning of "thus" *(tatha)* according to the Mahāyāna. The phrase "existent [dharmas]" clarifies the meaning of "come" *(āgata)*, for leaving mundane dharmas behind is an elucidation of what it means to "come" to the one mind. It is just as when one leaves behind the mundane, the five skandhas that are the objects of clinging do not reach the fruition-ground, for they "go" but do not "come." This thusness of the one mind still exists at the fruition-ground, for it can never be past. Therefore, it is said that the phrase "existent [dharmas]" reveals the meaning of "come." As the treatise [Buddha-Nature Treatise] says, "From [the first type of buddha-nature] that abides inherently [in deluded ordinary beings] . . . up through the [third type of buddha-nature that] is being achieved [and which will culminate in the fruition of buddhahood]. . . . "[127] This is exactly what is meant here.

In this wise, the one mind serves as the comprehensive support for all maculated and pure dharmas. "As the foundation of all dharmas" refers to the approach of original quiescence. There are none of the meritorious qualities as numerous as the sands of the Ganges with which it is not furnished; therefore, it says, "They are furnished with all dharmas." From the standpoint of its conditioned activities, there are none of the maculated dharmas as numerous as the sands of the Ganges with which it is not endowed; therefore, it says, "They are endowed with all dharmas." However, if we look at the mind's essence through these maculated dharmas, we will not be able to comprehend them completely; therefore, **[616a]** [those dharmas] will be separated and cut off [from one another]. But if we look at these maculated dharmas through the mind's essence, [that essence] will pervade all maculated dharmas so that there are none that will not be comprehended; therefore, it says, "They are neither separated nor cut off from mundane dharmas." This aspect of being "neither separated nor cut off" is the aspect of the concealed storehouse.

This third type [of tathāgatagarbha listed above in the *Neither Increase Nor Decrease Sūtra*] offers a concise clarification that the one mind pervades both motion and quiescence, and is the support for both maculations and purity. The second[128] type specifically elucidates that its active aspect serves as the support for maculated dharmas. The first type specifically elucidates that its quiescent aspect serves as the support for pure dharmas.

In the second [type], concerning the words "whose essences are dissociated from the original limit": the fact that all the defiled dharmas run counter to the mind's essence is what is meant by "dissociated." From the standpoint of its conditioned, active aspect, the essences of the one-mind is the support of those [defiled dharmas]; therefore, the essence of those [maculated] dharmas are dissociated [from the mind's essence]. Concerning the words "those impure dharmas that involve the bondage of defilements": those [maculated] dharmas that serve as the support evolve from out of the mind's essence, binding the essence of one's own mind and prompting one to remain associated with the maculations. Therefore, one clings to dharmas that are both the subject [the maculated dharmas] and the supported [the changes in accord with conditions]. This is the essence of the second type of tathāgatagarbha. "They can only be eradicated by the tathāgatas' bodhi-knowledge": only the path of liberation *(vimuktimārga)* can actually eradicate them. This aspect is as is fully explained in the *Essay on the Two Hindrances.*[129]

In the first [type], the phrase "[those pure dharmas] whose essences are associated with the original limit" means that the aspect of original quiescence contains meritorious qualities as numerous as the sands of the Ganges, which are associated with the mind. Therefore, this is the essence that is associated with meritorious qualities. The words "those pure dharmas" mean that the nature of the meritorious qualities that serve as the support remain far removed from the maculations; there, it embraces dharmas that serve as both the support and the object of support. This is the essence of the first [type of] tathāgatagarbha. "Those dharmas accord with reality, are neither false nor spurious, and are neither separated nor cut off [from reality]; they involve knowledge and are inconceivable dharmas": this line explicates the aspect of being "associated." This aspect of the dharmakāya is associated with all meritorious dharmas. Therefore, as a previous passage [in the *Śrīmālādevīsiṃhanāda-sūtra* (Lion's Roar of Queen Śrīmālā Scripture)] states, "That which is not separated, not cut off, not eradicated, not differentiated, and which is associated with the inconceivable dharmas of the buddhas is called the dharmakāya."[130]

What does this mean? The essence of this one mind has, in brief, five characteristics. What are the five? (1) **[616b]** It remains far removed from the differentiated characteristics of the objects to which one clings. (2) It is liberated from the discriminative grasping of the clinging subject. (3) It pervades all three time periods so that there is nothing with which it is not in equilibrium. (4) It is commensurate with the realm of empty space so that there is nothing that it does not pervade. (5) It does not fall into the extremes of existence and nonexistence, unity and difference; it passes beyond the loci of mental activities and surpasses the path of verbalization.

"It contains inherent meritorious qualities as numerous as the sands of the Ganges" also entails five aspects of its association with the essence. (1) Because each and every one of these meritorious qualities leaves behind characteristics that involve clinging, they are not separate from the dharmakāya. This is the first characteristic of association. Therefore, as the sūtra [the *Śrīmālādevīsiṃhanāda-sūtra*] says, "is not separated." (2) Because each and every one of these meritorious qualities is cut off from grasping at the objects of attachment, they are not cut off from the dharmakāya. This is the second characteristic of association. As the sūtra says, "not cut off." (3) Because each and every one of these meritorious qualities pervades the three time periods, temporally, it does not eradicate the limits of either past or future. This is the third characteristic of association. Therefore, it says "not eradicated." (4) Each and every one of these meritorious qualities is commensurate with the realm of empty space; spatially, there is no difference between this and that place. This is the fourth characteristic of association. Therefore, it says "not differentiated." (5) Each and every one of these meritorious qualities leaves behind all extremes and is an inconceivable object, for the pathways of verbalization are eradicated. This is the fifth characteristic of association. Therefore, as the sūtra says, "[It] is . . . inconceivable." All meritorious dharmas involve these five aspects, which are indistinguishable from the essence and which are interfused with the one taste; because of this rationale, they are termed "associated." It is not like the [mind] king and [mental] concomitants, which may have separate essences but remain associated with one another. Now in this [passage], the statement "[they] are neither separated nor cut off [from reality]; they involve knowledge and are inconceivable dharmas" means that we refer concisely to the aspect of enlightenment when referring to all the meritorious qualities and explain in brief these three aspects when referring to the five types of association. This is the first type [of tathāgatagarbha], the storehouse as the container.

The three types of storehouse can be briefly narrated in the above manner.

Concerning the twofold [account of] storehouse [II.A.2.b.ii.b.2.b], as the *Śrīmālādevīsiṃhanāda-sūtra* [Lion's Roar of Queen Śrīmālā Scripture] states:

> "The 'void tathāgatagarbha' is either separate, cut off, or differentiated; it is the storehouse of all the defilements. The 'nonvoid tathāgatagarbha' is neither separate, **[616c]** cut off, nor differentiated; it is the inconceivable dharma of the buddhas."[131]

Nota Bene: All the defiled dharmas are false and spurious. Because they involve the sense-spheres, which are unreal, they are "false." Because their essence involves distraction and agitation, they are "spurious." Because they are spurious, they are inauthentic. Because they are false, they are unreal. Because they are neither authentic nor real, they are called "void." Because it cloaks the tathāgata, it is termed the tathāgatagarbha. This is exactly the meaning of "void": to conceal and cloak what is authentic. All defiled sense-spheres are marked by unreality and are separated from the dharmakāya; therefore, they are said to be "separated." The essence of all the defilements is ensnared by spurious grasping and is cut off from the dharmakāya; therefore it is said to be "cut off." The term "differentiated" is used precisely because the preceding false and spurious distinctions and discriminations violate the impartial nature of the dharmakāya. Because of these three aspects, they are therefore "dissociated"; and the fact that they are neither true nor real is the aspect of "void." The term "nonvoid" means that all meritorious qualities are associated with the essence. Because that essence is not spurious, it is true; because that sphere is not false, it is real. Since it is true and real, it is termed "nonvoid." As the tathāgatas are cloaked there, it is called "tathāgatagarbha." The phrase "not separated, not cut off" explicates the aspect of "nonvoid." This aspect is as was explained in the threefold account of the storehouse. Nevertheless, in this [passage], the essence of the nonvoid tathāgatagarbha is identical to the first type among the three discussed above. The aspect of "void" in this [passage] is like the second type in the threefold account of tathāgatagarbha above, that is, the aspect of being concealed and cloaked, together with the third type there. Therefore, among these two preceding [types of tathāgatagarbha], we elucidate separately the two aspects of the container and the contained. Now, this twofold account of the tathāgatagarbha is intended to elucidate the aspect of voidness, which conceals and cloaks what is true and real. Therefore, we distinguish the two aspects of the container and the contained.

Furthermore, these two scriptures both elucidate specific aspects [of the tathāgatagarbha]. Therefore, we have separate explications based on twofold and threefold approaches.

I will now stop availing myself of the treatises and return to an exegesis of our text.

> **The Buddha replied, "The tathāgatagarbha is that characteristic of discriminative awareness that is subject to production and extinction, which conceals the principle so that it is not made manifest. [617a] This is [what is meant by the statement] 'as for this tathāgatagarbha, its nature is calm and motionless.' "**

"**That characteristic of discriminative awareness that is subject to production and extinction**" refers to the void tathāgatagarbha. Even while elucidating in this passage the aspect of the concealer, however, it does not say that this alone is the tathāgatagarbha. The statement "**the tathāgatagarbha is that . . . which conceals the principle so that it is not made manifest**" refers to the nonvoid tathāgatagarbha, which is a name for the tathāgatagarbha from the standpoint of what is concealed.

The words "**its nature is calm and motionless**" elucidates the fact that, although the nature of this storehouse may be concealed, it remains unaltered. This nature has five aspects, as explained in the *Wuxiang lun* [Treatise on Signlessness].[132] (1) The aspect of its varieties, which is an aspect of the nature. It is just like material dharmas, such as pots, clothes, and so forth, which all entail different varieties of the four great elements and thus all have the four great elements as their nature. In the same way, sentient beings are all ensconced in that one realm [of all sentient beings], and all their varieties emerge from that one realm. The *Mahāyānsaṃgraha* [Compendium of Mahāyāna Treatise] calls this the aspect of essential varieties,[133] while the *Buddha-Nature Treatise* calls it the aspect of self-nature.[134] The terminology may differ, but the meaning is identical. (2) The aspect of cause, which is an aspect of the nature. In the same way that wood contains the nature of fire and fire functions as its operative cause, [this aspect] is therefore termed "nature." In just the same way, the uncontaminated dharmas of the saints are perfected with this [nature] as their cause. In those other two treatises, this is referred to by the same term, "aspect of cause." (3) The aspect of production, which is an aspect of the nature. Just as in smelting true gold to produce a piece of jewelry, the piece of jewelry is produced with gold as its nature. This [dharma-] realm is also just the same: in producing the five aspects of dharmakāya[135] at the level of fruition, the production of that dharmakāya has this realm as its nature. In the *Compendium of Mahāyāna Treatise*, this is also called the "aspect of production."[136] In the *Buddha-Nature Treatise*, this is called the "aspect of being achieved,"[137] a separate aspect of cause. Because it appears on the doorstep to fruition and has therefore already been produced, it is called the aspect of "being achieved." (4) The aspect of unalterability, which is an aspect of the nature. Just as diamond, by its very nature, endures for a kalpa or more without increasing or decreasing, so too does this [dharma-] realm perdure throughout all three time periods, never decaying in this mundane world and never vanishing in the supramundane. In those other two treatises it is called the "aspect of being authentic and real."[138] **[617b]** The aspect of being authentic and real is this aspect of its unalterability. Therefore, while the terms may differ, the meaning is the same. (5) The aspect of secret storehouse, which is an aspect of the nature. It is just like yellow ore, which contains true gold by its very nature: if you do not mine that ore it is utterly without benefit, but by smelting it correctly, it may be put to use as precious metal. Therefore, its nature involves this aspect of a concealed storehouse. You should know that the nature of the tathāgatagarbha is also just the same: if you do not destroy its bonds, it will become externalized and maculated; but, as soon as you have destroyed those bonds, it will become internalized and pure. Therefore, know that this nature is the aspect of secret storehouse. In the *Buddha-Nature Treatise,* this is also called the "aspect of secrecy."[139] In the *Compendium of Mahāyāna Treatise,* it is called the "storehouse aspect."[140] It is transparently obvious that the idea is the same, even if the terms differ. Now, in this passage the reference to "nature" includes all five of these aspects. "Calm and motionless" is a brief elucidation of the last two aspects: "calm" is the aspect of secret storehouse; "motionless" is the aspect of unalterability.

We have finished with the preceding explicit and extensive treatments of the aspect of one enlightenment [II.A.2.b.ii.b.1–2].

> Haet'al Bodhisattva addressed the Buddha: "What is [meant by the statement] 'that characteristic of discriminative awareness that is subject to production and extinction'?"

From here onward there are six exchanges [viz. numbers 3 through 8] [II.A.2.b.ii.b.3–8], which resolve all remaining doubts and objections by elaborating on the original discussion *(illon saengnon).* The [question in this] first [viz. third] exchange [II.A.2.b.ii.b.3.a] seeks clarification of the characteristic of discriminative awareness that is the concealer.

> The Buddha replied: "Bodhisattva! This principle is free from either acceptance or rejection. If there were acceptance or rejection, then all kinds of thoughts would be produced. The thousands of conceptions and myriad of mentations are marked by production and extinction."

This answer [II.A.2.b.ii.b.3.b] is bifurcated into two portions:

initially [II.A.2.b.ii.b.3.b.I], a brief reply;
subsequently [II.A.2.b.ii.b.3.b.II], an extensive disquisition.

In the brief reply [II.A.2.b.ii.b.3.b.I], there are two passages. The first refers to the object of delusion. "This principle," which means the object of delusion, refers to the extinction of the loci of mental activities; therefore, it says, **"This principle is free from either acceptance or rejection." "Acceptance"** means approval; **"rejection"** means disapproval. This principle transcends all four antinomies [is, is not, both, neither] and is separate from all aspects of approval and disapproval, for it is not a locus for the activities of the discriminative mind.

The next [passage] elucidates the agent of delusion. **"If there were acceptance [617c] or rejection, then all kinds of thoughts would be produced"**: due to the presence of ignorance, one does not cognize impartiality. It is in fact the mind that discriminates between acceptance and rejection, because from this [mind] arises all six maculated states of mind. **"The thousands of conceptions and myriad of mentations are marked by production and extinction"**: although the six kinds of maculated states of mind[141] involve both coarse and subtle varieties, they are all antithetical to impartiality because they **"are marked by production and extinction."** As the *Awakening of Faith* says:

> Furthermore, concerning the phrase "discriminating the characteristics of [the realm of] production and extinction," this briefly is of two types. What are the two? (1) Coarse, because it is associated with mentation. (2) Subtle, because it is dissociated from mentation. Moreover, the coarsest of the coarse is the realm of ordinary beings. The subtlest of the coarse and the coarsest of the subtle are the realm of the bodhisattvas. The subtlest of the subtle is the realm of the buddhas. These two types of production and extinction exist in reliance on the permeation of ignorance. This is called the supporting cause and the coordinating conditions. It is called "supporting cause" because it involves the aspect of nonenlightenment and "coordinating conditions" because they involve the aspect that illusorily creates the sensory realms. If the cause is extinguished, then the conditions will be extinguished. Because the cause is extinguished, the mind dissociated [from mentation] will be extinguished. Because the condition is extinguished, the mind associated [with mentation] will be extinguished.[142]

Nota Bene: In this [excerpt], the line "coarse, because it is associated with mentation" refers to the three types of maculations associated [with mentation]. "Subtle, because it is dissociated from mentation" refers to the three types of maculations dissociated [from mentation]. "The coarsest of the coarse" refers to [1] the maculations associated with attachment and [2] the maculations associated with the uninterrupted [mind]. Because these both involve the sixth consciousness, this is the realm of ordinary beings. "The subtlest of the coarse" refers to [3] the maculations that are associated with discriminative awareness; this involves the seventh consciousness. "The coarsest of the subtle" are [4] the maculations dissociated from manifested materiality[143] [viz. the sense bases] and [5] the maculations dissociated from the perceiving subject. "The subtlest of the subtle" refers to [6] the maculations dissociated from the original activating [consciousness, *karmajāti[lakṣaṇa]vijñāna*].[144] These three [numbers 4–6] all entail the level of the eighth consciousness. In this [excerpt], the three types of subtle production and extinction refer to what is agitated by the winds of ignorance. Therefore, it says, "Because the cause is extinguished, the mind dissociated [from the maculations] is extinguished." Here, the three kinds of coarse production and extinction refer to that which is agitated by the winds of the sense-spheres. **[618a]** Therefore, it says, "Because the condition is extinguished, the mind associated [with the maculations] is extinguished." On this issue, the details are as explained in that treatise [viz. the *Awakening of Faith*].

Now, in this sūtra, "**the thousands of conceptions**" means that it comprehensively subsumes the subtle discriminations of the mind that are dissociated [from the maculations]. "**Myriad of mentations**" means that it comprehensively subsumes the coarse discriminations of the mind that are associated [with the maculations]. These two are both characterized by ratiocinative thought; for this reason, it says that they are "**marked by production and extinction.**"

> "Bodhisattva! Contemplate the characteristics of the original nature and the principle will be fulfilled in and of itself. The thousands of conceptions and myriad of mentations do not augment the principles of the path; instead, in vain they move and agitate [the mind] so that one forgets the original mind-king *(cittarāja)*."

From here onward is the extensive disquisition [II.A.2.b.ii.b.3.b.II], which is in three [subportions]:

one [II.A.2.b.ii.b.3.b.II.A], an elucidation that the principle is fulfilled in and of itself with regard to the characteristics of production and extinction;
two [II.A.2.b.ii.b.3.b.II.B], a clarification of the fact that the maculated faults are overcome in fulfillment of the principle;
three [II.A.2.b.ii.b.3.b.II.C], an analysis of the benefits that derive from extinguishing maculations in accordance with principle and leaving behind activity in order to enter into quiescence.

In the first [subportion, II.A.2.b.ii.b.3.b.II.A], "**bodhisattva**" is the term of address for Haet'al Bodhisattva. "**Contemplate the characteristics of the original nature**" means that the Buddha contemplates the nature of the tathāgatagarbha of original enlightenment. "**The principle will become perfected in and of itself**" means that the principle of the tathāgatagarbha of original enlightenment, which is the object of contemplation, is fully endowed with the immeasurable meritorious qualities of the nature. As the *Awakening of Faith* says,

> Moreover, the term "the characteristics of the essence itself of true thusness" means that . . . since time immemorial, the nature has itself been replete in all the meritorious qualities. This is to say, it means that the essence itself contains the aspect of the effulgence of great wisdom; the aspect of illuminating all the dharmadhātu; the aspect of authentic cognition; the aspect of the mind being pure in its self-nature; the aspects of permanence, bliss, selfhood, and purity; and the aspect of coolness, immutability, and autonomy. To be completely endowed in this wise with buddhadharmas more numerous than the sands of the Ganges, which are not separate, not eradicated, not differentiated, and which are inconceivable, and so on, up to . . . to be fully endowed with that aspect of being utterly free of deficiencies—this is called the tathāgatagarbha. It is also called the dharmakāya of the tathāgatas.[145]

Therefore this sūtra's statement here that "**the principle will become fulfilled in and of itself**" is a concise elucidation of the fact that [the tathāgatagarbha] is fully endowed in this wise with meritorious qualities. The first subportion of the passage is now complete.

The next [subportion, II.A.2.b.ii.b.3.b.II.B] **[618b]** clarifies the faults of thoughts that are agitated by production and extinction. In this [subportion], it concisely clarifies that [such thoughts] are worthless and injurious. This is just as in that treatise [the *Awakening of Faith*], where it extensively explicates this aspect:

> Question: You explained above that the essence, which is true thusness, is impartial and devoid of all characteristics. Why do you then go on to say that the essence has in this wise these different types of meritorious qualities?
>
> Answer: Although [its essence] actually does contain all kinds of meritorious qualities, being that it is free from any sign of differentiation, it is identical to this single taste and is just this one true thusness. What does this mean? As it is free from discrimination, it is devoid of any signs of discrimination; therefore, it is nondual.
>
> [Question:] How, then, is it that we may speak of differentiation?
>
> [Answer: Differentiation] may be inferred from the characteristics that are subject to extinction, which derive from the activating consciousness.

> [Question:] How can this be inferred?
>
> [Answer:] Since all dharmas are originally mind alone, in reality they are free from any conceptions about characteristics; but, owing to the existence of the spurious mind, thoughts arise from inattention and all the sense-spheres become visible. Therefore, we call it "ignorance." But if the nature of the mind does not give rise [to deluded thoughts], then it will in fact be the aspect of the effulgence of great wisdom. If the mind gives rise to [a specific] perception, there then will be [other] characteristics that cannot then be perceived; but if the nature of mind remains free from perception, this will in fact be "the aspect of illuminating all the dharmadhātu." Therefore, if the mind is active, this is not authentic conscious awareness, for where there is no self-nature, there is no permanence, bliss, selfhood, or purity.[146] . . . It is also the case that [the mind] will be completely endowed with spurious maculations more numerous than the sands of the Ganges. It is with reference to this aspect that it says that when the mind-nature is motionless, this will reveal all the characteristics of pure meritorious qualities more numerous than the sands of the Ganges. If the mind is subject to arising, and you furthermore cognize any previous dharmas that can be conceived, there will in fact be "deficiencies." In this wise, the immeasurable meritorious qualities associated with pure dharmas are in fact this one mind; there is nothing further to recollect. Therefore, it is "fully endowed." This is called the storehouse of the dharmakāya of the tathāgatas.[147]

Now, where this sūtra states "**instead in vain they move and agitate [the mind],**" this refers to [the *Awakening of Faith*'s statement] that "if the mind is active, this is not authentic conscious awareness, for where there is no self-nature, there is no permanence, bliss, selfhood, or purity"; therefore, it said "**move.**" "If the mind gives rise to [a specific] perception, there then will be [other] characteristics that cannot then be perceived"; therefore it said "**agitated.**" "**One forgets the original mind-king**": the immeasurable meritorious qualities are the one **[618c]** mind and that one mind is the host; therefore it is called the "**mind-king.**" The activities and agitations of production and extinction run counter to this mind-king so that one in turn is unable to take refuge in it; therefore it says "**forgets.**"

> **"If there are neither conceptions nor mentations, then production and extinction will vanish and will accordingly *(yathābhūta)* not be produced. All the consciousnesses will become peaceful and calm, the currents *(ogha)* will not be produced, and the five dharmas will be purified. This is called the Mahāyāna."[148]**

From here onward is the third [subportion, II.A.2.b.ii.b.3.b.II.C], on extinguishing maculations in accordance with principle and leaving behind activity in order to enter into quiescence. It is bifurcated into

an explicit elucidation [II.A.2.b.ii.b.3.b.II.C.1];
a reiterated conclusion [II.A.2.b.ii.b.3.b.II.C.2].

This is the explicit elucidation [II.A.2.b.ii.b.3.b.II.C.2], on leaving behind activity in order to enter into quiescence. "If there are neither conceptions nor mentations": initially, from the first bhūmi up until the [tenth] buddha-bhūmi, one gradually comes into conformity with the impartial dharmadhātu of the one mind until one is forever free from the discriminations of conceptions and mentations. "Then production and extinction will vanish": because the previous conceptions and mentations are characterized by production and extinction, now that one has become free from conceptions and mentations, one is forever free from discriminations and one remains forever removed from the two kinds of production and extinction [viz. coarse and subtle; see p. 617c above]. From this point on, one conforms to the principle and remains motionless and, throughout the future, one is never agitated again; therefore, it says "and will accordingly not be produced." When these two kinds of production and extinction are finally brought to an end, the agitations of the eight types of consciousnesses will all return to quiescence, and the currents of the six maculations (p. 617c above) will be forever extinguished, never to occur again; therefore, it says, "All the consciousnesses will become peaceful and calm, the currents will not be produced." Because the currents are not produced, the dharmadhātu will be perfectly effulgent, and because all the consciousnesses are peaceful and calm, the fourfold wisdom will be fully perfected; therefore, it says, "The five dharmas will be purified." Because there is no better merit than this that can be conveyed, he gives a general summation and says, "This is called the Mahāyāna." This completes the exegesis on the explicit clarification on leaving behind activity in order to enter into quiescence.

> "Bodhisattva! By accessing the purity of the five dharmas, the mind becomes free from deception. Once deception has vanished, one immediately accesses the stage of the tathāgatas' own enlightened, sanctified knowledge. One who accesses this stage of wisdom is well aware that all things have been unproduced since the beginning; and as he is aware that they originally are unproduced, he thence is free from deceptive conceptions."

This is the reiterated conclusion [II.A.2.b.ii.b.3.b.II.C.2], which is in three sentences. The first sentence, "By accessing the purity of the five dharmas, **[619a]** the mind becomes free from deception," means that, when one returns to the fountainhead of the mind, there then will no longer be any nonenlightenment [viz. deluded understanding] created by deceptive thoughts. The second sentence, "**Once deception has vanished, one immediately accesses the stage of the tathāgatas' own enlightened, sanctified knowledge,**" means that, when nonenlightenment has vanished, one immediately accesses the stage of the consummate wisdom of acquired enlightenment. This elucidates the fact that acquired enlightenment is perfected with respect to nonenlightenment. The third sentence—"**One who accesses this stage of wisdom is well aware that all things have been unproduced since the beginning; and as he is aware that they originally are unproduced, he thence is free from deceptive conceptions**"—means that, when the acquired enlightenment is fulfilled, one comes to know that the unenlightened activity of thought among the four characteristics [of production, maturation, decay, and extinction] is originally unproduced; hence, one knows that there originally are no deceptive conceptions. This elucidates the fact that acquired enlightenment is no different from original enlightenment. As the *Awakening of Faith* says:

> Sentient beings are presumed not to be enlightened because, since time immemorial, thought after thought has continued on interminably without ever leaving behind thought; therefore it is said they [are immersed in] beginningless ignorance. If a person gains no-thought, he then comes to know the characteristics of mind—production, maturation, decay, and extinction—because these are equivalent to no-thought. Nevertheless, in actuality, there are no such differences in acquired enlightenment, because the four characteristics exist simultaneously and are not independently established; they are originally impartial and are identical to the one enlightenment.[149]

Nota Bene: In this [passage], the line "if a person gains no-thought, he then comes to know the characteristics of mind—production, maturation, decay, and extinction" elucidates the phrase in this sūtra "**is well aware.**" "Nevertheless, in actuality, there are no such differences in acquired enlightenment" elucidates the line in this sūtra "**is well aware that [all things] have been unproduced since the beginning.**" "This is because the four characteristics exist simultaneously and are not independently established; they are originally impartial and are identical to the one enlightenment" elucidates the line in this sūtra "**as he is aware that they originally are unproduced, he thence is free from deceptive conceptions.**" The simile of crossing a river in a dream should be fully expounded in this context.[150]

> **Haet'al Bodhisattva addressed the Buddha: "Lord! One who is free from deceptive conceptions should have nothing that needs to be either tranquilized or brought to an end."**

From here onward is the second [viz. fourth] exchange [II.A.2.b.ii.b.4], which clarifies that there is nothing that needs to be either tranquilized or brought to an end. The implication of the question [II.A.2.b.ii.b.4.a] here is that if one says that **[619b]** originally there are no deceptive conceptions, there then would be nothing that needs to be tranquilized. Because there is no specific object to be tranquilized, the agent that tranquilizes [those objects] is also, then, nonexistent. And because there is no agent of tranquilization, there should be no acquired enlightenment. This is the kind of objection raised here.[151]

> **The Buddha responded: "Bodhisattva! Deceptions are originally unproduced; hence, there are no deceptions that need to be brought to an end. By knowing that the mind is actually no-mind, there then is no mind that needs to be tranquilized. Once [the mind] is free from differentiation and discrimination, the consciousnesses that manifest sensory objects are not produced. When there is nothing produced that needs to be tranquilized, this in fact would be nontranquilization—but also not nontranquilization. Why is this? Because it even tranquilizes nontranquilization."**

The intent of the answer [II.A.2.b.ii.b.4.b] is twofold:

initially [II.A,2.b.ii.b.4.b.I], acceptance of nontranquilization;
subsequently [II.A.2.b.ii.b.4.b.II], a rejection of nontranquilization.

"Acceptance" means that the acquired enlightenment does not differ from original enlightenment. "Rejection" means that the acquired enlightenment is not merely original enlightenment.

In the acceptance [subportion, II.A.2.b.ii.b.4.b.I], regarding the difference between bringing something to an end and tranquilization: since deceptions give rise to activity, they have to be brought to an end, and since the mind hurries toward agitation, it has to be tranquilized; but originally there is neither such arising nor such hurrying. Therefore, there [ultimately] is absolutely nothing that has to be brought to an end or tranquilized. "**Free from differentiation**" means that there is no perceived object *(sangbun)* that is different from the perceiving subject *(kyŏnbun)*. "**Free from . . . discrimination**" means that there is no perceiving subject that is different from the perceived object. Since both the perceived object and the perceiving subject are free from differentiation, the manifesting consciousnesses are originally unproduced. Because the foolish and the wise both understand that the past and future are unproduced, this clarifies that these also are originally unproduced from the standpoint of the present. Since nonenlightenment, the object that is to be tranquilized, is unproduced, [nonenlightenment] is indeed no different from acquired enlightenment, the agent of tranquilization. Given that there is no difference between them, [the Buddha] in this wise accepts [nontranquilization]. "But also not nontranquilization" means that it is also not the case that there is no acquired enlightenment that is not different from [original enlightenment]. "Because it even tranquilizes nontranquilization" means that one is able to tranquilize even deceptive states of mind that are not yet produced. Although production may be unascertainable, this is not to dismiss [the value of experiencing] nonproduction; and because [the value of] nonproduction cannot be dismissed, this is not to suggest that there are no objects that must be tranquilized. Accordingly, one cannot do without the [acquired] enlightenment, which serves as the agent of tranquilization. This is the intent of the answer.

> Haet'al Bodhisattva addressed the Buddha: "Lord! If one tranquilizes nontranquilization, then tranquilization would be produced. How then can you say it is unproduced?"

[619c] From here onward is the third [viz. fifth] exchange [II.A.2.b.ii.b.5], which elucidates the contemplation of nonproduction. The objection raised in the question [II.A.2.b.ii.b.5.a] is that, if one posits that [acquired] enlightenment is the agent of tranquilization, this then would produce a type of contemplation that serves as that agent of tranquilization. Although you may thereby dispel [the notion] that nonenlightenment occurs, you to the contrary end up validating the production of acquired enlightenment. How then can you say that you are able to realize the contemplation of nonproduction?

> The Buddha replied: "Bodhisattva! At the moment when tranquilization occurs it is produced, but after it is tranquilized there is no further tranquilization necessary. One should not linger in either nontranquilization or a nonabiding state. What then would be produced?"

The intent of the answer [II.A.2.b.ii.b.5.b] is twofold:

initially [II.A.2.b.ii.b.5.b.I], affirmation;
subsequently [II.A.2.b.ii.b.5.b.II], negation.

Affirmation [II.A.2.b.ii.b.5.b.I] accepts the [notion of] production. It involves the expedient contemplation, which serves as the agent that tranquilizes mental production. Moreover, it is just as when [one reaches the stage of] highest worldly dharmas *(laukikāgradharma):* although one may then tranquilize the production of consciousness but without clinging to consciousness, the mind that is the agent of tranquilization will still be produced but without clinging to anything. At the moment when this tranquilization occurs, it in fact is the acceptance of production. For this reason it says, "At the moment when tranquilization occurs it is produced."

[Negation, II.A.2.b.ii.b.5.b.II:] After this one thought has passed, it does not cling to nothingness. Because it does not cling to nothingness, the clinging mind is not produced. For this reason it says "**after it is tranquilized there is no further tranquilization necessary.**" At this time, because one leaves all discriminations far behind, one neither lingers in the nothingness of nontranquilization nor clings to this mind that is itself nonabiding. Both agent and object are annihilated forever and are utterly and completely impartial. What then, at such a time, would be able to be produced? This is the intent of the answer.

> **Haet'al Bodhisattva addressed the Buddha: "Lord! Concerning this mind that produces nothing: To what does it cling? What does it reject? In what characteristic of dharma does it linger?"**
>
> **The Buddha replied: "The mind that produces nothing does not cling to anything or reject anything. It lingers in no-mind and lingers in no-dharma."**

This is the fourth [viz. sixth] exchange [II.A.2.b.ii.b.6], which dispels the views of increase and decrease. All trainees still presume that the mind that accesses contemplation clings to the principle of signlessness and rejects all characteristics and qualities. In order to counter this view of increase, [the Buddha] therefore says "**does not cling to anything or reject anything.**" Alternatively, [trainees] presume that when one accesses contemplation, there are absolutely no dharmas that are the objects of abiding and also no mind that is the subject of abiding; it is in this wise no different from the ultimate uncompounded state *(asaṃskṛta)*. **[620a]** In order to remove this view of decrease, he therefore says, "**It lingers in no-mind and lingers in no-dharma.**" Although he may not be abiding in anything, he is not nonabiding; and because he is not nonabiding, we may say that he is abiding.

> **Haet'al Bodhisattva addressed the Buddha: "What do you mean by saying 'it lingers in no-mind and lingers in no-dharma'?"**
>
> **The Buddha replied: " 'Not producing states of mind' is what is meant by 'lingers in no-mind.' 'Not producing dharmas' is what is meant by 'lingers in no-dharma.' "**

From here onward is the fifth [viz. seventh] exchange [II.A.2.b.ii.b.7], which counters once again any remaining doubts.

[II.A.2.b.ii.b.7.a, Question:] The doubt expressed is this: "Since you referred to 'lingers,' then both mind and dharmas ought to exist. But if there is neither mind nor dharmas, you then should have said, 'not linger.' These words are extremely profound. How are we to believe and comprehend them?" Such is the doubt he has here.

[II.A.2.b.ii.b.7.b.I, Explicit Answer:] The intent behind the Buddha's response is not to validate the contemplating mind that is the agent of realization and not to validate the dharmas that reveal principles,[152] which are the objects of realization. Therefore, he says, "**Not producing states of mind [and] not producing dharmas.**" "Produce" is the same as "validate." Since one constantly avoids validating either mind or dharmas, it is not the "validation" that comes from getting lost in one's thoughts; therefore, it says, "**It lingers in no-mind and lingers in no-dharma.**" "Linger" is the same as "constancy": because one constantly refuses to withdraw from or to abandon it, it is called "lingering." The meaning of "linger" is explained in this manner. If you completely conform to this state of no-mind, how could they [mind and dharmas] be in opposition where they come into contact? Such is the explicit answer. Below is the reiterated elucidation.

> **"Oh son of good family! If one does not produce [a conception of] either mind or dharmas, [the mind] will then have no support *(apratiṣṭhita)*; not lingering over any compounded thing, the mind will be constantly void and calm, without any differentiated characteristics. It will be just like space, which is motionless and nonabiding, ungenerated and uncreated, and free from either that or this. Once one obtains the eye that is the voidness of mind and obtains the body that is the voidness of dharmas, the five skandhas and the six sense-bases will all become void and calm."**

From here onward is the second [portion, I.A.2.b.ii.b.7.b.II], the reiterated elucidation, which is in two [subportions]:

initially [I.A.2.b.ii.b.7.b.II.A], an elucidation of leaving behind all characteristics throughout all three time-periods;
subsequently [I.A.2.b.ii.b.7.b.II.B], an elucidation of perfecting one's cultivation of the six pāramitās by harmonizing with the dharmadhātu.

In the first [subportion, I.A.2.b.ii.b.7.b.II.A], there are three sentences:

an instruction [I.A.2.b.ii.b.7.b.II.A.1];
a simile [I.A.2.b.ii.b.7.b.II.A.2];
their correlation [I.A.2.b.ii.b.7.b.II.3].

[In the instruction subportion, I.A.2.b.ii.b.7.b.II.A.1], "**if one does not produce either mind or dharmas**" refers to the preceding line in the explicit-answer portion. "**[The mind] will then have no support**" **[620b]** means that, spatially, there is no differentiation between the agent and object of support; "**not lingering over any compounded thing**" means that, temporally, there are no compounded things manifesting in either past, future, or present. Because there is no past or future, "**the mind will be constantly void** and calm." Because there is no subject or object, it will be "without any differentiated characteristics."

From "it will be just like . . . " onward is the second [sentence, I.A.2.b.ii.b.7.b.II.A.2], a simile. "Motionless and nonabiding": it is just like empty space in this world, which is uncompounded and constantly abiding, without the activities of extinction in the past or production in the future; this is a simile for "not lingering over any compounded thing." Also not lingering over either the agent or the object of support may be compared to the line "[the mind] will then have no support." "Ungenerated and uncreated" is exactly the same as "the mind will be constantly void and calm." "Free from either that or this" is no different from "without any differentiated characteristics." For this reason, he brings up empty space as a simile for the contemplation of nonproduction.

In the correlation [I.A.2.b.ii.b.7.b.II.A.3], the line "once one obtains the eye that is the voidness of mind" means that, because one does not produce a state of mind that serves as the agent of contemplation, there is nothing that one is not able to contemplate. "Obtains the body that is the voidness of dharmas" means that, because one does not produce any dharmas that are the objects of contemplation, one achieves the impartial dharmakāya. "The five skandhas will become void" means that, because "one obtains the eye that is the voidness of mind," one penetrates to the voidness of the five skandhas throughout all three time periods. This can be correlated with the previous line that "space . . . [is] ungenerated and uncreated." "The six sense-bases will all become void" means that, because "one obtains the body that is the voidness of dharmas," one pervades this voidness of the six sense-bases both internally and externally. This correlates with the previous line "space . . . is . . . free from either that or this."

> "Oh son of good family! One who cultivates the dharma of voidness does not base himself on the three realms of existence and does not linger over the specific regulations of the Vinaya [the discipline]. Pure and free from thoughts, he neither appropriates nor releases anything. His nature is the same as adamant and is not deficient in the triratna [the three gems of the Buddha, Dharma, and Saṃgha]. His mind, emptied, is motionless and endowed with all the six pāramitās."

This is the second [subportion, I.A.2.b.ii.b.7.b.II.B], an elucidation of perfecting one's cultivation of the six pāramitās [by harmonizing with the dharmadhātu]. "One who cultivates the dharma of voidness" is a reference to the previous mind of void calmness. After this follows a specific elucidation of each of the six pāramitās. Because he "does not base himself on the three realms of existence" he has perfected the pāramitā of giving. Because he "does not linger over the specific regulations of the Vinaya," he has perfected the pāramitā of morality. Because he is "pure and free from thoughts," he has perfected the pāramitā of patient endurance. Because "he neither appropriates nor releases anything," he has perfected [the pāramitā of] vigorous effort. Because "his nature is the same as adamant," he has perfected [the pāramitā of] concentration. Because "[his nature] is not deficient in the triratna," he has perfected [the pāramitā of] prajñā. Why is this? Only this mind of one-pointed contemplation **[620c]** radiates everywhere and serves as the standard for resolving all points of controversy. Therefore, it is completely furnished with "the triratna." Since the import of all three jewels is fulfilled, it therefore says "not deficient." This one mind of voidness alone perfects the six pāramitās, without any specific action required; therefore, it says, "His mind, emptied, is motionless and endowed with all the six pāramitās."

> Haet'al Bodhisattva addressed the Buddha: "Lord! All the six pāramitās have characteristics. But how are dharmas that have characteristics capable of inducing transcendence?"
>
> The Buddha replied: "Oh son of good family! The six pāramitās of which I have spoken are signless and uncompounded."

From here onward is the sixth [viz. eighth] exchange [II.A.2.b.ii.b.8], which is a reiterated elucidation of the supramundane aspect of the six pāramitās.

[Question, II.A.2.b.ii.b.8.a:] Because the questioner seeks to resolve this issue by bringing up this doubt, he raises the issue of the phenomenal characteristics of the six mundane pāramitās in order to question whether the supramundane mind is also endowed with all six.

The answer [II.A.2.b.ii.b.8.b] is in two [portions]:

one [II.A.2.b.ii.b.8.b.I], a concise overview;
two [II.A.2.b.ii.b.8.b.II], an extensive explication.

This [sentence] is the concise overview [II.A.2.b.ii.b.8.b.I]. The term "signless" means that [each pāramitā] leaves behind all signs of the "three aspects" [*samnyun;* lit. "three wheels"]: [in the case of the pāramitā of giving, for example,] giver, recipient, and [the object given], and so forth. The term "uncompounded" means that it leaves behind the three [marks of] compoundedness, such as production, maturation, and so forth [viz. extinction]. As I explained previously, the fact that the one mind contains all six [pāramitās] means that each and every one [of the pāramitās] is "signless and uncompounded." Therefore these six pāramitās are supramundane; these are not the same as the characteristics and compoundedness associated with the mundane world.

> "Why is this? By accessing well [the mind-essence] and forsaking desires *(kāmavītarāgya)*, his mind will be constant and pure. His true speech, expedient devices, and original inspiration inspire others. This is *dānapāramitā* [perfection of giving]."

From here onward is the extensive explication [II.A.2.b.ii.b.8.b.II], which is in two [subportions]:

initially [II.A.2.b.ii.b.8.b.II.A], a specific explication [of each pāramitā]; subsequently [II.A.2.b.ii.b.8.b.II.B], a comprehensive clarification.

[The specific explication of each pāramitā, II.A.2.b.ii.b.8.b.II.A:] **"Why is this?"** raises this question: if there is an actual list of six [specific pāramitās], then how can they be **"signless"**?

[Explication of *dānapāramitā,* II.A.2.b.ii.b.8.b.II.A.1:] Initiating a transmutation of the basis *(āśrayaparivṛtti)* in true thusness is called **"forsaking desires,"** for this elucidates the fact that one forsakes desires for the three kinds of existence [the realms of desire, subtle materiality, and formlessness]. Because contemplating the mind-essence brings about comprehension, it says **"accessing well."** Because there is no further egress or access, it says **"his mind will be constant."** Because it forsakes the turbidity of the three wheels [viz. aspects, of each pāramitā], it says **"pure"**; this is identical to the preceding words **"[he] does not base himself on the three realms of existence"** (p. 620b). **[621a]** Because he speaks in accordance with principles, it says **"his true speech."** Because he guides through clever stratagems, it says **"expedient devices."** Although he is free from any active functioning, he edifies others in accordance with their capacity, just like the Heavenly Drum[153]—this is what is meant here. All sentient beings, through the one original enlightenment alone, prompt their fellow beings to take refuge together in the one enlightenment; for this reason, it says **"the original inspiration inspires others." This is** called the supramundane ***dānapāramitā.***

> **"As his earnest thoughts are tenacious and intent, his mind is constantly unabiding, pure and untainted, and he does not cling to the three realms. This is *śīlapāramitā* [perfection of morality]."**

[Explication of *śīlapāramitā,* II.A.2.b.ii.b.8.b.II.A.2:] He empathizes with sentient beings as if they were his only son; therefore, it says, **"As his earnest thoughts are tenacious and intent."** Because he dwells constantly in the world and does not linger in nirvāṇa, it says, **"His mind is constantly unabiding."** These [attitudes] guard against the errors of two-vehicle adherents. His contemplation of mind is lucid and intense, and not adulterated by any of the contaminants; therefore, it says **"pure and untainted."** Even while passing through all six destinies of life, he penetrates to the fact that they are all void and calm; therefore, it says, **"He does not cling to the three realms."** This brings a halt to the evil of ordinary beings and clarifies why he does not linger in the ethical characteristics of either ordinary persons or saints: this is identical to the preceding line "[he] **does not linger over the specific regulations of the Vinaya"** (p. 620b). **This is** called the supramundane **śīlapāramitā.**

> "Cultivating voidness and eradicating the fetters, he does not rely on any existing thing; he calms and quiets the three types of action and does not linger in either body or mind. This is *kṣāntipāramitā* [perfection of patient endurance]."

[Explication of *kṣāntipāramitā,* II.A.2.b.ii.b.8.b.II.A.3:] The first two passages ["cultivating voidness . . . existing thing"] means remaining quiescent in the principle of voidness and leaving behind the fetter of existence. The last two passages ["he calms and quiets . . . body or mind"] quiet the three types of action [via body, speech, and mind] and do away with body and mind. These are all aspects of the acquiescence to the nonproduction of dharmas, which is identical to the preceding line "pure and free from thoughts" (p. 620b).

> "Abandoning all numerical lists [of Buddhist concepts], he overcomes the views of both voidness and existence; he delves deeply into the voidness of the skandhas. This is *vīryapāramitā* [perfection of vigorous effort]."

[Explication of *vīryapāramitā,* II.A.2.b.ii.b.8.b.II.A.4:] The first two passages ["abandoning . . . voidness and existence"] is the aspect of leaving behind both coarse and subtle. "He delves . . . into the voidness" is the aspect of "advancing," which is identical to the preceding line "he neither appropriates nor releases anything" (p. 620b). This is the supramundane vīryapāramitā. **[621b]**

> "Abandoning completely void calmness [nirvāṇa], he does not linger in any type of voidness. The mind that resides in nothing dwells in great voidness.[154] This is *dhyānapāramitā* [perfection of meditation]."

[Explication of *dhyānapāramitā,* II.A.2.b.ii.b.8.b.II.A.5:] "Abandoning completely void calmness" means that one takes rebirth in order to edify [beings] throughout all the three realms of existence. "He does not linger in any type of voidness" means that he is not impeded by the five voidnesses [see below, p. 621b] and constantly proselytizes [all beings in] the ten directions; this clarifies the type of dhyāna that seeks to proselytize sentient beings. "The mind that resides in nothing": although his body may be immersed in the three realms of existence, his mind constantly resides in the emptiness of principle. "Emptiness of principle" is the principle that eradicates the characteristics of the three existences. "Dwells in great voidness": although he constantly proselytizes in all the ten directions, "his mind . . . dwells in great voidness." "Great voidness" is voidness as the principal characteristic of the ten directions; this elucidates the dhyāna that perfects the buddhadharmas. Although his body may go into action, his mind remains calm and motionless; this is identical to the preceding line "his nature is the same as adamant" (p. 620b).

Moreover, this aspect of "**great voidness**" involves, in brief, five types. (1) The two types of voidness, of person and of dharmas, is called "great voidness," as is explained in the *Mahāśūnyatā-sūtra* [Great Voidness Sūtra] of the *Saṃyuktāgama [Miscellaneous Āgama]*.[155] In the *Yogācārabhūmiśāstra* [Treatise on the Stages of Yoga Practice] the same explanation also appears.[156] (2) The voidness of the prajñāpāramitā is called "great voidness," as is explained in the *Mahāparinirvāṇa-sūtra* [Sūtra on the Great Decease].[157] The same explanation also appears in the *Laṅkāvatāra-sūtra* [Sūtra on the Entry into Laṅka].[158] (3) The voidness of the physical environment is called "great voidness," as is explained in the *Saṃdhinirmocana-sūtra* [Sūtra Elucidating the Hidden Connections].[159] The same explanation is found in the *Madhyāntavibhāgabhāṣya* [Distinguishing the Middle and Extremes].[160] (4) The voidness of the *ālayavijñāna* is called "great voidness," as is explained in the *Daśabhūmikasūtropadeśa* [Commentary on the Ten Bhūmis Sūtra].[161] (5) Voidness as the characteristic of the ten directions is called "great voidness," as is explained in the *Mahāprajñāpāramitā-sūtropadeśa* [Commentary to the Great Perfection of Wisdom Sūtra].[162] Now, the passage in this scripture refers to the fifth type and its explanation is given solely in accordance with that meaning.

> **"The mind is free from the characteristic of 'mind' and does not cling to empty voidness. No compounded things are produced and there is no realization of calm extinction. The mind has neither egress nor access, and the nature is constantly in equilibrium. The edge of reality of all dharmas has the nature of certitude. One does not rely on any of the bhūmis and does not linger in wisdom. This is [621c] prajñāpāramitā [perfection of wisdom]."**

[Explication of prajñāpāramitā, II.A.2.b.ii.b.8.b.II.A.6:] "**The mind is free from the characteristic of 'mind'** " means that one does not oneself validate internally any characteristic of a mind that contemplates. "**Does not cling to empty voidness**" means that one does not cling to the void nature that empties mind. This is the wisdom that derives from realizing the path [for oneself]. "**No compounded things are produced**" means that one penetrates to the fact that all compounded things are originally unproduced. "**There is no realization of calm extinction**" means that one perpetually proselytizes externally without being attached to nonproduction. This is the wisdom that derives from teaching the path [to others]. "**The mind has neither egress nor access and the nature is constantly in equilibrium**" means that the two previous [aspects of] the path are never separate from one another. Though active, they are constantly calm; though calm, they are perpetually active. Therefore, they have "**neither egress nor access.**" Both action and calmness are constant, and yet neither is impeded by either extreme; therefore, "**the nature is constantly in equilibrium.**" "**The edge of reality of all**

dharmas has the nature of certitude": this is a disquisition on the characteristic of the constant calmness that derives from realizing the path, which is identical to the true edge [of reality] because it is the same as the dharma-nature. **"One does not rely on any of the bhūmis and does not linger in wisdom"**: this is a disquisition on the reasons for the perpetual activity involved in teaching the path; one neither relies on nor is attached to the ten levels of the dharmadhātu,[163] and neither lingers in nor is impeded by the wisdom of calm radiance. Herein, [this passage] refers to the aspects of "the radiance of enlightenment" [of the sublime-enlightenment stage], "worthy of serving as a standard," and "resolving all points of controversy"; it is identical to the line above **"[his nature] is not deficient in the triratna"** (p. 620b). **This is** called the supramundane **prajñāpāramitā.**

The preceding subportion on the specific explication of the six pāramitās [II.A.2.b.ii.b.8.b.II.A] is finished.

> **"Oh son of good family! Since these six pāramitās all gain the original inspiration and access the nature of certitude, they supernally transcend the world. This is unobstructed liberation."**

From here onward is the second [subportion, II.A.2.b.ii.b.8.b.II.B], a comprehensive clarification, which is bifurcated into

initially [II.A.2.b.ii.b.8.b.II.B.1], a clarification that the six pāramitās are identical to liberation;
subsequently [II.A.2.b.ii.b.8.b.II.B.2], an elucidation that liberation is in fact nirvāṇa.

In the first [category, II.A.2.b.ii.b.8.b.II.B.1], the statement **"all gain the original inspiration and access the nature of certitude"** means that acquiring the practice of all six pāramitās is equivalent to original enlightenment. Because manifesting original enlightenment accomplishes the practice of original inspiration, one accesses the tathāgatagarbha, whose nature is originally calm and quiet, without beginning or end, and without change or evolution. Because in this wise the six pāramitās gain the original inspiration, they are far removed from characteristics that flow forth from deceptive conceptions; **[622a]** therefore, it says **"they supernally transcend the world."** Because [the six pāramitās] access the dharma-nature, they pervade the entire dharmadhātu, are signless and uncompounded, and are neither bound nor free; therefore, it says, **"This is unobstructed liberation."**

> **"Oh son of good family! In this way, dharmas that are marked by liberation are all free from signs and practices and are also free from both liberation and nonliberation. This is what is meant by liberation. Why is this? The characteristic of liberation means to be free from both signs**

and practices. It is motionless and undisturbed; it is calm and quiet nirvāṇa, but it also does not cling to the characteristics of nirvāṇa."

This is the second [category, II.A.2.b.ii.b.8.b.II.B.2], a clarification [*sic;* "elucidation" above] that liberation is in fact nirvāṇa. It is in two [subcategories]:

initially [II.A.2.b.ii.b.8.b.II.B.2.a], a clarification of liberation;
subsequently [II.A.2.b.ii.b.8.b.II.B.2.b], a reference to nirvāṇa.

In the first [subcategory, II.A.2.b.ii.b.8.b.II.B.2.a], the statement "**are all free from signs and practices**" means that the practice of all six pāramitās is in fact the original enlightenment. The characteristic of original enlightenment leaves behind both signs and nature; therefore, it says "**free from signs.**" The practice of the six pāramitās leaves behind both cultivation and practice; therefore, it says "**free from . . . practices.**" Because both practices and signs are eradicated, it says "**are all free from signs and practices.**" "**Dharmas that are marked by liberation**": since this is the case, how could there be either a freedom that derives from sloughing off bonds or a bondage that derives from a lack of freedom? Therefore, it says, "**They are also free from both liberation and bondage.**"

[In subcategory II.A.2.b.ii.b.8.b.II.B.2.b, a reference to nirvāṇa:] "**Why is this?**": that is, why is the practice of the six pāramitās said to be free of both characteristics and practice? In answer to this issue, he says that in this wise the six pāramitās are not merely liberation but are also nirvāṇa. Therefore, it says "**free from both signs and practices.**" "**The characteristic of liberation means to be free from both signs and practices**" is a description of the previous [subcategory of] liberation. "**It is motionless and undisturbed; it is calm and quiet nirvāṇa**": this clarifies that [the six pāramitās] are in fact nirvāṇa. He seeks here to clarify the explanation given above. The practice of the six pāramitās is free from both activity and motion, and also free from either distraction or agitation; it is nirvāṇa, which is originally calm and quiet. Since it is nirvāṇa, how can it involve either characteristics or practice? Because it leaves behind the signs of both motion and agitation, it says "**calm and quiet.**" But because it also leaves behind that nature of calm quiescence, "**it also does not cling to the characteristics of nirvāṇa.**" In this [passage], the six pāramitās, **[622b]** liberation, and nirvāṇa all apply from the first bhūmi up to and through the buddhabhūmi. As for the term "**nirvāṇa,**" of its four types, it here refers to the [first type of] nirvāṇa—that which is originally pure—which is identical to the inconceivable liberation.[164] Based on this sense that it is autonomous and unhindered, it therefore is called the unobstructed liberation.

Question: The meaning of liberation has myriads of implications. Liberation is included among the two paths.[165] Liberation is represented among the three points [of the Siddham letter i].[166] Liberation appears among the five aspects of the dharmakāya.[167] Liberation appears in a list of ten types of liberation.[168] Of all these various types, which is meant here?

Answer: Here it means the liberation among the three aspects,[169] because liberation in fact is nirvāṇa. He wishes to elucidate that the practice of the six pāramitās and the meritorious qualities of these three aspects, if explained according to reality, are already achieved at the first bhūmi and are ultimately consummated at the stage of sublime enlightenment. As a sūtra says, "If a bodhisattva abides in great nirvāṇa, he can accomplish great matters."[170] An extensive explanation appears there.

Haet'al Bodhisattva heard these words. His mind greatly pleased and elated, he gained what he never had before *(adbhūta)*. Wishing to proclaim the meaning and intent [of this sermon], he recited these gāthās:

1. That Lord who is replete in great enlightenment,
2. Has expounded the dharma for this congregation,
3. It has all been explained from the standpoint of the one vehicle,
4. Drawing nothing from the paths of either of the two vehicles.
5. The signless inspiration that has but a single taste,
6. Is like great space,
7. There is nothing it does not embrace.
8. According to the differences in each of their natures,
9. All things gain the original locus.

From this point onward is the second [subsection, II.B], reiterative verses. In this [subsection], it starts with a preface [II.B.1] proclaimed by the sūtra editor.

Among the verses themselves [II.B.2] there are seven quatrains [in twenty-eight lines], which are in two [subparts]:

initially [II.B.2.a], six specific quatrains;
finally [II.B.2.b], a summarizing quatrain.

In this first [subpart on specific quatrains] there are also two [divisions]:

one [II.B.2.a.i], two quatrains and one line [ll. 1–9] that give a concise overview in verse form of what has preceded;
two [II.B.2.a.ii], three quatrains and three lines [ll. 10–24] that give an extensive explication in verse form of what follows.

In the concise overview [II.B.2.a.i], the statement "the stage of wisdom of all the buddhas accesses the real characteristic of dharmas because of the nature of certitude. . . . [Their] expedients and spiritual powers are all the inspiration of signlessness" (p. 609b–c) [corresponds] to the first quatrain here [ll. 1–4]. "The explicit meaning of the one enlightenment [622c] is difficult to comprehend and difficult to access. . . . All [the tathāgatas] explain the single taste to those sentient beings who are capable of deliverance" (pp. 609c–610a): here, in these verses, it gives in verse form all three aspects [of instruction, simile, and correlation]: that is to say, the first line [l. 5] is the explanatory verse on the dharma instruction; the next two lines [ll. 6, 7] are the explanatory verses presenting the simile; and the last two lines [ll. 8, 9] are the verses that give the correlation with the simile.

10. Abandoning mind and self just as he has,
11. Is accomplished through the one dharma
12. Practices that involve identity and difference,
13. All gain the original inspiration,
14. And extirpate dualistic characteristics and views.

From this point on is the text of the verses that gives an extensive explication [II.B.2.a.ii], which is in two [subdivisions]:

initially [II.B.2.a.ii.a], five lines [ll. 10–14] that provide an extensive account in verse form of the signless contemplation;
subsequently [II.B.2.a.ii.b], two and a half quatrains [ll. 15–24] that provide an extensive account of the aspect of one enlightenment.

In the extensive account of signless [contemplation, II.B.2.a.ii.a] (see *KSGN*, p. 611a), there was an explicit explanation [of the inspiration of signlessness, II.A.2.b.ii.a.1] and a reiterated elucidation [of the mind of one enlightenment, II.A.2.b.ii.a.2]. Here, the first two lines [ll. 10, 11] present in verse form the text of the explicit explanation. That previous explicit account was also in two subsegments:

initially [II.A.2.b.ii.a.1.a], [an account of] expedient contemplation;
subsequently [II.A.2.b.ii.a.2.b], an explanation of the unmediated contemplation.

Now, this verse [ll. 10–14] presents in verse form the text on the unmediated contemplation. [A passage] there said, "It enables all those sentient beings to leave behind mind and self" (p. 611b), and so forth, continuing with an extensive explanation of leaving behind both subject and object. Now, these two lines [ll. 10, 11] are an explicit versification of that passage. The phrase "The one dharma" [in this verse] means that one leaves behind the extremes of both existence and nonexistence and contemplates just this middle way, because this enables one to leave behind the grasping at mind and self.

In the text of the reiterative elucidation [II.A.2.b.ii.a.2, a series of four dialogues that resolve doubts and objections (p. 612a ff.)], there were four exchanges. Now, these two lines [ll. 12, 13] versify the first two exchanges [II. A.2.b.ii.a.2.a, b]. The line "practices that involve identity and difference" [correlates with] the passage in the answer to that first exchange, "All the characteristics of the mind originally have no origin" (p. 612b). This sort of passage describes the "practice that involve[s] identity," which is the generic characteristic. In the second answer, it says, "If there is someone who retains a conception of self, he should be encouraged to contemplate the twelvefold chain of causal conditioning *(pratītyasamutpāda)*" (p. 613a). It also stated: "If there is a person who conceives of a self, he should be encouraged to abandon his view [that the self] exists. If there is a person who conceives that there is no self, he should be encouraged to abandon his view [that the self] does not exist. If a person conceives that the mind can be produced, he should be encouraged to abandon [his view that] the nature [of the mind] is subject to extinction. If a person conceives that the mind can be extinguished, he should be encouraged to abandon [his view that] the nature [of the mind] is subject to production" (p. 613a–b). This kind of passage describes this "practice . . . that involve[s] difference," a contemplation of the characteristics of particularity. Because these "practices that involve identity and difference" are no different regarding what they access, it said, "All gain the original [623a] inspiration" (p. 621c). As the end of the previous passage stated, "Once these views about the nature are extinguished, he will immediately approach the edge of reality" (p. 613b).

Furthermore, this verse's statement "and extirpate dualistic characteristics and views" is a versification of the subsequent two exchanges [viz. II. A.2.b.ii.a.2.a, b]. In that third answer appears the statement: "When a sentient being perceives that a dharma is produced, this causes the extinction of the view of nonexistence. When he sees the extinction of dharmas, this causes the extinction of the view of existence" (p. 614a). Now, here we have an explicit versification of this [passage] and it therefore says "extirpate dualistic . . . views." In the fourth answer, it said, "When production and extinction are both extinguished, production inherently would not be produced and the mind would be constantly void and calm; and that which is void and calm is nonabiding" (p. 614b). We now have an explicit versification of this [passage] and it therefore says "extirpate dualistic characteristics."

15. Of that nirvāṇa which is calm and tranquil,
16. One also neither lingers in, nor clings to, the realization.
17. Accessing that place of certitude,
18. There are neither characteristics nor practices.

The two verses and half a stanza [ll. 15–24] from here onward provide [in verse form an account of the subdivision on] an extensive explanation of the one enlightenment [II.A.2.b.ii.b]. In this extensive explanation of the one enlightenment, there was an explicit and extensive explanation [viz. two exchanges that treated the aspect of the tathāgatagarbha of one enlightenment, II.A.2.b.ii.b.1–2] and a reiteration [viz. six exchanges that resolved all the remaining doubts and objections by elaborating on the original discussion, II.A.2.b.ii.b.3–8]. Now, these stanzas only versify the reiteration. In the text of the reiteration there were six exchanges, here treated in two parts. The single quatrain above [ll. 15–18] gives a versification of the sixth answer; the subsequent one and a half quatrains that follow [ll. 19–24] versify the fifth answer. The prior four exchanges are elided and not versified here. In the sixth answer [II.A.2.b.ii.b.8.b], there appear the words "[Since these six pāramitās all . . .] access the nature of certitude, they supernally transcend the world. This is unobstructed liberation. . . . The characteristic of liberation means to be free from both signs and practices. It is motionless and undisturbed; it is calm and quiet nirvāṇa, but it also does not cling to the characteristics of nirvāṇa" (pp. 621c–622a). These stanzas here switch the order of versification.

19. In that stage of calm extinction where the mind is void,
20. The calm, extinct mind is unproduced.
21. It is identical to the adamantine nature,
22. Which is not deficient in the triratna.
23. Endowed with all six pāramitās,
24. One ferries across all sentient beings.

These lines give a versification of the fifth answer [II.A.2.b.ii.b.7.b]. The text there states: "If one does not produce either mind or dharmas, [the mind] will then have no support *(apratiṣṭhita)*; not lingering over any compounded thing, the mind will be constantly void and calm, without any differentiated characteristics. . . . His nature is the same as adamant and is not deficient in the triratna. His mind, emptied, is motionless and endowed with all the six pāramitās" (p. 620a–b). Now this verse here **[623b]** gives a versification in the proper sequence.

25. Supernally transcending the three realms of existence—
26. The Hīnayāna is never capable of any of it.
27. The dharma seal that has but a single taste,
28. This is what is perfected by the one vehicle.

This one quatrain is a summary versification of the principal intent of this whole preceding chapter [II.B.2.b]. The principal intent of this whole text is as has been explained above.

At that time, the whole congregation heard the exposition of these ideas. Their minds greatly pleased and elated, they were able to abandon mind and self. They accessed voidness and signlessness, which are broad and expansive, vacant and vast. All gained certitude, freeing

> themselves from the fetters and drying up the contaminants [*āsrava*; of existence, nonexistence, and speculative views].

In this chapter, there are three sections. The first two sections [viz. I, II] were finished with the above [verses], which constitute the main body [of the chapter]. This [passage] is the third section [III], when the congregation gains benefit.

"They were able to abandon [all conceptions of] mind and self" means that they realized the true thusness of the two types of voidness. "Freeing themselves from the fetters and drying up the contaminants" means that they eradicated these two types of delusions [that are eradicated on the path] of vision *(darśanamārga)* and [the path of] cultivation *(bhāvanāmārga)*. This [statement] seeks to elucidate the fact that when one has accessed the first bhūmi via the path of vision, one straightaway eradicates delusions regarding vision together with delusions regarding cultivation. The meaning here is as explained in the *Miluo suowen lun* [Treatise on the Questions Asked by Maitreya].[171] A detailed explanation appears in the *Essay on the Two Hindrances.*[172]

Exposition of the *Vajrasamādhi-Sūtra*

Roll Two

[Part Four: An Exegesis of the Text (cont.)]

[Section Two: Main Body (cont.)]

VAJRASAMĀDHI-SŪTRA, CHAPTER THREE: THE PRACTICE OF NONPRODUCTION

[623c] At the time when a bodhisattva perfects his contemplation practice, he cultivates according to principles that he has come to understand through his own personal contemplation of mind: namely, that the mind is neither produced nor unproduced and his practice also is neither existent nor nonexistent. It is only in order to leave behind the extreme of erroneous affirmation *(samāropikā)* [about the existence of things] that we provisionally refer to nonproduction. One should neither produce a thought in regard to production nor produce a thought in regard to nonproduction; therefore, in order to leave behind the extreme of denigration *(apavāda)*, we also provisionally refer to "practice."[173] Although this is not a practice that is conditioned, it also is not a practice that is unconditioned, either. For this reason, this chapter is titled "The Practice of Nonproduction."

Second Division of Contemplation Practice: Extinguishing the Mind Subject to Production in Order to Explain the Practice of Nonproduction

At that time, Simwang [Mind-King] Bodhisattva heard the Buddha's explanation of the dharma, which transcended the three realms of existence and was inconceivable. Arising from his seat, he joined his palms together in supplication and asked in gāthās:

Among the six divisions of the sequential elucidation of contemplation practices, the first—the [contemplation] Rejecting All Characteristics of Sense-Objects to Reveal the Signless Contemplation—has been completed as above. From this point on is the second [division of contemplation practice]: Extinguishing the Mind Subject to Production in order to Explain the Practice of Nonproduction.

The exegesis is in three [sections]:

One [I], an explicit explanation;
Two [II], praise;
Three [III], a clarification of hearing the explanation and gaining benefit.

In the initial [section], an explicit explanation, there are four [subsections]:

one [I.A], a series of dialogic exchanges;
two [I.B], a series of exchanges in which [the Buddha] scrutinizes [the bodhisattva];
three [I.C], the bodhisattva gains comprehension;
four [I.D], finalizing the Tathāgata's narrative.

The first [subsection] is in six [parts]:

one [I.A.1], a question;
two [I.A.2], an answer;
three [I.A.3], a problematic point;
four [I.A.4], a rebuttal;
five [I.A.5], a request;
six [I.A.6], an explication.

The initial [part, I.A.1] is in two [subparts]. This initial [subpart, I.A.1.a] is the preface of the sūtra editor. **[624a]**

"**Simwang [Mind-King] Bodhisattva**": his name is derived from his essential character. The meaning of "mind-king" is briefly of two types. One, the mind—that is, the eight consciousnesses—controls all the mental states *(caitta);* for this reason, it is called "mind-king." Two, the dharma of the one mind has comprehensive control over all the meritorious qualities *(guṇa);* for this reason, it is called "mind-king." Now, this bodhisattva has accessed the practice of nonproduction and has realized the [latter] one-mind king; hence, he derives his name from this experience. Now, in this chapter is clarified the practice of nonproduction and, therefore, it is Mind-King Bodhisattva who raises the questions.

"**[The Buddha's explanation . . .] transcended the three realms of existence and was inconceivable**": his questions derive from what he had just heard. This is the grounds for his question. What "he had just heard" was the explanation of the previous chapter.

I will now bring up the last [part of the last chapter] so as to tie it in with the first part [of this chapter].

The final verse said, "**Supernally transcending the three realms of existence**" [l. 25], and so on up to the completion of the narrative (p. 623b et passim).

The meaning of what the Tathāgata has said,
Transcends the world and is free from characteristics,
It enables all sentient beings,
To complete the annihilation of the contaminants.
Eradicating the bonds and emptying both mind and self,
This then will be [the state of] nonproduction.
But how, if there is nothing that is produced,
Will one gain the acquiescence to the nonproduction [of dharmas]?

These two verses are the expression of the question [second subpart, I. A.1.b]. Here, the initial verse expresses his comprehension of the preceding explanation. The first [two lines] demonstrate comprehension of the previous line [l. 27], "the dharma seal that has a single [taste]." The latter half expresses comprehension of the following line [l. 28], "Is perfected by the one vehicle."

The latter verse is the actual posing of [the bodhisattva's] question. There, the first half describes the meaning of nonproduction; the latter half is the question about the acquiescence to nonproduction. [This question is raised because], if there is no production, there should be no need to have any intention of acquiescing to it.

At that time, the Buddha proclaimed to Simwang Bodhisattva: "Oh son of good family! The acquiescence to the nonproduction of dharmas [means to realize that] dharmas are originally unproduced. Since all practices produce nothing, there is no way to practice this nonproduction. So achieving the acquiescence to nonproduction is in fact a deception."

This is the second part [I.A.2], the answer. There are two ideas presented in this answer. The former [I.A.2.a] points out the characteristics of the acquiescence to nonproduction. The latter [I.A.2.b] elucidates the fault of presuming that the acquiescence to nonproduction can actually be attained.

[I.A.2.a:] "The acquiescence to the nonproduction of dharmas" means to penetrate to the fact that dharmas are originally unproduced. Thus, concentration, wisdom, and all the compounded formations will also not be produced.

[I.A.2.b:] This is not to imply that **[624b]** there is some practice that catalyzes acquiescence to that nonproduction. For this reason it says, "There is no way to practice this nonproduction." During this [process], if one actually were to achieve some practice that is the agent of this acquiescence, this then would pervert the authentic acquiescence, which is nonabiding and uncompounded. For this reason, it says "[it] is in fact a deception."

Simwang Bodhisattva asked: "Lord! You say that 'achieving the acquiescence of nonproduction is in fact a deception.' [But is the converse

> then true: that] nonachievement and nonacquiescence perforce are not deceptions?"

This is the third [part, I.A.3], a problematic point. The issue behind the problem is this: if one were to presume that achievement and acquiescence are deceptions, then one should also say that "nonachievement and nonacquiescence perforce are not deceptions." Since, to the contrary, they too are deceptions, all those who train in the Mahāyāna and have nothing more to achieve would make this assumption and themselves presume that these are not deceptive. This problem is raised so that [the Buddha] may elucidate that deceptiveness.

> The Buddha replied: "Not so. Why is this? If nonachievement and nonacquiescence exist, then so would achievement. If achievement and acquiescence[174] exist, then so would production. If achievement is produced, there then would exist dharmas that are the objects of that achievement. So both [achievement and acquiescence] are deceptions."

This is the fourth [part, I.A.4], the rebuttal, which is in two [subparts].

"Not so" is the explicit rebuttal [I.A.4.a].

From "why is this?" onward is the second explanatory rebuttal [I.A.4.b]. The issue behind the rebuttal is this: [if that Bodhisattva believes that] there is "nonachievement and nonacquiescence," then, even though he may not achieve the state of existence in which achievement and acquiescence are present, he still might achieve that state of nonexistence in which achievement and acquiescence are absent. But since he does in fact achieve this nonexistence, his mind abides in nonexistence. Since the mind is abiding, it is subject to production. This means that the mind is produced with regard to something that is achieved. This also contradicts the fact of nonproduction and nonachievement. For this reason, he says, "So both are deceptions."

> Simwang Bodhisattva asked: "Lord! How is it that the mind may be free from either acquiescence or production and yet not be deceptive?"

This is the fifth [part, I.A.5], a request. [The bodhisattva] has attempted to follow the thread of the argument, but he still is unable to comprehend it. Therefore, he must beseech [the Buddha], requesting guidance. **[624c]**

> The Buddha replied: "The mind that is free from both acquiescence and production—that mind has neither form nor shape.[175] It is like heat [lit. the nature of fire], which, though latent in wood, cannot be found there.[176] Because its nature is fixed, [mind] is nothing more than a name and a word; its nature is unascertainable. Wishing to allude to this prin-

> **ciple, [the buddhas] have provisionally named it [mind], but this name is unascertainable. This is also the case for the characteristics of the mind: their location cannot be found. If one knows that the mind is like this, the mind will then not produce anything.**

This is the sixth [part, I.A.6], the explication. It is in four [subparts]:

first [I.A.6.a], analyzing the principle of nonattainment;
next [I.A.6.b], revealing the principle of nonproduction;
third [I.A.6.c], bringing up the negative aspects [of presuming that the mind-nature exists in reality];
fourth [I.A.6.d], clarifying the positive aspects [of understanding the mind-nature].

The initial [subpart] is in three [divisions]:

the instruction [I.A.6.a.i];
the simile [I.A.6.a.ii];
the correlation [I.A.6.a.iii].

In the first [division, I.A.6.a.i, the instruction], the statement "**the mind that is free from both acquiescence and production**" describes the mind that explicitly abides in the acquiescence to [the nonproduction of] dharmas. The statement "**that mind has neither form nor shape**" elucidates the fact that the mind is unascertainable. "**Form**" refers to "essence." "**Shape**" refers to "aspect." Since we search for the essential aspect of the mind in respect to all kinds of conditions, whether those [conditions] are identical or different, they are all unascertainable. This is why it says that [the mind] "**has neither form nor shape**"; this does not mean that it is without any material form, shape, or characteristic.

In the simile [division, I.A.6.a.ii], "**it is like heat [lit. the nature of fire], which, though latent in wood**" is a simile for the mind of acquiescence. Although it is latent within the principle, it "**cannot be found there.**" Since wood is comprised of all kinds of subtle particles, there is absolutely no place inside it where heat is latent; in just the same way, the principle contains approaches to dharma as numerous as the sands of the Ganges, but if one were to seek the mind therein, its abiding-place could never be found. And, just like the principle that heat has no place where it is latent, whether buddhas exist or not, the dharma-nature remains constant; therefore, it says "**because its nature is fixed.**" Despite the use of this word "**heat,**" there is no such aspect that can be ascertained; in this wise, although heat cannot be ascertained, this is not to say that there is no heat in wood. "**Wishing to allude to this principle,**" [the buddhas] use the term '**heat,**" but examining this term, it is merely like all other words. Examining in turn all words, they are all discovered to be unascertainable. The name and characteristics of the mind of acquiescence should also be understood in the same manner.

Next, the correlation [division, I.A.6.a.iii]: the line "**this is also the case for the characteristics of the mind**" means that a bodhisattva who attains acquiescence "**knows that the mind is [625a] like this.**" So how will he ever be able to produce a mind of clinging in regard to these [mental characteristics]? For this reason, it says "**the mind will then not produce anything.**"

> **"Oh son of good family! The nature and characteristics of the mind are like the *āmalaka* (myrobalan) fruit: they are not self-generated; they are not generated by some external agent; they are not produced symbiotically; they are not produced in the absence of a cause for that production.[177] Why is this? Because these conditions alternate successively. These conditions are generated, but there is no production; these conditions decay, but there is no extinction. Whether hidden or made manifest, they are signless. Their fundamental principle is calm and extinct. There is no place where they abide, nor is there seen anything that abides, because their natures are fixed."**

From here onward is the second [subpart, I.A.6.b], clarifying the principle of nonproduction. It is in two [divisions]:

first [I.A.6.b.i], a simile;
second [I.A.6.b.ii], a correlation.

The simile [I.A.6.b.i] is in two [subdivisions]:

initially [I.A.6.b.i.a], a clarification of the four negations;
subsequently [I.A.6.b.i.b], an elucidation of the eight negations.

Regarding "the four negations" [I.A.6.b.i.a]: because [the fruits] are dependent upon conditions [such as soil, water, and sunlight], "**they are not self-generated.**" Because [the fruits grow from] their own seeds, "**they are not generated by some external agent.**" [From the standpoint of absolute truth], because they are inactive *(akarmaka)*, "**they are not produced symbiotically.**" And yet, [from the standpoint of conventional truth,] because they are in fact able to function, they are not unproduced; thus, "**they are not produced in the absence of [a cause for that] production.**" Furthermore, at the time when they are not yet produced, they do not exist of their own accord and are therefore not self-generated. At the time when they have already been produced, they already exist and perforce are therefore not self-generated. Since it is impossible for them to be self-generated, upon what other thing would they depend [in order to be produced]? Since both they and others are nonexistent, how can they be produced in conjunction with one another? Since we cannot ascertain any production that occurs via a causal process, how much less so can we ascertain their production that occurs without a cause. In this wise, we seek out production, but it can never be ascertained. **"They are not produced in the absence of a cause for that production"**: this clarifies that they cannot be produced in the absence of a cause, which means that the fruition cannot have been produced in the absence of the efficient cause *(kāraṇahetu)*.

"**Why is this?**" onward provides additional explications that dispel the doubt [of Simwang Bodhisattva]. The idea behind his doubt is that perhaps there is a third possibility, which also is incorrect. What is that third possibility? His idea is that the fruit is produced through the conjunction of the primary cause— the seed—and the subsidiary conditions—soil and water. Through the conjunction of these two, the fruit is produced. How then can one say "**they are not produced in conjunction with something else**"? For this reason, he asks, "**Why is this?**" "**Because these conditions alternate successively**" clarifies that these two conditions alternate successively from beginning to end, without even a temporary respite. Since there is no moment of respite, they would consequently be devoid of function; and because they are devoid of function, together they could not **[625b]** produce the fruit. As a gāthā explains:

> All formations *(saṃskāra)* last but a *kṣaṇa* [an instant],
> They do not even linger, let alone function.[178]

Hence, despite exploring how they alternate successively, one finds that there is neither production nor extinction. This is because, since they do not perdure for even a moment, there can be no production; and because there is no production, there can be no extinction. Therefore, it says, "**These conditions are generated, but there is no production; these conditions decay, but there is no extinction.**" If you search for it in this same manner, "**whether hidden or made manifest,**" neither can be found. "**Hidden**" means that the seed is located beneath the soil. "**Made manifest**" means that the sprouts and the stem appear above ground.

"**Their fundamental principle is calm and extinct**": in examining the principle of the tree's root and trunk, despite seeking the cause that produces the fruit, it ultimately is ungenerated; therefore, it is "**calm and extinct. . . . There is no place where they abide, nor is there seen anything that abides.**" The reason for this is "**because their natures are fixed.**" The meaning of "**fixed nature**" is as was explained above.

> **"This fixed nature is neither unitary nor different; neither evanescent nor permanent; it has neither access nor egress; it is neither produced nor extinguished. It abandons all four of these antinomies *(catuṣkoṭi)*, for the pathways of words and speech are eradicated *(ŏnŏdodan)*.[179] This is**

the case as well for the unproduced nature of the mind: how can it be said that it is either produced or unproduced, either accepted or not accepted?"

This next [subdivision, I.A.6.b.i.b] clarifies the eight negations.[180] These would not normally be expected to be enumerated here, since the preceding four negations are sufficient in themselves to cover completely all of these eight, including unitary and different, and so on. The reason that [the eight negations are discussed] is that the seeds and the fruit are not unitary, because their characteristics are not identical; but they are also not different, because there is no fruit apart from the seed. Moreover, the seed and the fruit are not evanescent, because the fruit is what is formed from the seed; but they are also not permanent, because the seed vanishes once the fruit is formed. The seed does not access the fruit, because when the fruit is present there is no longer a seed; but the fruit also does not emerge from the seed, because when the seed is present there is as yet no fruit. Because "it has neither access nor egress," it is not produced. Because it is neither permanent nor evanescent, it is not extinguished. Because it is not extinguished, it cannot be described as nonexistent; but because it is not produced, it cannot be described as existent. Because it leaves far behind these two extremes, it cannot be said that it both exists and does not exist. Because none of these alternatives is correct, it cannot be said that it neither exists nor does not exist. For this reason, it says, "It abandons [625c] all four of these alternatives, for the pathways of words and speech are eradicated."

The Āmalaka fruit, in the same way, brings an end to the need for words. The mind that is immersed in the acquiescence to [the nonproduction of] dharmas is also not different from this. Therefore, it says, "This is the case as well for the unproduced nature of the mind."

"If a person claims that the mind may either achieve [something] or abide [somewhere] and takes this as his [wrong] view, then he will never attain *anuttarasamyaksaṃbodhi* [complete, perfect enlightenment] or prajñā. This is the 'long night.'"

This is the third [subpart, I.A.6.c], bringing up the negative aspects [of presuming that the mind-nature exists in reality]. This means that one who claims that the mind that acquiesces to nonproduction can be located in the mind-essence, abides in nonproduction, and is the subject that experiences the principle of nonproduction has not yet comprehended the mind-nature. It is precisely this deluded grasping that can hinder "bodhi" and its "prajñā." This clarifies that he attains neither the bodhi of the purity of the nature, nor the prajñā that is the agent of that realization. Furthermore, "bodhi" means the initial generation of [the thought of] bodhi. "Prajñā" means the cause of bodhi. Since one does not achieve the cause of awakening, there is a "long night"; this is because the deceptive conceptions, which are beginningless, are a great dream.

> "One who has comprehended the mind-nature knows that the mind-nature is thus and that this nature is also thus. This is the practice of nonproduction."

This is the fourth [subpart, I.A.6.d], clarifying the positive aspects [of understanding the mind-nature]. "One who has comprehended the mind-nature" means that he uses his own mind to comprehend his own mind-nature. As a sūtra says: "If one can use his attention *(manaskāra),* the perceiving subject, to penetrate instead that very attention, then sense-bases and sense-objects will in this wise be in a state of equilibrium. As they are in a state of equilibrium, the uncontaminated wisdom is produced and one completely penetrates to the noble truths."[181] Therefore, [one who] "knows that the mind-nature is thus" knows that the essence and nature of the contemplative mind are in a state of equilibrium. "This nature is also thus" means that the functioning of the agent of knowing and the nature of that functioning are in a state of equilibrium. In this wise, since the essence and function of the contemplative mind are in a state of equilibrium, they are neither produced nor extinguished and are without beginning or end. For this reason, it says, "This is the practice of nonproduction."

The preceding clarification of nonproduction in terms of the four negations elucidates the principle of nonproduction. **[626a]** This principle pervades both the profane and the sacred. This present clarification of nonproduction in terms of the knowledge of thusness clarifies the practice of nonproduction. This practice is unique to the saint. The practice at [the stage of] sanctity is of a single taste with that principle, and that principle of all-inclusiveness is commensurate with that knowledge. Because these are commensurate with this one taste, they are not something that the saints can differentiate; but because they are inclusive and distinctive, they are not something that the saints can amalgamate. "Cannot amalgamate" means that they are differentiated, while remaining amalgamated. "Cannot differentiate" means that they are amalgamated, while remaining differentiated. "Amalgamated" specifies that they are amalgamated in terms of differentiation; "differentiated" clarifies that they are differentiated in terms of amalgamation. "Specifies that they are amalgamated in terms of differentiation" does not mean to divide up an amalgamation into differences. "Clarifies that they are differentiated in terms of amalgamation" does not mean to fuse differences into an amalgamation. As a consequence, because amalgamation is not a fusion of differences, we cannot say that they are amalgamated; and because differences are not the dividing up of an amalgamation, we cannot say that they are differentiated. It is just that, because it cannot be explained as differentiation, it is possible to explain it as amalgamation; and because it cannot be explained as amalgamation, it is possible to explain it as differentiation. Whether explained or not explained, [the principle and practice of nonproduction] remain nondual and undifferentiated.

> Simwang Bodhisattva commented: "Lord! As the mind is originally thus, it will not produce such practices. As all practices are unproduced, there will be no practice that produces anything, and this nonproduction will then not need to be practiced. This in fact is the practice of nonproduction."

From here onward is [subsection I.B.], a series of exchanges in which [the Buddha] interrogates [the bodhisattva]. It is in eight [parts]:

one [I.B.1], [the bodhisattva] refers to practice in order to raise a problematic point concerning the principle;
two [I.B.2], [the Buddha's] interrogation on whether [the bodhisattva] has achieved realization;
three [I.B.3], [the bodhisattva's] respectful reply that he is free of [any attachment to] realization;
four [I.B.4], [the Buddha's] interrogation on whether [the bodhisattva] has attainment;
five [I.B.5], [the bodhisattva's] respectful reply that he is free of [any attachment to] attainment;
six [I.B.6], [the Buddha's concluding] narrative that he is free from both attainment and realization;
seven [I.B.7], [the bodhisattva] reiterates his doubts;
eight [I.B.8], [The Buddha] resolves [the bodhisattva's] doubts.

This is the first [part, I.B.1], in which [the bodhisattva] refers to practice in order to raise a problematic point concerning the principle. The statement "as the mind is originally thus, it will not produce such practices" refers to the preceding explanation of the idea that practice is unproduced. This corresponds to the preceding passage "[one] knows that the mind-nature is thus and that this nature is also thus. This is the practice of nonproduction." This means that **it will not produce** anything with regard to **practices** that involve production and extinction. This is an explicit reference to the characteristics of the practice of nonproduction. **[626b]** The statement "as all practices are unproduced" refers to the principle, that is, nonproduction. This means that all the practices [alt. formations, volitional actions; *saṃskāra*] involving the five aggregates of sentient beings are originally unproduced. "There will be no practice that produces anything" clarifies that the nonproduction of principle differs from the nonproduction of practices. This means that the practices that are generated through production are in fact void *(śūnya)* and unproduced; it is not because of realizing the principle that one extinguishes the mind so that it becomes unproduced. "There will be no practice that produces anything" elucidates the fact that the nonproduction of principle is the same as the nonproduction of practices. This means that the gateway of nonproduction is also free from any mental formations. [Question:] Is this like the acquiescence to the nonproduction [of dharmas], which, because it is free from any discriminative practices, will perforce be identical to the practice of nonproduction? [Answer:] If this were the case, there then would be no ordinary persons who would not already have realized and attained the acquiescence to the nonproduction [of dharmas].

> The Buddha asked: "Oh son of good family! Can you realize the practice of nonproduction by not producing anything?"

This is the second [part, I.B.2], [the Buddha's] interrogation of whether [the bodhisattva] has achieved realization. The import of this interrogation is this: "When you access the contemplation on the acquiescence to the nonproduction [of dharmas], do you therewith attain the practice of nonproduction by relying on the principle that all practices [alt. formations] are unproduced?" For this reason, if one were to ask why [the Buddha] scrutinizes [his view] through such a question, it is because that [bodhisattva], while distinguishing nonproduction in terms of practice from nonproduction in terms of principle, raises the issue of whether the nonproduction of principle is also in fact the nonproduction of practice. Hence, [the Buddha] now scrutinizes [this view] and asks, "When you access the contemplation [on the acquiescence to the nonproduction of dharmas], are principle and practice differentiated, and does the subject/object dichotomy remain?"

> Simwang Bodhisattva replied: "No. And why is this? In the actual practice of nonproduction, both nature and characteristics are void and calm. There is neither vision nor hearing, neither gain nor loss, neither words nor speech, neither cognition nor characteristics, neither clinging nor rejection. So how would one cling to this realization? If one clings to this realization, this would in fact serve [as the cause of] disputation and contention. Only when there is neither disputation nor contention is it the practice of nonproduction."

This is the third [part, I.B.3, the bodhisattva's] respectful reply that he is free of [any attachment to] realization. It is in three [subparts]:

initially [I.B.3.a], a clarification of his freedom from realization;
two [I.B.3.b], a reference to its negative attributes;
three [I.B.3.c], an elucidation of its positive attributes.

This initial [subpart] is also in two [divisions]:

the former [I.B.3.a.i], an overview;
the latter [I.B.3.a.ii], an explication.

"In the actual practice of nonproduction, both nature and characteristics are void and calm": this passage provides a general overview [I.B.3.a.i]. The statement "nature . . . [is] void and calm" means that the essential nature of the contemplative mind [626c] remains separate from the characteristics of production and extinction. This corresponds to the preceding explanation that "[one] knows that the mind-nature is thus." "Characteristics . . . are void and calm" means the awareness and functions of the contemplative mind, as well as the characteristics of those functions, are also thus. This corresponds to the preceding statement that "this nature is also thus."

From here onward is his explication [I.B.3.a.ii] of this general account in terms of ten negations. "There is neither vision nor hearing" means that the mind-nature is invisible and inaudible.[182] Because it is invisible, it brings an end to forms and is not represented by any image. Because it is inaudible, it brings an end to sounds and is not referenced by any doctrine. "Neither gain nor loss" means that, though elucidating voidness, there is nothing that it gains; and though rejecting production, there is nothing that it loses. In this wise, these four negations explicate [the statement] "nature [is . . .] void and calm." "Neither words nor speech" means that, since the activities of mind are calm, they do not generate words and speech. "Neither cognition nor characteristics" means that, since the activities of mind are calm and extinguished, he remains far removed from these two aspects [viz. cognition and characteristics]. "Neither clinging nor rejection" means that, since there is no discrimination, there is no nature to which one can cling and no characteristics that one should abandon. In this wise, these six negations explicate [the statement] "characteristics are void and calm."

The practice of nonproduction entails this sort of void calmness. So how, then, would one cling to realization with regard to [that practice]? Once this answer was delivered, [that bodhisattva] knew himself that the problematic point he raised earlier was no longer an issue. He raised its negative attributes [I.B.3.b] and elucidated of its positive attributes [I.B.3.c], which will both be obvious if you peruse them.

The Buddha said, "Have you attained *anuttarasamyaksaṃbodhi*?"[183]

This is the fourth [part, I.B.4, the Buddha's] interrogation of whether [the bodhisattva] has any attainments.

Question: If the bodhisattva has not yet attained ultimate bodhi, why would the Tathāgata have asked, "Have you attained [it]?"

Explanation: Although this [bodhisattva] may not yet have attained ultimate bodhi, he has already attained the realization of bodhi while on the first bhūmi. As it explains in the *Fahua lun* [Treatise on the *Lotus Sūtra*]:

> "To attain *anuttarasamyaksaṃbodhi* in [a period between] eight lifetimes and one lifetime" means to realize bodhi while on the first bhūmi. . . . They therewith leave behind the various types of existences within the three realms and, according to their individual capacity, are able to see true thusness, that is, the buddha-nature. This can be called "attaining bodhi." It does not imply that there is the ultimate fulfillment of the tathāgatas' expedients and nirvāṇa.[184]

Nota Bene: This **[627a]** is an explanation of the term "bodhi" from the standpoint of true thusness, viz. the buddha-nature. Because it is able to realize a vision [of that buddha-nature], it is called "attaining bodhi." As a sūtra says: "The voidness of the nature of all dharmas is in fact bodhi."[185] This is what is meant here.

> **Simwang Bodhisattva responded: "Lord! I am free from any attainment of *anuttarasamyaksaṃbodhi.* And why is this? The bodhi-nature has neither gain nor loss, neither thought nor awareness, for it is free from all differentiated characteristics. The pure nature actually exists in such nondiscrimination. This nature is free from any extraneous association or admixture. It is free from words and speech; it neither exists nor does not exist; it is neither aware nor nescient.**
>
> **"This is also the case for all the dharmas that can be cultivated. Why is this? All dharmas and practices have no loci that can be found, because their natures are fixed. Originally, they are free from any semblance of attainment or nonattainment. So how can one attain *anuttarasamyaksaṃbodhi?*"**

This is the fifth [part, I.B.5, the bodhisattva's] respectful reply that he is free of [any attachment to] attainment. It is in three [subparts]:

an overview [I.B.5.a; viz. the proposition "**I am free from any attainment of *anuttarasamyaksaṃbodhi***"];
an explication [I.B.5.b];
and a conclusion [I.B.5.c].

The explication is in two [divisions]:

initially [I.B.5.b.i], a clarification that the bodhi that is attained is free from any nature of attainment *[anupalabdhitva];*
subsequently [I.B.5.b.ii], an elucidation that all the practices that bring about this attainment are free from any characteristic of being an agent of attainment.

In this first [part I.B.5.b.i], the term "**bodhi-nature**" means that the nature of true thusness pervades empty space without hindrance and this nature leaves far behind dullness and stupidity; therefore it is called "bodhi." Herein, there is originally no true nature that needs to be validated and originally no deceptive conceptions that need be extinguished; therefore, it says, "[It] **has neither gain nor loss.**" In this wise, original enlightenment leaves far behind thoughts that involve plotting and scheming and also brings an end to awareness that is frivolous and agitated; therefore, it says, "[It has] **neither thought nor awareness.**" Since it is free from any discriminative views, it also leaves far behind all characteristics that are the objects of practice; therefore, it says, "**It is free from all differentiated characteristics.**" This being the case, it is not debased by deceptive characteristics, for the original nature leaves behind all taints; therefore, it says, "**The pure nature actually exists in such nondiscrimination.**" Temporally, it is not associated with either production or extinction; spatially, it is not confused by either subject or object; therefore, it says, "**This nature is free from any extraneous association or admixture.**" "**It is free from words and speech**" means that neither the speaker nor the words spoken are validated. "**It neither exists [627b] nor does not exist**": there is nothing that seems to exist, but also nothing that seems not to exist. "**It is neither aware nor nescient**": this is not original enlightenment, but also not nonenlightenment. The nature of bodhi is just so; this is the meaning of being free from attainment *(anupalabdhi).*

From the sentence "**for all the dharmas that can be cultivated**" is the ensuing explication [I.B.5.b.ii] of the fact that there are no practices that catalyze attainment. This refers to the previous chapter's statement that there are none of the practices of the six pāramitās that are not an authentic standard (cf. *KSGN,* p. 620c ff.). Hence, it says, "**dharmas that can [be cultivated].**" The statement "**this is also the case**" is the same as the preceding discussion on nonattainment. "**All dharmas and practices**" refers to such practices as the six pāramitās, and so forth. "**Have no loci that can be found**" means that he does not perceive any locus that should be the object of practice—such as gain and loss, thought and awareness, on up to existence and nonexistence, awareness and nescience, and so forth—for these are fully commensurate with bodhi. For this reason, [the bodhi-nature] is originally free from any sense that there is anything that either can or cannot be attained.

From "**so how**" onward is the comprehensive conclusion [I.B.5.c] regarding nonattainment.

> **The Buddha replied: "So it is, so it is. As you have said, all of the activities of mind are nothing but signlessness; their experience is calm and unproduced."**

From this point on is the sixth [part, I.B.6], the Tathāgata's concluding narrative [that he is free from both attainment and realization]. It is in three [subparts]:

one [I.B.6.a], the actual narration;
two [I.B.6.b], a reference to the negative aspects;
three [I.B.6.c], an elucidation of the positive aspects.

The first [subpart] is also in three [divisions]:

a general narrative [I.B.6.a.i];
a specific narrative [I.B.6.a.ii];
and finally a concluding summation [I.B.6.a.iii].

In the first [division, I.B.6.a.i, the general narrative] "so it is, so it is" refers to the preceding [discussion] on freedom from realization as well as the subsequent [treatment] of nonattainment.

From "all" onward is the second division [I.B.6.a.ii], the specific narrative:

initially [I.B.6.a.ii.a], a narration of [the concept of being] "unproduced";
subsequently [I.B.6.a.ii.b], he narrates [the aspect of] "calm" extinction.

[I.B.6.a.ii.a:] The term "unproduced" means the practice of nonproduction. This refers to the fact that there is neither an agent of realization nor an agent of attainment. [I.B.6.a.ii.b:] The term "calm" extinction refers to the principle of calm extinction [nirvāṇa]. This refers to the fact that there is neither an object of realization nor an object of attainment. The initial statement "all of the activities of mind" means that all the activities of mind that are associated with the supramundane nondiscriminative wisdom do not cling to any of the [discriminative] characteristics [of dharmas] and comprehend through realization that they are signless; therefore, it says "[they] are nothing but signlessness." Their experience of this void calmness is impassive and unproduced; therefore, it says "their experience is calm and unproduced."

> "It would also be the same as well with each and every type of consciousness. Why is this? [627c] The eye and visual contact are both void and calm. [Visual] consciousness is also void and calm: it is free from any characteristic of agitation or motionlessness. Since it is free internally of the three feelings [*vedanā;* painful, pleasurable, and neutral sensations], the three feelings are calm and extinct. So too is this the case for auditory, olfactory, gustatory, and tactile [consciousnesses], as well as mentality, mind-consciousness, *mano[vijñāna],*[186] and *ālaya[vijñāna]:* as all of them are also unproduced, they are the mind that is calm and extinct and the mind that produces nothing."[187]

This is the second [division, I.B.6.a.ii.b], in which he narrates the concept of calm extinction, that is, the void calmness of all the mundane eight consciousnesses. It is in two [subdivisions]:

one [I.B.6.a.ii.b.1], a sequential enumeration;
two [I.B.6.a.ii.2], an extensive explication.

In the initial [subdivision, I.B.6.a.ii.b.1], the statement "each and every consciousness" subsumes all the mundane eight consciousnesses, just as the statement "each and every place" subsumes all places. "It would also be the same" means that the principle of void calmness is identical to the preceding [reference to] the nonproduction of the supramundane mind.

From "why is this?" onward is the second [subdivision, I.B.6.a.ii.2], an extensive explication. "Eye" means the eye faculty *(cakṣurindriya)*. "Visual contact" means "contact" *(sparśa)* [in the list of ten] predominant mental factors *(mahābhūmika)*,[188] which is produced through the coming together of the three [factors of sense-base, sense-object, and sense-consciousness]. Since [all sensory contact] is caused by the coming together of these three [factors], he brings up only this partial example [of visual contact] because he wishes to clarify that they are all subject to dispersion and voidness. "[Visual] consciousness is also void" means that, since visual contact is void, visual consciousness is unproduced. Since there are no successive fluctuations [of consciousness] nor even a *kṣaṇa* of instability, it says that "it is free from any characteristic of agitation or motionlessness." The words "since it is free internally of the three feelings" means that the generation of the three feelings [*vedanā;* viz. pleasant, unpleasant, and neutral] is originally calm and extinct. Contact *(sparśa)* and feeling are proximate in all the mental factors *(caitta)* and possess great efficacy; therefore, [the Buddha] referred to these two in order to counter generally [the reality of] all remaining dharmas. "Auditory, olfactory, gustatory, tactile" refer to the ear, auditory object, auditory consciousness, and so forth [viz. olfactory, gustatory, and tactile bases, objects, and consciousnesses]. "Mentality, mind-consciousness": these both refer to the sixth consciousness. In the future period, [this consciousness] is called mind *(sim);* in the past, it is called mentality *(ŭi);* in the present, it is called mind-consciousness *(ŭisik)*. We derive these three names from the doctrine regarding the transformation of consciousness *(pravṛttivijñāna)*, in order to elucidate the fact that the three time periods are all void and calm. "*Mano[vijñāna]* and *ālaya[vijñāna]*," the seventh and eight [consciousnesses], are both identical to the visual consciousness in that they "are also unproduced." This completes the exegesis of the extensive explication.

Next [I.B.6.a.iii], the statement "the mind that is calm and extinct" is an abbreviated summation of the import that the eight consciousnesses **[628a]** are "void and calm." "And the mind that produces nothing" is an indirect summation of the import that the experience [of those consciousnesses] is calm and unproduced.

> "But if one produces a mind that is calm and extinct and if one produces a mind that produces nothing, this then would be practice that

> produces something, not the practice of nonproduction. Thus internally are generated three feelings, three karmic actions, and three moral restraints [of physical, verbal, and mental actions]."

This is the second [subpart, I.B.6.b], a reference to the negative aspects. Mahāyāna trainees who presume there is something to attain turn against calm extinction by not voiding the eight consciousnesses; therefore, it says, "one produces a mind that is calm and extinct." Not knowing about the nonproduction of the supramundane mind means that a state of mind is produced that realizes the principle of signlessness; therefore, it says, "One produces a mind that produces nothing." This is in fact a mundane practice that remains involved in saṃsāra, contravening the supramundane practice of the acquiescence to the nonproduction [of dharmas]; therefore, it says "this then is a practice that produces something," and so forth. The statement "three karmic actions" refers to the activities of body, speech, and mind, which subsume both the wholesome and the unwholesome. "Three moral restraints" refers to restrictions placed on body, speech, and mind, which ensure that one will cleave solely to what is wholesome. With the production of these three karmic actions and three moral restraints as cause, the three types of becoming *(bhava)* are produced, whereby one experiences all the "three feelings." In this wise, one remains involved [in saṃsāra] and does not attain liberation.

> "If these [three feelings, and so on] are already calm and extinct, the producing mind will not be produced and the mind will be constantly calm and extinct, without efficacy or function. He does not evince any characteristic of calm extinction; but he also does not insist on not corroborating [such a characteristic]. What is worth lingering in is the state of nonabiding, which encodes *(ch'ongji; dhārayati)* signlessness. Then, there will be none of these three, such as the three feelings, and so forth, for all will be calm and extinct, pure and nonabiding. He need not access samādhi; he need not persist in sitting in dhyāna. This is nonproduction and freedom from the need to practice."

This is the third [subpart, I.B.6.c], an elucidation of the positive aspects. The statement "if these are already calm and extinct, the producing mind will not be produced" counters the preceding statement "if one produces a mind that is calm and extinct." This means that one dispels all states of mind that are subject to production, for one does not cling to production. The line "the mind will be constantly calm and extinct, without efficacy or function" counters the preceding statement "if one produces [a mind that] produces nothing." This means that one leaves behind all characteristics of production, extinction, and activity, and one also is free from any discriminative function that involves intentionality *(manaskāra)*. "He does not evince any characteristic of calm extinction" means that, although he dispels [the notion that] states of mind are produced, he does not validate the characteristic of calm extinction. **[628b]** "He also does not insist on not corroborating [such a characteristic]" means that, although he is free from clinging to the characteristic of calm extinction, he does not succumb to the fault of assuming that realization is impossible. "What is worth lingering in is the state of nonabiding" is a general clarification of the fault of being attached [to the notion that] one is separate from any semblance of abiding; this is because any place worth lingering in will involve the state of nonabiding. As for "places worth lingering in," if one dispels the notion of generation, then wherever one lingers will be calm and extinct. If one dispels the notion of realization, then wherever one lingers will be free from realization. In this wise, "what is worth lingering in is in every case the state of nonabiding." "Encodes signlessness" is a general elucidation of all the meritorious qualities. This means that the mind of nonproduction, by encoding all types of merit achieved through practice, is identical to the single taste and is free of any discriminative characteristic. "Then, there will be none of these three, such as the three feelings, and so forth" counters the preceding statement "thus internally are generated three feelings," and so forth, because it leaves far behind any sign of saṃsāric [evolutionary process] cause and effect. "All will be calm and extinct" means that he penetrates to the fact that the three feelings, and so on, are originally void. "Pure and nonabiding" means that the mind that is the agent of such penetration is nonabiding and void. "He need not access samādhi" means that he is able to let go of the mundane state of mind that accesses concentration. "He need not persist in sitting in dhyāna" means that he also rejects the mundane tranquillity derived from lingering in dhyāna. Such a person is then free from all states of mind that generate anything and free from all discriminative practices; therefore, it says, "This is nonproduction and freedom from the need to practice."

> Simwang Bodhisattva asked: "Dhyāna can suppress all agitation and allay all illusory distractions. Why this negation of dhyāna?"

This is the seventh [part, I.B.7, in which the bodhisattva] reiterates his doubts. Harboring a doubt, he asks: all the usual types of dhyāna and samādhi can suppress thoughts of flurry and agitation, and can tranquilize scattered and distracted states of mind; so why is it that this state of mind involving the supramundane practice of nonproduction is also not able to access, and to linger in, this dhyāna and samādhi? Since dhyāna is thus negated, he therefore must be agitated. Because he has this sort of doubt, he raises this question.

> The Buddha replied: "Bodhisattva! Dhyāna in fact is agitation. Being neither agitated nor concentrated—this is the dhyāna of nonproduction. The nature of dhyāna is to produce nothing; it leaves far behind

the characteristics of the dhyāna that does produce something. The nature of dhyāna is to linger nowhere; [628c] it leaves far behind the agitation caused by trying to linger in dhyāna. Know that the nature of dhyāna is free from agitation and calmness, and you will immediately attain nonproduction and the prajñā that produces nothing. But also do not rely on, or linger over, this. Because of this knowledge, the mind also will not be agitated. For this reason, you will attain the prajñāpāramitā that produces nothing."

This is the eighth [part, I.B.8, in which the Buddha] resolves [the bodhisattva's] doubts. "Dhyāna in fact is agitation" means that, although mundane dhyāna is not scattered or distracted, it clings to the characteristic of the object [of concentration]; and the production of a thought that clings to characteristics in turn generates agitation. One who is able to leave behind the dhyāna that in this wise produces agitation will then be able to gain access to the noumenal concentration; therefore, it says "this is the dhyāna of nonproduction." In this wise, the nature of the noumenal concentration does not produce agitation; therefore, it says, "The nature of dhyāna is to produce nothing." It is not merely unproduced, but it also does not linger in quiescence; therefore it says, "The nature of dhyāna is to linger nowhere." If there is production, there then will be characteristics; where there is lingering in attachment, there then will be agitation. Now in order to contravene these [tendencies], it therefore says, "It leaves far behind the characteristics of the dhyāna that does produce something . . . ; it leaves far behind the agitation caused by trying to linger in dhyāna."

All the preceding passages clarify the characteristics of the noumenal concentration. From "Know that the nature of dhyāna" onward elucidates the characteristics of the noumenal knowledge. While [that noumenal knowledge] may have but a single essence, it involves two distinct aspects. "Know that the nature of dhyāna is free from agitation" means to know that "the nature of dhyāna is to produce nothing." "[Know that the nature of dhyāna] is free from calmness" means to know that "the nature of dhyāna is to linger nowhere." "You will immediately attain nonproduction" means that you will attain the principle, which is nonproduction. "The prajñā that produces nothing" means that you will attain the practice that produces nothing. "But also do not rely on, or linger over, this" means that the prajñā that produces nothing does not rely on, or linger over, the principle, because it leaves behind the subject-object dichotomy. "The mind also will not be agitated" means that, although one does not linger by relying on the principle, one does not produce any agitation of mind. Owing to this sort of knowledge, one is able to reach the other shore [of nirvāṇa]; therefore it says, "prajñāpāramitā."

The above eight parts together form the second [subsection, I.B], a series of exchanges that involve [the Buddha's] interrogation [of the bodhisattva].

Simwang Bodhisattva said: "Lord! The prajñā that produces nothing does not abide anywhere and is not absent anywhere. The mind has no abiding place and there is no [629a] mind that abides any place. When there is no abiding and no mind, the mind will then abide in nonproduction. The mind that so abides is in fact abiding in nonproduction.

"Lord! The mind's practice of nonproduction is inconceivable. In this inconceivability, it is both effable and ineffable."

This is the third [subsection, I.C, in which the bodhisattva] gains comprehension. "Anywhere" means in all loci, whether absolute or conventional, active or still, and so forth. "Does not abide" means that it is unascertainable in any of these [loci]. "Not absent" means there is nothing it does not ascertain in any of these [loci]. The reason this is the case is because, in all these loci, it is not-so and yet not not-so. "The mind has no abiding place" means that it has no locus that is the site of that abiding. " There is no mind that abides any place" means that there is no state of mind that is the subject of that abiding. "When there is no abiding and no mind" combines the previous two statements—that there is no mind that involves either a locus or any sense of abiding. "The mind . . . is . . . abiding in nonproduction" means that one is not devoid of a mind that produces nothing and lingers nowhere. "The mind that so abides" sums up the preceding [statement] "[the prajñā that produces nothing] does not abide anywhere" and so on, up to "and is not absent anywhere." This is because the aspect of being "not absent anywhere" is provisionally established in reference to abiding. "[This] is in fact abiding in nonproduction" sums up the preceding [statement] "the mind has no abiding place . . . the mind will then abide in nonproduction." This is because abiding is in fact nonabiding and nonabiding is in fact abiding. "The mind's practice of nonproduction is inconceivable" because it leaves behind speech and is cut off from thought. "In this inconceivability, it is both effable and ineffable" means that leaving behind speech is itself also distinct from any concept of leaving behind speech. Because it leaves behind speech, it is "ineffable." Because it is distinct from any concept of leaving behind speech, it is also "effable." "Effable" means that it is not not-so. "Ineffable" means that it is not-so. Therefore, covering both statements comprehensively, it says "it is both effable and ineffable." Just as when one says that verbalization and vocalization are both possible and yet impossible, so too should you know that conceptualization is also both possible and yet impossible. [The sūtra] refers only to one aspect [the inconceivable], while merely alluding to the other.

The Buddha said, "So it is, so it is."

This is the fourth [subsection, I.D], the completion of the Tathāgata's narrative. Since the preceding [subsection on] gaining comprehension did not provide explicit approval [629b], and since there is also a need to show reverence to the Buddha's words, [the Buddha] says, in reiteration, "So it is, so it is."

The explicit explanation [Section I] in the main outline is finished above.

> Simwang Bodhisattva heard these words and, praising its miraculousness, recited these gāthās:

From this point on is the second [section, II], [the bodhisattva's] praise [of the Buddha's] words in gāthās. It is in two [subsections]:

initially [II.A], a preface;
subsequently [II.B], verses.

"Heard these words": he heard the Buddha's words within this one chapter.

> That Lord who is replete in great knowledge,
> Has explained extensively the dharma of nonproduction,
> I have heard what has never been heard before,
> Now has been explained what had yet to be explained.

The three verses from here onward [II.B] are not versifications of specific qualities but are merely generic adulation. [This subsection] is in four [parts]:

instruction [II.B.1];
simile [II.B.2];
correlation [II.B.3];
summation [II.B.4].

This [verse] is the first [part, II.B.1], praise of the dharma that he has explained. "Now has been explained what had yet to be explained": although this may have been extensively explained before, now this sūtra's words are brief but its meaning fecund, its style terse but its principles complex. Therefore, this particular type of sublimity has never been explained before.

> It is like the pure sweet dew,
> That appears but once in a long while.
> [So too is this dharma] difficult to encounter and difficult to imagine,
> Difficult too is it to hear it,
> It is the unsurpassed, excellent field of merit *(puṇyakṣetra)*,
> The supremely efficacious, sublime medicine.
> It is in order to ferry across sentient beings,
> That it has now been proclaimed.

The first two lines here are the second [part, II.B.2], the simile. "Sweet dew" refers to the elixir of immortality, which is a simile for the fact that this sūtra can lead one out of birth and death.

The next four lines are the third [part, II.B.3], the correlation. "It is the unsurpassed, excellent field of merit" praises the hearer. "The supremely efficacious, sublime medicine" correlates [the simile] with the instruction that has been heard.

The concluding two lines are the fourth [part, II.B.4], the summation.

> At that time, all those in the congregation heard these words and attained the [acquiescence to] the nonproduction [of dharmas] as well as the prajñā that produces nothing.

[629c] This is the third [section, III], in which the congregation present at the time [hears the explanation and] gains benefit. This means that ordinary people *(pṛthagjana)* at the pre-bhūmi [stage] who hear this chapter preached will be able on the first bhūmi to attain the acquiescence to the nonproduction [of dharmas].

[Part Four: An Exegesis of the Text (cont.)]

[Section Two: Main Body (cont.)]

VAJRASAMĀDHI-SŪTRA, CHAPTER FOUR: THE INSPIRATION OF ORIGINAL ENLIGHTENMENT

Since time immemorial, all animate beings *(sattva)* have descended into the long night of ignorance and have dreamed the great dream of deluded conceptions. When bodhisattvas cultivate contemplation and gain nonproduction, they thoroughly penetrate to the fact that sentient beings are originally calm and quiescent, which is their original enlightenment. Lying on the couch of unitary thusness, they benefit sentient beings through this original inspiration [lit. benefit]. This chapter elucidates this principle and is therefore entitled the "Inspiration of Original Enlightenment" chapter.[189]

Third Division of Contemplation Practice: The Inspiration of Original Enlightenment

> At that time, Muju [Nonabiding] Bodhisattva heard what the Buddha said about the single taste being true and inconceivable. From far away, [Muju] drew close to the Tathāgata's seat and listened intently and with full attention. Accessing that pure, transparent place, his body and mind were motionless.[190]

In the systematic clarification of the six divisions of contemplation practice, from this point onward is the third division, which clarifies the Inspiration of Original Enlightenment.

By relying on the practice of nonproduction, one is able to experience original enlightenment. Then and only then will one gain the ability to proselytize everywhere, thereby benefiting everyone. This is why [the Buddha] next discusses this [inspiration of original enlightenment].

The exegesis [of this chapter] is in three [sections]:

One [I], an extensive clarification of the inspiration of original enlightenment;
Two [II], praising [the inspiration of original enlightenment] with gāthās;
Three [III], the congregation present at the time gains benefit.

In this first [section, I], there are two [subsections]:

one [I.A], clarifying quiescence through movement, which provides a brief overview of the theme of original inspiration;
two [I.B], progressing from the obscure to the evident, which is an extensive explanation of the aspect of original inspiration.

This initial [subsection, I.A] is in three [parts]:

one [I.A.1], prompting the body into action, so as to provide an overview of original inspiration;
two [I.A.2], an exchange of words, so as to provide an overview of original inspiration;
three [I.A.3], emitting rays of light and praising the original inspiration with verses.

In this initial [part, I.A.1], regarding the name "**Muju [Nonabiding] Bodhisattva**": although this being may have realized that original enlightenment originally does not generate action, he does not **[630a]** abide in calm quiescence but instead strives constantly to proselytize everywhere. His name is conferred because of this quality, and he is called "**Muju [Nonabiding].**" Since this quality of "**nonabiding**" corresponds to the original inspiration, this being is used to symbolize this theme. The statement "**the single taste being true and inconceivable**" correlates with the preceding chapter's explanations that "**the mind's practice of nonproduction is inconceivable**" (p. 629a), and so forth. "**From far away, [Muju] drew close to the Tathāgata's seat**": [this bodhisattva's] first seat was located far away from the Buddha's; but after hearing the preceding chapter, he moved it to a spot nearby. This symbolizes the fact that, before hearing the profound dharma, his status was that of an ordinary ignoramus who was far from the fruition of buddhahood; but now, having heard the

Buddha's sermon, he gained the inspiration of original enlightenment and knew for himself that he will soon gain the fruition of buddhahood. "[He] listened intently and with full attention. Accessing that pure, transparent place, his body and mind were motionless": once he had drawn near to the Buddha's seat, he gave "full attention" and "listened intently." "Accessing" that place which is originally pure and clean, transparent and clear, in accordance with the quiescence of original enlightenment, "his body and mind were motionless." This [passage] also symbolizes the fact that at the time that one accesses original enlightenment, one realizes the original motionlessness and gains that which is unascertainable *(anupalabdhi)*.

> At that time, the Buddha addressed Muju Bodhisattva: "Whence have you come? Where now have you arrived?"
>
> Muju Bodhisattva replied: "Lord! I come from where there is no origin and have now arrived where there is no origin."

From here onward is the second [part, I.A.2], an exchange of words, which is in three [subparts]:

a question [I.A.2.a];
an answer [I.A.2.b];
the conclusion of the narrative [I.A.2.c].

In the second [subpart, I.A.2.b], on the intent of the answer, it clarifies that, as a person approaches the stage of sanctity [after progressing from] the stage of an ordinary person *(pṛthagjana)* to the incipiency of sanctity, he reviews [his development] from past to present. In the past, when he was at the stage of an ordinary person and first aroused the intent [to seek enlightenment], he himself believed that his own mind was originally free from generating activity, because the origin of this generation of activity could not be found. Now that he has reached the stage of sanctity and attained nonproduction, he knows through realization that his own mind is originally unproduced, because an origin for such production cannot be found. Hence, he knows that he has first come from that place where there is no origin, and the place where he has now arrived is also where there is no origin. Since we have brought up this lack of any root [viz. anything fundamental], we should also understand that it is similarly free of **[630b]** branches [viz. derivatives]. Since there are no branches or roots, there is also ultimately no coming and no arrival. One can merely respond to the terms used in the Buddha's question and provisionally employ such words as "come" or "arrived." Although there is, furthermore, no actual coming or arriving, this is still not to say that there is absolutely no coming or arriving; hence, coming and arriving are used to elucidate the fact that there is no coming or arriving. This is because the place at which he arrives and the place whence he comes are both equally "where there is no origin."

> The Buddha said: "You originally came from nowhere and now you have also arrived nowhere. As you have gained the original inspiration (*polli*), which is inconceivable, you are a bodhisattva-*mahāsattva*."

This is the conclusion of the narrative [I.A.2.c]. The intent of this part is to explain that, since the place whence he comes and the place at which he arrives are both equally "where there is no origin," and since both are equally places that have no origin, there is then neither coming nor arriving. This is because the place whence he comes is no different from the place where he arrives; hence, there is originally no coming from anywhere. And the place where he arrives is identical to the place whence he comes; hence, there now is no place where he arrives. Furthermore, since the place whence he comes has no origin, there is neither coming nor not-coming. Since the place where he arrives now also has no origin, there is neither arriving nor not-arriving. Since he has no coming and no arriving and is originally calm and quiescent, it therefore says, "You have gained the original inspiration, which is inconceivable." Since he has obtained the original inspiration which inspires both oneself and others, it therefore says, "You are a great bodhisattva-*mahāsattva*."

> Then, emitting a great ray of light that illuminated the great chiliocosm, he recited gāthās:
>
> How great you are, oh bodhisattva,
> You who are replete in knowledge and wisdom.
> Constantly by means of the original inspiration,
> You inspire sentient beings.
> In all the four postures [walking, standing, sitting, lying],
> You constantly abide in the original inspiration,
> Guiding all the classes of beings,
> Without coming or going anywhere.[191]

This is the third [part, I.A.3], in which the Tathāgata emits rays of light to symbolize his praise for the bodhisattva. It is in two [subparts].

First [I.A.3.a] is the preface of the sūtra editor. The reason that [the Buddha was] "emitting a great . . . light that illuminated the great chiliocosm" was to symbolize that the effulgence of great wisdom illuminates the darkness of the world, causing it to be irradiated with brightness. This substantiates the Tathāgata's earlier praise.

"How great you are, oh bodhisattva" is the specific praise [subpart I.A.3.b] of Muju Bodhisattva. **[630c]** "You are replete in knowledge and wisdom" means that, because he knows nothing, there is nothing that he does not know. "In all the four postures,/You constantly abide in the original inspiration" parallels the passage earlier in the preface "from far away, [Muju] drew close to the Tathāgata's seat" (p. 629c). Through this [statement], he demonstrates the inspiration of original enlightenment. "Without coming or going anywhere" means that he is calm and yet constantly proselytizing. "**Without coming**" means, to the extent that [these sentient beings] are led and proselytized, they are rendered capable of transcending the world, a state whence they will never be able to backslide. "**[Without] going anywhere**" means, in accordance with this freedom from retrogression, he retires from making any kind of display and remains "well-gone" *(sugata)*.

> **At that time, Muju Bodhisattva addressed the Buddha: "Lord! Through what inspiring transformation may one transform all the affective consciousnesses of sentient beings so that they will access the *amala*[-*vijñāna;* immaculate consciousness]?"**[192]

From here onward is the second [subsection, I.B], an extensive disquisition [*sic;* "explanation" above] on the aspect of original inspiration. It is in two [parts]:

one, [I.B.1], an explicit and extensive account;
two, [I.B.2], a reiterated disquisition.

In this first direct and extensive account [I.B.1], initially [I.B.1.a], there is a question; and subsequently [I.B.1.b], an answer.

[I.B.1.a:] "**Through what inspiring transformation**": this question concerns the aspect of inspiration, which is the catalyst of transformation. It is a question regarding the previous statement "**guiding all [the classes of beings].**" "**May one transform . . . sentient beings**": this question concerns the aspect of the transmutation of all the consciousnesses, which are the objects of transformation. It is a question regarding the previous statement "**without . . . going anywhere.**" "**All the affective consciousnesses**" mean the eight consciousnesses. *Amala* means the ninth consciousness. Trepiṭaka Paramārtha's interpretation of the ninth consciousness is derived from this passage, as his treatise explains.[193]

> **The Buddha replied: "All the buddhas, the tathāgatas, constantly employ the one enlightenment to transform all the consciousnesses so that they will access the *amala*. Why is this? The original enlightenment of each and every sentient being is constantly enlightening all sentient beings by means of that one enlightenment, prompting them all to regain their original enlightenment. They become enlightened to the fact that all the affective consciousnesses are void, calm, and unproduced. Why is this? It is a given that the original natures [of the eight consciousnesses] are originally motionless."**

This answer [I.B.1.b] offers an explicit and extensive account of the aspect of original inspiration. It is in two [divisions]:

initially [I.B.1.b.i], an overview;
subsequently [I.B.1.b.ii], an explication.

[I.B.1.b.i, an overview:] "**All the buddhas, the tathāgatas, constantly employ the one enlightenment**": this statement provides an overview of the origin of the catalyst of transformation [viz. the aspect of inspiration]. "**To transform all the consciousnesses so that they will access the *amala***": **[631a]** this provides an overview of the transformation [of the consciousnesses], which are the objects of that transformation.

In the explication [division, I.B.1.b.ii], there are two [subdivisions]:

a direct explication [I.B.1.b.ii.a];
a reexplication [I.B.1.b.ii.b].

In the direct explication [I.B.1.b.ii.a], the statement "**the original enlightenment of each and every sentient being**" explicates the previous [reference] to the one enlightenment as being the origin of the catalyst of transformation. All sentient beings are equally endowed with this one, original enlightenment; therefore, it says, "**one enlightenment.**" All buddhas experience this [one enlightenment and] are then able to proselytize everywhere; therefore, it says, "**[They] constantly employ. . . .** " Since they employ this original enlightenment to catalyze the enlightenment of others, it therefore says "**[it] is constantly enlightening all sentient beings by means of that one enlightenment, prompting them all to regain their original enlightenment.**" This passage explicates the objects of proselytization, which are transformed so that they access [the *amalavijñāna*]. "**Original enlightenment**" is in fact the *amalavijñāna*. "**Regain their original enlightenment**": this explicates the aspect of "**access.**" At the time that one accesses the original enlightenment, one cognizes that the eight consciousnesses are originally calm and extinct. Because enlightenment is the ultimate *(niṣṭa)*, none of [these eight] consciousnesses are produced any longer. Therefore, it says, "**All the affective consciousnesses are void, calm, and unproduced.**" This passage is an explicit explication of the phrase "**to transform all the consciousnesses.**"

The text here offers a thorough elucidation of the two types of enlightenment: original and acquired. "**The original enlightenment of each and every sentient being**" is the aspect of original enlightenment. "**They cognize the fact that all the affective consciousnesses are void, calm, and unproduced**" is the aspect of acquired enlightenment. This [juxtaposition of phrases] elucidates the fact that acquired enlightenment is identical to original enlightenment.[194]

From "**why is this?**" onward is the second [division, I.B.1.b.ii.b], a reexplication. In the explication above, acquired enlightenment means that things to which one becomes enlightened are calm and extinct. Although all the eight consciousnesses evolve in accordance with conditions, even were one to seek out their given natures, they would all be unascertainable. Therefore, it says, **"It is a given that the original natures [of the eight consciousnesses] are originally motionless."** Because they are originally motionless, they are originally calm and extinct.

> **Muju Bodhisattva asked: "Each and every one[195] of the eight consciousnesses is generated with the sense-realms as condition. So how is it that they are motionless?"**

From here onward is the second [part, I.B.2], a reiterated disquisition. It is in two [subparts]:

initially [I.B.2.a], a disquisition on acquired enlightenment;
subsequently [I.B.2.b], a disquisition on original enlightenment.

The initial [subpart, I.B.2.a] is also in two [divisions]:

one [I.B.2.a.i], a disquisition on the fact that all the consciousnesses are void and calm;
two [I.B.2.a.ii], a disquisition on the fact that all the consciousnesses are unproduced.

The former [division, I.B.2.a.i] refers to the objects of enlightenment as the targets of acquired enlightenment; the latter [division, I.B.2.a.ii] refers to acquired enlightenment as the catalyst of enlightenment.

In this initial [division, I.B.2.a.i], there are a series of six exchanges, **[631b]** which are in three [subdivisions]:

one [I.B.2.a.i.a], the first set of two exchanges, which are an explicit clarification of void-calmness;
two [I.B.2.a.i.b], the third exchange, which clarifies the fact that the characteristics [of enlightenment and nonenlightenment] are not identical;
three [I.B.2.a.i.c], the last set of three exchanges, which clarify the fact that the characteristics [of enlightenment and nonenlightenment] are not different.

This first exchange [I.B.2.a.i.a.1] clarifies the fact that there is no generation of motion. The statement **"each and every one"** means "all"—that is, all the eight consciousnesses of all sentient beings. **"[Each] is generated with the sense-realms as condition"**: among the four types of conditions *(pratyaya)*, this refers to the objective-support condition *(ālambanapratyaya)* [viz. sensory objects],[196] which is used to critique [the notion that the consciousnesses] remain [unconditioned and thus] motionless.

> The Buddha answered: "All the sense-realms are originally void. All consciousnesses are originally void. Being void, their natures are not subject to conditions. So how are they produced by conditions?"

Here [the Buddha] rejects [the contrary notion that the consciousnesses] are conditioned by the sense-realms, elucidating the fact that the consciousnesses are not generated.

> Muju Bodhisattva retorted, "If all the sense-realms are void, then how can there be perception?"
>
> The Buddha replied: "Perception is in fact deceptive. Why so? All the myriad of existing things are unproduced and signless. Originally they have no names for themselves and are all void and calm. So too is this the case for all characteristics of dharmas. The bodies of all sentient beings are also just the same. And if even those bodies do not exist, then how much less so could perception!"

From here onward is the second exchange [I.B.2.a.i.a.2], which clarifies that perception is deceptive. Because it is deceptive, it is truly void. This means that, because the sense-realms are void, the perception that there are existent sense-objects is in fact deceptive; and because perception is also void, the assumption that things exist in reality is also deceptive. There are two [subsegments] to this explanation:

a general clarification [I.B.2.a.i.a.2.a];
a specific elucidation [I.B.2.a.i.a.2.b].

Regarding the general clarification [I.B.2.a.i.a.2.a], such putatively "existent" things as the skandhas (aggregates) and elements *(dhātu)* "originally . . . have no names for themselves" such as "I am materiality," and so forth. It is merely owing to the deceptive mind that these come to be named "materiality," and so forth. For this reason, these "are all void and calm."

In the specific elucidation [I.B.2.a.i.a.2.b], the statement "so too is this the case for all characteristics of dharmas" refers to the dharma-characteristics of the six sense-objects, such as the external mountains, streams, and so forth. "The bodies of all sentient beings are also just the same:" this refers to the body that is composed internally of the five skandhas, such as materiality, feeling, and so on; but if even that physical body is nonexistent, then how would the function of perception possibly exist?

> Muju Bodhisattva said, "If all sense-realms are void, all bodies are void, and all **[631c]** consciousnesses are void, then enlightenment too must be void."
>
> The Buddha replied: "Each and every enlightenment has a fixed na-

> ture that is not destroyed and not annihilated. They are not void and not nonvoid, for they are free from voidness or nonvoidness."

From here onward is the third exchange [I.B.2.a.i.b], which clarifies the fact that the characteristics of enlightenment and nonenlightenment are not identical. The import of the query "enlightenment too must be void" is that, since the conditionally produced consciousnesses are void, the conditionally generated enlightenment [viz. the acquired enlightenment] must also be void. Since the consciousnesses are void, sensory perception is deceptive. And because enlightenment also is void, the experience [of that enlightenment] must also be deceptive.

The implication of the Buddha's response, "each and every enlightenment," is that this principle that they are "not annihilated" means that these enlightenments cannot be voided; and since there is no nature of their own that is validated, they are also "not nonvoid." Therefore, while it may be that these enlightenments "are free from voidness or nonvoidness," it is not the same with all the consciousnesses, which by deceptively clinging to all dharmas and countering the true principle can be voided and negated. Since [enlightenment and consciousness] are in this wise different, how could they be classified as the same?

"Fixed nature" refers to the nature of true thusness *(bhūtatathatā),* which cannot be annihilated, because its nature is simply thus. "Not destroyed" means that [true thusness] does not cling to the characteristic of existence, because this would mar its void [aspect]. "Not annihilated" means that [true thusness] does not presume there is no nature, because this would mar its absolute [aspect]. This means that it is "not destroyed or annihilated" with respect to its "given nature."

> Muju Bodhisattva remarked: "It is the same too for all the sense-realms. They are not marked by voidness and yet they cannot but be marked by voidness."
>
> The Buddha assented: "So it is. The natures of all the sense-realms are originally fixed. The bases of their fixed natures are not located anywhere."
>
> Muju Bodhisattva said, "Enlightenment is also the same: it is not located anywhere."
>
> The Buddha assented: "So it is. Because enlightenment has no locus, it is pure. As it is pure, it is free from [any such limiting concept as] enlightenment. As material things have no locus, they are pure. As they are pure, they are free from [any such limiting concept] as materiality."

From this point onward is the third set [of three exchanges, I.B.2.a.i.c], which clarifies that the characteristics [of enlightenment and nonenlightenment] are not different. Herein, the first two exchanges [I.B.2.a.i.c.1, 2] clarify that enlightenment and the sense-realms have the same characteristics;

the latter single exchange [I.B.2.a.i.c.3] elucidates the fact that enlightenment and the consciousnesses have the same characteristics.

In the first [segment], the former exchange [I.B.2.a.i.c.1] clarifies the fact that the sense-realms are identical to enlightenment. This means that all the deceptive sense-realms **[632a]** are originally nonexistent. Since they are free from any semblance of existence, how would they involve any characteristics that void existence? And since they do not void existence, how would they achieve the voidness of nonexistence? Therefore, it says, "**They are not marked by voidness and yet they cannot but be marked by voidness.**" Explained from this standpoint, [the sense-realms] are then not different from enlightenment.

In the response, the statement "**the natures . . . are originally fixed**" clarifies that, because [the sense-realms] originally do not exist, they are not marked by voidness. "**The bases . . . are not located anywhere**" clarifies that, because they do not involve voidness, they are not devoid of voidness.

The latter exchange [I.B.2.a.i.c.2] clarifies the fact that enlightenment is the same as the sense-realms. "**Enlightenment is also the same**": enlightenment is also conditionally produced, because its original nature is void. In the response, the statement "**As it is pure, it is free from enlightenment**" means that cognizing the principle of voidness leaves behind all characteristics; thus, it says, "**it is pure.**" Since the nature of cognition is void, there is no cognition where there is voidness, in the same way that there is no characteristic of "materiality" in voidness. The preceding [exchange, I.B.2.a.i.c.1] clarified that the sense-realms were the same as enlightenment in order to demonstrate the parallels between the aspect of the sense-realms being "**not void and not nonvoid**" and the preceding aspect that enlightenment was "**not void and not nonvoid.**" Now, the present [exchange, I.B.2.a.i.c.2] clarifies that enlightenment is the same as the sense-realms in order to show that the enlightened nature's principle of being void and signless is the same as the sense-realms' aspect of being void and signless. The difference between these two passages should be understood in this manner.

> Muju Bodhisattva remarked: "The mind and the visual consciousness as well are similarly inconceivable."
>
> The Buddha said: "Yes, the mind and the visual consciousness as well are similarly inconceivable. Why is this? Materiality has no locus; it is pure and nameless. It does not intrude into the internal [sense-bases]. The visual [base] has no locus; it is pure and sightless. It does not go out into the external [sense-objects]. The mind has no locus; it is pure and unsurpassed; it has no locus whence it is produced. Consciousness has no locus; it is pure and motionless; it is not distinguished by conditions. Their natures are entirely void and calm.

This is the third exchange [I.B.2.a.i.c.3], which clarifies that consciousness is the same as enlightenment. The line "**the mind and the visual con-**

sciousness" refers to the mind that accumulates the seeds of the visual consciousness [viz. the *ālayavijñāna*] and the visual consciousness that derives from these seeds. He briefly alludes to these two to provide an overview of the fact that their natures are void and draws below on the four **[632b]** types of conditions to clarify the fact that the visual consciousness is void. "**Materiality has no locus**" means that the nature of materiality is itself void. "**It is pure and nameless**" means that, in voidness, there is no materiality. "**It does not intrude into the internal**" means that it does not become ar object of the visual faculty *(cakṣurindriya)*. This explains the fact that the objective-support condition *(ālambanapratyaya)* is void. "**The visual [base] has no locus; it is pure and sightless**" means that, where the nature of sight is void, there is no visual faculty. "**It does not go out into the external**" means that it does not function as the subject of sense perception with regard to the element of materiality. This clarifies that the predominant condition *(adhipatipratyaya)* [viz. the sense organ itself] is void. "**The mind has no locus; it is pure and unsurpassed**" means there are no seeds [of consciousness] where seeds are void. This is paramount among the four types of conditions. "**[The mind] has no locus whence it is produced**" means that it is not associated with any of the loci whence consciousness originates. This clarifies that the causal condition *(hetupratyaya)* is void. "**Consciousness has no locus; it is pure and motionless**" means that, since the three [preceding] types of conditions are nonexistent, visual consciousness does not originate. "**[Consciousness is] not distinguished by conditions**" means that there is no condition, for example, "materiality," by which to differentiate [the sensory] consciousnesses. This explains the fact that the antecedent condition *(samanantarapratyaya)* and the visual consciousness are void. "**Conditions**" refers to the conditions that precede extinction. "**Distinguished**" refers to the sensory distinctions that are produced subsequently. Because these two are both void, it says "**it is not.**"

Since, in this wise, the four types of conditions and the consciousnesses are both void, it says as a general summation that "**their natures are entirely void and calm.**" Just as we say that the four conditions are all void with regard to visual consciousness, so too should the same explanation be given for [all the consciousnesses] up to and including the "mentality"-consciousness: that is, dharmas [the objects of the mentality-consciousness] have no locus; they are pure and nameless. The mental [faculty] has no locus; it is pure and nameless. It does not intrude into the internal [sense-base]. The mental [base] has no locus; it is pure and free of perception. It does not go out into the external [realm of mental objects].

The mind has no locus; it is pure and unsurpassed. It has no place whence it originates. [Mind-]consciousness has no locus; it is pure and motionless; it is not distinguished by conditions. Its nature is entirely void and calm.

In this passage, "mentality" *(ŭi)* means the seventh consciousness *(kliṣṭ-*

manovijñāna); "mind" *(sim)* means the eighth consciousness [the *ālayavijñāna*]. This explains that the eight consciousnesses are all void and calm and, consequently, are the same as the voidness of all types of enlightenment.

> "That nature is free from any semblance of enlightenment, but if one becomes enlightened, [that nature too] will then be enlightened.
>
> "Oh son of good family! Once one realizes that there is no **[632c]** enlightenment, all the consciousnesses then access [the fountainhead of the mind].
>
> "Why is this? At the stage of adamantine knowledge, they [the consciousnesses] are eradicated on the path of liberation *(vimuktimārga)*. Once they are eradicated, you access the nonabiding stage [of sublime enlightenment] where there is neither egress nor access, that stage of certitude where the mind has no locus. That stage is pure, like transparent beryl.[197] That nature is constantly in equilibrium, like the great earth. Enlightened, sublime, contemplative investigation is like the effulgence of the sun of wisdom.[198] [One's ability to] inspire [others] is perfected and one gains original [enlightenment]; this is like the great rain of dharma.
>
> "Accessing this knowledge is accessing the buddhas' stage of knowledge [the sublime enlightenment where these four types of wisdom are perfected]. For one who has accessed this stage of knowledge, none of the consciousnesses is produced."

This is the second [division, I.B.2.a.ii], a clarification [*sic;* "disquisition" above, p. 631a] of the fact that all the consciousnesses are unproduced. It seeks to clarify that, originally, all the consciousnesses are produced in accordance with ignorance. Now, through the acquired enlightenment, [these consciousnesses] return to the fountainhead of the mind; and once they return to the fountainhead of the mind, none of the consciousnesses will any longer be generated. Because the consciousnesses are not generated, acquired enlightenment will be consummated.

This [division] is in two [subdivisions]:

a brief overview [I.B.2.a.ii.a];
an extensive explication [I.B.2.a.ii.b].

The overview [I.B.2.a.ii.a] is also in two [segments].

[In the first segment, I.B.2.a.ii.a.1], the statement "**that nature is free from any semblance of enlightenment, but if one becomes enlightened [that nature too] will then be enlightened**" offers an overview of the consummation of acquired enlightenment.

[In the second segment, I.B.2.a.ii.a.2], the statement "**once one awakens to the knowledge that there is no enlightenment, all the consciousnesses then access [enlightenment]**" offers an overview of the fact that all the consciousnesses are unproduced. The statement "**that nature is free from any semblance of enlightenment**" means not only that this nature of voidness is devoid of consciousness, but also that it is not associated in any way with acquired enlightenment. The principle that "**one realizes that there is no enlightenment**" then serves as the knowledge of acquired enlightenment; therefore, it says "**if one becomes enlightened, [that nature too] will then be enlightened.**" "**One awakens to the knowledge that there is no enlightenment**" describes the previous [account of] acquired enlightenment. Once acquired enlightenment is consummated, the eight consciousnesses will no longer be generated. This is because, to the extent that one awakens to the fact that there is no enlightenment, all the consciousnesses vanish; and, to the extent that one awakens to the ultimate, one returns to the fountainhead of the mind. Therefore, it says, "**All the consciousnesses then access [the fountainhead of the mind].**"

From "**why is this?**" onward is the [extensive] explanation [I.B.2.a.ii.b], which is in two [segments]:

initially [I.B.2.a.ii.b.1], a clarification of the fulfillment of the cause;
subsequently [I.B.2.a.ii.b.2], an elucidation of the consummation of the fruition.

[I.B.2.a.ii.b.1, a clarification of the fulfillment of the cause:] "**At the stage of adamantine knowledge**" refers to the *vajropamasamādhi,* which occurs at the stage of virtual enlightenment, where the cause of acquired enlightenment is fulfilled, as was explained previously (*KSGN,* p. 605c). Here is it called "**adamantine knowledge**" because it is explained from the standpoint of the cause of enlightenment.

"**Are eradicated on the path of liberation *(vimuktimārga)***" means that the cause of nonproduction is fulfilled. However, in this [line], "eradication" has two senses. [First, eradication] may be treated from the standpoint of the innate *(upapattilābhika)* ignorance that exists on the abiding stage; this means that the adamantine state of mind is the uninterrupted **[633a]** path *(ānantaryamārga),* and the initial thought-moment of sublime enlightenment is the path of liberation *(vimuktimārga).*[199] At the moment of the uninterrupted path, one remains associated with ignorance; it is only when the path of liberation is generated that there then can be actual "eradication." [Second, eradication] may be treated from the standpoint of the seeds of conceptual proliferation *(prapañca)* present in all the consciousnesses. Then, the thought-moments preceding [eradication] are the uninterrupted path, which is generated and extinguished in association with those seeds. The very last thought-moment, the *vajropamāsamādhi,* is the path of liberation, which is the actual eradication of those seeds. Now, [in this passage, "eradication"] should be taken in the [second] sense of eradication of these seeds [of *prapañca*]; therefore, it says, "**[At the stage of] adamantine [knowledge], they are eradicated on the path to liberation *(vimuktimārga).***" At this time, the present fruition consciousness *(*vipākavijñāna;* viz. the *ālayavijñāna)* is produced by the seeds of the past thought-moment, because the generation of cause and fruition does not occur simultaneously. This subsequent fruition is not again regenerated because at that time one has already eradicated all seeds. Therefore, we know that the statement "**eradicated on the path to liberation**" actually [explains] the cause for all the consciousnesses being unproduced.

Next [I.B.2.a.ii.b.2] is an elucidation of the fruition, which is in two [subsegments]:

initially [I.B.2.a.ii.b.2.a], a clarification that enlightenment is consummated;
subsequently [I.B.2.a.ii.b.2.b], an elucidation of the fact that the consciousnesses are unproduced.

In the first [subsegment, I.B.2.a.ii.b.2.a], the statement "**once they are eradicated, you access the nonabiding stage**" means that, after the adamantine liberation has eradicated the seeds [of *prapañca*], one immediately accesses the nonabiding stage of sublime enlightenment. Transcending the two truths [of absolute *(paramārtha)* and conventional *(saṃvṛtti)*], one abides independently in nonduality. For this reason it is called "**nonabiding.**" Because the nonabiding mind extinguishes both of the two truths, it makes no distinction between egressing from the conventional [truth] or accessing the absolute [truth]. Since "**there is neither egress nor access**" and no dwelling in either voidness or existence, it says "**the mind has no locus.**" In the place that has no locus, there is only the one mind. Because the essence of the one mind is originally calm and quiescent, it refers to "**that stage of certitude.**" At the time that the one mind is revealed, the eight consciousnesses are all transformed. Hence, at that time, the four wisdoms are consummated. This is because this one mind leaves darkness behind and perfects brightness. Clear and transparent, there are no shadows it does not illuminate; therefore, it says "**that stage is pure, like transparent beryl.**" This [statement] elucidates the aspect of the great perfect mirror wisdom *(ādarśanajñāna)*. This one mind leaves far behind the two extremes [of conventional and absolute] and penetrates to the fact that oneself and others are in a state of constant equilibrium and nonduality; therefore, it says "**that nature is constantly in equilibrium, like the great earth.**" **[633b]** This [statement] elucidates the aspect of impartial wisdom *(samatājñāna)*. In this wise, the one mind has no objects that it contemplates, and there are none of the approaches to dharma that it does not investigate; therefore, it says "**enlightened, sublime, contemplative investigation is like the effulgence of the sun of wisdom.**" This elucidates the aspect of the sublime-observation wisdom *(pratyavekṣanājñāna)*. In this wise, the one mind has nothing remaining to accomplish, and there is nothing it cannot accomplish with regard to acts of benefiting others; therefore, it says, "**[One's ability** to] inspire [others] is perfected and one gains original [enlightenment]; this is like the great rain of dharma." Just as the rain moistens the myriad things and causes them to form their fruits, so too is this the case with this knowledge. Accomplishing acts of benefiting others prompts one to gain original enlightenment. This clarifies the aspect of the wisdom that has accomplished what was to be done *(kṛtyānuṣṭhānajñāna)*.[200] Since the four wisdoms are consummated, acquired enlightenment is fulfilled.

From "accessing this knowledge" onward is the next [subsegment, I. B.2.a.ii.b.2.b], an elucidation of the fact that all the consciousnesses are unproduced. Obtaining these four wisdoms is precisely the stage of sublime enlightenment; therefore, it says, "[This] is accessing the buddhas' stage of knowledge." Since, at this time, one returns to the fountainhead of the one mind, all the waves of the eight consciousnesses will never arise again; therefore, it says, "For one who has accessed this stage of knowledge, none of the consciousnesses is produced."

The two subdivisions of the disquisition on acquired enlightenment [I.B.2.a.i, ii] are completed as above.

> Muju Bodhisattva said: "As the Tathāgata has explained, the sanctified dynamism of the one enlightenment and the stage of [sublime enlightenment where] the four vast wisdoms [are perfected] are in fact the enlightened inspiration that is innate in all sentient beings. Why is this? Because these are originally present in the bodies of all sentient beings."

From here onward is the second [subpart, I.B.2.b], a disquisition on the meaning of original enlightenment, which is in two [divisions]:

one [I.B.2.b.i], an explicit clarification;
two [I.B.2.b.ii], dispelling attachments.

The first [division] also has two [subdivisions]:

initially [I.B.2.b.i.a], a clarification of the principle of original enlightenment's nonduality;
subsequently [I.B.2.b.i.b], a revelation of the approach that accesses realization by removing hindrances.

This first [subdivision] is also in two [segments]:

initially [I.B.2.b.i.a.1], a question;
subsequently [I.B.2.b.i.a.2], an answer.

In the question [I.B.2.b.i.a.1], the statement "the sanctified dynamism of the one enlightenment and the stage of the four vast wisdoms" correlates with the preceding explanation of the meaning of the four wisdoms. The consummation of acquired enlightenment is identical to original enlightenment; since original and actualized are nondual, they are called "**one enlightenment.**" Because there is nothing that [the one enlightenment] cannot accomplish, reference was made to its "**sanctified dynamism.**" Because the one enlightenment subsumes all four great wisdoms, which contain all the meritorious qualities, it refers to its "**stage of . . . [633c] wisdom.**" In the same wise, the four wisdoms are of equal measure with the one mind, and there is nothing that they do not encompass; therefore, they are called "**vast wisdoms.**" In the same wise, the one enlightenment is the dharmakāya, and the dharmakāya is the original enlightenment of sentient beings; therefore, it says "**[these] are in fact the enlightened inspiration that is innate in all sentient beings.**" Since [the inspiration of original enlightenment] is originally endowed with the immeasurable meritorious qualities inherent in the nature, which influence the minds of sentient beings to perform the two kinds of action [benefiting self and others], it is called "**innate . . . inspiration.**" Following from this aspect of original enlightenment's nonduality, there is not a single sentient being who is isolated from the dharmakāya; therefore, it says "**these are present originally in the bodies of all sentient beings.**"

> **The Buddha replied: "So it is. And why is this so? Although all sentient beings are originally free from contaminants and all wholesome benefits are originally innate in them, they are being pricked by the thorn of desire, which they have yet to overcome [and thus do not realize that they are originally enlightened].**

This answer [I.B.2.b.i.a.2] narrates the [Buddha's] confirmation of the question. It clarifies that, in original enlightenment, the immeasurable meritorious qualities inherent in the nature are not tainted or affected by the three contaminants *(āsrava)*;[201] therefore, it says, "**[All sentient being] are originally free from contaminants.**" With these [meritorious qualities] as the foundation, one produces all wholesome actions and benefits; therefore, it says, "**All wholesome benefits are originally innate in them.**" Although one may be endowed with original enlightenment, one may still be overwhelmed by adventitious taints, that is, "**the thorn of desire.**" Therefore, at present, one has not yet gained one's own original enlightenment.

> **Muju Bodhisattva asked: "If there is a sentient being who has yet to draw on the original inspiration and who [continues to have the desire to] gather and accumulate [worldly experience], how then will he overcome that which is difficult to overcome?"**
>
> **The Buddha replied: "Whether discrimination and taints occur en masse or in isolation, if his spirit reverts to abide in the cave of voidness, he will overcome that which is difficult to overcome.[202] Liberated from the bonds of Māra [demonic forces personified], he will sit super-**

nally on the open ground, where the consciousness aggregate *(vijñāna-skandha)* [will be in a state of] *parinirvāṇa*."[203]

From here onward is the second [subdivision, I.B.2.b.i.b], a revelation of the approach that accesses realization by removing hindrances. It is in two [segments]:

initially [I.B.2.b.i.b.1], a question;
subsequently [I.B.2.b.i.b.2], the answer.

In the question [I.B.2.b.i.b.1], the statement "**gather and accumulate**" refers to the craving for the three types of existence [i.e., craving for the desire, form, and formless realms]. Because of this clinging to the fruits of birth and death [saṃsāra], it says, "**gather.**" Because these defilements are associated with mind, it says, "**accumulate.**" Since time immemorial, the manifestations of the defilements **[634a]** have never come to an end; therefore, it says "**difficult to overcome.**" Only when the counteracting paths *(pratipakṣamārga)* [which eradicate the afflictive hindrances *(kleśāvaraṇa)* and cognitive hindrances *(jñeyāvaraṇa)*] start does the power [of the hindrances] weaken; thus, the question here is, how will they be overcome? Such is the nature of [Muju Bodhisattva's] doubt.

In the answer [I.B.2.b.i.b.2], there are three [subsegments]:

initially [I.B.2.b.i.b.2.a], specifying what is to be subdued;
next [I.B.2.b.i.b.2.b], clarifying the agent that performs this subduing;
finally [I.B.2.b.i.b.2.c], elucidating the superior benefit that is obtained from the act of subduing.

[I.B.2.b.i.b.2.a:] "**Whether [discrimination and taints] occur en masse or in isolation**": the mental activities of sentient beings are coarse, subtle, and indeterminate *(avyākṛta)*. Since at certain times they are associated with defilements, they "**occur en masse.**" Since at other times those mental activities are separate from delusion, they "**occur in isolation.**" When [the mental activities] are separate from afflictions, they remain involved with [subtle] discrimination that grasps at dharmas, and when they are associated with afflictions, they are tainted by those afflictions; therefore, it says, "**Whether discrimination and taints occur.**"

Next [I.B.2.b.i.b.2.b] clarifies the agent that performs this subduing. Through relying on the Buddhist sūtras, one turns around one's mind and spirit, dispels the characteristics of both persons and dharmas, and abides in the principle of the two voidnesses [of persons and dharmas]; therefore, it says, "**His spirit reverts to abide in the cave of voidness.**" Then and only then will this mind be generated in conformity with the principles of the path; therefore, it has superior ability. Because those delusions have oppugned religious principles since time immemorial, they cannot be resisted; therefore, it says, "**[How] then will he overcome that which is difficult to overcome?**" This [passage] clarifies the stages before the bhūmis, where one subdues and removes the two [afflictive and cognitive] hindrances [i.e., the *pratipakṣamārga*]. Owing to this counteractive path, one enters the stage of the path of eradication, which gradually plucks out the seeds [of the defilements] until they are gone forever. Once they are gone forever, one leaves far behind the four Māras;[204] therefore, it says, "**Liberated from the bonds of Māra.**"

Next [I.B.2.b.i.b.2.c] is a clarification [*sic;* "elucidating" above] of the superior benefit gained from this act of subduing. There are two superior benefits: the fruition of bodhi and the fruition of the fruition. "The fruition of bodhi" means that, transcending that place where one accumulates the five skandhas that are associated with the contaminants, one sits at the *bodhimaṇḍa* and gains unsurpassed enlightenment; therefore, it says, "**He will sit supernally on the open ground.**" "The fruition of the fruition" means that he realizes great nirvāṇa through this unsurpassed enlightenment. His cognition will then be free from any semblance of perception, and all the consciousnesses will gain access [to nirvāṇa]; therefore, it says "**the consciousness aggregate [will be in a state of] *parinirvāṇa*.**"

> **Muju Bodhisattva remarked: "The mind that gains nirvāṇa is independent and singular as well as autonomous. It lingers perpetually in nirvāṇa and perforce is liberated."**

From this point on is the second [division, I.B.2.b.ii], dispelling attachments. It is in two [subdivisions]:

initially [I.B.2.b.ii.a], a clarification of nonabiding, **[634b]** which dispels the attachment to abiding;
subsequently [I.B.2.b.ii.b], a narration of nonattainment, which dispels the grasping at attainment.

The first [subdivision, I.B.2.b.ii.a] is also in two [segments]:

initially [I.B.2.b.ii.a.1], a question;
subsequently [I.B.2.b.ii.a.2], the answer.

In the question [I.B.2.b.ii.a.1], the statement "**independent and singular**" means that when the eight consciousnesses are transmuted *(pravṛtti)*, they become the one enlightenment. "**Autonomous**" means that one leaves far behind the two graspings at person and dharmas. This "**autonomous**" enlightenment "**lingers perpetually in nirvāṇa,**" and the wisdom that abides constantly therein "**is liberated**" from all bonds. [The bodhisattva] asks this question because this grasping [at nirvāṇa] still exists.

> The Buddha responded: "Lingering perpetually in nirvāṇa is the bondage of nirvāṇa. Why is this? Nirvāṇa is the inspiration of original enlightenment, and that inspiration is originally nirvāṇa. The enlightened aspects *(bodhyaṅga)* of nirvāṇa are in fact the aspects of original enlightenment. As the enlightened nature is undifferentiated, nirvāṇa is undifferentiated. As enlightenment is originally unproduced, nirvāṇa is unproduced. As enlightenment is originally free from extinction, nirvāna is free from extinction. Because nirvāṇa is innate, there is no attainment of nirvāṇa. And if nirvāṇa cannot be attained, then how can one linger therein?
>
> "Oh son of good family! One who is enlightened need not linger in nirvāṇa. Why is this? One who cognizes the original nonproduction remains far removed from the maculations *(mala)* of sentient beings. One who cognizes the original lack of calmness remains far removed from the activity of nirvāṇa. For one who abides at such a stage, his mind lingers nowhere. Free from both egress and access, it accesses the *amala*-consciousness."

This is the answer [I.B.2.b.ii.a.2], which explicitly dispels the grasping at abiding. It is in two [subsegments]:

initially [I.B.2.b.ii.a.2.a], a brief subversion of this grasping;
subsequently [I.B.2.b.ii.a.2.b], an extensive elucidation of the principle [of "nonabiding"].

In the first [subpart, I.B.2.b.ii.a.2.a], the statement "**lingering perpetually in nirvāṇa is the bondage of nirvāṇa**" means that, even though one may have realized eternal enlightenment, lingering in nirvāṇa is a type of clinging, which produces bondage to nirvāṇa; so how, then, can "**lingering perpetually**" be liberation?

From "**Why is this?**" onward is the extensive elucidation of the principle [of nonabiding] [I.B.2.b.ii.a.2.b]. Since this principle is "nonabiding," "abiding" goes against this principle. And how can a mind that violates this principle not be in "**bondage**"? This is the sort of explication that is appropriate for the import [of this passage]. This [subsegment] is in two [portions]:

initially [I.B.2.b.ii.a.2.b.I], it draws on the standpoint of original enlightenment to clarify nonabiding;
subsequently [I.B.2.b.ii.a.2.b.II], it draws on the standpoint of acquired enlightenment to elucidate nonabiding.

In this first [portion, I.B.2.b.ii.a.2.b.I], it draws on the standpoint of nondifferentiation to clarify nonattainment and nonabiding. This aspect of nondifferentiation **[634c]** is of four types.

First, the original principle is undifferentiated, as in the sūtra's statement "**Nirvāṇa is the inspiration of original enlightenment, and that inspiration is originally nirvāṇa.**" This clarifies that nirvāṇa is the inspiration of original enlightenment, and this inspiration of original enlightenment is originally nirvāṇa: that is, that acquired enlightenment is identical to original enlightenment. Therefore, because it is undifferentiated, it is unattained.

Second, the aspects of enlightenment *(bodhyaṅga)* are undifferentiated, as in the sūtra's statement "**The enlightened aspects of nirvāṇa are in fact the aspects of original enlightenment.**" This clarifies that all the meritorious qualities of nirvāṇa are in fact the meritorious qualities of original enlightenment; they are undifferentiated and are free from any semblance of attainment, as was explained previously.

Third, the single taste is undifferentiated, as in the sūtra's statement "**As the enlightened nature is undifferentiated, nirvāṇa is undifferentiated.**" This clarifies that the enlightened nature has but a single taste and is free from any sign of differentiation; it is in fact this nondifferentiation that is nirvāṇa.

Fourth, nondualism is undifferentiated, as in the sūtra's statement "**As enlightenment is originally unproduced, nirvāṇa is unproduced. As enlightenment is originally free from extinction, nirvāṇa is free from extinction.**" This clarifies that original enlightenment is originally free from production and extinction; it is in fact this freedom from production and extinction that is nirvāṇa.

Since these four aspects of the principle of undifferentiation are originally undifferentiated, "**there is no attainment of nirvāṇa.**" This clarifies that there is no subject that attains nirvāṇa or enlightenment. The next statement, "**there is no attainment of nirvāṇa,**" clarifies the aspect that nirvāṇa is unascertainable. Since there is neither a subject nor an object of attainment, how can there be a subject or an object of abiding? For this reason, it says, "**How can one linger therein?**" This elucidates the fact that "**lingering perpetually**" does not correspond to the principle [of nonabiding].

Next [I.B.2.b.ii.a.2.b.II], it draws on the standpoint of the acquired enlightenment to clarify [*sic;* "elucidate" above] nonabiding. [This portion is in two subportions:]

initially [I.B.2.b.ii.a.2.b.ii.A], an overview;
subsequently [I.B.2.b.ii.a.2.b.ii.B], an explication.

[In the overview [I.B.2.b.ii.a.2.b.ii.A], "**one who is enlightened**" refers to a person who has experienced the acquired enlightenment.

In the explication [I.B.2.b.ii.a.2.b.ii.B], "**one who cognizes the original nonproduction**" refers to the enlightened understanding that birth and death are originally unproduced, which prompts him to leave behind the maculations caused by grasping at birth and death. "**One who cognizes the original lack of calmness**" means the enlightened understanding that nirvāṇa is originally free from calmness and tranquillity, which prompts one to leave behind the activity of accessing nirvāṇa. **"His mind lingers nowhere"** means that he does not linger in saṃsāra or nirvāṇa. **"Free from both egress and access"** means that he does not perceive either mundane existence or true voidness. **"It accesses the *amala*-consciousness" [635a]** means that the essence of the one mind leaves behind the two extremes [of existence and voidness]. Since one returns to the fountainhead of the mind, it is called "accessing." One who in this wise is nonabiding will then attain liberation. Hence, lingering in nirvāṇa does not allow one to leave behind one's bonds.

> **Muju Bodhisattva asked, "If the *amala*-consciousness has some place where it can be accessed, [does this mean it is] something that is attained—that is, an attained dharma?"**

From this point on is the second [subdivision, I.B.2.b.ii.b], dispelling the grasping at attainment. It is in four [segments]:

one [I.B.2.b.ii.b.1], an explicit clarification of nonattainment;
two [I.B.2.b.ii.b.2], dispelling once again [the bodhisattva's] doubt;
three [I.B.2.b.ii.b.3], comprehension;
four [I.B.2.b.ii.b.4], the conclusion of the narrative.

The first [segment, I.B.2.b.ii.b.1] is in two [subsegments]:

initially [I.B.2.b.ii.b.1.a], a question;
subsequently [I.B.2.b.ii.b.1.b], the answer.

[In this first subsegment, I.B.2.b.ii.b.1.a], based on the preceding reference to accessing [the *amala*-consciousness], [Muju Bodhisattva] clings to the literal meaning of the words and presumes: if the *amala*-consciousness were something that could be accessed, at the time of gaining such access one would realize attainment; therefore, there must be something that is attained. [Muju Bodhisattva] harbors this doubt and therefore asks this question.

> The Buddha replied: "No, it does not. Why is this? It is like a deluded son who carries gold coins in his hands but does not know that he has them. Roaming throughout all the ten directions, he passes fifty years in poverty and destitution, hardship and suffering. Though he devotes all his efforts to eking out a living, he is unable to support himself.
>
> "Seeing his son in such dire straits, his father tells him, 'You're carrying around gold coins! Why don't you use them? Then you'll be free to satisfy your needs in every possible way.'
>
> "His son awakens and discovers the gold coins. His mind greatly joyous, he shouts, 'I found the gold coins!'
>
> "His father replies, 'My deluded son! You should not be elated [at

your good fortune]. The gold coins you've found have always been in your possession; they are not something you've "found." So how can you be happy?'"

This answer [I.B.2.b.ii.b.1.b] is an explicit clarification of the meaning of nonattainment. It is in three [portions]:

instruction [I.B.2.b.ii.b.1.b.I];
similes [I.B.2.b.ii.b.1.b.II];
correlations [I.B.2.b.ii.b.1.b.III].

In the first [portion, I.B.2.b.ii.b.1.b.I], the statement "no, it does not" is a sweeping rejection of the notion of attainment.

[I.B.2.b.ii.b.1.b.II:] From "why is this?" onward are the similes regarding this nonattainment. There are four similes:

one [I.B.2.b.ii.b.1.b.II.A], the simile about the deluded son not realizing that he possesses gold coins and ending up traveling about in poverty and destitution; **[635b]**
two [I.B.2.b.ii.b.1.b.II.B], the simile of his father revealing to his son that the son possesses these gold coins, thereby bringing him satisfaction;
three [I.B.2.b.ii.b.1.b.II.C], the simile of [the son's] joy at obtaining the gold coins;
four [I.B.2.b.ii.b.1.b.II.D], [the father's] statement that they are not something that he has obtained.

In the first simile [I.B.2.b.ii.b.1.b.II.A], the statement "deluded son" means that all sentient beings are deluded to the fountainheads of their own minds. The Tathāgata's great compassion is like [a father] looking out for his only son; hence, the simile is to a "deluded son." The destitute son in the *Saddharmapuṇḍarīka-sūtra* is a simile for the śrāvakas,[205] but here "deluded son" is a generic simile for various types of beings. "Carries gold coins in his hands" is a simile for the fact that all the deluded consciousnesses cling to and differentiate the five bonds *(bandhana)* and the afflictions *(kleśa)*. These shroud one's own pure mind until one is no longer aware that [that mind] even exists. "Roaming throughout all the ten directions" refers to one's biased imaginations *(parikalpita)* concerning the five characteristics and the five matters. "He passes fifty years" means that one receives the five aggregates and produces the fifty types of evil.[206] "In poverty" means that he has little worldly happiness. "Destitution" means that he completely lacks any supramundane wealth. "Hardship" means that he may fall into the three [evil] bournes and receive severe suffering. "Suffering" means that he may be born among men or gods and receive minor suffering. "Though he devotes all his efforts" means that, seeking worldly pleasures, he performs meritorious actions. "Eking out a living" means that he is rewarded by receiving the [sensual] pleasures of men and gods. "He is unable to support himself": receiving worldly pleasures only increases thirst and craving, and whatever flourishes will inevitably degenerate; therefore, [such worldly pleasures] are of no value or benefit.

In the second simile [I.B.2.b.ii.b.1.b.II.B], "seeing his son . . . , his father" means that the buddhas take refuge in the fountainhead of the mind, and, having the same essence of great compassion, they act as the loving father of all sentient beings. "In such dire straits" means that [the son] was involved in the events outlined in the first simile. "Tells him" means that [the Buddha] explains the Mahāyāna teaching to sentient beings. "'You're carrying around gold coins! Why don't you use them?'": he reveals that there is a pure mind in which one should have resolute faith *(adhimukti)*. "'Then you'll be free to satisfy your needs in every possible way'": if you make use of the superior inspiration of that pure mind's original enlightenment, then the dharmakāya and its life force of wisdom will be consummated.

In the third simile [I.B.2.b.ii.b.1.b.II.C], "his son awakens" means that, hearing the Mahāyāna teaching, he generates resolute faith and is positioned at the stage just before the bhūmis. "And [635c] discovers the gold coins" means that he gains access to the first bhūmi, the stage of actual penetration; this is because through realization he perceives the buddha-nature's inspiration of original enlightenment. "His mind greatly joyous": In the subsequently obtained wisdom *(pṛṣṭhalabdhajñāna)*,[207] he reflects upon what he is about to achieve and feels remarkable joy. "He shouts, 'I found the gold coins!'": emerging from his contemplation, he becomes distracted by mental states associated with the contaminants and, consequently, generates grasping at dharmas. This is because he presumes he has gained something.

In the fourth simile [I.B.2.b.ii.b.1.b.II.D], "'the gold coins you've found have always been in your possession'" reveals that the inspiration of original enlightenment that you realize originally belongs to you; it is not something you have only now obtained. "'They are not something you've "found." So how can you be happy?'": since these have originally belonged to you and are not something you have only now obtained, it is incorrect to give rise to thoughts that grasp at your attainments. "'So how can you be happy?'" neutralizes his discrimination: this means that, in presuming he has attainment, he is happy, even though he has actually become attached.

> "Oh son of good family! It is just the same with the *amala*-conscious. It originally is not something from which you have departed. It is not something that has now been accessed. Even though in the past you were unaware of it, it was not nonexistent. Even though now you have awakened to it, it is not accessed."

This is the third [portion, I.B.2.b.ii.b.1.b.III], the correlations, which is in two [subportions]:

a general correlation [I.B.2.b.ii.b.1.b.III.A];
a specific correlation [I.B.2.b.ii.b.1.b.III.B].

In the general correlation [I.B.2.b.ii.b.1.b.III.A], the term *amala* means "immaculate." This is because original enlightenment is originally pure; thus, its nature is free from change or alteration, just as the nature of that gold coin is also unchanging. Moreover, gold has four qualities that this simile adumbrates, which are termed permanence, bliss, selfhood, and purity in reference to original enlightenment;[208] these correlate with the gold coins in these four similes.

In the specific correlation [I.B.2.b.ii.b.1.b.III.B], there are four passages. "It originally is not something from which you have departed" correlates with the passage in the first simile where [the deluded son] "carries gold coins in his hands." "It is not something that has now been accessed" correlates with [the passage] in the third simile where he "discovers the gold coins." "Even though in the past you were unaware of it, it was not nonexistent" correlates with the second simile, "'You're carrying around gold coins! Why don't you use them?'" Because he was deluded in the past [to the existence of both the coins and the *amala*-consciousness] he may not have used them; but since he held them in his hands, they were not nonexistent. "Even though now you have awakened to it, it is not accessed" correlates with the fourth simile, "[The gold coins you've found] have always been in your possession; they are not something you've 'found.'" Now one cognizes that those things originally are not separate from one's own **[636a]** mind; and since they are originally not separate from it, how can they be accessed? And since it is not accessed, it is also not attained.

> Muju Bodhisattva asked, "If that father knew his son was deluded, why did he wait until [his son] had spent fifty years roaming throughout the ten directions in poverty and destitution, hardship and suffering, before he told him [about the gold coins he was carrying]?"
>
> The Buddha replied: "The passage of fifty years is but the agitation of a single moment of thought. Roaming throughout the ten directions is but the fantasy of distant travel."

From this point on is [the second segment, I.B.2.b.ii.b.2], dispelling once again [the bodhisattva's] doubt. It involves three exchanges, which progressively dispel his doubts.

This first exchange [I.B.2.b.ii.b.2.a] involves a question concerning a doubt deriving from the simile; the answer dispels [this doubt] in accordance with the dharma. The intent behind the answer is to suggest that "the passage of fifty years" is a simile for "the agitation of a single moment of thought" and "roaming throughout the ten directions" is a simile for "the fantasy of distant travel." These [statements], then, refer to the biased imaginations produced with regard to all dharmas during the period of a single moment of thought.

It was with regard to this very moment of thought that the father addressed [his son], and as soon as [the son] was told, he immediately awakened. Once his thoughts reached their climax, he achieved nonattainment: that is, although he saw his gold coins, he actually gained nothing. Therefore, his father told him a long period of time had not actually passed. The simile mentions **"fifty years"** in order to elucidate the fact that a single moment of thought involves the fifty types of evil. This is the intent expressed in the answer.

What does this mean? The four marks of existence [the *saṃskṛtalakṣaṇas*, of production, maturation, decay, and extinction] are generated through the power of ignorance. Owing to the power produced through this combination of the four marks of existence and ignorance, the one mind can be agitated into production, maturation, decay, and extinction. Since the one mind is agitated, it dons these four marks of existence. For this reason, it says **"the agitation of a single moment of thought."** As the *Awakening of Faith* says, "The pure mind of one's own nature is agitated by the wind of ignorance."[209] An extensive explanation appears there, the details of which are as explained in that account.

> **Muju Bodhisattva asked, "What is 'the agitation of a single moment of thought'?"**
>
> **The Buddha replied: "The five skandhas all arise in the agitation of a single moment of thought. In the arising of the five skandhas, all fifty evils are contained."**

[636b] This is the second exchange [I.B.2.b.ii.b.2.b], which dispels [Muju Bodhisattva's] second doubt. It elucidates the evils that are to be counteracted. Because [the Buddha] seeks to clarify that the four marks contained in a single moment of thought subsume all of birth and death, he notes that the five skandhas altogether include fifty evils. How is it that the five skandhas contain fifty evils? The consciousness skandha has eight evils: the eight consciousnesses. The feeling and perception skandhas both have eight apiece. The formations skandha has nine: eight that are associated with mind *(cittasaṃprayukta)* and one that is dissociated from mind *(cittaviprayukta)*. The materiality skandha has seventeen. Combined they make a total of fifty. The seventeen [evils of the materiality skandha are] the four great elements [*mahābhūta:* earth (solidity), water (cohesion or fluidity), fire (maturation), wind (motion)], which are the agents of production, and thirteen derivative elements, which are the objects of production; [these thirteen derivative elements are] the five sense-bases, the five sense-objects, and the three kinds of [unmanifested] materiality *([avijñapti-]rūpa)* included in the mind-object sense-field *(dharmayatana)*. As the *Āryaśāsanaprakaraṇa (Xianyang lun)* explains, [these three kinds of *avijñaptirūpa*] refer to the [unmanifest] materiality involving "restraint of the precepts" *(prātimokṣasaṃvara* *[avijñapti-]rūpa),* "nonrestraint" *(asaṃvara [avijñapti-]rūpa),* and "achievement of perceptionless trance" *(asaṃjñikasamāpatti).*[210] Now, through this one instruction, he establishes fifty [evils]. These fifty are, in this wise, genuinely evil because they all flow counter to nirvāṇa and because they all stand in opposition to nirvāṇa's genuine goodness.

> Muju Bodhisattva asked: "The fantasy of distant travel and roaming throughout the ten directions— both of these arise in a single moment of thought and contain all the fifty evils. How can one prompt those sentient beings not to give rise to a single thought [so that the fifty evils will not arise]?"
>
> The Buddha replied: "One should prompt those sentient beings to sit with their minds and spirits calm, abiding in the adamantine stage. Once thoughts are tranquilized so that nothing is generated, the mind will be constant, calm, and serene. This is what is meant by the absence of even a single thought."[211]

This is the third exchange [I.B.2.b.ii.b.2.c], which dispels the third doubt. It clarifies the counteractive path that dispels [these fifty evils]. "**Prompt those sentient beings**" means all sentient beings [on the stage] before the ten faiths [the preliminary level of the path]. "**To sit with their minds and spirits calm**": after one has left [the stage of] the ten abidings, "**to sit . . . calm[ly]**" means to settle the mind in the three voidnesses, where one is certain not to retrogress. "**Abiding in the adamantine stage**" refers to the first bhūmi onward, where one realizes the dharmakāya that, like adamant, is free from all extinction and annihilation. "**Once thoughts are tranquilized so that nothing is generated**" means that, at the stage of virtual enlightenment, one awakens to the fact that the agitation of thoughts is originally calm and quiescent, causing [thoughts] not to arise. "**The mind will be constant, calm, and serene**": **[636c]** reaching the stage of sublime enlightenment, one gains a vision of the fountainhead of the mind, which is free from generation or extinction, originally free from the agitation of thought, and without either beginning or end. Because it is free from generation or extinction, it is "**constant.**" Because it is free from the agitation of thought, it is "**calm.**" Because it is without either beginning or end, it is completely "**serene.**" In this wise, one's practice achieves ultimate enlightenment, which means that there is not a single moment of thought involving the four marks of existence in this realm of birth and death. Therefore, in order to elucidate this meaning, it says, "**This is what is meant by the absence of even a single thought.**" The *Awakening of Faith* explains:

> Bodhisattvas who have first aroused the thought [of enlightenment], and so forth [viz. Hīnayāna adherents], with regard to the changing state of thoughts, awaken to the fact that thoughts are devoid of any sign of differentiation. This [type of awakening] is

called "semblance enlightenment," because it abandons the clinging to characteristics derived from coarse discrimination.

The dharmakāya bodhisattvas, and so forth, with regard to the abiding state of thoughts, awaken to the fact that thoughts are devoid of any sign of abiding. This [type of awakening] is called "partial enlightenment," because it is free from the coarse signs of thoughts that are prompted by discrimination.

Bodhisattvas who have completed the bhūmis are endowed with all the expedients and are associated with a single moment of thought [viz. enlightenment]. They awaken to the fact that the initial arising of a moment of thought is devoid of any such starting sign, because they have left far behind even the subtlest of thoughts. Gaining such a vision of the mind-nature, in which the mind is constantly abiding, is called "ultimate enlightenment."[212]

Nota Bene: In this [excerpt], "gaining such a vision of the mind-nature, in which the mind is constantly abiding" explicates the passage in this sūtra which says, "**The mind will be constant, calm, and serene.**" The other statements are reiterations and should be understood as above.

The preceding major subpart on the disquisition on original enlightenment [I.B.2.b] is now finished *[sic]*.[213]

Muju Bodhisattva said: "This is inconceivable! When one is enlightened to the fact that thoughts are unproduced, one's mind becomes calm and serene. That is the inspiration of original enlightenment. That inspiration is motionless; it exists in perpetuity and is not nonexistent. But this does not mean that it is not nonexistent or that there is nothing to which it is not enlightened. Awakening to the knowledge that there is no enlightenment is the original inspiration and original enlightenment. Enlightenment is pure and immaculate, perdurable and unchanging, because its nature is fixed. It is inconceivable!"

The Buddha replied, "So it is."

This is the third [segment, I.B.2.b.ii.b.3], comprehension, and the fourth [segment, I.B.2.b.ii.b.4], the conclusion of the narrative.

"**This is inconceivable**" is a generic statement of comprehension [I.B.2.b.ii.b.3.a], praising the profundity [of the Buddha's statements].

What follows are specific points of comprehension [I.B.2.b.ii.b.3.b], which are in two [portions]: **[637a]**

initially [I.B.2.b.ii.b.3.b.I], comprehension of the words and phrases; subsequently [I.B.2.b.ii.b.3.b.II], comprehension of their meaning.

[I.B.2.b.ii.b.3.b.I:] "**When one is enlightened to the fact that thoughts are** unproduced, one's mind becomes calm and serene" expresses comprehension of the preceding statement "once thoughts are tranquilized so that nothing is generated, the mind will be constant, calm, and serene." This is the ultimate stage of acquired enlightenment.

From here onward is the comprehension of the meaning [I.B.2.b.ii.b.3.b.II]. "That is the inspiration of original enlightenment" expresses comprehension of the meaning that there is no distinction between acquired enlightenment and original enlightenment.[214] As a treatise *[Awakening of Faith]* states:

> If a person gains no-thought, he then comes to know the characteristics of mind—production, maturation, decay, and extinction—because these are equivalent to no-thought. Nevertheless, in actuality, there are no such differences in acquired enlightenment, because the four characteristics exist simultaneously and are not independently established; they are originally impartial and are identical to the one enlightenment.[215]

Nota Bene: "In actuality, there are no such differences in acquired enlightenment": this explicates the passage in this sūtra, "that is the inspiration of original enlightenment." "These four characteristics exist simultaneously and are not independently established; they are originally impartial": this explicates the passage in this sūtra "That inspiration is motionless." In this wise, because the acquired enlightenment's enlightened understanding is not different [from the original enlightenment], one is thereby able to achieve [a state in which] "it exists in perpetuity and is not nonexistent." The statement "exists in perpetuity" means exactly "not nonexistent."

Nevertheless, while here it says that [the inspiration of original enlightenment may exist] "in perpetuity," this does not mean that it exists in the future; therefore, it says, "But this does not mean that it is not nonexistent." Since there is no point at which you can claim the acquired enlightenment exists, then although this does not mean that there is no enlightenment, it also does not mean that there is enlightenment; therefore, it says, "There is nothing to which it is not enlightened." One who, in this wise, realizes that principle of nonenlightenment then knows that acquired enlightenment is not different from original enlightenment; therefore, "Awakening to the knowledge that there is no enlightenment is the original inspiration and original enlightenment." Because one who gains this sort of ultimate enlightened understanding leaves far behind the obscurations of ignorance, he is "pure and immaculate." He is "pure" because he is originally unsullied. He is "immaculate" because he has now left behind the maculations. Because he is forever free from production, maturation, decay, and extinction, he is "perdurable and unchanging." He is "perdurable" because he is free from production and maturation. He is "unchanging" because he is free from decay and extinction.

This sort of person is identical to the limit of truth and commensurate with the dharma-nature; therefore, it says "**because its nature is fixed.**" Since he is identical to equanimity, he leaves behind words and eradicates thoughts; therefore, it says, "**It is inconceivable!**" Previously, he had already said it was inconceivable; **[637b]** now, he repeats "**it is inconceivable,**" because this inconceivability is also inconceivable.

"**The Buddha replied, 'So it is'**": this is the fourth [segment, I.B.2.b.ii.b.4], the conclusion of the narrative. As with what was comprehended in the preceding [segment], this does not contravene the principle.

> **After Muju Bodhisattva heard these words, he gained what he had never had before and recited gāthās:**
> **The Lord is the Lord of Great Enlightenment,**
> **He explains the dharma that produces no-thought.**
> **The mind that is free of thoughts and is unproduced,**
> **That mind is produced in perpetuity and is never extinguished,**
> **The inspirations of one enlightenment and original enlightenment,**
> **Inspire all those who are endowed with original enlightenment.**
> **It is like he who [recovered] gold coins,**
> **But what he recovered was in fact not recovered at all.**

This is the second [section, II], praising [the inspiration of original enlightenment] with gāthās. The verses are in three [subsections]:

initially [II.A] the first two lines, which are a general praise of the preacher;
next [II.B], the following four lines, which praise the preceding explanation of the dharma;
finally [II.C], the last two lines, which praise the explanation in the simile.

In the first [subpart, I.A], the statement "**he explains the dharma that produces no-thought**" explains that all sentient beings perfect the dharma of no-thought, the ultimate enlightenment.[216]

[II.B] "**The mind that is free of thoughts and is unproduced**" means that the absence of thoughts that are associated with the realm of birth and death perfects the thought of nonproduction. The statement "**that mind is produced in perpetuity and is never extinguished**" is a brief versification of the prose passages from "**the mind will be constant, calm, and serene**" to "**it exists in perpetuity and is not nonexistent.**" "**Produced**" refers to "**exists**"; "**extinguished**" refers to "**nonexistent.**" "**The inspirations of one enlightenment and original enlightenment,/Inspire all those who are endowed with original enlightenment**": there are none of those sentient beings who are not endowed with original enlightenment; therefore, it says "all those who are endowed with original enlightenment."

[II.C] The last two lines praise the previous four similes. The verses can in this way be understood comprehensively.

> At that time, the congregation heard these words and all gained prajñāpāramitā, which is the inspiration of original enlightenment.

This is the third [section, III], [during which the congregation present at the time] hears the dharma and gains benefit, because they gained benefit according to the meaning of what was explained. "Gained [prajñāpāramitā, which is] the inspiration of original enlightenment" means that the "prajñā" of the acquired enlightenment is impartial and undifferentiated, as was explained previously.

[Part Four: An Exegesis of the Text (cont.)]

[Section Two: Main Body (cont.)]

VAJRASAMĀDHI-SŪTRA, CHAPTER FIVE: ACCESSING THE EDGE OF REALITY

[637c] The term "edge of reality" [*bhūtakoṭi;* lit. "reality limit," or "true end"] is the designation for leaving behind the spurious; it is a term of ultimate import. Because it is that ultimacy which leaves behind illusion, it is called "edge of reality." Because cultivating the principle while relying on the doctrinal teachings involves both the access of principle and the access of cultivation, [the chapter's title] includes the term "accessing." Nevertheless, the edge [lit. limit] of reality has limitlessness as its limit, and its two accesses have nonaccess as their access. Therefore, this chapter is titled "Accessing the Edge of Reality."

Fourth Division of Contemplation Practice: Abandoning the Spurious to Access Reality

> At that point, the Tathāgata made this statement: "All bodhisattvas and the rest [of the congregation], by being deeply affected by the original inspiration, are able to ferry across all sentient beings."

In the systematic clarification of the six divisions of contemplation practice, the third division, drawing on original [enlightenment] to inspire living things, is finished. From this point onward is the fourth [division], Abandoning the Spurious to Access Reality. Moreover, the previous chapter clarified the approach of the mind's production and extinction; now, this present chapter elucidates the approach of the mind's true thusness.

The exegesis is in four [sections]:

One [I], a brief overview of the principal intent;
Two [II], an extensive elucidation of the rationale;
Three [III], Śāriputra gains understanding;
Four [IV], the congregation present at the time gains benefit.

In the initial [section, I], there are two [subsections]:

initially [I.A], an analysis of the expedients that promote access;
subsequently [I.B], a revelation of the edge of reality, which is the object of that access.

In the analysis of the expedients [I.A], there is

a comprehensive overview [I.A.1];
a specific analysis [I.A.2].

This passage is the comprehensive overview [I.A.1], which prompts access to the principal idea.

> "If later, during an inappropriate time, one were to preach the dharma accordingly, the time and benefit would not match. Speech that is either accordant or discordant, neither identical nor different, would be speech that is in correspondence. [Such speech] guides all sensibilities and knowledges so that they flow into the sea of *sarvajña* [all-knowledge]. It prevents the assembly that is capable [of salvation] from being swept away by the empty breeze [of the sense realms] and prompts them to aspire to the spiritual cavern,[217] which has but a single taste."

This is the second [subsection, I.A.2], the specific analysis of the expedient. In this [subsection], it directly analyzes four types of expedients:

one [1.A.2.a], the expedient of knowing the time;
two [1.A.2.b], the expedient of recognizing the potential *(ki)*;
three [1.A.2.c], the expedient that guides one to the access;
four [1.A.2.d], the expedient that leaves everything behind.

[1.A.2.a] "The expedient of knowing the time" is like the sūtra's [statement] "**If later, during an inappropriate time, one were to preach the dharma accordingly, [638a] it would be neither timely nor beneficial.**" "Later" has three aspects: after the Buddha's *parinirvāṇa;* after the end of the right-dharma age; and the last five hundred years of five five-hundred-year cycles. "An inappropriate time" means a time that is neither innocent nor mature, a time when enlightenment does not come easily, or a time when heterodox views are rampant, for these are the signs of an inappropriate time. If, at such an inappropriate time, one were directly to preach the dharma according to true thusness, it would not be in accord with that time and would be utterly without benefit. Because the time and benefit are not corresponding, it says "[they] would not match." This is the expedient of knowing the time.

[1.A.2.b] The expedient of recognizing the potential is like the sūtra's [statement] "Speech that is either accordant or discordant, neither identical nor different, would be speech that accords with thusness." "Speech that is either accordant or discordant" means that if one speaks in direct accordance with that mind [of true thusness], then one will remain unmoved by perverted grasping. But were one to speak only discordantly, then one would not generate right faith. Because one seeks to prompt others to achieve the mind of right faith and to reject the original perverse grasping, one should speak either accordantly or discordantly. Furthermore, if one were to speak in direct accordance with the principle but not generate right faith, this would run contrary to that idea. But if one does not speak in accordance with the principle, then how would correct understanding arise, for [his speech] would contradict the rationale? In order to gain resolute faith *(adhimukti)*, one should speak either accordantly or discordantly.

When controversy is rampant among competing heterodox views, if one speaks in a way that is identical to the view of existence, then this will be different from the view of voidness; or if one speaks in a way that is identical to the grasping at voidness, this will then be different from grasping at existence. These identities and differences will only exacerbate these controversies. Furthermore, if you make these two things identical, then they will be disputing with one another inside oneself; but if you make those two things different, then they will be disputing directly with one another. For this reason, one should speak in a way that "is not identical and not different." As for the term "not identical," if we explain it literally, it means that nothing is sanctioned. As for the term "not different," if we explain it semantically, then there is nothing that it does not sanction. Because it is "not different," it does not contradict that sensibility. Because it is "not identical," it does not contradict the rationale. Because one remains in mutual conformity toward both sensibility and principle without contradicting them, it therefore refers to "speech that is in correspondence." "That is" in this passage is the contextual particle *i*.

[1.A.2.c] The expedient that guides one toward access is like the sūtra's [statement] "[Such speech] guides all sensibilities and knowledges so that they flow into the sea of *sarvajña*." [638b] "All sensibilities" refers to the differentiations in the great and small affective desires. "All knowledges" refers to the differentiations in the knowledge and vision of voidness and existence. [Such speech] guides all types of objects to flow in accordance with the path and prompts them to access the one enlightenment, the sea of *sarvajña,* which is the deep and expansive import of supreme bodhi. This is just like the hundreds of rivers and streams that together flow into the great sea; but despite the depth and expansiveness of that sea, it has but a single taste. Thus it is called "the expedient that guides one toward access."

[1.A.2.d] The expedient that leaves everything behind is like the sūtra's [statement] "It prevents the assembly that is capable [of salvation] from being swept away by the empty breeze [of the sense-realms] and prompts them to aspire to the spiritual cavern, which has but a single taste." "Swept away" (*ŭp;* lit. "to pour," "to extract") has the meaning of "measure" (or "conjecture") and conveys the sense of clinging. "Empty breeze" means the wind blowing through the sky, which can rouse all the waves. It is a simile for all the sense-realms, which agitate all the waves of the consciousnesses. Because the assembly of beings that is capable of salvation is swept away by the breeze of the sense-realms, the waves that have been roused previously by all the consciousnesses are transformed. Now, however, there is nothing that causes them to be swept away, for the waves of the consciousnesses are quiescent and calm. "Aspire for" [lit. "multitude"; "nearly"] means "seek" and has the sense of "wish/hope." "Spiritual cavern" refers to the grotto of the spiritually perfected, far removed from the cities and villages, which is an uneventful place of tranquillity and longevity. It is a simile for great nirvāṇa, the immortal refuge. Because it is consummately calm and uniform, it is said to have but "a single taste." It prompts those sentient beings to aspire to great nirvāṇa, to bring an end to all the waves of the consciousnesses, and to leave behind their evolutionary transformations *(pravṛtti).* Thus, it is called the expedient that leaves everything behind.

> "The world is not the world; an abiding place is not a refuge. In emerging from or accessing the five voidnesses [below, p. 639a], one neither clings to nor rejects anything. Why is this? All dharmas are marked by voidness, but the dharma nature is not nonexistent. That which lacks nonexistence [the principle of the dharma nature] is not nonexistent [in that it is not rejected by the practitioner], and that which is not nonexistent is not existent [for it is not clung to by the practitioner]. As it has no fixed nature [alt. "nature of certitude"; *niyatatā*], it does not linger in either existence or nonexistence. As long as there is that existence and nonexistence, the knowledge of ordinary persons and saints [two-vehicle adherents] will not be able to plumb that concealed [dharma-nature].[218] Once all bodhisattvas, and everyone else, are aware of this inspiration, they therewith attain bodhi."

This [subsection, I.B,] points out the principle [viz. the revelation of the edge of reality], which is the object of access. It is in four [parts]:

one [I.B.1], a brief clarification;
two [I.B.2], a reexplication;
three [I.B.3], the inappropriateness of grasping at either extreme;
four [I.B.4], the adept's **[638c]** superior inspiration.

In the initial [part, I.B.1, a brief clarification], "the world is not the world" means that there is nothing that exists among the mundane five [classifications of] dharmas.[219] "An abiding place is not a refuge" means that although one may constantly abide in nirvāṇa, it remains unascertainable. When one who cultivates contemplation practice penetrates to the five voidnesses, he emerges from existence and accesses voidness; therefore, it says "emerging from or accessing." At the time when he accesses voidness, he does not cling to the nature of voidness; and, although he does not cling to voidness, he also does not abandon voidness, either. For this reason, it says "one neither clings to nor rejects anything." Since he has accessed the five voidnesses, why would this not involve clinging? And if there is no more clinging, why would this not involve rejection? These are the questions to which he responds.

The second [part, I.B.2, on the reexplication,] explicates [the passage] "All dharmas are marked by voidness, but the dharma nature is not nonexistent." Therefore, it says that, upon accessing voidness, "that which lacks nonexistence is not nonexistent, and that which is not nonexistent is not existent." For this reason, "one neither clings to nor rejects anything." The passage "that which lacks nonexistence" refers to the principle of the dharma-nature, which is not the same as a rabbit's horn. "Not nonexistent" means that it is not negated by those engaged in contemplation practice. "Not negated" means that it is not without principle. "Not nonexistent" means that those engaged in contemplation practice also do not validate it. "Not validate" means that it does not involve principle. The dharma-nature, in this wise, is not fixed in either existence or nonexistence. For this reason, an adept does not linger in either of these two extremes; therefore, it says, "As it has no fixed nature, it does not linger in either existence or nonexistence." For this reason, "one neither clings to nor rejects anything."

In the third [part, I.B.3, on the inappropriateness of grasping at either extreme], the passage "As long as there is that existence and nonexistence, the knowledge of ordinary persons and saints [two-vehicle adherents]" means that the ordinary person validates existence but turns away from voidness, while the two-vehicle adherent turns away from existence but pursues the quiescence of voidness. It is in this wise impossible that they will ever be able to fathom the peaceful and concealed dharma-nature without leaving behind the knowledge of existence and nonexistence. This is why it says "not."

In the fourth [part, I.B.4, on the adept's superior inspiration], "all bodhisattvas" refers to bodhisattvas prior to the bhūmis. If they know that the dharma-nature is neither existent nor nonexistent, then, at the very moment of the initial arousal of the thought [of enlightenment; *bodhicittotpāda*], they will attain full enlightenment. Therefore it emphasizes the fact that "**they therewith attain bodhi.**" This means that, when one has just aroused the thought [of enlightenment] and comes to know the dharma-nature—at that very moment—**they instantly attain** [639a] the supreme **bodhi**. This notion derives from the chapter "The Meritorious Qualities of [Bodhisattvas Who have Initially] Aroused the Thought [of Enlightenment]" in the *Avataṃsaka-sūtra*.[220]

All of the preceding text referred always to the "fixed nature." Why then in this [passage] does it refer to "**no fixed nature**"? These [references] are not inconsistent, because "not fixed" means "unchanging stability."

> **At that time there was a bodhisattva in the assembly named Taeryŏk [Great Power; Mahābala]. Arising from his seat, he came before the Buddha and addressed him, saying: "Lord! In accordance with thusness, you have said, 'In emerging from or accessing the five voidnesses, one neither clings to nor rejects anything.' What are these five voidnesses? How is it that there is no clinging or rejection with regard to them?"**

From here onward is the second [section, II], an extensive elucidation of the rationale. It is divided into four subsections:

One [II.A], an elucidation of the aspect of the edge of reality;
Two [II.B], a clarification of the aspect of gaining access;
Three [II.C], an analysis of the stages of gaining access;
Four [II.D], revelation of the expedients for gaining access.

In the first [subsection, II.A], there are also four [parts]:

one [II.A.1], a clarification of the five voidnesses;
two [II.A.2], a clarification of the three voidnesses;
three [II.A.3], a clarification of the fact that voidness is truth;
four [II.A.4], a clarification of the fact that truth is thus.

This initial [part, II.A.1] is bifurcated between

initially [II.A.1.a], a question;
subsequently [II.A.1.b], the answer.

[II.A.1.a] The questioner's name is "**Taeryŏk [Great Power]**." This person has succeeded in gaining access to the teaching [lit. "dharma gateway"; *dharmaparyāya*] regarding the edge of reality, which pervades all the *dharmadhātu,* so that there is nothing that he cannot accomplish; because he has gained great autonomy, he is called "**Great Power.**" Therefore he opens, activates, elucidates, and disseminates this approach. "**In accordance with thusness**" means that the words the Buddha has spoken tally and accord with the principle. The first *yŏ* ["**in accordance with**"] has the meaning of "corresponds" and the second *yŏ* ["**thusness**"] has the meaning of "principle."

Initially [II.A.1.a.i], there is a restatement [of the Buddha's previous words];
subsequently [Ii.A.1.a.ii], there is the question itself.

The question has two aspects: one [II.A.1.a.ii.a], a question regarding the teaching regarding the five voidnesses; two [II.A.1.a.ii.b], a question regarding the idea of neither clinging to nor rejecting anything.

> **The Buddha replied: "Bodhisattva! The five voidnesses are**
>
> **[1.] the three [realms of] existence are void;**
> **[2.] the shadows [i.e., the karmic effects] of the six destinies [hell-denizens, animals, hungry ghosts, humans, asuras, and gods] are void;**
> **[3.] the characteristics of dharmas [the four *saṃskṛtalakṣaṇas* of production, subsistence, decay, and extinction] are void;**
> **[4.] nominal characteristics are void;**
> **[5.] the objects of the mental consciousnesses are void.**[221]
>
> **"Bodhisattva! In this wise, these [five kinds of voidness] may be all equally void but voidness does not linger in voidness, for voidness is not marked by voidness. And how can dharmas that are signless involve either clinging or rejection? Accessing that place which is free from clinging is identical to [639b] accessing the three voidnesses."**

Here he replies [II.A.1.b] in succession to the previous two questions. [The first division, II.A.1.b.i, the response to the first question, "**What are the five voidnesses?**"] elucidates the three types of true thusness. What are the three? (1) The true thusness of transmutation *(pravṛttitathatā)*, (2) the true thusness of the real characteristics *(lakṣaṇatathatā)*, (3) the true thusness of consciousness-only *(vijñaptitathatā)*. These types are like those thoroughly explained in the *Āryaśāsanaprakaraṇa*.[222] Among these [types], the first two voidnesses correspond to the first two [types of] true thusness, and the latter three voidnesses correspond to this third [type of] true thusness.

What does this mean? As for the first type, "**the three [realms of] existence are void**": the three realms of existence evolve out of the passion for those three types of existence [viz. desire, subtle materiality, and formlessness]. The evolution of these three realms of existence has neither past nor future qualities and does not linger for even a *kṣaṇa* [instant]. It is void and unascertainable. This is the approach of the true thusness of evolutionary transformation.

As for the second type, "**the shadows of the six destinies are void**": since there are two varieties of both wholesome and unwholesome karmic actions,[223] the fruitions of the six destinies are like the shadows manifested by forms. Shadows are not separate from their forms; they are void and unascertainable. This is in fact the approach of the true thusness of the characteristic of reality.

As for the last type [voidnesses numbers 3–5], which is the approach of the true thusness of mere-representation, the first two [types of voidnesses, viz. nos. 3 and 4] are concept and designation used for negating the object of clinging, but the designation and the concept are both subjective because they are not truly real. The last type [voidness no. 5] negates the mental consciousness that is the perceiving subject. But subject and object are each defined in terms of each other and cannot stand independently. The principle of mere-representation is the most difficult to comprehend. [The Buddha] therefore analyzes it in terms of three [different types of] voidness, in order to negate both subject and object. Because subject and object are both void, one gains [the state of] nondifferentiation.

From "**Bodhisattva!**" [in the second paragraph of the passage] is the response [II.A.1.b.ii] to the second question ["**How is it that there is no clinging or rejection with regard to them?**"]. "**In this wise, these may all equally be void**" is a general reference to the five voidnesses and refers to both principle and knowledge.[224] "**Voidness does not linger in voidness**" means that voidness and knowledge are nonabiding and are commensurate with principle. "**Voidness is not marked by voidness**" means that the principle of voidness is free of characteristics and is commensurate with knowledge. As principle and knowledge are commensurate, both subject and object vanish. So what need is there either to cling to or to reject their interrelationships? For this reason, accessing them "**is identical to accessing the three voidnesses.**" "**That place which is free from clinging**" refers to the ten bhūmis.

> Taeryŏk Bodhisattva asked, "What are the three voidnesses?"
>
> The Buddha replied: "The three voidnesses are [639c] [1] the characteristic of voidness is also void, [2] the voidness of voidness is also void, [3] that which is voided is also void.[225] These various kinds of voidness do not subsist in the three characteristics, and they are not devoid of true reality. The pathways of words and speech are eradicated and they are inconceivable."

This one exchange [II.A.2] is a clarification of the three[226] voidnesses.

[1] "**The characteristic of voidness is also void**": the "**characteristic of voidness**" is that characteristic of uniformity that negates conventional [truth] and reveals absolute [truth]. "**Is also void**" means that it fuses absolute with conventional.

[2] "**The voidness of voidness**" it is just like smelting real gold to make a piece of jewelry. As the *Mahāparinirvāṇa-sūtra* says, "This exists, that does not exist: this is called the voidness of voidness. This is real, that is not real:

this is called the voidness of voidness."[227] This [citation] clarifies that, from the standpoint of conventional truth, there exist the differentiated characteristics of existence and nonexistence, reality and unreality. The aspect of "**the voidness of voidness**" is that it is void with regard to the voidness of uniformity because it elucidates conventional differentiations. Therefore, these differentiations are called "**the voidness of voidness.**" "**The voidness of voidness is also void**": the voidness of voidness in fact refers to these differentiations of conventional truth. Voidness also means to fuse the conventional back into the absolute, just as if an item of jewelry were to be smelted back into a nugget of gold.

[3] As for this third type, "**that which is voided is also void**": in the first type of voidness, voidness is that which reveals conventional [truth]; in the second type of voidness, voidness is that which reveals absolute [truth]. Because these two [types of voidness] are nondual, it says that they are "**also void.**" This fuses [both conventional and absolute truths] into a single truth, which reveals the one *dharmadhātu*. The term "one *dharmadhātu*" means the one mind.[228]

Nevertheless, in the first type of voidness, the conventional [truth] that is negated refers to the characteristic [of the imaginary] objects of grasping *(parikalpita)*. In the second type of voidness, the conventional with which it is fused refers to the characteristic of being dependent on others *(paratantra)*. Because conventional [truth] involves these two types of characteristics, the acts of negation and fusion are not one.

Furthermore, in this first type, it refers to the absolute [truth] that is revealed by rejecting conventional [truth]. In this second type of voidness, it is the [absolute] truth that is revealed through this fusion with conventional [truth]. These two approaches involve absolute [truth]: they are only one, and not two. Absolute [truth] is of but a single **[640a]** type and is the nature of reality that is consummately perfected *(pariniṣpannasvabhāva)*. Therefore, that which is revealed through either rejection or fusion is only one. The third type of voidness is neither absolute nor conventional, neither two nor one.

Furthermore, as for these three types of voidness, the first type of voidness elucidates the middle way [from the standpoint] of conventional truth; the next type of voidness elucidates the middle way [from the standpoint] of absolute truth; and the third type of voidness elucidates the notion that the middle way is neither absolute nor conventional, neither at the extremes nor in the middle.

The passage "**these various kinds of voidness**" is a general designation for these three voidnesses. Because they do not subsist in either conventional characteristics, absolute characteristics, or nondualistic characteristics, it says that they "**do not subsist in the three characteristics.**" Since in this wise they do not subsist in any ultimate revelation of reality, it says that "**they are not devoid of true reality.**" Although they are not devoid of reality, they also are not real; this being the case, "**the pathways of words and speech are eradi-**

cated." But because one also should not cling to the statement "the pathways . . . are eradicated," it also says that "they are inconceivable."

> Taeryŏk Bodhisattva said, "If they 'are not devoid of true reality,' then it must be assumed that they do in fact exist."

From here onward is the third [part, II.A.3, a clarification of the fact that voidness is truth], which clarifies the notion that, while voidness is not devoid of [absolute] truth, it also does not involve [absolute] truth.

Initially [II.A.3.a], there is a question;
subsequently [II.A.3.b], an answer.

[II.A.3.a] If we were to explain the intent behind the question, ordinarily when we use the terms existence and nonexistence, they perforce are used in distinction to one another: whatever does not exist perforce is nonexistent, and whatever is not nonexistent is in fact existent. The principle behind the statement "they 'are not devoid of true reality'" then should mean that there exists this principle of true reality. All ordinary students typically make this assumption. He asks this question in order to dispel that attachment.

> The Buddha retorted: "Nonexistence does not linger in nonexistence.[229] Neither is nonexistent or existent. A nonexistent dharma does not in fact linger in nonexistence. A characteristic that is not nonexistent does not in fact linger in existence. One may not allude successfully to the principle in terms of either existence or nonexistence.
>
> "Bodhisattva! That characteristic which has neither name nor meaning is inconceivable. Why is this? The name that is nameless is not without name; the meaning that is meaningless is not without meaning."

The answer is in two [divisions]:

one [II.A.3.b.i], an explicit reply;
two [II.A.3.b.ii], praise for its profundity.

In the first [division, II.A.3.b.i], **[640b]** regarding the statement "nonexistence does not linger in nonexistence": the passage "they 'are not devoid of true reality'" in the previous question meant that the term "nonexistence" does not involve the aspect of nonexistence. Therefore the term "not nonexistent" also does not correspond to the aspect of "existence." For this reason, it says, "Neither is nonexistent or existent." This clarifies the notion that "the name that is nameless" does not correspond to the aspect of existence. "A nonexistent dharma does not in fact linger in nonexistence": although it fuses conventional with absolute, it does not validate the dharma of absolute nonexistence. "A characteristic that is not nonexistent does not in fact linger in existence": although it fuses absolute with conventional, it does not validate the characteristics of conventional existence. Because absolute and conventional do not linger over either existence or nonexistence, they are not devoid of the principle of the absolute, real nonduality. Because they are not devoid of the two truths of absolute and conventional, they do not entail the principle of the absolute, true nonduality. Therefore, it says, "One may not allude successfully to the principle in terms of either existence or nonexistence." This [statement] clarifies the fact that concepts that are free from conceptualization cannot be described by names that involve anything that can be named.

From "Bodhisattva!" onward is the second [division, II.A.3.b.ii], praise for its profundity. It is in two [subdivisions]:

explicit praise [II.A.3.b.ii.a];
explicatory praise [II.A.3.b.ii.b].

[II.A.3.b.ii.a, explicit praise, refers to the sentence "That characteristic which has neither name nor meaning is inconceivable"; *sic,* Wŏnhyo skips this section.]

[II.A.3.b.ii.b, explicatory praise":] "The name that is nameless is not without name": because the terms spoken by the Buddha do not correspond to concepts that involve conceptualization, he uses a "name that is nameless" to refer to concepts that are free from conceptualization. Therefore, he says it "is not without name." "The meaning that is meaningless is not without meaning": the meaning expressed by the Buddha cannot be described by names that involve something that can be named. A concept that is free from conceptualization may be described only by a name that is nameless; therefore, he says it "is not without meaning." In this wise, while it does not involve either name or concept, it is also not devoid of name or meaning. For this reason, it "is inconceivable."

> Taeryŏk Bodhisattva said: "Such names and meanings are true and are characterized by thusness; they are the tathāgatas' characteristic of thusness. Thusness does not linger in thusness: thusness has no characteristic of thusness, for its characteristic is to be free from thusness. Therefore, it could not help but 'come thusly' [=tathāgata]. As far as the mental characteristics of sentient beings are concerned, those characteristics are identical to those of the tathāgatas. So, should the minds of sentient beings also not involve any discrete sense-realms?"

From here onward is the fourth [part, II.A.4, a clarification of the fact that truth is thus], which clarifies the aspect that absolute truth is not thus, but it is also not devoid of thusness. **[640c]** It is in two [subparts]:

initially [II.A.4.a], a question;
subsequently [II.A.4.b], the answer.

The question is also in two divisions:

initially [II.A.4.a.i], he raises the principle;
subsequently [II.A.4.a.ii], he asks a question regarding his doubt.

[II.A.4a.i:] As for the statement "such names and meanings": as was explained previously regarding the inconceivability of the characteristics of name and meanings [viz. "that characteristic which has neither name nor meaning is inconceivable" (p. 640a)], the characteristics of names and meanings refer to the fact of being free of inversion or change; therefore they are called "true." In this wise, names and meanings leave far behind subject and object, have but a single taste, and are uniform; therefore, they are said to be "characterized by thusness." In this wise, names and meanings are characterized by uniformity and thusness, and are that which is experienced by all the buddhas, the tathāgatas; therefore, it says "they are the tathāgatas' characteristic of thusness." "Thusness does not linger in thusness": this clarifies that the name "thusness," which is nameless, corresponds to the meaning of thusness, which is free of thusness. "Thusness has no characteristic of thusness, for its characteristic is to be free from thusness": the characteristic of thusness, which is free of any characteristic of thusness, is designated by the name "thusness," which is nameless. Since this sort of designation is uniform with regard to subject and object, whether it is name or meaning, "it could not help but 'come thusly.'" "Its characteristic is to be free from thusness": the characteristic of thusness is to be free from thusness. Since the characteristic of thusness is in fact characterized by signlessness, you should know that "the thusness that is free from any characteristic of thusness" clarifies that [thusness] does not involve the signlessness of thusness; and the fact that "its characteristic is to be free from thusness" clarifies that it does not involve the thusness of signlessness. Although the [essence and characteristics of thusness] are not existent, it is also not the case that the essence and characteristics of thusness are nonexistent. In this wise, the characteristic of thusness, which is free of any characteristic of thusness, is then used to designate the name "thusness," which is nameless. "As far as the mental characteristics of sentient beings are concerned, those characteristics are identical to the tathāgatas": this means that, regarding the discriminative mental characteristics of all sentient beings, those characteristics are in fact free of characteristics; there are none that are not uniform. For this reason, those characteristics are also identical to the tathāgatas. The preceding statement directly raises the principle of uniformity.

[II.A.4.a.ii:] The next statement "So, should the minds of sentient beings also not involve any discrete sense-realms?" is a question regarding his doubt: since the mental characteristics of sentient beings are the same as those of the tathāgatas, then "**should the minds of sentient beings also not involve any discrete sense-realms?**" "**Not involve any discrete sense-realms**" means to be free of discrimination. Because [their minds] are free of discrimination, they should be unsullied. Because they are unsullied, **[641a]** they should transcend all three realms of existence. Since he had this doubt, he asks this question.

> **The Buddha said: "So it is. The minds of sentient beings are in reality free from any discrete sense-realms. Why is that? It is because the mind is originally pure and the principle unsullied. It is owing to being soiled by the dust [of sensory objects] that [this world] comes to be called the three realms of existence. The mind that is involved in these three realms of existence comes to be called the discrete sense-realms. These sense-realms are empty and deceptive, and are projections of the mind. If the mind is free from deception, there then will be no discrete sense-realms."**

This is the answer to his doubt [II.A.4.b]. It involves

initially [II.A.4.b.i], an affirmation;
subsequently [II.A.4.b.ii], a negation.

"Affirmation" means that, because of the purity of the self-nature, [the mind] is originally unsullied. "Negation" means that, from the standpoint of the maculations that arise adventitiously, the discrete sense-realms do exist.

[In II.A.4.b.i, the division on affirmation,] regarding the term "purity of the self-nature," as the *Baoxing lun* says, quoting a scriptural explanation [in the *Śrīmālādevīsiṃhanāda-sūtra*], "'If the wholesome mind is extinguished and unabiding, thought-moment after thought-moment, one will never be sullied by defilements. If the unwholesome mind is extinguished and unabiding, thought-moment after thought-moment, one will never be sullied by defilements. If one is never sullied by defilements, defilements will not touch the mind, and the mind will not be touched by defilements. In the absence of that dharma of touch, how would the sullied mind ever come to be?'"[230] An extensive explanation appears there. This is in fact the approach of being sullied while remaining unsullied. As for the term "the maculations that arise adventitiously," as the *Śrīmālādevī-sūtra* says, "The pure mind of the self-nature . . . is difficult to know thoroughly."[231] That mind which is sullied by defilements can also be difficult to understand thoroughly. This is in fact the approach of being sullied while remaining unsullied. "**It is because the mind is originally pure and the principle unsullied**": none of the dust or filth [of sensory objects] will intrude upon the pure mind of the self-nature and the principle of original enlightenment.

From "**it is owing to being soiled by the dust**" onward is the negation of the question [II.A.4.b.ii]. Here

initially [II.A.4.b.ii.a], he elucidates the maculated dust of unenlightenment;
subsequently [II.A.4.b.ii.b], he briefly makes reference to the acquired enlightenment in distinction to this unenlightenment.

In [subdivision II.A.4.b.ii.a, on] unenlightenment, the statement "**it is owing to being soiled by the dust [of sensory objects] that [this world] comes to be called the three realms of existence**" means that the predominant defilements *(kleśamahābhūmika)* are briefly of three types: the fundamental [defilements] associated with the craving *(tṛṣṇā)* for sensual desires, the craving for materiality, and the craving for existence. These predominants generate the craving for the three realms of existence. Because of that craving for the three realms of existence, states of mind associated with the three realms of existence are produced. Owing to these deceptive states of mind, the spurious sense-realms are contrived. For this reason, it says, "**[These sense-realms] . . . are projections of the mind.**"

Next [II.A.4.b.ii.b], he clarifies the acquired enlightenment. "**If the mind is free from deception**" **[641b]** means that, through contemplation practice based on this principle, the deceptive mind will not be produced. "**There then will be no discrete sense-realms**" means that these deceptively contrived sense-realms will be extinguished along with the mind.

The preceding four parts [II.A.1–4] together form the first [subsection, II.A], an extensive elucidation of the aspect of the edge of reality.

> **Taeryŏk Bodhisattva remarked: "If the mind remains pure, no sense-objects will arise. When this mind is pure, the three realms of existence will perforce no longer exist."**
>
> **The Buddha responded: "So it is. Bodhisattva! If the mind does not produce sense-objects, those sense-objects will not produce mind. Why is this? All visible objects are nothing but the mind that sees them. If the mind does not illusorily project them, there will be no visual objects."**

From here onward is the second subsection [II.B], an extensive treatment of the aspect of gaining access. It is in four [parts]:

one [II.B.1], a comprehensive clarification of gaining access;
two [II.B.2], a specific elucidation of gaining access;
three [II.B.3], leaving behind the faults associated with [the agent] of access;
four [II.B.4], leaving behind the extremes when gaining access.

The initial [part, II.B.1,] is in two [subparts]:

initially [II.B.1.a], a question;
subsequently [II.B.1.b], a response.

In the question [II.B.1.a], the statement "**when this mind is pure, the three realms of existence will perforce no longer exist**" means that [bodhisattvas] from the first bhūmi onward have direct perception *(pratyakṣa)* of original purity; therefore, the three realms of existence vanish in accordance with their level of attainment. The phenomenal characteristics of the three realms vanish either on the first bhūmi or the eighth bhūmi. The very nature of the three realms vanishes on the stage of virtual enlightenment. The propensities *(vāsanā)* of the three realms vanish only upon attaining the stage of sublime enlightenment. This notion is as is thoroughly explained in the *Essay on the Two Hindrances*.[232]

In the answer [II.b.1.b], because of his general assent, he says, "**So it is.**" When the three realms of existence vanish, neither mind nor sense-objects will be produced. Why is this? This is because the sense-realms are contrived merely by the deceptive perceptions of the mind; once the mind is free of deception, there then will be no sense-objects created. And because the sense-realms vanish, the mind [of the six sense-consciousnesses] will not be produced.

> **"Bodhisattva! If sentient beings have no existence internally and the three natures [internal, external, and medial] are void and calm, there then will be no personal aggregation [viz. things involving oneself] or impersonal aggregation [viz. things separate from oneself]. Even the two accesses will also not produce mind. For one who has been so inspired, there will then be no three realms of existence."**

From here onward is the second [part, II.B.2], a specific elucidation of gaining access. It is bifurcated into:

one [II.B.2.a], **[641c]** a general overview of various classifications;
two [II.B.2.b], a separate elucidation of each [of the two accesses (below)] through an exchange.

This is the text of the initial [subpart, II.B.2.a]. "**If sentient beings have no existence internally**" means that, at the stage of the ten abidings, one realizes the voidness of the person *(pudgala)* internally. "**The three natures are void and calm**" means that, at the stage of the ten practices, one realizes the voidness of dharmas internally. "**There then will be no personal aggregation or impersonal aggregation**" means that, at the stage of the ten transferences, one gains the impartial voidness that totally dispels all such aggregations as self and others, person and dharmas. As for the term "**aggregation**," "the aggregation of living things" [viz. sentient beings] is termed an "aggregation"; the dharmas of the five skandhas are also termed the five "aggregations." But these only involve apparent voidness, for there has not yet occurred any authentic realization [such as occurs on the ten bhūmis].

"Even the two accesses": these are a generic listing of the accesses involved in the stages before the bhūmis as well as on the bhūmis proper.

> Taeryŏk Bodhisattva asked: [II.B.2.b.i.a] "What do you mean by your statement 'the two accesses will also not produce mind'? [II.B.2.b.i.b] The mind is originally unproduced; so how can there be an access to it?"
>
> The Buddha replied: [II.B.2.b.ii.a.1] "There are two accesses: [II.B.2.b.ii.a.2] the first is called the access of principle *(iip)*; the second is called the access of practice *(haengnip)*.
>
> [II.B.2.b.ii.a.3] 'Access of principle' means one has deep faith that sentient beings are not different from the true nature, and thus are not identical and not commensurate.[233] [This true nature] is obscured and obstructed merely by adventitious sense-objects. Without either going or coming, one abides frozen in attentive contemplation *(ŭngju kakkwan)*.[234] One contemplates according to truth *(ch'egwan)* that the buddha-nature is neither existent nor nonexistent. It is neither self nor others and is no different in either ordinary person or sage. One abides firmly without wavering in the state of the adamantine mind, calm, quiet, inactive, and free from discrimination. This is called the access of principle."

From here onward is the second [subpart, II.B.2.b], a separate elucidation of each [of the two accesses] through an exchange. The question [division of this exchange, II.B.2.b.i,] is bifurcated into

initially [II.B.2.b.i.a], question ["What do you mean by your statement 'the two accesses will also not produce mind'?"];
subsequently [II.B.2.b.i.b], an objection ["The mind is originally unproduced; so how can there be an access to it?"].

The answer [division of this exchange, II.B.2.b.ii,] is also bifurcated into

initially [II.B.2.b.ii.a], an answer;
subsequently [II.B.2.b.ii.b], resolution [of the objection].

In the answer [subdivision, II.B.2.b.ii.a], there are also three [segments]:

a listing of the number [II.B.2.b.ii.a.1: viz. "There are two accesses"],
a roster of the names [II.B.2.b.ii.a.2: viz. "the first is called the access of principle *(iip)*; the second is called the access of practice *(haengnip)*"],
a systematic demarcation of their characteristics [II.B.2.b.ii.a.3, which is bifurcated into

a subsegment on the access of principle (II.B.2.b.ii.a.3.a);
a subsegment on the access of practice (II.B.2.b.ii.a.3.b)].

In this [subsegment, II.B.2.b.ii.a.3.a], "**access of principle**" means that it involves resolute faith *(adhimukti)* that is in accord with the principle but has not yet matured into the kind of practice that leads to realization; therefore, it is called "**access of principle.**" It is positioned before the bhūmis. [In subsegment II.B.2.b.ii.a.3.b], "**access of practice**" means that it is cultivation that involves realization of the principle and thus accesses the practice of nonproduction; therefore, it is called "**access of practice.**" It is positioned on the bhūmis.

In the text [of this subsegment, II.B.2.b.ii.a.3.a,] on the access of principle, there are four separate passages.

[II.B.2.b.ii.a.3.a.I] From "**one has deep faith . . . [through to] . . . adventitious sense-objects**" refers to the access via the ten faiths. "**Not identical**" means that, while the characteristic of sentient beings *(sattvalakṣaṇa)* does not differ from the true nature, **[642a]** it is also not identical to it. They are "**not commensurate**" because they are neither identical nor different.

[II.B.2.b.ii.a.3.a.II] The second passage "**without either going or coming, one abides frozen in attentive contemplation**" is the access via the ten abidings. Because one awakens to the fact that sentient beings are void, one is neither coming nor going. This is because one calms and settles one's mind via the experience of the voidness of the person, attentively examining the fact that the buddha-nature is free from either going or coming.

[II.B.2.b.ii.a.3.a.III] The third passage "**one contemplates according to truth that the buddha-nature is neither existent nor nonexistent**" is the access via the ten practices. Having already attained the voidness of dharmas, one relies on the experience of the voidness of dharmas to contemplate according to truth that the buddha-nature does not involve any characteristics of dharmas, but also is not devoid of the nature of voidness.

[II.B.2.b.ii.a.3.a.IV] The fourth passage "**it is neither self nor others and is no different in either ordinary person or sage**" clarifies the level of the ten transferences. Because the access of principle has already led to the achievement of the voidness that is impartial toward self and others, the mind becomes like adamant, abiding firmly without retrogressing. In the *Fanwang jing* [Book of Brahmā's Net] this is called the ten adamants.[235] In the *Renwang jing* [Book of Humane Kings] this is called the ten firm minds.[236] Both are different designations for the ten transferences.

> **"The 'access of practice' means that the mind has no bias or inclination; its shadows [the sense-objects] are free from flux. Wherever [the mind] finds itself, its tranquil thoughts seek nothing. It is not buffeted by the winds [of the sense-realms] and [remains still] like the great earth. It rejects [any notions of] mind and self and rescues sentient beings. It is not subject to production, has no characteristics, and is free from both clinging and rejection."**

This [subsegment on the access of practice, II.B.2.b.ii.a.3.b,] clarifies the access of realization that is positioned on the bhūmis. "The mind has no bias or inclination" means that the mind endowed with knowledge that is in accord with the principle is free from any mental disturbances, for the mind that experiences mental disturbances does not arise. "Its shadows are free from flux" means that objects that are in accord with the principle remain far removed from the three time periods, for the shadows of sense-objects, which are continually in flux, are never again made manifest. He does not wish for or seek anything—not worldly merits or pleasures, not even bodhi, the fruition of great nirvāṇa. Because he has penetrated to impartiality, which is free from any sense of this or that, he therefore "is not buffeted by the winds" of sense-objects. This clarifies the access of practice as it benefits oneself.

From "it rejects" onward is the practice that prompts others to this same access. Because he can leave behind all characteristics of person or dharmas by realizing the voidness of both, **[642b]** he can universally ferry across everyone. Although the mind is unproduced and is also free of any characteristics of objects, it nevertheless does not cling to that nature of calm extinction and never abandons any sentient being. For this reason, it says "it is free from both clinging and rejection." These two sorts of practices [i.e., to benefit both oneself and others] are called the access of practice.

> "Bodhisattva! The mind is free from both egress and access. Because the mind that is free from both egress and access accesses without accessing anything, I therefore referred to 'access.'"

This is the second [subdivision, II.B.2.b.ii.b], resolution of the objection. The mind that realizes the principle remains far removed from both production and extinction. Because it has neither beginning nor end, "the mind is free from both egress and access." Once it is free from both egress and access, the mind will have no sense that it was egressing or accessing anything in past times either. Therefore, "the mind . . . is free from both egress and access." Because it leaves behind that mind which in the past was subject to egress and access, and accesses this mind which is free from both egress and access, it says, "Because [the mind] accesses without accessing anything, I therefore referred to 'access.'" In this wise, the previous objection is resolved.

> "Bodhisattva! The characteristic of that dharma which in this wise accesses the dharma is not void; and the dharma that is not void—that dharma is not frivolously discarded. Why is this? Those dharmas that are not nonexistent are replete with all meritorious qualities. They are neither mind nor its shadows; they are naturally *(niyati)* pure."

From here onward is the third [part, II.B.3], on leaving behind the faults associated with the agent of access. It is in two [subparts]:

a brief clarification [II.B.3.a];
an extensive explication [of leaving behind the dangers; II.B.3.b].

This is the brief clarification [II.B.3.a]. "In this wise accesses the dharma" means that it accesses the edge of reality, the dharma that is free from both egress and access. "Those dharmas that are not nonexistent" are impartial with regard to both subject and object, are far removed from all dangers *(ādīnava)*, and "are replete with all meritorious qualities." "They are neither mind nor its shadows" means that mind and sense-objects are uniform because they have left behind both subject and object. "They are naturally pure" means that they have neither beginning nor end because they have left behind all characteristics.

> Taeryŏk Bodhisattva asked, "What is meant by your statements 'they are neither mind nor its shadows; they are naturally pure'?"
>
> The Buddha replied: "The dharma that is void and thus—it is not one of the dharmas of mind and consciousness; it is not one of the dharmas that drive the mind; it is not a dharma that is marked by space; it is not a dharma marked by materiality; it is not one of the dharmas dissociated from mind *(cittaviprayuktasaṃskāra)*; [642c] it is not a dharma that is associated with the unconditioned characteristics of the mind. It is not shadows that are cast; it is not that which is projected. It has no nature of its own; it is not differentiated. It is not name; it is neither characteristic nor object *(artha)*.
>
> "Why is this? Because [that dharma] is thus. Those dharmas that are not thus also do not lack thusness; there is nothing existent that lacks thusness. But it is not the case that there exists [any dharma] that lacks thusness. Why is this? The dharma of the root principle is neither principle nor root [viz. fundamental]. It is far removed from all controversy and manifests no characteristics.
>
> "Bodhisattva! This sort of pure dharma—its production is not produced by production; its extinction is not extinguished by nonextinction."

From here onward is the first [*sic;* second subpart, II.B.3.b], an extensive explication of leaving behind the dangers. [This subpart is in four divisions:]

initially [II.B.3.b.i], a question;
next [II.B.3.b.ii], an answer;
three [II.B.3.b.iii], a restatement;
four [II.B.3.b.iv], a conclusion to the narrative.

In the answer [division; II.B.3.b.ii], there are two [subdivisions]:

initially [II.B.3.b.ii.a], he explicates the statement "**they are neither mind nor its shadows**";
subsequently [II.B.3.b.ii.b], he explicates the statement "**they are naturally pure.**"

In the first [subdivision, II.B.3.b.ii.a], there are also two [segments]:

initially [II.B.3.b.ii.a.1], a clarification that accessing the dharma [of the edge of reality] leaves behind both mind and shadows;
subsequently [II.B.3.b.ii.a.2], a clarification that mind and shadows are not devoid of the principle of thusness.

In the first [segment, II.B.3.b.ii.a.1], the statement "**the dharma that is void and thus**" means that, at the time that one accesses the edge of reality, leaving far behind all characteristics is "voidness" and being impartial regarding subject and object is "thusness." In this wise, accessing the dharma [of the edge of reality] leaves behind both the mind and its shadows. The distinction between mind and shadows can briefly be elucidated in six dyads. First is the dyad of mind *(citta)* and mental concomitants *(caitta)*. Second is the dyad of space and materiality. Third is the dyad of dissociated forces *([citta]-viprayuktasaṃskāra)* and uncompounded [elements; *asaṃskṛtadharma*]. Fourth is the dyad of shadowy forms and fundamental matter. Fifth is the dyad of own-nature and differentiations. Sixth is the dyad of word and meaning. Of these six dyads, the first dyad is the type that involves the mind that is the subject of the objective supports; the latter five dyads are the type that involve the "shadows" that are the objective supports themselves. Apart from these six dyads, there is therefore neither mind nor its shadows. Thus, he systematically provides a statement describing each of these six dyads. "**It is not one of the dharmas of mind and consciousness**" because it remains far removed from the mind of the eight consciousnesses. "**It is not one of the dharmas that drive the mind**" because it remains far removed from the six categories of mental concomitants *(caitta)*.[237] "**It is not [643a] a dharma that is marked by space**" because it remains far removed from the [uncompounded] dharma of space *(ākāśa)*, which is free from all characteristics of materiality. "**It is not a dharma marked by materiality**" because it remains far removed from the three varieties of materiality: manifested [sense bases], forms [sense-objects], and unmanifested *(avijñaptirūpa)*.[238] "**It is not one of the dharmas dissociated [from mind]**" because it remains far removed from the twenty-four dissociated forces ***(cittaviprayuktasaṃskāra)***.[239] "**It is not a dharma that is associated with the unconditioned characteristics of the mind**" because it remains far removed from the seven remaining varieties of uncompounded dharmas *(asaṃskṛtadharma)*. Because they manifest in reliance on the mind, they are called "unconditioned characteristics of the mind." Because they are dharmas associated with the three types of unconditioned characteristics, they are called an "associated . . . dharma." Furthermore, the fact that they leave behind the three types of dharmas of true thusness means that, in the approach of the access of realization, there are no distinctions between these three.

"It is not shadows that are cast" means that they leave behind the fundamental forms that are revealed through the expedient contemplations. "It is not that which is projected" means that it also remains far removed from such basic material features as a skeleton, and so on, which are manifestations of these shadows. "It has no nature of its own" means that it remains far removed from the own-nature of materiality and mentality, and so forth. "It is not differentiated" means that it remains far removed from all differentiated characteristics, such as impermanence, and so on [viz. suffering, and non-self]. "It is not name" because it remains far removed from the descriptive signs of words *(nāmakāya)*, phrases *(padakāya)*, and syllables *(vyañjanakāya)*.[240] "It is neither characteristic nor object" because it remains far removed from the characteristics of the description and the described. Why so? Because one who remains far removed from the characteristics of these six dyads will be impartial toward and will make no distinctions between subject and object; therefore, it says, "Because [that dharma] is thus."

From the passage "those dharmas that are not thus" onward is the second [segment, II.B.3.b.ii.a.2], a clarification that the dharmas of mind and shadows are not devoid of the principle of thusness. "Those dharmas that are not thus" refers to the negation of the characteristics of the dharmas listed in the preceding six dyads. "Also do not lack thusness" means that the principle of thusness is all-pervasive. "There is nothing existent that lacks thusness" means that there is not a single dharma involving an existent characteristic that lacks the principle of thusness. "But it is not the case that there exists [any dharma] that lacks thusness": despite the fact that the existence of a dharma that lacks thusness may [from one standpoint] be presumed to exist, it is still not the case that dharmas that are not thus cannot be considered to exist.

From "Why is this?" onward explains the aspect of "not existent." "Root": the root of a tree is a simile for the seeds *(bīja)*. "Principle": the principle of wood is a simile for present dharmas, as was discussed previously in the simile of the *āmalaka* [myrobalan] fruit (p. 625a). "It is far removed from all controversy and manifests no [643b] characteristics": even were one to seek it with insight and wisdom, it would never be found. The above two segments have been an extensive [explication of the statement] "they are neither mind . . . nor its shadows."

From "this sort of pure dharma" onward is next an extensive [explication of the statement] "they are naturally pure" [II.B.3.b.ii.b]. "Its production is not produced by production" means that they remain far removed from the characteristic of production because their essence is unproduced. The same interpretation is valid for the latter statement as well: it means that they remain far removed from the characteristic of extinction because their essence is not extinguished. "This sort of pure dharma" means that they leave behind conditioned characteristics; they are unproduced and unextinguished; they have neither beginning nor end. It is because of these aspects that "they are naturally pure."

> Taeryŏk Bodhisattva remarked: "This is inconceivable! Such characteristics of dharmas are not produced in combination and are not produced independently. They are not bridled and not partnered. They are neither amassed [viz. materiality] nor scattered [viz. voidness]. They are neither produced nor extinguished. They are free from any characteristic of coming and from any characteristic of going. This is inconceivable!"

This is the third [division], a restatement [II.B.3.b.iii]. "Not produced in combination": they are neither mind nor mental concomitants because mind and mental concomitants are both associated with separate essences. "Not produced independently": they have neither an independent self-nature, nor are they differentiated from one another. These two aspects may be differentiated, but they do not involve two distinct essences. "Not bridled" means that they are neither name nor object because name and object are interdependent. "Not partnered" means that they are neither shadows nor matter because the characteristics of shadows and matter are in partnership with one another. "They are neither amassed nor scattered" means that they are neither voidness nor materiality. This is because that which is amassed and gathered is materiality, and that which is scattered and destroyed is voidness. "They are neither produced nor extinguished" means that they are neither dissociated [forces] nor uncompounded [dharmas]. This is because dissociated forces are subject to production, and all the uncompounded dharmas are made manifest through extinction. This is a restatement of the idea of leaving behind the six dyads, as was explained previously (pp. 642c–643a). "They are free from any characteristic of coming" means that they do not involve the production of anything that is produced by production. "And from any characteristic of going" means that they do not involve the extinction of anything that is extinguished by extinction. This is the restatement of the subsequent statement "they are naturally pure." The initial exclamation "This is inconceivable!" means that he could not even envisage a thusness that is not thus, because that [thusness] remains far removed from both thoughts and words. The subsequent exclamation **[643c]** "This is inconceivable!" means that the mind that leaves behind any sense of mentality also leaves behind duality.

> The Buddha said: "So it is. It is inconceivable. The inconceivable mind—that mind is also thus. Why is this? Thusness is not different from the mind, for the mind is originally thus."

This is the fourth [division, II.B.3.b.iv], a conclusion to the narrative, which provides a systematic summation of these two types of inconceivability. The term "**mind**" refers to the mind that accesses realization. Because the mind that is no-mind accesses that which is inaccessible, it is "**inconceivable.**" "**Thusness is not different from the mind**" explicates the former type of inconceivability. "**For the mind is originally thus**" explicates the latter type of inconceivability.

> **"Sentient beings and the buddha-nature are neither identical nor different. The natures of sentient beings are originally free from both production and extinction. This nature of production and extinction—that nature is originally nirvāṇa. The nature [of sentient beings] and the characteristics [of production and extinction] are originally thus, for thusness is motionless."**

From here onward is the fourth [part, II.B.4], on leaving behind extremes when gaining access. It is in two [subparts]:

initially [II.B.4.a], a clarification of the fact that the buddha-nature leaves behind the extremes of identity and difference;
subsequently [II.B.4.b], an elucidation of the fact that thusness leaves behind the extremes of existence and nonexistence.

The first [subpart] has two [divisions]:

a brief clarification [II.B.4.a.i];
an extensive elucidation [II.B.4.a.ii].

This [division] is the brief clarification, which is also in two [subdivisions]:

initially [II.B.4.a.i.a], the leaving behind of identity and difference;
subsequently [II.B.4.a.i.b], an explication of [the meaning of] leaving behind difference.

[II.B.4.a.i.a] "Leaving behind identity and difference" means that "**sentient beings and the buddha-nature are neither identical nor different.**" The term "**buddha-nature**" means the buddha-nature of true thusness. As the *Nirvāṇa Sūtra* says, "'Buddha-nature' means the absolute truth of voidness."[241] To claim that [the buddha-nature] involves either identity or difference would be erroneous.

[II.B.4.a.i.b] "**The natures of sentient beings are originally free from both production and extinction**": from this point on is explicated the meaning of leaving behind difference. Since the concept [that sentient beings and the buddha-nature] are not identical can be easily envisioned, this sentence instead clarifies that people are not different from the buddha-nature. "This nature of production and extinction—that nature is originally nirvāṇa": this clarifies the fact that production and extinction do not differ from nirvāṇa. "The nature and the characteristics are originally thus, for thusness is motionless": because the personal nature *(insŏng)* of sentient beings and the dharma characteristics of production and extinction are originally thus, they are not different [from the buddha-nature or nirvāṇa, respectively]. **[644a]**

> "All the characteristics of dharmas—none are generated by conditions, for the nature of this characteristic of generation *(utpādalakṣaṇa)* is thus and motionless. The characteristics of conditionality—those characteristics are originally void and nonexistent. As each and every condition is void, there is no conditioned generation *(pratītyasamutpāda)*. All conditioned dharmas are the deceptive visions of the deluded mind. Their appearance is originally unproduced, since the conditions [that produce them] are originally nonexistent. The mind involves the same dharma of principle, for its self-essence is void and nonexistent. It is like 'King Space,' which originally has no abode; the minds of ordinary people wrongly perceive [all-encompassing space] as differentiated [into this space and that space]."

From here onward is the second [division, II.B.4.a.ii.], an extensive elucidation [of the fact that the buddha-nature leaves behind the extremes of identity and difference]. Herein, it extensively [elucidates] only the concept of leaving behind the extreme of difference. "All the characteristics of dharmas" means that all the fruition-dharmas are generated by conditions; and since they come into existence through conditions, they are in fact ungenerated, for "the nature of this characteristic of generation is thus and motionless." Later the text will clarify the fact that all the conditions that are the agents of generation are also void. "The characteristics of conditionality—those characteristics are originally void and nonexistent": this means that causes and conditions, which serve as seeds *(bīja)*, are nonexistent. "As each and every condition is void, there is no conditioned generation" means that, while there is not one, but rather numerous, dharmas that serve as the objective-support condition *(ālambanapratyaya)*, there is not one of these that is not void; therefore, it says "each and every [one] is void." For this reason, there are no conditions that serve as the agent of generation. "All conditioned dharmas are the deceptive visions of the deluded mind": this refers to the predominant condition *(adhipatipratyaya)* and the antecedent condition *(samantarapratyaya)*; because these are merely the deceptive visions of the mind, they too are void. "Their appearance is originally unproduced, since the conditions [that produce them] are originally nonexistent": given these two types of voidness [viz. (1) voidness of the objective-support condition and (2) voidness of the predominant and antecedent conditions], the fruition that manifests through conditions originally is unproduced, and all the conditions that are the agents of generation are originally nonexistent. "**The mind involves the same principle of dharma, for its self-essence is void and nonexistent**": we have explained previously that cause and fruition are dharmas that are the perceived objects. Because dharmas that are the perceived objects are nonexistent, the mind that is the perceiving subject is also void. Just as we have explained the principle that dharmas that are the perceived objects are void, so too is this the case for the essence of the mind that is the perceiving subject.

The preceding has been an explanation of the dharma; below, this will be referenced in a simile. Regarding the term "**King Space**": "space" is of two types. One, it refers to the "realm of empty space" *(ākāśadhātu)*, which refers to the absence of materiality. Two, "King Space" refers to the dharma of space *(ākāśa)*, which is the support of all materiality in the same way that a king is **[644b]** the support of all his subjects; therefore, space is said to be "**King Space.**" In this wise, while King Space originally has no abiding place, the minds of ordinary people wrongly discriminate between space here and space there. But these are merely deceptive visions; there is no here and no there. You should know that all the causal and fruition dharmas are also just the same: they are perceived objects of the deluded mind; there is actually no cause and no fruition. This simile is made from the standpoint of the cause and fruition that are the objects of grasping when one perceives the seeming as real; they are the locus of deceptive vision.

> **"That characteristic of thusness originally neither exists nor does not exist. The characteristics of existence and nonexistence are perceived only by the mind and consciousness. Bodhisattva! So too is it with the nature of the mind: it is not devoid of self-essence, but that self-essence is [also] not existent, for nonexistence is actually not nonexistent. Bodhisattva! Those characteristics of both nonexistence and not nonexistence are not part of the stage of speech and language. Why is this? The dharma of true thusness is empty, vacant, and signless. It is not something that can be reached by dualities."**[242]

This is the second [subpart, II.B.4.b], which clarifies the fact that the dharma of thusness leaves behind the extremes of existence and nonexistence. It is in four [divisions].

[II.B.4.b.i] The initial passage ["**that characteristic of thusness originally neither exists nor does not exist**"] is an explicit clarification of the fact that thusness leaves behind extremes.

[II.B.4.b.ii] The next passage ["**the characteristics of existence and nonexistence are perceived only by the mind and consciousness**"] brings up to the contrary the fact that the extreme of existence is deceptive.

[II.B.4.b.iii] Three ["**Bodhisattva! So too is it with the nature of the mind: it is not devoid of self-essence, but that self-essence is [also] not existent, for** nonexistence is actually not nonexistent"] references an example of how the mind leaves behind extremes.

[II.B.4.b.iv] Four ["Bodhisattva! Those characteristics of both nonexistence and not nonexistence are not part of the stage of speech and language. Why is this? The dharma of true thusness is empty, vacant, and signless. It is not something that may be reached by dualities"] clarifies again that thusness leaves behind words.

In the third [division, II.B.4.b.iii], the statement "so too is it with the nature of the mind" means that it is just like the essential nature of the one mind. "It is not devoid of self-essence" means that it leaves behind the extreme of being devoid of self-essence, which is [illusory,] like a rabbit's horn. "But that self-essence is [also] not existent" means that it leaves behind the extreme of having a self-essence, [which is hollow], like an ox's horn; it does not mean that its other characteristics are nonexistent. It is only because it is "not existent" that it says "that self-essence is [also] not existent." "Nonexistence is actually not nonexistent": nonexistence is in fact not nonexistence, and not nonexistence is in fact nonexistence. For this reason, they once again are explained in correlation with one another. Just as the dharma of the one mind is both nonexistent and not nonexistent, so too should the principle of thusness be similarly explained. Therefore, the beginning of the passage says, "So too is it with . . . the mind."

From "those characteristics of both nonexistence and not nonexistence are not part of the stage of speech and language" onward is the fourth [division, II.B.4.b.iv], which clarifies again the principle that thusness leaves behind words. **[644c]** "Those characteristics of both nonexistence and not nonexistence" clarifies the passage in the initial sentence "[that characteristic of thusness] originally neither exists nor does not exist" because it may not be satisfactorily described through words. "It is not something that can be reached by dualities" means that it is not something that can be cultivated through such dualities as thought and imagination *(vitarkavicāra)*. These two dharmas of thought and imagination both involve verbalization. Because [thusness] is not something that can be cultivated through these two [dharmas], it is "not part of the stage of speech and language."

> "The realm of emptiness cannot be fathomed by either those inside or those outside [the Buddhist religion]. Only a master of the six practices may come to know of them."

From here onward is the third [subsection, II.C] of the main exegesis [viz. section II, the extensive elucidation of the rationale, an analysis of] the stages of gaining access. It is in four [parts]:

one [II.C.1], a clarification of the profundity of the object of access;
two [II.C.2], a listing of the stages of practice, which are the agents of access;

three [II.C.3], a specific elucidation of each of the stages;
four [II.C.4], an illuminating clarification of the mind that gains access [to the edge of reality].

In the initial [part, II.C.1], the statement **"the realm of emptiness"** means that the dharma of thusness is void, vast, and signless; therefore, it is called **"emptiness." "Cannot be fathomed by either those inside or those outside"** means the twenty-eight [assemblies of] saints within the [Buddhist] religion and the ninety-five types outside the religion.[243] These sorts of ordinary persons and saints cannot fathom [the realm of voidness].

In the second [part, II.C.2], the statement **"Only a master of the six practices may come to know of them"** refers to the bodhisattva stages associated with the two accesses.

> **Taeryŏk Bodhisattva asked: "What are these six practices? I beg of you to explain them."**
>
> **The Buddha replied: "First is the practice of the ten faiths. Second is the practice of the ten abidings. Third is the practice of the ten practices. Fourth is the practice of the ten transferences. Fifth is the practice of the ten bhūmis. Sixth is the practice of virtual enlightenment. One who practices these sorts of practices may then come to know [the realm of emptiness]."**

This is the third [part, II.C.3], a specific elucidation of each of the stages. It elucidates only the stages of practice and skips the stage of fruition; therefore, it does not include the bhūmi of sublime enlightenment. Among these six practices, the preceding four ranks involve the stage of the access of principle; the latter two ranks are distinctions of the access of practice. A précis of these is found in the *[Pusa yingluo] penye jing* [Book of the Original Acts That Serve as Necklaces for the Bodhisattvas]; an extensive analysis **[645a]** appears in the teachings of the *Avataṃsaka[-sūtra]*.[244]

> **Taeryŏk Bodhisattva asked: "The enlightened inspiration of the edge of reality has neither egress nor access. Through what sort of dharma or thought does one access the edge of reality?"**
>
> **The Buddha replied: "The dharma of the edge of reality—that dharma has no limit. The mind that is limitless thence accesses the edge of reality."**

This is the fourth [part, II.C.4], an illuminating clarification of the mind that gains access [to the edge of reality]. In the question, the statement **"the enlightened inspiration of the edge of reality has neither egress nor access"** refers to the fact that someone who is in accord with principle by having gained the two types of inspirational practice on the last two ranks [viz. the ten bhūmis and virtual enlightenment] will be subject to neither egress nor access. **"Through what sort of dharma or thought does one access the edge of reality?"** is an explicit query regarding the dharma or thought that serves as the agent of access. In the answer, the statement **"the dharma of the edge of reality—that dharma has no limit"** refers to the fact that the dharma that is accessed is naturally without limit. Temporally, it is free of the limits of past and future; this is because, having neither beginning nor end, it is independent of the three time periods. Spatially, it is free of the limits of here and there; this is because, having neither middle nor extremes, it is independent of the six directions [four cardinal directions plus the zenith and the nadir]. [1] It is exceedingly profound and limitless, [2] because it is independent of all extremes. [3] It is vast, great, and limitless, [4] because there is nothing it does not pervade. Because it subsumes all these four aspects, [the edge of reality] is said to have **"no limit."** Because the mind that is the agent of access also subsumes these four aspects, there is nothing of this edge of reality that it is unable to access. Therefore you should know that just as the edge of reality is independent of the extremes of agent and object, so too does the mind remain independent of the limitations of agent and object. Precisely when there is nothing to access there can be "gaining access." This is what is meant by "inconceivability."

> **Taeryŏk Bodhisattva asked: "The knowledge of this limitless mind—that knowledge is boundless. The boundless mind—that mind gains autonomy. Autonomous knowledge gains access to the edge of reality. This is also the case for ordinary persons, feeble-minded sentient beings—those whose minds are subject to severe panting *(ch'ŏn)*.[245] Through what dharma may they control that [panting], steady their minds, and gain access to the edge of reality?"**

From here onward is the fourth [subsection, II.D] of the main exegesis [viz. section II, an extensive elucidation of the rationale], [on the revelation of] the expedients for gaining access [to the edge of reality]. "The expedients for gaining access" are positioned on the four ranks before the bhūmis; these are the expedient contemplations involved with the approach of the access of principle. **[645b]** It is in two [parts]:

initially [II.D.1], a clarification of the expedients that serve as the agents of access;
subsequently [II.D.2], an elucidation of the supreme inspiration of those expedients.

The initial [part] is also in two [subparts]:

initially [II.D.1.a], a summary;
subsequently [II.D.1.b], an extensive elucidation.

In the summary, there is first a question [II.D.1.a.i], which is also in two [subdivisions]:

first [II.D.1.a.i.a], comprehension of the preceding [discussion];
second [II.D.1.a.i.b], a question regarding what comes next.

In the comprehension [subdivision, II.D.1.a.i.a], the term "limitless" means that the essence of the mind is limitless. "Boundless" means that the functioning of that knowledge is boundless.

> The Buddha replied: "Bodhisattva! This panting of the mind is driven both internally and externally. [The afflictions] flow along and form, following those drivers, until their drips become a sea. The heavenly[246] winds buffet the waves, startling the great dragon. Because the mind is startled and alarmed, one begins to pant severely.[247]
>
> "Bodhisattva! One should urge those sentient beings to preserve the three, guard the one, and access the tathāgatadhyāna.[248] Owing to this concentrated absorption, their minds will come to be free of panting."

In the answer [division, II.D.1.a.ii], there are two [subdivisions]:

initially [II.D.1.a.ii.a], a description of the characteristics of the obstructions that are to be resolved;
subsequently [II.D.1.a.ii.b], an account of the expedients that are the agents of this resolution.

In the initial [subdivision, II.D.1.a.ii.a], regarding the words "this panting of the mind": the mind that is startled is not at rest, and the increasing rapidity of one's inhalations and exhalations is termed "panting." It is used as a simile for the agitation of the six [sensory] consciousnesses, which are always active and never at rest. "[This panting] is driven both internally and externally": the four drivers[249] of the *[kliṣṭa]mano[vijñāna]* have the sense of a personal self as their internal conditions; the six drivers[250] of the mind-consciousness have sense-objects as their external conditions. "[The afflictions] flow along and form, following those drivers": this means that the [ten] minor afflictions *(upakleśabhūmika),* such as anger *(krodha)* and enmity *(upanāha);* the [eight] predominant afflictions *(upakleśamahābhūmika),* such as sloth *(styāna)* and agitation *(suddhatya);* and the [two] medial afflictions [viz. the predominant unwholesome dharmas *(akuśalamahābhūmika)*] of a lack of shame and blame *(āhrīkyānapatrāpya)*[251] "flow along . . . following those drivers" and form the manifesting consciousness *(khyātivijñāna).* "Until their drips become a sea": all the manifestations *(samudācāra),* including the fundamental drivers and the afflictions, suffuse the foundational consciousness [viz. the *ālayavijñāna*] because they are deeply and broadly amassed. "**The heavenly winds buffet the waves**": in response to karmic power, the six dusty realms [of the senses] manifest as is appropriate; therefore, they are termed "**the heavenly winds.**" They **buffet** the sea of the proclivities *(anuśaya)*, creating **the waves** of the seven consciousnesses; therefore, it says "**buffet the waves.**" "**Startling the great dragon**": the power of the abiding-ground of ignorance is immense. Because it dwells at the bottom of the sea of the fundamental *[ālaya]* consciousness's proclivities, it is called "**the great dragon.**" Because in this wise ignorance **[645c]** runs counter to calm quiescence and constantly fortifies the mind of crude activity, it says "**startling.**" Owing to all of these conditions, the mind "**begins to pant severely.**"

The [preceding] has been [a description of] what prompts awareness of the characteristics of the obstructions that are to be resolved. From this point on is an account of the expedients that catalyze this resolution [II. D.1.a.ii.b]. "**Preserve the three**": these are the expedients that can block **the heavenly winds** [of sense-objects]. "**Guard the one**": this is the expedient that can cause **the great dragon** [of ignorance] to capitulate. "**Access the tathāgatadhyāna**": this is the expedient that directly cures [the mind's tendency] **to pant severely.**"

> Taeryŏk Bodhisattva asked, "What do you mean by 'preserve the three, guard the one, and access the tathāgatadhyāna'?"
>
> The Buddha replied: "'Preserve the three' means to preserve the three liberations. 'Guard the one' means to guard the thusness of the one mind. 'Access the tathāgatadhyāna' means the noumenal contemplation *(igwan)* on the thusness of the mind. Accessing such a state is in fact what is meant by accessing the edge of reality."

From here onward is the second [subpart, II.D.1.b], an extensive elucidation of the expedients [that catalyze access], which involves three exchanges.

In this first exchange [II.D.1.b.i], he brings up various lists, to provide a general overview [of the appropriate expedients]. "**Guard the thusness of the one mind**": this dharma of the one mind has two aspects. Now, this first [expedient] guards that mind's aspect of true thusness, because it subdues the strength of **the great dragon** of ignorance. This is because ignorance directly deludes the thusness of the one mind.

In this [exchange], "**guard**" means that when one accesses [contemplation practice], one tranquilly guards the experience of the one thusness; but when one withdraws [from that contemplation], one does not lose the mind that has but a single taste; thus he says "**guard the one.**" This is as explained in the "Ten Practices" section of the *Benye jing*:

> Because these ten [practices] freely turn the great wheel of dharma, they are said to be the triratna of the bodhisattvas. For

> bodhisattvas at such a time, their very first knowledge of the middle way is the awakening-jewel [viz. the buddha]; the rule that all dharmas are unproduced and motionless is the dharma-jewel; constantly practicing throughout the six destinies together with the sentient beings who reside there is called the saṃgha-jewel. This is because [these triratna] transform all sentient beings so that they flow into the sea of buddhahood.[252]

Interpretation: Not losing the single taste of the middle way during all three time periods is exactly what is meant by this contemplation's function of guarding the one. This contemplation takes place at the level of the ten practices. The other [expedient, which protects the production-and-extinction aspect of the one mind,] will be elucidated later; it is not discussed here. **[646a]**

> Taeryŏk Bodhisattva asked: "What exactly are these three liberations? Through what dharma may one access this noumenal-contemplation samādhi?"
>
> The Buddha replied: "The three liberations are void liberation, adamantine liberation, and prajñā liberation. 'The mind that engages in noumenal contemplation' means that once the mind is pure in accordance with the principle, there is then nothing that cannot be the mind."
>
> Taeryŏk Bodhisattva asked: "How does one perform this act of preservation? How does one contemplate it?"
>
> The Buddha answered: "Preservation is put into operation when mind and objects are nondual. Whether withdrawing from or accessing internal practice or external practice, [these remain] nondual. One does not dwell on any particular characteristic, and the mind is free from gain or loss. The mind, purified, flows freely into the one-and-many bhūmi. This is what meant by 'contemplate it.'"

These are the second [and third] exchanges [II.D.1.b.ii, II.D.1.b.iii], a specific elucidation of contemplation practice.

In the answer to the first [exchange, II.D.1.b.ii], regarding the term "three liberations": since the three types of wisdom [wisdom gained through learning, reflection, and spiritual cultivation *(śrutacintābhāvanāmayīprajñā)*] subsume all eight liberations,[253] these are termed "liberations." As it says in the "Ten Abidings" chapter of the *Benye jing:*

> Since these six [contemplations] are protected by all the buddhas, they are called the contemplation of the eight liberations. The first liberation refers to the wisdom gained through learning, because the two characteristics of internal falsity and external falsity are unascertainable. The second liberation refers to the wisdom

> gained through reflection, because the dharmas of the five skandhas, internally, and all dharmas, externally, are unascertainable. By accomplishing the six contemplations involved with the wisdom gained through cultivation, the five skandhas of the [heavenly] realm of subtle materiality become void; this is the third liberation. Because the five skandhas associated with the four types of voidness [the four formless realms] and the contemplation of the trance of extinction *(nirodhasamāpatti)* are unascertainable, there are the thusness characteristics of the [last] five liberations.[254]

Nota Bene: The contemplation of the eight liberations involves, in brief, two approaches. If it involves only the contemplation of the wisdom gained through cultivation from the perspective of phenomenal characteristics, this is [the approach] common to the two-vehicle adherents, as is explained in various other places. If it involves the voidness of person and dharmas as derived from contemplation involving all three types of wisdom, then this is the Mahāyāna contemplation, as is explained in this passage.

The first type of liberation is "positing characteristics of materiality internally, he observes materiality externally." This means that, internally, he validates the reality of materiality, and so forth—that is, the characteristics of the dharmas of the five skandhas—and observes that, internally, the sense of self is void; externally, he validates materiality, and so forth, and contemplates the voidness of sentient beings. Because this voidness can be easily accessed, it is acquired through the wisdom gained from learning. Therefore, it says, "[The first liberation] involves the wisdom gained through learning, because the two characteristics of internal falsity and external falsity are unascertainable." Because it observes voidness without rejecting materiality, and so forth, it **[646b]** resembles space; but because it does not reject the characteristic of materiality, it is "**void liberation.**"

The second type of liberation is "there are no characteristics of materiality internally, but he observes materiality externally." Internally, he rejects materiality, and so forth—meaning the characteristics of the dharmas of the five skandhas—while externally he contemplates that all the mountains, rivers, and so forth, are void; there are none of the dharmas of the desire-realm that are not void. This type of voidness is difficult to comprehend but is perceived by the wisdom gained through reflection; therefore, it says, "[The second liberation involves] the wisdom gained through reflection, because the dharmas of the five skandhas, internally, and all dharmas, externally, are unascertainable." He seeks out a means of pulverizing all dharmas both internally and externally, just as adamant pulverizes all material dharmas; for this reason, it is called "**adamantine liberation.**"

The last six liberations are all derived from the wisdom gained through cultivation. Because one contemplates that all the dharmas of the two upper realms [subtle materiality and formlessness] are void, it refers to "the six contemplations involved with the wisdom gained through cultivation." These are all generated by the absorption derived from the wisdom gained through cultivation; therefore, they are given the general name of "**prajñā liberation.**" There are six specific characteristics of this type. The third [liberation] is called "he realizes with his body the liberation of purity." The five skandhas of the realm of subtle materiality are luminous, transparent, tranquil, and calm. Because he observes that these are all void, it is called "the liberation of purity." Since he himself realizes this internally, it is called "he realizes with his body." Therefore, it says "the five skandhas of the [heavenly] realm of subtle materiality become void; this is the third liberation." The fourth [liberation] is called "the liberation of the station of space," because he observes that the five skandhas are void in the station of endless space. It is just the same through [the liberations of (5) the station of infinite consciousness, (6) the station of nothing whatsoever, and (7)] the station of neither perception [nor nonperception]. Because the contemplation of the dharma of the absorption of extinction is also unascertainable, it is called [8] "the liberation of extinction," which gets its name from the fact that everything is negated there. Therefore, it says, "Because the five skandhas associated with the four types of voidness and the contemplation of the trance of extinction *(nirodhasamāpatti)* are unascertainable, these are the thusness characteristics of the five liberations." In this wise, the three wisdoms observe the voidness of person and dharmas, overcoming the two types of attachment and the two types of bondage of manifestations *(samudācāra);* therefore, they are called "**liberations.**" Since they reject all the false dharmas, both internally and externally, they can neutralize the heavenly winds that are blowing throughout all the realms of existence.

In [the discussion on] the noumenal contemplation, "**once the mind is pure in accordance with the principle, there is then nothing that cannot be the mind**" means the signless mind that conforms with the principle is free from discrimination. In the following answer, "**preservation is put into operation when mind and objects are nondual**" **[646c]** refers to the superior capability of the functioning of "preserving the three." If a person has not yet gained the functioning of "preserving the three," even though one quiets the mind and contemplates voidness, as soon as one is immersed in worldly affairs, one will lose one's composure and cling to self and objects of self; attached to both favorable and adverse objects, one will be buffeted by the heavenly winds so that mind and objects both become differentiated. But if one can mature one's cultivation of the three liberations, whenever one withdraws from contemplation or become immersed in worldly affairs, the strength of one's contemplation will still be preserved. One will not cling to characteristics of self and others, and will not be attached to wholesome or unwholesome objects. For this reason, one will not be buffeted by the heavenly winds, and, forgetting whether one has accessed or withdrawn [from contemplation], "**mind**

and objects are nondual." In this wise, this is called putting into operation "preserving the three." The cultivation of this contemplation occurs at the level of the ten faiths. The perfection of the function of preservation occurs on the level of the ten abidings. This contemplation appears in the section on the ten abidings in the *Benye jing*.[255]

From "**internal practice**" onward is the answer to the second question [in the third exchange, II.D.1.b.iii], which clarifies the characteristics of contemplation. "**Internal practice**" means the practice of calm radiance, which is generated when accessing contemplation. "**External practice**" means the practice of transforming objects, which occurs when withdrawing from contemplation. Whether withdrawing or accessing, one does not lose the middle way: therefore, it says "**[these remain] nondual.**" This is as has been explained in the "Ten Transferences" section of the *Benye jing:*

> Ten, one proselytizes all sentient beings through this autonomous wisdom; this is the so-called absolute truth of the middle way. One observes from the locus of prajñā and penetrates to the nonduality of all dharmas. Because this wisdom incessantly accesses the stage of sanctity, while its name resembles the contemplation of absolute truth, it is not true contemplation of the absolute truth of the middle way.[256]

A more extensive explanation appears there. "**One does not dwell on any particular characteristic**" means that one engages in the contemplation of the two truths. "**The mind is free from gain or loss**" means that one engages in the contemplation of impartiality. Based on these two varieties of expedient contemplation [viz. of the two truths and of impartiality; see below], one pushes forward into the flowing waters of the dharma of the first bhūmi; therefore, it says, "**The mind, purified, flows freely into the one-and-many bhūmi.**" As that sūtra *[Benye jing]* says,

> As for the "three contemplations": to access voidness from falsity is called "the contemplation of the two truths"; to access falsity from voidness is called "the impartial contemplation." These two contemplations are expedient paths. Owing to these two contemplations of voidness, one is able to gain **[647a]** access to the contemplation of the absolute truth of the middle way. By reflecting on both of these two truths, each and every state of mind is calm and extinct, and one pushes forward into the flowing waters of the dharma of the first bhūmi.[257]

An extensive explanation appears there.

Nota Bene: In this passage, "contemplation of the two truths" means that one dispels the conventional to observe the absolute; this is in fact the expedient of the essential knowledge [viz. *mūlajñāna*]. "Impartial contemplation" means that one contemplates the conventional while fusing it with the absolute; this is in fact the expedient of the knowledge that is acquired subsequently. It is called "impartial" because it contemplates the conventional as being illusory, without clinging to gain or loss and without either approving of or rejecting anything. "**The-one-and-many bhūmi**": this is an alternate name for the first bhūmi. This is because the first bhūmi in fact encompasses all ten bhūmis, for in one moment one may suddenly access the ten types of *dharmadhātus*. The ten bhūmis are in fact the first bhūmi, for all [ten] may instantly be completely fulfilled at this initial gate [of the first bhūmi]. Owing to the fact that the ten bhūmis are in fact the first bhūmi, [the first bhūmi] is called the "**one.**" But because the first bhūmi is in fact the ten bhūmis, it is also "**many.**" Consequently, [the first bhūmi] is called the "**one-and-many bhūmi.**" Through these two expedients, one purifies his mind and for this reason flows into the one-and-many bhūmi. For this reason it said, "**The mind, purified, flows freely into [the one-and-many bhūmi].**" This passage extensively explains only the first and last two contemplations; the middle contemplation must be inferred.

> **"Bodhisattva! Such a person does not linger over any dualistic characteristics. Although he does not go forth into homelessness *(pravrajita)*, he no longer dwells in the household. For this reason, although he wears no dharma-robes, does not fully observe the Prāṭimokṣa precepts [monk's disciplinary rules], and does not participate in the Poṣada [fortnightly religious observance], he can observe the Retreat-Ending Ceremony [Pravāraṇa] spontaneously *(muwi)* in his own mind and gain the fruition of sainthood. He does not linger over either of the two vehicles but instead accesses the bodhisattva path. Subsequently he will complete all the bhūmis and attain the bodhi of the buddhas."**

From here onward in the second [part, II.D.2] of [II.D, on the expedients for gaining access to the edge of reality] in the main exegesis [section II], [an elucidation of] the supreme inspiration [viz. benefits] of those expedients. It is in four [subparts]:

one [II.D.2.a], the supreme inspiration of gaining fruition;
two [II.D.2.b], the supreme inspiration of receiving offerings;
three [II.D.2.c], the supreme inspiration that derives from being free from distress;
four[II.D.2.d], the supreme inspiration that derives from being nonabiding.

This [passage] is the first [subpart], on the supreme inspiration of gaining fruition.

In this initial [subpart, II.D.2.a], there are four types of supreme inspiration. One [II.D.2.a.i] **[647b]** is the supreme inspiration of leaving behind all extremes. This means that one does not fall into the characteristics of the two extremes of sacred or secular. As the sūtra says: "Such a person does not linger over any dualistic characteristics. Although he does not go forth into homelessness, he no longer dwells in the household." Two [II.D.2.a.ii] is the supreme inspiration of autonomy. This means that he is not regulated by the precepts and discipline of the approach of the doctrinal teachings, but rather is able with his own mind to analyze the rationale so that, in perfect solitude, he accomplishes everything without doing anything. As the sūtra [says], "Although he wears no dharma-robes . . . [up to] . . . gain the fruition of sainthood." Three [II.D.2.a.iii] is the supreme inspiration of accessing the path. As the sūtra [says], "He does not linger over either of the two vehicles but accesses the bodhisattva path." Four [II.D.2.a.iv] is the supreme inspiration of gaining fruition. As the sūtra [says], "Subsequently he will complete all the bhūmis and attain the bodhi of the buddhas."

> Taeryŏk Bodhisattva remarked: "This is inconceivable! Even though such a person has not gone forth into homelessness, he cannot but have gone forth. Why is this? He has entered the domicile of nirvāṇa, where he dons the robe of the tathāgatas and sits on the bodhi-seat *(bodhimaṇḍa)*. Such a person should be worshiped respectfully even by śramaṇas [religious mendicants]."
>
> The Buddha said: "So it is. Why is this? Accessing the domicile of nirvāṇa, the mind generates[258] the three realms of existence.[259] Donning the robe of the tathāgatas, he accesses the site of the voidness of dharmas. Seated on the bodhi-seat, he ascends to the unique[260] bhūmi of right enlightenment. The mind of such a person transcends the two types of [belief in] selfhood [i.e., believing in the selfhood of the person and of dharmas]. So why wouldn't the śramaṇas worship him respectfully?"

From here onward is the second [subpart, II.D.2.b], on the supreme inspiration of receiving offerings. One who gains three superior meritorious qualities will be fit to serve as a field of merit *(puṇyakṣetra)* and will be worthy of offerings from all religious and laity. The passage is in three [divisions]:

initially [II.D.2.b.i], a clarification of the field of merit of bodhisattvas;
next [II.D.2.b.ii], an elucidation of the fact that the two-vehicle adherents cannot see it;
finally [II.D.2.b.iii], an elucidation of the fact that bodhisattvas are able to see it.

In this first [division, II.D.2.b.i], it reveals three fields of merit. "Accessing the domicile of nirvāṇa, the mind generates the three realms of existence":

this is the functioning of the three liberations, "preserving the three." The void-calmness of the three realms of existence is called "the domicile of nirvāṇa," because it is that locus of purity where one pacifies the mind and settles down. While accessing the voidness of the three realms of existence, the contemplation of the three liberations does not cling to that realization but instead generates the conventional mind, enabling one universally to proselytize all the three realms of existence. **[647c]** Therefore, it says "the mind generates the three realms of existence." While the mind generates the three realms of existence, it is not attached to maculations; this is precisely what is meant by the function of preserving [the three]. "Donning the robe of the tathāgatas, he accesses the site of the voidness of dharmas": this is the contemplation that guards the thusness of the one mind. That is to say, when he is involved in universally proselytizing all the three realms of existence, he dons the robes of patient endurance *(kṣānti)* without ever becoming exhausted; instead, he accesses the voidness of dharmas and guards the thusness of the one mind. As the *Lotus Sūtra* says, "The delicate [mind] of patient endurance is his clothes."[261] "Seated on the bodhi-seat, he ascends to the unique bhūmi of right enlightenment" refers to this mind of noumenal contemplation of the tathāgatadhyāna. This is to say, seated amid the voidness of dharmas, one proceeds to cultivate expedients until he succeeds in climbing up to the first bhūmi's absolute contemplation of right enlightenment. As the *Lotus Sūtra* says, "The voidness of all dharmas is his seat."[262] In this wise, each of these three ranks involves the contemplation on the two voidnesses. Because he subdues and extinguishes the two types of grasping—to the selfhood of person and the selfhood of dharmas—it says, "transcends the two types of selfhood." Because he transcends the two types of selfhood, he is fully endowed with the meritorious quality of letting go *(prahāṇa)*. And because he cultivates the three contemplations, he also is equipped with the meritorious quality of knowledge. Therefore, he is fit to serve as a field of merit for religious and laity.

> Taeryŏk Bodhisattva remarked, "Adherents of the two vehicles do not see such a unique bhūmi or the sea of voidness."
>
> The Buddha responded: "So it is. Those two-vehicle adherents savor samādhi and gain the samādhi-body. With regard to that unique bhūmi and the sea of voidness, they become like alcoholics who stay drunk and never sober up. Continuing through numerous kalpas [eons], they remain unable to gain enlightenment. But once the liquor has worn off and they first awaken, they will then be able to cultivate these practices and subsequently gain the body of a buddha."

From here onward is the second [division, II.D.2.b.ii, which elucidates the fact that] two-vehicle adherents cannot see [that unique bhūmi and the sea of voidness]. It has two [subdivisions]:

initially [II.D.2.b.ii.a], a question;
subsequently [II.D.2.b.ii.b], an answer.

In the question [subdivision, II.D.2.b.ii.a], the term "**unique bhūmi**" means that bhūmi to which one ascends, in which the ten bhūmis are identical to the first bhūmi; this is called the "**unique bhūmi.**" "**Sea of voidness**" means that the voidness one has accessed through the preceding three contemplations is extremely deep, expansive, and vast; therefore it is called a "**sea.**"

In the answer [subdivision, II.D.2.b.ii.b], the response "**so it is**" confirms the fact that [two-vehicle adherents] do not see it. Following that [exclamation], he explicates the reasons why two-vehicle adherents **[648a]** do not see it. "**Those two-vehicle adherents savor samādhi**" means that, in enjoying tranquil absorption, they end up pursuing quiescence. "**Gain the samādhi-body**": through this enjoyment and pursuit they access the concentration in which the mind is extinguished [viz. *nirodhasamāpatti*]; because of having accessed nirvāṇa, they scorch their bodies and extinguish their knowledge. At the point where they know the mind is extinguished, the experience of this trance of extinction occurs, which neutralizes both mind and mental concomitants. In this wise, it is called "**gain the samādhi-body.**" Their enjoyment of quiescence suffuses the foundational consciousness; owing to this, they do not awaken to the sea of voidness, the unique bhūmi. "**They become like alcoholics who stay drunk and never sober up. Continuing through numerous kalpas, they remain unable to gain enlightenment**": the *śrotāpanna* [stream-enterer; the first stage of sanctity in the Hīnayāna] abides [in nirvāṇa] for eighty thousand kalpas . . . on up to arhats [the fourth, and last, stage of sanctity] abide for twenty thousand kalpas. Pratyekabuddhas [solitary buddhas who do not teach] abide for ten thousand kalpas. All are abiding in nirvāṇa but never awakening. Now, he describes this generic characteristic by saying "**continuing through numerous kalpas.**" "**But once the liquor has worn off and they first awaken, they will then be able to cultivate these practices**": depending on the extent to which the suffusion of their attachment to enjoyment is heavy or light, their feelings of attachment will eventually dissipate so that they may instead generate the mind [of enlightenment]. Once they have generated that mind, they dedicate their minds to accessing the Great [Vehicle]. **They will then be able to cultivate** the three types of contemplation **practice** discussed above. As a verse in the *Laṅkāvatāra-sūtra* says, "It is like a drunkard,/ Whose liquor wearing off, later awakens,/He gains the supreme essence of buddhahood,/Which is my true dharma-body."[263] An extensive explanation appears there.

> **"From the moment that such a person abandons the [status of the] *icchantika* [a person who is blocked from ever attaining enlightenment], he may access the six practices. On those stages of practice, his mind is purified in a single moment of thought and he gains absolute clarity and brightness.**

> The power of his adamantine knowledge renders him *avaivartaka* [not subject to spiritual retrogression]. He ferries sentient beings across to liberation and has inexhaustible friendliness and compassion."[264]

This [is the third division, II.D.2.b.iii, an elucidation of the fact that bodhisattvas are able to see it and become enlightened. It] explicates the fact that, from the moment when a person who is endowed with the lineage *(gotra)* of the bodhisattva abandons the *icchantika*'s obstacle of disbelief, he immediately accesses the ten faiths, the initial level of the six practices. At that stage of practice, he then arouses one thought-moment of purity of mind, which is the initial arousal of the thought [of enlightenment, on the first stage] of the ten abidings. "He gains absolute clarity and brightness" means that on the level of the ten practices all practices become clear and pure. "The power of his adamantine knowledge" refers to the firm power of knowledge [he develops on] the ten transferences. "*Avaivartaka*" means that, from the first bhūmi onward, **[648b]** his true realization is irreversible. "He ferries sentient beings across to liberation and has inexhaustible friendliness and compassion" means that, on the preceding levels he practiced so as to benefit others, which is something that the unrelated two-vehicle adherents cannot practice.

> Taeryŏk Bodhisattva said, "But such a person would not have to maintain the moral codes and he should not show respect to the śramaṇas."
>
> The Buddha replied: "Those who recite the Prāṭimokṣa precepts do so because of their unwholesome haughtiness and because of the waves and swells of the sea. On the mind-ground, the sea of the eighth consciousness is limpid and the flow of its ninth consciousness is pure. The winds cannot buffet them, so waves and swells do not arise.[265] The nature of the moral codes is equanimous and void; [the śrāvakas] who hold fast to them are deluded and confused.
>
> "For such a person, the seventh and sixth [consciousnesses] will not be produced, and all origination ceases [for he has achieved] meditative absorption. Remaining close to the three buddhas [below, p. 649a], he arouses bodhi. His compliant mind mysteriously accesses the three [types of] signlessness. He deeply reveres the triratna, he does not neglect his dignified demeanor *(īryāpatha)*, and he would not show disrespect toward the śramaṇas.
>
> "Bodhisattva! That humanhearted person will not linger over any worldly dharmas, whether active or motionless. [Rather,] he will access the three types of voidness and extinguish the mind that is involved with the three realms of existence."

This is the third [subpart, II.D.2.c], on the supreme inspiration that derives from being free from distress, because it refers to being free from the distress of the causes and fruitions that afflict the ordinary person.

Herein, initially [in the question, II.D.2.c.i.], the remark "but such a person would not have to maintain the moral codes" refers to the preceding line "[he does] not observe all the Prātimokṣa precepts" (p. 647a). "He should not show respect to the śramaṇas": since he does not have to keep the precepts, he should not have to respect [the śramaṇas] who do need to keep the precepts.

The answer [division, II.D.2.c.ii], is in two [subdivisions]:

initially [II.D.2.c.ii.a], assenting to the previous query;
next [II.D.2.c.ii.b], negation of the subsequent remark.

In the initial [subdivision, II.D.2.c.ii.a], regarding the statement "those who recite the Prātimokṣa precepts": those people who recite the Prātimokṣa precepts refers to all the śrāvakas [disciples of the Buddha]. Because they are conceited about their own adherence to the precepts and hold in contempt all those who break the precepts, it says "because of their unwholesome haughtiness." Because this person has yet to realize the voidness of all dharmas, the waves of the seven consciousnesses are churning on the sea of the latent proclivities *(anuśaya);* therefore, it says "because of the waves and swells of the sea." This [passage] alludes to the faults of people who adhere to the precepts. "On the mind-ground" means that the mind of the bodhisattva realizes the voidness of all dharmas and accesses the great **[648c]** bhūmi. The discriminations in the eighth consciousness that are generated, such as the two types of attachments [to person and dharmas] and the latent proclivities, all vanish without a trace; therefore, it says "the sea of the eighth consciousness is limpid." "Limpid" means "clear." The wisdom of nondiscrimination accesses through realization the original enlightenment and, progressing through all the bhūmis, leaves behind the various sorts of maculations; therefore, it says, "The flow of its ninth consciousness is pure." "Original enlightenment" refers explicitly to this "ninth consciousness." Because the mind is free of discriminations and unmoved by sense-objects, it says, "The winds cannot buffet them." Because [the mind] cannot be moved, the maculated seven [consciousnesses] are not produced; therefore, it says, "Waves and swells do not arise." Since this person realizes that all dharmas are void and penetrates to the fact that the nature of the seven strictures of the precepts[266] is void and quiescent, it says, "The nature of the moral codes is equanimous and void." But since śrāvakas do not realize that dharmas are void, they are attached to the notion that the moral codes actually have a "nature" that exists in reality and are conceited about their own ability to adhere [to the precepts]; therefore, it says "[those] who hold fast to them are deluded and confused." This answers the initial query [II.D.2.c.i.a, "but such a person would not need to maintain the codes of morality"], clarifying that there is no fault in not adhering to the precepts.

From "for such [a person]" onward is the next [subdivision, II.D.2.c.ii.b], answering the subsequent remark [II.D.2.c.i.b, "he would not show disrespect toward the śramaṇas"], which clarifies why there should be no haughtiness. "The seventh and sixth [consciousnesses] will not be produced" means that the four defilements *(kleśa)* of the *mano[vijñāna]* are no longer made manifest, and the seeds of the defilement of [wrong] view are already eradicated completely. "All origination ceases [for he has achieved] meditative absorption": all the consciousnesses that are generated, as well as the origination of mind and mental concomitants, vanish without a trace, for he has already achieved the meditative absorption that derives from accessing the principle. "Remaining close to the three buddhas, he arouses bodhi" clarifies that with the arousal of the thought [of enlightenment], he universally reveres the tathāgatagarbha-buddha produced in the mind. This is because, based on that arousal of the thought [of enlightenment], none of these sentient beings will casually exhibit haughtiness. "His compliant mind mysteriously accesses the three [types of] signlessness": at the time that one has perfected the access of practice, he uproots the root of ignorance, as was explained previously. He accesses deeply the three types of liberation by complying with the dharma of the one mind. For this reason, "he deeply reveres the triratna," which means that he cannot but venerate the buddha as image, the dharma written on paper, white silk, and so forth, and the fourfold saṃgha [monks, nuns, laymen, laywomen]. Therefore, "he would not show disrespect toward the śramaṇas," because he has aroused the thought [of enlightenment] by relying on those three buddhas and has eradicated the root of pride and conceit and the seeds of ignorance. **[649a]**

The preceding [discussion] clarifies that he leaves behind the distress prompted by all types of causes. From this point on, he elucidates the need to leave behind the distress prompted by all types of fruitions. "[He] will not linger over any worldly dharmas, whether active or motionless": meritorious and pleasurable fruitions [derive from rebirth among] humans or heavenly beings in the desire-realm are called "active dharmas," because they are the fruition of wholesome actions performed in distraction; quiescent and tranquil fruitions [deriving from rebirth in the heavenly] realms of subtle materiality and formlessness are called "motionless dharmas," because they are the fruition of wholesome actions performed in stability. Because he is not attached to these, it says "will not linger." "He will access the three types of voidness": as discussed previously, he progressively works his way toward this access; therefore, these are called "types." By not directly trying to be unattached, he is also able to prompt [the existent mind] to be unproduced; for this reason, it says "extinguish the mind that is involved with the three realms of existence."

> Taeryŏk Bodhisattva stated: "That virtuous one arouses the thought of bodhi at the sites of the [three] buddhas: that is, [1] the buddha endowed with all meritorious qualities of the fruition, [2] the tathāgatagarbha-buddha, and [3] the buddha as image. He accesses the three codes of

morality [see *KSGN*, p.650b/651b below] but does not linger over their characteristics. He extinguishes all thoughts of the three realms of existence but does not reside in that calm place. Not forsaking the assembly that is capable [of salvation], he reenters the untamed stage. It is inconceivable!"

This is the fourth [subpart, II.D.2.d], on the supreme inspiration of being nonabiding. It is in two [divisions]:

initially [II.D.2.d.i], comprehension of the preceding discussion;
subsequently [II.D.2.d.ii], [an explicit] elucidation of [the supreme inspiration of] nonabiding.

In the comprehension [division, II.D.2.d.i], there are two passages.

The initial [passage, division II.D.2.d.i.a] expresses comprehension of the line "**remaining close to the three buddhas.**" "**The buddha endowed with all the meritorious qualities of the fruition**" means that, with the consummation of acquired enlightenment, he is fully endowed with myriad meritorious qualities. "**The tathāgatagarbha-buddha**" means the original enlightenment inherent in all sentient beings. "**The buddha as image**" means the gold, bronze, clay, and wood that can be shaped into representations of [the buddha's] venerated image. ["**(He) remain(s) close to the three buddhas**"] because he neglects nothing of either cause and fruition or principle and phenomena.

"**He accesses the three codes of morality but does not linger over their characteristics**": this [second passage, II.D.2.d.i.b] expresses comprehension of the line "**the nature of the moral codes is equanimous and void.**" This means that the four conditions [see p. 651a below] for accessing the precepts do not cling to the characteristics of the precepts. The three moral codes and the four conditions will be explained in the following chapter.

From here onward is [the second division, II.D.2.d.ii], an explicit elucidation of the supreme inspiration of nonabiding. Although, furthermore, "**he will access the three types of voidness and extinguish the mind that is involved with the three realms of existence,**" he "**does not abide in that calm place.**" Instead, he passes through all the places where sentient beings who **pant severely** in the six destinies reside; **[649b]** this is called "**the untamed stage.**" Owing to the latent proclivities, he takes rebirth through karma that does not subject him to further bondage [viz. indeterminate karma; *avyākṛta-karman*]; therefore, it says "**he reenters.**" The term "latent proclivities" means that they do not quickly vanish, which is the case with Hīnayānists, who gradually eradicate them over three infinitely long great kalpas but for whom they are extinguished only when they finally gain bodhi. It does not mean that they remain uneradicated up until [the stage] of the adamantine [samādhi]; therefore, they are termed "latent."

At that time, Śāriputra rose from his seat, came forward, and recited these gāthās:

He perfects the sea of prajñā,
And he does not dwell in the city of nirvāṇa,
Just as the exotic lotus blossom,
Does not grow in the high plains.[267]
All the buddhas over immeasurable kalpas,
Did not forsake all the defilements,
Only after saving the world did they gain [nirvāṇa],
Like the lotus rising from the mud.
Just as those six stages of practice,
Are what are cultivated by the bodhisattvas;
So too are those three types of voidness,
The true path to bodhi.

From here onward is the third [section, III], in which Śāriputra gains understanding. It is intended to help the lesser congregation [of Hīnayānists] arouse the great mind [of enlightenment]. It is in two [subsections]:

one [III.A], gaining understanding;
two [III.B], a conclusion to the narrative.

The initial [subsection] is also in two [parts]:

[III.A.1] the preceding three verses versify what was discussed previously;
[III.A.2] the subsequent two verses explain one's personal arousal of the thought [of enlightenment].

The first [part] has three [subparts]:

one [III.A.1.a], the preceding two verses versify the path of nonabiding;
next [III.A.1.b] are two lines that versify the levels of the six practices;
[III.A.1.c] the last two lines versify the three types of voidnesses.

In the first [subpart, III.A.1.a], the line "He perfects the sea of prajñā" means that the three liberations subsume the three types of wisdom. "He does not dwell in the city of nirvāṇa" means that "he extinguishes all thoughts of the three realms of existence but does not reside in that calm place." "Does not grow in the high plains": it is just as is the case with those two-vehicle adherents, who may leave behind the mud of the defilements but will still not arouse the mind [of enlightenment] for eighty thousand kalpas. "Did not forsake all the defilements": unlike two-vehicle adherents, [the buddhas] quickly eradicate [the defilements] completely in four[268] lifetimes [two to master the śrāvaka, or disciple, stage and two, the pratyekabuddha, or nonteaching buddha, stage]. "Like the lotus rising from the mud": owing to the latent proclivities, "he reenters the untamed stage" and there completes the cultivation of the bodhisattva practices. Owing to this [cultivation], **[649c]** he is able to realize the fruition of bodhi; therefore, it says he practices "those three types [of voidness]." This is obvious from the passage.

> I now abide in nonabiding,
> Just as the Buddha has explained.
> I will return again to this place whence I came,
> And discard [these bodies] only after completion.
> Furthermore, I will urge all sentient beings,
> To join with me [in pursuing this same vow] and not remain apart.
> May those who came before and those who will come afterward,
> All be encouraged to climb to right enlightenment.

This is the second [part, III.A.2], on the personal arousal of the thought [of enlightenment]. It is in two [subparts]:

initially [III.A.2.a], two lines explain the present rank of arousing the thought [of enlightenment];
subsequently [III.A.2.b], a verse and a half represent the practice of the cultivation that follows [arousing the thought of enlightenment].

[III.A.2.a] "I now abide in nonabiding": now, having heard the Buddha's words, I have aroused the great mind [of enlightenment] and instantly abide in the mind that "does not reside in that calm place." "I will return again to this place whence I came": after transmigrating among them since time immemorial, I now once again return to those places that I initially left behind and reenter the three realms of existence in order to ferry across sentient beings; I manifest as is appropriate the bodies I have received through the power of my absorption in this extreme limit [viz. the edge of reality]. ["And discard them only after completion"]: after completing all the bodhisattva practices, I discard these bodies and gain a buddha's body. "Those who came before" means those in the past whose wholesome faculties *(kuśalamūla)* had already matured. "Those who will come afterward" means those whose [wholesome faculties] will finally mature only in a future age. The implication is that, to the end of time, he will never rest.

> At that time, the Buddha proclaimed to Śāriputra: "This is inconceivable! You are certain subsequently to complete the path to bodhi. Innumerable sentient beings will transcend the sea of birth and death."

This is the second [subsection, III.B], a conclusion to the narrative, which sanctions what [Śāriputra] said.

At that time, the great congregation all awakened to bodhi, and all the lesser congregation, and so forth, accessed the sea of the five voidnesses.

This is the fourth [section, IV,] of the main exegesis, in which the congregation present at the time gains benefit. The term "great congregation" **[650a]** refers to the Mahāyāna congregation. "Awakened to bodhi" means that, on the first bhūmi, they awakened and accessed the mind of bodhi. "Lesser congregation" refers to the congregation of śrāvakas, who succeeded in accessing the approach of the three types of true thusness.

Exposition of the *Vajrasamādhi-Sūtra*

Roll Three

[Part Four: An Exegesis of the Text (cont.)]

[Section Two: Main Body (cont.)]

VAJRASAMĀDHI-SŪTRA, CHAPTER SIX: THE VOIDNESS OF THE TRUE NATURE

[650b] The dharma of true thusness subsumes all meritorious qualities and serves as the original nature of all the qualities gained through spiritual practice; for this reason, it is called "true nature." The true nature in this wise neutralizes all names and characteristics; for this reason, it is called "the voidness of the true nature." Moreover, this true nature leaves behind both characteristics and nature: "leaves behind characteristics" means that it stays far removed from deceptive characteristics; "leaves behind nature" means that it stays far removed from any sense of a "true nature." Because it stays far removed from deceptive characteristics, these deceptive characteristics are void. Because it stays far removed from true nature, that true nature is also void. For this reason, it is called "the voidness of the true nature." Now, in this chapter, these two meanings are elucidated; and, based on these aspects, the title of the chapter is given.

Fifth Division of Contemplation Practice: Sanctified Practices Emerge from the Voidness of the True Nature

> At that time, Śāriputra addressed the Buddha, saying: "Lord! The cultivation of the bodhisattva path is free from both names and characteristics. The three [codes of] morality do not demand a dignified demeanor. How should we receive and keep these [codes] so that we may then preach them to sentient beings? I beg that the Buddha may proclaim this for us, out of his compassion."

Among the six divisions of contemplation practice that are being explained sequentially, the fourth division, Abandoning the Spurious to Access Reality, has been completed above. From here onward is the fifth division, a clarification that All the Sanctified Practices Emerge from the

Voidness of the True Nature. The main outline of this chapter is in two [sections]:

One [I], for those with sharp faculties, there are numerous passages offering extensive explanations;
Two [II], for those with dull faculties, there are just a few passages offering a brief synopsis.

The initial extensive explanation [section] is in six subsections:

one [I.A], clarification that the three moral codes are perfected through the true nature;
two [I.B], clarification that the practices included among the constituents of the path *(bodhipakṣikadharma)* are established through the voidness of the true nature;
three [I.C], clarification that the teachings of the Tathāgata are spoken in accordance with principle;
four [I.D], clarification that the bodhisattva ranks emerge from the original inspiration;
five [I.E], clarification that great prajñā neutralizes **[650c]** all causes and conditions;
six [I.F], clarification that great dhyānic absorption transcends all names and classifications.

In the first [subsection, I.A], on the three moral codes, the text is in five parts:

one [I.A.1], a question;
two [I.A.2], a [brief] answer;
three [I.A.3], a [reiterated] query;
four [I.A.4], an [extensive] explanation;
five [I.A.5], gaining understanding.

This is the first [part, I.A.1]. The passage "**the cultivation of the bodhisattva path is free from both names and characteristics**" is a generic allusion to all practices. "**The three [codes of] morality do not demand a dignified demeanor**" describes sequentially the practice of morality. As the previous chapter said (p. 649a), "**He accesses the three codes of morality but does not linger over their characteristics.**" This means that the three moralities are signless and "**do not demand a dignified demeanor.**" "**How should we**" ourselves "**receive and keep these [codes] so that we may preach them**" to others? Since Śāriputra has just entered the Great [Vehicle] and was just beginning to engage in spiritual cultivation with morality at its root, he therefore asks about the initial practice among the three trainings [morality, meditation, wisdom]. Furthermore,

"Body Son" [the literal translation of Śāriputra] is born from the body. Now, this chapter explains that all the practice dharmas are born from the dharma body. Therefore, "Body Son" is deputed to ask the question.

> The Buddha replied: "Oh son of good family! May you now listen well and I will proclaim this for you.
>
> "Oh son of good family! Both wholesome and unwholesome dharmas are projections of the mind. All the sense-realms are but the discriminations of ratiocination and verbalization. Control this [discrimination through] one-pointedness of mind and all conditioning will be brought to an end.
>
> "Why is this? Oh son of good family! The one is originally not generated. The functioning of the three is inoperative. Abiding in that principle of thusness, the gates leading to the six destinies are closed, and the four conditions that accord with thusness become imbued with the three moral codes."

This is the second [part, I.A.2], a brief answer, which is in two [subparts]. The first [subpart, I.A.2.a] is the answer to the general question. "**Both wholesome and unwholesome dharmas are projections of the mind**" means that the causes and activities of the three types of karma [via body, speech, and mind] are all created by the mind. "**All the sense-realms are but the discriminations of ratiocination and verbalization**" means that none of the objects coming to fruition in the six destinies [hell-denizens, hungry ghosts, animals, humans, asuras, gods] are not transformations of thought. Because [these objects] are initiated chaotically by the mind and cannot be controlled, they come to serve as the causes and effects that prompt one to travel continually over the sea of suffering. For this reason, one who wishes to cross over the sea of suffering should cultivate the bodhisattva path. By controlling the mind so that it becomes one-pointed and [absorbed in] thusness, "**all conditioning will be brought to an end.**" Therefore the cultivation of the bodhisattva is nameless and signless.

From "**Why is this?**" **[651a]** onward is [the second subpart, I.A.2.b], a follow-up answer to [the Buddha's own] separate question. Although a summary explanation has already been given, Śāriputra has not yet heard about specific practices. Therefore, [the Buddha] asks again, "**Why is this?**" "**The one is originally not generated**" means that the **one** original enlightenment, which is the basis of the three moral codes, **is originally** calm and tranquil; therefore, it says "**not generated.**" "**The functioning of the three is inoperative**": since **the functioning of the three** moral codes is perfected by relying on the original enlightenment, this functioning is independent from maintaining a dignified demeanor and from any operative characteristics; therefore, it **is inoperative.** Since it abides harmoniously in the one original [enlightenment], it says "**Abiding in that principle of thusness.**" Since it abides in that principle of thusness, it extinguishes all causation; therefore, it says "the gates leading to the six destinies are closed." The power of the four conditions is subsumed in this principle of unitary thusness; and since one who is able to remain in harmony with this unitary thusness is then imbued with the three moral codes, it says, "The four conditions that accord with thusness become imbued with the three moral codes."

> Śāriputra asked, "How is it that 'the four conditions that accord with thusness become imbued with the three moral codes'?"

This is the third [part, I.A.3], the reiterated query.

> The Buddha replied: "The four conditions are (1) The condition that keeps [the precepts] through the power of the analytical suppression *(pratisaṃkhyānirodha);* it corresponds to the moral code that maintains both the discipline and the deportments. (2) The condition that is generated through the power of the pure basis of original inspiration; it corresponds to the moral code that accumulates wholesome dharmas. (3) The condition that is the power of the great compassion of original wisdom; it corresponds to the moral code that aids all sentient beings.[269] (4) The condition that is the power of the penetrative knowledge of the one enlightenment; it accords with abiding in thusness. These are called the four conditions. Oh son of good family! In this wise, the great power of the four conditions does not linger over phenomenal characteristics and does not lack efficacious functioning. As it remains separate from any one locus, it cannot be sought.
>
> "Oh son of good family! In this wise, the one phenomenon [viz. the one enlightenment] completely subsumes the six practices. It is the buddhas' sea of bodhi and *sarvajña.*"

This is the fourth [part, I.A.4], an [extensive] explanation. It is in two [subparts]:

one [I.A.4.a], an explicit answer, which clarifies the causes and conditions of morality;
two [I.A.4.b], he avails himself of the opportunity to offer a generic overview of all [the myriads of] spiritual practices.

In the initial [subpart, I.A.4.a, on the explicit answer; this is the general import division, I.A.4.a.i.], "The four conditions" means that four powerful functions are contained within the one mind's inspiration of original enlightenment, which serve as the conditions for the three moral codes. These are (1) the condition that is based on suppression, (2) the condition based on production, (3) the condition based on assistance, (4) the condition based on separation. **[651b]**

[1] "Based on suppression" means that, in original enlightenment, the meritorious qualities engendered by the tranquillity of the nature are in their own-nature diametrically opposed to all the defilements. Through this condition, one perfects the moral code that subsumes both the discipline and the deportments *(saṃvaraśīla)*.

[2] "Based on production" means that, in original enlightenment, the meritorious qualities engendered by the wholesomeness of the nature are all commensurate in their own natures with the wholesome faculties *(kuśalamūla)*. Through this condition, one perfects the moral code that subsumes all wholesome dharmas *(kuśaladharmasaṃgrāhakaśīla)*.

[3] "Based on assistance" means that, in original enlightenment, the nature produces great compassion that by its very nature does not abandon even a single sentient being. Through this condition, one perfects the moral code that assists all sentient beings *(sattvārthakriyāśīla)*.

[4] "Based on separation" means that, in original enlightenment, the nature produces prajñā that by its very nature stays far removed from all phenomenal characteristics. Through this condition, one is able to keep the three moral codes separate from phenomenal characteristics and to abide in accordance with thusness.

The first three conditions have a specific application; the last one is a condition that is of comprehensive application. When a bodhisattva arouses the thought [of enlightenment] and receives the three moral codes, he receives and keeps these while remaining in harmony with the inspiration of original enlightenment; hence these four conditions are replete with the three moral codes. This has been the general import [of this passage].

Next [I.A.1.a.ii] is the exegesis of the text itself.

"**(1) The condition that keeps [the precepts] through the power of the analytical suppression**": original enlightenment originally leaves behind the bonds of the defilements. It produces the *pratisaṃkhyānirodha* liberation by maintaining its own essence and is endowed with that force which is able to keep the specific liberating precepts [viz. the Prātimokṣa precepts]. Like a magnet attracting a needle, this powerful function occurs even without any specific intention. We should know that this is also the case with the principle of the middle way. "**(2) The condition that is generated through the power of the pure basis of original inspiration**": the original enlightenment is originally endowed with the meritorious qualities derived from the purity of the nature, which have as their basis all the qualities engendered through spiritual practice. Owing to this fundamental power, it produces all the wholesome dharmas and serves as the condition for the accumulation and production of those wholesome dharmas. It is this very condition that "**accumulates wholesome dharmas.**" "**(3) The condition that is the power of the great compassion of original wisdom; it corresponds to the moral code that aids all sentient beings**": the wisdom inherent in original enlightenment that illuminates the mundane world is in fact the great compassion that constantly soothes sentient beings. It is through this condition that one perfects "**the moral code that aids all sentient beings.**" "**(4) The condition that is the power of the penetrative knowledge of the one enlightenment; it accords with abiding in thusness**": **[651c]** the knowledge inherent in original enlightenment that irradiates one's very nature brings all three moral codes into accord "**with abiding in thusness.**" In this wise, the four conditions pervade all dharma-realms and their functions subsume all the myriads of spiritual practices; therefore, it says that they have "**great power.**" Although they have great power, they all have the same one taste. Because they stay far removed from all names and characteristics and from the discriminative functions of phenomena, it said that they do "**not linger over phenomenal characteristics.**" Although they are free of phenomenal characteristics, they are endowed with superior capabilities that enable them to subsume all supramundane meritorious qualities that derive from spiritual practice; therefore, it said that they do "**not lack efficacious functioning.**" For this reason, only original enlightenment has no such implication with regard to conventional dharmas; therefore, it says, "**As it remains separate from any one locus, it cannot be sought.**"

The preceding has been [the explicit answer], which clarifies sequentially the conditions that generate the three moral codes. From here onward is [I.A.4.b], a clarification of the generic overview of [all] the myriads of spiritual practices. Each and every one of the practices on all the six stages—from the ten faiths through virtual enlightenment—are all subsumed by the one enlightenment. Therefore, it says, "**The one phenomenon completely subsumes the six practices.**" It is not merely the bodhisattvas who take refuge in this original enlightenment. All the buddhas too, through their consummate knowledge, together take refuge in this sea; therefore, it says, "**It is the buddhas' sea of bodhi and *sarvajña*.**"

> **Śāriputra remarked: "[You said that] it 'does not linger over phenomenal characteristics and does not lack efficacious functioning.' Such a dharma would be true voidness, which is permanent, blissful, selfhood, and pure. As it transcends [the attachment to] the two types of selfhood [viz. the selfhood of person and of dharmas], it is great parinirvāṇa. That mind has no bonds: it is a contemplation that has great power.**

This is the fifth [part, I.A.5], on gaining understanding. It is in two [subparts].

Initially [I.A.5.a], he recognizes that the one thusness with which he is in conformity is in fact the dharma-body. It is fully endowed with four meritorious qualities [viz. it "**is permanent, blissful, selfhood, and pure**"] and transcends the characteristics of person and of dharmas. It is great nirvāṇa.

Subsequently [I.A.5.b], he recognizes that the mind that conforms with thusness leaves behind all bonds by conforming to that thusness and has nothing that it cannot accomplish. It is endowed with that great autonomous power.

"All the thirty-seven constituents of the path *(bodhipakṣikadharma)* are necessarily contained in this contemplation and enlightenment."

The Buddha said: "So indeed does it contain the thirty-seven constituents of the path.

"What are these? They are the four loci of mindfulness *(smṛtyupasthāna)*; the four right efforts *(samyakprahāṇa)*; the four bases of psychic power *(ṛddhipāda)*; the five faculties *(indriya)*; the five powers *(bala)*; the seven aspects of enlightenment *(bodhyaṅga)*; **[652a]** and the eightfold noble path *(mārgāṅga)*. These several classifications have but a single aspect, for they are neither identical nor different. Being numerical lists, they are merely names and merely letters;[270] those dharmas are unascertainable *(anupalabdhi)*. An unascertainable dharma has but a single aspect and is free from locution. That characteristic of being free from locution is the nature of true and real voidness. The meaning of that void nature accords with reality *(yathābhūta)* and is thus. That principle which is thus contains all dharmas. Oh son of good family! A person who abides in that principle of thusness crosses over the sea of the three sufferings."[271]

This is the second [subsection] in the main outline [I.B], clarification that the practice of the constituents of the path *(bodhipakṣikadharma)* are established through the voidness of the true nature. It is in two [parts]:

initially [I.B.1], a question;
subsequently [I.B.2], an answer.

In the question [part, 1.B.1], the passage "in this contemplation and enlightenment" refers to the contemplation that is the agent of harmonization and the original enlightenment that is the object of harmonization. "In this contemplation and enlightenment," which balances agent and object, one perforce will be fully endowed with the practices of all the thirty-seven constituents of the path.

In the answer [part, I.B.2], there are two [subparts]:

initially [I.B.2.a], assent ["So indeed does it contain the thirty-seven constituents of the path."];
subsequently [I.B.2.b], the explication.

From "what are these?" onward is the second [subpart, I.B.2.b], on the explication, which is in two [divisions]:

a direct explication [I.B.2.b.i];
a reiterated elucidation [I.B.2.b.ii].

In the first [division, I.B.2.b.i], the words "these many classifications have but a single aspect" mean that the aspects categorized in the thirty-seven constituents involve merely this solitary contemplation and enlightenment; they are not dualistic dharmas. "They are neither identical nor different" means that contemplation and enlightenment are neither identical nor different. From the standpoint of their being "not different," it says that they "have but a single aspect."

From the words "but because their designations are manifold" onward is the reiterated elucidation [I.B.2.b.ii], which is in four [subdivisions]:

initially [I.B.2.b.ii.a], a rejection of the aspect of difference;
next [I.B.2.b.ii.b], an elucidation of the aspect of being identical;
three [I.B.2.b.ii.c], a clarification that the aspect of being identical subsumes all dharmas;
four [I.B.2.b.ii.d], a clarification that the aspect of being identical leaves behind all dangers *(ādīnava).*

In the initial [subdivision, I.B.2.b.ii.a], the passage "but because their designations are manifold, they are merely names and merely letters; those dharmas are unascertainable *(anupalabdhi)*" means that the mundane practice dharmas listed among the constituents of the path are classified into thirty-seven listings according to their designations. Bodhisattvas, through their enlightened wisdom, seek those aspects enumerated in these thirty-seven dharmas but find them all to be unascertainable.

In the second [subdivision, I.B.2.b.ii.b], the passage "an unascertainable dharma has but a single aspect and is free from locution" means that, when one seeks those specific dharmas but finds that they are unascertainable, this [unascertainable] dharma will then have but a single taste because it neutralizes all locution and verbalization.

In the third [subdivision, I.B.2.b.ii.c], the passage "that characteristic of being free from locution is the nature of true and real voidness" means that, **[652b]** since one cannot ascertain any mind that actually contemplates specific dharmas, one neutralizes all locution and verbalization and leaves behind all differentiated characteristics. "The meaning of that void nature accords with reality and is thus": the mind that is the agent of contemplation leaves behind all characteristics and aspects, for it is not different from the true characteristic's principle of thusness. In this wise, original enlightenment's principle of thusness in fact contains all the dharmas that perfect cultivation, including the constituents of the path, just as smelted gold inherently contains all the [thirty-two] major and [eighty] minor marks of a [buddha-] image. For this reason, it says, "That principle which is thus contains all dharmas."

Since abiding in this principle of thusness, which subsumes all meritorious qualities, leaves behind the dangers of the various types of maculations, it says, "A person who abides in that principle of thusness crosses over the sea of the three sufferings." This is the fourth [subdivision, I.B.2.b.ii.d], on leaving behind all dangers.

If we were briefly to clarify the meaning of the constituents of the path in this passage, we could divide them into four alternatives:

1. subsume the thirty-seven [constituents of the path] into ten dharmas;
2. subsume the ten dharmas into four dharmas;
3. subsume the four dharmas into one aspect;
4. clarify that this one aspect subsumes all thirty-seven *[bodhipakṣikadharmas]*.

As the *[Da]zhidu lun* says, "These thirty-seven constituents have ten dharmas as their basis."[272] An extensive explanation is provided there. We should know that these ten are expanded to make the thirty-seven, but if we discuss the essence of those [thirty-seven] dharmas, there are only these ten dharmas. What are the ten? (1) Morality *(śīla)*, [five of the ten predominant factors *(mahābhūmika)*, viz.] (2) volition *(cetanā)*, (3) sensation *(vedanā)*, (4) mindfulness *(smṛti)*, (5) absorption *(samādhi)*, and (6) wisdom (*mati*=prajñā); [and four of the ten predominant wholesome dharmas *(kuśalamahābhūmika)*, viz.] (7) faith *(śraddhā)*, (8) vigor *(vīrya)*, (9) tranquillity *(praśabdhi)*, (10) equanimity *(upekṣā)*.

[First,] how are these ten expanded to make thirty-seven? Morality is expanded into three: right speech, action, and livelihood. The listing for intention is just one: right intention. Sensation is also just one: the "bliss" aspect of enlightenment *(prītibodhyaṅga)*. Mindfulness is expanded into four: the faculty of mindfulness, the power of mindfulness, the mindfulness aspect of enlightenment, and right mindfulness. Absorption is expanded into eight: the four bases of psychic power [*ṛddhipāda;* viz. desire-to-be, vigor, thought, analysis], the faculty of absorption, the power of absorption, the absorption aspect of enlightenment, and right absorption. Wisdom also becomes eight: the four loci of mindfulness [*smṛtyupasthāna;* viz. with regard to body, sensations, thought, and dharmas], the faculty of wisdom, the power of wisdom, the investigation-into-dharmas aspect of enlightenment *(dharmapravicayabodhyaṅga)*, and right view. Vigor also becomes eight: the four right efforts *(samyakprahāṇa)*,[273] the faculty of vigor, the power of vigor, the vigor aspect of enlightenment, and right vigor. Faith becomes two: the faculty of faith and the power of faith. **[652c]** Tranquillity and equanimity are each one: the tranquillity aspect of enlightenment and the equanimity aspect of enlightenment. In summary, there are five categories. (1) Three [dharmas] are expanded into eight: viz. the twenty-four [separate aspects of] absorption, wisdom, and vigor are subsumed in these three [dharmas]. (2) One is expanded into four: viz. the four [loci of] mindfulness are compressed in this one [dharma of] mindfulness. (3) One is expanded into three: viz. the three aspects of morality are compressed in that one [dharma of] morality. (4)

One is expanded into two: viz. the two aspects of faith are compressed in that one [dharma of] faith. (5) Four are listed singly: viz. intention, sensation, tranquillity, and equanimity each embraces its own nature. In this wise, ten dharmas subsume the thirty-seven.

Second, we may compress the ten dharmas into four dharmas. First, morality is included in the dharmas of materiality, both manifested *(vijñapti)* and unmanifested *(avijñapti)*. Second, intention and feeling are included among the predominant factors *(mahābhūmika)* of the mental constituents *(caitta/caitasika)*. Third, mindfulness, absorption, and wisdom are included among the mental constituents that involve specific objects *(anyajātīyālambana)*. Faith and so on [viz. vigor, tranquillity, and equanimity] are included among the wholesome dharmas *(kuśalamahābhūmika)*.

Third, we may compress the four dharmas into one aspect. Through one's enlightened wisdom, one investigates in this wise these four dharmas. The first dharma, of materiality, is unascertainable, regardless of whether or not its existence can be located. The latter three mental constituents are all unascertainable, regardless of whether or not they exist in the present moment. Although this does not mean that they are nonexistent dharmas, no ascertainable dharmas can be found. They are impartial and have but a single taste. Therefore, you should know that these four dharmas have but one aspect. For this reason, it says, "These many classifications have but a single aspect."

Fourth, we may clarify that this one aspect subsumes all thirty-seven [constituents of the path]. This refers to the aspect of the single taste, in which subject and object are in equilibrium. Observing the voidness of the body, and so forth, are the four loci of mindfulness. Leaving behind all sloth and torpor is the four right efforts. Calming and extinguishing all distracted thoughts are the bases of psychic power. Leaving behind a lack of faith, and so forth, is what is meant by the faculty of faith, [etc.]. Extinguishing ignorance, and so forth, are the seven aspects of enlightenment. Leaving behind the eight perverted dharmas is the eightfold noble path. In this wise, this one aspect, in which one leaves far behind all the various types of maculations, is fully endowed with immeasurable meritorious qualities. Therefore, it says, "All the thirty-seven [653a] constituents of the path are necessarily contained in this contemplation enlightenment." It also says, "That principle which is thus contains all dharmas."

> Śāriputra asked: "Each and every one of the myriads of dharmas is but verbalization and locution. These things that are characterized by verbalization and locution in fact have no meaning and a meaning that accords with reality cannot be explained verbally. So why now does the Tathāgata preach the dharma?"

From here onward is the third [subsection] in the main outline [I.C], a clarification that the words and teachings of the Buddha are spoken in accordance with the principle of thusness.

Initially [I.C.1], there is a question;
subsequently [I.C.2], an answer.

In the question [I.C.1], the passage "each and every one of the myriads of dharmas" refers to dharmas that are established according to conventional speech, for dharmas that are explained in accordance with words are all unascertainable. Only "verbalization and locution in fact have no meaning" means that the real meaning of all dharmas neutralizes all locution and verbalization. Now, if the Buddha's preaching of the dharma were all verbalization and locution, it then in fact would have no real meaning, and if it had real meaning, it necessarily would be free of verbalization and locution. Therefore, [Śāriputra] asks the question, "Why . . . preach the dharma?"

> The Buddha replied: "I preach the dharma because you sentient beings persist in needing explanations. I preach what cannot be spoken of. This is why I preach on it.
>
> "My speech consists of meaningful words, not mere locution. Sentient beings' speech consists of verbalization and locution and is not meaningful.
>
> "Meaningless words are all spurious and worthless; spurious and worthless words say nothing about meaning.
>
> "Anything that does not convey meaning is all false speech.
>
> "Concerning speaking in accordance with meaning, the real is void and yet not void; voidness is real and yet unreal. [Speaking in accordance with meaning] remains separate from dualistic characteristics, but also is not centered in between. The dharma that is not so centered remains far removed from these three characteristics [voidness, reality, and the nonduality of both]; its location cannot be found.
>
> "[Those words that remain separate from these three characteristics] are spoken in accordance with thusness.
>
> "Thusness does not make existence nonexistent, for how in nonexistence would existence be made nonexistent? Thusness does not make nonexistence existent, for how in existence would nonexistence be made to exist? Neither existence nor nonexistence applies. Because such statements are inapplicable, [the concept 'thusness' too] is inapplicable. Thusness is not said to be either a thusness that is existent or a thusness that is nonexistent."

This is the second [part, I.C.2], the answer, which is in two [subparts]:

initially [I.C.2.a], the motive behind the Buddha's speech;
subsequently [I.C.2.b], an elucidation of the difference between locution and meaning.

In the first [subpart, I.C.2.a], concerning the passage "**I preach the dharma because you sentient beings persist in needing explanations**": "**you**" refers to Śāriputra; "**sentient beings**" refers to all **[653b]** ordinary persons. Were I to preach about uncompounded [dharmas, you] then would presume this implied the existence of a dharma-essence. Were I to preach about compounded [dharmas, you] then would presume these implied the production of the characteristics of dharmas. The sort of speech that is associated with "existence" and "production" cannot explain real meaning. Mine is different from that type of speech, and "**this is why I preach on it.**" This is the motive behind the Buddha's speech and teachings.

Next, in [subpart I.C.2.b], an elucidation of the differing characteristics of locution and meaning, there is

Initially, an overview, in two sentences [I.C.2.b.i];
subsequently, the explication, in two sentences [I.C.2.b.ii].

In the overview [division, I.C.2.b.i], [the first sentence, "**My speech consists of] meaningful words, not mere locution**" means that speech should have real meaning, not just be spurious locution. [The second sentence, "**Sentient beings' speech consists of] verbalization and locution and is not meaningful**" means that speech is mired in spurious locution and is unrelated to real meaning.

In the second [division, I.C.2.b.ii], the explication, he initially explicates the latter sentence. "**[Meaningless words] are all spurious and worthless**" means that, as spurious locution, they have no real meaning; this explicates the passage ["**Sentient beings' speech consists of] verbalization and locution. . . .** " "**[Spurious and worthless words] say nothing about meaning**" means that they are unable either to refer to or to discuss anything regarding the meaning that accords with reality; this explicates the passage "**and is not meaningful.**"

What follows is a summation [viz. I.C.2.b.iii].[274] The sentence "**[Anything that does not convey meaning] is all false speech**" means that, although [a phrase] may be semantically correct, it can be contrary to fact, such as saying you see when you don't or saying you don't see when you do.

From "**[concerning speaking] in accordance with meaning**" onward is the succeeding explication of the initial sentence [in the overview: viz. "**My speech consists of meaningful words, not mere locution.**"] It is in two [subdivisions]:

a direct explication [I.C.2.b.ii.a];
a reiterated elucidation [I.C.2.b.ii.b].

The initial [direct explication subdivision, I.C.2.b.ii.a] is also in two [segments]:

initially [I.C.2.b.ii.a.1], an explication of "**not mere locution**";
subsequently [I.C.2.b.ii.a.2], an explication of "**meaningful words.**"

The explication of "not mere locution" [I.C.2.b.ii.a.1] means that [meaningful words] are not "spurious and worthless," for they are not spurious locution and are not meaningless. The explication of "meaningful words" [I.C.2.b.ii.a.2] means that meaning corresponds to words and words conform to meaning.

In the initial explication [of "not mere locution," I.C.2.b.ii.a.1], the words "the real is void and yet not void" means that we say the real characteristic of true thusness is also void. As was said previously, "the characteristic of voidness is also void" (p. 639c). While it says that "the real is void," it does not obviate the principle of its real characteristic; therefore, it says "and yet not void." Although it does not involve the real, it also is not devoid of the real; therefore, it says that "voidness is real and yet unreal." This means that explaining the principle of true voidness involves the real; therefore, it says "voidness is real"; but because it does not linger in this principle of true voidness, it therefore says "and yet unreal." This is because, although it is not devoid of voidness, it does not involve voidness. "[It] remains separate from dualistic characteristics, but also is not centered in between": [653c] locution that is not void is far removed from the characteristic of voidness, and locution that is unreal is far removed from the characteristic of reality; therefore, it says, "[It] remains separate from dualistic characteristics." Nevertheless, it does not linger in this state of nonduality between these two characteristics of voidness and reality; therefore, it says "but [it] also is not centered in between." Since it stays far removed from these two extremes, without also falling in between, it therefore says, "[The dharma that is not so centered] remains far removed from these three characteristics." The loci of thought, speech, and action do not extend beyond these three characteristics. However, the words of the Buddha leave far behind these three characteristics and at their intersection the pathways of thoughts and words are eradicated; therefore, it says, "Its location cannot be found." In this wise, [the words of the Buddha] sublimely tally with this aspect in which words are eradicated and consequently are not the same as meaningless locution. This has explicated "not mere locution."

"[Those words that remain separate from these three characteristics] are spoken in accordance with thusness *(yŏ yŏyŏ sŏl)*": this is the explication of "meaningful words" [I.C.2.b.ii.a.2]. The first *yŏ* [in accordance with] means "in correspondence with." The last two *yŏ*s [thusness] refer to meaning and principle. This is just like the previous line "[it] remains far removed from these three characteristics," which was spoken in correspondence with meaning and principle. Consequently, the Buddha's speech involves "meaningful words"; it is not the same as the meaninglessness of ordinary words.

From "thusness is nonexistent" onward is the second [subdivision], the reiterated elucidation [I.C.2.b.ii.b].

Initially [I.C.2.b.ii.b.1], it elucidates "not mere locution";
subsequently [I.C.2.b.ii.b.2], it elucidates "meaningful words."

In the first [segment, I.C.2.b.ii.b.1, on the elucidation of "**not mere locution**"], the passage "**thusness does not make nonexistence existent, for how in existence would nonexistence be made to exist**" means that, although the principle of true thusness may not be existent, nevertheless the original nonexistence of thusness causes its state of existence not to exist; that is to say, it causes any existent dharmas within those nonexistent dharmas not to exist. The reason for this is that thusness is originally not existent; so from what state of existence would nonexistence fall into nonexistence? Hence, this is a statement that synthesizes the voidness and nonvoidness of reality. "**Thusness does not make nonexistence existent, for how in existence would nonexistence be made to exist**": although the principle of true thusness is not nonexistent, nevertheless the original nonexistence of thusness causes its nonexistence to exist; that is to say, it causes nonexistent dharmas within those existent dharmas to exist. The reason for this is that thusness is originally not nonexistent; so from what state of nonexistence would existence fall into existence? Hence, this is a statement that synthesizes the reality and unreality of voidness. "**Neither existence nor nonexistence applies**": because "**thusness is nonexistent and makes existence nonexistent,**" existence is inapplicable; because "**thusness is nonexistent and makes nonexistence existent,**" nonexistence is inapplicable. **[654a]** Since these two do not apply, how can one find anything in between? These are words that correlate with [this notion of] "**remain[ing] far removed from these three characteristics.**" Since this is also the case with the idea of thusness, it correlates with [this notion of] "**meaningful words.**" Therefore the Buddha's words in reality are "**not mere locution.**" This has been the reiterated elucidation of the explication of "**not mere locution.**"

Because the concepts and words spoken by the Buddha correspond in this wise with the principle, the subsequently obtained wisdom *(tatpṛṣṭalabdhajñāna)* is embellished with these sorts of concepts. By reflecting on true thusness, one then succeeds in observing intimately the essence of the principle of true thusness; therefore, among the [four] alternatives [of same, different, both, and neither], this is the alternative of 'both.'

In this second [segment, I.C.2.b.ii.b.2], on the reiterated elucidation of "**meaningful words,**" the line "**because such statements are inapplicable, [the concept 'thusness' too] is inapplicable**" means that the Buddha's words are spoken without being applicable to either existence or nonexistence. Existence and nonexistence are inapplicable to the principle of true thusness. [The Buddha's words] are inapplicable to existence because thusness is not existent; they are inapplicable to nonexistence because thusness is not nonexistent. Consequently, [the Buddha] speaks in accordance with that thusness which is neither existent nor nonexistent. Therefore, it says, "**Thusness is not said to be either a thusness that is existent or a thusness that is nonexistent.**" For this reason, the preceding line "**[those words] are spoken in accordance with thusness**" in this wise offers a reiterated elucidation of the explication of [the sentence] "**[my speech consists of] meaningful words, [not mere locution].**"

This completes the third subsection [I.C, clarification that the teachings of the Tathāgata are spoken in accord with thusness] of the six subsections [of the main outline].

> **Śāriputra said: "All sentient beings begin as *icchantikas*. On what levels should the *icchantika*'s thoughts abide in order to reach the [level of] the tathāgatas and the tathāgatas' real characteristic?"**
>
> **The Buddha said, "From the [level of] the *icchantika*'s mind up until one reaches the tathāgatas and the real characteristic of the tathāgatas, one passes through five ranked levels."[275]**

From here onward is the fourth subsection of the main outline [I.D], clarification that the bodhisattva ranks emerge from the original inspiration. It is in two [parts]:

initially [I.D.1], a question;
subsequently [I.D.2], the answer.

The answer is in three [subparts]:

one [I.D.2.a], a listing of the classifications in a summary overview;
two [I.D.2.b], a sequential explication;
three [I.D.2.c], a summary clarification.

This [statement] is the general overview [I.D.2.a]. "**Five ranked levels**": "**ranked**" means "stage." "**From the [level of] the *icchantika*'s mind**": those who have yet to arouse the mind of supreme bodhi are called *icchantikas* because they do not have decisive faith in the Mahāyāna. However, *icchantikas* are, in brief, of two types.[276] (1) *Icchantikas* who have make a great vow: they are those who **[654b]** refuse ever to access nirvāṇa. (2) *Icchantikas* who do not have great faith, which are also in two subtypes. One [2a], disjoined *icchantikas*, meaning those who, by generating great perverse views, have eradicated their wholesome faculties *(samucchinnakuśalamūla)* [and fallen into the hells]. Two [2b], conjoined *icchantikas*, meaning those who have not yet aroused the great mind [the thought of enlightenment] and thus lack great faith; everyone [at stages] up through the four fruitions of two-vehicle adherents [viz. stream-enterer, once-returner, non-returner, arhat] is included at this level of *icchantikas*.

Now, because this passage is given from the standpoint of this very last [type, the conjoined *icchantikas*], it states, "**From the [level of] the *icchantika*'s mind up until one reaches the tathāgatas, [there are] five ranked levels.**" This is because anyone who has not yet accessed the ten faiths is called an *icchantika*.

With regard to these [rankings], let me first clarify the ordering system of the five levels.

The first level, faith, involves the practice of the ten faiths. Although [practitioners on this level] have yet to achieve nonretrogression, they have aroused the great mind [the thought of enlightenment]. In the *Benye jing* [Original Acts of the Bodhisattva], this is called a bodhisattva characterized by faith.[277]

The second level, consideration [viz. the three levels of the ten abidings, ten practices, and ten transferences], involves thirty states of mind. Here, one reflects upon the principle that all dharmas are consciousness-only but has not yet achieved cultivation involving authentic realization that is free from discrimination.

The third level, cultivation, involves the practice of the ten bhūmis. Here, one achieves cultivation involving authentic realization that counteracts the ten obstructions.[278]

The fourth level, practice, involves the practice of virtual enlightenment. Here, the causal practices are already fulfilled, but one has not reached the stage of fruition.

The fifth level, relinquishment, involves the stage of sublime enlightenment. Here, one does not cling to calm extinction but instead proselytizes everyone with great compassion.

For this reason, we establish these "five ranked levels" in order to elucidate the distinctions between levels that involve retrogression and nonretrogression, realization and nonrealization, integration and nonintegration, the fulfillment of the appropriate causes, and the consummation of fruition. In accordance with their sequential order, we establish "five ranked levels."

The general meaning is as above. Next is an explication of the text.

> "First is the level of faith [viz. the ten faiths]. [The practitioner] has faith that in this body there is a seed of true thusness,[279] which is obscured by deception. By relinquishing the deceptive thoughts and leaving them far behind, the pure mind will become clear and transparent. One will then know that all the sense-realms are just the discriminations of ratiocination and verbalization."

From here onward is the second [subpart, I.D.2.b], a sequential explication. It is in two [divisions]:

initially [I.D.2.b.i], [a clarification of] faith;
subsequently [I.D.2.b.ii], [a clarification of] comprehension. **[654c]**

First [I.D.2.b.i], the clarification of faith. "Faith" involves three aspects of the buddha-nature. "[The practitioner] has faith that in this body there is a seed of true thusness" means the faith that [1] the buddha-nature abides in one's own nature, [2] true thusness is in fact absolute voidness, and [3] the seed is in fact the middle way of *anuttara[samyaksaṃ]bodhi*. One's own nature's purity of mind is foundational and maintains its own natural state; therefore, it is called "true thusness." Because it serves as the direct cause for the fruition of the three bodies [of the buddhas, viz. the dharma, enjoyment, and transformation bodies], it is called a "seed." Abiding in that state in which one has not yet aroused the mind [of enlightenment] is called "abiding in one's own nature." Not yet overcoming all the hindrances is to be "obscured by the deceptions." The passage "by relinquishing the deceptive thoughts and leaving them far behind" means to have faith in the guidance of the buddha-nature. This means that, from the level of the ten faiths up through virtual enlightenment, one gradually removes the hindrances of incredulity and nescience and accordingly relinquishes the coarse and deceptive discriminations of mind. "The pure mind will become clear and transparent" refers to faith that one will successfully reach the buddha-nature. This means that, after [consummating] the path, one leaves behind all the maculations so that the pure mind of one's own nature will become clear and transparent. The use of the character "faith" in the first passage carries over into the last two passages. "One will then know that all the sense-realms are just the discriminations of ratiocination and verbalization": since one has faith in the three types of buddha-nature, one also understands the principle of consciousness-only. Therefore, one knows that all the sense-realms to which the mind clings are merely created by "the discriminations of ratiocination and verbalization," and will no longer exist if one leaves behind discrimination.

> "Second is the level of consideration. 'Consideration' means to contemplate the fact that all the sense-realms are nothing more than ratiocination and verbalization. Through the discriminations of ratiocination and verbalization, [those sense-realms] manifest according to one's mind *(manas)*, but the sense-realms that are perceived are not my foundational consciousness. I know that the foundational consciousness is neither a dharma, nor its object, nor [the perceived objects] to which one clings, nor that [perceiving subject] which clings."

[Now begins the second division, I.D.2.b.ii, the clarification of comprehension, which is in four subdivisions: I.D.2.b.ii.a, clarification of the level of consideration; I.D.2.b.ii.b, clarification of the level of cultivation; I.D.2.b.ii.c, clarification of the level of practice; I.D.2.b.ii.d, clarification of the level of relinquishment.[280]]

[The first subdivision, I.D.2.b.ii.a,] clarification of the level of consideration, which involves two passages:

initially [I.D.2.b.ii.a.1], a clarification of the contemplation on the [four] aspirations *(paryeṣaṇā)*, which involves signlessness;
subsequently [I.D.2.b.ii.a.2], an elucidation of the [four] wisdoms that accord with reality *(yathābhūtaparijñāna)*, which involves nonproduction.

In the initial [passage, I.D.2.b.ii.a.1], "**to contemplate**" means to reflect on and investigate. "**[All the sense-realms] are nothing more than ratiocination and verbalization**" means that the external sense-spheres, which are the perceived objects, are unascertainable. **[655a]** "**[Those sense-realms] manifest according to one's mind**" means that characteristics that appear to be external are not separate from one's subjective view. "**[The sense-realms that are perceived] are not my foundational consciousness**": since those sense-realms that are perceived to be separate from my consciousness are not my foundational consciousness, they therefore are unascertainable. In this [sentence], the term "**foundational consciousness**" means the sixth consciousness that is the origin of the three realms of existence. As a gāthā recited by [Ārya] Deva Bodhisattva says,

> The mind-consciousness is the basis of the three realms of existence.
> And all the dusty sense-objects are its causes.
> If one perceives that these dust motes do not exist,
> Its seeds will spontaneously be extinguished.[281]

The preceding has been a generic elucidation of the aspirations that involve signlessness and the wisdoms that accord with reality. From here onward is a [specific] clarification [of the wisdoms that accord with reality, which involve] the principle of nonproduction [I.D.2.b.ii.a.2]. "**I know that the foundational consciousness is neither a dharma, nor its object**" means that it is neither a dharma, which is description, nor an object, which is the described, for he knows that concept and object are both subjective. "**Nor [is the foundational consciousness . . . the perceived objects] to which one clings, nor that [perceiving subject] which clings**": since the dusty sense-objects, the perceived objects, are nonexistent, [mentality], the perceiving subject, cannot occur. The perceiving subject is perforce dependent on the perceived objects, and since there are no objects that are dependent, there is in fact no subject that is dependent.

This has been a generic elucidation of the aspirations that involve nonproduction and the wisdoms that accord with reality. Starting from the ten types of comprehension up through the highest worldly dharmas *(laukikāgradharma)*, one cultivates this contemplation of the aspirations and these wisdoms that accord with reality. Although one also cultivates wisdom and investigation during this [stage], one never leaves behind the discriminations prompted by reflection. Therefore, it is given the general name "**level of consideration.**"

> **"Third is the level of cultivation. 'Cultivation' involves constant training in the catalysts of spiritual development [i.e., calmness *(śamatha)* and insight *(vipaśyanā)*]. Training and cultivation are to be simultaneous and initially guided by knowledge. Eliminating all hindrances and difficulties, one removes all restraints and fetters and stays far removed from them."**

This clarification of the "**level of cultivation**" [I.D.2.b.ii.b] is also in two passages:

initially [I.D.2.b.ii.b.1], a clarification of the characteristics of cultivation;
subsequently [I.D.2.b.ii.b.2], an elucidation of the causes of cultivation.

The term "characteristics of cultivation" [in this first segment, I.D.2.b.ii.b.1] refers to knowledge of the actual essence. Because the simultaneous operation of calmness *(śamatha)* and contemplation *(vipaśyanā)* involves no further egress or access, it refers to "**constant training.**" The term "**catalysts**" means calmness as the catalyst, for it can catalyze contemplation. Next, the term "**training**" refers to the contemplation that is the object of training. Because these are not separate from calmness and contemplation, it says that these "**are to be simultaneous.**" This is because the characteristics of calmness and the contemplation of thusness perforce are to be simultaneous.

This [passage] has clarified the characteristics of cultivation; next [I.D.2.b.ii.b.2] is an elucidation of the **[655b]** causes [of cultivation] For this reason, one gains this cultivation in which [calmness and contemplation] are simultaneously operative because one's initial preparatory practice has "**eliminat[ed] all hindrances.**" The phrase "**guided by knowledge**" refers to the preparatory knowledge *(saṃbhārajñāna)*. Because "**the discriminations of ratiocination and verbalization**" are not separate from concepts and verbalization, they therefore are called "preparatory knowledge." All the [bodhisattva] bhūmis up to the seventh bhūmi involve preparatory practice because they initially must subdue the hindrances. "**Eliminating all hindrances and difficulties**" means that one overcomes the debilitating [afflictions; *dauṣṭhūlya*].[282] "**One removes all restraints and fetters and stays far removed from them**" means that one does not generate any fetters in the present.

> **"Fourth is the level of practice. Practice means to leave behind all the stages of practice. The mind that is free from both clinging and rejection [manifests] the extremely pure, fundamental inspiration. The thusness of the mind will be motionless and the real nature will become fixed. This is great parinirvāṇa; its very nature is void and vast."**

The [clarification of] the level of virtual enlightenment [I.D.2.b.ii.c] is also in two passages:

initially [I.D.2.b.ii.c.1], a clarification of the qualities of this level;
subsequently [I.D.2.b.ii.c.2], an elucidation of its practices.

In the initial [segment I.D.2.b.ii.c.1], the passage "**to leave behind all the stages of practice**" means that this practice has surmounted all ten bhūmis. "**The mind that is free from both clinging and rejection**" means that one's comprehension is equivalent to that of the buddhas. Therefore, it is said that this level is called the practice of virtual enlightenment. Next is a summation. The phrase "the extremely pure, fundamental inspiration" refers to the mind of original enlightenment because it elucidates the fact that all causes [of enlightenment] have been completely fulfilled.

Next [I.D.2.b.ii.c.2], in the clarification of its practices, the passage "the thusness of the mind will be motionless and the real nature will become fixed" means that this level succeeds in accessing the vajrasamādhi. "This is great parinirvāṇa; its very nature is void and vast" means it is calm extinction and uncompounded; it has a single characteristic and is signless. As the *Benye jing* says, "Upon accessing the vajrasamādhi, its one characteristic is to be signless. Calm extinction is uncompounded, and it therefore is called the immaculate stage."[283]

> "Fifth is the level of relinquishment [viz. sublime enlightenment, the stage of buddhahood]. 'Relinquishment' means that not lingering in the voidness of the nature, right knowledge flows freely. Great compassion is characterized by thusness, but that characteristic does not linger in thusness. *Samyaksaṃbodhi* empties the mind so that there is nothing to realize. As the mind is boundless and limitless, it does not focus on a single, limited spot. This is reaching tathāgatahood."

This is [subdivision I.D.2.b.ii.d], clarification of the bhūmi of buddhahood, which is also in two passages.

First [I.D.2.b.ii.d.1] is the clarification of the meaning of relinquishment. **[655c]** It offers three aspects by which to elucidate the characteristics of relinquishment. [1] "Not lingering in the voidness of the nature, right knowledge flows freely": by not lingering in nirvāṇa, one incinerates the physical body and extinguishes [discriminative] knowledge. But because [right] knowledge is not extinguished, measured knowledge continues to flow and changes freely in accordance with the faculties, performing the acts of the buddhas. [2] "Its great compassion is characterized by thusness, but that characteristic does not linger in thusness": the great compassion that is free of conditions does not cling to the discriminative signs of person and dharmas; therefore, it says it is "characterized by thusness." Because he has never come to rest in any of the six destinies, which are as numerous as the sands of the Ganges, it says "that characteristic does not linger in thusness." [3] *Samyak* means "right." *Saṃ* means "commensurate." "Bodhi" means "enlightenment." All together, the term means "right, commensurate enlightenment," which is the consummate, unsurpassed enlightenment. But even there, there is no lingering, so one "empties the mind so that there is nothing to realize." Of these three aspects, the first two are the relinquishment that derives from not lingering in nirvāṇa; the last one is the relinquishment that derives from not clinging to bodhi.

Next [I.D.2.b.ii.d.2] is the clarification of the qualities of this level. "As the mind is boundless and limitless": returning to the fountainhead of the one mind, the mind-essence becomes all-pervasive and extensive. Because it pervades the ten directions, it is "boundless." Because it extends through the three time periods, it is "limitless." Even though it extends through the three time periods, it recognizes no distinction between past and present; even though it pervades the ten directions, it recognizes neither this place nor that place. For this reason, it says, "It does not focus on a single, limited spot." In this wise, the ultimate fruit [of buddhahood] is nothing like that associated with other types of persons. It is something that is reached only by availing oneself of thusness. For this reason, it says, "This is reaching tathāgatahood."

The sequential clarification of each of the five ranked levels [viz. I. D.2.b.i and I.D.2.b.ii.a–d] is finished as above.

> "Oh son of good family! These five levels are but one enlightenment; they are accessed through the original inspiration. The proselytization of sentient beings must derive from that original locus."

From here onward is the second [*sic,* third, subpart, I.D.2.c], a summary clarification, which is in two [divisions]:

one [I.D.2.c.i], an explicit clarification of what proceeds from original [enlightenment];
two [I.D.2.c.ii], a reiterated elucidation through a set of exchanges.

This [passage] is the first gateway [viz. I.D.2.c.i, an explicit clarification of what proceeds from original enlightenment]. None of the practices of the five levels are separate from original enlightenment; none of them are not perfected through the original inspiration. At the time that those practices are perfected, one moves from the preceding [level] to the succeeding one; therefore, it is called an "access." "Access" means benefiting oneself; "proselytization" means benefiting others. In this wise, these two practices both **[656a]** "derive from the original locus."

> Śāriputra asked, "What do you mean by 'must occur from that original locus'?"
>
> The Buddha replied: "Originally there is no original locus: on the brink of voidness, which has no locus, one accesses reality. Arousing bodhi, one completes the sanctified path. Why is this? Oh son of good family! Like a hand grabbing at air, it is neither obtained nor not obtained."

This is the reiterated elucidation [I.D.2.c.ii]. [It is in two subdivisions: I.D.2.c.ii.a, Śāriputra's question; and I.D.2.c.ii.b, the Buddha's answer.]

In the answer [subdivision, I.D.2.c.ii.b], there are two [segments]:

initially [I.D.2.c.ii.b.1], an instruction;
subsequently [I.D.2.c.ii.b.2], a simile.

In the instruction [I.D.2.c.ii.b.1], there are four passages. The first two passages clarify that the original locus has no locus [viz. "**Originally there is no original locus; on the brink of voidness, which has no locus, one accesses reality**"]. The latter two passages elucidate that [practice] is perfected through cause and effect [viz. "**Arousing bodhi, one completes the sanctified path**"].

"**Why is this?**" is asked in response to a doubt. "**Why**" means that, if originally there is no locus, one should not be able to gain access to it; and if one is able to gain access to it, then this could not occur without that original locus.

In order to resolve this doubt, he therefore brings up a simile [I.D.2.c.ii.b.2] in order to explicate it. "**Like a hand grabbing at air**": "**a hand grabbing**" is a simile for practice, the catalyst of access; "**air**" is a simile for that origin which is the object of access. "**Neither obtained**" means that the air has no form that can be grasped. "**Nor not obtained**" means that air is present inside that grasping fist. The original inspiration is also just the same: because originally it has no nature of being an original locus, it cannot be ascertained; but because the origin that is originless is not nonexistent, it cannot not be ascertained.

> **Śāriputra remarked: "As the Lord has explained, at the inception of one's vocation, one should cleave to the original inspiration. Such a state of mind is calm and extinguished, and that calm extinction is thus. [Thusness] encodes all the meritorious qualities and collects the myriad of dharmas so that they are consummately interfused and nondual. It is inconceivable!**
>
> **"We should know that this dharma is in fact *mahāprajñāpāramitā*. It is the great spiritual spell, the spell of great clarity, the unsurpassed spell, the unequaled spell."**[284]

From here onward is the fifth [subsection, I.E], clarification that great prajñā [neutralizes all causes and conditions and] is consummately interfused and free from duality. It is in two [parts]:

one [I.E.1], Śāriputra's respectful remark;
two [I.E.2], completion of the Tathāgata's **[656b]** narrative.

The first [part] also has two [subparts]:

initially [I.E.1.a], comprehension of the Buddha's explication that the original inspiration is consummately interfused;
subsequently [I.E.1.b], an elucidation that this is in fact the great perfection of prajñā.

The line [in subpart I.E.1.a] "**at the inception of one's vocation, one should cleave to the original inspiration**" is the comprehension of the Buddha's words. When ordinary people are about to mention the acts of the buddhas, they first should always cleave to the inspiration of original enlightenment. Thoughts that involve birth and death originally are calm and extinguished; and that which, in this wise, is calm and extinguished is in fact the principle of thusness. This principle comprehensively subsumes all the meritorious qualities of both original and acquired [enlightenments] and also then amalgamates all the myriad dharmas involved in birth and death "**so that they are consummately interfused and nondual.**" Since it is extremely profound, "**it is inconceivable!**"

[I.E.1.b] Although this [thusness that subsumes both original and acquired enlightenments] is replete with immeasurable meritorious qualities, in its essence, it is nothing more than that original enlightenment and acquired enlightenment, which are in equilibrium and nondual. Therefore, it says, "**[This dharma] is in fact *mahāprajñāpāramitā*.**" Because, in this wise, prajñā plumbs the fountainhead and exhausts its nature, it is called a "**pāramitā**" [perfection]. Explaining it separately according to its two destinations, at the level of virtual enlightenment, [prajñā] reaches the other shore of [viz. perfects] the myriad practices; while at the time of sublime enlightenment, it reaches the other shore of the myriad meritorious qualities.

At the level of virtual enlightenment, [prajñā] has, in brief, two destinations. (1) [Prajñā] has great spiritual power, which can vanquish the enemy, the three *māras*;[285] this is like the sūtra's "**great spiritual spell.**" (2) [Prajñā] has great clarity and radiance, which can scrutinize pervasively all the realms [seen by] the four eyes;[286] this is like the sūtra's "**spell of great clarity.**"

At the level of sublime enlightenment, [prajñā] also has two destinations. (1) It is fully endowed with the four knowledges[287] and completely fulfills all the five eyes.[288] It radiates throughout all the *dharmadhātu* and has nothing further that needs to be sustained; this is like the sūtra's "**the unsurpassed spell.**" (2) It makes manifest the three bodies [of the buddhas].[289] There is nothing that equals unsurpassed bodhi, which is identical in all the buddhas; this is like the sūtra's "**the unequaled spell.**"

"**Spell**" means "supplication." Worldly spells have great awesome power: for one who makes supplication to spirits by reciting spells, there is no merit that is not invited and no misfortune that is not expelled. It is exactly the same with this ***mahāprajñāpāramitā*:** it contains the above four qualities [the four types of spells above] and has great spiritual power. Internally, there are no meritorious qualities with which it is not endowed and, externally, **[656c]** there are no calamities that it does not leave behind. If one recites the words of this spell with a mind of utmost sincerity and makes supplication to all the buddhas, bodhisattvas, spirits, and [enlightened] persons, there then will be nothing that you seek or for which you pray that will not be accomplished. This is why it is called a "**spell.**" It is just like Śakra, the Emperor of Heaven, who recited the words of this spell and vanquished the hordes of asuras: this is the appropriate explanation here.

> The Buddha said, "So it is, so it is!
>
> "True thusness has voidness as its nature. As its nature is void, its knowledge is empyreal, incinerating all the fetters. In an equipoised and balanced manner, the three stages of virtual enlightenment and the three bodies of sublime enlightenment radiate brilliantly in the ninth consciousness so that there are no shadows."[290]

From here onward is the second [part, I.E.2], the Tathāgata's narrative, which is in three [subparts]:

initially [I.E.2.a], a summary narrative;
next [I.E.2.b], a sequential narrative [about reaching the other shore];
finally [I.E.2.c], the summary conclusion.

The "summary narrative" [I.E.2.a] is the line "So it is, so it is!"

The specific [narrative, subpart I.E.2.b] is also in two [divisions]:

initially [I.E.2.b.i], a narrative about the fulfillment of the cause;
subsequently [I.E.2.b.ii], a narrative about the consummation of the fruition.

In the first [division, I.E.2.b.i], it elucidates "the three stages of virtual enlightenment." What are "the three stages of virtual enlightenment"? (1) the level of one hundred kalpas [eons], (2) the level of one thousand kalpas, (3) the level of myriad kalpas. As the *Benye jing* states:

> Sons of the buddhas! One who receives the designation "Necklace of Maṇi [Jewels]" is a person who is ensconced within the nature of virtual enlightenment; his name is Jin'gang Hui [Adamantine Wisdom] Bodhisattva. He abides in the absorption of supreme calmness and, through the power of his great vow, he lives for a hundred kalpas. After cultivating a thousand samādhis, he accesses the vajrasamādhi and is identical to the nature of all dharmas, the two truths [conventional and absolute], the one truth [the absolute], and the single common characteristic *(piṇḍagrāha)*. Next, he lives for a thousand kalpas, training in the dignified demeanor of the buddhas until he practices like a buddha, sitting at a buddha's *bodhimaṇḍa* [seat of enlightenment] and overcoming the three *māras*. Next, he lives for myriad kalpas, transforming himself into a buddha, until he manifests himself identically to all the buddhas of antiquity; while constantly practicing the middle way and enjoying

> immensely the unconditioned, he still recognizes the distinction between production and cessation.[291]

Now, in this passage [in our sūtra], the phrase "**true thusness has voidness as its nature**" is a reference to being "identical . . . to **[657a]** the single common characteristic." This means that [true thusness] is common in all existent and nonexistent dharmas—that is, both of the two truths are identically fused in the one truth and this one truth is in fact identical to this single common characteristic. In this wise, it is said that "**true thusness has voidness as its nature.**" "**As its nature is void, its knowledge is empyreal, incinerating all the fetters**": this is the second [stage of virtual enlightenment], "transcending the three *māras*." "**Incinerating all the fetters**" means to extinguish the *māra* of the defilements. Because he extinguishes the defilements, the *māra* of the skandhas will not bind him. Because he extinguishes these two *māras*, the Māra of Heaven [the devil] will be naturally vanquished. Only the *māra* of death, who governs inconceivable change, will remain. "**In an equipoised and balanced manner**" *(p'yŏngdŭng p'yŏngdŭng):* this is the third [stage of virtual enlightenment], "constantly practicing the middle way." Because he does not fall into either of the two extremes, it is said to be *p'yŏngdŭng* [**equipoised**]. Because it elucidates constant practice, it repeats the term *p'yŏngdŭng* [**balanced**]. "**The three stages of virtual enlightenment**" includes these above three stages. Among these, the first two refer to "**the great spiritual spell**"; the third one refers to "**the spell of great clarity.**"

From "**sublime enlightenment**" onward clarifies the consummation of the fruition [I.E.2.b.ii]. "**The three bodies**": the first is called the dharma-body; the second, the response [viz. reward] body; the third, the transformation body. The path to these three bodies is the same for all the buddhas. This refers to the phrase "**the unequaled spell.**" "**[The three bodies of sublime enlightenment] radiate brilliantly in the ninth consciousness so that there are no shadows**": this refers to the phrase "**the unsurpassed spell.**" The previous stage of virtual enlightenment is still involved with birth and death and has not yet uncovered the fountainhead of the mind; for this reason, it is located among the eight consciousnesses. But upon reaching sublime enlightenment, one forever leaves behind birth and death and fully returns to the fountainhead of the one mind of original enlightenment. Hence, he accesses the radiant purity of the ninth consciousness.

Furthermore, the previous causal level [of virtual enlightenment] involves the aspect of relying on conditions; therefore, the shadowy images manifest in the mind. But returning now to the fountainhead of the mind, one experiences their original substance and, consequently, all the characteristics of those shadows vanish. For this reason, it says "**there are no shadows.**" As the *Benye jing* says:

> Sons of the buddhas! The necklace of crystal radiates strikingly both internally and externally; the constant abiding in sublime en-

> lightenment radiates brilliantly. This is called the stage of all-embracing wisdom *(sarvajñā;* alt. *sarvākārajñāna).* Constantly residing in the middle way **[657b]**, one transcends the four *māras* while remaining involved in all dharmas. Being neither existent nor nonexistent, all characteristics vanish and one suddenly understands great enlightenment. One recognizes illusion and experiences the spirit. The two bodies abide constantly, so as to transform everything that is conditioned.[292]

Nota Bene: That *[Benye]* sūtra mentions two bodies: (1) the body of the dharma-nature [=dharmakāya], (2) the dharma-body of responsive transformation, which combines the two remaining bodies [the *saṃbhoga-* and *nirmāṇa-kāyas*] into one body. Now in this *[Vajrasamādhi]* sūtra, this [second body] is bifurcated back into two; therefore, it refers to "**three bodies.**" Whether three or two, they are "**equipoised and . . . balanced.**"

The preceding has been the sequential narrative [I.E.2.b] about reaching the other shore.

> **"Oh son of good family! This dharma is not a cause and not a condition, because it is just the spontaneous functioning of wisdom. It is neither moving nor still, because the nature of that functioning is void. Its meaning neither exists nor does not exist, because the characteristic of voidness is void.**
>
> **"Oh son of good family! If one proselytes sentient beings, one should make those sentient beings access this meaning through contemplation. One who accesses this meaning will see the tathāgatas."**

This is [the third subpart, I.E.2.c,] the summary conclusion, which concerns [the phrase] "**they are consummately interfused and nondual**" (p. 656a). The preceding [subpart, the sequential narrative, I.E.2.b,] gave an explanation that proceeded from the superficial to the profound in order to elucidate the distinction between cause being fulfilled and fruition consummated. If instead we give an explanation that proceeds from the standpoint that the one dharma is nondual, then cause and fruition are free from duality and mind and sense-objects are undifferentiated. Because cause and fruition are free from duality, it says "**not a cause.**" Because mind and sense-object are undifferentiated, it says "**not a condition.**" The reason for this is as explained previously: cause and fruition and mind and sense-objects are all simply the "**spontaneous functioning**" of the one, consummate "**wisdom.**" Since it is just **spontaneous functioning**, what causes or conditions could there be? Furthermore the functioning of this wisdom is called "radiant and calm wisdom" at the level of virtual enlightenment, because it has not yet left behind the active characteristics of production and cessation. Upon reaching the sublime-enlightenment level, it is called "calm and radiant wisdom," because it has returned to the ultimate stillness of the ninth consciousness.

However, now, from the standpoint of this instruction on nonduality, there is neither activity initially nor calmness subsequently. The functioning of calmness and activity occurs "**because the nature of that functioning is void.**" If, from this standpoint, it were presumed that the voidness of the nature is nonexistent because "**it is neither moving nor still,**" this also would be wrong. Therefore, it says, "**[Its object] neither exists nor does not exist.**" If it is correct to say that it does not exist, **[657c]** then how can it not not-exist? This is "**because the characteristic of voidness is void.**" Thus is the summary conclusion regarding [the phrase] "**they are consummately interfused and nondual.**"

From "**if one proselytes**" onward, [the Buddha] encourages him to "**access this meaning.**"

> Śāriputra remarked: "Contemplation of the tathāgatas' meaning does not linger in any of the currents. One should leave behind the four dhyānas and transcend the summit of existence *(bhavāgra)*."[293]
>
> The Buddha said, "So it is.
>
> "Why is this? All dharmas are but names and classifications; this is also the case with the four dhyānas.
>
> "If one sees the tathāgatas, [one's own] tathāgata-mind will become autonomous *(aiśvarya)* and remain eternally in a state of extinction, neither withdrawing from [that state] nor accessing it. This is because both internal and external will be in equilibrium."

From here onward is the sixth [subsection, I.F] in the main outline, clarification that great dhyānic absorption transcends all names and classifications. It is in two [parts]:

initially [I.F.1], a question;
subsequently [I.F.2], an answer.

In the question [I.F.1], "**any of the currents**" refers to the three realms of existence [desire, subtle materiality, formlessness], for one continually drifts between these states without ever resting. "**Summit of existence**" refers to the sphere of [neither perception nor] nonperception *(naivasaṃjñānāsaṃjñāyatana)*, which is the summit of the three realms of existence.

The answer [I.F.2] is in two subsections:

a general assent [I.F.2.a, viz. "**So it is**"];
and a sequential analysis [I.F.2.b].

The sequential analysis is also in two [divisions]:

a brief clarification [I.F.2.b.i];
an extensive explanation [I.F.2.b.ii].

In the brief [clarification, I.F.2.b.i], there are two passages:

initially [I.F.2.b.i.a], a clarification that the mundane dhyānas are not separate from **names and classifications**;
subsequently [I.F.2.b.i.b], an elucidation that supramundane dhyāna transcends those names and classifications.

[I.F.2.b.i.b:] **"If one sees the tathāgatas"**: as explained previously (p. 657b), this means that one accesses the tathāgatas' contemplation. **"[One's own] tathāgata-mind will become autonomous"** means that contemplating the mind of the tathāgatas leaves behind all the bonds. **"Remain eternally in a state of extinction"** means that the dharmas of mind *(citta)* and mental concomitants *(caitta)* are unproduced. **"Neither withdrawing from [that state] nor accessing it"** means that the mind-essence's principle of thusness neither arises nor is extinguished. For this reason, one who is able to gain this state of neither egress nor access impartially observes both the **"internal,"** the mind, and the **"external,"** sense-objects. The exegesis of the brief clarification [I.F.2.b.i] is finished.

> "Oh son of good family! In the same way, all dhyānic contemplations are absorptions that involve past conceptions. But this thusness, furthermore, is not the same as those [types of dhyāna]. Why so? One who contemplates thusness according to reality perceives no sign that he is 'contemplating thusness.' All signs are already calm and extinct. Calm extinction is in fact the meaning of thusness.
>
> "In the same way, that dhyānic absorption which involves such conceptions is active and is not dhyāna.[294] Why is this? The nature of dhyāna **[658a]** is separate from all movement. It neither taints nor is tainted; it is neither a dharma nor its shadow.
>
> "It remains far removed from all discrimination, because it is the meaning of the original meaning.[295]
>
> "Oh son of good family! This sort of contemplative absorption alone deserves to be called dhyāna."

This is the second [division], the extensive explanation [I.F.2.b.ii]. It is in four [subdivisions:]

one [I.F.2.b.ii.a], a clarification from the standpoint of characteristics of how to leave behind characteristics;
two [I.F.2.b.ii.b], an elucidation from the standpoint of activity of how to leave behind activity;

three [I.F.2.b.ii.c], a conclusion regarding these aspects;
four [I.F.2.b.ii.d], a conclusion regarding the names.

In the first [subdivision, I.F.2.b.ii.a], it initially alludes to the characteristic of clinging to all the types of dhyāna. "**All dhyānic contemplations**" mean the mundane eight dhyānas [the four *rūpa-* and four *ārūpya*-dhyānas]. The words "**that involve past conceptions**" mean that one does not leave behind the past grasping at the beginningless delusive conceptions that cling to all types of characteristics. He next elucidates [the meaning of] leaving behind characteristics. "**But this thusness, furthermore, is not the same as those [types of dhyāna]**" means that accessing the tathāgatas' contemplation, in which subject and object are in equilibrium, is called "**thusness.**" "**One who contemplates thusness according to reality**" means that this knowledge of equanimity penetrates to that which accords with reality *(yathābhūta)*. "**[He] perceives no sign that he is 'contemplating thusness'**" means that he does not perceive any characteristic differentiating the knowledge that is the agent of contemplation from the thusness that is the object of contemplation; for these are in equilibrium and have but a single taste. Since he has forgotten subject and object, a perceiving subject and perceived objects do not arise; therefore, it says, "**All signs are already calm and extinct.**" Because they are calm, extinct, and undifferentiated, this is in fact "**the meaning of thusness.**"

From "**in the same way, that**" onward is [the second subdivision, I.F.2.b.ii. b], an elucidation from the standpoint of activity of how to leave behind activity. It initially brings up [the meaning of] this "activity": that is, the arising of a mind that clings to the characteristics of mundane dhyānas in fact involves active thought. Because active thought is not still, it "**is not** true **dhyāna.**" He next elucidates the fact that true dhyāna leaves behind all characteristics of activity. "**It neither taints**" means that it does not serve as an agent of tainting, for it is not active thought. "**Nor is tainted**" means that it is not tainted by activity, for it is originally still. "**It is neither a dharma**" means that it is not a mental dharma, which would function as the objective support of sensory impressions. "**Nor its shadow**" means that it is not the shadowy images [of sense-objects] that are made manifest. Owing to these aspects, [true dhyāna] leaves behind all types of activity.

"**It remains far removed from all discrimination, because it is the meaning of the original meaning**" is the third [subdivision, I.F.2.b.ii.c], a conclusion regarding these aspects. "**It remains far removed from . . . discrimination**" is the conclusion regarding the aspect of leaving behind characteristics, since by remaining far removed from discrimination, one will not cling to characteristics. "**The meaning of the original meaning**" is the conclusion regarding the aspect of leaving behind activity, **[658b]** because the original stillness does not give rise to activity.

"**This sort of contemplative absorption alone deserves to be called dhyāna**" is the fourth [subdivision, I.F.2.b.ii.d], a conclusion regarding the names.

Only by leaving behind both characteristics and activity does it earn the name "dhyāna," because dhyāna is the designation for still pensiveness. As for those mundane absorptions that are called dhyānas: these are provisional designations for dhyāna; they are not true dhyāna.

In the two major sections of this chapter, we have now completed the six sections [of section I], which has provided numerous passages offering extensive explanations for those with sharp faculties.

> Śāriputra asked: "It is inconceivable! The tathāgata constantly proselytes sentient beings by means of that which accords with reality *(yathābhūta).* In this wise, the real meaning has many locutions and vast import. Sentient beings of sharp faculties alone are able to cultivate it; sentient beings of dull faculties find it difficult to recall the ideas. Through what expedient device may we prompt those of dull faculties to gain access to this truth?"

From here onward is the second [section, II], which provides just a few passages offering a brief synopsis for those of dull faculties.

Nevertheless, there are two standpoints regarding extensive and brief [accounts] among those who are of sharp and dull [faculties]. [First,] if we were to discuss the means by which they gain understanding, the sharp prefer brief and the dull prefer extensive. This is because the sharp hear one and understand ten,[296] while the dull must hear ten to be able to understand ten. [Second,] if we were to categorize them according to how their understanding is expressed in words, then the sharp prefer extensive and the dull prefer brief. The sharp gain much understanding by learning much, while the dull memorize the gist by reciting a few brief lines. Here, this passage should be understood from the latter standpoint.

In this section, there are five [subsections]:

one [II.A], a question;
two [II.B], the answer;
three [II.C], an entreaty;
four [II.D], an explanation;
five [II.E], the congregation hears the explanation and gains benefit.

This [passage] is the first subsection. It is in two [parts]:

initially [II.A.1], comprehension of the preceding explanation;
subsequently [II.A.2], a question regarding a doubt.

"To recall" means "to keep in mind." The shallow erudition of people of dull faculties makes it difficult for them to retain the ideas found in lengthy passages involving extensive meanings.

> The Buddha replied: "One should encourage those people of dull faculties to receive and keep one four-line gāthā; this will then allow them access to the real truth. All of the buddhadharmas are contained within a single[297] gāthā."

This is the second [subsection, II.B], the answer. The Tathāgata's erudition is unhindered and autonomous. Therefore when he speaks one gāthā, it subsumes all the buddhadharmas. The essentials of the buddhadharma are contained even within a **[658c]** four-line verse. "One should encourage . . . those of dull faculties to recite and keep one . . . gāthā" and constantly recollect and reflect upon it, until they have pervasive knowledge of all the buddhadharmas: these are called the skillful stratagems and expedients of the tathāgatas.

> Śāriputra asked: "What is this four-line gāthā? I beg you to recite it."

This is the third [subsection, II.C], an entreaty.

> Thereupon, the Lord recited the gāthā:
>
> Objects[298] that are produced by causes and conditions,
> Those objects are extinguished and unproduced.
> Extinguish all objects subject to production and extinction,
> And those objects will be produced and unextinguished.[299]

This is the fourth [subsection, II.D], an explanation. The meaning of these four lines involves both specific and comprehensive [standpoints]. From a specific [standpoint], it clarifies the meaning of the two aspects [of mind]. From a comprehensive [standpoint], it elucidates the dharma of the one mind. In this wise, there are none of the buddhadharmas that are not subsumed within the two aspects of the one mind. What does this mean? The first two lines fuse the conventional with the absolute to elucidate the meaning of uniformity. The latter two lines fuse the absolute with the conventional to elucidate the aspect of differentiation. But explaining these comprehensively, true and conventional, while nondual, do not guard the one. Since they are nondual, they are in fact identical to the one mind. But because they do not guard the one, we say that their essences are dualistic. In this wise, we call them the one mind and its two aspects. Such is the main import [of the passage]. Next, I explicate the text.

"Objects that are produced by causes and conditions": this alludes to all dharmas that are associated with conventional truth. "Those objects are extinguished" fuses conventional with absolute; this means that the aspect of production is originally calm and extinct. "Unproduced" elucidates the reason why the aspect of production in fact involves extinction. Since the aspect of production is in fact "unproduced," one will never succeed in discovering this aspect of production. Therefore, the aspect of production is identical to calm extinction (viz. nirvāṇa).

"**Extinguish all objects subject to production and extinction**": this refers to the dharma of calm extinction, which is associated with absolute truth. "**And those objects will be produced**" fuses absolute with conventional; this means that the dharma of calm extinction is produced from conditions. "**Unextinguished**" **[659a]** elucidates why this calm extinction is in fact production. Since this calm extinction is not calm and extinct, one may try to discover this aspect of calm extinction, but it can never be ascertained. For this reason, calm extinction is produced from conditions. "This calm extinction is in fact production" refers to the production that is unproduced. "The aspect of production is in fact extinction" refers to the extinction that is unextinguished. Because it is the extinction that is unextinguished, extinction is in fact production. Because it is the production that is unproduced, production is in fact extinction. To describe them synthetically *(hap)*, while production is in fact calm extinction, it does not validate [lit. guard] that extinction; and while extinction is in fact production, it does not linger in production. Production and extinction are nondual; action and calmness are undifferentiated. It in this wise comes to be called the dharma of the one mind. Although in reality they are nondual, they do not "guard the one." Thus, this suggests that the essence produces action in accord with conditions and, in accord with conditions, the essence becomes calm extinction. For this reason, production is calm extinction and calm extinction is production. They are unobstructed and unhindered, not one and not different. This is what is meant by the comprehensive and specific aspects of this one gāthā.

> **At that time, the great congregation heard this gāthā and all were utterly rapturous. Everyone gained comprehension of extinction and production, the prajñā that comprehends extinction and production, and the sea of the knowledge that the nature is void.**

This is the fifth [subsection, II.E], [the congregation] hears the explanation and gains benefit. This elucidates the fact that they gain understanding of the principle from both comprehensive and specific perspectives. Here the term "**extinction**" means extinction from the standpoint of production in the first two lines [of the gāthā]. The next term, "**production**," refers to production from the standpoint of extinction in the last two lines. This clarifies that they comprehend both aspects. "**The prajñā that comprehends extinction and production**": this elucidates the fact that they gain these two types of understanding, inspired by relying on this approach involving specifics. "**The sea of the knowledge that the nature is void**" means to contemplate this from comprehensive perspective. Whether production or extinction, neither guards its own nature. This knowledge that their natures are void is profound, vast, and limitless; it is in this wise called "**the sea of the knowledge that** the nature is void." This means that they gain benefit by relying on this comprehensive approach.

[Part Four: An Exegesis of the Text (cont.)]

[Section Two: Main Body (cont.)]

VAJRASAMĀDHI-SŪTRA, CHAPTER SEVEN: THE TATHĀGATAGARBHA

There is one true dharma, in which absolute and conventional are nondual; as it is that to which all the buddhas return, it is called **[659b]** the tathāgatagarbha [storehouse of the tathāgatas]. Now, in this chapter, [the Buddha] clarifies that there are none of the immeasurable dharmas or practices that do not end up accessing the tathāgatagarbha; therefore, the title [of this chapter] is derived from the object that is accessed.

Sixth Division of Contemplation Practice: Immeasurable Dharmas Access the Tathāgatagarbha

> At that time, the elder Pŏmhaeng arose from the original limit *(ponje)* and addressed the Buddha: "Lord! The object that is produced is not extinguished; the object that is extinguished is not produced. The object that in this wise is thus is in fact the bodhi of the buddhas. The nature of bodhi is in fact free from differentiation and discrimination. The nondiscriminative knowledge cannot be fathomed by discrimination. This characteristic of being unfathomable is simply the extinction of discrimination.[300] In this wise, both objects and characteristics are inconceivable, and in this inconceivability there is accordingly no discrimination."

In the six divisions of the sequential clarification of contemplation practice, the elucidation that All Practices Derive from the Voidness of the True Nature is finished as above. From here onward is the sixth division [of contemplation practice]: a clarification that Immeasurable Dharmas Access the Tathāgatagarbha. The text is in two [sections]:

One [I], a clarification that all dharmas and all practices together access the locus of oneness;
Two [II], an elucidation of the distinctions between the causes and fruitions of the practices that bring about access and the knowledges gained through access.

The initial [section] is also in two [subsections]:

the former [I.A] clarifies the aspect that all dharmas access the one reality;
the latter [I.B] clarifies that all practices access the one path to buddhahood.

The initial [subsection] has four [parts]:

one [I.A.1], a question;
two [I.A.2], the answer;
three [I.A.3], comprehension;
four [I.A.4], a conclusion to the narrative.

In the question [part, I.A.1], there are two [subparts]:

initially [I.A.1.a], comprehension of the preceding sermon;
subsequently [I.A.1.b], a question regarding a doubt.

In this [chapter], the questioner is named "**Pŏmhaeng**" [Moral Practice; Brahmacarya]. Although this person's body appears to be that of an ordinary householder, his mind abides in the single taste, for this single taste absorbs all tastes. Although he may seem to be a sullied layman who commingles all kinds of tastes, he in fact does not neglect that moral and pure practice that has but a single taste. Since this chapter elucidates this aspect, it therefore has him serve as the interlocutor.

[I.A.1.a] "**[The elder Pŏmhaeng] arose from the original limit**": hearing what the Buddha had preached, he had accessed the "**original limit**"; now, wishing to ask a question, he "**arose**" from that [state]. "**The object that is produced is not extinguished**": this demonstrates his comprehension of the latter half [of the gāthā in the previous chapter, (p. 658c)], that is, "**those objects will be produced and unextinguished.**" "**The object that is extinguished is not produced**": this demonstrates comprehension of the former half [of the gāthā], that is, "**those objects are extinguished and [659c] unproduced.**" "**The object that in this wise is thus**" demonstrates thorough comprehension of the whole gāthā: the idea that nonextinction and nonproduction are nondual. In this wise, because the idea of nonduality is the path to which all the buddhas awaken, it says, "**[It] is in fact the bodhi of the buddhas.**" Because awakening conforms to nonduality, which is undifferentiated and undiscriminating, it says, "**[It] is in fact free from differentiation and discrimination.**" Since there is nothing that it discriminates, there then is nothing that it is not able to discriminate; therefore, it says, "**The nondiscriminative knowledge cannot be fathomed by discrimination.**" For this reason, that which "**cannot be fathomed by discrimination**" derives solely from the extinction of all discrimination; therefore, it says, "**This characteristic of being unfathomable is just the extinction of discrimination.**" Because it is far removed from words and eradicates thought, it is "in-

conceivable." Because both mind and words vanish in this inconceivability, he is then free from discrimination. In this wise, he demonstrates his comprehension of the ideas in the gāthā that was preached previously.

> **"Lord! All the classifications of dharmas are immeasurable and limitless, but that limitless characteristic of dharmas has the nature of having but one real meaning. They merely abide in that one nature: How can that be?"**

This is [the second subpart, I.A.1.b], an explicit question regarding his doubt. The doctrine of the Hīnayāna involves eighty thousand aggregations of dharma *(dharmaskandha)*, and each single aggregation measures some one thousand classifications in size. Now, because the doctrine of the Great Vehicle is not limited to these eighty thousand, it says, "**The classifications of dharmas are immeasurable and limitless.**" The terminology, meanings, and characteristics of those limitless doctrinal teachings have no extraneous significance: they involve only the "**one real meaning.**" The doctrinal teachings may be multitudinous, but "**they merely abide in that one nature.**" This is extremely difficult to comprehend, so "**how can that be?**"

> **The Buddha replied: "Elder! It is inconceivable! I preach all the dharmas out of concern for those who are deluded and because it is an expedient way. All the characteristics of dharmas are but the knowledge of this one real meaning. Why is this? It is just like four gates that open upon a single city: one may return to that single city through any of those four gates.[301] And just as the populace [of that city] may freely enter [through any gate], just so is it the same with the taste of the various types of dharmas [all of which have but a single taste]."** **[660a]**

This is the second [part, I.A.2], the answer, which is in three [subparts]:

[I.A.2.a] an instruction;
[I.A.2.b] a simile;
[I.A.2.c] their correlation.

In the initial instruction [subpart, I.A.2.a], the phrase "**I preach all the dharmas**" refers to the teaching of the three vehicles and the teaching of the one vehicle. "**Out of concern for those who are deluded**": I speak out of concern for those who have not yet penetrated to the single taste. "**Because it is an expedient way**" means that [teachings] are all expedients for accessing the single taste. This is because, when one accesses right contemplation, there is no need for verbal teachings. "**All the characteristics of dharmas are but the knowledge of this one real meaning**" means that the characteristics that are accessed through the doctrinal teachings are only the one real meaning's knowledge of right contemplation.

In the simile [subpart, I.A.2.b], "a single city" is a simile for this "one real meaning." "Four gates" is a simile for the four types of teachings, that is, the teachings of the three vehicles and the teachings of the one vehicle. "One may return to that single city through any of those four gates": this is said because all those who rely on the four teachings will return to the one reality. "And just as the populace may freely enter [through any gate]": based on the shallowness or depth of one's faculties, one accordingly accesses the one teaching. The reason "'a single city' is used as a simile for this 'one real meaning'" is that it is that which is accessed by all the people [lit. the "hundred surnames"] and that to which all sentient beings return.

In the correlation [subpart, I.A.2.c], the words "the various types of dharmas" correlate with the "four gates." The last reference to "taste" means the taste that is imbibed, which correlates with the "single city."

> The elder Pŏmhaeng remarked, "If this is indeed how dharmas are, I should be able to imbibe each and every taste while lingering in that single taste."

This is the third [part, I.A.3], on gaining comprehension. "To imbibe . . . every taste" means to imbibe the tastes of all the doctrines and to return to the one reality.

> The Buddha replied: "So it is, so it is! Why is this? The true meaning of the single taste—its taste[302] can be compared to that of the one ocean: none of the myriad of streams does not flow into it. Elder! The tastes of all the dharmas are just like those streams: while their names and classifications may differ, that water is indistinguishable.[303] And once [those streams] have flowed into the ocean, [that seawater] then[304] absorbs all those streams.[305] [In the same way,] if one lingers in the single taste, then all tastes are imbibed." **[660b]**

This is the fourth [part, I.A.4], a conclusion to the narrative, which is in two [subparts]:

[I.A.4.a] a generic statement [viz. "So it is, so it is!];
[I.A.4.b] a specific conclusion.

The specific conclusion [I.A.4.b] is in three [divisions]:

[I.A.4.b.i] an instruction [viz. "The true meaning of the single taste"];
[I.A.4.b.ii] a simile [viz. "its taste can be compared to that of the one ocean"];
[I.A.4.b.iii] their correlation.

The correlation [I.A.4.b.iii] is in two [subdivisions]. First [I.A.4.b.iii.a] is the correlation with "those streams," where [the streams] are initially correlated with the teachings and subsequently illustrated with a simile. Second [I.A.4.b.iii.b] is the correlation with "absorbs all those streams," where it initially brings up the simile and subsequently correlates it with the instruction.

> The elder Pŏmhaeng asked: "If all dharmas are of a single taste, then how is it that there are [separate] paths for the three vehicles? Does their knowledge have distinctions?"

From here onward is the second [subsection, I.B], the clarification that all practices access the one path to buddhahood. There is

initially [I.B.1], a question;
subsequently [I.B.2], an answer.

The question [I.B.1] concerns "distinctions" [in the understanding of adherents of the three vehicles].

> The Buddha replied: "Elder! It is like the [Chang]jiang [Yangtze River], the [Huang]he [Yellow River], the Huai [River], and the ocean: because there are variations in their size, disparities in their depth, and differences in their names, when water is in the [Chang]jiang it is called Jiang water, when it is in the Huai it is called Huai water, and when it is in the He it is called He water. But once all these types [of water] enter the ocean, they are just called seawater.[306] The dharmas [i.e., the three vehicles] are also the same: once they all abide in true thusness they are just called the path to buddhahood."

This is the second [part, I.B.2], the answer. It includes:

a simile [I.B.2.a];
the correlation [I.B.2.b].

In the first [simile subpart, I.B.2.a], "the Jiang, the He, the Huai" are similes for the practices of the three vehicles. "The ocean" is a simile for the path to buddhahood. "Variations in their size" is a simile for dissimilarities in the breadth or narrowness of the minds of three vehicle adherents. "Disparities in their depth" is a simile for differences in the superiority or inferiority of the knowledge of three-vehicle adherents. In accordance with the preceding two aspects, they are each given separate names. "But once all these types [of water] enter the ocean, they are just called seawater" is a simile for the fact that, at the stage of the ten bhūmis, these three vehicles access together the "true thusness" of the voidness of dharmas. "They are just called the path to buddhahood," which makes superfluous separate names for the three vehicles.

You should know that the distinctive practices of the three vehicles are all part of the path of expedients, which precedes the bhūmis. There are none of them that do not ultimately access the right contemplation of true thusness. For this reason, when the three vehicles reach their culmination, they have no separate refuge, just as all the doctrinal teachings together access the single taste. The words of the simile and the correlation can be found in the text itself. **[660c]**

> "Elder! One who abides in the one path to buddhahood then comprehends three practices."
>
> The elder Pŏmhaeng asked, "What are those three practices?"
>
> The Buddha replied: "First is the practice that cleaves to phenomena. Second is the practice that cleaves to consciousness. Third is the practice that cleaves to thusness."

From here onward is the second [section, II,] of the main exegesis, the distinctions between the causes and fruitions of the practices that bring about access and the knowledges gained through access. It is in four [subsections]:

one [II.A], distinctions in the practices that bring about access;
two [II.B], distinctions in the knowledge gained through accessing [the tathāgatagarbha];
three [II.C], the operation and functioning of the causes that bring about access;
four [II.D], constantly abiding in the fruition gained through accesss.

The initial [subsection, II.A,] is in three [parts].

one [II.A.1], a generic proposition. "**One who abides in the one path to buddhahood**": the first bhūmi on up is called "abiding in the path to buddhahood," because by fulfilling three types of knowledge, one penetrates to the three practices.
two [II.A.2], a question ["**What are those three practices?**"].
three [II.A.3], the answer.

The answer is in two [subparts]:

a specific clarification [II.A.3.a];
a general explication [II.A.3.b].

In the specific clarification [II.A.3.a], the line "**the practice that cleaves to phenomena**" means that, while relying on the four noble truths and the twelve links of conditioned generation, and in accordance with phenomena [that are governed by] cause and fruition, one cleaves to the practice of the [thirty-seven] constituents of the path. "The practice that cleaves to consciousness" means that all sentient beings are created by the one mind alone and, in accordance with that principle of consciousness-only, they cleave to the practice of the four means of conversion *(saṃgrahavastu)*.[307] "The practice that cleaves to thusness" means that all dharmas are impartial and uniform; in accordance with that impartial thusness, one cleaves to the practice of the six pāramitās. "Cleaves" means that it accumulates practices and assimilates them in the mind; it does not refer to the clinging that discriminates subject from object.

> "Elder! In this wise, the three practices subsume completely all approaches; there are no approaches to dharma that are not accessed thereby. One who accesses these practices does not produce the characteristic of voidness. And one who accesses [these practices] in this manner can be said to have accessed the tathāgata. One who accesses the tathāgata accesses that access at nonaccess."

This is the general explication of the three practices [II.A.3.b]. "The practice that cleaves to phenomena" is an approach that is associated with the Hīnayāna. "The practice that cleaves to consciousness" is the approach that is exclusive to the Mahāyāna. These two are distinct approaches; the third [the practice that cleaves to thusness] is an impartial approach. Thanks to this principle, [these three approaches] "subsume completely all approaches."

Furthermore, the practice of the [thirty-seven] constituents of the path does not linger in the production-and-extinction aspect, and the practice of the four **[661a]** means of conversion does not linger in the nirvāṇa aspect. The soteriological practice that is in accordance with thusness is the approach of impartiality and nonduality. Therefore "there are no approaches to dharma that are not accessed thereby." "One who accesses these practices does not produce the characteristic of voidness" means that, although one practices in accordance with thusness, one also constantly practices in accordance with phenomena and consciousness as well. For this reason, while not clinging to the characteristic of voidness, one abides in calm extinction. "Can be said to have accessed the tathāgata": although one remains in accord with phenomena and consciousness, one constantly remains in accord with thusness and cleaves to the practice of impartiality. This is what can be termed the capacity to access the sea of the tathāgatagarbha. "Accesses that access at nonaccess": since nonaccess is what is accessed by the mind that gains access, the agent and object of access are uniform and are indistinguishable; hence, it says "nonaccess." Although they are not different or distinguished, they are, however, not one; hence, from the standpoint of the mind that contemplates, it is provisionally called "the mind that gains access." In this wise, the mind that gains access does not preserve this characteristic of gaining access; hence, one "accesses that access at nonaccess."

> The elder Pŏmhaeng asked: "This is inconceivable! Accessing the tathāgatagarbha has no access point; it is like a sprout that matures into a fruit. Through the power of the fundamental inspiration, that inspiration will bring about the recovery of the original [edge of reality]. In attaining that original edge of reality, how many kinds of knowledge would one have?"

From here onward is the second [subsection, II.B], distinctions in the knowledge gained through accessing [the tathāgatagarbha].

Initially [II.B.1], there is a question;
subsequently [II.B.2], an answer.

In the question [part, II.B.1], there are two [subparts]:

initially [II.B.1.a], comprehension of the preceding sermon;
subsequently [II.B.1.b], a question concerning his doubt [viz. "In attaining that original edge of reality, how many kinds of knowledge would one have?"]

[In subpart II.B.1.a, comprehension of the preceding sermon:] "It is like a sprout that matures into a fruit": just as when a sprout matures into an ear of grain, there is no thing that is the agent of access and no place that is the object of access [i.e., there is nothing that causes the seed to sprout and no viable way of explaining how the sprouting of a seed can lead to an ear of grain]. You should know it is just the same with "accessing the tathāgatagarbha." "Sprout" is a simile for the inspiration of original [enlightenment]. "Fruit" is a simile for attaining that original [enlightenment]. At the time one gains access, [the essence and function of original enlightenment] are in equilibrium, for there is no place that is the object of access.

> The Buddha replied: "His knowledge would be unfathomable. Explaining it briefly, he has four types of knowledge. What are the four? First is decisive knowledge: that is, [knowledge that] accords with thusness. Second is adaptable knowledge: that is, [knowledge that], through expedients, neutralizes and rebuts [concepts]. Third is nirvāṇa knowledge: that is, [knowledge that] removes lightning[-like] sensory awareness. Fourth is ultimate knowledge: that is, **[661b]** [knowledge that] accesses reality and perfects the path.
>
> "Elder! In this wise, the operation of these four great matters has been explained by all the buddhas of antiquity as being a great bridge

> and a great ford. If you are to proselyte sentient beings, you should make use of these knowledges."

This is the second [part, II.B.2], the answer, which is in three [subparts]:

[II.B.2.a] a general overview;
[II.B.2.b] a specific explication;
[II.B.2.c] a comprehensive clarification.

In the general overview [II.B.2.a], the statement "**his knowledge would be unfathomable**" means that, because his penetration is limitless, his knowledge also would be unfathomable. It is merely in terms of their respective range of meanings that [these knowledges] are explained both comprehensively and briefly as having just four types.

In the specific explication [II.B.2.b], the term "**decisive knowledge**" means impartial wisdom *(samatājñāna)*. Because it involves direct perception alone and makes no use of expedients, it is called "**decisive knowledge.**" [This type of knowledge] counteracts the *mano[vijñāna]* and the clinging to "I" and "mine," and regardless of whatever it perceives, it remains impartial; therefore, it says that it is "**[knowledge that] accords with thusness.**"

"**Adaptable knowledge**" is the wisdom of marvelous observation *(pratyavekṣanājñāna)*. At the level of the sixth consciousness [viz. mentality], it generates progress by applying expedients; therefore, it is called "**adaptable.**" On the path of applying expedients, it thoroughly pursues ways to neutralize and rebut concepts and phenomena; therefore, it says "**neutralizes and rebuts.**" This knowledge in reality incorporates both expedient [contemplation] and direct contemplation [perception]; but, because it is distinguished from decisive knowledge, it is referred to summarily as involving "**expedients.**"

"**Nirvāṇa knowledge**" is the wisdom of having accomplished what was to be done *(kṛtyānuṣṭānajñāna)*. By being able to make manifest the eight episodes [the stereotypical events in the life of a buddha],[308] one masters the tasks of the buddhas and demonstrates the final sign [of passing into parinirvāṇa]; this is called "**nirvāṇa knowledge.**" Bringing an end to the five sensory consciousnesses produces this type of knowledge; for this reason, it is called "**[knowledge that] removes lightning[-like] sensory awareness.**" "**Lightning[-like] sensory awareness**" refers to the five consciousnesses, which abruptly arise and abruptly vanish, like flashes of lightning.

"**Ultimate knowledge**" is the great perfect mirror wisdom *(ādarśanajñāna)* because it is only at that ultimate level that one achieves this knowledge. Since there are no realms it is unable to fathom, it accesses the one real meaning. Therefore it is called "**[knowledge that] accesses reality.**" Since there are no realms that it is unable to make manifest, it is called "**[knowledge that] perfects the path.**"

In the comprehensive clarification [II.B.2.c], "**the operation of these four**

great matters" means that there are no operations that have not been completed. "**[This] has been explained by all the buddhas of antiquity**" means that it has been identical in all the buddhas' dispensations. They are a "**great bridge**" because these four wisdoms convey three-vehicle adherents across to the other shore of the one vehicle. **[661c]** They are a "**great ford**" because the operation of these four wisdoms pervades all the six destinies and reveals that transcendental path which crosses over the river of craving. For this reason, one who seeks "**to proselyte . . . should make use of these knowledges.**"

> "Elder! Their functions are great functions. These, furthermore, involve three great matters. First, in the three samādhis (p. 662a below), the internal and the external do not mutually encroach[309] on one another. Second, in the great object matrix (p. 662b below), the analytical suppression *(pratisaṃkhyānirodha)* occurs in accordance with the path. Third, in the wisdom and concentration that are thus, these are both inspired by compassion. In this wise, these three matters perfect bodhi. One who does not practice these matters will then be unable to flow into the sea of the four knowledges and will be subject to the whims of all the great *māras*.
>
> "Elder! Until all of you in the congregation attain buddhahood, you ought constantly to cultivate and train, without even a temporary respite."

From here onward is the third [subsection, II.C], the operation and functioning of the causes that bring about access [to the tathāgatagarbha], which is in two [parts]:

[II.C.1] a prose explanation;
[II.C.2] reiterative verses.

In the first [part, II.C.1], there are three [subparts]:

[II.C.1.a] a concise clarification;
[II.C.1.b] a repeated elucidation [II.C.1.b];
three [II.C.1.c], gaining comprehension.

The initial[subpart, II.C.1.a,] is in four [divisions]:

one [II.C.1.a.i], a general overview;
two [II.C.1.a.ii], specific understanding;
three [II.C.1.a.iii], a synthetic clarification;
four [II.C.1.a.iv], a concluding inducement.

In the general overview [II.C.1.a.i], the statement "**their functions are great functions**" refers to the great functioning of the four knowledges, as explained previously (p. 661b above). These are positioned [at stages ranging] from the bhūmis through the fruition of buddhahood.

[II.C.1.a.ii, specific understanding:] **"[These,] furthermore, involve three great matters"**: there are three [matters] that serve as catalysts that perfect the four wisdoms. For one who practices these three matters on the four levels of the path that precede the bhūmis [viz. the ten faiths, ten abidings, ten transferences, and ten practices], the initial concentration, the succeeding wisdom, and the third joint practice of concentration and wisdom all have compassion as their essence. The initial reference to "concentration" here means **"the three samādhis."** There are several different lists of these [three samādhis], which offer varying explanations from a variety of standpoints, including voidness *(śūnya)*, signlessness *(ānimitta)*, and wishlessness *(apraṇihita)*; wishlessness, signlessness, and the voidness of voidness *(śūnyaśūnyatā)*; or voidness, wishlessness, and signlessness. These [three samādhis] can be established as is appropriate, without any hindrances or obstructions. They may be termed the three [gates to] liberation *(vimokṣadvāra)*, because they exist only where there are no contaminants. They may also be termed **"the three samādhis," [662a]** because they also incorporate that which involves the contaminants. Each of their specific meanings will be explained in the following passage.

[II.C.1.a.iii, a synthetic clarification:] **"The internal and the external do not mutually encroach on one another"** means that the internal consciousnesses and the external sense-realms make each other manifest and create clinging to the favorable and the unfavorable, both encroaching on [lit. snatching away] all the wholesome faculties. Now, penetrating to the fact that all is voidness, such encroachment will no longer be allowed to occur. **"In the great object matrix, the analytical suppression *(pratisaṃkhyānirodha)* occurs in accordance with the path"** means that one analyzes the four great elements [viz. earth, air, fire, water] and the three main classifications of dharmas [viz. skandha, *dhātu*, and *āyatana*] in accordance with the principle, eradicating all signs and bringing to an end the seeds of conceptual proliferation *(prapañca)* inherent in the foundational consciousness [viz. the *ālayavijñāna*]. The preceding three samādhis overcome the snares *(paryavasthāna)*[310] that have currently appeared; this wisdom that derives from analysis eradicates their seeds. Because of this, at the time that one accordingly perfects the four wisdoms, one can dig up the seeds and transmute the eight consciousnesses [into the ninth immaculate consciousness]. **"In the wisdom and concentration that are thus, these are both inspired by compassion"**: the preceding wisdom and concentration both accord with the principle of thusness; therefore, [the text] refers to **"the wisdom and concentration that are thus."** This [matter] is also associated with the cultivation of great compassion, which inspires both oneself and others; therefore, it says **"these are both inspired."** This is because, if one cultivates samādhi and wisdom directly but is devoid of great compassion, one will fall into the stage of two-vehicle adherents and find the bodhisattva path blocked. And were one merely to give rise to compassion but not cultivate samādhi and wisdom, one would fall into the distress that ordinary people face, which is not the bodhisattva path. Therefore, cultivating these three matters allows one to remain far removed from these two extremes, to cultivate the bodhisattva path, and to perfect supreme enlightenment. Therefore, it says, "**In this wise, these three matters perfect bodhi.**" If one does not practice together all three of these matters, one inevitably will linger in birth and death (saṃsāra) and be attached to nirvāṇa; one "**will then be unable to flow into the great sea of the four knowledges and will be subject to the whims of the four *māras*.**" This has been the synthetic clarification [II.C.1.a.iii].

Following is the fourth gateway [II.C.1.a.iv], the inducement to cultivate [viz. "**Elder! Until all of you in the congregation attain buddhahood, you ought constantly to cultivate and train, without even a temporary respite**"].

> **The elder Pŏmhaeng asked, "What are the three samādhis?"**
>
> **The Buddha replied: "The three samādhis are the samādhi of voidness *(śūnyasamādhi)*, the samādhi of wishlessness *(apraṇihitasamādhi)*, and the samādhi of signlessness *(ānimittasamādhi)*.[311] These are the samādhis."**

This is the second [subpart, II.C.1.b], a repeated elucidation. It involves two exchanges, which elucidate the first two of the three gateways [viz. the first two of the three matters listed in subsection II.C (p. 661c above)]. **[662b]**

This [passage] elucidates the first gateway [of the three samādhis, II. C.1.b.i]. The differences among these three [samādhis] can briefly be described in terms of three categories: (1) essence, function, and characteristics; (2) mind, cause, and fruition; (3) consciousness, sensory awareness, and [external] characteristic. [One,] essence, function, and characteristics: None of the ordinary dharmas involve anything other than these three. Because the essence of dharmas is void, we establish the samādhi of voidness. Because they involve no active functioning, they are the samādhi of wishlessness. Because they have no characteristics or attributes, they are the samādhi of signlessness. [Two,] mind, cause, and fruition: The arising of cause and fruition proliferates the activities of mind. Because the activities of mind are void, we establish the samādhi of voidness. Because all causes are nonexistent, we establish the samādhi of wishlessness. Because all fruitions are unascertainable, we establish the samādhi of signlessness. [Three,] consciousness, sensory awareness, and [external] characteristic: Because the own-essences of all the consciousnesses are void, we establish the samādhi of voidness. Because it abandons the aspect of sensory awareness, we establish the samādhi of wishlessness. Because it abandons the aspect of [external] characteristics, we establish the samādhi of signlessness.

This third gateway accords with the previous line "the internal and the external do not mutually encroach on one another."

> The elder Pŏmhaeng asked, "What is the great object matrix?"
>
> The Buddha replied: "'Great' means the four great elements. 'Object' means the aggregates (skandha), sense-elements *(dhātu),* sense-fields *(āyatana),* and so forth. 'Matrix' means the foundational consciousness. This is called the great object matrix."

This [passage] elucidates the second gateway [viz. the second matter, the great object matrix, II.C.1.b.ii]. The reason that "the four great elements" are established separately is in order to elucidate the elementary cultivation for neophytes, which initially investigates coarse sensory realms. This means that, among all dharmas, the dharmas of materiality are the coarsest. These include the physical body, and so forth, internally, and the mountains, rivers, and so forth, externally. One observes that these sorts of dharmas are not separate from the four great elements. One [also] observes that all these four great elements are unascertainable, because regardless of the direction in which one looks, they all are unformed. After finishing this sort of general investigation, one moves on to observe the subtler "object" [of materiality], which means the aggregates (skandha), sense-elements *(dhātu),* and sense-fields *(āyatana).*" These involve brief, extensive, and average listings. "Brief" means to observe the five [skandhas]. "Extensive" means to observe the eighteen *[dhātu].* Averaging the brief and extensive [listings] means to observe the twelve *[āyatana].* One observes that all of these are unascertainable. The next words "and so forth" refer to other dharma lists, such as the twelvefold chain of conditioned generation, and so forth. In this wise, because of the power of analytical observation **[662c]** and investigation, one immediately obliterates the beginningless seeds of conceptual proliferation and conceptualization that are inherent in the foundational consciousness. At the inception [of this type of practice], these are obliterated, which culminates in the absorption of suppression. Therefore, it said previously, "The analytical suppression *(pratisaṃkhyānirodha)* occurs in accordance with the path" (p. 661c).

> The elder Pŏmhaeng said: "It is inconceivable! In this wise, the knowledges and matters inspire both oneself and others, transcend the lands of the three realms of existence, do not linger in nirvāṇa, and access the bodhisattva path.
>
> "These sorts of characteristics of dharmas are dharmas that are subject to production and extinction, because they involve discrimination. If one stays far removed from discrimination, these dharmas ought not to be subject to extinction."

This is the third [subpart, II.C.1.c], gaining comprehension, which is in two [divisions]:

initially [II.C.1.c.i], comprehension of contemplation practice;
subsequently [II.C.1.c.ii], understanding their experiential realms.

[II.C.1.c.i: comprehension of contemplation practice:] "In this wise, the knowledges and matters" means the functioning of the three types of matters that in this wise are able to perfect the four knowledges. "Inspire both oneself and others" means the preceding two types that inspire oneself [viz. concentration and wisdom] and the third type that inspires other people [viz. great compassion]. "Transcend the lands of the three realms of existence" refers to the preceding two [stages] of concentration and wisdom, which are distinct from ordinary persons. "Do not linger in nirvāṇa" refers to the third [stage] of great compassion, which is distinct from two-vehicle adherents; by remaining far removed from these two extremes, one will "access the bodhisattva path."

From "these sorts" onward explains [division II.C.1.c.ii,] understanding their experiential realms. This means that at the realm of the initial stage of concentration, [one comes to know] the sensory perceptions and characteristics of all the consciousnesses, while at the next realm of knowledge, [one comes to know] the dharmas of the great object matrix. "These sorts of characteristics of dharmas are all dharmas that are subject to production and extinction": this is because the mind's sea is moved due to deceptive discrimination. From the standpoint of the original quiescence, "if one stays far removed from discrimination" there will no longer be any causes, so whence would production and extinction arise? For this reason, it says, "These dharmas ought not to be subject to extinction."

Wishing to proclaim this idea, the Tathāgata then recited this gāthā:
Dharmas are produced by discrimination,
And in turn are extinguished owing to discrimination,
Extinguish all dharmas that are subject to discrimination,
And those dharmas will be neither produced nor extinguished.

From here onward is the second [part, II.C.2], reiterative verses in gāthās, which is in two [subparts]:

one [II.C.2.a], a brief pronouncement by the Tathāgata;
two [II.C.2.b], an extensive disquisition [in verses] by the elder.

[II.C.2.a: a brief pronouncement by the Tathāgata:] Now, in this verse, **[663a]** the word "dharmas" means the dharma of the one mind, for if there is deceptive discrimination, the mind's sea will begin to move. There is not a single characteristic that, whether produced or extinguished, is not created from discrimination. From the standpoint of the original quiescence of original enlightenment, if one stays far removed from all discrimination, then these dharmas will be neither produced nor extinguished. This means that through the original extinction of all types of discrimination, there will be no causes that give rise either to production or extinction, and therefore "[those dharmas] will be neither produced nor extinguished." If production and extinction both come to be created through discrimination, how will this be reconciled with the explanation given in the Yogācāra school? As the "Bhūmi on Being Perfected by Thought" [in the *Yogācārabhūmi-śāstra*] explains, "There is no function [whereby dharmas] extinguish any other thing; and no function [whereby dharmas] are self-extinguished."[312]

Question: Just as things are produced through the amalgamation of many conditions, would not they also be extinguished through an amalgamation of many conditions?

Answer: Things are produced through the amalgamation of many conditions, but after being produced, they are naturally extinguished.

How do we reconcile this contradiction?

Explanation: The principle of causes and conditions is as explained in that śāstra. The principle of consciousness-only is as explained in this sūtra. Therefore these two explanations both involve correct principles.

At that time, the elder Pŏmhaeng heard the recitation of this gāthā, and his mind was jubilant and elated. Wishing to proclaim its meaning, he recited gāthās:

> **All dharmas are originally calm and extinguished,**
> **But this calm extinction is also unproduced,**
> **All those dharmas that are subject to production and extinction,**
> **Those dharmas are not unproduced.**
> **Those are thence not associated with these,**
> **Because each is subject to either annihilationism or eternalism,**
> **This [verse spoken by the Buddha above] thence leaves behind all such dualities,**
> **But it also does not persist in lingering in oneness.**

From this point on is [subpart II.C.2.b], an extensive [disquisition in] verses by the elder. There are eight quatrains of gāthās in five divisions.

one [II.C.2.b.i], the first two quatrains, which are an explicit disquisition on the preceding aspect;
two [II.C.2.b.ii], the next two verses, which eliminate all types of perverse understanding;
three [II.C.2.b.iii], one verse that personally declares the right type of grasping;
four [II.C.2.b.iv], two verses that honor those who preach appropriately;
five [II.C.2.b.v], one [verse] that invites [the Buddha] to speak what has not been heard before.

This [passage] is the first [division, II.C.2.b.i], an explicit disquisition on the preceding verses [*sic;* aspect]. It is in three [subdivisions]: **[663b]**

one [II.C.2.b.i.a], two lines that explain that last half [of the above discussion];
two [II.C.2.b.i.b], two lines the explain the first half;
three [II.C.2.b.i.c], one verse that provides a comprehensive disquisition on both aspects.

In the initial [subdivision, II.C.2.b.i.a], the line "all dharmas are originally calm and extinguished" means that the dharmas of the skandhas, *dhātus*, and so forth, are originally calm and extinct. "But this calm extinction is also unproduced" means that it is not just all dharmas that are originally calm and extinct, for this principle of calm extinction is also unproduced.

In the second [subdivision, II.C.2.b.i.b], the statement "all those dharmas that are subject to production and extinction" refer to the worldly, mundane dharmas of the skandhas, *dhātus*, and so forth. "Those dharmas are not unproduced" means that they come into existence through the activity of discrimination. This [line] elucidates, from the standpoint of the approach that absolute and conventional [truths] are not one, the aspect that activity and rest are not to be confused indiscriminately.

In the third [subdivision, II.C.2.b.i.c], the statement "those are thence not associated with these" means that those dharmas that are calm, extinct, and unproduced are not associated with these dharmas that are subject to production and extinction. "Because each is subject to either annihilationism or eternalism" means that, if "those" exist in tandem with "these," then "these" dharmas that are subject to production and extinction would thence be subject to annihilationism and "those" dharmas that are constantly calm and extinct would thence be subject to eternalism. Since it violates the middle way, this is the same mistake made by two-vehicle adherents. Nevertheless, because the idea explained by the Buddha in his single gāthā [above] does not fall into either annihilationism or eternalism, "this thence leaves behind all such dualities"; but because it is not devoid of both activity and rest, "it also does not persist in lingering in oneness." "It . . . does not persist in lingering in oneness" means that it does not guard the nature of the one mind, the one reality. That it "leaves behind all such dualities" refers to the fact that the essence's activity and rest are not dualistic dharmas. You therefore should know that this matter is inconceivable.

If it is said that dharmas are one,
This characteristic will be like a hairnet,[313]
It is like mistaking heat waves for water,
This is because all [such conceptions] are false and deceptive.[314]
If you perceive the nonexistence of dharmas,

Those dharmas will be identical to voidness,
Just like a blind man who mistakenly believes that the sun is nonexistent,
Your preaching of the dharma would be as [deceptive as] the [nonexistent] hair of a tortoise.

This is the second [division of the verses, II.C.2.b.ii], which eliminates all types of perverse understanding. Although perverse understandings may be many, there are two types that are the worst, for in relying on the most profound of teachings and clinging literally to their meaning, they claim that these are the ultimate. **[663c]** Therefore, these are the most difficult to correct. The first is, having heard the Buddha's explanation that activity and rest are nondual, someone then claims that they are one—that is, they are the one mind that is the one reality—and, accordingly, he slanderously repudiates the principle of the two truths. The second is, having heard the Buddha's explanation that voidness involves two aspects, someone presumes that they do not involve one reality but instead are dualistic dharmas, and, accordingly, he slanderously repudiates the principle of the middle way of nonduality. These two types of perverse understanding are like ingesting a medicine that instead ends up making you ill: they are extremely difficult to cure. [The elder Pŏmnang] now exposes these faults and, in these two verses, systematically elucidates them.

In the opening [verse], "if it is said that dharmas are one": as explained above, this statement means that one presumes there is a single reality and, based on this presumption, advocates that there is but a single dharma. "This characteristic will be like a hairnet" means that the characteristic of that one real dharma which is presumed to exist is like a hairnet seen by someone suffering from conjunctivitis [i.e., blurred vision]. "It is like mistaking heat waves for water": just as a thirsty deer sees heat waves and, thinking there is water, bounds over to find it but is completely confused and mistaken, so too is it the same with presuming there is one mind. "This is because all [such conceptions] are false and deceptive": whether it is a thirsty deer seeing "water," a person suffering from conjunctivitis seeing a "[hair]net," or an exegete presuming there is but "one" [mind], all these sorts of presumptions are equally deceptive and false.

Next, he eliminates the view of nonexistence. "If you perceive the nonexistence of dharmas": as explained above, this means to presume that there are two truths but not the dharma of the one mind. "Those dharmas will be identical to voidness": this means that one presumes that the one mind is identical to the principle of voidness, for apart from the principle of voidness there originally is no other single reality. "Just like a blind man who mistakenly believes that the sun is nonexistent" means that he is like a poor, destitute beggar who is congenitally blind and has never seen the effulgence of the orb of the sun: the sighted may refer to the sun, but the blind man will not believe a sun can exist, for he is utterly deluded. One who posits [that the one mind is nonexistent] will be just the same: since he originally learned only about voidness and existence and has never heard of the middle way of nonduality, even were it to be explained to him, he would never believe or accept it. Accordingly, the orb of the sun is a simile **[664a]** for the middle way: the sun's orb is perfectly round and emits great effulgence; except for the blind, there is no one who cannot see it. The one mind is also just the same: it is completely perfect and flawless, and radiates with the great effulgence of original and acquired enlightenments; except for the incredulous, there is no one who cannot access it. "**Your preaching of the dharma would be as [deceptive as] the [nonexistent] hair of a tortoise**": the person who clings to the view of nonexistence explains that the dharma of the one mind refers only to that which has no essence, like the hair of a tortoise; he is no different from a blind person who says that the orb of the sun is nonexistent.

> **I have now heard the Buddha say,**
> **Knowledge of the dharma is not [perceived through] dualistic views,**
> **It also does not depend on remaining in between,**
> **It therefore is grasped by not abiding anywhere.**

This is the third [division, II.C.2.b.iii], where he personally declares the correct type of grasping. "**Knowledge of the dharma is not [perceived through] dualistic views**" means he knows the dharma of the middle way is not perceived through understanding existence or nonexistence. This is leaving behind the second misconception, that the sun does not exist. "**It also does not depend on remaining in between**": although one leaves behind the two extremes, one does not linger on, guarding the one reality of the middle way. This is leaving behind the first delusion, of [misperceiving] a hairnet or water. Because one, in this wise, leaves behind the errors of both these extremes, one is able to comprehend the import of the referent "nonabiding" through the reference made to "nonabiding" in the Buddha's teachings. Thus, it says, "**It therefore is grasped by not abiding anywhere.**"

> **The dharma spoken by the tathāgatas,**
> **Derives completely from this nonabiding,**
> **It is from that nonabiding place,**
> **That I worship the tathāgatas.**
> **Respectfully worshiping the characteristic of the tathāgatas—**
> **That motionless wisdom which is equal to empty space,**
> **At that place which is free from grasping and which does not exist,**
> **I respectfully worship their nonabiding bodies.**

This is the fourth [division, II.C.2.b.iv], honoring the preachers. It is in three [subdivisions]:

one [II.C.2.b.iv.a], one verse honoring the preachers;
two [II.C.2.b.iv.b], two lines honoring the knowledge of the preachers;
three [II.C.2.b.iv.c], two lines honoring the bodies of the preachers.

In the first [subdivision, II.C.2.b.iv.a, honoring the preachers], the statement "The dharma spoken by the tathāgatas,/Derives completely from this nonabiding" means that the dharma of the Buddha's teachings are derived in accordance with nonabiding. "It is from that nonabiding place,/That I worship the tathāgatas" **[664b]** means that, at this nonabiding place which is derived from relying on these teachings, one knows still further that the tathāgatas are the most worthy of honor and respect; therefore, at that place one worships the preachers. In this [passage], the term "nonabiding" means not abiding in the two truths, but also not lingering in between. While not lingering in between, one leaves behind the two extremes; in this wise, it comes to be called the "nonabiding place."

In the second [subdivision, II.C.2.b.iv.b, honoring the knowledge of the preachers], concerning the statement "the characteristic of the tathāgatas": we do not consider the [thirty-two] major and [eighty] minor characteristics [of the buddhas' bodies] to be "the characteristic of the tathāgatas." Rather, the "motionless wisdom" is the characteristic of the tathāgatas. The statement "equal to empty space" means that the knowledge of the tathāgatas is immeasurable and limitless and, like the realm of empty space, there is no place it does not pervade. The word "motionless" means that it universally penetrates all the three time periods without limitation; though there may be an ebb and flow of those time periods, the functioning of that knowledge is unchanging.

In the third [subdivision, II.C.2.b.iv.c, honoring the bodies of the preachers], the statement "free from grasping" means that the dharmakāya leaves behind the two extremes. "At that place which . . . does not exist" means that it does not abide in between. Therefore it says, "I respectfully worship their nonabiding bodies."

I, in all places,
Constantly see all the tathāgatas,
I wish only that all the tathāgatas,
Will explain the perpetual dharma to me.

This is the fifth [division, II.C.2.b.v], asking [the Buddha to speak] what has not been heard before. In this [division], the first half is a personal declaration regarding his constant companions [viz. the buddhas]; in the following two lines he requests that [the Buddha] explain the perpetual dharma. As for the idea behind a personal declaration: because I leave behind all extremes and gain that knowledge of nonabiding, I am able in each and every dust mote to perceive perpetually all the numberless buddhas of the ten directions; and, in all the dust motes of the world systems of the ten directions, there is no place where I do not perceive numberless buddhas. Therefore, it says, "[I,] in all places,/Constantly see all the tathāgatas." As the *Avataṃsaka-sūtra* says,

> In a single dust mote,
> I see buddhas without number everywhere.
> And just as with that one dust mote,
> So too is it the same with all dust motes.[315]

Since he has this sort of power, he is worthy of hearing the perpetual dharma. Therefore, he wishes to hear [the Buddha] "explain the perpetual dharma."

> At that time the Tathāgata made this statement: "All you good men! [664c] Listen well and I will explain for all of you the perpetual dharma."

From here onward is the fourth [subsection, II.D], the perpetual dharma, which is the fruition gained through access *[sic]*.[316] It is in three [parts]:

one [II.D.1], the Tathāgata's explanation;
two [II.D.2], the elder's disquisition;
three [II.D.3], the congregation gaining benefit.

In the first [part], there are two [subparts]:

[II.D.1.a] consent to speak;
[II.D.1.b] an explicit explanation.

This [passage] is the consent to speak.

> "Oh son of good family! The perpetual dharma is not a perpetual dharma; it is neither the spoken nor the written word; it is neither truth nor liberation. It is neither nonexistence nor the [sense-] realms and remains far removed from the limits of deception and annihilationism. But this dharma is also not impermanent, for it remains far removed from either eternalism or annihilationism. [At the moment of] cognition, the consciousnesses are permanent. These consciousnesses are perpetually calm and extinct; but that calm extinction is also calm and extinct.

From here onward is the second [subpart, II.D.1.b], the direct explanation. It is in two [divisions]:

initially [II.D.1.b.i], an explanation of "perpetual" from the standpoint of fruition;
subsequently [II.D.1.b.ii], a revelation of "perpetual" from the standpoint of cause.

The initial [division, II.D.1.b.i,] is in two [subdivisions]:

the perpetuity of the dharma [II.D.1.b.i.a];
the perpetuity of the buddhas [II.D.1.b.i.b].

As for this first [subdivision, II.D.1.b.i.a, the perpetuity of the dharma], the statement "**the perpetual dharma is not a perpetual dharma**" means that the essence of the dharmakāya, which is the teacher of the buddhas, remains far removed from the characteristics of production and extinction; therefore, it is called the "**perpetual dharma.**" But because it remains far removed from that nature of constant abiding, it "**is not a perpetual dharma.**" "**It is neither the spoken nor the written word**" means that it neutralizes all terms of reference. "**It is neither truth nor liberation**" means that it transcends the real meaning of those referents. "**It is neither nonexistence nor the [sense-] realms and remains far removed from the limits of deception and annihilationism**" means that it is not ultimately nonexistent, but also does not involve the sense-realms. Because it does not involve the sense-realms, it remains far removed from any experience that involves deceptive grasping; but because it is not nonexistent, it remains far removed from any experience of annihilationism. "**Limits**" is a synonym for "realm." "**But this dharma is also not impermanent, for it remains far removed from either eternalism or annihilationism**": because it is "**not impermanent,**" it leaves behind all annihilationist views. But because it is "**this dharma,**" it leaves behind all eternalist views; this is because "**this dharma**" is not something that can be grasped by eternalist views.

I have already clarified the perpetuity of the dharma; next [II.D.1.b.i.b], I elucidate the perpetuity of the buddhas. "**[At the moment of] cognition, the consciousnesses are permanent**" refers to the ultimate cognition of that perpetual dharma. At that moment of cognition, all "**the consciousnesses are permanent.**" This is because the mind of original quiescence may be moved initially in accordance with ignorance; but now, in accordance with that cognition, one returns to that original quiescence. "**These consciousnesses are perpetually [665a] calm and extinct**" means that all the consciousnesses are originally free from production or extinction; and because they are free from production and extinction, their natures are perpetually calm and extinct. Now, because at the moment of cognition one extinguishes forever the consciousnesses that in this wise are calm and extinct, it therefore says "**but that calm extinction is also calm and extinct.**" This is because those calm and extinct consciousnesses are these impermanent dharmas; and it is only after their extinction that one gains permanence. This idea will be elucidated in the following "Dhāraṇī" [Codes] chapter. Furthermore, this nature that is originally calm and extinct does not linger in constant abiding; therefore, it says "[that calm extinction] is also calm and extinct."

> "Oh son of good family! Since he who knows that dharmas are calm and extinct need not make his mind calm and extinct, his mind remains constantly calm and extinct. The mind of one who attains calm extinction constantly engages in absolute contemplation."

From here onward is the second [division, II.D.1.b.ii], which reveals "perpetual" as [from the standpoint of] cause. It is in two [subdivisions]:

a specific clarification [II.D.1.b.ii.a];
a comprehensive summation [II.D.1.b.ii.b].

The specific [clarification] is also in two [segments]:

initially [II.D.1.b.ii.a.1], contemplation from the standpoint of absolute realization;
subsequently [II.D.1.b.ii.a.2], contemplation according to expedients.

In this initial [segment, II.D.1.b.ii.a.1], the line "he who knows that dharmas are calm and extinct" means that adepts from the first bhūmi onward know that all dharmas are originally calm and extinct. Since they know [the dharmas] are not generated, they need not extinguish the mind. "Not extinguish the mind" means that [the mind] is "constantly calm and extinct." Because it is "constantly calm and extinct," it therefore elucidates that calm extinction which is the object of knowledge. "The mind of one who attains calm extinction constantly engages in absolute contemplation": this clarifies that the mind that is the agent of realization is constantly abiding and, in accordance with the principle that is realized, leaves far behind the characteristics of production and extinction but without ever neglecting the contemplation that illuminates the absolute.

> "He knows that all mentality and materiality are nothing but the ignorant mind. The discriminations of the ignorant mind differentiate all the dharmas; [all the dharmas] are nothing apart from name and materiality. If in this wise one knows dharmas and does not pursue written and spoken language, the mind will think only of meaning and will not distinguish a self."

This is the second [segment, II.D.1.b.ii.a.2], which clarifies contemplation according to expedients. It is in two [subsegments]:

initially [II.D.1.b.ii.a.2.a], a clarification that applied thought *(vitarka)* is consciousness-only;

subsequently [II.D.1.b.ii.a.2.b], an elucidation of the knowledge that accords with reality.

In the first [subsection, II.D.1.b.ii.a.2.a], in the line "**[all the dharmas] are nothing apart from name and materiality,**" "name" refers to the four [mental] skandhas and "materiality" refers to the skandha of materiality. All of the dissociated [dharmas] are established hypothetically and **[665b]** have no discrete essence apart from name and materiality. All compounded phenomena are constructed from name and materiality. In this wise, all dharmas are created by mind-alone: there are no objects apart from mind and no mind apart from objects. In this wise, "name" means the applied thought that is consciousness-only. As the *Avataṃsaka-sūtra* [Flower Garland Sūtra] says,

> The mind is like a painter,
> Who paints all aspects of the five skandhas.
> Throughout everything of this world,
> There are no dharmas it does not create.
> As it is with the mind, so too is it with the buddhas,
> As it is with the buddhas, so too is it the same with sentient beings,
> The mind, the buddhas, and sentient beings,
> These three are not differentiated.[317]

I have already clarified applied thought; next [II.D.1.b.ii.a.2.b], I elucidate the knowledge that accords with reality. "**If in this wise one knows dharmas and does not pursue written and spoken language**": this explains that the knowledge that accords with reality is realized through applied thought. "**The mind will think only of meaning and will not distinguish a self**": "meaning" here refers to the fact that the knowledge that accords with reality is realized through applied thought. Therefore the two types of selfhood—of person and of dharmas—are both meaningless. For this reason, one does "**not distinguish**" either of them.

> **"Knowing that the self is a hypothetical name is in fact the attainment of calm extinction. If one attains calm extinction, one then attains *anuttarasamyaksaṃbodhi*."**

This is the second [subdivision, II.D.1.b.ii.b], a comprehensive summation. The preceding two [segments] achieved the contemplation of the absolute by consummating the preceding [contemplation according to] expedients [viz. segment II.D.1.b.ii.a.2] and, moreover, achieved the fruition of bodhi by consummating the contemplation of the absolute [viz. segment II.D.1.b.ii.a.1].

Once the elder Pŏmhaeng had heard this speech, he recited gāthās:
Nominal characteristics and discriminative phenomena,
Together with dharmas—these are called the three,
True thusness and right and sublime knowledge:
Together with those make five.[318]
I now know that these dharmas,
Are fettered by annihilationism and eternalism,
And access the path of production and extinction,
This is annihilationism, not eternalism.

The dharmas of voidness spoken by the Tathāgata,
Remain far removed from annihilationism and eternalism.

From this point on is the second [part, II.D.2], the elder's disquisition, which contains eight verses that convey three ideas.

The first two and a half verses [II.D.2.a] analyze the idea of the buddha's teaching.

Next, there are five verses [II.D.2.b] that break down the grasping at the two extremes.

The final two lines [II.D.2.c] also involve this contemplation of nonduality. **[665c]**

In this first [set of verses, II.D.2.a]:

the first two verses [II.D.2.a.i] describe a teaching that falls into the two extremes;
the last two lines [II.D.2.a.ii] elucidate the teaching that leaves behind these two extremes.

In the first [subset, II.D.2.a.i], the term "**nominal characteristics**" refers to words *(nāmakāya)*, phrases *(padakāya)*, and syllables *(vyañjanakāya)*.[319] Phrases are formed from words, and syllables are the constituents of words. Since all of these factors make words manifest, together they are called "**nominal characteristics.**" "**Discriminative phenomena**" refer to all states of mind that are subject to the contaminants as well as to the dharmas and phenomena that are constituents of mind. The words "**together with dharmas**" mean all the characteristics of dharmas, apart from the previous two. These are all the referents of words and sentences and the products of discrimination. These refer to all the characteristics of dharmas, such as the ten constituents of materiality [the ten material sense-bases and sense-objects] and those [dharmas associated with mentality] among the list of dharmas, which are dissociated from materiality. These three are of a single type, which clarifies that they are all characteristics that involve miscellaneous types of maculations. For this reason they are explained separately and "**are called the three.**" "**True thusness**" refers to the object of right knowledge. "**Right and sublime knowledge**" refers to the two wisdoms, fundamental *(mūla)* and subsequently obtained *(pṛṣṭalabdhajñāna)*.[320] "Together with those": together with those previous three, these two and those three together make five matters. These refer to the characteristics of dharmas in the teachings of the three vehicles. "I now know that these dharmas,/Are fettered by annihilationism and eternalism": this clarifies that the five matters explained in those teachings inevitably involve the attachment to the two views of annihilationism and eternalism. The reason for this is that those four types of dharmas [all except "true thusness"] all entail the characteristics of production and extinction and thus inevitably involve the experience of attachment to the view of annihilationism; this dharma of true thusness has the nature of constant abiding and thus inevitably involves the experience of clinging to the view of eternalism. "And access the path of production and extinction,/This is annihilationism, not eternalism": the preceding three that were discussed separately as well as the right and sublime knowledge all involve the four [compounded] characteristics [of production, subsistence, decay, and extinction] that are part of the path of production and extinction; these directly involve the extreme of annihilation and are distinct from the extreme of eternalism. The elucidation of true thusness is part of the path of eternal existence; it directly involves the extreme of eternalism and is distinct from the extreme of annihilationism.

"The dharmas of voidness spoken by the Tathāgata,/Remain far removed from annihilationism and eternalism": this [half-verse, II.D.2.a.ii,] clarifies the teaching of the one vehicle. It explains that the three dharmas of voidness remain far removed from the errors of the two extremes of annihilationism and eternalism. The reason for this is, as explained previously (p. 639c), "the characteristic of voidness is also void; the voidness of voidness is also void; that which is voided is also void." In this wise, the three voidnesses neither **[666a]** obviate absolute and conventional nor preserve absolute and conventional. Although one leaves behind both activity and rest, one does not linger in between them, either. Therefore, they remain far removed from the extremes of annihilationism and eternalism.

Causal conditions are nonexistent and unproduced,
And because they are unproduced, they are not extinguished,[321]
Grasping at the existence of causal conditions,
Is like reaching for flowers in the sky,
Or expecting a barren woman's child—
Ultimately it is unascertainable.[322]

From here onward is the second [set of five verses, II.D.2.b], which breaks down the grasping at the two extremes. It is in two [divisions]:

first [II.D.2.b.i], four verses that break down the grasping at the extreme of existence;

second [II.D.2.b.ii], one verse that removes the attachment to the extreme of voidness.

The first [division] is in two [subdivisions]:

the preceding two and a half verses [II.D.2.b.i.a], which break down the attachment to existence;
the latter verse and a half [II.D.2.b.i.b], which reveals the true voidness.

This first [subdivision] is also in two [segments]:

the initial verse and a half [II.D.2.b.i.a.1], which breaks down the grasping at causal conditions *(hetupratyaya);*
the next verse [II.D.2.b.i.a.2], which breaks down the remaining three kinds of conditions.

In this first [segment, II.D.2.b.i.a.1], "**causal conditions are nonexistent and unproduced**" means that, whether identical or different, all the seeds present in the foundational consciousness, along with the fruition consciousness *(vipākavijñāna;* viz. the *ālayavijñāna)* itself, are all unascertainable. If they are "identical," then they are like things that ripen entirely on their own; if they are "different," then they are like a rabbit's horn. If they are neither identical nor different, they would also be nonexistent, like a "jar" or a "house," which have merely nominal reality. Owing to this principle, even though there is neither production nor extinction, a student who relies on the instructions and teachings of the three vehicles would grasp firmly at the notion that the seeds of causal conditioning exist in reality. Just like an idiot, he would be "**reaching for flowers in the sky**" or "**expecting a barren woman's child.**" It is the same with the causal condition: it is forever "**unascertainable.**" In this [passage], "**flowers in the sky**" are a simile for striving to eradicate maculated seeds. "**A barren woman's** son" is a simile for seeking to nurture pure seeds.

> **One leaves behind all clinging to causal conditions,**
> **But [one] also does not [presume that] it is because of anything else that extinction [occurs],**
> **Or [because of] the selfhood of the [threefold matrix of] meaning and the [four] great [elements],**
> **Because of relying on thusness one attains reality,**

This is [segment II.D.2.b.i.a.2,] breaking down the remaining three kinds of conditions. If one leaves behind all the seeds, that is, the causal condition, but clings to the remaining three types of conditions and presumes that production occurs because of them, then developing this sort of grasping would also not accord with the principle; as the sūtra says, "**But [one] also** does not [presume that] it is because of anything else that extinction [occurs]." "Anything else" here **[666b]** refers to the predominant condition *(adhipatipratyaya)* and the objective-support condition *(ālambanapratyaya).* It is just like the production of visual consciousness, which requires materiality to serve as the condition for the visual sense-base; but even when in this wise there is the coming together of the eye, materiality, and [visual] consciousness, there still is no nature of consciousness. Therefore, it is called "anything else." Even though the antecedent condition *(samanatarapratyaya)* shares this quality of consciousness, its essence has already been extinguished; therefore, it is called "extinction." Whether "anything else" or "extinction," [these three conditions] are all devoid of self-nature. Therefore the production of consciousness also does not derive from something else.[323]

As for the next line, "Or [because of] the selfhood of the [threefold matrix of] meaning and the [four] great [elements]": one moreover assumes that the dharmas of the skandhas, elements *(dhātu),* and so forth, all have their own essences that exist in the future but have not yet been produced in the present; and that they will be produced in the present thanks to this own essence. In order to counter this assumption, it therefore says, "But [it is] also not . . . [because of] the selfhood of the [threefold matrix of] meaning and the [four] great [elements]." The words "not . . . because of" in the preceding line continues into the latter line as well. As was explained above (p. 662b), "object" here refers to the [five] aggregates (skandhas), the [eighteen] elements *(dhātu),* and the [twelve] sense-fields *(āyatana);* and "great" refers to the four great elements. One assumes that these sorts of dharmas originally have their own self-essences and for this reason it refers to "the selfhood of the [threefold matrix of] meaning and the [four] great [elements]."

"Because of relying on thusness one attains reality" means that, were I one who was able to break down the grasping at all types of existence, it is because this destruction occurred by relying on the principle of thusness that one attains the aspect of reality.

> For this reason, the dharma of true thusness,
> Is constantly autonomous and thus;
> All the myriads of dharmas,
> Are transformations of those consciousnesses that are not thus.
> That dharma which remains separate from consciousness is void,
> Hence it is explained from the standpoint of voidness.

This is the second [subdivision, II.D.2.b.i.b, the latter verse and a half], which reveals the dharma of true voidness. As for the words "for this reason": this preceding grasping at existence is all illusory and deceptive; and for this reason that which serves as the agent of its annihilation is what achieves the real. Since true thusness is motionless, deceptive dharmas are not created. "Transformations of those consciousnesses": [all dharmas] are the suppositions of consciousness, and that characteristic of supposition is, in principle, unascertainable but derives directly from affective existence. Therefore it says that [all dharmas are] "**transformations.**" Because "**all . . . dharmas,/Are transformations of those consciousnesses that are not thus,**" that **dharma which remains separate from consciousnesses is void** and unascertainable. Therefore I [Elder Pomhaeng] **explain** thusness **from the standpoint of voidness. [666c]**

> One who extinguishes all those dharmas that are subject to production and extinction,
> And thence dwells in nirvāṇa,
> He will be snatched away by the great compassion [of the buddhas],
> So that nirvāṇa is extinguished and he will not linger there.

[This is the second division (II.D.2.b.ii), one verse that removes the attachment to the extreme of voidness.] The passage above has already broken down the ordinary person's grasping at existence. This verse also counters the tendency of two-vehicle adherents to linger in voidness. This means that followers of the two vehicles access extinction through the dharma of the production and extinction of the body of cognition. Lingering therein for eighty thousand kalpas or even for ten thousand-fold kalpas, they are snatched away from that nirvāṇa owing to the great compassion that is identical in all the buddhas and are prompted instead to arouse the thought [of enlightenment]. At the very time they arouse that thought, nirvāṇa is extinguished. It is just like a great merchant, who extinguishes that conjured city and does not linger therein ever again.[324] When that state of mind no longer exists, there is no need for any explicit annihilation [of clinging]. This explicitly elucidates the fact that all the buddhas negate that nirvāṇa, neutralizing thereby that person's presumption that he has not yet accessed [nirvāṇa]. With the above is completed the breaking down of the two extremes of existence and nonexistence.

> Transmuting *(parivṛtti)* both the subject and object of clinging [mind and sensory objects],
> He accesses the tathāgatagarbha.

This is the third [subpart, II.D.2.c], which reveals the contemplation of nonduality. He has already broken down the grasping at the two extremes of ordinary persons and saints. Now he transmutes those two congregations of ordinary persons and saints, and prompts them to access that contemplation in which subject and object are uniform. The preceding eight verses have been the disquisition of the elder [II.D.2].

> At that time the great assembly heard this meaning and all attained right vocation *(samyagājīva)* and accessed the tathāgatas and the sea of the tathāgatagarbha.

This is the third [part, II.D.3], the congregation gaining benefit. **"Attained right vocation"**: leaving behind the extremes of existence and nonexistence, they gained the middle way's livelihood of right wisdom. **"Accessed the tathāgatas"** means that they have already accessed a share of the tathāgatas' knowledge. **"Accessed . . . the sea of the tathāgatagarbha"** means that they have accessed the profound and vast aspect of the original enlightenment.

[Part Four: An Exegesis of the Text (cont.)]

VAJRASAMĀDHI-SŪTRA, CHAPTER EIGHT: DHĀRAṆĪ [CODES]

In this [chapter] are resolved all the doubts remaining from the previous chapters. It comprehensively encodes *(dhārayati)* their important meanings, without **[667a]** forgetting them; this is why [this chapter] is titled "Dhāraṇī." Moreover, because Chijang (Earth-Store; Skt. Kṣitigarbha) Bodhisattva had already attained the dhāraṇī that encodes both text *(grantha)* and meaning *(artha)*, he comprehensively encodes the meaning of all the passages in the preceding chapters and recalls the points on which the congregation had doubts. Next, he asks questions in order to resolve skillfully all those doubts. Because of his ability to pose these questions, [this chapter] is titled "Dhāraṇī."[325]

Section Three (A): Dhāraṇī [Codes] and Section Three (B): Dissemination

> At that time, Chijang (Earth-Store; Kṣitigarbha) Bodhisattva arose from amid the congregation and came before the Buddha. Joining his palms together and genuflecting in foreign fashion, he addressed the Buddha: "Lord! I observe that the congregation entertains doubts that have yet to be resolved. The Tathāgata is now about to dispel those doubts. I will now ask questions on behalf of this congregation concerning the doubts that remain; I beg that the Tathāgata, out of his friendliness and compassion, will take pity on us and grant this request."
>
> The Buddha replied: "Bodhisattva-*mahāsattva*! That you are interested in rescuing sentient beings shows that your great compassion and empathy is inconceivable. You should question me extensively, and I will answer you."

In the main body [of the exegesis], there were two major sections [*sic;* "three" at p. 607b]. The sequential clarification of contemplation practice [section 2; viz. *VS*, chapters 2–7] ended with the previous [chapter]. From here onward is the second section [section 3 (A, B), viz. *VS*, chapter 8], which completely resolves all remaining doubts.

There are four [sections] in this chapter:

Initially [I], a request;
Next [II], consent;
Three [III], resolution;
Four [IV], comprehension.

This exchange represents the request and consent [sections I, II].

[Section I:] The questioner here is named **Chijang [Earth-Store]**, because this person attains the great compassion that comes from viewing himself as being identical in essence with all others and because he matures the wholesome faculties of all sentient beings, just as the great "**earth**" *(chi)* nurtures all plants and trees. He retains all meritorious qualities through dhāraṇīs, and though he generously offers them to everyone, they are never exhausted, just as the precious gems in a great "**store**" *(-jang)* of jewels are inexhaustible. Because of these two aspects, he is called "**Earth-Store**" (**Chijang**). Now, in this chapter, he resolves all his remaining doubts and confusions and produces resolute faith and understanding *(śraddhādhimukti),* exposing the jewels of resolution and offering them to the congregation that is seeking the dharma. Because these aspects correspond to his name, [Chijang] is therefore called upon to serve as the interlocutor.

Section Three (A): Completely Resolving All Remaining Doubts

> Chijang Bodhisattva asked, "How is it that all dharmas are not conditionally produced?" **[667b]**
>
> Wishing to proclaim this meaning, the Tathāgata then recited a gāthā:
>
> If dharmas are produced by conditions,
> Then no dharmas could exist apart from conditions.
> How is it that conditions can produce dharmas,
> When the dharma-nature is nonexistent?

From here onward is the third [section, III], an explicit resolution of all remaining doubts. It is in two [subsections]:

one [III.A], six doubts remaining from the six chapters, which are resolved in contrary order;
two [III.B], three doubts remaining from one chapter, which are dispelled in direct order.

The first [subsection] is also in two [parts]:

one [III.A.1], a sequential resolution;
two [III.A.2], a general clarification.

In the first [part] on the sequential resolution, he sequentially resolves six doubts remaining from the last [chapter] back to the first [III.A.1.a–f], resolving them in contrary order.

Now, this exchange [III.A.1.a] resolves a doubt remaining from the "Tathāgatagarbha" chapter. There it said, "Causal conditions are nonexistent and unproduced,/And because they are unproduced, they are not extinguished" (p. 666a). In this [passage], there remains some clinging to the notion that the causal condition *(hetupratyaya)* is the agent of production, and thus a doubt remains as to why the fruition [of that causal process] would not be conditionally produced. Hence, [Chijang] avails himself of this doubt in order to ask about conditioned generation *(pratītyasamutpāda)*. The Tathāgata's single verse explicitly resolves this doubt. In it, the first half determines the nature of that fundamental clinging; the second half makes use of that to subvert the idea of conditioned generation. This idea explicitly sets up the notion that dharmas are not produced by conditions. Looking for the state in which "no dharmas could exist" is like looking for a rabbit's horn. Thanks to this inference *(anumāna)*, that doubt has been resolved.

> At that time, Chijang Bodhisattva asked, "If dharmas are unproduced, then how is it that in your preaching of dharma [you say that] dharmas are produced by the mind?"
>
> Thereupon, the Lord recited a gāthā:
> Dharmas that are produced by the mind,
> These dharmas cling to subject and object,
> They are like sky-flowers in a drunkard's eyes,
> These dharmas are just-so and not otherwise.

From here onward is the second [exchange, III.A.1.b], which resolves a doubt remaining from the "Voidness of the True Nature" chapter. There it said, "I preach the dharma because you sentient beings persist in needing explanations. . . . This is why I preach on it" (p. 653a). Given this [statement], his doubt is this: based on this passage, the dharmas that are explained in the Buddha's preaching of the dharma arise from the Buddha's mind; so, how, then, can we say that dharmas are unproduced? There are two levels at which to rebut this doubt: **[667c]**

one [III.A.1.b.i], an explicit rebuttal [of the doubt];
two [III.A.1.b.ii], a reiterated resolution.

This [passage] is the explicit rebuttal [of the doubt, III.A.1.b.i]. "Dharmas that are produced by the mind,/These dharmas cling to subject and object": those dharmas that you now presume to be produced by the mind are in fact the deluded mind's subjects and objects of clinging. They are like sky-flowers seen in an intoxicated drunkard's eyes. "These dharmas are just-so and not otherwise": these dharmas that you presume have been produced by the mind are like those sky-flowers. These dharmas are also just-so; they are not dharmas spoken otherwise by him [the Buddha] but are identical to those that you presume were produced. This idea explicitly clarifies that the dharmas you presume to exist are void and unascertainable. Because they serve as objects of clinging, they are like sky-flowers. But the dharmas that I preach leave behind speech and dispel ratiocination; they cannot be described as either subjects or objects of clinging.

> At that time, Chijang Bodhisattva remarked: "If this is what dharmas are like, then those dharmas would have no analogues.[326] Dharmas that have no analogues—those dharmas ought to be generated spontaneously [viz. without causes]."
>
> Thereupon the Lord recited a gāthā:
>
> Dharmas are originally free from both existence and nonexistence,
> So too is this the case for self and others,
> As [these dharmas] have neither beginning nor end,
> Both accomplishment and failure are in fact nonabiding.

This is the second [division, III.A.1.b.ii], the reiterated resolution. It is in two [subdivisions]:

initially [III.A.1.b.ii.a], a criticism;
subsequently [III.A.1.b.ii.b], its resolution.

The gist of the criticism [III.A.1.b.ii.a] is as follows. If it were the case that the dharmas of the verbal teachings preached by the Buddha are not objects of clinging, they are not the same as sky-flowers, which ultimately do not exist. If this were so, then "those dharmas ought to be generated spontaneously"; and since they "would have no analogues," they would be like true thusness.

[III.A.1.b.ii.b, its resolution:] In order to rebut this criticism, [the Buddha] therefore recited a gāthā. The idea of the gāthā is this: because the dharmas I preach dispel names and words, they are "originally free from both existence and nonexistence," "self and others," or "beginning" and "end." Whether they are subject to "accomplishment and failure," both "are in fact nonabiding." How, then, are you able to say that they are "generated spontaneously?" This elucidates the fact that that cause contains the flaw of mutual contradiction: namely, that dharmas are free from either creation or destruction because they are without analogues. Thus, they have nothing to which one may cling and, furthermore, are like **[668a]** true thusness. Thanks to this principle, that criticism is not upheld; and because it is not upheld, his doubt is resolved.

> At that point Chijang Bodhisattva said: "The characteristics of each and every dharma are originally nirvāṇa. This is also the case with nirvāṇa and the characteristic of voidness. The dharma that remains once these types of dharmas are nonexistent ought to be thus."
>
> The Buddha replied, "Once there are no such dharmas, that [remaining] dharma will be thus."

From here onward is the third [exchange, III.A.1.c], which resolves a doubt remaining from the "Accessing the Edge of Reality" chapter. There it said: "Taeryŏk Bodhisattva said . . . 'As far as the mental characteristics of sentient beings are concerned, those characteristics are identical to those of the tathāgatas. So, should the minds of sentient beings also not involve any discrete sense-realms?' The Buddha said: 'So it is. The minds of sentient beings are in reality free from any discrete sense-realms. Why is that? It is because the mind is originally pure and the principle unsullied'" (pp. 640b, 641a). Based on this passage, [the bodhisattva] thinks, "The mind that is originally pure is in fact the principle of thusness; and that which is originally pure—its own-nature is nirvāṇa. But if nirvāṇa is assumed to be void and nonexistent, then this perforce would have to be a spurious conception of nonexistence, not the principle of thusness. In order to rebut this doubt, he therefore says that all [the characteristics of dharmas] are thus.

This passage can be divided into four [divisions]:

initially [III.A.1.c.i], a question;
next [III.A.1.c.ii], assent;
three [III.A.1.c.iii], comprehension;
four [III.A.1.c.iv], a narrative conclusion.

The idea in the initial question [division, III.A.1.c.i,] is that, if through the idea of voidness, "the characteristics of each and every dharma" are realized to be the "originally pure nirvāṇa," this in effect would then conflate nirvāṇa and the characteristic of voidness, rendering moot the distinction between nirvāṇa and voidness. As for this dharma that has but a single taste—"the dharma . . . ought to be thus." In order to counter that sort of grasping, he therefore asks this question.

In the second answer [division, III.A.1.c.ii], [the Buddha] assents to the premise of this question.

> Chijang Bodhisattva said: "This is inconceivable. The characteristic of thusness is in this wise neither associated nor dissociated. Clinging to mentality and clinging to action are in fact both void and calm. The void and calm mind-dharma may not cling to both [saṃsāra and nirvāṇa] or neither, for it too is perforce calm and extinct."

This is the third [division, III.A.1.c.iii], on gaining comprehension, which is intended to rebut the point of criticism. Having heard the preceding explanation, [the bodhisattva] raises this problematic point: since the original nirvāṇa is this one thusness, if **[668b]** one conflates nirvāṇa and the characteristic of voidness, one would have to posit a second type of thusness. In this wise, these two types of thusness would be either "associated or dissociated." If we say they are "associated," this could not in fact refer to the principle of thusness, for these two would have to exist side by side. If we say that are "dissociated," this would mean that there is nothing further that could be made void, for they would both be merely a single thusness. In order to rebut this point of criticism, it therefore says, "[The characteristic of thusness is in this wise] neither associated nor dissociated." "Neither associated" means that it is nondual and thus. Neither . . . dissociated" means that both alternatives are rebutted. Although what is rebutted are these two alternatives, the points that are rebutted are nondual. Therefore the criticisms he has raised are perforce all illogical. "Clinging to mentality and clinging to action are in fact both void and calm": this elucidates the fact that the two alternatives that are rebutted as well as the points that are rebutted are nondual. "Clinging to mentality" refers to nirvāṇa, for that is the condition to which void calmness clings. "Clinging to action" refers to saṃsāra, because that is the object to which all defiled actions cling. These two are both void, and this void calmness is nondual. "The void and calm mind-dharma may not cling to both [saṃsāra and nirvāṇa] or neither, for it too is perforce calm and extinct": this clarifies that the one mind-dharma also does not guard the one. Saṃsāra and nirvāṇa are void, calm, and nondual. This point of nonduality is the one mind-dharma. Based on this one mind-dharma, there are two types of approaches. Nevertheless, if one clings to both these two approaches, one will never realize the mind, for these are two, not one. If one abrogates these two approaches, clinging to neither of them, one also will not realize the mind, for there is nothing that is not the mind. Owing to these aspects, the nondual mind-dharma "may not cling to both [saṃsāra and nirvāṇa] or neither, for it too is perforce calm and extinct."

Thereupon, the Lord recited a gāthā:

All void and calm dharmas,
Those dharmas are calm but not void,
When the mind is not void,
That will bring about the nonexistence of the mind.

This is the fourth [division, III.A.1.c.iv], a conclusion to the narrative [in the third exchange]. "All void and calm dharmas" means all the void and calm dharmas in both saṃsāra and nirvāṇa. "Those dharmas are calm but not void" means that this nondual mind-dharma is not entirely a nonexistent dharma. Although **[668c]** [the mind-dharma] may not be this nonexistent dharma, this does not mean it is existent, either. Therefore, when one understands that the mind is not void, one understands at that time the mind's nonexistence. Therefore the previous explanation that one "may not cling to both [saṃsāra and nirvāṇa] or neither, for it too is perforce calm and extinct" (p. 668a) does not contradict this principle.

> At that point, Chijang Bodhisattva said: "This dharma [of the one mind] does not involve the three truths, for [the three truths of] materiality, voidness, and mind are also extinguished. When these [three] dharmas are originally extinguished, that dharma [of the one mind] ought also to be extinguished."
>
> Thereupon the Lord recited a gāthā:
>
> Dharmas are originally devoid of own-nature,
> They are produced by that,
> While not found in this sort of loci,
> They are involved in this wise with that.

This is the fourth [exchange, III.A.1.d], which resolves a doubt remaining from the "Inspiration of Original Enlightenment" chapter. There it said: "Muju Bodhisattva said, 'If all the sense-realms are void, all bodies are void, and all consciousnesses are void, then enlightenment too must be void.' The Buddha replied: 'Each and every enlightenment has a fixed nature that is not destroyed and not annihilated. They are not void and not nonvoid, for they are free from voidness or nonvoidness'" (p. 631b–c). He has the following doubt deriving from this passage: if this one mind is also not existent and therefore is calm and extinct, why is it that in the preceding explanation not one single [type of] enlightenment is annihilated? This is not the same as the voidness of the mind that is associated with materiality. Now, availing himself of this doubt, he therefore asks this question. "This dharma does not involve the three truths": as a previous gāthā explained, this one mind-dharma is not the voidness of the mind that is associated with materiality; therefore it does not involve the three truths. However, this approach of the three truths is, in brief, of three types:

one, the truth of materiality, the truth of mentality, and absolute truth;
two, the truth of existence, the truth of nonexistence, and the absolute truth of the middle way;
three, as in this chapter, [a listing] that is explained in a subsequent passage (p. 672c below).

Now, the idea behind this question is derived from the first approach. "Materiality, voidness, and mind are also extinguished": since this dharma [of the one mind] is not subsumed among the three truths, the characteristics of materiality are originally void, and the mind is also calm and extinct. At the time that these dharmas of materiality and mind are originally calm and extinct, this dharma of the one mind also should be identical to calm extinction. As the previous **[669a]** gāthā explained (p. 668b), this brings about "the nonexistence of the mind." The previous explanation that it is not the same as voidness is vacuous conversation made in vain—this is the sort of doubt he has.

Regarding this [doubt] he clarifies in the verses that these are not the same. "Dharmas are originally devoid of own-nature": the dharmas of materiality and mentality are originally devoid of own-nature. "They are produced by that": they are produced by that mind of original enlightenment. The materiality and mind that are produced are marked by discrimination, but that mind of original enlightenment stays far removed from both characteristics and nature. While not found in this sort of discriminative loci, they are involved in this wise with that one enlightenment that stays far removed from characteristics. Therefore, even at the time that one voids these discriminative characteristics of materiality and mind, it is not the same as neutralizing that one enlightenment that leaves behind characteristics. Owing to this principle, the preceding is not a spurious explanation.

> At that time, Chijang Bodhisattva asked: "All dharmas are neither produced nor extinguished. So how is it that they are not all one?"
>
> Thereupon, the Lord recited a gāthā:
>
> An abiding place for dharmas does not exist,
> Both characteristics and classifications are void and therefore nonexistent.
> These two—name and locution—together with dharmas,
> These in fact involve grasping at subject and object.

This is the fifth [exchange, III.A.1.e], which resolves a doubt remaining from the "Practice of Nonproduction" chapter. There it said, "These conditions are generated, but there is no production; these conditions decay, but there is no extinction. . . . There is no place where they abide, nor is there seen anything that abides, because their natures are fixed. . . . This fixed nature is neither unitary nor different" (p. 625a–b). Based on this passage, he has the following doubt. Dharmas of materiality, mentality, and so forth, are neither produced nor extinguished; they are in fact equipoised and are the fixed, real nature. This being the case, from a spatial perspective, they are free of distinctions between materiality and mentality, and, from a temporal perspective, they are free of discriminations between production and extinction. Being without distinctions or discriminations, they perforce have but a single taste. Since there is no differentiation that can be sanctioned, why are they not unitary?

In response to this, the verses elucidate the aspect of being nonunitary. "An abiding place for dharmas does not exist" means that there cannot be found either the abiding of or an abiding place for any dharma. "Both characteristics and classifications are void and therefore nonexistent" means that the characteristics of materiality, mind, and so forth, and the classifications of unitary, differentiated, and so forth, are void and therefore nonexistent. Since characteristics and classifications are nonexistent, how [669b] would either of them be unitary? Furthermore, because materiality is nonexistent, there is therefore no characteristic of mind; and since these are not differentiated, why would they be unitary? And yet, if these two—name and locution—together with dharmas, which have been discussed, are presumed to exist, these in fact involve grasping at subject, the deluded mind, and object; in accordance with reality, they are not unitary, dualistic, and so forth. Such names and locutions refer to the function of referencing and are objects to which the mind-consciousness clings. Locutions are the sounds of speech and are cognized by the auditory consciousness. If you say these are unitary, they in fact involve both of these two [speech and consciousness], and there would exist various dharmas among them that are the objects of reference. These sorts of classifications are the deluded mind's objects of clinging; they do not involve the aspect of reality. Given these sorts of classifications, how would they all involve but a single taste?

At that point, Chijang Bodhisattva remarked: "All the characteristics of dharmas—there are none that linger on either of the two shores [of saṃsāra or nirvāṇa]; they also do not linger in the current between them. Mind and consciousness are also just the same [in being free from both production and extinction]; so how is it that all the sense-realms are produced by consciousness? If consciousness is the cause of that production, then consciousness too must be produced from [something else]. So how then can consciousness be unproduced? If there is production, then there must be a product."

Thereupon, the Lord recited a gāthā:

These two things—product and production,
These two are causality and the caused,
Both are originally [mere] names and are themselves nonexistent,
Clinging to their existence is like a sky-flower or a mirage.

When consciousness has not yet been produced,
Objects then are not produced either,
When objects have not yet been produced,
Consciousness is then also extinguished.
These are both originally nonexistent,
They also do not exist and do not not-exist,
Consciousness that is unproduced is also nonexistent,
So how is it that objects exist on account of it?

This is the sixth [exchange, III.A.1.f], which resolves a doubt remaining from the "Signless Dharma" chapter. There it said: "'What is [meant by the statement] "that characteristic of discriminative awareness which is subject to production and extinction"?' The Buddha replied: '... The principle is free from either acceptance or rejection. If there were acceptance or rejection, then all kinds of thoughts would be produced. The thousands of conceptions and myriad of mentations are marked by production and extinction'" (p. 617b). Now, given the subsequent explanations, he in turn has a doubt about this passage. If the consciousnesses are able to produce sense-realms that are subject either to acceptance or rejection, then those sense-realms in turn should produce consciousness of all kinds of thoughts. This would explicitly suggest that the mind and consciousnesses are subject to production and extinction. So how would one say that "there are none that linger on either of the two shores"? **[669c]** But if the mind and consciousnesses are all free from production and extinction, how then would all the consciousnesses be able to produce the sense-realms? Availing himself of this kind of doubt, he raises this sort of question.

"There are none that linger on either of the two shores" means that they are free from production and extinction. "They also do not linger in the current between them" means that they also are not unitary. Since mind and consciousness are the same in that they are both free from production or extinction, how is it that... sense-realms that are subject to acceptance or rejection would be produced by consciousness? If consciousness is able to produce the sense-realms, and the consciousnesses are also produced from the sense-realms, then how would they be unproduced? Since consciousness is the agent of production, existence would be the object of that production.

In order to dispel this doubt, [the Buddha] therefore speaks these three verses. The text of these three verses can be divided into two:

the first verse [III.A.1.f.i] reveals the principle;
the last two verses [III.A.1.f.ii] eradicate the grasping that is produced with regard to characteristics.

In the first verse [III.A.1.f.i], the line "these two are causality and the caused" means that your presumption that the consciousnesses are the agent of production and the sense-realms are the objects of production is a deceptive clinging to both causality and the objects produced by causal processes. Both are originally mere names and devoid of own [nature]. If you cling to them as existing, it would be like clinging to a sky-flower and clinging to a mirage, as if they existed in reality. For this reason, this is no different from being free from production or extinction.

In the rebuttal [III.A.1.f.ii], the lines "When consciousness has not yet been produced,/Objects then are not produced either" clarifies that consciousness—when it is serving as the agent of production— does not yet exist, and the sense-realms that are the objects of production are not then produced. "When objects have not yet been produced,/Consciousness is then also extin-

guished": this clarifies that the sense-realms—when they are serving as the agents of production—do not yet exist, and the consciousness that is the object of production is also then extinguished. **"Extinguished"** means calm extinction—that is, original nonexistence. **"These are both originally nonexistent,/ They also do not exist and do not not-exist"** means that **these** two—when they are serving as the agents of production—**are both originally nonexistent**; and since there are no agents of production, they also are nothing that can be caused to exist. Therefore, it says **"they . . . do not exist."** Because there is nothing that can be caused to exist, throughout the future, they remain unproduced; therefore, it says **"they . . . do not not-exist." "Consciousness that is unproduced is also nonexistent"**: given this aspect of nonproduction, how could consciousness ever exist? Because consciousness does not exist, the sense-realms **[670a]** do not correspondingly come to exist.

In this passage, there are two syllogistic inferences. The first syllogism:

> Consciousness is unproduced,
> Because it is not subject to production,
> Like expecting a scorched seed [to sprout].

The second syllogism:

> The sense-realms are not generated,
> Because there is nowhere where they are found,
> Like finding hair on a tortoise's back.[327]

The preceding six divisions on the specific resolution of each doubt are now finished.

> **At that time, Chijang Bodhisattva remarked: "The characteristics of dharmas, in this wise, are void both internally and externally. These two groups—sensory objects and sensory awareness—are originally calm and extinct. As the Tathāgata has explained, a dharma that in this wise is the real characteristic and true voidness would not be subject to origination."**

From here onward is the second [part, III.A.2], a summary determination of what has been explained. It is a summary determination of the fact that these six resolutions are not diseases but medicines. It is in two [subparts]:

initially [III.A.2.a], a clarification that these [characteristics of dharmas] are not diseases;
subsequently [III.A.2.b], a clarification that this [dharma of voidness] is a medicine.

The initial [subpart] is also in two [divisions]:

a query [III.A.2.a.i];
[the Tathāgata's] assent [III.A.2.a.ii].

In the query [division, III.A.2.a.i], the words "**the characteristics of dharmas, in this wise**" suggest the summary comprehension of the characteristics of dharmas brought up in the preceding discussion of these six divisions [of contemplation practice]. The words "**internally and externally**" mean the sense-consciousnesses, internally, and the sense-realms, externally. "**These two groups**" mean the manifold types of **sensory objects and sensory awareness.** "**Would not be subject to origination**" means that it would not originate the various maculations and tribulations present in saṃsāra. This is because [true voidness] is not the same as wrongly clinging to voidness, which in turn originates all types of tribulations.

> **The Buddha responded: "So it is. Dharmas that accord with reality are formless and nonabiding. They are not originated, nor do they prompt origination. They are not objects and not the great [elements]. They are the aggregation of the profound, meritorious qualities [inherent in] the dharma of the matrix of the one original [enlightenment]."**

This is the Tathāgata's assent [III.A.2.a.ii]. The word "**formless**" means that [such dharmas] do not produce the disease of attachment to existence. "**Nonabiding**" means that they also leave behind any mistaken clinging to voidness or to tribulations. "**They are not originated**" means that the [first noble] truth of suffering is void. "**Nor do they prompt origination**" means that the [second noble] truth of origination is void. "**They are not objects**" means that they leave behind the distinctive categories of the skandhas, *dhātus*, and so forth [viz. the *āyatanas*]. "**They are . . . not the great**" means that they leave behind the creative characteristics of earth [solidity], water [fluidity], and so forth. "**The dharma of the matrix of the one original [enlightenment]**" refers to the one original enlightenment because, with that as the root, it can catalyze the production of all the formations *(saṃskāra)* and all types of meritorious qualities *(guṇa)*. However, this matrix is of two types. The first **[670b]** is the matrix that involves various maculations, that is, the foundational consciousness, the meaning of which was explained above (p. 662a–c). The second is the matrix of pristine purity, that is, the one original enlightenment, as is explained in this passage. In that foundational consciousness, all the seeds of the various maculations are accumulated; but in this original enlightenment, only those meritorious qualities that are extremely profound in nature are aggregated. They are called "**profound**" because they leave behind both characteristics and nature. They are called "**aggregation**" because their numbers surpass that of the sands of the Ganges.

> Chijang Bodhisattva said: "It is inconceivable! This is an inconceivable aggregation! The seventh [consciousness] and the five [sensory consciousnesses] are not produced. The eighth and sixth [consciousnesses] are calm and extinct. The characteristic of the ninth [consciousness] is to be void and nonexistent. Existence is void and nonexistent. Nonexistence is void and nonexistent. As the Lord has explained, dharmas and phenomena are both void. Accessing voidness, there are no remaining practices, but one also does not neglect any actions. There are neither self nor objects-of-self, neither subject nor object, nor the false view of selfhood *(satkāyadṛṣṭi)*. All the internal and external bonds and defilements are calm and still. Accordingly, wishes are also assuaged. In this wise, contemplation of principle is the true thusness that involves wisdom and concentration. The Lord constantly explains that, in this wise,[328] the dharma of voidness is a superb medicine."

From here onward is the second [subpart, III.A.2.b], a clarification that [the dharma of voidness] is a medicine. It also is in two [divisions]:

initially [III.A.2.b.i], the bodhisattva's query;
[subsequently (III.A.2.b.ii), the Tathāgata's assent and approval.][329]

In this query [division], there are three [subdivisions]:

one [III.A.2.b.i.a], comprehending the previous reference to "**the aggregation of the profound, meritorious qualities**";
two [III.A.2.b.i.b], availing himself of and elucidating the profound access to the contemplation of principle;
three [III.A.2.b.i.c], a query regarding the superior qualities of this superb medicine.

The first [subdivision] is also in three [segments]:

a summary overview [III.A.2.b.i.a.1];
a sequential elucidation [III.A.2.b.i.a.2];
finally [III.A.2.b.i.a.3], a summary conclusion.

"**This is an inconceivable aggregation!**" is the summary overview [III.A.2.b.i.a.1] of the meritorious qualities that leave behind both characteristics and nature.

In the sequential elucidation [III.A.2.b.i.a.2],

initially [III.A.2.b.i.a.2.a], he clarifies leaving behind characteristics;
subsequently [III.A.2.b.i.a.2.b], he elucidates leaving behind the nature.

In the initial [subsegment, III.A.2.b.i.a.2.a], the line "The seventh [consciousness] and the five [sensory consciousnesses] are not produced" is a joint explanation of the voidness of the two kinds of subsidiary consciousness. This means that, within the consciousnesses that are constantly active [viz. the *kliṣṭamanovijñāna* and the *ālayavijñāna*], the seventh *[kliṣṭamanovijñāna]* is the subsidiary [consciousness]; but within the consciousnesses that are not constantly active [the five sensory consciousnesses and the *manovijñāna*], the five [sensory] consciousnesses are the subsidiary ones. "The eighth and sixth [consciousnesses] are calm and extinct" is a joint explanation of the calmness of the two kinds of foundational consciousness. This means that, within the consciousnesses that are constantly active, the eighth *[ālayavijñāna]* is the foundational [consciousness]; but within the consciousnesses that are not constantly active, the sixth *[manovijñāna]* is the foundational [consciousness].

Next [III.A.2.b.i.a.2.b], he elucidates leaving behind the nature. "The characteristic of the ninth [consciousness] is to be void and nonexistent" means that the characteristic of the ninth consciousness **[670c]** also does not guard its own nature. "Existence is void and nonexistent" is a reiteration of the aspect of leaving behind characteristics; this means that the dharmas of the eight consciousnesses, which involve characteristics, are void and unascertainable. "Nonexistence is void and nonexistent" is a reiteration of the aspect of leaving behind the nature; this means that the nature of the ninth consciousness, which is signless, is void and unascertainable. The one mind, in this wise, leaves behind both characteristics and the nature. It is in fact an aggregation of immeasurable meritorious qualities and, in this wise, is called "an inconceivable aggregation."

"As the Lord has explained, dharmas and phenomena are both void": this is the third [segment, III.A.2.b.i.a.3], a summary conclusion to [this discussion of the aspects of] leaving behind characteristics and leaving behind the nature.

Next [III.A.2.b.i.b], he clarifies the contemplation of principle. It is in two [segments]:

a sequential clarification [III.A.2.b.i.b.1];
a summary conclusion [III.A.2.b.i.b.2].

In the sequential clarification [III.A.2.b.i.b.1], there are three passages.

"Accessing voidness, there are no remaining practices, but one also does not neglect any actions": this refers to the samādhi of voidness [viz. the gate to liberation of voidness]. This means that in accessing voidness through the contemplation of principle, there are no remaining subjects or objects of practice; but even though there are no remaining subjects or objects, one does not neglect the actions of the six perfections, and so forth.

The next [passage] clarifies the samādhi of signlessness [viz. the gate to liberation of signlessness]. "There are neither self nor objects-of-self, neither subject nor object views": this means that one leaves behind all the defiled characteristics that are associated with views, the characteristics that are affiliated with self and objects-of-self, and the characteristics of seer and seen. "All the internal and external bonds and defilements are calm and still": this means that one leaves behind all the characteristics of the bonds and defilements that are associated with craving, including all the internal bonds and all the external defilements. This is because all the characteristics of the defilements that are affiliated with the three realms of existence are void. In this wise, it is called the samādhi of signlessness.

"Accordingly, wishes are also assuaged": this clarifies the samādhi of wishlessness [viz. the gate to liberation of wishlessness]. Since all dharmas in the three realms of existence are calm and still, the mind that wishes and seeks for things is spontaneously assuaged forever. In this wise, it is called the samādhi of wishlessness.

"In this wise, contemplation of principle is the true thusness that involves wisdom and concentration": this sentence is the summary conclusion [III. A.2.b.i.b.2]. This means that, just as the preceding three types [of samādhis or gates to liberation] are all included in the contemplation of principle, they are unbiased toward either calmness or contemplation, and nondualistic with regard to subject or object.

"The Lord constantly explains that, in this wise, the dharma of voidness is a superb medicine": this is the third query [subdivision, III.A.2.b.i.c, regarding the superior qualities of this superb medicine]. In this wise, the dharma of voidness is fully endowed with all types of meritorious qualities and counteracts **[671a]** all the defilements. Therefore [he asks], "Should this be a superb medicine?"

> The Buddha replied: "So it is. Why is this? Because of voidness. As this void-nature is unproduced, the mind is perpetually unproduced. As this void-nature is not extinguished, the mind is perpetually unextinguished. As the void-nature is nonabiding, the mind is also nonabiding. As the void-nature is inactive *(muwi)*, the mind is also inactive.
>
> "Voidness is free from both egress and access, and leaves behind both gain and loss. The skandhas, *dhātus*, and *āyatanas*, and so forth, are also all nonexistent. So too is this the case with the mind, which likewise is unattached.
>
> "Bodhisattva! I have discussed the several classifications of voidness in order to refute all existence."

This is the Tathāgata's assent and approval [III.A.2.b.ii]. It is in three [subdivisions].

One [III.A.2.b.ii.a], is the summary assent. As for the line "because of voidness": the reason that [voidness] serves as a superb medicine is simply because it is void, for existence instantly gives rise to disease.

From "void-nature" onward is the second [subdivision, III.A.2.b.ii.b], a sequential approval. It is in two [segments].

initially [III.A.2.b.ii.b.1], he clarifies that, by ingesting the medicine of voidness, one is able to leave behind the tribulations that are the results of wandering on in saṃsāra.
subsequently [III.A.2.b.ii.b.2], he elucidates that, by ingesting the medicine of voidness, one cures the diseases that are the causes of clinging and attachment.

In this first [segment, III.A.2.b.ii.b.1], the sentence "**as this void-nature is unproduced, the mind is perpetually unproduced**" means that the mind that accesses voidness is unproduced, just as is the case with voidness. Furthermore, in accord with this freedom from extinction, the mind is constantly unextinguished; and, because being subject to production and extinction is what is meant by "impermanence," these two by contrast are therefore called "permanent." "**The mind is also nonabiding**": not merely is [the mind] free from any past or future characteristics, but there also is no characteristic of abiding in the interstice between them [viz. the present]. This is a sequential clarification of leaving behind the three characteristics [of past, present, and future]. "**The mind is also inactive**": this is a summary elucidation of leaving behind the three characteristics of compounded objects *(saṃskṛtalakṣaṇa)*. This clarifies that ingesting [the medicine of] voidness frees one from the disease of impermanence.

The next [segment, III.A.2.b.ii.b.2] clarifies that [ingesting the medicine of voidness] also cures the diseases of clinging and attachment. "**[Voidness] is free from both egress and access**" means that it makes no distinction between withdrawing from contemplation or accessing contemplation. "**Leaves behind both gain and loss**" means that [voidness] also leaves behind the characteristics of gaining the new and losing the old. "**So too is this the case with the mind, which likewise is unattached**": the mind that is the agent of contemplation, like the principle of voidness, also does not cling to the characteristics of egress and access, or gain and loss, and is unattached to such dharmas as the **skandhas, *dhātus*, *āyatanas*, and so forth**. This clarifies that ingesting voidness cures the disease of clinging and attachment.

"**I [671b] have discussed the several classifications of voidness in order to destroy all existence**": this is the third [subdivision, III.A.2.b.ii.c], the concluding assent. Discussed from the standpoint of reality, the principle of voidness is nondual, [but the Buddha] explains that there are **several classifications of voidness**, such as the five, the three, and so forth, in order to heal the diseases of people's attachment to existence. Just as there are many such diseases, so too must there be many explanations of voidness. Moreover, the principle is in reality not void; although it is not void, we force the name "voidness" on it merely in order to refute existence. This is because the concept "voidness" does not validate the nature of voidness. Through these two ideas, he concludes the instruction on the various classifications of voidness.

> Chijang Bodhisattva said: "Lord! Would that person be considered wise who knows that existence is unreal, like heat waves that are [not] water, and that reality is not nonexistent, like the sovereignty of fire that is inherent [in wood]?[330]

The [subsection, III.A,] on the six doubts remaining from the six chapters that were to be resolved in contrary order, including a sequential resolution [III.A.1] and a summary clarification [IIII.A.2], has been completed as above.

From here onward is the second [subsection, III.B], on three doubts remaining from one chapter, which are rebutted in sequential order. It is in three [parts]. This means that there were three additional doubts regarding just the "Tathāgatagarbha" chapter, which will be rebutted sequentially.

As for the first doubt [III.B.1], as Elder Pŏmhang's verses state (p. 663b):

> If it is said that dharmas are one . . .
> It is like mistaking heat waves for water . . .
> If you perceive the nonexistence of dharmas . . .
> [You are] just like a blind man who mistakenly believes that the sun is nonexistent.

[Chijang Bodhisattva] has a doubt about this explanation: since the elder is merely a layperson, is his analysis a wrong view, or is it authentic wisdom? Since he has this sort of doubt, he is unwilling to accept in faith [the elder's explanation]. In order to rebut this doubt, he brings up a question [III.B.1.a] regarding that matter. The simile of "**heat waves**" has already been explained above (p. 663c). "**That reality is not nonexistent**" means that one is able to know that the nature that involves the aspect of the one reality is not nonexistent. Someone who presumes that there is no such reality is "**just like a blind man who mistakenly believes that the sun is nonexistent.**" He recognizes that the elder "**knows . . . that reality is not nonexistent.**" This aspect of being "**not nonexistent**" is "**like the sovereignty of fire that is inherent [in wood]**": the nature of the great element of fire is innate in wood, but if one splits [that wood] in order to find that [fire nature], one will never discover its characteristic of heat. Even so, that nature of fire is in fact not nonexistent in wood, because if one uses friction to find it, **[671c]** that fire perforce will appear. It is just the same with the one mind: one cannot find the nature of the mind simply by splitting it into all its characteristics. Even so, that mind is in fact not nonexistent in all those dharmas, and if one cultivates the path in order to find it, the one mind will appear. In this wise, as far as the nature of fire is concerned, its characteristic [of heat] may be hidden, but its efficacy is still great, just like the sovereign of a kingdom; hence, it mentions "sovereignty." If the elder, in this wise, leaves behind the two extreme views, "would that person be considered wise"? This is the sort of question raised.

> The Buddha replied: "So it is. Why is this? This person's true contemplation contemplates the calm extinction of the one [mind]. Signs and signlessness are grasped as being equally void, and since voidness is cultivated, one does not lose one's vision of the buddhas. Because one sees the buddhas, one does not flow along with the three currents."

From here onward is the Tathāgata's resolution of this doubt [III. B.1.b]. It is in two [divisions]:

an explicit resolution [III.B.1.b.i];
a resolution through an explication [III.B.1.b.ii].

"So it is" is the [explicit] resolution [III.B.1.b.i], that such a person would in fact be considered wise.

From "Why is this?" onward explicates [III.B.1.b.ii] the quality of his wisdom. It is in two [subdivisions]:

a brief explication [III.B.1.b.ii.a];
an extensive disquisition [III.B.1.b.ii.b].

In the first [subdivision, III.B.1.b.ii.a], "contemplates the calm extinction of the one" means that he contemplates the calm and extinct aspect of the dharma of the one mind. "Signs and signlessness are grasped as being equally void" means that he contemplates that the mundane truth of signs and the absolute truth of signlessness are equally invalid and conflated into one. In this wise, "since voidness is cultivated" and one verily accords with the buddha-mind, one constantly sees the body of the buddhas without ever losing [that vision]; therefore, it says, "One does not lose one's vision of the buddhas." Since one constantly sees the buddhas, one intensifies one's contemplation of voidness. And as one's contemplation of voidness develops still further, one turns against all aspects of existence; therefore, it says "one does not flow along with the three currents." "The three currents" subsume all the defilements of the three realms of existence, meaning the three currents *(ogha)* of greed for sensual experience *(kāmarāga)*, greed for existence *(bhavarāga)*, and ignorance *(avidyā)*. The meaning of these so-called three currents is as is commonly explained.

> "In the Mahāyāna, the three paths to liberation [voidness, signlessness, wishlessness] have but a single essence and are devoid of nature. Be-

cause they are devoid of nature, it is void; because it is void, it is signless; because it is signless, it is wishless; because it is wishless, it seeks nothing; because it seeks nothing, it is free from anticipation. Owing to this action, the mind is purified. Because the mind is purified, one sees the buddhas. Because one sees the buddhas, one then will be reborn in the Pure Land. **[672a]**

"Bodhisattva! Diligently cultivate the three transformations[331] with regard to this profound dharma. Wisdom and concentration will be completely perfected, and one will immediately transcend the three realms of existence."

This is the second [subdivision, III.B.1.b.ii.b], an extensive disquisition. It is in two [segments]:

initially [III.B.1.b.ii.b.1], a clarification of the superior benefit of the "three paths to liberation";
subsequently [III.B.1.b.ii.b.2], an elucidation of the superior benefit of "diligently cultivat[ing] the three transformations."

In the first [segment, III.B.1.b.ii.b.1], "have but a single essence and are devoid of nature" means that [the Mahāyāna account of the three paths to liberation] is distinct from the three paths to liberation of the Hīnayāna, which have natures that involve distinctive essences. This elucidates the fact that they are of a single essence with the contemplation practice of Mahāyāna bodhisattvas. During one's contemplation of the mind, when one realizes that these are "devoid of nature," one can still provisionally describe them in accordance with their aspects and posit three separate types of liberation. Voidness liberation is posited with regard to the aspect of forgetting their essential nature; signless liberation is posited with regard to the aspect of forgetting their essential characteristics; and the liberation that is free of anticipation—also known as the wishless liberation—is posited with regard to the aspect of forgetting their essential functions. By elucidating this contemplation that [these three liberations] are singular and undifferentiated, there will be none of the essential natures, characteristics, and functions of all dharmas that will not be neutralized and none that will not be assimilated. It is for this reason that three gates to liberation are posited. "Due to this action, the mind is purified": by forgetting all aspects of essence, characteristics, and function, one is able to purify the mind that becomes immersed in the mundane after withdrawing from contemplation and leave behind all the tainted attachments. By leaving behind this mind which is subject to tainted attachments, one is able to see the reward [body] of the buddha; and because one sees this reward buddha, one is able to be "reborn in the Pure Land." This is the superior benefit that derives from the three paths to liberation.

[In the second segment, III.B.1.b.ii.b.2,] the line "diligently cultivate the three transformations with regard to this profound dharma" means diligently to cultivate the three voidnesses with regard to that dharma of voidness. What are these? The voidness of the characteristic of voidness is the cultivation of the first transformation. The voidness of voidness itself is the cultivation of the second transformation. The voidness of that which is voided is the cultivation of the third transformation. The meanings of these are as was explained previously (p. 639a), and they are therefore not discussed separately here. "Diligently cultivat[ing] the three transformations" means to penetrate to the one mind. By penetrating to the one mind, "wisdom and concentration will be completely perfected," and, at that point of complete perfection, "one will immediately transcend the three realms of existence." This is the superior benefit that derives from diligently cultivating the three transformations.

> Chijang Bodhisattva asked: "As the Tathāgata has said, nonproduction and nonextinction **[672b]** are impermanent, so extinguish this production and extinction. Once production and extinction have been extinguished, this calm extinction will be permanent. Because it is permanent, it cannot be excised. That dharma which cannot be excised remains far removed from all the active and motionless dharmas of the three realms of existence. [One should avoid] the conditioned dharmas as if avoiding a fiery pit. Through relying on what dharma may one admonish oneself and access that one approach [to dharma]?"

From this point on, he dispels a second doubt [III.B.2] remaining from the "Tathāgatagarbha" chapter. There, it says: "[At the moment of] cognition, the consciousnesses are permanent. These consciousnesses are perpetually calm and extinct, but that calm extinction is also calm and extinct" (p. 664c). He has this doubt regarding this passage: although the dharma of calm extinction, which in this wise is perpetually abiding, can be enjoyed, it is exceedingly rare; it would be difficult to fathom with the shallow minds of sentient beings. So how can we train the mind so that we can approach that gateway? Given this doubt, he asks this question.

The question is in two [subparts]:

initially [III.B.2.a], he brings up how distant the fruition [of nirvāṇa is from its cause];
subsequently [III.B.2.b], he asks about the causes of access.

In the first [subpart, III.B.2.a], the words "nonproduction and nonextinction are impermanent" express comprehension of the preceding line "these consciousnesses are perpetually calm and extinct" (p. 664c). Because [these consciousnesses] are originally calm and extinct, they are in a state of "nonproduction and nonextinction"; but because they are originally not permanent, they are "impermanent." "Extinguish this production and extinction. Once production and extinction have been extinguished, this calm extinction will be permanent": this expresses comprehension of the preceding line "that calm extinction is also calm and extinct" as well as of the sentence "[At the moment of] cognition, the consciousnesses are permanent."

From "the conditioned dharmas" onward is the second explicit question concerning the expedients that will help one to access that gateway [III.B.2.b.i]. Although previously he explained the explicit expedient contemplations, they were explained only briefly. He asks here for a more extensive explanation.

> The Buddha replied: "Bodhisattva! Admonish your mind concerning the three great matters; access this practice via the three great truths."
>
> Chijang Bodhisattva asked: "How may one admonish one's mind in regard to these three matters? How may one access the one practice via the three truths?"
>
> The Buddha replied: "As for the three great matters: the first is cause; the second is fruition; the third is consciousness. These three matters are, in this wise, void and nonexistent from their inception; they are not the self, but instead are true self. So how is it [672c] that the taint of craving *(tṛṣṇā)* arises concerning them? Contemplate these three matters as being bound[332] by the bonds and being aimlessly adrift in the sea of suffering. It is because of such matters that one must constantly admonish oneself.
>
> "As for the three truths: the first truth is that the path to bodhi is impartial, not unimpartial. The second truth is that great enlightenment is gained through the orthodox knowledge [of the Buddhists], not through the perverse knowledge [of the non-Buddhists]. The third truth is that truth is accessed by not differentiating the practices of wisdom and concentration; truth is not accessed by practicing them randomly. Cultivating the path to buddhahood by means of these three truths—that person cannot but attain right enlightenment concerning these dharmas. Gaining the knowledge of right enlightenment, one spreads immense friendliness.
>
> "Benefiting both oneself and others, one achieves the bodhi of the buddhas."

This passage [which continues the discussion on the expedients that will help one to access that gateway, III.B.2.b,] has four [divisions]:

initially [III.B.2.b.i], the [preceding] question;
next [III.B.2.b.ii], the answer;
three [III.B.2.b.iii], a query;
four [III.B.2.b.iv], the explanation.

In the explanation [III.B.2.b.iv], there are two [subdivisions; *sic*]:

initially [III.B.2.b.iv.a], an explanation of the expedient of admonishment;
subsequently [III.B.2.b.iv.b], a narration of the expedients that bring about access;
[three (III.B.2.b.iv.c), a summary conclusion.][333]

In the first [subdivision, III.B.2.b.iv.a], the term "**cause**" means the cause of the five precepts and the ten wholesome [ways of] actions. "**Fruition**" means the fruition of the merits that bring about rebirth among humans and gods. "**Consciousness**" is that which retains these causes and fruitions—that is, the foundational consciousness. Although sentient beings misconstrue this [foundational consciousness] as being their own internal self, its nature is void; therefore, they are **not the self.** This principle of nonself *(anātman)* is expediently [termed] the "**true self.**" Therefore, one should not produce the "**taint of craving**" regarding that which is "**not the self.**" "**Contemplate these three matters as being bound by the bonds**": since the four bonds obstruct the mind that in this way becomes concentrated, they induce these three matters [cause, fruition, and consciousness] to be "**aimlessly adrift in the sea of suffering.**"

What are these four bonds? As the "Truths" chapter of the *Abhidharmasamuccaya [Duifa lun,* viz. *Da Abidamo zaji lun]* states:

> There are four types of bonds *(kāyagrantha).* These are the physical bonds of covetousness, ill will, attachment to mere rules and rituals, and clinging to [the self] as being real [viz. dogmatic fanaticism]. Because these can obstruct and hinder the mind-made body *(manomayakāya)* produced through meditation, they are called "bonds." What is the reason for this? Since these can obstruct the mind-made body produced through concentrated thought, they are called "bonds" not because they can obstruct the physical body. Why is this? It is because they serve as four causes of mental agitation. **[673a]** Covetousness toward possessions serves as causes of mental agitation. Conflict, disputation, and other inappropriate actions serve as a cause of mental agitation. Tormenting oneself with rules and rituals that are difficult to cultivate serves as a cause of mental agitation. Seeking truth in invalid principles [such as the belief in an eternal soul] serves as a cause of mental agitation. Based on those [principles], each creates a subjective viewpoint. Therefore, various sorts of miscalculations occur regarding the invalid principles that derive from these subjective points of views, mistakenly producing grasping and attachment. This means that they presume that their [own personal views] alone are correct, and all others are foolish and false. This serves as a cause of mental

agitation. Regardless of the kind of agitation that might be present, knowledge and vision that accords with reality *(yathābhūtajñānadarśana)* will lead to a concentrated mind.[334]

"It is because of such matters that one must constantly admonish oneself": this means that one admonishes oneself concerning the four bonds that bind and loathes the three matters in which one is adrift. This completes the explanation of the expedient of admonishment.

What are the expedients that bring about access [III.B.2.b.iv.b]? They involve the careful scrutiny of the three truths. **"The first truth is that the path to bodhi is impartial, not unimpartial"**: this means that there is nothing of the bodhi of the purity of the nature realized by the buddhas that is not fully probed; therefore, it is called a "**path**." All living creatures are identical in this nature, and there is not a single one who does not return to it—this is the ultimate path. Therefore, it says it is "**impartial, not unimpartial**." This serves as the antidote to the separate byways taken by two-vehicle adherents. **"The second truth is that great enlightenment is gained through the orthodox knowledge [of the Buddhists], not through the perverse knowledge [of the non-Buddhists]"**: this means that the fruition of the great enlightenment of omniscience solely involves the realization of impartiality and is the product of orthodox [Buddhist] knowledge. It is not conditioned by the products of perverse [non-Buddhist] knowledge, including such factors as the principle of unmanifest potentiality *(myŏngch'e; avyakta,* viz. *prakṛti)* or the property of genericness *(taeyu; sāmānyapadārtha)*.[335] This is the antidote to the attachments of those who are outside the path [of Buddhism]. **"The third truth is that truth is accessed by not differentiating the practices of wisdom and concentration; truth is not accessed by practicing them randomly"**: this means that, when one gains orthodox knowledge and accesses impartiality, wisdom and concentration will be consummately interfused and it will be impossible to differentiate specific characteristics of practice. This will then be the authentic access to the truth of impartiality. It will be quite unlike the worldly mind-king's tendency toward discrimination, which enumerates separate essences and distinguishes the practices of concentration and wisdom. These sorts of random practices are not an authentic access. **[673b]** This is the antidote to worldly contemplation practice, that worst form of conceit *(abhimāna)* in which one presumes one has achieved realization, when in fact one has not.

As to why these three sorts of penetration are generically termed "truths," they are the objects perceived by the contemplation that entails careful scrutiny. Curing each of these three different kinds of grasping will then enable one to cultivate correctly the one way to buddhahood; therefore, it says "**cultivating the path to buddhahood by means of these three truths.**"

Next, he elucidates the fruition gained by cultivating the path. **"That person cannot but attain right enlightenment concerning these dharmas"**: this elucidates the fruition of the meritorious quality of knowledge, which benefits oneself. **Cultivating the path to buddhahood . . . concerning these dharmas** of the three [truths], it will be impossible not to obtain the fruition of right enlightenment. "**Gaining the knowledge of right enlightenment, one spreads immense friendliness**": this elucidates the fruition of the meritorious quality of empathy, which benefits others. One universally spreads immense, unconditional friendliness, pervading the dharma-realm, so that there are none who are not benefited thereby.

"**Benefiting both oneself and others, one achieves the bodhi of the buddhas**": this is a summary conclusion [III.B.2.b.iv.c] to the previous two [subdivisions of the explanation], which means that the two types of benefit are consummately fulfilled and one achieves perfect enlightenment.

> **Chijang Bodhisattva asked: "Lord! Such a dharma would in fact be free from causes and conditions. If a dharma is unconditioned, there then would be no causes that are generated. So how can such a motionless dharma prompt access to the Tathāgata[garbha]?"**

From here onward, he rebuts a third doubt [III.B.3] remaining from the "Tathāgatagarbha" chapter. As a verse at the end of that chapter states: "**Transmuting both the subject and object of clinging,/ He accesses the tathāgatagarbha**" (p. 666c). Based on this account, [Chijang Bodhisattva] has a doubt about this [statement, III.B.3.a]: in this [passage], the path to bodhi and the truth of impartiality are in fact the tathāgatagarbha. Without availing himself of the power of causes and conditions, how would he transmute both subjective and objective causes and be able to gain access to the tathāgatagarbha-dharma? Because he has this doubt, he brings up this question. "**[Such a dharma] would in fact be free from causes and conditions**": because [dharmas] are impartial, they do not derive from causal conditions *(hetupratyaya)*. Furthermore, because they are impartial, they do not involve any additional conditions. Since there are also no additional conditions, causes could not be generated. So how would ungenerated, motionless dharmas draw on causes and conditions to gain **[673c]** access to the tathāgata[garbha]? If one were to gain access by making use of causal power, then this would be availing oneself of causes and conditions, not motionlessness.

Wishing to proclaim this meaning, the Tathāgata then recited these gāthās:

> **The characteristics of all dharmas,**
> **Their natures are void, nonexistent, and motionless.**
>
> **These dharmas, in this time,**
> **Are not generated in this time,**
> **But dharmas do not involve another time,**
> **And are not generated in another time either.**[336]

Dharmas are neither moving nor motionless,
As their natures are void, they are calm and extinct.

Only at the time when their natures are void, calm, and extinct,
Will those dharmas then appear.
As they leave behind all characteristics, they abide calmly,
And as they abide calmly, they are unconditioned.

From here onward is the Tathāgata's explicit resolution of the doubt [III.B.3.b]. It describes how, through impartiality and motionlessness, one succeeds at gaining access. These eight verses are in two divisions:

the initial three [verses] are the brief explanation [III.B.3.b.i];
the subsequent five are the extensive proclamation [III.B.3.b.ii].

In the brief [explanation division, III.B.3.b.i], there are two [subdivisions]:

the initial two[337] verses clarify the aspect of motionlessness [III.B.3.b.i.a];
the subsequent single verse elucidates the aspect of gaining access [III.B.3.b.i.b].

In the initial [subdivision], there are three [segments]:

overview [III.B.3.b.i.a.1];
explication [III.B.3.b.i.a.2];
conclusion [III.B.3.b.i.a.3].

This means that the first two lines [The characteristics of all dharmas,/Their natures are void, nonexistent, and motionless] provide an overview of the aspect of motionlessness; the next four lines [These dharmas, in this time,/ . . . And are not generated in another time either] explicate the aspect of motionlessness.

[In the explication (III.B.3.b.i.a.2)] concerning the lines "These dharmas, in this time,/Are not generated in this time": "this time" means "this time period." "This time period" is the present. The present time does not stop for even a moment. There is no interval between past and future, just as there is no space between light and shadow. Therefore, in this present time, nothing is able to be generated. "But dharmas do not involve another time,/And are not generated in another time either": "another time" means past and future. Because the future has not yet come into existence, it involves the aspect of being ungenerated; but because the past has already passed out of existence, it as well involves the aspect of being ungenerated. For this reason, dharmas are devoid of the activity of generation; and since they are devoid of the activity of production, they also are neither constantly abiding nor motionless.

For this reason, it says, "Dharmas are neither moving nor motionless,/As

their natures are void, [674a] they are calm and extinct." These two lines are the conclusion [III.B.3.b.i.a.3] regarding this aspect of motionlessness.

The next verse clarifies the aspect of gaining access [III.B.3.b.i.b]. "**Only at the time when their natures are void, calm, and extinct**": at the time when there is the clear vision that "**their natures are void, calm, and extinct,**" the dharma of motionlessness will then appear. The appearance of [motionlessness] in the mind is therefore called "gaining access." In this wise, the first half [of the verse] clarifies the aspect of gaining access. Nevertheless, this apparent dharma leaves behind all characteristics; and because it leaves behind all characteristics, it abides in calm stillness. Because it abides in calm stillness, it is never again subject to conditions. For this reason, although access is possible, it does not abrogate this aspect of leaving behind conditioning. In this wise, the second half [**As they leave behind all characteristics, they abide calmly,/And as they abide calmly, they are unconditioned**] elucidates the aspect of leaving behind conditioning.

> **All these conditionally produced dharmas,**
> **Those dharmas are not produced by conditions.**
>
> **Because there is no production or extinction due to causes and conditions,**
> **The natures of production and extinction are void and calm.**
> **The nature of conditions involves both the subject and object conditions,**
> **These conditions arise from the original condition.**
>
> **Hence, the production of dharmas is not due to conditions,**
> **This is also the case with the nonproduction of conditions.**
>
> **Dharmas that are produced according to causes and conditions,**
> **These dharmas [in turn function as] causes and conditions.**
> **[Those dharmas that] are characterized by being produced and extinguished according to causes and conditions,**
> **Those are in fact free from production and extinction.**

From here onward is the second [division, II.B.3.b.ii], an extensive proclamation. It is in two [subdivisions]:

the first three verses [II.B.3.b.ii.a] are an extensive explanation of the meaning of motionlessness;
the last two verses [II.B.3.b.ii.b] proclaim the aspect of gaining access.

The first [subdivision] also has two [segments]:

the first two verses [II.B.3.b.ii.a.1] explore [the idea that causes and

conditions] are originally unascertainable, thereby elucidating motionlessness;
the last single verse [II.B.3.b.ii.a.2] examines [the idea that causes and conditions] are ultimately unascertainable, thereby elucidating motionlessness.

This first [segment] has three [subsegments]:

overview [II.B.3.b.ii.a.1.a];
explication [II.B.3.b.ii.a.1.b];
conclusion [II.B.3.b.ii.a.1.c].

In the first [subsegment, II.B.3.b.ii.a.1.a], the lines "**All these conditionally produced dharmas,/Those dharmas are not produced by conditions**" offer an overview of the fact that, for all dharmas that have come to fruition, their conditions are unproduced.

Next [II.B.3.b.ii.a.1.b], there are four lines that explicate the aspect of nonproduction. "**Because there is no production or extinction due to causes and conditions**" clarifies that all causes and conditions are being produced and extinguished without respite; therefore, they have no efficacy to produce a fruition. "**The natures of production and extinction are void and calm**": because there is no abiding, there is in fact no production or extinction. Because their natures are void and calm, there are also no fruitions that are produced. "**The nature of conditions involves both the subject and object conditions**": the hidden potency inherent in the seeds that serve as causes and conditions is called "**nature.**" That faculty, which is the predominant condition *(adhipatipratyaya)*, has the capacity to serve as the counterpart of the sensory realms; therefore, it is called **[674b]** the "**subject . . . condition.**" The sensory realms, which are the objective-support condition *(ālambanapratyaya)*, are the objective counterpart of that faculty; therefore, they are called the "**object . . . condition.**" Because sequentially conditioned dharmas are extinguished, they are not discussed here. In this wise, seeds—the "**nature of conditions**"—together with the two conditions of subject and object, are all generated by the original condition. Therefore, it says, "**These conditions arise from the original condition.**" Since these are in fact the origin of all conditions, it is just as was explained previously: because "**the natures of production and extinction are void,**" the function of production does not occur. Owing to these three aspects, we can refer to the nonproduction aspect of conditions.

"**Hence, the production of dharmas is not due to conditions**": this conclusion [II.B.3.b.ii.a.1.c] states that the arising of fruition dharmas is not produced by conditions. "**This is also the case with the nonproduction of conditions**": this conclusion states that the nonproduction of conditions is also identical to that fruition.

Next [II.B.3.b.ii.a.2] is a single verse that examines [the idea that causes and conditions] are ultimately unascertainable, thereby elucidating motionlessness. "Dharmas that are produced according to causes and conditions,/These dharmas [in turn function as] causes and conditions": this clarifies that all fruition dharmas also serve as the causal condition *(hetupratyaya)* because they operate as the conditions for those dharmas that are expected to be produced later. Since all these fruition dharmas serve as causal conditions, it is just as was explained previously: "the natures of production and extinction are void." Therefore, it says, "[Those dharmas that] are characterized by being produced and extinguished according to causes and conditions,/Those are in fact free from production and extinction."

When the previous brief explanation [III.B.3.b.i] was given, it explicitly elucidated the fact that the fruition is void. Now, since this extensive proclamation [III.B.3.b.ii] explained the causal condition, it sought to elucidate the fact that the causes and fruitions of all dharmas are motionless and that this in fact is the impartial path to bodhi.[338] One should not seek for bodhi apart from this dharma. This explains the main idea of these verses. As Dharma Master [Seng]zhao (384–414) said: "How distant is the path? Truth is in the things you touch. How distant are the saints? One's spirit is what experiences them."[339]

Those characteristics that are thus, true, and real,
Originally make no appearance,
All dharmas in the present moment,
Produce their appearances themselves.

Accordingly that consummately pure origin,
Is originally not caused by the multitude of forces.

Precisely where this is subsequently obtained,
One reattains the original attainment.

These two verses are the proclamation of the aspect of gaining access [II.B.3.b.ii.b]. It is in three [segments]:

one [II.B.3.b.ii.b.1], the first verse elucidates that all things that are subject to motion are thus and motionless;
two [II.B.3.b.ii.b.2], **[674c]** the next two lines clarify that the motionless origin does not avail itself of the mass of conditions;
three [II.B.3.b.ii.b.3], the last two lines clarify that leaving behind conditioned dharmas is the aspect of gaining access.

"Where this is subsequently obtained" means that point after the completion of the path. In the preceding brief explanation [division, III.B.3.b.i], the statement "at the time when [their natures are] . . . calm, and extinct" (p. 673c) corresponds to the line "where this is subsequently obtained." Since they are calm and extinct, how would there be either place or time? Only by leaving behind time and place would one be able to take advantage of time and place. "One reattains the original attainment": the culmination of the acquired enlightenment is called "attainment" because it can catalyze attainment. At the culmination of acquired enlightenment, it turns into the original enlightenment; for this reason, "one reattains the original attainment."

The preceding part [III.B.3], on the third resolution of doubt, is now complete.

> At that time, Chijang heard what the Buddha said and his mind-ground became enraptured. At that time, there was no one in the congregation who entertained any further doubts. Once [Chijang] had known all their minds, he recited gāthās:
>
> I knew the doubts in all their minds,
> And accordingly questioned cordially and sincerely,
> Through his virtue of great friendliness, the Tathāgata
> Has analyzed [these doubts] and left none remaining.
> Everyone in these two congregations,
> Has clearly understood everything.
>
> Through my understanding, I now
> Proselyte universally all sentient beings.
> Just as the great friendliness of the Buddha,
> Does not allow him to abandon his original vow,
> Hence at that "only-child stage,"
> [The bodhisattva continues to] linger in defilement.

This is the fourth [section, IV], on gaining comprehension. These three verses are in two subsections:

The first verse and a half [IV.A] provide the conclusion to the preceding [account] of the benefit of resolving doubts;
the last verse and a half [IV.B] declare the subsequent practice of universal proselytization.

[IV.B: The subsequent practice of universal proselytization:] "Only-child stage" *(ilcha chi):* from the first bhūmi on up, [a bodhisattva] has already realized that all sentient beings are equal and he regards each and every sentient being as if they were his only child. This is called the pure predominant intention *(āśaya).* He employs a simile to allude to this state of mind and calls it the "only-child stage." "Linger in defilement": although a bodhisattva realizes the impartiality of all dharmas, owing to the power of his expedients, he refuses to abandon defilements *(kleśa)*. This is because, if he were to abandon all defilements and proclivities *(anuśaya)* and thence access nirvāṇa, he would be turning his back on his original vow. As it states in the analysis of *samāhita* [concentrated absorption] in the *Yogācārabhūmiśāstra:* **[675a]**

> The "analytical suppression" *(nirodhasamāpatti)* is called "uncontaminated" *(anāsrava)* because it is dissociated from the defilements. Because it is not so associated, it is free from any coordinating conditions; and because it is not produced in conjunction with any defilements, it is supramundane. It is not something that ordinary beings can practice, except for those bodhisattvas who have already accessed the [seventh] Far-Reaching Bhūmi. Although bodhisattvas have the capacity to generate supramundane dharmas and make them manifest, nevertheless, owing to the power of their expedients and skillful stratagems, they choose not to abandon defilements.[340]

Nota Bene: In this passage, "choose not to abandon" does not mean ultimate abandonment, like that of the arhats, and so forth; therefore, it says, "choose not to abandon." But because it is not complete nonabandonment, it says, "choose not to abandon." A detailed treatment of this can be found in the *Essay on the Two Hindrances.*[341] Because [defilements] are not abandoned, it says that [bodhisattvas continue to] "linger in defilement." But because they do not access nirvāṇa, they universally proselyte the world-systems of the ten directions.

In the three major sections of this one-roll-long sūtra, Section Two: The Main Body, is completed as above.

Section Three (B): Dissemination

> **At that time, the Tathāgata addressed the congregation: "This bodhisattva is inconceivable! He constantly relieves sentient beings from their suffering through his great friendliness. If there is a sentient being who keeps the dharma [taught in] this sūtra or keeps this bodhisattva's name, he then will not fall into the evil destinies, and all obstructions and difficulties will completely vanish. If there are sentient beings who have no extraneous thoughts remaining, but reflect exclusively on the dharma of this sūtra and cultivate and train in it, then this bodhisattva will constantly manifest a transformation body and speak the dharma to them. He will guard and protect those persons, never abandon them even for a moment, and prompt them quickly to attain *anuttarasamyaksaṃbodhi.***

From here onward is Section Three (B): Dissemination [in part 4: An Exegesis of the Text]. It is in six [sections]:

One [I], dissemination through praising the interlocutor;
Two [II], dissemination through encouraging the congregation;
Three [III], dissemination through assigning a title [to the sūtra];
Four [IV], dissemination through receiving and keeping [the sūtra];
Five [V], dissemination through repentance;
Six [VI], dissemination through practicing respectfully [the teachings of the sūtra].

This is the first [section, I], dissemination through praising the interlocutor, **[675b]** which praises the four kinds of superior meritorious qualities of the bodhisattva who is this sūtra's agent of dissemination:

1. the meritorious quality of universally proselytizing everyone through great friendliness;
2. the meritorious quality of the special benefit that comes from keeping this sūtra;
3. the meritorious quality of speaking the dharma via transformation bodies;
4. the meritorious quality that prompts them to gain the ultimate fruition.

> "All of you bodhisattvas! When you proselyte sentient beings, you should encourage all of them to cultivate and train in this decisive, definitive meaning *(nitārtha)* of the Mahāyāna."

This is the second [section, II], dissemination through encouraging the congregation. "Decisive, definitive meaning" elucidates the fact that this is the most profound and ultimate [truth], which needs no augmentation.

> At that time, Ānanda arose from his seat and, coming forward, addressed the Buddha: "As the Tathāgata has said, the Mahāyāna's aggregate of merits is certain to eradicate the fetters. The inspiration of the enlightenment, which is unproduced, is inconceivable.
>
> "What sūtra title should such a teaching be given? How much merit will be forthcoming from receiving and keeping such a sūtra? I beg the Buddha to explain this for us, out of his friendliness and compassion."

From here onward is the third [section, III], dissemination through assigning a title [to the sūtra, which has two subsections]:

initially [III.A], a question;
subsequently [III.B], an answer.

In the question [subsection], there are two [parts]:

initially [II.A.1], comprehension;
subsequently [III.A.2], a question.

In the comprehension [part, II.A.1,] are elucidated the four superior capacities of this sūtra. The first capacity is that [this sūtra] can prompt one who keeps it to gain immeasurable merit, as in the sūtra [passage] "**the Mahāyāna's aggregate of merits.**" The second capacity is that it can prompt one who keeps it to eradicate forever all the fetters, as in the sūtra [passage] "**is certain to eradicate the fetters.**" Three, the principal idea to which it refers is the inspiration of original enlightenment, as in the sūtra [passage] "**the inspiration of the enlightenment, which is unproduced.**" Four, the teaching that provides such references is difficult to conceptualize, as in the sūtra [passage] it "**is inconceivable.**"

Next, in the question [part, III.A.2], he asks about two matters. Initially [III.A.2.a], he asks about the sūtra's title, in order to know the essential point of the sūtra. Subsequently [III.A.2.b], he asks about the merit that derives from keeping [the sūtra], since one keeps a sūtra in order to seek merit.

> **The Buddha replied: "Oh son of good family! The name of this sūtra is inconceivable. It has been protected by all the buddhas of antiquity.**
>
> **"It is able to catalyze access into the sea of the tathāgatas' all-embracing knowledge. [675c] If there is a sentient being who keeps this sūtra, then in all other sūtras he will have nothing more to seek. The dharma of this scripture encodes all dharmas and includes the essentials of all sūtras. It is the unifying thread of the dharmas of all these sūtras.**
>
> **"As far as the title of this sūtra is concerned, it is named *Sŏp taesŭng kyŏng (Mahāyānasaṃgraha-sūtra; Compendium of Mahāyāna Scripture); Kŭmgang sammae (Vajrasamādhi),* and *Muryangŭi chong (Anantanirdeśasiddhānta; Source of Immeasurable Doctrines).*"**

From here onward, in this answer [subsection, III.B], there are two [parts, III.B.1, III.B.2], which answer in sequence the two questions. In the first [part, III.B.1], there are also two [subparts]:

initially [III.B.1.a], he praises its name and significance;
subsequently [III.B.1.b], he assigns specifically its titles.

This first [subpart] is also in two [divisions]:

initially [III.B.1.a.i], summary praise of its title [**The name of this sūtra is inconceivable. It has been protected by all the buddhas of antiquity**];
subsequently [III.B.1.a.ii], specific elucidation of its significances.

From "**it is able to catalyze access**" onward is the specific elucidation of its significances [III.B.1.a.ii], which elucidates three significances.

[1.] "**It is able to catalyze access into the sea of the tathāgatas' . . . knowledge. . . . he will have nothing more to seek**": this elucidates the significance of the title *Kŭmgang sammae (Vajrasamādhi)*. There is no dharma that [the *vajrasamādhi*] cannot pulverize and no principle that it cannot probe. Owing to these [qualities], it can prompt "**access into the sea of the tathāgatas' . . . knowledge,**" for there is nothing further that one will anticipate.

[2.] "**The dharma of this scripture encodes all dharmas and includes the essentials of all sūtras**": this elucidates the significance of the title *Sŏp taesŭng kyŏng (Mahāyānasaṃgraha-sūtra; Compendium of Mahāyāna Scripture)*.

[3.] "**It is the unifying thread of the dharmas of all these sūtras**": this elucidates the significance of the title *Muryangŭi chong (Anantanirdeśasiddhānta; Source of Immeasurable Doctrines)*.

Concerning the distinction in the significance of these [last] two titles, the former *[Sŏp taesŭng kyŏng]* clarifies the denotation of "extensively incorporating all the sūtras"; the latter *[Muryangŭi chong]* elucidates that ultimacy which threads through all the sūtras.

Next [III.B.1.b], he assigns its three titles. The details have already been extensively explained in the two divisions [III.B.1.a.i, ii] of the preceding exegesis.

> **"If there is a person who receives and keeps this scripture, he will be called one who welcomes and serves [lit., receives and keeps] hundreds of thousands of buddhas. Such meritorious qualities may be compared to the limitlessness of space, which is inconceivable. It is this sūtra alone with which I now charge you."**

This is the answer [III.B.2] to the second question, which elucidates four types of superior meritorious qualities. **[676a]** One [III.B.2.a], the superior meritorious quality of serving the buddhas. This means that this sūtra is able to subsume the minds of all the buddhas, as in the sūtra [passage] that he "**welcomes and serves hundreds of thousands of buddhas.**" Two [III.B.2.b], the superior meritorious quality of being extensive and vast, as in the sūtra [passage] "**the limitlessness [of space].**" Three [III.B.2.c], the superior meritorious quality of being extremely profound, as in the sūtra [passage] "**is inconceivable.**" Four [III.B.2.d], the meritorious quality of being incomparable, as in the sūtra [passage] "**It is this sūtra alone.**"

> **Ānanda asked: "As for receiving and keeping this scripture: What sort of mental attitude does he maintain? What sort of person does it?"**

The Buddha replied: "Oh son of good family! For the person who receives and keeps this scripture, his mind is free from gain or loss and constantly cultivates the religious life *(brahmacarya)*. If he constantly gladdens and purifies his mind of conceptual proliferation *(prapañca)*, then even amidst the crowded masses, his mind will remain ever concentrated; even if he dwells in the household life, he will not grasp at the three realms of existence."

From here onward is the fourth [section, IV], dissemination through receiving and keeping [the sūtra]. It is in two [subsections]:

one [IV.A], an explicit clarification of "receiving and keeping":
two [IV.B], a reiteration through a series of exchanges.

The initial [subsection] is in two [parts]:

initially [IV.A.1], a question;
subsequently [IV.A.2], an answer.

The question [part] is in two [subparts]:

initially [IV.A.1.a], a question regarding the mental attitude of the person who receives and keeps this sūtra;
subsequently [IV.A.1.b], a question regarding the meritorious benefit coming to one who receives and keeps this sūtra.

In the answer [part, IV.A.2], he answers in sequence these two questions.
In the initial [answer subpart, IV.A.2.a], he [answers question IV.A.1.a, "What sort of mental attitude does he maintain?"] by clarifying five kinds of mental attitude. (1) "His mind is free from gain or loss" means that he does not notice the strengths and shortcomings of other people. (2) He "constantly cultivates the religious life *(brahmacarya)*" means that he cultivates internally that pure practice which remains separate from characteristics. (3) "He constantly gladdens and stills[342] his mind" means that he is motionless amid action. (4) "His mind will remain ever concentrated" means that he is undistracted amid distraction. (5) "He will not grasp at the three realms of existence" means that he is untainted even while residing amid the taints.

"There are five types of merits accruing from this person's appearance in the world. First, he will be honored by the congregation. Second, he will not die an untimely death. Third, he will eruditely rebut perverse opinions. Fourth, he will joyfully ferry across sentient beings. Fifth, he will be able to access the sanctified path. It is this sort of person who will receive and keep this scripture." **[676b]**

This is the answer [IV.A.2.b] to the second question [IV.A.1.b, "What sort of person does it [viz. receiving and keeping this sūtra]?"]. In accordance with the preceding five [mental] attitudes, one gains these five merits. [1] "He will be honored by the congregation" because he does not notice the congregation's strengths and shortcomings. [2] "He will not die an untimely death" because he constantly cultivates that practice which remains separate from characteristics. [3] "He will eruditely rebut perverse opinions" because he gladdens and stills his mind. [4] "He will joyfully ferry across sentient beings" because he is ever concentrated even amid distraction. [5] "He will be able to access the sanctified path" because he does not grasp at the three realms of existence.

> Ānanda asked, "Will those who ferry across all sentient beings be as worthy of receiving offerings as that person or not?"
>
> The Buddha replied: "Such people are able to become a great field of merit *(puṇyakṣetra)* for sentient beings, to practice constantly great knowledge, and to articulate both expedients and truth; they are the saṃghas of the four types to be relied on *(pratisaraṇa)*. They receive all manner of offerings, including even heads, eyes, marrow, and gray matter; so how could they not but receive clothes and provisions? Oh son of good family! Such a person is your spiritual mentor, your bridge; how could an ordinary person not but worship him?"

From here onward is a reiteration through a series of exchanges [IV.B], which is in two [parts]:

initially [IV.B.1], a clarification regarding the essence of a field of merit;
subsequently [IV.B.2], an elucidation of his ability to produce merit.

This [exchange] is the first [subpart, IV.B.1]. "The saṃghas of the four types to be relied on": the first type of reliance involves a defiled nature and is located before the bhūmis; the remaining three types of reliances are located on the bhūmis. This is as is extensively explained in the *Nirvāṇa Sūtra*.[343]

> Ānanda asked, "If, at that person's place, one receives and keeps this sūtra and worships that person, how much merit will one accrue?"
>
> The Buddha answered: "If, furthermore, there is a person who gives a cityful of gold and silver, it would not measure up to the inconceivable amount [of merit] forthcoming from receiving and keeping one four-line gāthā of this scripture at that person's place or from worshiping that person. Make offerings to this person!"[344]

This is the second [section, IV.B.2], a clarification that one who keeps this sūtra has the ability to produce much merit. The merit accrued from giving "a cityful [676c] of gold and silver" to a person who does not keep this sūtra does not even compare to the merit that accrues from making offerings of even one meal or an article of clothing to a person who keeps even one of its four-line gāthās.

> "Oh son of good family! The mind of a person who encourages all sentient beings to keep this sūtra will be constantly concentrated; he will never forget his original mind. If he forgets his original mind, he then must repent. This practice (dharma) of repentance produces clarity and coolness *(śītībhūta)*."

From here onward is the fifth [section, V], dissemination through repentance, which is in two [subsections]:

initially [V.A], praising the meritorious quality of repentance;
subsequently [V.B], reiteration through exchanges.

In the first [subsection, V.A], regarding the term "clarity and coolness": "clarity" means to bring an end to the turbidities *(kaṣāya)*,[345] which are the causes of unwholesome action; "coolness" means to leave behind the afflictions, which come to fruition as birth and death.

> Ānanda stated, "Repenting of previous evil deeds does not mean that they have receded into the past."
>
> The Buddha responded: "So it is. It is like bringing a bright lamp into a dark room: that darkness instantly vanishes. Oh son of good family! We do not say that we have repented from all previous evil deeds; and yet we still say that they have receded into the past."

From here onward is the second [subsection, V.B], reiteration through exchanges. It contains two dialogues:

initially [V.B.1], an exchange that elucidates the logic behind repentance;
subsequently [V.B.2], an exchange that elucidates the dharma of practicing repentance.

In this [first exchange, V.B.1], the intent of the question is to ask about "repenting of previous evil deeds." Doesn't the term "repentance" imply that previous evil deeds have yet to recede into the past? If they are "previous," then they are "not of the present." But if they have already in fact "receded into the past," then what need would there be to repent of an evil deed that no longer exists?

In the answer, the sentence "so it is" means "so it is" that "previous evil deeds have . . . not receded into the past"; therefore, one does not repent from something that is nonexistent. Why is this? Evil deeds that one has performed previously suffuse the foundational consciousness [the *ālayavijñāna*] so that their seeds constantly flow out into the present. By this logic, they have not yet receded into the past. Moreover, by repenting now, one can control the moment of their production, prompting those seeds of evil deeds **[677a]** to stop flowing into the present. Just as when a lamp is lit, the darkness of a room vanishes, [so too] the seeds of evil deeds will not reach the present moment. At that time, while we then explain that [those seeds] have been prompted to recede into the past, "**we do not say that we have repented from all previous evil deeds.**" "**All previous [evil deeds]**" cannot be repented from because we cannot cause them not to exist in the past; we merely ensure that their past existence does not reach into present. "Not reaching into the present" is a product of repentance. This differs from the sense of eradicating the fetters, in that that [viz. eradication of the fetters] draws upon the principle of disjunction [lit. production and cessation] to cause what has yet to be produced not to reach the present; while this [viz. repentance] draws upon the principle of continuity *(saṃtati)* to prompt what has previously existed not to reach again into the present. Furthermore, eradicating the fetters eradicates forever the seeds [of evil deeds], while repenting from previous evil deeds subdues the potential functioning of those seeds so that they do not reach into the present. From this standpoint, we may "**say that they have receded into the past.**"

> **Ānanda asked, "What is meant by 'repentance'?"**
>
> **The Buddha replied: "By relying on the teachings of this sūtra, one accesses the contemplation of true reality. As soon as one accesses that contemplation, all evil deeds will vanish completely. Leaving behind all evil destinies, one will be reborn in the Pure Land, where one will quickly achieve *anuttarasamyaksaṃbodhi*."**

This is the second [exchange, V.B.2], which elucidates the dharma of practicing repentance. This answer is in two [subparts]:

initially [V.B.2.a], a clarification of the dharma to be practiced;
subsequently [V.B.2.b], a revelation of its superior benefit.

In this first [subpart, V.B.2.a], the sentence "**By relying on the teachings of this sūtra, one accesses the contemplation of true reality**" means that, based on the purport of the teachings of the *Vajrasamādhi*, one destroys all the characteristics of dharmas; this is called "**accesses the [contemplation] of true reality.**" This refers to the contemplation of apparent reality, which occurs before the bhūmis. "**As soon as one accesses that contemplation, all evil deeds will vanish completely**": all evil obstructions are produced from dubious conceptions. Now, by destroying all characteristics and accessing the contemplation of true reality, one suddenly destroys all the objects of those dubious conceptions. Therefore, **all evil deeds** will in an instant **vanish completely.**

Next [V.B.2.b], he elucidates its superior benefit, which appears in two passages. **"Leaving behind all evil destinies, one will be reborn in the Pure Land"**: this clarifies his elegant reward [of rebirth inside a lotus flower in the Pure Land]; **"one will quickly achieve [677b] *anuttarasamyaksaṃbodhi*"**: this reveals the reward of the fruition [of enlightenment].

> **When the Buddha had finished preaching this sūtra, Ānanda, the bodhisattvas, and the great fourfold congregation were all enraptured and elated, and their minds achieved certitude. Worshiping the Buddha's feet with their foreheads, they were enraptured and elated, and practiced [his teaching] respectfully.**

This is the sixth [section,VI], dissemination through practicing respectfully [the teachings of the sūtra], which is discussed in four passages. [1] **"Were all enraptured and elated"** means that they were enraptured and elated by hearing the dharma. [2] **"Their minds achieved certitude"** means that they left behind all perplexity *(vicikitsā)*. [3] **"Worshiping the Buddha's feet with their foreheads"** means that they revered the dharma and venerated its speaker. [4] **"They were enraptured and elated, and practiced [his teaching] respectfully"** means that they became elated when they practiced [his teaching].

> This most profound and sublime teaching of the *Vajra[samādhi]*,
> Receiving it in reverence and in faith, I have now commented briefly upon it.
> May the wholesome roots [produced by writing this commentary] pervade the dharma-realm,
> Universally inspiring everyone, without remainder!

Appendix

A Schematic Outline of Wŏnhyo's *Exposition of the Vajrasamādhi-Sūtra*

The appendix offers the complete outline of the exegetical sections I have proposed in my English translation of Wŏnhyo's *Exposition* included in Part 2 of this book. I include it here as a separate appendix so that the reader can glean at a glance the complexity of Wŏnhyo's commentary. This outline follows the numbering schemata I adopt in my translation and does not, of course, occur in Wŏnhyo's original text. Page and register numbers marking the beginning of each category, which are included in brackets in this English translation, correspond to the edition of Wŏnhyo's *Kumgang sammaegyŏng non* published in the *Han'guk Pulgyo chŏnsŏ.*

Part One: A Statement of its Main Idea 604b

Part Two: An Analysis of the Themes of the Sūtra 604c

I. Synthetic standpoint 604c
II. Analytical standpoint 604c

Part Three: An Explanation of the Title 605a

I. Explication of *vajra* 605b
  I.A. Connotations [of the word *vajra*] 605b
  I.B. An analysis [of the compound vajrasamādhi] 605b
    I.B.1. An examination of samādhi and prajñā 605b
    I.B.2. Distinguishing [three] related concentrations 605c
II. Explication of the term samādhi 606a
  II.A. Explication of the meaning of samādhi 606a
  II.B. Overview of different types of concentration 605c

II.B.1. Distinguishing the different designations [of concentration] 606a
II.B.2. An overview of their general categories 607a

Part Four: An Exegesis of the Text 607a

Section One: Prologue

I. Generic [prologue] 607b
II. Specific [prologue] 607c
II.A. The setting 607c
II.B. Preaching the sūtra 607c
II.B.1. A prologue that gives the sūtra's title 607c
II.B.2. Praise for the sūtra's efficaciousness 607c
II.C. Accessing samādhi 608a
II.D. Reiterative verses 608a
II.D.1. Prologue 608a
II.D.2. Verses 608a
II.D.2.a. Versifying the preaching of the sūtra 608a
II.D.2.a.i. Succinct clarification 608b
II.D.2.a.ii. Specific elucidations [viz. praises of the questions and the responses] 608b
II.D.2.a.ii.a. Praising the breadth and depth of the questions 608b
II.D.2.a.ii.b. [Praising the superlative inspiration behind the Buddha's response] 608b
II.D.2.b Versifying the access to samādhi 608b

Section Two: Main Body, the Sequential Elucidation of Contemplation Practice

FIRST DIVISION OF CONTEMPLATION PRACTICE: REJECTING ALL CHARACTERISTICS OF SENSE-OBJECTS TO REVEAL THE SIGNLESS CONTEMPLATION

I. Emerging from samādhi 609b
I.A. The perfection of the time for preaching the dharma 609b
I.B. The perfection of the preacher of the dharma 609b
I.C. The perfection of his autonomy 609b
II. Starting to speak 609b
II.A. Extended prose narration 609b
II.A.1. Concise overview 609c
II.A.1.a. Overview of the signless contemplation 609c

II.A.1.a.i. Overview of the fact that the Tathāgata himself accesses the signless contemplation 609c
II.A.1.a.ii. Overview of the fact that he prompts others to access the signless contemplation 609c
II.A.1.b. Overview of the dharma that is contemplated 609c
II.A.1.b.i. An explicit overview of the profundity of the dharma that is contemplated 610a
II.A.1.b.ii. Explaining this profound dharma to others 610a
II.A.2. Extensive explanation 610b
II.A.2.a. Initial request 610b
II.A.2.a.i. Prologue involving personal etiquette 610b
II.A.2.a.i.a. Referring to both the time and the speaker 610b
II.A.2.a.i.b. Prologue involving personal etiquette 610b
II.A.2.a.ii. Clarification in the form of an address 610b
II.A.2.a.ii.a. he alludes to the era 610b
II.A.2.a.ii.b. he requests that [the Buddha] speak to them 610b–c
II.A.2.b. Subsequent explanation/proclamation 610c
II.A.2.b.i. The Buddha's proclamation to them 610c
II.A.2.b.i.a. Praising the question 610c–611a
II.A.2.b.i.b. Consenting to preach 611a
II.A.2.b.ii. Explicit proclamation in response to the request 611a
II.A.2.b.ii.a. Clarification regarding the signless contemplation 611a
II.A.2.b.ii.a.1. An explicit explanation of the characteristics of this contemplation practice 611a
II.A.2.b.ii.a.1.a. Expedient contemplation 611a–b
II.A.2.b.ii.a.1.b. Unmediated contemplation 611b–612a
II.A.2.b.ii.a.2. A series of dialogues that resolves all doubts and objections 612a
II.A.2.b.ii.a.2.a. First exchange 612a
II.A.2.b.ii.a.2.a.I. Question 612a–b
II.A.2.b.ii.a.2.a.II. Answer 612b
II.A.2.b.ii.a.2.a.II.A. Explicit answer 612b–c
II.A.2.b.ii.a.2.a.II.B. Answer that resolves [a doubt] 612c
II.A.2.b.ii.a.2.b. Second exchange 612c
II.A.2.b.ii.a.2.b.I. Question 613a
II.A.2.b.ii.a.2.b.II. Answer 613a
II.A.2.b.ii.a.2.b.II.A. Treatment for the grasping at personality 613a
II.A.2.b.ii.a.2.b.II.A.1. Generic [treatment] 613a
II.A.2.b.ii.a.2.b.II.A.1.a. Contemplation of conditioned production as uncreated 613a

characteristics throughout all three time periods 620a
II.A.2.b.ii.b.7.b.II.A.1. Instruction 620a–b
II.A.2.b.ii.b.7.b.II.A.2. Simile 620b
II.A.2.b.ii.b.7.b.II.A.3. Correlation 620b
II.A.2.b.ii.b.7.b.II.B. Elucidation of perfecting one's cultivation of the six pāramitās by harmonizing with the dharmadhātu 620b–c
II.A.2.b.ii.b.8. Sixth [viz. eighth] exchange [containing a reiterated elucidation of the supramundane aspect of the six pāramitās] 620c
II.A.2.b.ii.b.8.a. Question 620c
II.A.2.b.ii.b.8.b. Answer 620c
II.A.2.b.ii.b.8.b.I. Concise overview 620c
II.A.2.b.ii.b.8.b.II. Extensive explication 620c
II.A.2.b.ii.b.8.b.II.A. Specific explication [of each pāramitā]
II.A.2.b.ii.b.8.b.II.A.1. Explication of *dānapāramitā* 620c–621a
II.A.2.b.ii.b.8.b.II.A.2. Explication of *śīlapāramitā* 621a
II.A.2.b.ii.b.8.b.II.A.3. Explication of *kṣāntipāramitā* 621a
II.A.2.b.ii.b.8.b.II.A.4. Explication of *vīryapāramitā* 621a
II.A.2.b.ii.b.8.b.II.A.5. Explication of *dhyānapāramitā* 621b
II.A.2.b.ii.b.8.b.II.A.6. Explication of prajñāpāramitā 621b–c
II.A.2.b.ii.b.8.b.II.B. Comprehensive clarification 621c
II.A.2.b.ii.b.8.b.II.B.1. Clarification that the six pāramitās are identical to the liberation 621c–622a
II.A.2.b.ii.b.8.b.II.B.2. Elucidation that liberation is in fact nirvāṇa 622a
II.A.2.b.ii.b.8.b.II.B.2.a. Clarification of liberation 622a
II.A.2.b.ii.b.8.b.II.B.2.b. Reference to nirvāṇa 622a–b
II.B. Reiterative verses 622b
II.B.1. Preface [proclaimed by the editor of the sūtra] 622b
II.B.2. Verses themselves [seven quatrains in twenty-eight lines] 622b
II.B.2.a. Six specific quatrains 622b

II.B.2.a.i. Concise overview in verse form of what has preceded [two quatrains and one line, ll. 1–9] 622b–c
II.B.2.a.ii. Extensive explication in verse form of what follows [three quatrains and three lines, ll. 10–24] 622c
II.B.2.a.ii.a. Extensive account in verse form of the signless contemplation [five lines, ll. 10–14] 622c
II.B.2.a.ii.b. Extensive account in verse form of the aspect of one enlightenment [two and a half quatrains, ll. 15–24] 622c
II.B.2.b. One summarizing quatrain [ll. 25–28] 623b
III. The congregation gains benefit 623b

Section Two: Main Body (cont.)

SECOND DIVISION OF CONTEMPLATION PRACTICE: EXTINGUISHING THE MIND SUBJECT TO PRODUCTION IN ORDER TO EXPLAIN THE PRACTICE OF NONPRODUCTION

I. An explicit explanation 623c
I.A. Series of dialogic exchanges [first subsection] 623c
I.A.1. Question 623c
I.A.1.a. Preface of the sūtra editor 623c–624a
I.A.1.b. Expression of the question 624a
I.A.2. Answer 624a
I.A.2.a. Pointing out the characteristics of the acquiescence to nonproduction 624a
I.A.2.b. Elucidating the fault of presuming that the acquiescence to nonproduction can actually be attained 624b
I.A.3. Problematic point 624b
I.A.4. Rebuttal 624b
I.A.4.a. Explicit rebuttal 624b
I.A.4.b. Explanatory rebuttal 624b
I.A.5. Request 624b–c
I.A.6. Explication 624c
I.A.6.a. Analyzing the principle of nonattainment 624c
I.A.6.a.i. Instruction 624c
I.A.6.a.ii. Simile 624c
I.A.6.a.iii. Correlation 624c–625a
I.A.6.b. Revealing the principle of nonproduction 625a
I.A.6.b.i. Simile 625a
I.A.6.b.i.a. Clarification of the four negations 625a–b
I.A.6.b.i.b. Clarification of the eight negations 625b–c
I.A.6.b.ii. Correlation 625a
I.A.6.c. Bringing up the negative aspects [of presuming that the mind-nature exists in reality] 625c

I.A.6.d. Clarifying the positive aspects [of understanding the mind-nature] 625c–626a
I.B. Series of exchanges in which the [the Buddha] scrutinizes [the bodhisattva] 626a
  I.B.1. [The bodhisattva] refers to practice in order to raise a problematic point concerning the principle 626a–b
  I.B.2. [The Buddha's] interrogation on whether [the bodhisattva] has achieved realization 626b
  I.B.3. [The bodhisattva's] respectful reply that he is free of [any attachment to] realization 626b
    I.B.3.a. Clarification of his freedom from realization 626b
      I.B.3.a.i. Overview 626b–c
      I.B.3.a.ii. Explication 626c
    I.B.3.b. Raising its negative attributes 626c
    I.B.3.c. Elucidating its positive attributes 626c
  I.B.4. [The Buddha's] interrogation of whether [the bodhisattva] has attainment 626c–627a
  I.B.5. [The bodhisattva's] respectful reply that he is free of [any attachment to] attainment 627a
    I.B.5.a. Overview 627a
    I.B.5.b. Explication 627a
      I.B.5.b.i. Clarification that the bodhi that is attained is free from any nature of attainment *[anupalabdhitva]* 627a–b
      I.B.5.b.ii. Elucidation that all the practices that bring about this attainment are free from any characteristic of being an agent of attainment 627b
    I.B.5.c. Conclusion 627b
  I.B.6. [The Buddha's concluding] narrative that he is free from both attainment and realization 627b
    I.B.6.a. Actual narration 627b
      I.B.6.a.i. General narrative 627b
      I.B.6.a.ii. Specific narrative 627b
        I.B.6.a.ii.a. Narration of [the concept of being] "unproduced" 627b
        I.B.6.a.ii.b. Narration of [the aspect of] "calm" extinction 627b–c
          I.B.6.a.ii.b.1. Sequential enumeration 627c
          I.B.6.a.ii.b.2. Extensive explanation 627c
      I.B.6.a.iii. Concluding summation 627c–628a
    I.B.6.b. Reference to the negative aspects 628a
    I.B.6.c. Elucidation of the positive aspects 628a–b
  I.B.7. [The bodhisattva] reiterates his doubts 628b–c
  I.B.8. [The Buddha] resolves [the bodhisattva's] doubts 628c
I.C. The bodhisattva gains comprehension 628c–629a

- I.D. Completion of the Tathāgata's narrative 629a–629b
- II. [The bodhisattva's] praise [of the Buddha's] words in gāthās 629b
  - II.A. Preface 629b
  - II.B. Verses 629b
    - II.B.1. Instruction 629b
    - II.B.2. Ṣimile 629b
    - II.B.3. Correlation 629b
    - II.B.4. Summation 629b
- III. Hearing the explanation and gaining benefit 629b–c

[Section Two: Main Body (cont.)]

THIRD DIVISION OF CONTEMPLATION PRACTICE: THE INSPIRATION OF ORIGINAL ENLIGHTENMENT

- I. Extensive clarification of the inspiration of original enlightenment 629c
  - I.A. Clarifying quiescence through movement, which provides a brief overview of the theme of original enlightenment 629c
    - I.A.1. Prompting the body into action, so as to provide an overview of original enlightenment 629c–630a
    - I.A.2. Exchange of words, so as to provide an overview of original inspiration 630a
      - I.A.2.a. Question 630a
      - I.A.2.b. Answer 630a–b
      - I.A.2.c. Conclusion of the narrative 630b
    - I.A.3. Emitting rays of light and praising the original inspiration with verses 630b
      - I.A.3.a. Preface of the sūtra editor 630b
      - I.A.3.b. Specific praise of Muju Bodhisattva 630b–c
  - I.B. Progressing from the obscure to the evident, which is an extensive explanation of the aspect of original inspiration 630c
    - I.B.1. Explicit and extensive account 630c
      - I.B.1.a. Question 630c
      - I.B.1.b. Answer 630c
        - I.B.1.b.i. Overview 630c–631a
        - I.B.1.b.ii. Explication 631a
          - I.B.1.b.ii.a. Direct explanation 631a
          - I.B.1.b.ii.b. Reexplication 631a
    - I.B.2. Reiterated disquisition 631a
      - I.B.2.a. Disquisition on acquired enlightenment 631a
        - I.B.2.a.i. Disquisition on the fact that all the consciousnesses are void and calm 631a–b
          - I.B.2.a.i.a. First set of two exchanges explicitly clarifying void-calmness 631b

I.B.2.b.i.b.1. Question 633c–634a
I.B.2.b.i.b.2. Answer 634a
I.B.2.b.i.b.2.a. Specifying what is to be subdued 634a
I.B.2.b.i.b.2.b. Clarifying the agent that performs this subduing 634a
I.B.2.b.i.b.2.c. Elucidating the superior benefit that is obtained from the act of subduing. 634a
I.B.2.b.ii. Dispelling attachments 634a–b
I.B.2.b.ii.a. Clarification of nonabiding 634b
I.B.2.b.ii.a.1. Question 634b
I.B.2.b.ii.a.2. Answer [that explicitly dispels the grasping at abiding] 634b
I.B.2.b.ii.a.2.a. Brief subversion of this grasping 634b
I.B.2.b.ii.a.2.b. Extensive elucidation of the principle [of "nonabiding"] 634b
I.B.2.b.ii.a.2.b.I. Drawing on the standpoint of original enlightenment to clarify nonabiding 634b–c
I.B.2.b.ii.a.2.b.II. Drawing on the standpoint of actualized enlightenment to elucidate nonabiding 634c
I.B.2.b.ii.a.2.b.II.A. Overview 634c
I.B.2.b.ii.a.2.b.II.B. Explication 634c–635a
I.B.2.b.ii.b. Narration of nonattainment 635a
I.B.2.b.ii.b.1. Explicit clarification of nonattainment 635a
I.B.2.b.ii.b.1.a. Question 635a
I.B.2.b.ii.b.1.b. Answer 635a
I.B.2.b.ii.b.1.b.I. Instruction 635a
I.B.2.b.ii.b.1.b.II. Similes 635a
I.B.2.b.ii.b.1.b.II.A. Simile about the deluded son not realizing that he possesses gold coins, traveling about in poverty and destitution 635a–b
I.B.2.b.ii.b.1.b.II.B. Simile of the father revealing to his son that the son possesses these gold coins 635b
I.B.2.b.ii.b.1.b.II.C. Simile of [the son's] joy at obtaining the gold coins 635b–c
I.B.2.b.ii.b.1.b.II.D. [The father's] statement that they are not something that he has obtained 635c
I.B.2.b.ii.b.1.b.III. Correlations 635c
I.B.2.b.ii.b.1.b.III.A. General correlation 635c
I.B.2.b.ii.b.1.b.III.B. Specific correlation 635c–636a
I.B.2.b.ii.b.2. Dispelling again [the bodhisattva's] doubts 636a
I.B.2.b.ii.b.2.a. First exchange [involving a question concerning a doubt deriving from the simile and an answer dispelling this doubt] 636a

I.B.2.b.ii.b.2.b. Second exchange [dispelling the Bodhisattva's second doubt and elucidating the evils that are to be counteracted] 636a–b
I.B.2.b.ii.b.2.c. Third exchange [dispelling the third doubt and clarifying the path that serves as the counteragent]. 636b–c
I.B.2.b.ii.b.3. Comprehension 636c
I.B.2.b.ii.b.3.a. Generic statement of comprehension 636c
I.B.2.b.ii.b.3.b. Specific points of comprehension. 636c–637a
I.B.2.b.ii.b.3.b.I. Comprehension of the words and phrases 637a
I.B.2.b.ii.b.3.b.II. Comprehension of their meaning 637a–b
I.B.2.b.ii.b.4. Conclusion of the narrative 637b
II. Praising [the inspiration of original enlightenment] with gāthās 637b
II.A. General praise of the preacher—first two lines [of verse] 637b
II.B. Praising the preceding explanation of dharma—next four lines [of verse] 637b
II.C. Praising the explanation in the simile—last two lines [of verse] 637b
III. Congregation present at the time gains benefit 637b

Section Two: Main Body (cont.)

FOURTH DIVISION OF CONTEMPLATION PRACTICE: ABANDONING THE SPURIOUS TO ACCESS REALITY

I. Brief overview of the principal intent 637c
I.A. Analysis of the expedients that promote access 637c
I.A.1. Comprehensive overview 637c
I.A.2. Specific analysis [of four types of expedients] 637c
I.A.2.a. Expedient of knowing the time 637c–638a
I.A.2.b. Expedient of recognizing the potential *(ki)* 638a
I.A.2.c. Expedient that guides one to the access 638a–b
I.A.2.d. Expedient that leaves everything behind 638b
I.B. Revelation of the edge of reality, which is the object of access 638b
I.B.1. Brief clarification 638c
I.B.2. Reexplication 638c
I.B.3. Inappropriateness of grasping at either extreme 638c
I.B.4. Adept's superior inspiration 638c–639a
II. Extensive elucidation of the rationale 639a
II.A. Elucidation of the aspect of the edge of reality 639a
II.A.1. Clarification of the five voidnesses 639a

II.A.1.a. Question 639a
II.A.1.a.i. Restatement [of the Buddha's previous words] 639a
II.A.1.a.ii. Question itself 639a
II.A.1.a.ii.a. Question regarding the teaching regarding the five voidnesses 639a
II.A.1.a.ii.b. Question regarding the idea of neither clinging to nor rejecting anything 639a
II.A.1.b. Answer 639a–b
II.A.1.b.i. Response to the first question [elucidating the three types of true thusness] 639b
II.A.1.b.ii. Response to the second question 639b
II.A.2. Clarification of the three voidnesses 639b–640a
II.A.3. Clarification of the fact that voidness is truth 640a
II.A.3.a. Question 640a
II.A.3.b. Answer 640a–b
II.A.3.b.i. Explicit reply 640b
II.A.3.b.ii. Praise for its profundity 640b
II.A.3.b.ii.a. Explicit praise 640b
II.A.3.b.ii.b. Explicatory praise 640b
II.A.4. Clarification of the fact that truth is thus 640b–c
II.A.4.a. Question 640c
II.A.4.a.i. He raises the principle 640c
II.A.4.a.ii. He asks a question regarding his doubt 640c–641a
II.A.4.b. Answer to his doubt 641a
II.A.4.b.i. An affirmation 641a
II.A.4.b.ii. A negation 641a
II.A.4.b.ii.a. Elucidating the maculated dust of unenlightenment 641a
II.A.4.b.ii.b. Briefly making reference to the acquired enlightenment in distinction to this unenlightenment 641a–b
II.B. Clarification of the aspect of gaining access 641b
II.B.1. Comprehensive clarification of gaining access 641b
II.B.1.a. Question 641b
II.B.1.b. Answer 641b
II.B.2. Specific elucidation of gaining access 641b–c
II.B.2.a. General overview of various classifications 641c
II.B.2.b. Separate elucidation of each [of the two accesses] through an exchange 641c
II.B.2.b.i. Question 641c
II.B.2.b.i.a. A question [concerning a statement]. 641c
II.B.2.b.i.b. Objection. 641c
II.B.2.b.ii. Answer 641c
II.B.2.b.ii.a. Answer [consisting of three segments] 641c
II.B.2.b.ii.a.1. A listing of the number 641c

II.D.2.b.iii. Elucidation of the fact that bodhisattvas are able to see it [and become enlightened] 648a–b
II.D.2.c. The supreme inspiration that derives from being free from distress 648b
II.D.2.c.i. A remark 648b
II.D.2.c.ii. Answer 648b
II.D.2.c.ii.a. Assent to the initial query 648b–c
II.D.2.c.ii.b. Negation of the subsequent remark 648c–649a
II.D.2.d. The supreme inspiration of being nonabiding 649a
II.D.2.d.i. Comprehension of the preceding discussion 649a
II.D.2.d.i.a. Initial passage 649a
II.D.2.d.i.b. Second passage 649a
II.D.2.d.ii. Explicit elucidation of the supreme inspiration of nonabiding 649a–b
III. Śāriputra gains understanding 649b
III.A. Gaining understanding 649b
III.A.1. Versifying what was discussed previously—first three verses 649b
III.A.1.a. Versifying the path of nonabiding 649b–c
III.A.1.b. Versifying the levels of the six practices 649c
III.A.1.c. Versifying the three types of voidnesses 649c
III.A.2. Explaining one's personal arousal of the thought [of enlightenment]—subsequent two verses 649c
III.A.2.a. Explaining the present rank of arousing the thought [of enlightenment] 649c
III.A.2.b. Representing the practice of cultivation that follows [arousing the thought of enlightenment] 649c
III.B. Conclusion to the narrative 649c
IV. Congregation present at the time gains benefit 649c–650a

Section Two: Main Body (cont.)

FIFTH DIVISION OF CONTEMPLATION PRACTICE: SANCTIFIED PRACTICES EMERGE FROM THE VOIDNESS OF THE TRUE NATURE

I. Extensive explanations for those with sharp faculties 650b
I.A. Clarification that the three codes of morality are perfected through the true nature 650c
I.A.1. Question 650c
I.A.2. [Brief] answer 650c
I.A.2.a. Answer to the general question 650c
I.A.2.b. Follow-up answer to [the Buddha's own] separate question 651a
I.A.3. [Reiterated] query 651a

- I.A.4. [Extensive] explanation 651a
  - I.A.4.a. Explicit answer 651a
    - I.A.4.a.i. General import 651a–b
    - I.A.4.a.ii. Exegesis of the text itself 651b–c
  - I.A.4.b. Clarification of the generic overview of [all] the myriads of spiritual practices 651c
- I.A.5. Gaining understanding 651c
  - I.A.5.a. Recognizing that the one thusness with which he is in conformity is in fact the dharma-body 651c
  - I.A.5.b. Recognizing that the mind that conforms with thusness leaves behind all bonds by conforming to that thusness and has nothing that it cannot accomplish 651c

I.B. Clarification that the practices included among the constituents of the path *(bodhipakṣikadharma)* are established through the voidness of the true nature 651c–652a

- I.B.1. Question 652a
- I.B.2. Answer 652a
  - I.B.2.a. Assent 652a
  - I.B.2.b. Explication 652a
    - I.B.2.b.i. Direct explication 652a
    - I.B.2.b.ii. Reiterated elucidation 652a
      - I.B.2.b.ii.a. Rejection of the aspect of difference 652a
      - I.B.2.b.ii.b. Elucidation of the aspect of being identical 652a
      - I.B.2.b.ii.c. Clarification that the aspect of being identical subsumes all dharmas 652a–b
      - I.B.2.b.ii.d. Clarification that the aspect of being identical leaves behind all dangers *(ādīnava)* 652b–653a

I.C. Clarification that the teachings of the Tathāgata are spoken in accordance with principle 653a

- I.C.1. Question 653a
- I.C.2. Answer 653a
  - I.C.2.a. Motive behind the Buddha's speech 653a–b
  - I.C.2.b. Elucidation of the difference between locution and meaning 653b
    - I.C.2.b.i. Overview 653b
    - I.C.2.b.ii. Explication 653b
      - I.C.2.b.ii.a. Direct explication 653b
        - I.C.2.b.ii.a.1. Explication of "not mere locution." 653b–c
        - I.C.2.b.ii.a.2. Explication of "meaningful words" 653c
      - I.C.2.b.ii.b. Reiterated elucidation 653c
        - I.C.2.b.ii.b.1. Elucidation of "not mere locution" 653c–654a
        - I.C.2.b.ii.b.2. Elucidation of "meaningful words" 654a

I.D. Clarification that the bodhisattva ranks emerge from the original inspiration 654a

- I.D.1. Question 654a
- I.D.2. Answer 654a
  - I.D.2.a. Listing of the classifications in a summary overview 654a–b
  - I.D.2.b. Sequential explication 654b
    - I.D.2.b.i. [Clarification of] faith 654c
    - I.D.2.b.ii. [Clarification of] comprehension 654c
      - I.D.2.b.ii.a. Clarification of the level of consideration 654c
        - I.D.2.b.ii.a.1. Clarification of contemplation on the four aspirations 654c–655a
        - I.D.2.b.ii.a.2. Elucidation of the four wisdoms that accord with reality 655a
      - I.D.2.b.ii.b. Clarification of the level of cultivation 655a
        - I.D.2.b.ii.b.1. Clarification of the characteristics of cultivation 655a
        - I.D.2.b.ii.b.2. Elucidation of the causes of cultivation 655a–b
      - I.D.2.b.ii.c. Clarification of the level of practice 655b
        - I.D.2.b.ii.c.1. Clarification of the qualities of this level 655b
        - I.D.2.b.ii.c.2. Elucidation of its practices 655b
      - I.D.2.b.ii.d. Clarification of the level of relinquishment 655b
        - I.D.2.b.ii.d.1. Clarification of the meaning of relinquishment 655b–c
        - I.D.2.b.ii.d.2. Clarification of the qualities of this level 655c
  - I.D.2.c. Summary clarification 655c
    - I.D.2.c.i. Explicit clarification of what proceeds from original [enlightenment] 655c
    - I.D.2.c.ii. Reiterated elucidation through a set of exchanges 656a
      - I.D.2.c.ii.a. Śāriputra's question 656a
      - I.D.2.c.ii.b. [The Buddha's] answer 656a
        - I.D.2.c.ii.b.1. An instruction 656a
        - I.D.2.c.ii.b.2. A simile 656a

I.E. Clarification that great prajñā neutralizes all causes and conditions 656a

- I.E.1. Śāriputra's respectful remark 656b
  - I.E.1.a. Comprehension of the Buddha's explication that the original inspiration is consummately interfused 656b
  - I.E.1.b. Elucidation that this is in fact the great perfection of prajñā 656b–c
- I.E.2. Completion of the Tathāgata's narrative 656c
  - I.E.2.a. Summary narrative 656c
  - I.E.2.b. Sequential narrative [about reaching the other shore] 656c
    - I.E.2.b.i. Narrative about the fulfillment of the cause 656c–657a
    - I.E.2.b.ii. Narrative about the consummation of the fruition 657a–b
  - I.E.2.c. Summary conclusion 657b–c

I.F. Clarification that great dhyānic absorption transcends all names and classifications 657c
  I.F.1. Question 657c
  I.F.2. Answer 657c
    I.F.2.a. General assent 657c
    I.F.2.b. Sequential analysis 657c
      I.F.2.b.i. Brief clarification 657c
        I.F.2.b.i.a. Clarification that the mundane dhyānas are not separate from names and classifications 657c
        I.F.2.b.i.b. Elucidation that supramundane dhyāna transcends those names and classifications 657c
      I.F.2.b.ii. Extensive explanation 657c–658a
        I.F.2.b.ii.a. Clarification from the standpoint of characteristics of how to leave behind characteristics 658a
        I.F.2.b.ii.b. Elucidation from the standpoint of activity of how to leave behind activity 658a
        I.F.2.b.ii.c. Conclusion regarding these aspects 658a–b
        I.F.2.b.ii.d. Conclusion regarding the names 658b

II. Brief synopsis for those with dull faculties 658b
  II.A. Question 658b
    II.A.1. Comprehension of the preceding explanation 658b
    II.A.2. Question regarding a doubt 658b
  II.B. Answer 658b–c
  II.C. Entreaty 658c
  II.D. Explanation 658c–659a
  II.E. Congregation hears the explanation and gains benefit 659a

Section Two: Main Body (cont.)

SIXTH DIVISION OF CONTEMPLATION PRACTICE: IMMEASURABLE DHARMAS ACCESS THE TATHĀGATAGARBHA

I. Clarification that all dharmas and all practices together access the locus of oneness 659b
  I.A. Clarifies that aspect that all dharmas access the one reality 659b
    I.A.1. Question 659b
      I.A.1.a. Comprehension of the preceding sermon 659b–c
      I.A.1.b. Explicit question regarding his doubt 659c
    I.A.2. Answer 659c–660a
      I.A.2.a. An instruction 660a
      I.A.2.b. A simile 660a
      I.A.2.c. Their correlation 660a
    I.A.3. Comprehension 660a
    I.A.4. Conclusion to the narrative 660a–b

I.A.4.a. Generic statement 660b
I.A.4.b. Specific conclusion 660b
I.A.4.b.i. An instruction 660b
I.A.4.b.ii. A simile 660b
I.A.4.b.iii. Their correlation 660b
I.A.4.b.iii.a. Correlation with "**those streams**," where [the streams] are initially correlated with the teachings and subsequently illustrated with a simile 660b
I.A.4.b.iii.b. Correlation with "**absorbs all those streams**," where it initially brings up the simile and subsequently correlates it with the instruction 660b
I.B. Clarifies that all practices access the one path to buddhahood 660b
I.B.1. Question concerning "distinctions" [in the understanding of adherents of the three vehicles] 660b
I.B.2. Answer 660b
I.B.2.a. A simile 660b
I.B.2.b. The correlation 660b
II. Elucidation of the distinctions between the causes and fruitions of the practices that bring about access and the knowledges gained through access 660c
II.A. Distinctions in the practices that bring about access 660c
II.A.1. Generic proposition statement 660c
II.A.2. Question 660c
II.A.3. Answer 660c
II.A.3.a. Specific clarification 660c
II.A.3.b. General explication [of the three practices] 660c–661a
II.B. Distinctions in the knowledge gained through accessing [the tathāgatagarbha] 661a
II.B.1. Question 661a
II.B.1.a. Comprehension of the preceding sermon 661a
II.B.1.b. Question concerning his doubt 661a
II.B.2. Answer 661a–b
II.B.2.a. General overview 661b
II.B.2.b. Specific explication 661b
II.B.2.c. Comprehensive clarification 661b–c
II.C. Operation and functioning of the causes that bring about access 661c
II.C.1. Prose explanation 661c
II.C.1.a. Concise clarification 661c
II.C.1.a.i. General overview 661c
II.C.1.a.ii. Specific understanding 661c–662a
II.C.1.a.iii. Synthetic clarification 662a
II.C.1.a.iv. Concluding inducement 662a
II.C.1.b. Repeated elucidation 662a

II.D.1.b.ii.a.2. Contemplation according to expedients 665a
II.D.1.b.ii.a.2.a. Clarification that applied thought *(vitarka)* is consciousness-only 665a–b
II.D.1.b.ii.a.2.b. Elucidation of the knowledge that accords with reality 665b
II.D.1.b.ii.b. Comprehensive summation 665b
II.D.2. The elder's disquisition (eight verses total) 665b
II.D.2.a. Analyzing the idea of the buddha's teaching (two and a half verses) 665b–c
II.D.2.a.i. Two verses that describe a teaching that falls into the two extremes 665c
II.D.2.a.ii. Two lines that elucidate the teaching that leaves behind these two extremes 665c–666a
II.D.2.b. Breaking down the grasping at the two extremes (five verses) 666a
II.D.2.b.i. Four verses that break down the grasping at the extreme of existence 666a
II.D.2.b.i.a. Preceding two and a half verses, which break down the attachment to existence 666a
II.D.2.b.i.a.1. Initial verse and a half, which breaks down the grasping at causal conditioning *(hetupratyaya)* 666a
II.D.2.b.i.a.2. Next verse, which breaks down the remaining three kinds of conditions 666a–b
II.D.2.b.i.b. Latter verse and a half, which reveals the true voidness 666b
II.D.2.b.ii. One verse that removes the attachment to the extreme of voidness 666c
II.D.2.c. Contemplation of indivisibility (two lines) 666c
II.D.3. The congregation gains benefit 666c

Section Three (A): Dhāraṇī (Codes)

I. Request 667a
II. Consent 667a
III. Resolution 667b
III.A. Six doubts remaining from the six chapters, which are resolved in contrary order 667b
III.A.1. Sequential resolution 667b
III.A.1.a. Resolving a doubt remaining from the "Tathāgatagarbha" chapter 667b
III.A.1.b. Resolving a doubt remaining from the "Voidness of the True Nature" chapter 667b
III.A.1.b.i. Explicit rebuttal [to the doubt] 667c
III.A.1.b.ii. Reiterated resolution 667c

III.A.1.b.ii.a. Criticism 667c
III.A.1.b.ii.b. Resolution 667c–668a
III.A.1.c. Resolving a doubt remaining from the "Accessing the Edge of Reality" chapter 668a
III.A.1.c.i. Question 668a
III.A.1.c.ii. Assent 668a
III.A.1.c.iii. Comprehension 668a–b
III.A.1.c.iv. Conclusion to the narrative 668b–c
III.A.1.d. Resolving a doubt remaining from the "Inspiration of Original Enlightenment" chapter 668c–669a
III.A.1.e. Resolving a doubt remaining from the "Practice of Non-production" chapter 669a–b
III.A.1.f. Resolving a doubt remaining from the "Signless Dharma" chapter 669b–c
III.A.1.f.i. One verse that reveals the principle [in order to rebut this doubt] 669c
III.A.1.f.ii. Two verses that eradicate the grasping that is produced with regard to characteristics 669c–670a
III.A.2. Summary clarification [of the fact that these six resolutions are not diseases but medicines] 670a
III.A.2.a. Clarification that these [characteristics of dharmas] are not diseases 670a
III.A.2.a.i. Query 670a
III.A.2.a.ii. Assent [of the Tathāgata] 670a–b
III.A.2.b. Clarification that this [dharma of voidness] is a medicine 670b
III.A.2.b.i. Bodhisattva's query 670b
III.A.2.b.i.a. Comprehending the previous reference to "the aggregation of the profound, meritorious qualities" 670b
III.A.2.b.i.a.1. Summary overview [of the meritorious qualities that leave behind both characteristics and nature] 670b
III.A.2.b.i.a.2. Sequential elucidation 670b
III.A.2.b.i.a.2.a. He clarifies leaving behind characteristics 670b
III.A.2.b.i.a.2.b. He elucidates leaving behind the nature 670b–c
III.A.2.b.i.a.3. Summary conclusion 670c
III.A.2.b.i.b. Availing himself of and elucidating the profound access to the contemplation of principle 670c
III.A.2.b.i.b.1. Sequential clarification 670c
III.A.2.b.i.b.2. Summary conclusion 670c
III.A.2.b.i.c. Query regarding the superior qualities of this superb medicine 670c– 671a

III.A.2.b.ii. Tathāgata's assent and approval 671a
III.A.2.b.ii.a. Summary assent 671a
III.A.2.b.ii.b. Sequential approval 671a
III.A.2.b.ii.b.1. The bodhisattva clarifies that, by ingesting the medicine of voidness, one is able to leave behind the tribulations that are the results of wandering on in saṃsāra 671a
III.A.2.b.ii.b.2. The bodhisattva elucidates that, by ingesting the medicine of voidness, one cures the diseases that are the causes of clinging and attachment 671a
III.A.2.b.ii.c. Concluding assent 671b
III.B. Three doubts remaining from one chapter, which are rebutted in sequential order 671b
III.B.1. First doubt [concerning Elder Pŏmhang's explanation (cf. 663b)] 671b
III.B.1.a. Question 671b–c
III.B.1.b. The Tathāgata's resolution of this doubt 671c
III.B.1.b.i. Explicit resolution 671c
III.B.1.b.ii. Resolution through an explication 671c
III.B.1.b.ii.a. Brief explanation 671c
III.B.1.b.ii.b. Extensive disquisition 671c–672a
III.B.1.b.ii.b.1. Clarification of the superior benefit of the "three paths to liberation" 672a
III.B.1.b.ii.b.2. Elucidation of the superior benefit of "diligently cultivat[ing] the three transformations" 672a–b
III.B.2. Second doubt remaining from the "Tathāgatagarbha" chapter 672b
III.B.2.a. Question regarding how distant the fruition [of nirvāṇa is from its cause] 672b
III.B.2.b. Question concerning the expedients that will help one to access the gateway 672b–c
III.B.2.b.i. Question 672b
III.B.2.b.ii. Answer 672c
III.B.2.b.iii. Query 672c
III.B.2.b.iv. [The Buddha's] explanation
III.B.2.b.iv.a. Explanation of the expedient of admonishment 672c–673a
III.B.2.b.iv.b. Narration of the expedients that bring about access 673a–b
III.B.2.b.iv.c. Summary conclusion 673b
III.B.3. Third doubt remaining from the "Tathāgatagarbha" chapter 673b–c
III.B.3.a. Statement 673c
III.B.3.b. Explicit resolution of the doubt 673c

III.B.3.b.i. Brief explanation in three verses 673c
III.B.3.b.i.a. Clarifying the aspect of motionlessness—initial two verses 673c
III.B.3.b.i.a.1. Overview 673c
III.B.3.b.i.a.2. Explication 673c
III.B.3.b.i.a.3. Conclusion 673c–674a
III.B.3.b.i.b. Elucidating the aspect of gaining access—last verse 674a
III.B.3.b.ii. Extensive proclamation in five verses 674a
III.B.3.b.ii.a. Extensive explanation of the meaning of motionlessness—first three verses 674a
III.B.3.b.ii.a.1. Two verses that explore [the idea that causes and conditions] are originally unascertainable, thereby elucidating motionlessness 674a
III.B.3.b.ii.a.1.a. Overview 674a
III.B.3.b.ii.a.1.b. Explication 674a–b
III.B.3.b.ii.a.1.c. Conclusion 674b
III.B.3.b.ii.a.2. Single verse that examines [the idea that causes and conditions] are ultimately unascertainable, thereby elucidating motionlessness 674b
III.B.3.b.ii.b. Proclaiming the aspect of gaining access—last two verses 674b–c
III.B.3.b.ii.b.1. First verse elucidating that all things that are subject to motion are thus and motionless 674b
III.B.3.b.ii.b.2. Two lines [of last verse] clarifying that the motionless origin does not avail itself of the mass of conditions 674c
III.B.3.b.ii.b.3. Last two lines [of last verse] clarifying that leaving behind conditioned dharmas is the aspect of gaining access 674c
IV. Gaining comprehension—three verses 674c
IV.A. Providing the conclusion to the preceding [account] of the benefit of resolving doubts (first verse and a half) 674c
IV.B. Declaring the subsequent practice of universal proselytization (last verse and a half) 674c–675a

Section Three (B): Dissemination 675a

I. Dissemination through praising the interlocutor 675a–b
II. Dissemination through encouraging the congregation 675b
III. Dissemination through assigning a title [to the sūtra] 675ab
III.A. Question 675b
III.A.1. Comprehension, in which the four superior capacities of this sūtra are elucidated 675b

III.A.2. Question [concerning] two matters 675b
III.A.2.a. [Concerning] the sūtra's title 675b
III.A.2.b. [Concerning] the merit that derives from keeping [the sūtra] 675b
III.B. Answer 675b–c
III.B.1. Answer [concerning the sūtra's title] 675c
III.B.1.a. Praising its name and significance 675c
III.B.1.a.i. Summary praise of its title 675c
III.B.1.a.ii. Specific elucidation of its significance 675c
III.B.1.b. Assigning its titles 675c
III.B.2. Answer [concerning the merit that derives from keeping the sūtra] 675c–676a
III.B.2.a. The superior meritorious quality of serving the buddhas 676a
III.B.2.b. The superior meritorious quality of being extensive and vast 676a
III.B.2.c. The superior meritorious quality of being extremely profound 676a
III.B.2.d. The meritorious quality of being incomparable 676a
IV. Dissemination through receiving and keeping [the sūtra] 676a
IV.A. Explicit clarification of "receiving and keeping" 676a
IV.A.1. Question 676a
IV.A.1.a. Question regarding the mental attitude of the person who receives and keeps this sūtra 676a
IV.A.1.b. Question regarding the meritorious benefit coming to one who receives and keeps this sūtra 676a
IV.A.2. Answer 676a
IV.A.2.a. Answer to the first question [IV.A.1.a] 676a
IV.A.2.b. Answer to the second question [IV.A.1.b] 676a–b
IV.B. Reiteration through a series of exchanges 676b
IV.B.1. Clarification regarding the essence of a field of merit 676b
IV.B.2. Elucidation of [the fact] that one who keeps this sūtra has the ability to produce merit 676b–c
V. Dissemination through repentance 676c
V.A. Praising the meritorious quality of repentance 676c
V.B. Reiteration through exchanges 676c
V.B.1. Exchange that elucidates the logic behind repentance 676c–677a
V.B.2. Exchange that elucidates the dharma of practicing repentance 677a
V.B.2.a. Clarification of the dharma to be practiced 677a
V.B.2.b. Revelation of its superior benefit 677a–b
VI. Dissemination through practicing respectfully [the teachings of the sūtra] 677b

Notes

Notes to Part I

1. *Kŭmgang sammaegyŏng non,* in 3 rolls *(kwŏn), HPC* 1.604b–677b; *T* 1730: 34.961a–1008a. An exquisite modern vernacular Korean translation of the *Exposition,* which constitutes a major step forward in interpreting the text, has been made by Ŭn Chŏnghŭi and Song Chinhyŏn, trans., *Wŏnhyo ŭi Kŭmgang sammaegyŏng non* (Seoul: Ilchisa, 2000). The pioneering Korean translation of the *Exposition* was made by the premier Korean Buddhist scholar of the last generation, Rhi Ki-yong (Yi Kiyŏng), trans., *Kŭmgang sammaegyŏng non,* Han'guk myŏngjŏ taejŏnjip (The great works of Korea) (Seoul: Taeyang Sŏjŏk, 1973), 331 pp. Still useful is Kim Talchin, trans., *Kŭmgang sammaegyŏng non, Wŏnhyo chŏnjip* (Collected works of Wŏnhyo), vol. 1 (Seoul: Yŏrŭmsa, 1986), 403 pp. Satō Shigeki has made an extensive study of the entire text of the *Exposition* in his *Wŏnhyo ŭi hwajaeng nolli: Mui pulsuil sasang* (Wŏnhyo's Logic of Doctrinal Reconciliation: "Nondual without guarding the one" thought) (Seoul: Minjoksa, 1996). The sūtra itself has also been the subject of a modern translation and exposition; see Kim Chaegŭn (Mubyŏn), *Kŭmgang sammaegyŏng sin'gang* (New lectures on the *Vajrasamādhi-sūtra*) (Seoul: Poryon'gak, 1980).

2. Sung-bae Park's translation of this treatise will appear in a later volume of the Collected Works of Wŏnhyo series.

3. In this regard, tathāgatagarbha builds on an ancient strand in Buddhist thought, of which the locus classicus is the oft-quoted statement in *Aṅguttara-nikāya* 1.10 "The mind, oh monks, is luminous but defiled by adventitious defilements" *(pabhassaraṃ idam bhikkhave cittaṃ, tañ ca kho āgantukehi upakkilesehi upakkiliṭṭhaṃ).* While this passage is discussed in much of the relevant secondary literature, its implications for Buddhist spiritual cultivation are brought out best in two classic books by Bhikkhu Ñāṇananda: *Concept and Reality in Early Buddhist Thought: An Essay on "Papañca" and "Papañca-Saññā-Saṅkhā"* (Kandy, Sri Lanka: Buddhist Publication Society, 1971), esp. p. 58; and *The Magic of the Mind: An Exposition of the Kalākārāma Sutta* (Kandy, Sri Lanka: Buddhist Publication Society, 1974), pp. 83–88. Similar passages can also be found in other Mahāyāna materials. The *Aṣṭasāhasrikāprajñāpāramitā-sūtra* (1.5) says, for example; "When a Bodhisattva courses in perfect wisdom and develops it, he should so train himself so that he does not pride himself on that thought of enlightenment. That thought is no thought, since in its essential original nature thought is transparently luminous." See Edward Conze, trans., *The Perfection of Wisdom in Eight Thousand Lines and Its Verse Summary* (Bolinas, Calif.: Four Seasons Foundation, 1975), p. 84.

4. See Takasaki Jikidō, trans., *A Study on the Ratnagotravibhāga (Uttaratantra): Being a Treatise on the Tathāgatagarbha Theory of Mahāyāna Buddhism,* Serie Orientale Roma 33 (Rome: Istituto Italiano per il Media ed Estremo Oriente, 1966), pp. 22–23. A number of Tathāgatagarbha sūtras and śāstras state that enlightenment, or

the absolute aspect of existence *(paramārtha),* is accessible only through faith *(adhimukti);* see David Seyfort Ruegg, "On the Knowability and Expressibility of Absolute Reality in Buddhism," *Indogaku Bukkyōgaku kenkyū* 20 (1971): 495–489 *[sic].*

5. Wŏnhyo takes the first half of the definition ("that characteristic of discriminative awareness, subject to production and extinction") as the void tathāgatagarbha and the second half ("conceals the principle so that it is not made manifest") as the nonvoid tathāgatagarbha. *KSGN,* p. 617a.

6. The seminal text of the doctrine, the *Tathāgatagarbha-sūtra,* for example, says, "All sentient beings have the tathāgatagarbha . . . which is covered over and hidden by all the defilements." See *Dafangdeng rulaizang jing, T* 666:16.457c25–26. Another early Tathāgatagarbha scripture, *Śrīmālādevīsiṃhanāda-sūtra,* offers a similar interpretation of tathāgatagarbha: "this dharmakāya of the tathāgata when not free from the store of defilement *(avinirmuktakleśakośa)* is referred to as the tathāgatagarbha." See *Shengman jing, T* 353:12.221c11; rendering by Alex Wayman and Hideko Wayman, trans., *The Lion's Roar of Queen Srīmālā* (New York: Columbia University Press, 1974), p. 98. This passage need not imply that dharmakāya and tathāgatagarbha are identical; rather both should be viewed instead as variant aspects of the unitary thusness, where defiled thusness is tathāgatagarbha and undefiled thusness dharmakāya. See Wayman and Wayman, *Lion's Roar,* p. 98, n. 83.

7. *Dasheng qixin lun, T* 1666:32.576a24–26; Yoshito S. Hakeda, trans., *The Awakening of Faith, Attributed to Aśvaghosha* (New York: Columbia University Press, 1967), p. 34.

8. See, for example, *Shengman jing (Śrīmālādevīsiṃhanāda-sūtra), T* 353:12.221c16–18; Wayman and Wayman, trans., *Lion's Roar,* p. 99.

9. Takasaki, trans., *Ratnagotravibhāga,* p. 187; cf. *Jiujing yisheng baoxing lun* 2, *T* 1611:31.827a1–4.

10. *Dasheng qixin lun, T* 1666:32.465b8–9; after Peter Gregory's translation in "The Problem of Theodicy in the *Awakening of Faith,*" *Religion* 22 (1986): 73.

11. *Dasheng qixin lun, T* 1666:32.465b8.

12. *Dasheng qixin lun, T* 1666:32.577c2–3; cf. Hakeda, *Awakening of Faith,* p. 50.

13. For the passage, see *KSGN,* p. 608a.

14. *KSGN,* pp. 608a–609a.

15. Original enlightenment, in fact, is an indigenous Chinese term, which appears in sūtra literature only in Sinitic apocrypha; for background on the term, see Lewis R. Lancaster, "Buddhist Apocryphal Words" (Paper delivered at panel on Chinese Buddhist Apocrypha, American Academy of Religion annual meeting, November 24, 1986). See also Jacqueline I. Stone, *Original Enlightenment and the Transformation of Medieval Japanese Buddhism,* Kuroda Institute Studies in East Asian Buddhism, no. 12 (Honolulu: University of Hawai'i Press, 1999), pp. 5–10.

16. Yuancheng (*Jin'gang sanmei jing zhujie, ZZ* 1, 55, 2–3, p. 199b13–16) takes a somewhat different tack in his interpretation of this passage: "Because the previous fifth, sixth, and seventh consciousnesses are [marked by] mundane characteristics, they are affective consciousnesses. The eighth consciousness then contains both the mundane and the transcendental. The ninth consciousness alone is transcendental. This passage means that one transmutes these mundane affective consciousnesses so that they access the transcendental pure nature." Yuancheng's reading of this passage is an apparent attempt to resurrect the southern Dilun school's bifurcation of the ālayavijñāna into both pure and impure aspects. This reading cannot really be

supported by *VS,* however, since in the following exchange Muju Bodhisattva states unequivocally that all eight consciousnesses are mundane ("Each and every one of the eight consciousnesses arises conditioned by the sense-spheres"). Cf. also Zhuzhen, *Jin'gang sanmei jing tongzong ji, ZZ* 1, 55, 3, pp. 256d–257a.

17. See *KSGN,* p. 631a, *supra;* and cf. *Dasheng qixin lun, T* 1666:32.576b15; Hakeda, *Awakening of Faith,* p. 37.

18. *Dasheng qixin lun, T* 1666:32.576c1–4; cf. Hakeda, p. 40. Wŏnhyo cites this same passage also at *KSGN,* p. 619a.

19. For the *tiyong* distinction in the *Awakening of Faith,* see *Dasheng qixin lun, T* 1666:32.575c; Hakeda, *Awakening of Faith,* pp. 29–30. For Wŏnhyo's use of this distinction in explicating the treatise, see Sung Bae Park, "A Comparative Study of Wŏnhyo and Fa-tsang on the Ta-Ch'eng Ch'i-hsin lun," in *Cheil hoe Han'gukhak Kukche haksurhoe ŭi nonmunjip (Papers of the First International Conference on Korean Studies)* (Sŏngnam, Korea: Academy of Korean Studies, 1979), pp. 579–597.

20. See Zhanran's account of Paramārtha's role in developing the *amalavijñāna* concept in *Chiguan quanxing quanhong jue* 3a, *T* 1912:46.221c2–9; quoted in Diana Y. Paul, *Philosophy of Mind in Sixth-Century China: Paramārtha's "Evolution of Consciousness"* (Stanford: Stanford University Press, 1984), p. 70. It is principally in an anthology of Paramārtha's own works, the *Wuxiang lun,* that the amalavijñāna is treated; see Paul, *Philosophy of Mind,* p. 94. For a convenient survey of the theory of amalavijñāna as attributed to Paramārtha, see ibid., pp. 6–7, 108–111, 160; and for background on the controversy within Chinese Yogācāra concerning the various schemes of consciousnesses, see pp. 46–71, summarizing the work of Yūki Reimon, Fukaura Seibun, and Sakaino Kōyō (for which see pp. 196–197, n. 55). Other summaries of amalavijñāna doctrine appear in David S. Ruegg, *La théorie du Tathāgatagarbha et du Gotra: Études sur la sotériologie et la gnoséologie du Bouddhisme,* Publications de l'École Française d'Extrême-Orient, vol. 70 (Paris, 1969), pp. 439–444, and Eric Frauwallner, "Amalavijñānam und ālayavijñānam," *Beitrage zur Indischen Pilologie und Alterumskunde: Festschrift W. Schubring,* (Hamburg: Cram, 1951), pp. 148–159. Pehaps the most complete treatment of the meaning and significance of the amalavijñāna is found in Fukaura Seibun, *Yuishikigaku kenkyū* (Studies in Yogācāra teachings) (2nd ed., Kyoto, 1977), vol. 1, pp. 188–228. For other sources and Liebenthal's thoughts on the topic with reference to the *Vajrasamādhi,* see Walter Liebenthal, "Notes on the 'Vajrasamādhi,'" (hereafter Liebenthal), *T'oung Pao* 1956: 268–269n.

21. *VS,* chap. 5; *KSGN,* p. 648b. My interpretation here follows Wŏnhyo.

22. "Original enlightenment is precisely the amalavijñāna"; *KSGN,* p. 631a.

23. *Kisillon pyŏlgi* 1, *T* 1845:44.230a19–21.

24. *Pusa yingluo benye jing, T* 1485:24.1012c27–1013a9. For the Chinese provenance of this text, see Mochizuki Shinkō, *Bukkyō kyōten seiritsu shiron* (Studies on the history of the composition of Buddhist scriptures) (Kyoto: Hōzōkan, 1946), pp. 471–484.

25. See *Pusa yingluo benye jing* 2, *T* 1485:24.1017a3, 1010b278, 1022b13; cited in Liebenthal, "Vajrasamādhi," p. 362, n.1.

26. Cf. also Zhuzhen, *Tongzong ji* 9, p. 277c; Yuancheng, *Zhujie* 2, p. 212a–b.

27. See *Cullavagga* ix.14; for "single taste," see also *Jieshenmi jing (Sandhinirmocana-sūtra)* 1, *T* 676:16.692a25.

28. Wŏnhyo provides alternate analyses of the significance of each chapter of the scripture in *KSGN,* pp. 608c–609b.

29. Ko Ikchin gives convenient charts outlining these four schemata; "Wŏnhyo ŭi sasang ŭi silch'ŏn wŏlli" (Praxis in Wŏnhyo's thought), in Sungsan Pak Kilchin Paksa Hwagap Kinyŏm Saŏphoe, eds., *Han'guk Pulgyo sasangsa, Sungsan Pak Kilchin paksa hwagap kinyŏm* (History of Korean Buddhist thought, presented in commemoration of the sixtieth birthday of [Sungsan] Dr. Pak Kilchin) (Iri: Wŏn Pulgyo Sasang Yŏn'guwŏn, 1975).

30. *Kŭmgang sammae kyŏng (Jin'gang sanmei jing), T* 273:9.365c–374b; the sūtra is embedded here in my translation of Wŏnhyo's *Exposition.* I have translated the sūtra in full in an earlier work, Robert E. Buswell Jr., *The Formation of Ch'an Ideology in China and Korea: The "Vajrasamādhi-Sūtra," a Buddhist Apocryphon,* Princeton Library of Asian Translations (Princeton: Princeton University Press, 1989).

31. *Tang Xinluoguo Huanglongsi Yuanxiao zhuan* (Biography of Wŏnhyo of Hwangnyongsa in the Tang Dominion of Silla), in *Song Gaoseng zhuan* 4, *T* 2061: 50.730a6b–29. I have translated both this biography and the later hagiography by Iryŏn in my article "The Hagiographies of the Korean Monk Wŏnhyo (617–686)," in *Buddhism in Practice,* ed. Donald S. Lopez Jr. (Princeton: Princeton University Press, 1995), pp. 553–562.

32. The identity of this Trepiṭaka is another of the mysteries of this biography. The most probable candidate for the person referred to in our story would seem to be the third Huayan patriarch Fazang (643–712), who was widely referred to as *fanjing dade,* as his biography notes (*T* 2054:50.280c17). Fazang is well known to have been familiar with Wŏnhyo's work and to have held him in great respect.

33. The term *lun* was generally reserved by Chinese translators for independent treatises and expositions presumed written by Indian bodhisattva-masters; translated from Sanskrit, such texts were accorded canonical status on a par with scriptures attributed to the Buddha himself. Indigenous treatises on translated sūtras were usually given the appellation *shu* (Kor. *so*), "commentary," and had only semicanonical status. Hence, conferring such a designation would have been equivalent to placing Wŏnhyo on a par with his Indian predecessors. See also discussion in Kim Yŏngt'ae, "Chŏn'gi wa sŏrhwa rŭl t'onghan Wŏnhyo yŏn'gu" (A Study of Wŏnhyo from the standpoint of biographies and legends), *PGHP* 17 (1980): 31. Robert Shih's statement (*Biographies des moines éminents [Kao seng tchouan] de Houei-kiao* [Louvain: Institut Orientaliste, 1968], p.169) concerning the Liang *Gaoseng zhuan* that *lun* refers to a Chinese composition is not necessarily valid for later texts; indeed, many of the interpretation of terms given by Shih in the appendix to his book should be followed cautiously for post-sixth-century materials.

34. Buswell, *Ch'an Ideology,* chapter 4.

35. Kim Yŏngt'ae, "Silla esŏ iruktoen *Kŭmgang sammae kyŏng*" (The *Vajrasamādhi-sūtra* composed in Silla), *PGHP* 25 (1988): 35–36.

36. *Samguk yusa* 4, *T* 2039:49.1004c26.

37. Yanagida Seizan, "*Kongōzammaikyō* no kenkyū" (A study of the *Vajrasamādhi-sūtra*), *Paengnyŏn Pulgyo nonjip* 3 (1993): 440 (Korean translation, p. 467).

38. Han T'aesik, "Kanbantō de tsukurareta gigi kyō ni tsuite" (On apocryphal scriptures produced on the Korean Peninsula), *IBK* 45:1 (1996).

39. Buswell, *Ch'an Ideology,* p. 172.

40. Ibid., p. 173.

41. Ishii Kōsei, "*Kongōzammaikyō* no seiritsu jijō," *IBK* 46:2 (1998), 31–37.

42. Buswell, *Ch'an Ideology,* p. 177.

43. This section is adapted from my article "The Chronology of Wŏnhyo's Life and Works: Some Preliminary Considerations," in *Wŏnhyo yŏn'gu nonch'ong: kŭ ch'ŏrhak kwa in'gan ŭi modŭn kŏt* (Wŏnhyo studies: various aspects of his philosophy and humanism), ed. Kim Chigyŏn (Seoul: Kukt'o T'ongirwŏn, 1987), pp. 932–964. See also my *Ch'an Ideology,* pp. 60–73.

44. See the fragments of the *P'an piryang non* edited by Kim Chigyŏn, in Cho Myŏnggi, ed., Wŏnhyo *taesa chŏnjip* (Collected works of the great master Wŏnhyo), (Seoul: Poryŏn'gak, 1978), pp. 674, 683; and *HPC* 1.817a. The *P'an piryang non* will be translated by Cuong Tu Nguyen in a later volume of the Collected Works of Wŏnhyo series.

45. For this continuity in the citations that appear in Wŏnhyo's works, see Rhi Ki-yong (Yi Kiyŏng), "Kyŏngjŏn inyong e nat'anan Wŏnhyo ŭi tokch'angsŏng" (The uniqueness of Wŏnhyo as manifested in his citations of scriptures), in Pak Kilchin Festschrift, pp. 192–223.

46. For this biography, see *Samguk yusa, T* 2039:49.1006a7–b29. I have also translated this biography in full in my article "The Hagiographies of the Korean Monk Wŏnhyo," pp. 559–562.

47. Iryŏn came from Changsan (the old Amnyanggun mentioned in Wŏnhyo's biography), which might account for his familiarity with the *hyangjŏn* materials on Wŏnhyo. See Kim Pusik, *Samguk sagi, k.* 34, p. 539a; *Sinjung Tongguk yŏji sŭngnam, k.* 27, fol. 1a–b.

48. The *Chinyŏk Hwaŏmgyŏng so* is to be translated by Pokan Chou in a later volume of the Collected Works of Wŏnhyo series.

49. See, for example, *Samguk yusa* 3, *T* 2039:49.997a10–11, where Iryŏn attempts to clarify the problematic chronological relationship between Wŏnhyo, Ŭisang, and Pŏmil (810–889).

50. There have been a number of attempts to establish a chronology of Wŏnhyo's career, all of which should be used cautiously (including my own). That of Motoi Nobuo ("Shiragi Gangyō no denki ni tsuite" [On the biography of Wŏnhyo], *Ōtani gakuhō* [Ōtani University reports] 41 [1961]: 50–51) is especially problematic, since he often interpolates dates for the events described in Wŏnhyo's two major hagiographies without any apparent evidence. See also Sung Bae Park, "Wŏnhyo's Commentaries on the *Awakening of Faith in Mahāyāna*" (Ph.D. diss., University of California, Berkeley, 1979), p. 71.

51. For fuller details of the complete chronology of Wŏnhyo's life, see my *Ch'an Ideology,* pp. 60–73.

52. The *Yu simallak to* (Wandering the path to mental peace and bliss) is translated by Richard McBride in a later volume of the Collected Works of Wŏnhyo series; his introduction will also provide an extensive discussion of the doubts scholars have raised concerning Wŏnhyo's authorship of this text. As Etani Ryūkai (Shiragi Gangyō no *Yūshinanrakudō* wa gisaku ka," *IBK* 23 [1974]: 16–23) notes, for example, the issues include the dearth of catalogue entries for this text until the Kamakura period, its quotation of passages from two works not translated until after 713, and the similarities between its first half and another of Wŏnhyo's works, the *Muryangsu chongyo* (Thematic essentials of the Amitābha-sūtra). McBride proposes that the work was compiled by a Tendai adept in tenth-century Japan as an overview of contemporary debates concerning Pure Land doctrines.

53. See discussion in Kim Yŏng'tae, "Chŏn'gi wa sŏrhwa rŭl t'onghan Wŏnhyo yŏn'gu," 56.

54. *Samguk yusa* 2, p. 1006b14.

55. Mizuno Kōgen ("Bodaidaruma no *Ninyūshigyō setsu* to *Kongō sammaikyō*" [Bodhidharma's *Explanation of the two accesses and four practices* and the *Vajrasamādhi-sutra*] (hereafter cited as Mizuno), *Komozawa daigaku kenkyū kiyō* 13 [1995]: 40), Motoi Nobuo ("Gangyō no denki," p. 51), Rhi Ki-yong (*Kŭmgang sammaegyŏng non,* p. 331), Etani Ryūkai ("Shiragi Gangyō no *Yūshinanrakudō* wa gisaku ka," p. 19), and Kim Yŏngt'ae ("Wŏnhyo yŏn'gu," p. 59) all accept that *Hwaŏmgyŏng so* was Wŏnhyo's last work.

56. Only the preface and third *kwŏn* of Wŏnhyo's *Chin'yŏk Hwaŏmgyŏng so* are extant; see *HPC* 1.495a–497c (*T* 2757:85.234c–236a). This text is first listed in Buddhist scriptural catalogues, though without comment, in the Japanese Kegon catalogue, *Kegonshū shōsho byō immyōroku* (*T* 2177:55.1133a19), compiled in 914 by Enchō (d.u.). Ŭich'ŏn lists it in his 1090 catalogue, *Sinp'yŏn chejong kyojang ch'ongnok* (*T* 2184: 55.1166b4), as a ten-*kwŏn* work. His interlinear note adds: "Originally this [commentary] was in eight *kwŏn*. Now, its fifth *kwŏn* has been divided [*kae;* lit. 'opened up'] and [Wŏnhyo's *Hwaŏmgyŏng*] *chongyo* combined with it, to make [a total of] ten *kwŏn*." Ŭich'ŏn's notice suggests that the entire commentary was extant at least through the early eleventh century.

57. See Sung Bae Park, "Wŏnhyo's Commentaries," p. 71. I have speculated elsewhere that Wŏnhyo's anomalous *Palsim suhaeng chang* (Arouse your mind and practice!) may well have been one of these songs he sang while on the road as a missionary; see the introduction to my translation of this text in *Sourcebook of Korean Civilization,* volume 1: *From Early Times to the Sixteenth Century,* ed. Peter H. Lee (New York: Columbia University Press, 1993), p. 154. This work will also be included in a later volume of the Collected Works of Wŏnhyo series.

58. See the convenient chart of Wŏnhyo's extant works and the texts they cite in Rhi Ki-yong, "Kyŏngjŏn ŭi nat'anan Wŏnhyo ŭi tokch'angsŏng" (The uniqueness of Wŏnhyo as manifested in his citations of scriptures), in *Pak Kilchin Festschrift,* pp. 220–223.

59. The Buddhist newspaper *Taehan Pulgyo* (Korean Buddhism), in its February 10, 1979 (Pulgi 2524, p. 2) issue, carries an illustration of a xylograph of Wŏnhyo's *Kŭmgang sammaegyŏng non* in the Haeinsa monastic library, which is said to date to the sixth year of the Silla King Sinmun's reign (680). I have not seen the xylograph, but if this dating is correct, it fits perfectly with the chronology I have proposed here.

60. This section is adapted from my article "Did Wŏnhyo Write Two Versions of His *Kŭmgang sammaegyŏng-ron* [Exposition of the *Book of Adamantine Absorption*]?: An Issue in Korean Buddhist Textual History," *Papers of the Fifth International Conference on Korean Studies: Korean Studies, Its Tasks and Perspectives* (Sŏngnam, Korea: Academy of Korean Studies, 1988), vol. 2, pp. 585–601.

61. *Samguk yusa, T* 2039:49.1006b21–24.

62. *Sinp'yŏn chejong kyojang ch'ongnok* 1, *T* 2184:55.1171b10. I might note too that Ŭich'ŏn mentions in his catalogue a Korean commentary to the *Vajrasamādhi* by Sŭngdun (alt. Toryun or Tullyun), titled *Kŭmgang sammaegyŏng chu* (Notes to the *Vajrasamādhi-sūtra*); see *Sin'yŏn chejong kyojang ch'ongnok* 1, *T* 2184:55.1171b11. We know little about this Sŭngdun except that he lived at Hŭngnyunsa during the Silla

period. While this text is no longer extant, it is cited under the listing for *amalavijñāna* (immaculate consciousness) in *Fanyi mingyi ji* 6, *T* 2131:54.1158b–c, indicating that it may have remained in circulation at least through 1143, the composition date of that lexicon.

63. Ŭich'ŏn's memorial inscription mentions that he dispatched agents throughout China, Japan, and the Khitan Liao regions of northeast Asia to scout for indigenous Buddhist writings; see the inscription in Yi Nŭnghwa, *Chosŏn Pulgyo t'ongsa* (A comprehensive history of Korean Buddhism) (1918; reprint ed., Seoul: Poryŏn'gak, 1979), vol. 3, p. 310, l. 2. For Ŭich'ŏn's role in compiling the catalogue and *Supplement* to the canon, see Lewis R. Lancaster and Sung Bae Park, eds., *The Korean Buddhist Canon: A Descriptive Catalogue* (Berkeley and Los Angeles: University of California Press, 1979), pp.xiii–xiv; Cho Myŏnggi, *Koryŏ Taegak kuksa wa Ch'ŏnt'ae sasang* (National Master Ŭich'ŏn of Koryŏ and Ch'ŏnt'ae thought) (Seoul: Tongguk Munhwasa, 1964), pp. 78–103.

64. Ishida Mosaku, *Shakyō yori mitaru Narachō Bukkyō no kenkyū* (Nara Buddhism as reflected in manuscript copies), *Tōyō bunko ronshū,* vol. 11 (Tokyo: Tōyō Bunko, 1930), p.111; the catalogue of manuscripts appears in the appendix, pp. 1–156.

65. Wŏnhyo cites his own *Yijang chang* at five places in the *Exposition;* see *KSGN,* pp. 613a, 616a, 623b, 641b, and 675a. The *Yijang ŭi* is translated by Charles Muller in a later volume of the Collected Works of Wŏnhyo series.

66. See Stanley Jeyraja Tambiah, *The Buddhist Saints of the Forest and the Cult of Amulets: A Study of Charisma, Hagiography, Sectarianism, and Millennial Buddhism* (Cambridge: Cambridge University Press, 1984), pp. 28–29.

67. This conclusion is not meant to suggest that the information appearing in the Buddhist bibliographical catalogues is consistently trustworthy; nothing in fact could be further from the truth. For the limitations on the evidence found in Buddhist catalogues, see Kyoko Tokuno, "The Evaluation of Indigenous Scriptures in Chinese Buddhist Bibliographical Catalogues," in *Chinese Buddhist Apocrypha,* ed. Robert E. Buswell Jr. (Honolulu: University of Hawai'i Press, 1990), pp. 31–74. This caveat should not, however, deter us from using catalogue references as the starting point in any research on the indigenous texts of Korean Buddhism—or indeed on the texts of any of the East Asian traditions. Uncritical acceptance of hagiographic accounts, without checking them against the catalogues, could easily lead us astray in understanding the textual history of a Buddhist author's writings, as we have seen here is the case with Wŏnhyo.

68. The first Buddhist exegetical work said to have been written in Silla was the *Sabunnyul kalma ki* (Commentary to the *Karman* section of the *Dharmaguptaka-Vinaya*), by Chimyŏng (d.u.), ca. early seventh century, but this work is no longer extant. Wŏnhyo's friend Ŭisang wrote but two or three shorter exegeses contemporaneously with Wŏnhyo, but Wŏnhyo still remains the earliest, and most prolific, of Silla's Buddhist exegetes. See discussion in Rhi Ki-yong, "Wŏnhyo and His Thought," *Korea Journal* 11:1 (January 1971), 5.

69. See Zanning's definition of "doctrinal exegetes," the second of the ten categories of monks listed in the *Song gaoseng zhuan,* at *T* 2061:50.710a. Wŏnhyo is also listed among "doctrinal exegetes" in the Koryŏ-period *Samguk yusa.* For the role that Koreans played in developing the indigenous Sinitic schools of Buddhism, see my edited volume *Currents and Countercurrents: Korean Influences on the East Asian Buddhist Traditions* (Honolulu: University of Hawai'i Press, 2005).

70. John B. Henderson, *Scripture, Canon, and Commentary: A Comparison of Confucian and Western Exegesis* (Princeton: Princeton University Press, 1991), p. 1.

71. See José Ignacio Cabezón's discussion about the contemporary mistrust of exegesis in his edited volume *Scholasticism: Cross-Cultural and Comparative Perspectives* (Albany: State University of New York Press, 1998), introduction. Note also Edward Conze's denigration of the new in his *Buddhist Thought in India* (London: George Allen and Unwin, 1962), preface, p. 8.

72. An intriguing suggestion proposed in Jörg Plassen, "Another Inquiry into the Commentarial Structure of Wŏnhyo's Works, Focussing on *Kŭmgang sammaegyŏng non*," *Proceedings of the Twenty-First Conference of the Association for Korean Studies in Europe,* ed. Antonetta Bruno and Federica Baglioni (Frascati: AKSE, 2003), pp. 270–275.

73. K. R. Norman, *A Philological Approach to Buddhism,* The Buddhist Forum, vol. 5 (London: School of Oriental and African Studies, University of London, 1997), chap. 9, "Buddhism and the Commentarial Tradition," pp. 156–157.

74. *Majjhima-nikāya,* no. 133; see the fascinating treatment in Bhikkhu Ñāṇananda, *Ideal Solitude: An Exposition of the Bhaddekaratta Sutta,* The Wheel Publication, no. 188 (Kandy: Buddhist Publication Society, 1973).

75. Norman, *Philological Approach,* p. 149. This frequent usage of synonyms in exegesis is all the more plausible given the wide range of dialectical variation used in the various regions in which Buddhism was taught and the need to gloss words that would be difficult or impossible to comprehend in different dialects. For example, Norman (ibid.) cites a passage from the Pāli canon where the Buddha gives seven different dialectical forms (what he calls "country language" [*janapadanirutti*]) of the words for "bowl," as an example of this tendency to replace words with synonyms.

76. The *Nidessa,* however, does display some incipient attempts to analyze even lengthier sections of the text in order to demonstrate how a term is used not just in the text of the *Sutta-nipāta* proper but in a wider context. See Norman, *Philological Approach,* p. 150.

77. See Norman, *Philological Approach,* p. 159.

78. See discussion in ibid., p. 161.

79. See Luis O. Gómez, "Buddhist Literature: Exegesis and Hermeneutics," in *Encyclopedia of Religion* (New York: Macmillan, 1987), vol. 2, p. 532.

80. See the treatment of Vasubandhu's commentary (*T* 1510:25.757a–766a), in Giuseppe Tucci, *Minor Buddhist Texts,* part 1 (Rome: Istituto Italiano per il Medio ed Estremo Oriente, 1956), pp. 129–171.

81. See George D. Bond, *The Word of the Buddha: The Tipiṭaka and Its Interpretation in Theravāda Buddhism* (Colombo: M. D. Gunasena and Co., 1982); and the brief summary of the *Netti* schema in Gómez, "Buddhist Literature," p. 531.

82. *Prayojanaṃ sapiṇḍārthaṃ padārthaḥ sānusaṃdhikaḥ/sacodyaparihāraś ca vācyaḥ sūtrārtha vādibhiḥ// Abhisamayālaṁkārāloka Prajñāpāramitāvyākhyā,* by Haribhadra, ed. U. Wogihara (Tokyo: Tōyō Bunko, 1934), p. 15; quoted in José Ignacio Cabezón, "Vasubandhu's *Vyākhyāyukti* on the Authenticity of the Mahāyāna *Sūtras,*" in *Texts in Context: Traditional Hermeneutics in South Asia,* ed. Jeffrey R. Timm (Albany: State University of New York Press, 1992), pp. 237–238, n. 16.

83. The Western scholar who has undertaken the most sustained study of this important text is José Ignacio Cabezón. See his "Vasubandhu's *Vyākhyāyukti.*" The quote is taken from p. 224 of this article. See also José Ignacio Cabezón, *Buddhism*

and Language: A Study of Indo-Tibetan Scholasticism (Albany: State University of New York Press, 1994).

84. For background on the early Han commentarial tradition, see see Rudolf G. Wagner, *The Craft of a Chinese Commentator: Wang Bi on the "Laozi"* (Albany: State University of New York Press, 2000), pp. 31–51.

85. Daniel K. Gardner, "Confucian Commentary and Chinese Intellectual History," *Journal of Asian Studies* 57:2 (May 1998), 400, 401. East Asian Buddhist commentary is an area of the tradition that has been much neglected by scholars to date, and my treatment here has benefited greatly from several recent works on commentary within the Chinese Confucian tradition. I am particularly indebted to Daniel K. Gardner's insightful article cited above and to John B. Henderson's *Scripture, Canon, and Commentary*. This neglect of Buddhist commentary by modern scholars is all the more reason to anticipate publication of Alexander L. Mayer's Habilitation thesis at Heidelberg University on Tang dynasty Buddhist commentary: "Das *Vajracchedikā-sūtra* und die chinesische Auslegung der prajñā: Ein Beitrag zur Expositorik, Exegese under Hermeneutik im sino-buddhistischen Sūtra-Kommentar" (Habilitation-Schrift, Heidelberg University, 1999), which was not available to me. See also Alexander L. Mayer's article on "Commentarial Literature," in Robert E. Buswell Jr., editor-in-chief, *Encyclopedia of Buddhism* (New York: Macmillan, 2004), vol. 1, pp. 166–169.

86. See my definition of the meaning of "Buddhist apocrypha" in my article "Prolegomenon to the Study of Buddhist Apocryphal Scriptures," in *Chinese Buddhist Apocrypha,* ed. Robert E. Buswell Jr. (Honolulu: University of Hawai'i Press, 1990), pp. 3–8.

87. For this and other exegetical categories, see the comprehensive article by Luis O. Gómez, "Buddhist Literature: Exegesis and Hermeneutics," in Buswell, *Encyclopedia of Religion.* Gómez notes that this threefold schema is not attested until some three centuries later in India.

88. See Kōgen Mizuno, *Buddhist Sutras: Origin, Development, Transmission* (Tokyo: Kōsei Publishing Co., 1982), p. 143. For further information on the Tiantai exegetical and hermeneutical schemata, see David W. Chappell, "Introduction to the 'T'ien-t'ai ssu-chiao-i,'" *Eastern Buddhist,* n.s. 9 (May 1976): 72–86. The *Tiantai sijiao yi* is attributed by the tradition to Zhiyi but is now generally presumed to have been written by Guanding.

89. For the importance of this interlocking style in Chinese classical literature, see Wagner, *The Craft of a Chinese Commentator,* chap. 3.

90. For an interesting discussion of the ways in which Wŏnhyo seeks to unify the contents of the scripture into an organic whole, see Plassen, "Another Inquiry."

91. As John Henderson says in *Scripture, Canon, and Commentary,* "The canon is self-consistent, [and] internal contradictions in it are only apparent" (p. 115; discussion, pp. 115–121); and the canon is "well ordered and coherent, arranged according to some logical, cosmological, or pedagogical patterns" (p. 106 and discussion, pp. 106–115).

92. See discussions on the tendency toward categorization as being a general feature of scholastic traditions in José Ignacio Cabezón, *Buddhism and Language: A Study of Indo-Tibetan Scholasticism* (Albany: State University of New York Press, 1994), chap. 1, "Scholasticism," pp. 11–26; and Cabezón, *Scholasticism,* "Introduction," pp. 1–17.

93. A term suggested to me by my colleague Robert Gimello.

94. Alexander Mayer, "Commentarial Literature," in Buswell, *Encyclopedia of Buddhism.*

95. Satō Shigeki, *Wŏnhyo ŭi hwajaeng nolli,* appendix, pp. 315–321. See also a similar type of exegetical chart included with Ŭn Chŏnghŭi and Song Chinhyŏn, trans. *Wŏnhyo ŭi Kŭmgang sammaegyŏng non,* which is more readable because of its larger scale.

96. Mayer, "Das *Vajracchedikā-sūtra* und die chinesische Auslegung der prajñā."

97. For an early example, see the elaborate outline, down to some four levels of subheading, in E. Obermiller's *Analysis of the Abhisamayālaṃkāra,* Calcutta Oriental Series, no. 27 (Luzac and Co., 1933). For East Asian commentaries, note Paul L. Swanson's use of an outline format in translating Zhiyi's *Fahua xuanyi;* see his *Foundations of T'ien-t'ai Philosophy: The Flowering of the Two Truths Theory in Chinese Buddhism* (Berkeley: Asian Humanities Press, 1989), pp. 159–163.

98. As Gardner ("Confucian Commentary," p. 404), remarks: "The commentator wishes to 'fix' the meaning of the text he is commenting on, to persuade others to read and understand the text just as he has."

99. See discussion in my *Ch'an Ideology,* p. 58, following Michael Rogers' characterization of Korean needs to repudiate Tang suzerainty over their land in his seminal article "*P'yŏnnyŏn T'ongnok:* The Foundation Legend of the Koryŏ State," *Korean Studies* (University of Washington), 4 (1982–1983): 42.

100. Gardner, "Confucian Commentary," p. 404.

101. Paraphrasing ibid., p. 404.

102. One of the best treatments of the close connections between Buddhism and the state in ancient Korea appears in Ko Ikchin, "Han'guk kodae ŭi Pulgyo sasang" (Buddhist thought in Ancient Korea), in *Ch'ogi Han'guk Pulgyo kyodansa ŭi yŏn'gu* (History of Buddhist sectarianism in early Korea), *Pulgyohak nonjip* (Essays in Buddhist Studies) (Seoul: Minjoksa, 1986), pp. 11–106. For accessible treatments of the role of Buddhism in state formation in Three Kingdoms Korea, see An Kyehyŏn, "Silla Buddhism and the Spirit of the Protection of the Fatherland," *Korea Journal* 17: 4 (April 1977), 27–29; Hee Sung Keel, "Buddhism and Political Power in Korean History," *Journal of the International Association of Buddhist Studies* 1 (1978): 10–12; Enchō Tamura, "Japan and the Eastward Permeation of Buddhism," *Acta Asiatica* 47 (1985): 10–12. For the *hwarang* system, see Richard Rutt, "The Flower Boys of Silla (Hwarang): Notes on the Sources," *Transactions of the Korea Branch of the Royal Asiatic Society* 38 (1961): 1–66. The legend of Ich'adon appears in the biography of Pŏpkong in *Haedong kosŭng chŏn* (*T* 2065:50.1018c–1019a); see Peter H. Lee, trans., *Lives of Eminent Korean Monks: Haedong Kosŭng Chŏn,* Harvard-Yenching Institute Studies, no. 25 (Cambridge: Harvard University Press, 1969), pp. 58–63.

103. See *Hwaŏm ilsŭng pŏpkye to* (*T* 1887A:45.711a). For the importance of Hwaŏm Buddhism in Silla national ideology, see Ki-Baek Lee, *A New History of Korea,* trans. Edward W. Wagner, with Edward J. Shultz (Cambridge: Harvard University Press, 1984), p. 81.

104. Both *kae* and *hap* are hermeneutical terms that occur frequently in East Asian Buddhist commentarial exegesis. For Wŏnhyo's use of these terms, see Pak Chonghong, "Wŏnhyo ŭi chŏrhak sasang," in *Han'guk sasang sa* (History of Korean Thought) (Seoul: Ilsinsa, 1966), pp. 59–88; reprinted in Pak's *Han'guk sasang sa: Pulgyo sasang p'yŏn* (History of Korean Thought: Buddhist Thought," Sŏmun mun'go,

no. 11 (Seoul, 1972), pp. 85–127. I have translated this article as "Wŏnhyo's Philosophical Thought," *in Assimilation of Buddhism in Korea: Religious Maturity and Innovation in the Silla Dynasty,* Studies in Korean Religions and Culture, vol. 4, ed. Lewis R. Lancaster and C. S. Yu (Berkeley: Asian Humanities Press, 1991), pp. 47–103. Sung Bae Park, who has been critical of Pak Chonghong's interpretation, has proposed the renderings "opening" *(kae)* and "sealing" *(hap)* for these terms; see his article "Silla Buddhist Spirituality," in *Buddhist Spirituality: Later China, Korea, Japan and the Modern World,* World Spirituality, an Encyclopedic History of the Religious Quest, vol. 9, edited by Takeuchi Yoshinori et al. (New York: Crossroad Publishing Company, a Herder and Herder Book, 1999), p. 63. Cf. also Fa-tsang, *Huayan wujiao zhang* 2, *T*1866:45.482a–b; Yŏndam Yuil (1720–1799), *Pŏpchip pyŏrhaengnok chŏryo kwamok pyŏngip sagi* (Taehungsa xylograph, dated 1916, in the Tongguk University archives), fol. 8b10.

105. *Taesŭng kisillon so, HPC* 1:698c7–8.

106. Daisetz Teitaro Suzuki, *Studies in the Laṅkāvatāra Sūtra* (1932; reprint, Boulder: Prajñā Press, 1978), p. 17; and note also Suzuki's *Essays in Zen Buddhism,* series 1 (London: Routledge and Kegan Paul, 1970), p. 75.

107. For a similar attempt by the Qing dynasty commentator Zhuzhen (d.u.) to present a systematic and complete outline of the *Vajrasamādhi,* see Buswell, *Ch'an Ideology,* p. 255.

108. A suggestion made to me by my UCLA colleague Gregory Schopen.

109. A listing derived from the *Adhyāśayasañcodana-sūtra;* see the discussion in Ronald M. Davidson, "An Introduction to the Standards of Authenticity in Indian Buddhism," in *Chinese Buddhist Apocrypha,* ed. Robert E. Buswell Jr. (Honolulu: University of Hawai'i Press, 1990), p. 310.

110. This is not to deny José Ignacio Cabezón's rather more sanguine view of this decision ("Vasubandhu's *Vyākhyāyukti,*" p. 233) as being not "an instance of hermeneutical naiveté . . . [but] in fact, the result of a considerable critical reflection."

111. See Cabezón, "Vasubandhu's *Vyākhyāyukti,*" p. 233.

112. I am drawing here from my treatment of the premodern understanding of the Buddhist tradition in East Asia; see my article "Imagining 'Korean Buddhism': The Invention of a National Religious Tradition," in *Nationalism and the Construction of Korean Identity,* ed. Hyung Il Pai and Timothy R. Tangherlini, Korea Research Monograph, no. 26 (Berkeley: Institute of East Asian Studies, 1998), pp. 83–84.

113. For Wŏnhyo's contributions to the developing East Asian tradition of *panjiao,* see Rhi Ki-yong (Yi Kiyŏng), "Kyop'ansasang aesŏ pon Wŏnhyo ŭi wich'i (Wŏnhyo's place in the history of doctrinal taxonomies), in *Han'guk Pulgyo yŏn'gu* (Seoul: Han'guk Pulgyo Yŏn'guwŏn, 1982), pp. 345–358.

114. Even the Indian exegete Vasubandhu bewails this difficult of establishing the veracity of the textual transmission based on historicity; as he states in his *Vyākhyāyukti:* "How can *all* of those mutually inconsistent expositions be considered the Buddha's word?" (translated in Cabezón, "Vasubandhu's *Vyākhyāyukti,* p. 228).

Notes to Part 2

1. The three voidnesses: (1) voidness of characteristics (conventional voidness), (2) voidness of voidness (absolute voidness), (3) voidness of both. *VS,* chap. 5 (p. 369b15–17); *KSGN,* p. 639b24–c3; see also Wŏnhyo's comments at *KSGN,* p. 639c.

2. Wŏnhyo's abundant usage of symmetry and chiasmus throughout part 1 suggests that the main idea he seeks to highlight here is the rhetorical, or perhaps "exegetical," method employed in the sūtra, i.e., the pattern of interlocking correspondences, in which all propositions are shown to intersect. Wŏnhyo defers most of discussion of emblematic doctrines or teachings contained in the sūtra itself until the following part 2. See the interpretation in Plassen, "Another Inquiry into the Commentarial Structure of Wŏnhyo's Works," p. 157; but cf. Satō Shigeki, *Wŏnhyo ŭi hwajaeng nolli*, pp. 48–58, which highlights the importance of the fountainhead of the one mind and the sea of three voidnesses in understanding part 1.

3. *Hwanjung* is also used metaphorically to allude to the sphere of absolute reality beyond all relative discrimination and is commonly used to refer to the *dharmadhātu*. See *Zhao lun*, *T* 1858:45.157a16.

4. These are the three titles the sūtra is given in chapter 8 of *VS* (p. 374a28–29) at the conclusion of the discourse; *KSGN*, p. 675c4–5.

5. Literally, *kae* (to open) means "to open up" for detailed analysis the intricate relationships between different doctrinal categories; *hap* (to combine) means "to combine" or "to bring together" via a synthetic approach the foundational qualities fundamental to all such doctrinal categories. For discussion, see the section "Wŏnhyo's Hermeneutical Strategy," in the Study part of this book.

6. The "single taste" is explained in chapter 7 of *VS* (p. 371c22–25). See *KSGN*, p. 660a.

7. "Spatial dimension . . . temporal perspective" are free renderings for what is literally "horizontal discourse" *(hoengnon)* and "vertical viewing" *(sumang)*: e.g., "Horizontally penetrating the ten directions . . . vertically piercing the three time limits" (*Jin'gang jing zuanyao kanding ji* 4, *T* 1702:33.201a16–17; and *Qixin lun pi xue ji*, *T* 1848: 44.299a5–8). In their Buddhist usage, "horizontal" and "vertical" often refer respectively to unsystematic and systematic treatments of doctrinal questions; see *Youqieshi di lun (Yogācārabhūmiśāstra)* 11, *T* 1579:30.330b15. Their directional senses are conveyed in such usages as "vertically piercing, horizontally pervading, perfect interfusion is unimpeded" (*Qixin lun shu bi xue ji*, *T* 1848:44.297b10) and "horizontally and vertically it radiates universally; its opening and its combination (*kaehap;* see note 5 above) are perfectly free" (*Miaofa lianhua jing wenju* 3b, *T* 1718:34.43b21–22). Finally, and in their least technical usages, the terms are used simply to convey two contrasting ideas, e.g., "on the one hand . . . on the other hand": cf. "On the one hand, it reveals the qualities of action. . . . On the other hand, it reveals the characteristics of action" (*Taesŭng Kisillon naeŭi nyakt'am ki*, *T* 1849:44.415b20–21); "Expounded upon from one standpoint (lit. horizontally), the principle transcends eight affairs; from the other standpoint (lit. vertically), the four antinomies *(catuṣkoṭi)* are all negated" (*Zhongguan lun shu* 2b, *T* 1824:42.30c16–18); or, "The Tathāgata, on the one hand, takes the medicine of gracious response, and his wisdom accords with the profound principle. Because he, on the other hand, takes the medicine of absolute truth, he benefits [living] things everywhere" (*Miaofa lianhua jing wenju* 9b, *T* 1719:34.327b2–3; and note *Fahua xuanyi shiqian* 18, *T* 1717:33.943c29–944a1).

8. The five dharmas: the pure *dharmadhātu*, which is the manifestation of the ninth *amalavijñāna;* and the four wisdoms into which the remaining eight consciousnesses develop. Along with the exegesis that immediately follows, see also *KSGN* 1, p. 618c; and see note 11 below.

9. Six practices: The cultivation of (1) the ten faiths, (2) ten abidings, (3) ten

practices, (4) ten transferences, (5) ten bhūmis, (6) virtual enlightenment. Along with the following exegesis, see *KSGN,* p. 651c; *VS,* chap. 4 (p. 370a12–14).

10. In these last sentences, Wŏnhyo has outlined the core chapters of the sūtra. "Practices which are unproduced" refer to chapter 3 of the sūtra. "The signless dharma" is chapter 2, which is the first chapter of the main body of the scripture itself. "Original inspiration" refers to chapter 4, "The Inspiration of Original Enlightenment." "Edge of reality" alludes to the fifth chapter, "Accessing the Edge of Reality." "Is devoid of any nature of its own, the authentic edge is also void" refers to chapter 6, "The Voidness of the True Nature." Finally, "accessing the tathāgatagarbha" refers to the seventh chapter, "The Tathāgatagarbha."

11. The transformations of the eight consciousnesses into the four wisdoms of the buddhas is a common theme in Yogācāra texts. First, the great perfect mirror wisdom *(mahādarśanajñāna),* which is a transformation of the eighth consciousness, the *ālayavijñāna,* sees the perfect interfusion of all things as if everything were simultaneously reflected in a great mirror. Second, the impartial wisdom *(samatājñāna),* a transformation of the seventh *kliṣṭamanovijñāna,* rises above all distinctions and sees all things impartially without coloring by the ego. Third, the sublime-observation wisdom *(pratyavekṣanājñāna),* a transformation of the sixth *manovijñāna,* is the wisdom that contemplates the unique and common characteristics of all dharmas. Fourth, the perfection in action wisdom, or the wisdom that has accomplished what was to be done *(kṛtyānuṣṭhānajñāna),* a transformation of the five sensory consciousnesses, accomplishes actions that benefit both oneself and others. See *Cheng weishi lun* 10, *T* 1585:31.56a12–28, 56b2–3; *Fodi jing lun* 3, *T* 1530:26.302b23–c11; for all four wisdoms, see also *KSGN,* p. 633b. In an innovation found only in this sūtra (*VS,* p. 372a8–12), however, designations that differ from the standard names are given to the four wisdoms into which the consciousnesses evolve. The revised list, along with the standard wisdoms to which they correspond (in parentheses) in Wŏnhyo's interpretation: (1) decisive wisdom (impartial wisdom), (2) adaptable wisdom (sublime observation wisdom), (3) nirvāṇa wisdom (wisdom that has accomplished what was to be done), (4) ultimate wisdom (great perfect mirror wisdom). See *KSGN,* p. 661b–c;.

12. The three bodies: commonly, the law body (dharmakāya), enjoyment body *(saṃbhogakāya),* and transformation body *(nirmāṇakāya).* The *VS* listing once again differs slightly: the fruition buddha who is endowed with all meritorious qualities (equivalent to the *saṃbhogakāya*); the tathāgatagarbha buddha (equal to the dharmakāya); and the form buddha (the *nirmāṇakāya*). See *VS,* p. 370b29; the passage, along with Wŏnhyo's explanations of these terms, appears in *KSGN,* pp. 657a.

13. The term "one enlightenment: is used in *VS,* p.366b15. Wŏnhyo explains, "Because original and actualized [enlightenments] are nondual, they are called one enlightenment"; *KSGN,* p. 633b.

14. "Two kinds of selfhood": the selfhood of person *(pudgala)* and dharmas; *VS,* p. 370b13; and *KSGN,* p. 647c.

15. "Two extremes": specifically, the extreme views *(antagrāhadṛṣti)* that the self continues after death ("eternalism," or *śāśvatavāda*) or that are brought to an end forever after one's demise ("annihilationism," or *ucchedavāda*).

16. "Two accesses": the accesses of principle and practice are discussed in chapter 5 of *VS* (p. 369c7 ff); see *KSGN,* pp. 641b–642b.

17. "Three buddhas": identical to the *VS* listing given in note 12 above.

18. "Three moral codes": the rules of conduct and deportment, the cultivation

of all wholesome dharmas, aiding all sentient beings. *VS*, chap. 6 (p. 370c25–27); *KSGN*, p. 651a.

19. "Three great truths": (1) the path to bodhi is all-embracing, (2) enlightenment is attained via correct wisdom, (3) one enters enlightenment by not differentiating between the practices of samādhi and prajñā. *VS*, chap. 8 (p. 373c9–12); *KSGN*, p. 672c–673b; and cf. Leon Hurvitz, "Chih-i (538–597): An Introduction to the Life and Ideas of a Chinese Buddhist Monk," *Mélanges chinois et bouddhiques* 12 (1962): 315.

20. "Three liberations": this list is unique to *VS:* (1) empty-space liberation, (2) adamantine liberation, (3) prajñā liberation; *VS*, chap. 5 (p. 370a29). Wŏnhyo correlates them with the more common group of eight liberations; *KSGN*, p. 646a–b.

21. "Three levels of virtual enlightenment" appear in chapter 6 of *VS* (p. 371b15); they involve abiding on the virtual-enlightenment stage for (1) one hundred kalpas, (2) one thousand kalpas, (3) myriad kalpas. *KSGN*, p. 656c. The idea has been adopted from the apocryphal *Pusa yingluo benye jing* 1, *T* 1485:24.1012c27–1013a9.

22. "Three bodies of sublime enlightenment" are noted but not listed in chapter 6 of *VS* (p. 371b15). Wŏnhyo interprets them as simply the dharmakāya, *saṃbhogakāya*, and *nirmāṇakāya; KSGN*, p. 657a.

23. "Three groups of voidness": see note 1 above.

24. The three existences are the equivalents of the three realms of existence *(traidhātuka):* (1) the desire realm, (2) the subtle-materiality realm, (3) the formless realm; *Apidamo dabiposha lun (Abhidharmamahāvibhāṣā)* 60, *T* 1545:27.310b9–12; *Abidamo zhiyimen zulun (Abhidharmasaṃgītiparyāya)* 4, *T* 1536:26.383b25–c1.

25. Four right efforts: (1) to avoid unwholesome states that have not yet arisen, (2) to overcome unwholesome states that have already arisen, (3) to develop wholesome states that have not yet arisen, (4) to maintain wholesome states that have already arisen. These constitute the sixth stage of the eightfold path and the second category of the thirty-seven limbs of enlightenment.

26. Four bases of supranormal power: (1) concentration of will, (2) concentration of mind, (3) concentration of effort, (4) concentration of investigation. These constitute the third category of the thirty-seven constituents of enlightenment *(bodhipākṣkadharma)*.

27. Four great conditions: Wŏnhyo explains that these are four powers inherent in original enlightenment; they act as the conditions for the observation of the three moral codes (see note 18 above). They are (1) suppression, which acts as the condition for perfecting the rules of conduct and deportment; (2) its pure basis, which acts as the condition for cultivating all wholesome dharmas; (3) compassion, which acts as the condition for encouraging one to aid all sentient beings; (4) penetrating knowledge, which acts as the condition for freeing the mind from all attachments to the phenomenal characteristics of the above three moral codes so that they will conform to thusness *(tathatā)*. VS, chap. 6 (p. 370c25–28); *KSGN*, p. 651a–c.

28. Four postures *(īryāpatha):* walking, standing, sitting, and lying down.

29. Four dhyānas: The four stages of meditation that are associated with the realm of subtle-materiality, each of which is accompanied by specific mental concomitants. (1) The absorption that is accompanied by thought and imagination, born of detachment, and associated with joy and ease. (2) The absorption free from thought and imagination, born of concentration, and associated with

joy and ease. (3) The absorption free from thought, imagination, and joy; and associated with ease. (4) The absorption free from ease and associated only with equanimity.

30. Denigration *(apavāda)* is an aspect of wrong view *(mithyādṛṣṭi),* the "denigration" of that which really exists; see discussion in *KSGN,* p. 623c, and the relevant note there (note no. 173).

31. "Stage of the four vast [wisdoms]": this term is used chapter 4 of *VS* (p. 368c14), which Wŏnhyo interprets as the four wisdoms (for which see note 11 above); *KSGN,* p. 633b.

32. Five skandhas: materiality, sensation, perception, impulses, consciousness.

33. The fifty evils are another unusual listing found in *VS* (chap. 4; *VS,* p. 369a14). The consciousness aggregate *(vijñānaskandha)* includes eight evils—the eight consciousnesses—as do both the sensation and perception skandhas. The impulse skandha possesses nine evils: eight associated with mind *(cittasaṃprayukta)* and one disassociated therefrom *(cittaviprayukta).* The materiality skandha possesses seventeen evils: the four primary elements and the thirteen derivative forms. These make a total of fifty evils. See *KSGN,* p. 636a–b.

34. Five moral faculties: faith, exertion, mindfulness, concentration, wisdom. These are the fourth category in the thirty-seven constituents of enlightenment.

35. Five powers: the preceding five moral faculties once they have developed into potent forces. These are the fifth of the categories in the thirty-seven constituents of enlightenment.

36. Five voidnesses: another peculiar listing in *VS* (chap. 5, p. 369b12–13). (1) The three realms of existences (see note 24 above) are void; (2) the shadows of the six destinies are void; (3) dharma characteristics are void; (4) nominal characteristics are void; (5) the objects of mental consciousness are void. See *KSGN,* p. 639a.

37. The five ranked levels are discussed in chapter 6 of *VS* (p. 371a23–b5): (1) faith, (2) consideration, (3) cultivation, (4) practice, (5) relinquishment. Wŏnhyo correlates these ranked levels with the following stages of the standard bodhisattva path: (1) the ten faiths; (2) ten abidings, ten practices, and ten transferences; (3) ten bhūmis; (4) virtual enlightenment; (5) sublime enlightenment; see his interpretation at *KSGN,* p. 654a–655c.

38. Quoted from *VS* (chap. 2, p. 366c23); see *KSGN,* p. 618c.

39. The five realms of existence: divinities, humans, animals, hungry ghosts, denizens of hell.

40. Six pāramitās: giving, moral discipline, patience, exertion, mental absorption, wisdom.

41. Six sense-bases: eye, ear, nose, tongue, body, mind.

42. Seven aspects of enlightenment: mindfulness, investigation of dharmas, exertion, joy, serenity, concentration, equanimity.

43. The "great object matrix" is another classification peculiar to *VS* (chap. 7, p. 372a21–23). The term is parsed as follows: "great" means the four great elements of solidity (earth), cohesion of fluidity (water), maturation (fire), and motion (air); "object" refers to the three sūtra classifications of dharmas, as skandhas, *dhātus*, and *āyatanas*; "matrix" means the foundational consciousness *(mūlavijñāna).* Wŏnhyo interprets these as contemplations on the four coarse phenomena (the four great material elements) as well as the contemplation of three subtler categories of dharmas (skandhas, etc.), yielding seven meanings. These contemplations lead to the destruc-

tion of the beginningless seeds *(bīja)* of conceptual proliferation *(prapañca)* within the *mūlavijñāna*. See *KSGN*, p. 662b–c.

44. This sentence is quoted from *VS* (chap. 5, p. 370b23); see Wŏnhyo's interpretation at *KSGN*, p. 648c.

45. Ten faiths: the preliminary level of the bodhisattva path, consisting of (1) faith, (2) mindfulness, (3) effort, (4) wisdom, (5) concentration, (6) nonretrogression, (7) transferences, (8) dharma-protection, (9) moral discipline, (10) vows. *Pusa yingluo benye jing* 1, *T* 1485:24.1011c4–5.

46. Ten bhūmis: the final stages of the bodhisattva path: (1) Joyful, (2) Stainless, (3) Illuminating, (4) Radiant, (5) Difficult to Conquer, (6) Liberation, (7) Far-Reaching, (8) Unshakable, (9) Intelligence, (10) Dharma-Cloud. *Dafangguang fo huayan jing (Avataṃsaka-sūtra)* 23, *T* 278:9.542c27–543a1, gives the standard *Daśabhūmika-sūtra* tabulation. The list is considerably different in the apocryphal *Pusa yingluo benye jing* 1, *T* 1485:24.1014c16–18.

47. "Next part" here means part 4 of *KSGN*, the extended discussion on passages in the text itself; for these titles, see *KSGN*, pp. 607c and 675c.

48. Much of the material in this section of Wŏnhyo's treatise is reminiscent of Jingying Huiyuan's (523–592) treatment of the term "vajrasamādhi" in his *Dasheng yi zhang* 9, *T* 1851:44.637c–641a. There can be little doubt that Wŏnhyo drew heavily upon it here in preparing his exposition.

49. *VS*, chap. 1, p. 366a28.

50. Ibid., p. 366a29.

51. *Mohe boruo boluomi jing* 5, *T* 223:8.251b27–28; quoted in *Dazhidu lun* 47, *T* 1509:25.397a13–14. The implication is that vajrasamạdhi is the concentration that produces mastery over all other types of samādhis; note *Dabanniepan jing (Mahāparinirvāṇa-sūtra)* 24, *T* 374:12.509b14–c6.

52. *Dazhidu lun* 47, *T.* 1509:25.399b2–5.

53. Virtually the same exchange appears in *Dasheng yi zhang* 9, *T* 1851:44.638b4 ff.

54. See *Dazhidu lun* 47, *T.* 1509:25.400b26–27.

55. *Mohe boruo boluomi jing* 5, *T* 223:8.251c19–20 and 252a29–b2; quoted in *Dazhidu lun* 47, *T* 1509:25.397b4–5 and 397c12–13. Both of these qualities are attributed to vajrasamādhi in *Dabanniepan jing* 24, *T* 374:12.509b–c.

56. The text of *Dazhidu lun* seems corrupt here, both in the original and in Wŏnhyo's citation. I would transpose "the Buddha said" with *vajropamasamādhi* and make this and the following two sentences direct quotations from the *Pañca*.

57. For the legend of Indra destroying the asuras, see Joseph Campbell, *The Masks of the Gods II: Oriental Mythology* (New York: Viking Press, 1962), pp. 182–183, 184–187; quoting *Ṛg-Veda* I.32a and *Mahābhārata* 12.281.1–12.282.20. *Vajra* in this context should be taken as a thunderbolt, the mythical weapon of Indra, king of the gods. The asuras are fallen gods and constitute a sixth realm of existence supplementing the five listed above (note 39).

58. According to *Vijñaptimātratāsiddhi-śāstra*, even upon attaining the tenth bhūmi, there still remains a trace of subtle *jñeyāvaraṇa* (cognitive hindrances) and the seeds *(bīja)* of *kleśāvaraṇa* (afflictive hindrances); it is through the *vajropamasamādhi* that these are both excised so that one may enter the tathāgatabhūmi. See *Cheng weishi lun* 10, *T* 1585:31.54a ff; Tat Wei, trans., *Ch'eng Wei-Shih Lun: The Doctrine of Mere-Consciousness* (Hong Kong: Ch'eng Wei-Shi Lun Publication Committee, 1973), pp. 740–743. See also *Apidamo jushe lun (Abhidharmakośabhāṣya)* 24,

T 1558:29.126b, and *ch.* 28, p. 150a–b; Prahlad Pradhan, ed., *Abhidharmakośabhāṣyam of Vasubandhu* (Patna: K. P. Jayaswal Research Institute), pp. 364–366 and 451–452.

59. For these three bodhis, see *Xianyang shengjiao lun (*Āryaśāsanaprakaraṇa)* 3, *T* 1602:31.496b1–5.

60. *Anuttarasamyaksaṃbodhi;* it is defined in *Yuqieshi di lun (Yogācārabhūmiśāstra)* 38, *T* 1779:30.498c–499a and especially p. 499a9–11.

61. *Dabanniepan jing* 24, *T* 374:12.509b4.

62. Eighteen special buddhadharmas *(aṣṭādaśa āveṇikā buddhadharmāḥ)* are said to be unique to the buddhas. The list includes such things as being free from error or distraction, never regressing, having all their actions motivated by pristine cognition, and so on. See *Mohe boruo boluomi jing* 24, *T* 223:8.395b20–28. A different listing of 140 such dharmas is given in *Yuqieshi di lun* 38, *T* 1779:30.499a11–14.

63. *Dazhidu lun* 47, *T* 1509:25.400b17–29.

64. The first of the seven precious things unique to the cakravartin, or wheel-turning emperor; the list also includes his wealth, queen, ministers, elephants, generals, and horses.

65. Following the interpretation at *Dazhidu lun* 17, *T* 1509:25.180c22.

66. Vajrasamādhi is also said to be able to shatter all defilements in *Dabanniepan jing* 24, *T* 374:12.509c18–21.

67. *Yŏ kŭmgang;* the equivalency for *vajropama* adopted by Kumārajīva and Paramārtha.

68. *Kŭmgang yu;* the rendering of *vajropama* used by Xuanzang.

69. Adapted from *Laozi* 48: "Keep on diminishing and diminishing again, until you reach the state of nonaction."

70. The implication here is that *vajropamasamādhi* corresponds to the pseudo-enlightenment of the two-vehicle adherents that only involves the abandonment of the gross attachments resulting from conceptualization. See *Dasheng qixin lun*, *T* 1666:32.576b20–22; Hakeda, trans., *Awakening of Faith*, p. 38.

71. Known in our present recensions as the *Foshuo jin'gang sanmei benxing qingjing buhuai bumie jing*, *T* 644:15.697a–699b.

72. For the technical implications of these types of Sanskrit compounds, see M. S. Narayana Murti, *Sanskrit Compounds: A Philosophical Study* (Varanasi: Chowkhamba, 1973); and Johan F. Staal, "Room at the Top in Sanskrit: Ancient and Modern Descriptions of Nominal Composition," *Indo-Iranian Journal* 9 (1966): 165–198. Note that the Chinese interpretation of the denotation of these compounds was not always consistent with the Indian.

73. This quotation appears to be a paraphrase of a passage in Huiyuan's *Dasheng yi zhang* 13, *T* 1851:44.718a7–8; this identification seems plausible given that so much of Wŏnhyo's exposition on the meaning of *Vajrasamādhi* is drawn from Huiyuan's earlier treatment.

74. *Yuqieshi di lun* 11, *T* 1579:30.329b1–2.

75. This section also parallels closely the treatment found in *Dasheng yi zhang* 13, *T* 1851:44.718a.

76. This description is adapted from *Yuqieshi di lun* 11, *T* 1579:30.329a4–5.

77. Cf. *Yuqieshi di lun* 11, *T* 1579.30.328c19–27; *Abidamo dabiposha lun* 141, *T* 1545:27.727b8–10, for parallel descriptions.

78. *Yuqieshi di lun* 11, *T* 1579:30.329a1–3.

79. Ibid., *T* 1579:30.328c12–15.

80. Ibid., *T* 1579:30.330b22–25; and cf. p. 504a7–12.

81. See *Hebu Jin'guangming jing* (Composite Suvarṇaprabhāsottama-Sūtra) 3, *T* 664:16.375a12–23, for the list to which Wŏnhyo is referring. Unfortunately for Wŏnhyo's thesis, Yijing's later translation of the same text (made in 703, some seventeen years after Wŏnhyo's death) gives the same list but with all ten concentrations transliterated using only one scheme, not two. See *Jin'guangming (cuishengwang) jing (Suvarṇaprabhāsottamarāja-sūtra)* 4, *T* 665:16.420a18–27. Hindsight thus shows us clearly that the different transcriptions in the earlier text were, in fact, nothing more than variant equivalencies for the identical term, samādhi. The confusion there is perhaps due to the composite nature of that edition, which might have led to two different transcriptions for the same term appearing in the text. See discussion in Rhi Ki-yong (Yi Kiyŏng), "Kyŏngjŏn inyong nat'anan Wŏnhyo ŭi tokch'angsŏng," pp. 188–191.

82. Wŏnhyo's analysis in this section has its antecedent in Xuanzang's translation of Jinaputra's *Yuqieshi di lun shi (Yogācārabhūmiśāstrakārikā)*, *T* 1580:30.887a8–16.

83. Distraction *(vikṣepa)* is included among the twenty subsidiary afflictions *(upakleśa)* in the Yogācāra listing. See *Dasheng bofa mingmen lun*, *T* 1614:31.855c6; *Cheng weishi lun* 6, *T* 1585:31.34b28–c14; Tat Wei, trans., *Mere-Consciousness*, pp. 448–449.

84. *Dasheng bofa mingmen lun*, *T* 1614:31.855b24; *Cheng weishi lun* 5, *T* 1585:31.28b25–c11; Tat Wei, trans., *Mere-Consciousness*, pp. 378–379.

85. The second of the four samādhis recognized in the Tiantai school; it is also known as the "constantly walking samādhi." This samādhi is developed through walking constantly in a clockwise direction for ninety days, until all the present buddhas of the ten directions appear before you *(pratyutpanna)* in attestation of your accomplishment. See *Mohe zhiguan* 2a, *T* 1911:46.12a–13a; and Hurvitz, "Chih-i," p. 322.

86. Nine varieties of mental absorption culminating in equanimous retention (samādhi). See *Yuqieshi di lun* 30, *T* 1579:30.450c18–451a19; *Dasheng apidamo caji lun (Abhidharmasamuccayavyākhyā)* 10, *T* 1606:31.741b9–23.

87. The first of the two major subdivisions of the three samādhis (see below n. 90); it is the stage at which liberation is still not achieved and the mind is occasionally distracted and disturbed. See *Yuqieshi di lun* 12, *T* 1579:30.337b24–c3; and cf. *Xianyang shengjiao lun (*Āryaśāsanaprakaraṇa)* 19, *T* 1602:31.575a1–18.

88. The eighth of the wholesome mental concomitants *(kuśalāścaitasikā dharmāḥ)* listed in the *Dasheng bofa mingmen lun*, *T* 1614.31.855b29; *Cheng weishi lun* 6, *T* 1585.31.30b5–7; Tat Wei, trans., *Mere-Consciousness*, pp. 400–401.

89. I believe that Wŏnhyo may be referring here to the four penetrating practices *(catasraḥ pratipādāḥ)* mentioned in the *Abhidharmakośabhāṣya*, which are practices based, first, on the four dhyānas and, second, on dispassion toward the five skandhas; each of these is then subdivided into slow and rapid aspects for those of inferior and superior capacity, respectively. They lead ultimately to nirvāṇa. See *Apidamo chü-she lun* 25, *T* 1558.29.132a19–28; Pradhan, *Abhidharmakośabhāṣyam*, p. 382; and note *Abidamo dabiposha lun* 93, *T* 1545.27.482a26–484a18.

90. For the three samādhis, see *VS*, chap. 7 (p. 372a19–21); and the discussion at *KSGN*, pp. 661c–662b.

91. Wŏnhyo's division of the text is anomalous here. In the opening of his exegesis of chapter 8 (p. 667a), Wŏnhyo explicitly separates the dissemination section of the chapter from the preceding parts of the chapter. For this reason, I designate

most of chapter 8 as section 3 (A) and call the dissemination portion section 3 (B). See the discussion in note no. 325 in the translation of chapter 8 in the *Vajrasamādhi* (*KSGN*, p. 667a) for the rationale behind this subdivision of section 3.

92. I translate this stock opening to Buddhist scriptures following Wŏnhyo's analysis below, in which the line "thus have I heard at one time" is treated as an interconnected unit. John Brough has advocated this same interpretation ("Thus Have I Heard . . . ," *Bulletin of the School of Oriental and African Studies* 13 (1950): 416–426), following the Tibetan commentarial tradition.

93. As Mizuno Kōgen has noted, these would be unusual personal names for Indians, and their use provides a significant clue of the East Asian origin of the scripture itself. See Mizuno's "Bodaidaruma no *Ninyūshigyō setsu* to *Kongōzammaikyō* (Bodhidharma's *Explanation of the Two Accesses and Four Practices* and the *Vajrasamādhi-sūtra*), *Komazawa Daigaku kenkyū kiyō* (Research report of Komazawa University) 13 (1955): 42.

94. Wŏnhyo's interpretation here parallels the *Dazhidu lun*'s analysis of a sixfold division of a sūtra's opening; see Luis Gómez, "Buddhas Literature," p. 533.

95. *Miaofa lianhua jing (Saddharmapuṇḍarīka-sūtra)*, T 262:9.2b7 ff; Leon Hurvitz, trans., *Scripture of the Lotus Blossom of the Fine Dharma (The Lotus Sūtra)* (New York: Columbia University Press, 1976), p. 3. I have sought to show through this connection between these two scriptures the strong influence exerted by the structure of the *Lotus Sūtra* on the composition of the *VS*. The author or editor of the *VS* shows that he attempted to frame his text in such a way that it would compare with one of the most popular, and undeniably authentic, Indian scriptures ever translated into Chinese; see my *Ch'an Ideology*, pp. 29–33 and table 1.1 (pp. 31–32), where I give a comparative translation of the prologues to both scriptures. See also Zhuzhen's *Jin'gang sanmei jing tongzong ji* (pp. 226b–227a), where he discusses various theories concerning the placement of the *VS* within the Tiantai fivefold temporal taxonomy of the teachings and seeks to prove that the *VS* was preached after the *Lotus Sūtra*—the *Lotus* being intended to excise the initial doubts and regrets of the congregation, the *VS* instead being directed toward those adepts who had already completed all the bodhisattva bhūmis.

96. See Wŏnhyo's *Pŏphwa chongyo, HPC* 1, 492b–493c, section 4, "An Explanation of the Title."

97. The Koryŏ II/Taishō edition reads "reiterate" for "proclaim": *VS*, p. 366a13.

98. *Agada* is a generic Sanskrit term for herbal medicines and cure-alls; the term is mentioned everywhere from Pāli materials (*Apadāna* 41, 46, 508; *Majjhimanikāya* ii.216) to later Sanskrit texts, such as *Mahāyānasūtrālaṃkāra* vi.9 (Lévi ed., p. 24); *Dasheng zhuangyan jing lun* 2, *T* 1604:31.599b1. See also *Fanyi mingyi ji* 3, *T* 2131:54.1108a–b, for other references. An Agada *xian* (transcendent or sage) is mentioned as appearing in chap. 35 of the *Mahāparinirvāṇa-sūtra;* noted in *Fan fanyu* 5, *T* 2130:54.1013b4.

99. Alluding to the famous simile of the rain of dharma that nurtures all living things. See *Miaofa lianhua jing (Saddharmapuṇḍarīka-sūtra)* 3, *T* 262:9.19a–20b; Hurvitz, *Lotus*, pp. 101–103.

100. The Koryŏ II/*Taishō* recension misprints *ch'al (kṣetra)* for *i* (inspiration, benefit); *KSGR* 1, p. 963c6.

101. The five penetrations are an alternate listing of the five superknowledges *(abhijñā):* (1) heavenly eye (viz. clairvoyance), (2) heavenly ear (clairaudience), (3)

cognition of others' states of mind (telepathy), (4) recollection of past lives, (5) magical powers. Sometimes a sixth (cognition of the extinction of the contaminants) is added.

102. These superpowers correspond to the six superknowledges *(abhijñā),* as listed in the previous note.

103. These are the eight stereotypical events in any buddha's life. Between the first and last events that Wŏnhyo lists (the bodhisattva's descent from Tuṣita Heaven to be reborn and his parinirvāṇa), the intervening events are entering the womb for his final birth, birth, leaving the home life, subduing Māra and his minions, achieving enlightenment, and turning the wheel of the dharma. See *Sijiao yi* 7, *T* 1929:46.745c5–7 ff. Sometimes the fifth event (subduing Māra) is replaced by a different third event, that of gestation in the womb.

104. *Ru Lengqie jing (Laṅkāvatāra-sūtra)* 1, *T* 670:16.519a1–2.

105. *Miaofa lianhua jing youbotishe (Saddharmapuṇḍarīkasūtropadeśa), T* 1520: 26.14b8–9.

106. In the following exegesis, Wŏnhyo construes this passage as referring to *VS*'s audience: the preceding expanded *(vaipulya)* sūtra was intended for the period of *saddharma,* while *VS* targets the needs of beings in the semblance-dharma age. Actually *VS* here jumbles the transition period of *pratirūpakadharma* and the final age of *saddharma-vipralopa.* For a survey of different Chinese Buddhist eschatological schemes, see David Chappell, "Early Forebodings of the Death of Buddhism," *Numen* 27:1 (1980), 122–154; and Jan Nattier, *Once upon a Future Time: Studies in a Buddhist Prophecy of Decline,* Nanzan Studies in Asian Religions, no. 1 (Berkeley: Asian Humanities Press, 1991).

107. The five turbidities are five events that mark the gradual decay of the universe; they appear during the abiding period of an eon, or kalpa. (1) Turbidity of the kalpa, marking the beginning of the declining period of the kalpa; (2) turbidity of views, that is, the wrong views of egoism and so on; (3) turbidity of defilements; (4) turbidity of sentient beings, that is, the decline in their behavior; (5) turbidity of the lifespan, or the decreasing length of life.

108. *Miaofa lianhua jing (Saddharmapuṇḍarīka-sūtra), T* 262:9.7a21–22; Hurvitz, *Scripture of the Lotus Blossom of the Fine Dharma,* p. 30. The citations to the *Lotus* in the commentary that follows are all from the same section of that sūtra.

109. *Miaofa lianhua jing youbotishe* 2, *T* 1519:26.7a20–b4.

110. The four wholesome faculties, or roots of goodness, refer to the four aids to penetration *(nirvedhabhāgīya-kuśalamūla),* of heat, climax, acceptance, and highest worldly dharmas, which initiate access to the path of vision *(darśanamārga).* See Robert E. Buswell, Jr., "The 'Aids to Penetration' *(Nirvedhabhāgīya)* According to the Vibhāṣika School," *Journal of Indian Philosophy* 25 (1997): 589–611, and especially 591–593, which treat why these faculties might have been considered *kuśalamūlas.*

111. *Dasheng qixin lun, T* 1666:32.576b15.

112. The "Benfen" section of the *Shidi jing lun (Daśabhūmikaśūtropadeśa)* appears in the first roll of the treatise (*T* 1522:26.126b–127b), but the line Wŏnhyo quotes is not found there. Wŏnhyo is probably quoting secondhand a citation to the passage appearing in some other treatise.

113. *Dasheng qixin lun, T* 1666:32.575b15, 575c21, 576a5.

114. *Ru Lengqie jing (Laṅkāvatāra-sūtra), T* 671:16.519a1–2.

115. The equation drawn here between "nonproduction" *(anutpatti)* and "void calmness" (a synonym of nirvāṇa) is standard in the earliest stratum of Tathā-

gatagarbha materials. See William Grosnick, "Nonorigination and *Nirvāṇa* in the Early *Tathāgatagarbha* Literature," *Journal of the International Association of Buddhist Studies* 4:2 (1981), 33–43.

116. "Efficient cause," or "comprehensive cause," refers to causation in its broadest sense, namely, that all conditioned dharmas serve as the "efficient cause" for the production of all other dharmas. For this type of causation, see also *Yinming ru zhengli lun shu* 1, *T* 1840:44.101c.

117. See *Cheng weishi lun* 4, *T* 1585:31.19b.

118. See Wŏnhyo's *Yijang ŭi, HPC* 1.807b20 ff; the full text will be translated by A. Charles Muller in a later volume of the Collected Works of Wŏnhyo Series. (Wŏnhyo consistently refers to this work as the *Yijang chang* [Essay on the two hindrances], not the *Yijang ŭi* [Doctrine of the two hindrances], as the text is now known in the literature). Wŏnhyo explains there that "bond through association" means that, when defilements are associated with the mind, the mind will be in bondage to those defilements. "Bond through sense objects" means that, when these defilements become attached to sense objects, the mind will be bound by those objects.

119. See *Dazhidu lun* 5, *T* 1509:25.100c4–7.

120. The Yuan and Ming editors of the scripture (*VS*, p. 366, nn. 13, 14) have attempted to make some sense out of this problematic passage by transposing the clauses as follows: "If a person conceives that the mind can be produced, he should be encouraged to abandon [his view that] the nature [of the mind] is subject to production. If a person conceives that the mind can be extinguished, he should be encouraged to abandon [his view that] the nature [of the mind] is subject to extinction." Wŏnhyo, as we shall see in the analysis that follows here, tries to wring some sense out of this passage by interpreting each statement as meaning its exact opposite. His understanding of the passage's import, however, ends up being quite close to these later emendations, possibly suggesting that the Yuan and Ming editors may have derived their emendations from Wŏnhyo's interpretation.

121. Only Wŏnhyo's recension reads "not" *(pu)* for "originally" *(pon)* here; this is almost certainly a dittography from the following line and is best corrected according to all other editions (*VS*, p. 366c1) to read as "originally, production is not extinguished"; see the alternative rendering in Buswell, *Ch'an Ideology*, p. 191.

122. The Three Editions (of the Song, Yuan, and Ming dynasties) add a line that is missing in the Wŏnhyo and K'ai-pao editions: "What view is extinguished when a sentient being perceives that a dharma ceases." See *VS*, p. 366, n. 16; Buswell, *Ch'an Ideology*, p. 191.

123. Previously Wŏnhyo designated this subdivision (II.A.2.b.ii.a) a clarification on the "signless contemplation," not the "contemplation of nonproduction"; see *KSGN*, p. 611a.

124. *Buceng bujian jing, T* 668:16.467b–c, with slight differences. See also Buswell, *Ch'an Ideology*, p. 78, n8, for an exhaustive list of sources on this scripture.

125. See the discussion in the *Foxing lun* (Treatise on the buddha-nature) 2, *T* 1610:31.795c–796a. Authorship of this treatise is traditionally attributed to the Indian scholiast Vasubandhu (fl. ca. mid-fourth–mid-fifth centuries), with the Chinese translation by the Indian monk Paramārtha (499–569). It is now generally accepted, however, that the text displays the heavy editorial hand of Paramārtha and may actually have been written by the famed translator and exegete. See my *Ch'an Ideology*, p. 90, n. 38, for a discussion and further references to the authorship issue surround-

ing this text. See also the extended treatment of this text in Sallie B. King, *Buddha Nature* (Albany: State University of New York Press, 1991), and see pp. 48–54 for her discussion of the text's interpretation of tathāgatagarbha.

126. *Foxing lun* 4, *T* 1610:31.812b3–10.

127. *Foxing lun* 2, *T* 1610:31.795c27, and cf. 794a18–21. Wŏnhyo elides only the second type of buddha-nature, which "emerges" as a result of practice, which is initiated with the first generation of the thought of enlightenment *(bodhicittotpāda)*. See the discussion in Sallie King, *Buddha Nature*, p. 40–56.

128. *HPC* misprints "one" for the correct "two" here (p. 816a5); see *T* 1730: 34.968b15.

129. *Yijangŭi*, *HPC* 1.805a–c, 811a.

130. *Shengman shizihu yisheng dafangbian fangguang jing*, *T* 353:12.221c9–10; cf. Wayman and Wayman, *Lion's Roar*, p. 98.

131. *Shengman shizihu yisheng dafangbian fangguang jing*, *T* 353:12.221c16–18; cf. Wayman and Wayman, *Lion's Roar*, p. 98.

132. *Wuxiang lun*, *T* 1618:31.881c25–882a9. See also the treatment in Satō Shigeki, *Wŏnhyŏ ŭi hwajaeng nolli*, p. 114 and n. 41.

133. *She Dasheng lun* 1, *T* 1595:31.156c16–23.

134. *Foxing lun* 2, *T* 1610:31.796b6–c29.

135. The five aspects of the dharmakāya, also called the uncontaminated skandhas, are morality, concentration, wisdom, liberation, and the knowledge and vision of liberation.

136. *She Dasheng lun* 1, *T* 1595:31.156c20.

137. *Foxing lun* 2, *T* 1610:31.795c27, 794a18–21; and see *KSGN*, p. 615a above.

138. *Foxing lun* 4, *T* 1610:31.810b12; cf. *She Dasheng lun* 1, *T* 1595:31.156c.

139. This aspect does not appear in the *Foxing lun* but is noted in *Xianshi lun*, *T* 1618:31.882a8.

140. *She Dasheng lun* 1, *T* 1595:31.156c.

141. *Dasheng qixin lun*, *T* 1666:32.577c; cf. Hakeda, *Awakening of Faith*, pp. 51–52. These six maculated states of mind will be discussed just below by Wŏnhyo.

142. *Dasheng qixin lun*, *T* 1666:32.577c26–578a4; cf. Hakeda, *Awakening of Faith*, pp. 54–55.

143. The first of the three types of materiality, which will be discussed below in *KSGN*, p. 643a. For these three, see *Abhidharmakośabhāṣyam* 4.4a–b; La Vallée Pousin, *Abhidharmakośabhāṣyam*, vol. 2, p. 560 ff.

144. The activating consciousness is the first of the five types of consciousness discussed in the *Awakening of Faith*. Owing to the power of ignorance, the one mind of true thusness is disturbed, thereby activating the dualistic processes of thought. See *Dasheng qixin lun*, *T* 1666:32.577b7; Hakeda, *Awakening of Faith*, pp. 47–48.

145. *Dasheng qixin lun*, *T* 1666:32.579a12–20; Hakeda, *Awakening of Faith*, pp. 64–65.

146. The text alludes here to the *Nirvāṇa Sūtra*'s portrayal of nirvāṇa as selfhood, permanence, bliss, and purity; see *Dabanniepan jing* 2, *T* 374:12.377b.

147. *Dasheng qixin lun*, *T* 1666:32.579a21–579b ; cf. Hakeda, *Awakening of Faith*, pp. 65–67.

148. Following Wŏnhyo's interpretation below. Wŏnhyo takes the five dharmas as the pure dharmadhātu, which derives from the ninth *amalavijñāna*, along with the four wisdoms into which the other eight consciousnesses transmute.

149. *Dasheng qixin lun, T* 1666:32.576b29–576c4; cf. Hakeda, *Awakening of Faith,* p. 40. Wŏnhyo quotes the same passage in his exposition of chapter 4 of the *VS* below; see *KSGN,* p. 637a.

150. A well-known simile from the *Suvarṇaprabhāsottama-sūtra* (Simile of golden light sūtra): "This is like a man who sees himself in a dream floating down a big river. By using his hands and kicking his feet, he is able to cross the river and reach the far shore, because his body and mind would not give up out of laziness. But once he awakens from his dream, he no longer sees any river, or either this shore or the far shore." *Jin'guangming jing [Hebu]* 1, T 664:16.364c1–3; *Jin'guangming Zuishengwang jing* 2, *T* 665:16.410a29–b3.

151. As Wŏnhyo explains here, the issue raised in this question is that someone who has realized the state of nonconceptualization would be unable to conceive either of any mental concept that needs to be controlled or of any conception of a person who actually performs such controlling. Such a position would imply that there was no such thing as actualized enlightenment—that is, a process of spiritual development by which enlightenment is achieved.

152. "Dharmas that reveal principles" are one of the four types of dharmas, along with doctrinal dharmas, practice dharmas, and fruition dharmas. This type refers to the principles that are revealed in the teachings of the Buddha. See discussion in Ŭn and Song, *Kŭmgang sammaegyŏng non,* p. 186, n. 1.

153. An epithet for the Buddha, after the Heavenly Drum in Indra's Heaven of the Thirty-Three (Trayastriṃśa), which sounds spontaneously, inspiring all heavenly beings to enlightenment. As Jizang explains: "In foreign countries, they call the Buddha the 'Heavenly Drum.' When thieves come, the heavenly drum sounds . . . emboldening the minds of all heavenly beings . . . and frightening away the asuras. Should sentient beings become defiled, the Buddha will then expound the Dharma . . . , emboldening the minds of those sentient beings . . . and frightening all the Māras." *Fahua yishu* 1, *T* 1721:34.455c22–27.

154. The Koryŏ II/Taishō recension reads instead: "The mind that resides nowhere does not reside in great voidness"; *VS,* p. 367a23.

155. The *Dakong jing* (*Mahāśūnyatā-sūtra;* equivalent to the Pāli *Mahāsuññatā-sutta* [*Majjhima-nikāya,* no. 122]) appears in the *Za Ahan jing [Saṃyuktāgama]* 49, *T* 26:1.738a–740c. The *Dakong jing* emphasizes the need to focus on voidness internally, externally, and then both internally and externally, by avoiding all attention to characteristics. I should note that the term "great voidness" does not in fact appear in the text, because the title actually means the *Great Sūtra on Voidness,* not the *Sūtra on Great Voidness.* Wŏnhyo derives his reference not directly from the *Za Ahan jing* recension of the *Dakong jing* but from a citation to a *Za Ahan jing Dakong jing* that appears in the *Mahāprajñāpāramitā-sūtropadeśa;* see *Dazhidu lun* 31, *T* 1509: 25.388a12–13. The *Dazhidu lun*'s citation here is either incorrect or refers to a nonextant recension of the sūtra.

156. I have been unable to locate a precise reference to this explanation in the *Yuqieshi di lun (Yogācārabhūmiśāstra),* but cf. *Yuqieshi di lun* 77, *T* 1579:30.726c–727a, and 833b20. Wŏnhyo may instead be thinking of similar references found in two texts that he has frequently cited in this chapter of his *KSGN;* see *Foxing lun* 1, *T* 1610:31.787b4–5; and *She Dasheng lun shi* 10, *T* 1575:31.222b1 and 245c18–28. This interpretation is also found in *Shengtianwang buoluo buoluomi jing* 7, *T* 231:8.723c19.

157. *Dabanniepan jing* 16, *T* 374:12.461b6–8; for this precise citation, see p. 461c22: "Prajñāpāramitā is called 'great voidness.'" This is the last of the eleven kinds of voidness listed in that sūtra.

158. *Ru Lengqie jing* 3, *T* 671:16.529a8–10; *Lengqieaboduoluo jing* 1, *T* 670:16.488c8, c18–20. In this sūtra, it is termed the "great voidness of ultimate sagacious knowledge."

159. *Jieshenmi jing* 3, *T* 676:16.700a5. The sūtra also mentions great voidness in reference to voidness' standard role as one of the three gates of deliverance; see *Jieshenmi jing* 1, *T* 676:16.688b15. Note also Nāgārjuna's account of eighteen types of voidness, which lists as the fourth type "the great voidness of the physical environment"; see *Shibakong lun, T* 1616:31.861b.

160. See Vasubandhu's *Zhong bian fenbie lun [Madhyāntavibhāgabhāṣya], T* 1599:31.452c25–26.

161. See *Shidi jing lun, T* 1522:26.172b16. This notion that the *ālayavijñāna* is "great voidness" may also derive from a line in the *Laṅkāvatāra-sūtra:* "Upon leaving behind the *ālayavijñāna,* there will be neither production nor extinction"; *Ru Lengqie jing, T* 671:16.556c29.

162. *Dazhidu lun* 31, *T* 1509:25.288a15; and see the explanation at p. 288a 15–22.

163. Ten levels of the dharmadhātu: (1) hell denizens, (2) hungry ghosts, (3) animals, (4) asuras, (5) human beings, (6) heavenly beings, (7) arhats, (8) pratyekabuddhas, (9) bodhisattvas, (10) buddhas.

164. The four types of nirvāṇa are (1) nirvāṇa that is originally pure by nature, (2) nirvāṇa with remainder, (3) nirvāṇa without remainder, (4) nirvāṇa that has no fixed abode; see *Cheng weishi lun* 10, *T* 1585:31.55b.

165. That is, the *ānantaryamārga* (immediate path), which constitutes the penultimate eighteen of the thirty-four moments of the path of vision leading up to final enlightenment in the Sarvāstivāda path schema, followed by the final eighteen moments of the *vimokṣamārga* (path of liberation).

166. The Sanskrit Siddham letter for the high front vowel *i* was an arrangement of three dots in a triangular shape; hence, if any point was out of place or missing, the letter was not formed properly. The simile is taken from the *Nanben Niepan jing, T* 375:12.616b. For an example of the orthography of the letter, see *Xita zi ji, T* 1232:54.1187c3. Here, this letter is being used as a simile for the three aspects of liberation: the meritorious qualities of dharmakāya (alt. nirvāṇa), liberation, and wisdom. See also Chengguan's description in *Dafanghuang fo huayan jing suishu yanyi chao* 7, *T* 1736:36.47a–b.

167. See *KSGN,* p. 617a above.

168. The ten types of liberation, based on the *Avataṃsaka-sūtra:* (1) the inconceivable liberation of the bodhisattvas, (2) unobstructed liberation, (3) pure-practice liberation, (4) the liberation of understanding universal dharma-gates, (5) liberation of the tathāgatagarbha, (6) liberation of unobstructed eloquence, (7) liberation of accessing all three time periods, (8) liberation of the storehouse of the dharma-nature, (9) the liberation of cognition, (10) liberation of successful progress. See *Dafangguan fo huayan jing* 27, *T* 278:9.573a3–6. For an alternate list, see *Shidi jing* 8, *T* 287:10.569c29–b4.

169. The three aspects here refer to the three aspects of of nirvāṇa: dharmakāya, liberation, and wisdom.

170. Wŏnhyo here transposes two lines from *Dabanniepan jing* 4, *T* 375:12.628a18–19, 20. The sūtra explains that a bodhisattva who abides in mahāparinirvāṇa has complete control over his dominion (e.g., he can make the trichiliocosm, the entire universe, enter into a mustard seed or a single pore of the skin).

171. *Miluo Pusa suowen jing lun [Maitreyaparipṛcchopadeśa]* 1, *T* 1525:26.238a9–11.

172. *Yijang ŭi,* section 5, *HPC* 1:802b–811b.

173. "Erroneous affirmation" *(samāropikā)* and "denigration" *(apavāda)* are two extreme aspects of wrong views. Wrong views *(mithyādṛṣṭi)* themselves are the "denigration" of that which really exists, such as the truth of suffering; all other types of wrong views are an "erroneous affirmation" of things that do not in fact exist in reality. See *Apidamo jushe lun* (*Abhidharmakośabhāṣya,* v. 7) 19, *T* 1558:29.100a17. Four types are mentioned in the *Abhidharmamahāvibhāṣā.* Denigration of (1) cause, which is countered by understanding the noble truth of origination; (2) effect, which is countered by the noble truth of suffering; (3) the path (mārga), which is countered by the noble truth of the path; (4) extinction, which is countered by the noble truth of extinction. See *Apidamo dabiposha lun* 198, *T* 1545:27.988a–c.

174. The Koryŏ II/Taishō edition reads *in* (acquiescence) for *zhu* (abiding) here; see *VS,* p. 367, n. 8.

175. See Baozhi's *Shisike song,* in *Jingde chuandeng lu* 29, *T* 2076:51.451b5: "The mind-essence has neither form nor shape."

176. For this simile, see *Guang Bolun ben, T* 1570:31.185b21–26; and *VS,* chapter 8 below. To paraphrase Wŏnhyo's explanation that follows, heat may be latent in wood, but that "heat" can never be isolated from "wood." In the same way, innumerable dharmas may be latent inside the principle, but they cannot be isolated from that principle. While heat therefore may ultimately be unascertainable, we know that heat nevertheless exists; in the same way, while the vast numbers of wholesome qualities inherent in the principle may ultimately be unascertainable, the adept can draw upon them in his spiritual practice.

177. The rendering of the last alternative follows Wŏnhyo's interpretation below. The myrobalan is used in *Mahāparinirvāṇa-sūtra* as a metaphor for the perfect clarity of insight that comes about through accessing the vajrasamādhi. "If there is a bodhisattva who abides in this vajrasamādhi, he will see that all dharmas have no obstructions, just as if they were myrobalans in one's palm *(kāratalāmalakavat).*" *Dabanniepan jing* 24, *T* 374:12.509c5–8, noted in Liebenthal, p. 371. For other references to the myrobalan in Buddhist literature, see Alex Wayman, "Notes on the Three Myrobalans," *Phi Theta Annual* 5 (1954–1955): 63–77.

178. This same gāthā is quoted in Huihong's (1071–1128) *Zhizheng lun* (Treatise on Wisdom and Realization) (*XZJ* 1235:63.185a19), but since this is a Song dynasty text, it obviously could not have been Wŏnhyo's own source. I have been unable to trace any other reference to this gāthā in the literature.

179. The locus classicus for this phrase is *Sutta-nipāta,* v. 1076, describing the state of nirvāṇa: "There is no means of knowing him who has gone to rest,/He has nothing that could be named. /When all dharmas are eradicated,/All pathways of speech are also eradicated" *(attan-gatassa na pamāṇam atthi; yena naṁ vajju, taṁ tassa n'atthi; sabbesu dhammesu samuhatesu; samuhatā vādapathā pi sabbe ti).* For discussion of the significance of this verse, see Luis Gómez, "Proto-Mādhyamika in the Pāli Canon," *Philosophy East and West* 26 (1976): 146, and for further references to the phrase in Sanskrit literature, p. 158, n. 5.

180. For these eight negations, see *Zhonglun [Mūlamadhyamakakārikā]* 1, *T* 1564: 30.1c8–9; that treatise, however, replaces "neither access nor egress" with "neither coming nor going" and changes the order of the eight.

181. I have been unable to trace this sūtra quotation.

182. Alluding to *Laozi* 14: "What cannot be seen is called evanescent;/what cannot be heard is called rarified." D. C. Lau, trans., *Lao Tzu Tao Te Ching* (New York: Penguin Books, 1963), p. 70.

183. For a similar exchange, cf. *Jin'gang boruo boluomi jing (Vajracchedikāprajñāpāramitā-sūtra), T* 235:8.749b11–15 and 751c20–27.

184. See Vasubandhu's *Miaofa lianhua jing youbotishe [Saddharmapuṇḍarīkopadeśa]* 2, *T* 1519:26.9c28,10a4–5; and cf. Jizang's *Fahua lun shu* 3, *T* 1818:40.823c27–29.

185. I have been unable to find an exact match to Wŏnhyo's citation. The passage most resonates with a discussion in the *Da zhuangyan famen jing* (*j.* 1, *T* 818: 17.826c28–29): "Furthermore, if the essence and nature of the visual faculty is void, then visual objects cannot be spoken of. This void essence and nature of visual objects is in fact bodhi. So too is it the case with the eye, ear, nose, tongue, body, and mind: if their essences and natures are void, then all dharmas cannot be spoken of. *The void essence and nature of dharmas are in fact bodhi*" (emphasis added). There is also a close parallel in the *Foshuo dasheng ru zhufo jingjie zhiguangming zhuangyan jing* (*j.* 3, *T* 359:12.259a2): "One understands that the voidness of the nature is in fact bodhi."

186. "Mental [consciousness]" *(ŭi)*, "mind-consciousness" *(ŭisik)*, and *manovijñāna (malna [sik])* are actually the translations and transliteration of the same sixth consciousness (the *manovijñāna*), obvious indications that the author of the sūtra was not working from Sanskrit materials. Wŏnhyo tries to resolve the reiteration by specifying that both "mental" and "mind-consciousness" refer to the sixth consciousness—that consciousness being called *ŭi* (=mentation) when it is past, *ŭisik* (mental consciousness) when it is present, and *sim* (mind) when it is future. *Manovijñāna* then refers instead to the seventh consciousness, the governing consciousness *(kliṣṭamanovijñāna)*. See Wŏnhyo's explanation below.

187. This passage, especially as it is elucidated in Wŏnhyo's interpretation, closely parallels statements concerning the meaning of nonproduction made by Jingjue (683–750?), the Northern school adept who compiled *Lengqie shizi ji* (Record of successive masters and disciples of the Laṅka school) in his *Boruo xinjing zhujie* (Annotation and explication of the *Heart Sūtra*): "Thus we know that all dharmas are tranquil and calm, unproduced and unextinguished." The text is reproduced in Yanagida Seizan, *Shoki Zenshū shisho no kenkyū* (Research on early Ch'an historiographical works) (Kyoto: Hōzōkan, 1967), p. 602.

188. In the dharma listings of the Sarvāstivāda, contact *(sparśa)* is the fourth of the ten *mahābhūmika*-dharmas along with feeling, perception, volition, zeal, intelligence, mindfulness, attention, resolution, and concentration; these ten are the predominant mental factors that are conjoined with any conditioned state of consciousness. In the Yogācāra listing, *sparśa* is the first of the five mental concomitants *(caitta)* that are said to be always active *(sarvatraga)*.

189. According to Wŏnhyo's exegesis below chapter 4 is concerned with the phenomenal, production-and-extinction aspect of the one mind's two aspects. The absolute, true-thusness aspect will be treated in the following chapter of the sūtra, "Accessing the Edge of Reality."

190. "Motionless" *(acala)* is not only the attribute of samādhi, as seen before in

the sūtra with reference to the vajrasamādhi, but also a samādhi in its own right; see sources listed in Franklin Edgerton, *Buddhist Hybrid Sanskrit Dictionary* (New Haven: Yale University Press, 1953), p. 6, s.v. "acala."

191. An alternate reading given in the *HPC* edition (p. 630b, l. 19) is "Without either coming or going." I follow the reading above since this is the one that Wŏnhyo obviously prefers.

192. The affective consciousnesses, in Wŏnhyo's interpretation, refer to the eight consciousnesses, all of which are subject to the interplay of the defilements. Only the ninth consciousness, the *amalavijñāna,* is unaffected thereby, thus earning its designation as the "immaculate consciousness." Wŏnhyo presumes that this passage was the source for Paramārtha's theory of a ninth consciousness; see discussion below. The transcription *ammara* (Ch. *anmoluo*) for the Sanskrit word *amala,* as used here, is generally described as being peculiar to the Tiantai tradition and especially to Zhiyi's (539–597) writings (see Mizuno, pp. 45–46; Liebenthal, p. 371, n. 1). It is not, however, exclusive to that tradition. The same transcription is found, for example, in Chinese Pure Land works (Chuandeng's *Jingtu sheng wusheng lun, T* 1975: 47.38lc17), Chan materials (Yanshou's *Zongjing lu* 90, *T* 2016:48.907bl6), Korean Yogācāra commentaries (Tullyun's *Yugaron ki* 13A, *T* 1828:42.605b22), and Japanese exegeses (Jōnen's *Gyōrinshō* 50, *T* 2409:76.352c7). The transcription is also used frequently in East Asian apocryphal compositions, such as *Shoulengyan jing* 4, *T* 745: 19.123cl5. This rendering antedates Paramārtha's own works, which adopt the alternate *amoluo.*

193. Wŏnhyo is referring here to Paramārtha's *Foxing lun;* see discussion in part 1, Study, chapter 1, "Wŏnhyo's Analysis of 'Immaculate Consciousness' and the Innate Purity of Mind."

194. Yuancheng (*Zhujie* 2, p. 199b13–16) takes a somewhat different tack in his interpretation of this passage from the *VS:* "Because the previous fifth, sixth, and seventh consciousnesses are [marked by] mundane characteristics, they are affective consciousnesses. The eighth consciousness then contains both the mundane and the transcendental. The ninth consciousness alone is transcendental. This passage means that one transmutes these mundane affective consciousnesses so that they access the transcendental pure nature." Yuancheng's reading of this passage is an apparent attempt to resurrect the southern Dilun school's bifurcation of the *ālayavijñāna* into both pure and impure aspects. This reading cannot really be supported by *VS,* however, since in the following exchange Muju Bodhisattva states unequivocally that all eight consciousnesses are mundane ("**Each and every one of the eight consciousnesses is generated with the sense realms as condition**"). Cf. also Zhuzhen, *Tongzong ji,* pp. 256d–257a.

195. Wŏnhyo glosses *kail* as *ilch'e* (each and every). *KSGR* 2, p. 978b7. The Yuan and Ming editions have simply changed the following "eight" to *ch'e* to bring out the same sense; *VS,* p. 368bl8, n. 13.

196. The objective-support condition refers to the sensory objects that serve as a necessary condition in the process of perception. For these four types of conditions, see *Abhidharmakośabhāṣya* ii.61c–65; La Vallée Poussin, *Abhidharmakośabhāṣyam,* vol. 1, pp. 296–304; F. I. Stcherbatsky, *Buddhist Logic* (New York: Dover, 1962), pp. 138–139. Wŏnhyo discusses all four conditions in *KSGN,* p. 632b.

197. In Buddhist texts, the nominal binome *yuri* (Ch. *liuli*) should be translated as "beryl," from Pāli *veluriyam,* not with the more common rendering of "glass." See

Edward Schafer, "Combined Supplements to *Mathews*," mimeographed (University of California, Berkeley, Department of Oriental Languages, n.d.), s.v. *"liuli."*

198. Cf. the description of *pratyavekṣanājñāna* in *Cheng weishi lun* 10, *T* 1585: 31.56a21–25.

199. *Ānantaryamārga* and *vimuktimārga* are two of the four soteriological paths outlined in the *Abhidharmakośabhāṣya* (*AKB* vi.65). The *Abhidharmamahāvibhāṣā* distinguishes the two by specifying that the *ānantaryamārga* overcomes the defilements (e.g., through the *vajropamasamādhi*), while the *vimuktimārga* realizes extinction; see *Abidamo dabiposha lun* 90, *T* 1545:27.465c10–11. Wŏnhyo's exegesis here conforms with that interpretation.

200. For these four wisdoms, see *Cheng weishi lun* 7, *T* 1585:31.39a. All four are discussed above in part 2 of the *Exposition,* n. 11.

201. The three contaminants *(āsrava)* are sensual desire, becoming, and ignorance; wrong views are commonly added as a fourth.

202. This sentence is adapted from a citation to the *Udānavarga* (*Faji yaosong jing* 4, *T* 213:4.799a26–27) appearing in the *Mahāyānasaṃgraha;* see *She Dasheng lun* 2, *T* 1593: 31.119al8–19. Noted by Liebenthal, p. 364, though his citation to *T* 212 is wrong.

203. The phrase "sit supernally on the open ground" is cited also in *Lidai fabao ji* (*T* 2075:51.193a8), the Baotang doxography compiled in the late eighth century, and appears to derive from a passage in the *Lotus Sūtra* (*Miaofa lianhua jing, T* 262:9.12cl4–15). The entire sentence appears also in the biography of the Korean Sŏn monk Sunji (fl. 858); see *Chodang chip* 20, p. 356c24–25.

204. The four Māras are defilements *(kleśa),* the aggregates of existence (skandha), death *(mṛtyu),* and evil personified *(devaputra).*

205. *Miaofa lianhua jing [Saddharmapuṇḍarika-sūtra], T* 262:9.16b–17c; Hurvitz, *Lotus,* pp. 85–90. Liebenthal (p. 363, n. 3) has suggested that the attempts by Wŏnhyo below to trace this simile to the allegory of the compassionate father and his ignorant son in the *Lotus Sūtra* are dubious. Liebenthal instead proposes to trace it to a simile in the *Nirvāṇa Sūtra* (*Dabanniepan jing* 24, *T* 374:12.510bl) about a destitute person who finds a diamond (=adamant), though I find Liebenthal's argument unconvincing. As we will see below, Wŏnhyo treats this passage as a simile for the delusion of any sentient being ("a deluded son") whose grasping at defilements obscures the original purity of his mind ("carries gold coins in his hands but does not know that he has them"). The buddhas are able to arouse resolute faith *(adhimukti)* in such a being through the Mahāyāna teachings ("You're carrying around gold coins!"), and finally that being is able to access the first bhūmi ("[he] discovers the gold coins"). But he then grasps at the achievement of that state ("I found the gold coins!"), which the buddhas must counter by admonishing him, "The gold coins you've found have always been in your possession; they are not something you've 'found.' So how can you be happy?" See also Zhuzhen's explanation in *Tongzong ji* 6, p. 260a.

206. See Wŏnhyo's account below at p. 636b; see also Buswell, *Ch'an Ideology,* p. 208, n. 46.

207. See *Cheng weishi lun, T* 1589.45.73a24.

208. The four attributes of nirvāṇa, which Wŏnhyo discussed previously at *KSGN,* p. 618b.

209. *Dasheng qixin lun, T* 1665:32.576c13–14; Hakeda, *Awakening of Faith,* p. 41.

210. *Avijñaptirūpa,* "unmanifest materiality" or more freely "invisible forcefield," refers to three divisions of the eleventh class of derivative material dharmas

in the Abhidharma. *Prātimokṣasaṃvara* (restraint of the precepts) refers to the precepts as a physical force that dissuades the ordained monk from wrongdoing. *Asaṃvara* (nonrestraint) are vows that do not dissuade one from evil but instead actively encourage wrongdoing, such as the vow to kill someone. *Asaṃjñikasamāpatti* (achievement of perceptionless trace) involves an advanced level of meditative equipoise associated with the formless realm of existence. There is a discussion of the three types of *avijñaptirūpa* in Asaṅga's *Xianyang lun [Āryaśāsanaprakaraṇa]*; see *T* 1602:31.484a. Interestingly, however, the particular translation for *asaṃjñikasamāpatti* that Wŏnhyo cites here is not found in the *Āryaśāsanaprakaraṇa* but instead in Asaṅga's *Dasheng Apidamo ji lun [Abhidharmasamuccaya]* 1 (*T* 1605.31.663c), suggesting that Wŏnhyo may have consulted an intermediary source for his citation. For an overview of this peculiar type of materiality, see William Montgomery McGovern, *A Manual of Buddhist Philosophy* (New York: E. P. Dutton, 1923), p. 118.

211. Zhuzhen (*Tongzong ji* 6, p. 260c) construes this paragraph as presenting the major meditation technique of *VS.* He also relates it to various passages in Chan writings attributed to Bodhidharma, Sengcan, and Huineng to illustrate its affinities with Chan praxis.

212. *Dasheng qixin lun, T* 1666:32.576b20–26; cf. Hakeda, *Awakening of Faith,* pp. 38–39.

213. This subpart actually continues through segments I.B.2.b.ii.b.3 and 4, below.

214. See *KSGN,* p. 631a ff, above; and cf. *Dasheng qixin lun, T* 1666:32.576b15; Hakeda, *Awakening of Faith,* p. 37.

215. *Dasheng qixin lun, T* 1666:32.576c1–4; cf. Hakeda, *Awakening of Faith,* p. 40. Wŏnhyo cited this same passage previously at *KSGN,* p. 619a.

216. See *Dasheng qixin lun, T* 1666:32.576b; cf. Hakeda, *Awakening of Faith,* p. 38.

217. Following the Wŏnhyo and Kaibao recensions; Koryŏ II/Taishō replaces *kong* (cavern) with the near-homographic *yü* (milk), which might be better considering its characterization as having a single taste. See *VS,* p. 369b5, n. 5.

218. My translation here follows Wŏnhyo's interpretation below. The Kaibao and Three Editions read instead: "Neither ordinary nor sanctified knowledge is distressed by existence or nonexistence." *VS,* p. 369, n. 7.

219. This list is sometimes given as (1) the three realms of existence, (2) the images of the six destinies, (3) dharma characteristics, (4) nominal characteristics, (5) mind and consciousness; see Ŭn and Song, *Kŭmgang sammaegyŏng non,* p. 327, n. 1. Wŏnhyo may also be suggesting the five characteristics of name *(nāma)* from the *Laṅkāvatāra-sūtra:* characteristics, name, discrimination, right knowledge, and true thusness; see *Ru Lengqie jing, T* 671:16.514c16, 527c16–17 558a26–27 (and see Suzuki, *Laṅkāvatāra-sūtra,* p. 60). Alternatively, Wŏnhyo may simply be alluding to the five major categories of dharmas found in the Abhidharma systems: mind, mental concomitants, materiality, factors dissociated from thought, and unconditioned elements; see discussion below.

220. Chapter 13 ("Chu faxin pusa gongde pin") of *Dafangguang fo huayan jing, j.* 9, *T* 278:9.449c–458c; see also *Dafangguang fo huayan jing* 10, *T* 279:10.89a–95a.

221. As Wŏnhyo explains below, the first two of the five types of voidness are intended to counter the deception that phenomenal objects, which are the perceived objects, are real; the latter three are designed to counter the deceptions produced by the consciousnesses that are the catalysts for that clinging.

222. These three types of true thusness are discussed in *Xianyang lun [Āryaśāsanaprakaraṇa]* 3, *T* 1602:31.493b11, 14, 18, respectively. The "true thusness of transmutation" is also discussed in the *Yuqieshi di lun [Yogācārabhūmi-śāstra]* 77, *T* 1579:30.725b18; it does not, however, mention the other two types.

223. These two types are the mundane and supramundane types of wholesome and unwholesome karmic action. See *Xianyang lun [Āryaśāsanaprakaraṇa], T* 1602:31574c17–18.

224. The logograph for "knowledge" *(chi)* is missing in the *HPC* edition of *KSGN* (p. 638b19) and is supplied from the *Taishō* edition, *T* 1730:34.983c1.

225. As Wŏnhyo will explain below, the first of these three types of voidness shows that negating the reality of mundane objects ("characteristic of voidness") is in turn to be rejected as well, thereby reconciling absolute truth with conventional truth. The second type suggests that descriptions of existence or nonexistence made according to conventional truth are also to be rejected; this reconciles conventional truth with absolute truth. The last demonstrates that both of the two preceding accounts of the significance of voidness are also void; this fuses both conventional and absolute truths into a single truth and reveals the one *dharmadhātu*, which is the one mind.

226. Reading "three" for "two," following the editor's emendation; see *KSGN*, p. 639, n. 3.

227. *Dabanniepan jing [Mahāparinirvāṇa-sūtra]* 16, *T* 374:12.461c16–17, and *T* 375:12.704A24–25. The sūtra explains that the "this is real, that is not real," and so on, refer to the dualistic types of understanding in which śrāvakas and pratyekabuddhas are trapped.

228. This is a crucial equivalency, which reveals how Wŏnhyo seeks to establish an inherent relationship between the *VS* and the *Awakening of Faith*. See Rhi, *Kŭmgang sammaegyŏng non*, p. 179a.

229. The Taishō edition of the scripture adds here one line omitted in the Wŏnhyo and Kaibao recensions: "Existence does not linger in existence." *VS*, p. 369b19 and n. 9.

230. *Jiujing yisheng baoxing lun* 3, *T* 1611:31.802a26–28, quoting with slight modifications, *Shengman jing [Śrīmālādevīsiṃhanāda-sūtra], T* 353:12.222n25–27.

231. *Shengman jing, T* 353:12.222b28–29; and cf. Jizang's *Shengman baoku* 3b, *T* 1744:37.86c22–23.

232. Wŏnhyo's *Yijang ŭi, HPC* 1:811c7–812a21.

233. "Commensurate" *(kong)* may be a mistake for "different" *(i)*, the top portion of the latter logograph somehow having been deleted. This emendation is not corroborated in any of the recensions but is suggested in Wŏnhyo's exegesis below.

234. "Attentive contemplation" *(kakkwan)* replaces Bodhidharma's renowned, but problematic, term "wall contemplation" *(biguan)*. The precise denotation of this term as used in *VS* is somewhat unclear, since *kakkwan* (Ch. *jueguan*) as the *dvandva* "attention and contemplation" is the equivalent in older Chinese translations of "thought and imagination" *(vitarkavicāra)*—the scourge of any meditation deeper than the first dhyāna. Wŏnhyo's interpretation seeks to give the term a rather more salutary connotation, taking it as "attention and examination" or "attentive examination" *(kakch'al;* Ch. *juecha)*, adopting the rendering of *vitarkavicāra* used in the translation of the *Laṅkāvatāra;* see discussion in Mizuno, p. 53, and for the *Laṅkāvatāra*'s translation of *vitarkavicāra* as *jueguan*, see Suzuki, *Studies*, p. 442. All in all,

VS's gloss seems to suggest that "wall contemplation" is a form of detached but nevertheless vigilant awareness, in which the adept remains constantly focused on the utter ineffability of the buddha-nature. This is extremely close, as we shall see, to *VS*'s interpretation of "guarding the one."

There is also an interesting allusion in Huisi's (515–576) *Suiziyi sanmei* to a type of samādhi that combines the vajrasamādhi and wall contemplation. This is the "adamantine-wall samādhi" *(jin'gangbi ding sanmei).* Huisi's explication of this samādhi draws on an *Ekottarāgama* story of a demon who attacked the Buddha's disciple Śāriputra: the power of Śāriputra's achievement of the vajrasamādhi (what Huisi terms instead "adamantine-wall samādhi") was such that Śāriputra was completely unaware he had been struck a deadly blow over the head by a demon. His experience illustrates that samādhi's ability to leave one totally senseless to the external world. See *Zengi ahan jing* 45, *T* 125:2.793a–c, for this story; and for additional discussion, see my *Ch'an Ideology,* p. 105. Somewhat the same connotation is brought out in the reference to "abiding frozen" in either "wall contemplation" or "attentive contemplation" in the two corresponding passages of *VS* and *Erru sixing lun.* See *Suiziyi sanmei* 1, *ZZ* 1, 98, 350d–51a; discussed in John A. Jorgensen, "The Earliest Text of Ch'an Buddhism: The *Long Scroll*" (M.A. thesis, Australian National University, 1979), p. 194; and John R. McRae, *The Northern School and the Formation of Early Ch'an Buddhism,* Studies in East Asian Buddhism, no. 3 (Honolulu: University of Hawai'i Press, 1986), p. 306, n. 21.

235. *Fanwang jing* 10b, *T* 1484:24.1003c3, 1004b1, and so on.

236. *Renwang boluomi jing* 1, *T* 245:8.826c10, 827b18.

237. The six categories of mental concomitants *(caitta)* are (1) the ten predominant mental states *(mahābhūmika),* such as contact and attention; (2) the eight wholesome mental states *(kuśalamahābhūmika),* including faith and shame; (3) the six defiled mental states *(kleśamahābhūmika),* such as delusion and indolence; (4) the two unwholesome mental states *(akuśalamahābhūmika)* of lack of shame and blame; (5) the ten subsidiary defiled mental states *(parīttakleśabhūmika),* such as anger and deceit; and (6) the eight indeterminate mental states *(aniyata),* such as thought, imagination, and worry. For the listings, see *Abhidharmakośabhāṣyam* 2.23–27; La Vallée Poussin, *Abhidharmakośabhāṣyam,* vol. 1, pp. 188–196.

238. For the three types of materiality, see *Abhidharmakośabhāṣyam* 4.4a–b; Le Vallée Pousin, *Abhidharmakośabhāṣyam,* vol. 2, p. 560. For unmanifest materiality *(avijñaptirūpa),* see note 210 above at *KSGN,* p. 636b.

239. The twenty-four forces dissociated (from mind), or *(citta)viprayuktasaṃskara,* refer to various anomalous forces posited first by the Sarvāstivāda Ābhidharmikas, and adapted later by the Yogācāra, to provide consistent analyses of particularly complex or anomalous moral and mental processes. They include possession *(prāpti),* vitality *(jīvita),* and words, phrases, and syllables (see below). For the full list of twenty-four, see Vasubandhu's *Dasheng bofa mingmen lun (Mahāyānaśatadharmaprakāśamukha-śāstra), T* 1614:31.855c10–16. For detailed studies on the category, see Padmanabh S. Jaini, "The Development of the Theory of the *Viprayukta-Saṁskāras,*" *Bulletin of the School of Oriental and African Studies* 22 (1959): 531–547; the monumental study by Collett Cox, *Disputed Dharmas: Early Buddhist Theories of Existence, an Annotated Translation of the Section on Factors Dissociated from Thought from Saṅghabhadra's "Nyāyānusāra,"* Studia Philological Buddhica Monograph Series, 11 (Tokyo: International Institute for Buddhist Studies, 1995); Robert E. Buswell, Jr.,

"The Proliferation of *Cittaviprayuktasaṃskāra*-s in the Vaibhāṣika School," *Journal of Indian Philosophy* 25 (1997): 451–466.

240. These three dissociated forces *(viprayuktasaṃskāra)* constitute an early Buddhist analysis of the nature and operation of language; see Cox, *Disputed Dharmas,* chap. 10; and Padmanabh S. Jaini, "The Vaibhāṣika Theory of Words and Meanings," *Bulletin of the School of Oriental and African Studies* 22 (1959): 95–107.

241. *Da banniepan jing (Mahāparnirvāṇa-sūtra)* 25, *T* 375:12.767c18–19.

242. Following the Wŏnhyo and Kaibao recensions. Koryŏ II/Taishō has "it is not reached by two-vehicle [adherents]," which is also plausible; *VS,* p. 370all.

243. The twenty-eight assemblies of saints within Buddhism refers to the fourfold assembly (monks, nuns, laymen, laywomen) in each of the six directions (north, south, east, west, zenith, and nadir), giving twenty-four assemblies plus one assembly at each of the four cardinal directions, for a total of twenty-eight. The terms appears at *Qianshou qian'an Guanshiyin pusa guangda yuanman wu'ai dabeixin tuoluoni jing, T* 1060:19.108b19; for the explanation see *Jin'guangming jing wenju 5, T* 1785:39.77a12–13. The ninety-five non-Buddhist religious *(tīrthika)* appear in the *Dabaoji jing (Mahāratnakuṭa-sūtra)* 113, *T* 310:11.640b29; a list of ninety-six, which includes the six traditions founded by contemporary competitors of the historical Buddha and each of their fifteen branch schools, is rather more common in the literature.

244. This is the expanded outline of the Buddhist path (mārga) as found in such Chinese apocryphal compositions as the *Pusa yingluo benye jing,* the *Fanwang jing,* and the *Renwang jing.* Wŏnhyo himself notes that the outline of this mārga comes from *Pusa yingluo benye jing* (which Wŏnhyo cites here; *T* 1485), and its full explication appears in the *Avataṃsaka-sūtra.* He then correlates the first four stages of this mārga (the ten faiths through the ten transferences) with the access of principle and the latter two (the ten bhūmis and virtual enlightenment) with the access of practice. For a listing of the comprehensive Hwaŏm/Huayan interpretation of the bodhisattva path, in fifty-three stages, see Robert E. Buswell Jr. and Robert M. Gimello, "Introduction," in *Paths to Liberation: The Mārga and Its Transformations in Buddhist Thought,* Kuroda Institute Studies in East Asian Buddhism, no. 7 (Honolulu: University of Hawai'i Press, a Kuroda Institute Book, 1992), p. 9; and for a survey of the influence of Buddhist path systems in Chinese religion, see Stephen R. Bokenkamp, "Stages of Transcendence: The *Bhūmi* Concept in Taoist Scripture," in *Chinese Buddhist Apocrypha,* ed. Robert E. Buswell Jr. (Honolulu: University of Hawai'i Press, 1990), pp. 119–147.

245. Wŏnhyo explains in the next paragraph [II.D.1.a.ii] that "panting" means rapid inhalations and exhalations, which is used as a simile for the agitation of the six sense-consciousnesses. See also the comments of Yuancheng (*Zhujie* 3, p. 208a), who seeks to trace the idea of "panting" to the *Laṅkāvatāra-sūtra.* The term "panting" appears commonly in early Chinese translations of dhyāna texts. One of An Shigao's translations associates panting with the rapid breath that accompanies the onset of the dying process; see *Mayi jing, T* 732:17.533b14. Panting is also equated with distracted thought in Zhu Fahu's translations; see *Faguan jing, T* 611:15.241a24.

246. Following Wŏnhyo's reading (*KSGN* 2, p. 987b13). All other editions read the near-homograph *tae* (great) for *ch'ŏn* (heavenly); see *VS,* p. 370a22.

247. The glosses for this simile are drawn from Wŏnhyo's explanations that follow; this passage would be all but unintelligible without the glosses.

248. The last, and most profound, of the four types of dhyāna mentioned in the

Laṅkāvatāra-sūtra, in which the person is able to go out into the world to aid sentient beings while still maintaining the full depth of his concentration; see *Lengqie jing* 2, *T* 670:16.492a22–24; *Dasheng ru Lengqie jing* 3, *T* 672:16.602al2; Suzuki, *Lankāvatāra,* pp. 85–86; it is discussed in Suzuki, *Studies,* pp. 367–368.

249. The four drivers refer to the four attachments *(upādāna):* that is, to sense-objects, wrong views, rites and rituals, and self.

250. The six drivers refer to the six afflictions *(upakleśa):* that is, of craving, anger, ignorance, pride, doubt, and wrong views.

251. Wŏnhyo here is referring to Yogācāra analysis of twenty afflictions into ten minor, two medial, and eight predominant types; see Vasubandhu's *Dasheng bofa mingmen lun (Mahāyānaśatadharmaprakāśamukha-śāstra), T* 1614:31.855c.

252. *Pusa yingluo benye jing, T* 1485:24.1014a2–6.

253. The traditional list of the eight liberations *(vimokṣa)* is (1) having materiality, he perceives materiality; (2) not perceiving inward materiality, he perceives outward materiality; (3) he becomes resolved on what is pure; (4) the station of endless space; (5) the station of infinite consciousness; (6) the station of nothing whatsoever; (7) the station of neither perception nor nonperception; (8) the extinction of perception and feeling. Wŏnhyo will give his own interpretation of these eight liberations in the explanation that follows.

254. *Pusa yingluo benye jing, T* 1485:24.1013b7–11. As Wŏnhyo clarifies, this indigenous Chinese interpretation of the eight liberations correlates rather closely with the traditional list given in the previous note.

255. *Pusa yingluo benye jing, T* 1485:24.1013a.

256. *Pusa yingluo benye jing, T* 1485:24.1014b15–18.

257. *Pusa yingluo benye jing, T* 1485:24.1014b19–22.

258. The Koryŏ II/Taishō edition reads *wŏl* (to transcend) for *ki* (to activate). *VS,* p. 370b12.

259. Liebenthal (p. 366 and n. 2) traces this phrase to allusions in Paramārtha's translation of *Shibakong lun* (*T* 1616), though I believe the page and line numbers are miscited; apparently, he means to refer to *T* 1616:31.86lc28, 862al.

260. Lit., "single" *(il).* This word is missing in the Koryŏ II/Taishō recension but is included in the Wŏnhyo, Kaibao, and Three Editions; *VS,* p. 370b 13, n. 11.

261. Paraphrasing *Miaofa lianhua jing, T* 262:9.31c26.

262. Paraphrasing *Miaofa lianhua jing, T* 262:9.31c26–27.

263. *Ru Lengqie jing (Laṅkāvatāra-sūtra)* 4, *T* 671:16.540b7–8. The Sanskrit is somewhat different (as rendered in Suzuki, *Laṅkāvatāra,* p. 116, v. 210): "Like unto the drunkard who, being awakened from his intoxication, regains his intelligence, [the Śrāvakas] will have the realization of the Buddha's truth, which is his own body."

264. *VS*'s correlation of the *icchantika* with two-vehicle adherents who are hopelessly attached to samādhi is without parallel in other scriptures, so far as I am aware Mahāyāna texts have, however, frequently equated *icchantikas* with Hīnayānists. For example, of the two types of *icchantika* discussed in the *Laṅkāvatāra-sūtra,* the first type—those who are *icchantika* "because they have abandoned all the roots of merit" *(sarvakuśalamūlotsargataḥ)*—are defined as "those who have abandoned the Bodhisattva canon, making the false accusation that they are not in conformity with the sūtras, the codes of morality, and emancipation. By this they have forsaken all the stock of merit and will not enter into Nirvāṇa"; see Suzuki, *Laṅkāvatāra,* p. 59. The

Mahāyāna conception of *icchantika* is discussed by Suzuki in his companion volume, *Studies*, pp. 217–221; and see the citations to other Mahāyāna texts in Takasaki Jikidō, *A Study on the Ratnagotravibhāga*, introduction, p. 40, and translation, p. 205. I have also discussed the relationship between *icchantika* and the related *samucchinna-kuśalamūla* ('those whose wholesome roots are eradicated') in my article "The Path to Perdition: The Wholesome Roots and Their Eradication," in *Paths to Liberation: The Mārga and Its Transformations in Buddhist Thought*, ed. Robert E. Buswell Jr. and Robert M. Gimello, Kuroda Institute Studies in East Asian Buddhism, no. 7 (Honolulu: University of Hawai'i Press, 1992), pp. 118–123; many relevant citations to major Mahāyāna discussions of *icchantika* are included there. See also my recent entry on "Icchantika" in the *Encyclopedia of Buddhism*, vol. 1, p. 351.

265. Cf. the simile of waves and water in *Dasheng qixin lun*, *T* 1666:32.476c.

266. By the seven strictures of the precepts Wŏnhyo is probably referring to the three kinds of unskillful actions perpetrated by the body (killing, stealing, and sexual misconduct) and the four kinds perpetrated by the mouth (disparagement, duplicity, obsequiousness, and lying). Alternatively, Wŏnhyo may also be referring to the seven principal categories of the monastic rules of conduct in the Prātimokṣa: (1) offenses requiring expulsion from the Order *(pārājika)*, (2) offenses requiring suspension *(saṃghāvaśeṣa)*, (3) offenses of indeterminate type *(aniyata)*, (4) offenses entailing forfeiture *(niḥsargikapācittiya)*, (5) transgressions requiring confession (variously termed *prāyaścittika*, *pātayantika*, or *pācittiya*), (6) offenses requiring acknowledgement *(pratideśanīya)*, (7) minor rules of good behavior *(śaikṣa)*. The number of rules listed in each category varies in the different Vinaya recensions.

267. Taken from the *Weimojie suoshuo jing (Vimalakīrtinirdeśa-sūtra)* 2, *T* 475:14.549b6; cf. Robert A. F. Thurman, trans., *The Holy Teaching of Vimalakīrti: A Mahāyāna Scripture* (University Park: Pennsylvania State University Press, 1976), p. 66. The locus classicus for this lotus metaphor is *Dhammapada* (Pupphavagga), vols. 58, 59.

268. Lit. "two twos." Kim Talchin (p. 164) translates this number as "twenty-two"; Rhi Ki-yong (p. 216b) translates it as simply "two."

269. These three moral codes are common in Yogācāra and Yogācāra-influenced literature and have been adopted frequently in Sinitic Buddhist apocrypha. Their Sanskrit equivalents are (1) *saṃvaraśīla*, (2) *kuśaladharmasaṃgrāhaka*, (3) *sattvārtha-kriyā*. See *Yuqieshi di lun (Yogācārabhūmi-śāstra)* 40, *T* 1579:30.511a15, and explication at pp. 511a–c. The first type helps to calm one's mind, the second to mature one's own buddhadharmas, and the third to mature other sentient beings; ibid., p. 523a2–4. This same division of the precepts appears in such Chinese apocryphal sūtras as *Zhancha shan'e yebao jing* 1 (*T* 839:17.904c7–8) and *Pusa yingluo benye jing* (*T* 1485:24.1019b17). Liebenthal (p. 365 and cf. p. 380, n. 1) gives a useful comparative listing of other relevant citations; to his listings add *Dasheng zhuangyan jing lun (Mahāyānasūtrālaṃkāra-śāstra)* 8 (*T* 1604:31.630c13–14), which is the closest to the wording of *VS*; *Dasheng apidamo zaji lun (Abhidharmasamuccaya)* 12, *T* 1606:31.749c4–5; and cf. *Huayan jing* 27, *T* 279:10.149b22 and *j.* 49, p. 258a22–23.

270. See *Mohe boruo boluomi jing* 1 (*T* 223:8.221c19), where the Buddha also addresses Śāriputra, telling him that all concepts "are merely explained with names and letters."

271. The "three sufferings" are physical pain, suffering caused by change, and the suffering inherent in all compounded things.

272. *Dazhidu lun* 19, *T* 1509:25.198b8.

273. Not to produce evil and unwholesome dharmas that have not yet been produced, to forsake evil and unwholesome dharmas that have already been produced, to produce wholesome dharmas that have not yet been produced, and to develop further those wholesome dharmas that have already been produced.

274. Although Wŏnhyo does not designate this summation as a separate division in his exegesis, I believe it should be added as division I.C.2.b.iii.

275. The following section outlines the five major stages of the bodhisattva path found in many Sinitic apocryphal scriptures, such as *Pusa yingluo benye ching* (*T* 1485:24.1017a3, 1010b27, 1022b13). The correlations Wŏnhyo draws between the *VS* schema and the more standard list found in other scriptures are bracketed in the translation.

276. *Icchantika* refers to a class of beings who for various reasons are rendered forever unable to attain nirvāṇa. Wŏnhyo's analysis here invokes the *Laṅkāvatāra-sūtra*'s division of *icchantikas* into two subclasses: (1) those who are *icchantikas* because "they have abandoned all the wholesome faculties" *(sarvakuśalamūlotsargata)*; and (2) those who are so because "they cherish certain vows for all beings since beginningless time" *(sattvānādikālapraṇidhānata)*. The former are defined as those "who have abandoned the bodhisattva collection [of the Buddhist canon], making the false accusation that they are not in conformity with the sūtras, the codes of morality, and emancipation. By this they have forsaken all the stock of merit *(kuśalamūla)* and will not enter into nirvāṇa." See Suzuki, trans., *Laṅkāvatāra Sūtra*, pp. 58–59; Suzuki, *Studies*, pp. 217-221. This is a common Mahāyāna polemical definition of the term, to describe those who lack conviction in the truth of the Mahāyāna teachings. For discussion of this and other interpretations of the *icchantika*, see Buswell, "Path to Perdition," pp.118–123.

277. *Pusa yingluo benye jing* 2, *T* 1485:24.1017a13 and 1021b24–25, with a change of one homophonous logograph.

278. Wŏnhyo is referring here to counteracting the obstructions that hinder realization of each of the ten bhūmis; see Chengguan's *Dafangguang fo huayan jing shu* 34, *T* 1735:35.769c12–13. Wŏnhyo's language recalls a citation in Chengguan's *Dafangguang fo huayan jing shu yanyi chao* 57, *T* 1736:36.450a6–8: "On each of the ten bhūmis, bodhisattvas courageously cultivate the ten kinds of superior practice, eradicating the ten kinds of obstructions and realizing the ten kinds of true thusness."

279. See the discussion of the significance of this passage in the development of the buddha-nature concept in Tokiwa Daijō, *Busshō no kenkyū* (Studies on the buddha-nature) (Tokyo: Kokusho Kankōkai, 1973), p. 406.

280. Wŏnhyo here embarks on an exegesis of the next four levels of the bodhisattva path but neglects to mention that these are all subdivisions of this second division I.D.2.b.ii, the clarification of comprehension; see at p. 654b. This omission may have led to his error below (p. 655c) in mistakenly listing I.D.2.c, the summary clarification, as the second, rather than the third, subpart.

281. I have been unable to locate the precise verse cited here by Wŏnhyo. However, a similar verse appears in *Guang Bolun ben [*Śataśāstra]*, *T* 1570:30.185c10–11; and see exegesis at *Dasheng guang Bolun shilun* 9, *T* 1571:30.236a.

282. See Wŏnhyo's *Yijang ŭi*, *HPC* 1:793a–b.

283. *Pusa yingluo benye jing*, *T* 1485:24.1018b9–10.

284. This passage is taken from the final line of Xuanzang's rendering of the

Prajñāpāramitāhṛdaya (Heart sūtra), (*T* 251:8.848c14–15), which was made on July 8, 649 (Lancaster and Park, *Korean Buddhist Canon,* p. 11). This date provides the terminus a quo for the composition of *VS.*

285. The three *māras,* or personifications of evil, are the *māra* of defilements, the *māra* of the constituents of existence (the five skandhas), and the *māra* of the devil himself.

286. The four eyes refer to the visual sense organ (the fleshy eye), the heavenly eye of supranormal powers, the wisdom eye, and the dharma-eye.

287. The four wisdoms refer to a Yogācāra classification of the four types of knowledge exclusive to the buddhas (viz. the sublime-enlightenment level). (1) Great perfect mirror wisdom *(ādarśanajñāna):* the wisdom that perceives the perfect interfusion of all things, as if everything were simultaneously being reflected in a great mirror. (2) Impartial wisdom *(samatājñāna):* the wisdom that rises above all distinctions and sees all things impartially without coloring by the ego. (3) Wisdom of marvelous observation *(pratyavekṣanājñāna):* the wisdom of profound intellectual discrimination. (4) Wisdom of the accomplishment of what was to be done *(kṛtyānuṣṭānajñāna):* the wisdom that perfects actions that benefit both oneself and others. See *Cheng weishi lun, T* 1585:31.39.

288. The five eyes: (1) fleshy eye; (2) heavenly eye; (3) wisdom eye; (4) dharma-eye; (5) buddha-eye.

289. The three bodies of the buddhas: (1) the dharma-body (dharmakāya), the absolute body of thusness; (2) the enjoyment or reward body *(saṃbhogakāya),* the body endowed with all the regalia of the buddhas, formed as a result of the vast merits achieved during practice on the bodhisattva path, and the body that only bodhisattvas can perceive; (3) the transformation body *(nirmāṇakāya),* the body of the historical buddhas, expediently assumed in order to instruct ordinary beings. See Wŏnhyo's explanation at p. 657a below.

290. "The three stages of virtual enlightenment" are distinct levels in which the lifespan of the bodhisattva lasts for respectively a hundred kalpas, a thousand kalpas, and myriad (lit. ten thousand) kalpas. On the first level, the bodhisattva practices all the samādhis and finally enters the vajrasamādhi. On the second level, he practices all the deportments of a buddha, until he finally sits at the *bodhimaṇḍa* and overcomes *Māra's* hordes. On the final level, he leads the life of a fully enlightened buddha. These derive from *Pusa yingluo benye jing* 1, *T* 1485:24.1012c27–1013a9. The three bodies of sublime enlightenment are the three buddha-bodies: the dharmakāya, *saṃbhogakāya,* and *nirmāṇakāya.*

291. *Pusa yingluo benye jing* 1, *T* 1485:24.1012c27–1013a8.

292. *Pusa yingluo benye jing* 1, *T* 1485:24.1013a9–13.

293. The summit of existence refers to the last of the four formless dhyānas, the absorption of neither perception nor nonperception *(naivasaṃjñānāsaṃjñāyatana).* See Wŏnhyo's explanation immediately following.

294. A parallel phrase ("activity is not dhyāna") appears in the apocryphal *Dharmapada, pin* no. 11, *Faju jing, T* 2901:85.1435a22. That *pin* is frequently cited in Chan writings; see discussion in Mizuno Kōgen, "Gisaku no Hokkukyō ni tsuite" pp. 17–20. (On the apocryphal Dharmapāda), *Komazawa Daigaku Bukkyōgakubu kenkyū kiyō* 19 (1961): 11–33.

295. Following the Wŏnhyo, Kaibao, and Three Editions, which all read here "because it is the meaning of the original meaning," a probable dittography of the

first "meaning." The Koryŏ II/Taishō recension reads instead "because it is the meaning of the original inspiration," which makes better sense. See *VS*, p. 371b27, n. 7.

296. Alluding to *Lunyu* 5.8, James Legge, trans., *The Chinese Classics* (1935; reprint edition, Taipei: n.p., 1976), vol. 1, p. 176.

297. The Koryŏ II/Taishō recension adds "four-line" after "single"; *VS*, p. 371c4 and n. 8.

298. "Objects" here renders the logograph *ŭi* (Skt. *artha*), which can refer to either meaning or object; both senses are probably implicit in the gāthā. "Dharma" is used for "object" in the text from which this gāthā derives (see next note).

299. The first line of this gāthā is taken, with minor modifications, from Kumārajīva's translation of the *Madhyamakakārikā* (*Zhong lun, T* 1654:30.33bll–12, *Mūlamadhyamakakārikā* xxiv.19); see also *Zhongguan lun shu* (*T* 1824:42.152b1); *Ru Dasheng lun, T* 1634:32.41b; *Fozu tong ji* 37, *T* 2035:49.352a4–5; *Mohe zhiguan, j.* la, *T* 1911a:46.lb29–cl. These and other sources are cited in Liebenthal (pp. 375–376, 375 n. 3, and 382). For the import of this gāthā, see Ko Ikchin, Wŏnhyo ŭi sasang ŭi silch'ŏn wŏlli," pp. 246–247.

300. This passage, the earliest quotation from *VS* to appear in Chinese materials, is cited in Fazang's *Huayan jing yihai bomen* (*T* 1875:45.628c21–22), from the early eighth century. See discussion in Buswell, *Ch'an Ideology*, p. 177.

301. This trope appears prominently in the *Yuanjue jing;* see *T* 842:17.917c2. A similar simile of a single city with four gates appears also in Wŏnhyo's *Pŏmmanggyŏng posal kyebon sagi* (Personal exposition on the "Bodhisattva Precepts" text of the *Fanwang jing*) 1, *HPC* 1:586b18; this text will be translated by Eunsu Cho in a later volume of the Collected Works of Wŏnhyo series. The wording Wŏnhyo uses in that treatise to relate the simile differs substantially from the version found here, so it would be difficult to conclude that the *Posal keybon sagi* was therefore written after the *Vajrasamādhi-sūtra*'s appearance in Silla Korea.

302. "Taste" appears in Wŏnhyo's edition but is missing in the Koryŏ II/Taishō edition (*VS*, p. 371c22).

303. For this common metaphor of the "single taste" of the ocean, which is often used to explain the soteriological purport of the teachings of Buddhism, see the Pāli *Cullavagga* ix.14: "As the vast ocean, oh monks, is impregnated with a single taste, the taste of salt, so too, monks is my Dharma and Vinaya impregnated with but a single taste, the taste of liberation." See *also Jieshenmi jing (Sandhinirmocana-sūtra), T* 676: 16.692a25.

304. Following the Koryŏ II/Taishō recension, which reads *chŭk* (then) for Wŏnhyo's *chŭk* (is in fact); *VS*, p. 371c24; and passim throughout chapters 7 and 8 of the sūtra.

305. An allusion to this passage appears in *Platform Sūtra:* "It is like the great sea which gathers all the flowing streams, and merges together the small waters and large waters into one." *Liuzu tan jing*, T 2007:48.340b1, 8–19; Philip Yampolsky, trans., *The Platform Sūtra of the Sixth Patriarch* (New York : Columbia University Press, 1967), p. 150.

306. Compare the Pāli *Udāna* 5.4: "Whatsoever great rivers there are—namely, Gaṅgā, Yamunā, Aciravatī, Sarabhū, Mahī—these, when they reach the mighty ocean, abandon their former names and lineage, and go henceforth by the name of just 'mighty ocean.'" Translation from F. L. Woodward, *The Minor Anthologies of the Pali Canon* (London: Oxford University Press, 1948), p. 64. The use of native geo-

graphical names in this passage is a strong piece of textual evidence suggesting the non-Indian origin of this scripture; see Mizuno, pp. 42–43; Liebenthal, p. 361.

307. The four means of conversion: giving, kind words, helpfulness, consistence between words and deeds (or, alternatively, cooperation).

308. The eight archetypal events in a buddha's life: (1) rebirth in Tuṣita heaven for his penultimate life before becoming a buddha, (2) entry into his mother's womb for his final life, (3) gestation, (4) birth, (5) renunciation (viz. leaving home to become a monk), (6) attaining enlightenment, (7) turning the wheel of the dharma at the first sermon, (8) passing into parinirvāṇa. See *Dasheng qixin lun, T* 1666:32.581a6–8; Hakeda, *Awakening of Faith,* p. 85.

309. "Encroach" is literally "to snatch away." Cf. the celebrated usage of this term by Linji Yixuan (d. 866) in his four approaches to practice (snatch away the man, but don't snatch away the objects; etc.); see *Linji lu, T* 1985:47.497a.

310. The "snares" are an alternate name for the *kleśa*s or *upakleśa*s (afflictions). The number varies, but a common list includes eight: lack of shame *(āhrīkya),* lack of blame *(anapatrāpya),* envy *(īrṣyā),* selfishness *(mātsarya),* remorse *(kaukṛtya),* torpor *(middha),* agitation *(auddhatya),* sloth *(styāna).*

311. Here and in the Kaibao recension of the sūtra, these last two types of samādhis are transposed from the usual listing; see *VS,* p. 372a20, nn. 6, 7. For this common list, see *Mohe boruo boluomi jing* 24, *T* 223:8.394c26–27.

312. Wŏnhyo adapts this passage from *Yuqieshi di lun (Yogācārabhūmi-śāstra)* 16, *T* 1579:30.364b28–29.

313. For "hairnet" *(moryun)* as a metaphor for something "gossamery," viz. illusory, see *Ru Lengqie jing (Laṅkāvatāra-sūtra)* 9, *T* 671:16.565cl 6; *Renwang jing* 1, *T* 246:8.839a23.

314. The last two lines of this verse derive from *Laṅkāvatāra-sūtra;* see *Ru Lengqie jing* 3, *T* 671:16.532b28; and cf. *Dasheng ru Lengqie jing* 3, *T* 672:16.601cl 1; both noted (though the first citation is misprinted) in Liebenthal, pp. 367–368. Cf. also Suzuki's rendering of the Sanskrit in *Laṅkāvatāra-sūtra,* p. 83, v. 150.

315. *Dafangguang fo Huayan jing (Avataṃsaka-sūtra)* 33, *T* 278:9.609a10–12 (with one slight change). Cf. also *T* 279:10.425a22, 259c20, 294c26–27; *T* 293: 10.847a6–7.

316. Wŏnhyo had previously titled this section "constantly abiding in the fruition gained through access," with "constantly abiding" replacing "perpetual dharma"; see p. 660c above.

317. *Dafangguang fo huayan jing (Avataṃsaka-sūtra)* 10, *T* 278:9.465c26–29; and cf. *T* 279:10.102a21–24.

318. This verse also is adapted from *Laṅkāvatāra-sūtra.* See *Ru Lengqie jing* 3, *T* 671:16.527cl6–17; cf. *Dasheng ru Lengqie jing* 2, T 672:16.598a6; all noted by Liebenthal, pp. 366–367. See also Suzuki, *Laṅkāvatāra Sūtra,* p. 60, v. 134.

319. For these three dissociated forces that govern language, see *KSGN,* p. 643a above.

320. These two types of wisdom are described in the *Cheng weishi lun* (*T* 1585: 31.73a24). Fundamental wisdom is the innate wisdom that is in direct conformity with truth and devoid of any distinctions between subject and object. This wisdom is the foundation upon which other aspects of wisdom arise and is the basis upon which the subsequently obtained wisdom is developed. Subsequently obtained wisdom is the wisdom that allows one to save other sentient beings. Whereas fundamen-

tal wisdom leads to enlightenment for oneself, subsequently obtained wisdom gives one the ability to help others to enlightenment.

321. Adapted from *Laṅkāvatāra-sūtra; Ru Lengqie jing* 3, *T* 671:16.529b5–6, 530c8–9; noted by Liebenthal, p. 367. See Suzuki, *Laṅkāvatāra Sūtra,* p. 68, v. 137, and p. 75, v. 140, though the Sanskrit differs radically.

322. Adapted from *Laṅkāvatāra-sūtra;* see *Ru Lengqie jing* 3, *T* 671:16.530c14–15; see Liebenthal, p. 367; Suzuki, *Laṅkāvatāra Sūtra,* p. 75, v. 143.

323. The locus classicus for these four types of conditions is *Abhidharmakośabhāṣyam* ii.61c–62d; La Vallée Poussin, *Abhidharmakośabhāṣyam,* vol. 1, pp. 296–304. Wŏnhyo has discussed all four types of conditions previously at *KSGN,* p. 632b.

324. Alluding to the famous simile of the conjured city in the *Lotus Sūtra; Miaofa lianhua jing* 3, *T* 262:9.26a, 27a11ff.; Hurvitz, *Lotus,* pp. 148–149, 153–154.

325. Wŏnhyo's explanation of the following exegetical structure is anomalous. In his opening remarks to part 4. An Exegesis of the Text (see p. 607b above), Wŏnhyo says that part 4 consists of three sections: section 1, the prologue (viz. chap. 1); section 2, "the main body" of the sūtra (viz. the sequential clarification of contemplation practice, chaps. 2–7); and section 3, the Dhāraṇī chapter (viz. chap. 8) and the sūtra's dissemination. As Wŏnhyo opens his exegesis of this chapter, he states that the sequential clarification of contemplation practice ended with the previous chapter and from this point on is "the second section, which completely resolves all remaining doubts" (p. 667a). By "second section" here, Wŏnhyo means the second of the two sections that follow the prologue (viz. section 2 and section 3 of part 4). At the conclusion of the Dhāraṇī portion of chapter 8 as well, Wŏnhyo states: "In the three major sections of this one-roll sūtra, Section Two: The Main Body, is completed as above" (p. 675a). This division of the sūtra contradicts Wŏnhyo's initial analysis, which clearly states (p. 607b) that chapter 8 follows the "main body" of the sūtra. By including the Dhāraṇī chapter with "the main body," however, Wŏnhyo indicates that he sought to distinguish the major portion of the Dhāraṇī chapter from that chapter's concluding dissemination section. In order to represent this division, I have designated most of the exegesis of chapter 8 as Section Three (A): Completely Resolving All Remaining Doubts (viz. pp. 667a–675a), and the concluding portions of chapter 8 as Section Three (B): Dissemination (viz. pp. 675a–677b).

326. "Analogue" *(tae)* here might also be rendered as "counterpart" or "complementarity." The sense is that the production of those dharmas would not be dependent on the existence of any other dharma—that is, they would not be conditionally generated.

327. Wŏnhyo here follows the standard three-membered syllogistic form of Indian logic in arguing his thesis, with his statement of the *probandum,* or subject *(pakṣa),* justified by a reason *(hetu),* and illustrated in an exemplification *(dṛṣṭānta; sapakṣa);* see Musashi Tachikawa, "A Sixth-Century Manual of Indian Logic (A Translation of the *Nyāyapraveśa*)," *Journal of Indian Philosophy* 1 (1971): 111–145; Joseph M. Bochenski, *A History of Formal Logic,* trans. and ed. Ivo Thomas (Notre Dame, Ind.: Notre Dame University Press, 1961), pp. 416–450. Perhaps the most rigorous attempt to date to describe Buddhist logic in India and China in the formalistic terms of the West is found in R. S. Y. Chi, *Buddhist Formal Logic,* Dr. B. C. Law Trust Fund, vol. 1 (London: Royal Asiatic Society of Great Britain and Ireland, 1969).

328. Following Wŏnhyo's gloss (p. 670c below).

329. I add this division following Wŏnhyo's exegesis below at p. 671a.

330. For this simile see *Guang Bolun ben, T* 1570:31.185b21–26. The translation follows Wŏnhyo's interpretation below.

331. The "three transformations" *(samhwa)* are glossed by Wŏnhyo just below (p. 672a) as the three voidnesses: i.e., the voidness of the characteristic of voidness; the voidness of voidness itself; and the voidness of that which is voided. There is also a proselytic listing: (1) past transformation: previous preachings of the Mahāyāna; (2) adaptable transformation: the bodhisattva entering into saṃsāra in order to rescue beings from their plight; (3) ultimate transformation: prompting those beings to attain complete buddhahood. See *Fahua xuan lun* 7, *T* 1720:34.417a; *Fahua yishu* 7, *T* 1721:34.546a.

332. Following the Koryŏ II/Taishō reading of *pak* (to bind) et passim. Wŏnhyo and the K'ai-pao recension wrongly dittograph the following character *p'yo* (to whirl; to be adrift); *VS,* p. 373c8, n. 14.

333. I add this third subdivision following Wŏnhyo's exegesis below, p. 673b.

334. *Da Abidamo zaji lun (Abhidharmasamuccaya)* 7, *T* 1606:31.724c16–26.

335. These two types of non-Buddhist knowledge refer to the foundational doctrines of two of the important schools of Indian philosophy. In the Sāṃkhya school, "unmanifest potentiality" *(avyakta)* is the primary quality of the primal nature or potentiality *(mūlaprakṛti)* from which the entire material world evolves; it is the first of Sāṃkhya's twenty-five cardinal principles. In the Vaiśeṣika school, the property of genericness *(sāmānyapadārtha)* is the fourth of the seven categories of existents around which reality is structured; it is that quality of inherence that is common to an entire class of entities *(jāti)*, e.g., the generic property "horseness" that is common to all individual horses.

336. Adapted from *Mūlamadhyamakakārikā* (vii.28); see *Zhonglun* 2, *T* 1564: 30.11c11–12. Noted in Liebenthal, p. 366.

337. Reading "two" for "three," following the *Kap* edition; *KSGN* 3, *HPC* 1: p. 673, n. 3.

338. Wŏnhyo alludes here to the first of the three truths that are to be cultivated: "the first truth is that the path to bodhi is impartial"; see p. 672c above.

339. *Zhao lun, T* 1858:45.153a4–5; cf. Walter Liebenthal, trans., *Chao Lun: The Treatises of Seng-chao* (Hong Kong: Hong Kong University Press, 1968), p. 63: "Is the Tao far away? This life of ours is reality. Is the Sage far away? Recognize him as in truth he is, and you are the (cosmic) spirit."

340. *Yuqieshi di lun (Yogācārabhūmi-śāstra)* 62, *T* 1579:30.646b16–21.

341. *Yijang ŭi, HPC* 1:807a22 ff.

342. Wŏnhyo misreads "stills" *(chŏng)* for "purifies" *(chŏng)* in his quotation of the passage; *KSGN* 3, p. 676a18.

343. This term derives from the *Nirvāṇa Sūtra's* listing of four reliances *(pratisaraṇa)* regarding human beings: (1) The educated *pṛthagjana* (ordinary person) who keeps the precepts and preaches the dharma but still retains a defiled nature; he has not yet reached the first bhūmi. (2) The *śrotāpanna* (streamwinner) and *sakṛdāgāmin* (once-returner); these are bodhisattvas who have reached the first bhūmi and received prediction of their future buddhahood but have not yet reached the second or third bhūmi. (3) The *anāgāmin* (nonreturner), who has received this prediction and is destined soon to attain *anuttarasamyaksaṃbodhi.* (4) The arhat, who has achieved the tenth bhūmi. When any of these types appear, they benefit living creatures and become people on whom the world relies; hence, they are called the

"four reliances." See *Dabanniepan jing* 6, *T* 375:12.637c; *Dabannihuan jing* 4, *T* 376: 12.875–876b.

344. The Koryŏ II/Taishō recension reads "It is inconceivable!" for "Make offerings to this person!" See *VS,* p. 374b17.

345. The five turbidities are the turbidity of life span, of views, of defilements, of living beings, and of the kalpa. See Edgerton, *Buddhist Hybrid Sanskrit Dictionary,* p. 174, s.v. "kaṣāya."

Glossary of Sinitic Logographs

Ado *hwasang* 阿道和尚
ammara 菴摩羅
Amnyanggun 押梁郡
amolo 阿摩羅
An Shigao 安世高
anmoluo 菴摩羅
Ansimsa 安心寺
anxin 安心
anzhu 安住
Baotang 保唐
baoyi 抱一
baoyuanxing 報寃行
Beiliang 北涼
Beizong 北宗
benjue 本覺
ben shiji 本實際
bianben 辨本
biguan 壁觀
Boruo xinjing zhujie 般若心經注解
budong 不動
budongdi 不動地
busiyi sanmei 不思議[義]三昧
Caodong 曹洞
Chajang 慈藏
Chakchegŏn 作帝建
chan 禪
Chang'an 長安
Changsan 章山
Chanmen jing 禪門經
chaŭn purhyŏn 自隱不現
ch'e 體
Ch'egwan 諦觀
chengfaxing 稱法行
Chengguan 澄觀
chi (knowledge) 智
chi (stopping) 止
chiana 持阿那
Chidŏk 智德
chigwan 止觀
ch'im 斟
Chimyŏng 智明
Chinhŭng (king) 眞興
Chinul 知訥
chinyŏ 眞如
Chisŏn Tohŏn 智詵道憲
Ch'oe Ch'iwŏn 崔致遠
Ch'ogae 初開
chŏlp'il 絶筆
chon 存
ch'ŏn (heavenly) 天
ch'ŏn (panting) 喘
chong 宗
chŏng (concentration) 定
chŏng (purifies) 淨
chŏng (stills) 静
ch'ongji 總持
chŏngnyŏ 靜慮
chŏngsa 正思
Chŏngt'o 淨土
chongyo 宗要
chonsim 存心
chonsin 存神
chuan 喘
Chuan'ao *dashi* 傳澳大師
Chuanfabaoji 傳法寶紀[記]
Chuhaengsa 住行寺
chŭk (is in fact) 卽
chŭk (then) 則
Chunbŏm 遵範
chung 中
Chunqiu 春秋
cun 存
cunsan 存三
danben shiyi 單本失譯
Dao'an 道安
Daosheng 道生
Daoshi 道世
Daoshun 道舜

Daoxin 道信
Daoxuan 道宣
Daoxuan 道璿
Dapin jing 大品經
Dazhao Zhikong 大照志空
dengjue 等覺
Dilun 地論
Dongshan famen 東山法門
Dongshan wusheng famen 東山無生法門
Du Zhenglun 杜正倫
Duifa lun 對法論
duizhi 對治
dunjiao 頓教
dunwu 頓悟
Eichō 永超
Enchō 圓超
Ennin 圓仁
erru 二入
Erru sixing lun 二入四行論
Fajing 法經
fan 返
fanjing dade 翻經大德
Fanxing pin 梵行品
fanyuan kan 返源看
fanzhao 返照
Farong 法融
Faru 法如
Fashang 法上
Fawang jing 法王經
Faxiang 法相
Fayan 法眼
fayundi 法雲地
Fazang 法藏
Fazhong 法忠
Feichangfang 費長房
fenbie 分別
foji shixin 佛卽是心
Foxing lun 佛性論
Fu *dashi* 傅大師
Fujian 符堅
Fuxi 傅翕
gong (associated) 共
gong (cavern) 孔
gong'an 公案
guanxin 觀心
guanxing 觀行
Guanxin lun 觀心論
guyijing 古異經
Haedong ko Sinhaeng sŏnsa chi pi 海東故信行禪師之碑
Haengjang 行狀
Haengmyŏngsa 行名寺
haengnip 行入
Haet'al 解脫
hap 合
hehe 和合
hoegwang panjo 廻光返照
hoesin 廻神
Hogŏ 胡踞
hoguk pulgyo 護國佛敎
hogwe 胡跪
Hongren 弘忍
Hongzhou 洪州
huatou 話頭
Huayan 華嚴
Huayan jin'guan chao 華嚴錦冠鈔
Huguo pin 護國品
Huiguan 慧觀
huiguang fanzhao 廻光返照
Huihong 慧洪
Huijiao 慧皎
Huike 慧可
hŭimang 希望
Huineng 慧能
huishen 廻神
Huisi 慧思
Hŭiyangsan 曦陽山
hwadu 話頭
hwahap 和合
hwangnyong 黃龍
Hwangnyongsa 皇龍寺[黃龍寺]
hwanjung 環中
Hwaŏm 華嚴
Hwaŏm chongyo 華嚴宗要
Hwaŏmgyŏng chongyo 華嚴經宗要
Hwaŏmgyŏng so 華嚴經疏
hwarang 花郎
Hyangjŏn 鄉傳
Hyet'ong 惠通
Hyeŭn 惠隱
Hyoso (king) 孝昭王
i (contextual particle) 而
i (different) 異
i (inspiration) 利
i (principle) 理

Ich'adon 異次頓
igwan 理觀
iip (access of principle) 理入
iip (two accesses) 二入
ilcha chi 一子地
ilch'e 一切
illon saengnon 因論生論
Ilmi chinsil musang musaeng kyŏlchŏng silche pon'gangnihaeng 一味眞實無相無生決定實際本覺利行
ilmi kwanhaeng 一味觀行
il pŏpkye 一法界
ilsim 一心
Imok 璃目
in (acquiescence) 忍
insŏng 人性
Inwang kyŏng 仁王經
ip 入
Iryŏn 一然
Jiangnan 江南
jianjiao 漸敎
jianxing 見性
jimieren 寂滅忍
jin'gangbi ding sanmei 金剛壁定三昧
Jin'gang sanmei jing 金剛三昧經
Jin'gang shangwei jing 金剛上味經
Jingjue 淨覺
Jingtu 淨土
Jingying Huiyuan 淨影慧遠
Jingzhong 淨衆
Jizang 吉藏
juan 卷
juecha 覺察
Juefan Huihong 覺範慧洪
jueguan 覺觀
Jueguan lun 絶觀論
jueyong 覺用
kae 開
Kaesŏng 開城
kagyong 覺用
kahaeng chi 加行地[智]
kail 可一
Kajisan 迦智山
kakch'al 覺察
kakkwan 覺觀
Kaksŭng (Enlightenment Vehicle) 覺乘
Kaksŭng (Horn Rider) 角乘
kan 看
kanhua 看話
kanhwa 看話
Kanhye chi 乾慧地
kanxin 看心
Kegon engi emaki 華嚴緣起繪卷
kepan 科判
ki (to activate) 起
Kim Hŏnjŏng 金獻貞
Kim *hwasang* 金和尙
Kim Pusik 金富軾
Kim Wŏn 金遠
Koguryŏ 高句麗
kong (cavern) 孔
kong (commensurate) 共
Kongōzammaikyōgi 金剛三昧經記
Kongōzammaikyō ronso 金剛三昧經論疏
Kongōzammaikyō shiji 金剛三昧經指事
Kongōzammaikyō shiki 金剛三昧經私記
Koryŏ 高麗
Kosŏnsa Sŏdang hwasang t'appi 高仙寺誓幢和上塔碑
Kuiji 窺基
kŭmgang sammae 金剛三昧
Kŭmgang sammaegyŏng chu 金剛三昧經注
Kŭmgang sammaegyŏng non 金剛三昧經論
Kŭmgang sammae kyŏng 金剛三昧經
kŭmgang yu 金剛喩
Kusan Sŏnmun 九山禪門
kwamun 科文
kwanhaeng 觀行
kwŏn 卷
kyejong 繫宗
kyŏlchŏng sŏng 決定性
kyŏnbun 見分
kyŏngga 經家
Kyŏngju 慶州
kyŏnsŏng 見性
Kyunyŏ 均如
Lengqie renfa ji 楞伽人法記
li (inspiration) 利
li (principle) 理
Liangtu yijing lu 涼土異經錄

Liangzhou 涼州
Liaodong 遼東
ligou sanmei 離垢三昧
Linji 臨濟
Linji Yixuan 臨濟義玄
liru 理入
liuli 琉璃
liuru famen 六入法門
liuxing 六行
lüeshu 略疏
lun 論
lunyong 論用
malna [sik] 末那識
miaojue 妙覺
miaojuedi 妙覺地
miaoxue 妙學
Mich'u (king) 味鄒
mingzong 明宗
moryun 毛輪
Muae 無礙
mubunbyŏl chi 無分別智
Mugu chi 無垢地
Muju 無住
Mukhoja 墨胡子
Munmu (king) 文武
munŭi darani 文義陀羅尼
munyŏm 無念
Muryangsu chongyo 無量義宗要
Muryangŭi chong 無量義宗
Muryangŭijong kyŏng 無量義宗經
Musang 無相
musoŭi 無所爲
Muyŏm 無染
myogak 妙覺
myohak 妙學
myŏngch'e 冥諦
Myŏngnang 明朗
Naksansa 洛山寺
Namak 南岳
Nangji 朗智
ningran 凝然
Niutou 牛頭
non 論
Nulchi (king) 訥祇
ŏnŏdodan 言語道斷
Paekche 百濟
pak (to bind) 縛
p'alsang pangp'yŏn 八相方便
pangoe 方外
panjiao 判教
panjo 返照
P'an piryang non 判比量論
panwŏn kan 返源看
pin 品
polli 本利
Pŏmhaeng 梵行
Pŏmil 梵日
Pŏmnang 法朗
pon'gak 本覺
pon silche 本實際
Pongnimsan 鳳林山
Pŏphŭng (king) 法興
Poyang 寶壤
pudong 不動
Puji 普寂
Puksan 北山
Pulchi 佛地
punbyŏl 分別
pun'gu paeksong 分軀於百松
Punhwangsa 芬皇寺
Pusŏksa 浮石寺
Putidamo 菩提達摩
p'yo (to whirl; to be adrift) 飄
p'yŏngdŭng 平等
p'yŏn kyŏngjong 辨經宗
Qingyuan Xingsi 青原行思
queben 闕本
Renwang jing 仁王經
ru 入
rudao 入道
Rudao anxin yao fangbian famen 入道安心要方便法門
ruding 入定
ruguan 入觀
Rulai guangmingjue pin 如來光明覺品
runiepan 入涅槃
ruocun guanxin 若存觀心
Ruzanglu 入藏錄
ruzheng dingwei 入正定位
Sabunnyul kalma ki 四分律羯磨記
saengmyŏl 生滅
Sagulsan 闍崛山
Sajasan 獅子山
sajong hyehaeng 四種慧行
Samguk sagi 三國史記

samhwa 三化
sammae 三昧
sammaje 三摩提
sanfen kejing 三分科經
sangbun 相分
sanjing 散經
sanmeijing 三昧經
sanmeijing lei 三昧經類
Sanyi 三一
sanzang 三藏
Sengcan 僧璨
Sengyou 僧祐
Sengzhao 僧肇
Shandong 山東
shanhuidi 善慧地
Shanwuwei 善無畏
Shelun 攝論
shengmie 生滅
Shenhui 神會
Shenxiu 神秀
shenyi 神異
sheyibianru 拾遺編入
shi 世
Shihuixiang pin 十廻向品
shijue 始覺
shiming 釋名
shishiwuai 事事無礙
shixing 十行
shouben zhenxin 守本眞心
shouxin 守心
shouyi 守一
shouyi buyi 守一不移
shouyi dedu 守一得度
shouyi ningran 守一凝然
shouzhen baoyi 守眞抱一
shouzhi 守直
shouzhong 守中
shouzi benxin 守自本心
shu 蜀
shu (commentary) 疏
sibi 是非
Sidan 始旦
sigak 始覺
Silla 新羅
Silla kuk Muju Kajisan Porimsa si Pojo sŏnsa yŏngt'ap pimyŏng 新羅國武州迦智山寶林寺普照禪師靈塔碑銘
sim 心
sim ilgyŏngsŏng 心一境性
Simmun hwajaeng non 十門和諍論
Simwang 心王
Sinhaeng 信行/神行/愼行
sini 神異
Sinmun (king) 神文
Sinp'yŏn chejong kyojang ch'ongnok 新編諸宗敎藏總錄
siphaeng 十行
so 疏
sŏ 庶
sŏk 釋
Sokchang 續藏
sŏk chemok 釋題目
Sŏl Ch'ong 薛聰
Sŏndŏk 善德
sŏng 性
Sŏngdŏk 聖德
Sŏngjusan 聖住山
sŏnna 禪那
Sŏp taesŭng kyŏng 攝大乘經
suil 守一
suiyan 隨緣
suiyanxing 隨緣行
Suje 樹提
sul taeŭi 述大意
Sumisan 須彌山
sun 旬
Sŭngdun 僧遁
Sŭngnang 僧朗
Sunji 順之
Suro 首露
susim 守心
suyŏn 隨緣
Suzong 肅宗
tae (analogue) 待
tae (great) 大
Taean 大安
Taebŏmhaeng 大梵行
taeyu 大有
Taishang Laojun 太上老君
Taiyi 太一
Taizong 太宗
Tang 唐
Tang Xinluoguo Huanglongsi Yuanxiao chuan 唐新羅國皇龍寺元曉傳
Tanlin 曇林

ti 體
Tiantai 天台
tianzun 天尊
Tiwei Boli jing 提謂波利經
t'ongdal 通達
T'ongdosa 通度寺
Tongnisan 桐裡山
t'ong Pulgyo 通佛教
Toryun 道倫
Toŭi 道義
Tullyun 遁倫
tŭnggak 等覺
tŭngin 等引
tŭngji (equanimous arrival) 等至
tŭngji (equanimous retention) 等持
ŭi ("idea") 意
ŭi (object) 義
Ŭich'ŏn 義天
ŭihae 義解
Ŭisang 義湘
ŭisik 意識
ŭnbok 隱覆
ŭngju kakkwan 凝住覺觀
ŭn i purhyŏn 隱而不顯
Unjŏng 運精
ŭp (to pour) 挹
Waiyu 外域
Wang Kŏn (king) 王建
Wang Bi 王弼
weijing 僞經
Weishi 唯識
wŏl (to transcend) 越
Wŏlch'ung 月忠
Wŏnch'ŭk 圓測
Wŏnhyo 元曉
Wŏnhyo pulgi 元曉不羈
wŏnsŏng 圓聲
wŏnyung 圓融
Wu Yue 吳越
wufa 無法
Wufangbian 五方便
wufenbie zhi 無分別智
Wugou di 無垢地
wunian 無念
wushengfa 無生法
wushi 無時
wusuo qiuxing 無所求行
wusuowei 無所爲
wuxing 無性
wuzhong xuanyi 五種玄義
Wuzhu 無住
Xiangfa 像法
xianqiandi 現前地
xin 信
xin'an 心安
xinbuqi 心不起
xing 行
xingru 行入
Xinwang 心王
Xinwang jing 心王經
Xinwang pusa shuo toutuo jing 心王菩薩說投陀經
xinxiang 心相
Xiuxin yaolun 修心要論
Xuanzang 玄奘
Xuanzong (emperor) 玄宗
xufeng 序分
xun 旬
yak chon kwansim 若存觀心
yak kisul 略記述
yakso 略疏
Yan Fotiao 嚴佛調
Yancong 彥琮
Yangzhou Gaoliseng Zhide 楊州高麗僧智德
Yanshou 延壽
yi (different) 異
yi (one) 一
yichu 異出
Yijang chang 二障章
yijie 義解
yijing (anomalous sūtras) 異經
yinfu 隱覆
yinyang 陰陽
yiqie 一切
yiwei guanxing 一味觀行
yizidi 一子地
yo 要
yŏ kŭmgang 如金剛
yong 用
Yonghui 永徽
Yongŏ i 龍魚異
yŏ yŏyŏ sŏl 如如如說
yu (milk) 乳
Yu Tang Silla kuk ko Hŭiyangsan Pongamsa kyo si Chijŭng taesa Chŏk-

cho chi t'ap pimyŏng 有唐新羅國故曦陽山鳳巖寺教謚智證大師寂照之塔碑銘
yuan 緣
Yuancheng 圓澄
yuanrong 圓融
yuansheng 圓聲
yuanxingdi 遠行地
yukhaeng 六行
yuri 琉璃
Yusik 唯識
Yu simallak to 遊心安樂道
Zanning 贊寧
Zhanran 湛然
zhengzongfen 正宗分
zhenru 眞如
zhenshifa 眞實法
zhi 知
zhiguan 止觀
Zhisheng 智昇
Zhiyan 智儼
Zhiyi 智顗
Zhizhou 智周
zhong 中
zhongshu 忠恕
zhongyao 宗要
zhu 住
Zhuangzi 莊子
zhuanshi 轉識
Zhuzhen 誅震
Zixuan 子璿
ziyin buxian 自隱不現
zong 宗
Zongmi 宗密
zongyao 宗要
Zuimiaoshengding jing 最妙勝定經
zun 尊
zuochan 坐禪

Bibliography

Works in Buddhist Canonical Collections

Apidamo dabiposha lun 阿毘達磨大毘婆沙論. *T* 1545:27.1a–1004a.
Apidamo jushe lun 阿毘達磨俱舍論. *T* 1558:29.1a–159b.
Apidamo zaji lun 阿毘達磨雜集論. *T* 1606:31.694b–774a.
Baozang lun 寶藏論. *T* 1857:45.143b–150a.
Beihua jing 悲華經. *T* 157:3.167a–233c.
Buduizhuan falun jing 不退轉法輪經. *T* 267:9.226a–254b.
Chanyuan zhuquanji duxu 禪源諸詮集都序. *T* 2015:48.397b–413a.
Cheng weishi lun 成唯識論. *T* 1585:31.1a–59a.
Chinyŏk Hwaŏmgyŏng so 華嚴經疏. *T* 2757:85.234c–236a.
Ch'oesangsŭng non 最上乘論. *T* 2011:48.377a–379b.
Chu sanzang jiji 出三藏記集. *T* 2145:55.1a–114a.
Da'aidao biqiuni jing 大愛道比丘尼經. *T* 1478:24.945b–955a.
Dabanniepan jing 大般涅槃經. *T* 374:12.365a–603c.
Dabanniepan jing jijie 大般涅槃經集解. *T* 1763:37.377a–611a.
Dabannihuan jing 大般泥洹經. *T* 376:12.853a–899c.
Dabaoji jing 大寶積經. *T* 310:11.1a–658a.
Dafangdeng daji jing 大方等大集經. *T* 397:13.1a–407a.
Dafangdeng rulaizang jing 大方等如來藏經. *T* 666:16.457a–460b.
Dafangguang fo huayan jing 大方廣佛華嚴經. *T* 278:9.395a–788b; *T* 279.10.1a–444c.
Dafangguang fo huayan jing shu 大方廣佛華嚴經疏. *T* 1735:35.503a–963a.
Dafangguang fo huayan jing shu yanyi chao 大方廣佛華嚴經疏演義鈔. *T* 1736: 36.1a–701a.
Dapilouzhe'na chengfo jing shu 大毘盧遮那成佛經疏. *T* 1796:39.579a–689c.
Dasheng apidamo zaji lun 大乘阿毘達磨雜集論. *T* 1606:31.694b–774a.
Dasheng bei fentuoli jing 大乘悲分陀利經. *T* 158:3.233c–289a.
Dasheng bofa mingmen lun 大乘百法明門論. *T* 1614:31.855b–c.
Dasheng guang Bolun shilun 大乘廣百論釋論. *T* 1571:30.187a–250b.
Dasheng qixin lun 大乘起信論. *T* 1666:32.352a–583b.
Dasheng qixin lun yishu 大乘起信論義疏. *T* 1843:44.175a–201c.
Dasheng rudao cidi 大乘入道次弟. *T* 1864:45.449b–467c.
Dasheng ru Lengqie jing 大乘入楞伽經. *T* 672:16.1a–640c.
Dasheng yi zhang 大乘義章. *T* 1851:44.465a–875c.
Dasheng zhuangyan jing lun 大乘莊嚴經論. *T* 1604:31.589b–661c.
Da-Tang neidian lu 大唐典錄. *T* 2149:55.219a–342a.
Dazhidu lun 大智度論. *T* 1509:25.57a–756c.
Da-Zhou lu 大周錄. *T* 2153:55.373b–476a.
Da zhuangyan famen jing 大莊嚴法門經. *T* 818:17.825a–833c.
Faguan jing 法觀經. *T* 611:15.240b–242a.
Fahua xuan lun 法華玄論. *T* 1720:34.361a–450c.

Fahua yishu 法華義疏. *T* 1721:34.451a–633b.
Faji yaosong jing 法集要頌經. *T* 213:4777a–799c.
Faju jing 法句經. *T* 2901:85.1432b–1435c.
Fanwang jing 梵網經. *T* 1484:24.997a–1010a.
Fanyi mingyi ji 翻譯名義集. *T* 2131:54.1055a–1185b.
Fangguang boruo jing 放光般若經. *T* 221:8.1a–146c.
Foshuo dasheng ru zhufo jingjie zhiguangming zhuangyan jing 佛說大乘入諸佛境界智光明莊嚴經. *T* 359:12.253c–265b.
Foshuo pusa neixi liu boluomi jing 佛說菩薩內習六波羅密經. *T* 778:17.714b–715a.
Fo wei Xinwang pusa shuo toutuo jing 佛爲心王菩薩說投陀經. *T* 2886:85.1401c–1403b.
Foxing lun 佛性論. *T* 1610:31.787a–813a.
Foyijiao jing 佛遺教經. *T* 389:12.1110c–1112b.
Fozu tong ji 佛祖統紀 . *T* 2035:49.129a–475c.
Guang Bolun ben 廣百論本. *T* 1570:29.182a–187a.
Guangbo yanjing butuizhuanlun jing 廣博嚴淨不退轉輪經. *T* 268:9.254b–285c.
Guangzan jing 光讚經. *T* 222:8.147a–216b.
Gyōinshō 行林抄. *T* 2409:76.1a–501c.
Haedong kosŭng chŏn 海東高僧傳. *T* 2065:50.1015a–1023a.
Huayan jing. See *Dafangguang fo huayan jing*.
Huayan jing neizhang men dengza kongmu zhang 華嚴經內章門等雜孔目章. *T* 1870:45.536c–589b.
Huayan jing shu. See *Dafang guang fo huayan jing shu*.
Huayan jing yihai bomen 華嚴經義海百門. *T* 1875:45.627a–636c.
Huayan wushi yao wenda 華嚴五十要問答. *T* 1869:45.519a–536b.
Huiyin sanmei jing 慧印三昧經 . *T* 632:15.460c–568a.
Hwaŏm ilsŭng pŏpkye to 華嚴一乘法界圖. *T* 1887A:45.711a–716a.
Jieshenmi jing 解深密經. *T* 676:16.688b–711b.
Jieshenmi jing shu 解深密經疏. *ZZ* 1, 34, 291a–476c, *ZZ* 1, 35, 1a–55d.
Jin'gang boruo boluomi jing 金剛般若波羅密經. *T* 235:8.748c–752c.
Jin'gangding jing da yuqie bimi xindi famen yijue 金剛頂經大瑜伽祕密心地法門義訣. *T* 1798:39.808a–821a.
Jin'gang sanmei benxing qingjing buhuai bumie jing 金剛三昧本性清淨不壞不滅經. *T* 644:15.697a–699b.
Jin'gang sanmei jing. See *Kŭmgang sammae kyŏng*.
Jin'gang sanmei jing tongzong ji 金剛三昧經通宗記. *ZZ* 1, 55, 3, 223a–299a.
Jin'gang sanmei jing zhujie 金剛三昧經注解. *ZZ* 1, 55, 2–3, 186a–222a.
Jingde chuandeng lu 景德傳燈錄. *T* 2076:51.196a–467a.
Jinglü yixiang 經律異相. *T* 2121:53.1a–268c.
Jingtu sheng wusheng lun 淨土生無生論. *T* 1975:47.381a–384a.
Jin'guangming jing 金光明經. *T* 663:16.335a–359b; *T* 664:16.359b–402a; *T* 665:16.403a–456c.
Jin'guangming jing wenju 金光明經文句. *T* 1785:39.46b–83b.
Jin'guangming jing xuanyi 金光明經玄義. *T* 1783:39.1a–12a.
Jiujing yisheng baoxing lun 究竟一乘寶性論. *T* 1611:31.813a–848a.
Juedingzang lun 決定藏論. *T* 1584:30.1018b–1035b.
Kaiyuan Shijiao lu 開元釋教錄. *T* 2154:55.477a–723a.
Kegonshū shōshū byō immyō roku 華嚴宗章并因明錄. *T* 2177:55.1132c–1135b.
Kŭmgang sammaegyŏng non 金剛三昧經論. *T* 1730:34.961a–1008a.

Kŭmgang sammae kyŏng 金剛三昧經. *T* 273:9.365c–374b.
Lengqieaboduoluo bao jing 楞伽阿跋多羅寶經. *T* 670:16.479a–514b.
Lengqie jing. See *Lengqieaboduoluo bao jing*.
Lengqie shizi ji 楞伽師資記. *T* 2837:85.1283a–1290c.
Lianhuamian jing 蓮華面經. *T* 386:12.1070b–1077c.
Lidai fabao ji 歷代法寶記. *T* 2075:51.179a–196b.
Linji lu 臨濟錄. *T* 1985:47.495a–506c.
Liuzu tan jing 六祖壇經. *T* 2007:48.237a–345b.
Mayi jing 罵意經. *T* 732:17.530a–534c.
Miaofa lianhua jing 妙法蓮華經. *T* 262:9.1a–62b.
Mohe boruo boluomiduo xin jing 摩訶般若波羅密多心經. *T* 251:8.848c.
Mohe boruo boluomi jing 摩訶般若波羅密經. *T* 223:8.217a–424a.
Mohe zhiguan 摩訶止觀. *T* 1911:46.1a–140c.
Pŏmmang kyŏng bosal kyebon sagi 梵網經菩薩戒本私記. *XZJ* 95:108a–121b.
Pŏpkye toji ch'ongsurok 法界圖記叢髓錄. *T* 1887B:45.716a–767c.
Pusa cong Doushuaitianjiang shenmutai shuo guangpu jing 菩薩從兜率天降神母胎說廣普經. *T* 384:12.1015a–1058b.
Pusa yingluo benye jing 菩薩瓔珞本業經. *T* 1485:24.1010b–1023a.
Qianshou qianyan Guanshiyin pusa guangda yuanman wu'ai dabeixin tuoluoni jing 千手千眼觀世音菩薩廣大圓滿無礙大悲心陀羅尼經. *T* 1060:19.106a–111c.
Renwang boruo boluomi jing 仁王般若波羅密經. *T* 246:8.834c–845a.
Renwang boruo jing shu 仁王般若經疏. *T* 1707:33.314b–359a.
Renwang huguo boruo jing shu 仁王護國般若經疏. *T* 1705:33.253a–286a.
Ru Dasheng lun 入大乘論. *T* 1634:32.36a–49c.
Ru Lengqie jing 入楞伽經. *T* 671:16.514c–586b.
Samguk yusa 三國遺事. *T* 2039:49.953c–1019a.
Sanlun xuanyi 三論玄義. *T* 1852:45.1a–15a.
Shanhaihui pusa jing 山海慧菩薩經. *T* 2891:85.1405c–1409c.
She Dasheng lun 攝大乘論. *T* 1593:31.112b–132c.
Shengman jing 勝鬘經. *T* 353:12.217a–323b.
Shibakong lun 十八空論. *T* 1616:31.861a–867a.
Shi chan boluomi cidi famen 釋禪波羅蜜次弟法門. *T* 1916:46.475c–548c.
Shidi jing 十地經. *T* 286:10.497c–535a; *T* 287:10.535a–574c.
Shidi jing lun 十地經論. *T* 1522:26.123a–203b.
Shidi yiji 十地義記. *T* 2758:85.236a–239c.
Shimen guijing yi 釋門歸敬儀. *T* 1896:45.854c–868c.
Shimen Hung Juefan linjian lu 石門洪覺範林間錄. *ZZ* 2b, 21, 4.
Shi Moheyan lun. See *Sŏk Mahayŏn non*.
Shokyō yōshō 諸經要抄. *T* 2819:85.1192c–1197c.
Shoulengyan jing 首楞嚴經. *T* 945:19.105b–155b.
Shoulengyan yishu zhujing 首楞嚴義疏注經. *T* 1799:39.823a–976c.
Sinp'yŏn chejong kyojang ch'ongnok 新編諸宗教藏總錄. *T* 2184:55.1165b–1178c.
Sŏk Mahayŏn non 釋摩訶衍論. *T* 1668:32.591c–668c.
Song Gaoseng zhuan 宋高僧傳. *T* 2061:50.709a–900a.
Suiziyi sanmei 隨自意三昧. *XZJ* 98:344a–354a.
Taesŭng kisillon pyŏlgi 大乘起信論別記. *T* 1845:44.226a–240c.
Taesŭng kisillon so 大乘起信論疏. *T* 1844:44.202a–226a.
Tang Dajianfusi gusizhu fanjing dade Fazang heshang

zhuan 唐大薦福寺故寺主翻經大德法藏和尙傳. *T* 2054:50.280a–289c.
Tiantai sijiao yi 天台四教儀. *T* 1931:46.774c–780c.
Tōiki dentō mokuroku 東域傳燈目錄. *T* 2183:55.1145c–1165b.
Wanshan tonggui ji 萬善同歸集. *T* 2017:48.957b–993c.
Weimojie suoshuo jing 維摩詰所說經. *T* 475:14.537a–557b.
Weimojing lüeshu 維摩經略疏. *T* 1778:38.562c–710a.
Weimo jing shu 維摩經疏. *T* 2772:85.375c–423c.
Wuliangyi jing 無量義經. *T* 276:9.383b–389b.
Wumen guan 無門關. *T* 2005:48.292a–299c.
Wushangyi jing 無上依經. *T* 669:16.468a–477c.
Xinxin ming 信心銘. *T* 2010:48.376b–377a.
Xiuxin yao lun 修心要論. See *Ch'oesangsŭng non.*
Xu Gaoseng zhuan 續高僧傳. *T* 2060:50.425a–707a.
Yŏlban kyŏng chongyo 涅槃經宗要. *T* 1769:38.239a–255c.
Youpọsai jie jing 優婆塞戒經. *T* 1488:24.1034a–1075c.
Yuanjue jing 圓覺經. *T* 842:17.913a–922a.
Yuanjue jing lüeshu zhu 圓覺經略疏注. *T* 1795:39.523b–578a.
Yugaron ki 瑜伽論記. *T* 1828:42.311a–868b.
Yuqieshi di lun 瑜伽師地論. *T* 1579:30.279a–882a.
Zengyi ahan jing 增一阿含經. *T* 125:2.549a–830b.
Zhancha shan'e yebao jing 占察善惡業經. *T* 839:17.901c–910c.
Zhao lun 肇論. *T* 1858:45.150c–161b.
Zhiguan fuxing chuanhong jue 止觀輔行傳弘決. *T* 1912:46.141a–446c.
Zhizheng zhuan 智證傳. *XZJ* 1235:63.
Zhongguan lun shu 中觀論序. *T* 1824:42.1a–169b.
Zhongjing mulu 眾經目錄. *T* 2147:55.150a–180b.
Zhong lun 中論. *T* 1564:30.1a–39b.
Zhuanshi lun 轉識論. *T* 1587:31.61c–63c.
Zhu Weimojie jing 註維摩詰經. *T* 1775:38.327a–419c.
Zimen jingxun 緇門警訓. *T* 2023:48.1041c–1097c.
Zongjing lu 宗鏡錄. *T* 2016:48.417b–957b.
Zuishangsheng lun. See *Ch'oesangsŭng non.*

Other Works in Asian Languages

An Kyehyŏn 安啓賢. *Silla Chŏngt'ogyo sasangsa yŏn'gu* 新羅淨土思想史研究 (Research on the history of Silla Pure Land thought). 1976; reprint ed., Seoul: Hyŏnŭmsa, 1987.

Bonaben ershisi shi 百衲本二十四史 (Bona edition of the twenty-four histories). *Sibu congkan* 四部叢刊 edition. Shanghai: Commercial Press, 1920–1922.

Ch'ae Inhwan 蔡印幻. *Shiragi Bukkyō kairitsu shisō kenkyū* 新羅佛教戒律思想研究 (Studies in Silla Buddhist Vinaya thought). Tokyo: Kokusho Kankōkai, 1975.

Chang Wŏn'gyu 張元圭. "Hwaŏm kyohak wansŏnggi ŭi sasang yŏn'gu" 華嚴教學完成期의 思想研究 (A study of Hwaŏm scholastic thought during its mature period). *PGHP* (Buddhist Studies Review) 11 (1974): 11–43.

Chodang chip 祖堂集 (Collection from the basilica of the patriarchs). In *Hyosŏng Cho Myŏnggi paksa hwagap kinyŏm pulgyo sahak nonch'ong* 曉城趙明基博士華甲記

念: 佛教史學論叢 (Essays on Korean Buddhist history, in honor of Prof. Cho Myŏnggi's sixtieth birthday), Appendix, pp. 1–129. Seoul, 1965.

Cho Myŏnggi 趙明基. *Koryŏ Taegak kuksa wa Ch'ŏnt'ae sasang* 高麗大覺國師와 天台思想 (National Master Ŭich'ŏn of Koryŏ and Ch'ŏnt'ae thought). Seoul: Tongguk Munhwasa, 1964.

———. *Silla Pulgyo ŭi inyŏm kwa yŏksa* 新羅佛敎의理念과 歷史 (The ideology and history of Silla Buddhism). Seoul: Sin T'aeyangsa, 1962.

———. *Wŏnhyo taesa chŏnjip* 元曉大師全集 (The complete works of Wŏnhyo). Seoul: Poryŏn'gak, 1978.

Ch'oe Pyŏnghŏn 崔柄憲. "Silla hadae Sŏnjong Kusanp'a ŭi sŏngnip: Ch'oe Chiwŏn ŭi sasan pimyŏng ŭl chungsim ŭro" 新羅下代禪宗九山派의 成立: 崔致遠의 四山碑銘을 中心으로 (The establishment of the Nine Mountains Sŏn lineage during the latter Silla, focusing on Ch'oe Chiwŏn's stelae inscriptions from four mountains). In Yŏksa Hakhoe 歷史學會, ed., *Han'guk sa nonmun sŏnjip (Kodae p'yŏn)* 韓國史論文選集 (古代篇) (Essay collection on Korean history: ancient period), vol. 2, 265–321. Seoul: Ilchogak, 1976.

Chōsen Sōtokufu 朝鮮總督府, eds. *Chōsen kinseki sōran* 朝鮮金石總覽 (Collection of Korean metal and lithic inscriptions). Keijō (Seoul): Chōsen Sotokufu, 1919.

Chuan An 船菴. "Wuzu Hongren chanshi" 五祖弘忍禪師 (The Fifth Patriarch, Ch'an master Hung-jen). *Xiandai foxue* 現代佛學 82 (June, 1957): 26–29.

Dai-Nihon zokuzōkyō 大日本續藏經 (The Japanese supplement to the Buddhist canon). Kyoto: Zōkyō Shoin, 1905–1912.

Etani Ryūkai 惠谷隆戒. "Shiragi Gangyō no Jōdokyō shisō" 新羅元曉の浄土教思想 (The Pure Land thought of Wŏnhyo of Silla). In *Jōdokyō no shin kenkyū* 浄土教の新研究 (New research on Pure Land Buddhism), pp. 71–92. Tokyo: Sankibō Busshorin, 1976.

———. "Shiragi Gangyō no *Yūshinanrakudō* wa gisaku ka" 新羅元曉の「遊心安樂道」は僞作か (Is Wŏnhyo's *Yu simallak to* apocryphal?). *IBK* 23 (1974): 16–23.

Fukaura Seibun 深浦正文. *Yuishikigaku kenkyū* 唯識學研究 (Studies in Yogācāra teachings). 2 vols. 1954; 2nd ed., Kyoto, 1977.

Han Kidu 韓基斗. *Silla sidae ŭi Sŏn sasang* 新羅時代의 禪思想 (Sŏn thought during the Silla). Han'guk Sŏn sasang yŏn'gu 韓國禪思想研究 (Studies in Korean Sŏn thought), no. 1. Iri: Wŏn'gwang Taehakkyo Ch'ulp'anbu, 1974.

Han T'aesik (Pogwang) 韓泰植 (普光). "Kanbantō de tsukurareta gigikyō ni tsuite" 韓半島で作られた 疑僞經 について(On apocryphal scriptures produced on the Korean Peninsula) *IBK* 45:1 (1996), 315, 332.

Hattori Masaaki 服部正明. "Zen to Indo Bukkyō" 禪とインド佛教 (Zen and Indian Buddhism). In *Zen no honshitsu to ningen no shinri* 禪の本質と人間の眞理 (The essence of Zen and human truth), ed. Hisamatsu Shin'ichi 久松眞一 and Nishitani Keiji 西谷啓治, 509–524. Tokyo: Sōbunsha, 1969.

Hayashi Taiun 林岱雲. "Bodaidarumaden no kenkyū" 菩提達摩傳の研究 (Studies in the biography of Bodhidharma). *Shūkyō kenkyū* 宗教研究 (Religious studies) 9 (1932): 62–72.

Hayashiya Tomojirō 林屋友次郎. *Kyōroku kenkyū* 經錄研究 (Studies on scriptural catalogues). Tokyo: Iwanami Shoten, 1941.

Hirakawa Akira 平川彰 et al., eds. *Index to the Abhidharmakośabhāṣya* (*Kusharon* sakuin 俱舍論索引). Tokyo: Daizō Shuppan Kabushikikaisha, 1977.

Hong Yunsik 洪潤植. "Koryŏ Pulgyo ŭi sinang ŭirye" 高麗佛敎의 信仰儀禮 (Koryŏ Buddhism and religious observances). In *Pak Kilchin Festschrift,* 655–698.

———. "Samguk yusa wa Pulgyo ŭirye" 三國遺事와佛敎儀禮 (Samguk yusa and Buddhist ceremonies). *PGHP* 16 (1979): 221–246.

Hongmun'gwan 弘文館, eds. *(Chŭngbo) Munhŏn pigo* 增補文獻備考 (Comprehensive references to documentary materials, revised and expanded edition). P'yŏngyang: Sahoe Kwahagwŏn Ch'ulp'ansa, 1967.

Hwang Suyŏng 黃壽永. "Silla Sŏdang hwasang pi ŭi sinp'yŏn" 新羅「誓幢和上碑」의 新片 (New fragments of the memorial inscription to Sŏdang Upādhyāya of Silla). *Kogo misul* 考古美術 (Archaeology and art) 108 (1970): 1–6.

Inoue Hideo 井上秀雄. "Chōsen ni okeru Bukkyō juyō to shinkan'nen" 朝鮮における佛教受容と神觀念 (The reception of Buddhism in Korea and the concept of spirits). *Nihon bunka kenkyūsho kenkyū hōkoku* 日本文化研究所研究報告 (Research reports of the Japanese Cultural Research Center) 13 (1977): 45–69.

Ishida Mosaku 石田茂作. *Shakyō yori mitaru Narachō Bukkyō no kenkyū* 寫經より見たる奈良朝佛教の研究 (Nara Buddhism as reflected in manuscript copies). *Tōyō bunko ronshū* 東洋文庫論集, vol. 11. Tokyo: Tōyō Bunko, 1930.

Ishii Kōsei 石井公成. "*Kongōzammaikyō* no seiritsu jijō" 金剛三昧經の成立事情. *IBK* 46: 2 (1998), 31–37.

Jan Yün-hua (Ran Yunhua) 冉雲華. "Donghai dashi Wuxiang zhuan yanjiu" 東海大師無相傳研究 (A study of the biography of the Korean monk Musang). *Dunhuang xue* 敦煌學 (Dunhuang studies) 4 (1979): 47–60.

Kamata Shigeo 鎌田茂雄. *Chōsen Bukkyō no tera to rekishi* 朝鮮佛教の寺と歷史 (The history and monasteries of Korean Buddhism). Tokyo: Daihōrinkaku, 1980.

———. *Chūgoku Kegon shisōshi no kenkyū* 中國華嚴思想史の研究 (Studies in the history of Chinese Huayan thought). Tokyo: Tokyo University Press, 1965.

Kamata Shigeo and Ueyama Shunpei 鎌田茂雄, 上山春平. *Bukkyō no shisō VII (Chūgoku Zen)* 佛教の思想 7 (中國禪) [(Buddhist thought: Chinese Chan)]. Tokyo, 1969.

Kameda Tsutomu 龜田孜. *Kegon engi* 華嚴緣起 (The foundation of Huayan.) *Nihon emakimono zenshū* 日本繪卷物全集 (Anthology of Japanese scroll-paintings), vol. 8. Tokyo: Kadokawa Shoten, 1976.

Kashiwagi Hiroo 柏木弘雄. *Daijō kishinron no kenkyū: Daijō kishinron no seiritsu ni kansuru shiryōron teki kenkyū* 大乘起信論の研究: 大乘起信論の成立に關する資料論的研究 (Studies on *Dasheng qixin lun:* Text-critical research concerning the composition of *Awakening of Faith in Mahāyāna*). Tokyo: Shunchōsha, 1981.

Kim Chaegŭn (Mubyŏn) 金栽根 (無邊). *Kŭmgang sammaegyŏng sin'gang* 金剛三昧經論 新講 (New lectures on the *Vajrasamādhi-sūtra*). Seoul: Poryŏn'gak, 1980.

Kim Chigyŏn 金知見. "Silla Hwaŏmhak ŭi churyu ko" 新羅華嚴學의主流考 (Investigation of mainstream of Silla Hwaŏm studies). In *Pak Kilchin Festschrift,* 257–275.

———. "Silla Hwaŏmhak ŭi kyebo wa sasang" 新羅華嚴學의系譜와思想 (The thought and lineage of Silla Hwaŏm). *Haksurwŏn nonmunjip* 學術院論文集 (Essay collection of the Academy of Arts and Sciences) 12 (1973): 31–65.

Kim Chigyŏn and Ch'ae Inhwan 蔡印幻, eds. *Shiragi Bukkyō kenkyū* 新羅佛教研究 (Studies in Silla Buddhism). Tokyo: Sankibō Busshorin, 1973.

Kim Hyŏnghŭi 金炯熙. "Hyŏnjon ch'anso rŭl t'onghae pon Wŏnhyo ŭi Hwaŏmgyŏng kwan" 現存撰疏를 通해본 元曉의 華嚴經觀 (Wŏnhyo's view of the

Avataṃsaka-sūtra according to his extant commentaries). M.A. thesis, Tongguk University, 1980.

Kim Ingsŏk 金仍石. *Hwaŏmhak kaeron* 華嚴學概論 (An outline of Hwaŏm studies). Seoul: Pŏmnyunsa, 1974.

Kim Kangmo 金彊模. "Shiragi Gangyō no bungakukan" 新羅元曉の文學觀 (The literary perspectives of the Silla monk Wŏnhyo). In *Shiragi bukkyō kenkyū,* ed. Kim Chigyŏn and Ch'ae Inhwan, 111-136. Tokyo: Sankibō Busshorin, 1973.

Kim Pusik (1075-1151) 金富軾. *Samguk sagi* 三國史記 (Historical records of the three kingdoms). Ed. Sin Sŏkho 申奭鎬, trans. Kim Chonggwŏn 金鐘權. Seoul: Sŏnjin Munhwasa, 1960.

Kim Sanggi 金庠基. "Song-dae e issŏsŏ ŭi Koryŏbon ŭi yut'ong e taehayŏ" 宋代에 있어서의 高麗本의 流通에 對하여 (The transmission of Koryŏ books during the Song period). *Asea yŏn'gu* 亞細亞研究 (Asian studies) 8:2 (1965), 273-279.

Kim Sanghyŏn 金相鉉. *Wŏnhyo yŏn'gu* 元曉研究 (Studies on Wŏnhyo). Seoul: Minjoksa, 2000.

Kim Talchin 金達鎭, trans., with Ko Ikchin 高翊晉. *Kŭmgang sammaegyŏng non* 金剛三昧經論 (Exposition of the *Vajrasamādhi-sūtra*). *Wŏnhyo ch'ŏnjip* 元曉全集 (The Collected works of Wŏnhyo), vol. 1. Seoul: Yŏrŭmsa, 1986.

Kim Unhak 金雲學. "Wŏnhyo ŭi hwajaeng sasang" 元曉의和諍思想 (Wŏnhyo's thought on reconciling doctrinal controversies). *PGHP* 15 (1978): 173-182.

Kim Yŏngt'ae 金煐泰. "Chŏn'gi wa sŏrhwa rŭl t'onghan Wŏnhyo yŏn'gu" 傳記와說話를 通한 元曉研究 (A study of Wŏnhyo from the standpoint of biographies and legends). *PGHP* 17 (1980): 33-76.

———. "Hŭiyangsan Sŏnp'ae ŭi sŏngnip kwa kŭ pŏpkye e taehayŏ" 曦陽山 禪派의 成立과 그 法系에 대하여 (The foundation of the Hŭiyang-san Sŏn school and its dharma lineage). *Han'guk Pulgyohak* 韓國佛教學 (Korean Buddhist studies) 4 (1979): 11-38.

———. "Ogyo Kusan e taehayŏ" 五教九山에 對하여 (On the Five Scholastic Sects and the Nine Mountains of Sŏn). *PGHP* 16 (1979): 59-77.

———. "Silla esŏ iruktoen *Kŭmgang sammae kyŏng*" 新羅에서 이룩된 金剛三昧經 (The *Vajrasamādhi-sūtra* composed in Silla). *PGHP* 25 (1988): 11-37.

———. "Silla Pulgyo e issŏsŏ ŭi yongsin sasang: Samguk yusa rŭl chungsim ŭro" 新羅佛教에있어서의 龍神思想: 三國遺事를中心으로 (The ideology of dragon spirits in Silla Buddhism: Focusing on the *Samguk yusa*). *PGHP* 11 (1974): 123-154.

———. "Silla Pulgyo sasang" 新羅佛教思想 (Silla Buddhist thought). In *Pak Kilchin Festschrift,* 89-132.

———. "Silla Pulgyo taejunghwa ŭi yŏksa wa kŭ sasang yŏn'gu" 新羅佛教大衆化의 歷史와 그 思想研究 (A study of the history and ideology of the popularization of Buddhism in Silla). *PGHP* 6 (1969): 145-191.

Kimura Senshō 木村宣彰. "*Kongōzammaikyō* no shingi mondai" 金剛三昧經の眞僞問題 (The issue of the authenticity of the *Vajrasamādhi-sūtra*). *Bukkyo shigaku kenkyū* 佛教史學研究 (Buddhist historical studies) 18 (1976): 106-117.

Ko Ikchin 高翊晉. "Han'guk kodae ŭi Pulgyo sasang" 韓國古代의佛法思想 (Buddhist thought in Ancient Korea). In *Ch'ogi Han'guk Pulgyo kyodansa ŭi yŏn'gu* 初期韓國佛教教團史의 研究 (History of Buddhist sectarianism in early Korea), *Pulgyohak nonjip* 佛教學論集 (Essays in Buddhist Studies), pp. 11-106. Seoul: Minjoksa, 1986.

———. "Wŏnhyo ŭi sasang ŭi silch'ŏn wŏlli" 元曉의思想의實踐原理 (Praxis in Wŏnhyo's thought). In *Pak Kilchin Festschrift,* 225-255.

Koryŏ taejanggyŏng (Tripiṭaka Koreana *[sic]*) 高麗大藏經. Photolithographic edition. Seoul: Tongguk University Press, 1976.

Kwŏn Sangno 權相老. "Han'guk kodae sinang ŭi illan" 古代信仰의一覽 (A cross-section of ancient Korean beliefs). *PGHP* 1 (1963): 81–108.

———. "Han'guk Sŏnjong yaksa" 韓國禪宗略史 (A brief history of the Korean Sŏn school). In *Paek Sŏnguk Festschrift,* 265–298.

Makita Tairyō 牧田諦亮. *Gikyō kenkyū* 疑經研究 (Studies on apocryphal scriptures). Kyoto: Jinbun Kagaku Kenkyūsho, 1976.

———. "Tendai daishi no gikyō kan" 天台大師の疑經觀 (Zhiyi's view of apocryphal scriptures). In *Shikan no kenkyū* 止觀の研究 (Studies in calmness and insight), ed. Sekiguchi Shindai 關口眞大, 201–215. Tokyo: Iwanami Shoten, 1975.

Masunaga Reihō 增永靈鳳. "Shoki Zenshi to Dōgen zenshi no buppō" 初期禪史と道元禪師の佛法 (Early Ch'an history and the teachings of Zen master Dōgen). *Komazawa daigaku kenkyūkiyō* 駒澤大學研究紀要 (Research reports of Komazawa University) 13 (1955): 58–75.

Matsubayashi Kōshi. 松林弘之 "Shiragi Jōdokyō no ichikōsatsu: Gangyō no Jōdokyō shisō o megutte" 新羅淨土教の一考察: 元曉の淨土教思想をめぐって (An examination of Silla Pure Land teachings, with reference to Wŏnhyo's Pure Land thought). *IBK* 15:1 (1966), 196–198.

Matsumae Takeshi 松前健. "Kodai Kanzoku no ryūda sūhai to ōken" 古代韓族の龍蛇崇拜と王權 (Royal authority and the ancient Korean people's worship of dragons and snakes). *Chōsen gakuhō* 朝鮮學報 (Korean studies report) 57 (1970): 53–68.

Min Yŏnggyu 閔泳珪. "Iryŏn ŭi Sŏn Pulgyo: Silla wa Koryŏ ŭi Kusan Sŏnmun ŭn Nanjong i anigo Pukchong ida" 一然의禪佛敎—新羅와高麗의 九山禪門은 南宗이아니고 北宗이다. (Iryŏn's Sŏn Buddhism: The Silla and Koryŏ Nine Mountains school of Sŏn was not the Southern school but the Northern school). In *Han'guk kojŏn simp'ojium* 韓國古典심포지움 (Symposium on Korean classical texts), vol. 1, ed. Chindan Hakhoe, 2–9. Seoul: Ilchogak, 1980.

Minamoto Hiroyuki 源弘之. "Shiragi Jōdokyō no tokushoku" 新羅淨土教の特色 (The special characteristics of Silla Pure Land thought). In *Shiragi bukkyō kenkyū,* ed. Kim Chigyŏn and Ch'ae Inhwan, 285–317.

Mishina Akihide 三品彰英 (a.k.a. Shōei). "Shiragi no Jōdokyō" 新羅の淨土教 (Silla Pure Land teachings). In *Bukkyō shigaku ronshū, Tsukamoto hakushi shōju kinen* 佛教史學論集, 塚本博士頌壽記念 (Essays on the history of Buddhism, presented to Professor Tsukamoto Zenryū on his retirement from the Research Institute for Humanistic Studies), 727–745. Kyoto: Kyoto University, 1961.

Mitomo Kenyō 三友健容. "*Muryōgikyō* Indo senjutsu setsu" 無量義經インド撰述說 (The Indian provenance of the *Wuliangyi jing*). *Nichiren kyōdan no shomondai* 日蓮教團の諸問題 (Issues in the Nichiren Sect) 1983: 1119–1145.

Mizuno Kōgen 水野弘元. "Bodaidaruma no *Ninyūshigyō setsu* to *Kongōsammaikyō*" 菩提達摩の二入四教說と金剛三昧經 (Bodhidharma's *Explanation of the Two Accesses and Four Practices* and the *Vajrasamādhi-sūtra*). *Komazawa daigaku kenkyū kiyō* 駒澤大學研究紀要 13 (1955): 33–57.

———. "Gisaku no *Hokkugyō* ni tsuite" 僞作の法句經について (On the apocryphal Dharmapāda). *Komazawa daigaku Bukkyōgakubu kenkyū kiyō* 駒澤大學佛教學部研究紀要 19 (1961): 11–33.

Mochizuki Shinkō 望月信亨. *Bukkyō kyōten seiritsu shiron* 佛教經典成立史論 (Studies on the history of the composition of Buddhist scriptures). Kyoto: Hōzōkan, 1946.

Motoi Nobuo 本井信雄. "Shiragi Gangyō no denki ni tsuite" 新羅元暁の傳記について (On the biography of Wŏnhyo). *Ōtani gakuhō* 大谷學報 (Ōtani University reports) 41 (1961): 33–52.

Naitō Ryūō 内藤龍雄. "*Shutsu sanzō kishū* no senshū nenji ni tsuite" 出三藏記集の撰集年次について (The completion date of *Chu sanzang jiji*). *IBK* 7 (1958): 162–163.

———. "Sōyū no chosaku katsudō" 僧祐の著作活動 (Sengyou's literary activities). *IBK* 20 (1971): 284–287.

Nam Tongsin 南東信. "Silla chungdae Pulgyo ŭi sŏngnip e kwanhan yŏn'gu: *Kŭmgang sammae kyŏng* kwa *Kŭmgang sammaegyŏng non* ŭi punsŏk ŭl chungsim ŭro" 新羅 中代佛教의 成立에관한 硏究: 金剛三昧經과 金剛三昧經論의 분석을 중심으로 (A Study on the establishment of medieval Buddhism during the Silla: Focusing on an analysis of the *Vajrasamādhi-sūtra* and *Exposition of the Vajrasamādhi-sūtra*). *Han'guk munhwa* 韓國 文化 (Korean culture) 21 (June 1998): 113–142.

———. *Wŏnhyo* 원효 (Wŏnhyo). Seoul: Saenuri, 1999.

Ninomiya Keinin 二宮啓任. "Chōsen ni okeru Ninnōkai no kaisetsu" 朝鮮における仁王會の開設 (The establishment of *Renwang jing* assemblies in Korea). *Chōsen gakuhō* 朝鮮學報 (Korean studies) 14 (1959): 155–163.

Nishitani Keiji 西谷啓治 and Yanagida Seizan 柳田聖山, eds. *Zenke goroku II* 禪家語錄 (The recorded sayings of Zen). Tokyo: Chikuma Shobō, 1974.

Nukariya Kaiten 忽滑谷快天. *Zengaku shisōshi* 禪學思想史 (History of Zen thought). Vol. 1. Tokyo: Genkōsha, 1923.

Obata Hironobu 上畠宏允. "Chibetto no Zenshū to *Rekidai hōbōki*" チベットの禪宗と歷代法寶記 (The Tibetan Chan school and *Lidai fabao ji*). *Zen bunka kenkyūsho kiyō* 禪文化研究所紀要 (Research reports of the Zen Cultural Institute) 6 (1974): 139–176.

Ogawa Kan'ichi 小川貫弌. *Bukkyō bunkashi kenkyū* 佛教文化史硏究 (Studies in the history of Buddhist culture). Kyoto: Nagata Bunshōdō, 1973.

Okabe Kazuo 岡部和雄. "Sōyū no gigikyō-kan to shōkyō-kan" 僧祐疑僞經觀と抄經觀 (Sengyou's views on apocryphal sūtras and abbreviated scriptures). *Komazawa daigaku Bukkyōgakubu ronshū* 駒澤大學佛教學部論集 (Essay collection of the Komazawa University Buddhist Studies department) 2 (1971): 63–74.

———. "Zensō no chūshō to gigi kyōten" 禪僧の注抄と疑僞經典 (Scriptural citations by Chan monks and apocryphal scriptures). In *Tonkō butten to Zen* 敦煌佛典と禪 (Dunhuang Buddhist texts and Chan). *Kōza Tonkō* 講座敦煌, vol. 8, ed. Shinohara Hisao 篠原壽雄 and Tanaka Ryōshō 田中良昭, 351–376. Tokyo: Daitō Shuppansha, 1980.

Okimoto Katsumi 沖本克己. "Chibetto yaku *Ninyūshigyōron* ni tsuite" チベット譯「二入四行論」について (On the Tibetan translation of the *Treatise on the Two Accesses and Four Practices*). IBK 24 (1976): 999–992 *[sic]*.

Ōminami Ryūshō 大南龍昇. "Sanmai kyōten no yakushutsu to juyō" 三昧經典の譯出と受容 (The translation and reception of samādhi sūtras). *Bukkyō bunka kenkyū* 佛教文化硏究 (Studies on Buddhist culture) 21 (1976).

Paek Sŏnguk Paksa Songsu Kinyŏm Saŏp Wiwŏnhoe 白性郁博士頌壽記念事業委員會, eds. *Pulgyohak nonmunjip: Paek Sŏnguk paksa songsu kinyŏm* 白性郁博士頌壽

記念: 佛教學論文集 (Essay collection in Buddhist studies: Festschrift in honor of Dr. Paek Sŏnguk's sixtieth birthday). Seoul: Tongguk University, 1957.

Pak Chonghong 朴鍾鴻. *Han'guk sasang sa: Pulgyo sasang p'yŏn* 韓國思想史: 佛教思想篇 (History of Korean thought: Buddhist thought). Sŏmun mun'go, no. 11. Seoul: Sŏmun Mun'go 瑞文文庫, 1972.

Pak Kilchin Festschrift. See Sungsan Pak Kilchin Paksa Hwa'gap Kinyŏm Saŏphoe, eds. *Han'guk Pulgyo sasangsa: Sungsan Pak Kilchin paksa hwa'gap kinyŏm.*

Rhi Ki-yong (Yi Kiyŏng) 李箕永. *Han'guk ŭi Pulgyo sasang* 韓國의 佛教思想 (Korean Buddhist thought). *Segye sasang chŏnjip* 世界思想全集, vol. 11, 138–240. Seoul: Samsŏng Ch'ulp'an Sa, 1977.

———, trans. "*Inwang panyagyŏng* kwa hoguk pulgyo" 仁王般若經과 護國佛教 (The *Renwangjing* and national-protection Buddhism). In *Han'guk Pulgyo yŏn'gu, Puryŏn Yi Kiyŏng paksa hwagap kinyŏm* 韓國佛教研究—不然李箕永博士華甲紀念 (Studies on Korean Buddhism, in commemoration of the sixtieth birthday of [Puryŏn] Dr. Rhi Ki-yong), 163–193. Seoul: Han'guk Pulgyo Yŏn'guwŏn, 1982.

———, trans. *Kŭmgang sammaegyŏng non* 金剛三昧經論 (Exposition of the *Vajrasamādhi-sūtra*). Han'guk myŏngjŏ taejŏnjip 韓國名著大全集 (The great works of Korea). Seoul: Taeyang Sŏjŏk, 1973.

———. "Kyŏngjŏn inyong e nat'anan Wŏnhyo ŭi tokch'angsŏng" 經典引用에나타난 元曉의獨創性 (The uniqueness of Wŏnhyo as manifested in his citations of scriptures). In *Pak Kilchin Festschrift,* 177–224.

———. "Kyop'ansasang aesŏ pon Wŏnhyo ŭi wich'i" 教判史上애서 본 元曉의 位置 (Wŏnhyo's place in the history of doctrinal taxonomies). In *Han'guk Pulgyo yon'gu* 韓國佛教研究 (Korean Buddhist Studies), 345–358. Seoul: Han'guk Pulgyo Yŏn'guwŏn, 1982.

———. *Wŏnhyo sasang: segye kwan* 元曉思想: 世界觀 (Wŏnhyo's thought: His world view). Seoul: Hongbŏbwŏn, 1967.

Satō Ken 佐藤健. "*Anrakushū* to gikyō" 安樂集と僞經 (The *Anluoji* and apocryphal scriptures). *Bukkyō daigaku kenkyū kiyō* 佛教大學研究紀要 60 (1976): 79–134.

Satō Shigeki 佐藤繁樹. *Wŏnhyo ŭi hwajaeng nolli: Mui pulsuil sasang* 元曉의和諍論理: 無二不守一思想 (Wŏnhyo's logic of doctrinal reconciliation: "Nondual but without guarding the one" thought). Seoul: Minjoksa, 1996.

Sekiguchi Shindai 關口眞大. *Bukkyō no jissen genri* 佛教の實踐原理 (The principles of Buddhist practice). Tokyo: Sankibō Busshorin, 1977.

———. *Tendai shikan no kenkyū* 天台止觀の研究 (Studies in the calmness and insight meditations of the Tiantai school). Tokyo: Iwanami Shoten, 1969.

Shisanjing zhushu 十三經注疏 (Annotations and commentaries to the Thirteen Classics). Taipei: Chengwen Chubanshe, 1966.

Sinjŭng Tongguk yŏji sŭngnam 神增東國輿地勝覽 (Revised survey of Korean geography). Ed. No Sasin 盧思愼. Photolithographic reprint of 1530 revised and enlarged edition. Seoul: Tongguk Munhwasa, 1959.

Shimizu Yōkō 清水要晃. "*Nyūryōgakyō* no shiki no sansōetsu ni tsuite: Nyōraizō to arayashiki no dōshi o megutte" 入楞伽經の識の三相說について—如來藏とアーラヤ識の同視をめぐって (The theory of the three characteristics of consciousness in the *Laṅkāvatāra-sūtra:* With special reference to the identification of tathāgatagarbha and *ālayavijñāna*). *IBK* 25 (1976): 162–163.

Shinohara Hisao 篠原壽雄 and Tanaka Ryōshō 田中良昭, eds. *Tonkō butten to Zen* 敦

煌佛典と禪 (Dunhuang Buddhist scriptures and Chan). *Kōza Tonkō* 講座敦煌, vol. 8. Tokyo: Daitō Shuppansha, 1980.

Shiratori Kiyoshi 白鳥清. "Rei to tatsu tono kankei o ronjite Lingism no setsu o teishōsu" 靈と龍との關係を論じて'Lingism'の說を提唱す (Proposing the theory of "Lingism" [Numinosity] with special reference to the relation between *ling* [numinosity] and *long* [dragons]). In *Tōyōshi shūsetsu, Katō hakushi kanreki kinen* 東洋史集說, 加藤博士還曆記念 (Essays on Oriental history, presented in commemoration of Dr. Katō's sixtieth birthday), 363–397. Tokyo, 1941.

Shizutani Masao 靜谷正雄. "Indo Bukkyōshi to Nāga (tatsu)" インド佛教史とナーガ(龍) (Indian Buddhist history and Nāgas [dragons]). *Ryūkoku shidan* 龍谷史壇 (Historical circle of Ryūkoku University) 73:4 (1978), 131–146.

Sŏng Nakhun 成樂熏, trans. *Wŏnhyo, Wŏnch'ŭk, Ŭisang, Hyech'o, Chegwan, Ŭich'ŏn* 元曉 圓測 義湘 慧超, 諦觀 義天. *Han'guk ŭi sasang taejŏnjip* 韓國의思想大全集, vol. 1. Seoul: Tonghwa Ch'ulp'an Kongsa, 1972.

Sungsan Pak Kilchin Paksa Hwagap Kinyŏm Saŏphoe 崇山朴吉眞博士華甲紀念事業會, eds. *Han'guk Pulgyo sasangsa: Sungsan Pak Kilchin paksa hwagap kinyŏm* 韓國佛教思想史, 崇山朴吉眞博士華甲紀念 (History of Korean Buddhist thought: Presented in commemoration of the sixtieth birthday of [Sungsan] Dr. Pak Kilchin). Iri (Chŏlla Pukto): Wŏn Pulgyo Sasang Yŏn'guwŏn, 1975.

Suzuki Daisetsu 鈴木大拙. "Daruma no Zenbō to shisō oyobi sono ta" 達摩の禪法と思想及びその他 (Bodhidharma's Zen teachings, thought, and so forth). In *Kōkan Shōshitsu issho oyobi kaisetsu* 校刊少室逸書及解說 (Fragments from Bodhidharma's chambers, with explication). Osaka: Ataka Bukkyō Bunko, 1936.

———. *Zen shisōshi kenkyū* 禪思想史研究 (Studies in the history of Zen thought). *Suzuki Daisetsu zenshū* 鈴木大拙全集 (The complete works of D. T. Suzuki), vol. 2. Tokyo, 1968.

Taishō shinshū daizōkyō 大正新修大藏經 (Revised Tripiṭaka compiled during the Taishō reign period). Ed. Takakusu Junjirō 高楠順次郎 and Watanabe Kaikyoku 渡邊海旭. Tokyo: Daizōkyōkai, 1924–1935.

Takamine Ryōshū 高峯了州. *Kegon shisōshi* 華嚴思想史 (History of Huayan thought). Revised ed., Kyoto: Hyakkaen, 1963.

———. *Kegon to Zen to no tsūro* 華嚴と禪との通路 (The convergence of Huayan and Chan). Nara: Nanto Bukkyō Kenkyūkai, 1956.

Takasaki Jikidō 高崎直道. *Nyoraizō shisō no keisei* 如來藏思想の形成 (The formation of Tathāgatagarbha thought). Tokyo: Shunjusha, 1974.

Tamura Enchō 田村圓澄. *Kodai Chōsen Bukkyō to Nihon Bukkyō* 古代朝鮮佛教と日本佛教 (Ancient Korean Buddhism and Japanese Buddhism). Tokyo: Yoshikawa Kōbunkan, 1980.

Tanaka Ryōshō 田中良昭. "Gisaku no *Hokkukyō* to sono ihon ni tsuite" 僞作の「法句經」と疏の異本について(The apocryphal *Dharmapada:* its commentaries and editions). IBK 23:1 (1974), 122–129.

Tatsuzawa Toshiaki 瀧澤俊亮. "Chūgoku minzoku to ryūda no densho" 中國民族と龍蛇の傳承 (The Chinese people and legends of dragons and snakes). *Tōyō bungaku kenkyū* 東洋文學研究 (Studies on Oriental literature) 9 (1961): 81–106.

Tokiwa Daijō 常盤大定. *Busshō no kenkyū* 佛性の研究 (Studies on the buddha-nature). Tokyo: Kokusho Kankōkai, 1973.

Tongbang Sasang Nonch'ong Kanhaeng Wiwŏnhoe 東方思想論叢刊行委員會, eds. *Tongbang sasang nonch'ong, Yi Chongik paksa hagwi kinyŏm nonmunjip* 東方思想論

叢, 李鐘益博士學位紀念論文集 (Essays in Oriental thought, presented in commemoration of Dr. Yi Chongik's doctoral degree). Seoul: Poryŏn'gak, 1975.

Tongguk Taehakkyo Pulgyo Munhwa Yŏn'guso 東國大學校佛教文化硏究所, eds. *Han'guk Pulgyo ch'ansul munhŏn ch'ongnok* 韓國佛教撰述文獻總錄 (A comprehensive catalogue of Korean Buddhism materials and literature). Seoul: Tongguk Taehakkyo Ch'ulp'anbu, 1976.

Ui Hakuju 宇井伯壽. *Zenshūshi kenkyū* 禪宗史硏究 (Studies in the history of the Zen sect). 3 vols. Tokyo: Iwanami Shoten, 1939/1941/1943.

Ŭn Chŏnghŭi 은정희 and Song Chinhyŏn 송진현, trans. *Wŏnhyo ŭi Kŭmgang sammaegyŏng non* 원효의 금강삼매경론 (Wŏnhyo's *Exposition of the Vajrasamādhi-sūtra*). Seoul: Ilchisa, 2000.

Wang Zhongmin 王重民. *Dunhuang yishu congmu suoyin* 敦煌遺書總目索引 (General index to the catalogues of the manuscript remains from Dunhuang). Peking, 1962.

Yabuki Keiki 矢吹慶輝. *Meisha yoin* 鳴沙餘韻 (Echoes of the desert). Tokyo: Iwanami Shoten, 1930.

———. *Meisha yoin kaisetsu* 鳴沙餘韻解說 (Annotation to *Echoes of the Desert*). Tokyo: Iwanami Shoten, 1933.

———. "Tonkō shutsudo gigi kobutten ni tsuite" 敦煌出土疑僞古佛典に就いて (Ancient apocryphal Buddhist scriptures from Dunhuang). *Shūkyō kenkyū* 宗教硏究 (Religious studies) 3:10 (1919), 41–121.

Yamaguchi Zuihō 山口瑞鳳. "Chibetto Bukkyō to Shiragi Kin oshō" チベット佛教と新羅金和尙 (Tibetan Buddhism and Reverend Kim). In *Shiragi Bukkyo kenkyū* (Studies on Silla Buddhism), ed. Kim Chigyŏn and Ch'ae Inhwan, 1–36. Tokyo: Sankibō Busshorin, 1973.

Yanagida Seizan 柳田聖山. *Daruma no goroku* 達摩の語錄 (The records of Bodhidharma), *Zen no goroku* 禪の語錄 (Recorded sayings of Chan), vol. 1. Tokyo: Chikuma Shobō, 1969.

———. "*Kongōzammaikyō* no kenkyū" 金剛三昧經の硏究 (A study of the *Vajrasamādhi-sūtra*). *Paengnyŏn Pulgyo nonjip* 百蓮佛教論集 3 (1993): 433–460 (Korean translation, pp. 461–487).

———. *Shoki no Zenshi 1: Ryōga shijiki, Denhōbōki* 初期の禪史: 楞伽師資記, 傳法寶紀 (Early Chan histories: The *Lengqie shizi ji* and *Zhuan fabao ji*). *Zen no goroku* 禪の語錄, vol. 2. Tokyo: Chikuma Shobō, 1971.

———. *Shoki no Zenshi 2: Rekidai hōbōki* 初期の禪史2: 歷代法寶記 (Early Chan histories: The *Lidai fabao ji*). *Zen no goroku* 禪の語錄, vol. 3. Tokyo: Chikuma Shobō, 1976.

———. *Shoki Zenshū shisho no kenkyū* 初期禪宗史書の硏究 (Research on early Chan historiographical works). Kyoto: Hōzōkan, 1967.

Yi Chongik 李鐘益. "Han'guk Pulgyo chejongp'a sŏngnip ŭi yŏksa chŏk koch'al" 韓國佛教諸宗派成立의 歷史的 考察 (A historical investigation of the foundation of Korean Buddhist sects). *PGHP* 16 (1979): 29–58.

———. "Silla Pulgyo wa Wŏnhyo sasang" 新羅佛教와 元曉思想 (Silla Buddhism and Wŏnhyo's thought). In *Tongbang sasang nonch'ong, Yi Chongik paksa hagwi kinyŏm nonmunjip* 東方思想論叢—李鐘益博士學位紀念論文集 (Essays in Oriental thought, presented in Commemoration of Dr. Yi Chongik's doctoral degree), 183–197. Seoul: Poryŏn'gak, 1975.

———. *Wŏnhyo ŭi kŭnbon sasang: Simmun hwajaeng-non yŏn'gu* 元曉의根本思想: 十門

和諍論硏究 (Wŏnhyo's fundamental thought: Research on *Ten Approaches to the Reconciliation of Doctrinal Controversy*). Seoul: Tongbang Sasang Yŏn'guwŏn, 1977.

———. "Wŏnhyo ŭi saengae wa sasang" 元曉의 生涯와 思想 (The life and thought of Wŏnhyo). In *Tongbang sasang nonch'ong,* 198–239.

Yi Hŭisu 李喜秀. *T'och'ak-hwa kwajŏng esŏ pon Han'guk pulgyo* 土着化過程에서본韓國佛敎 (The adaptation of Korean Buddhism to indigenous culture). Seoul: Pulsŏ Pogŭpsa, 1971.

Yi Kiyŏng 李箕永. See Rhi Ki-yong.

Yi Nŭnghwa 李能和. *Chosŏn Pulgyo t'ongsa* 朝鮮佛敎通史 (A comprehensive history of Korean Buddhism). 3 vols. 1918; reprint ed., Seoul: Poryŏn'gak, 1979.

Yi Pyŏngdo 李丙燾, trans. *Samguk sagi* 三國史記 (Historical records of the Three Kingdoms). 2 vols. Seoul: Ŭryu Munhwasa, 1977.

———, trans. *Samguk yusa* 三國遺事 (Memorabilia and mirabilia of the Three Kingdoms). Seoul: Tongguk Munhwasa, 1962.

Yi Pyŏngdo and Kim Chaewŏn 金載元. *Han'guk-sa 1: Kodae pyŏn* 韓國史: 古代篇 (History of Korea: Ancient period). Seoul: Ŭryu Munhwasa, 1959.

Yi Usŏng 李佑成. "*Samguk yusa* sojae Ch'ŏyong sŏrhwa ŭi ilbunsŏk" 「三國遺事」所在處容說話의 一分析 (An analysis of the Ch'ŏyong story contained in *Samguk yusa*). In *Kim Chaewŏn paksa hoe'gap kinyŏm nonch'ong* 金載元博士回甲紀念論叢 (Essays presented in commemoration of Dr. Kim Chaewŏn's sixtieth birthday), 89–127. Seoul, 1969.

Yoritomi Motohiro 頼富本宏. "Gokoku kyōten to iwareru mono: *Ninnōkyō* o megutte" 護國經典と言われるもの一「仁王經」をめぐって(The national-protection class of scriptures: On the *Renwangjing*). *Tōyō gakujutsu kenkyū* 東洋學術研究 (Oriental scholarship) 14 (1975): 45–62.

Yoshimura Shuki 芳村修基. "The Denkar-Ma, an Oldest Catalogue of the Tibetan Buddhist Canons." In *Indo Daijō Bukkyō shisō kenkyū: Kamarashīra no shisō* インド大乘佛教思想研究–カマラシーラの思想 (Studies on Indian Buddhist Mahāyāna thought: The Thought of Kamalaśīla), 99–199. Kyoto: Hyakkaen, 1974.

Yoshioka Yoshitoyo 吉岡義豊. "Bukkyō no zenpō to Dōkyō no shuitsu" 佛教の禪法と道教の守一 (Buddhist meditation techniques and Daoism's guarding the one). *Chisan gakuhō* 智山學報 27–28 (Nov. 1964): 109–125. Reprinted in *Dōkyo to Bukkyō* 道教と佛教 (Taoism and Buddhism), vol. 3, 287–314. Tokyo: Kokusho Kankōkai, 1976.

———. "Shoki Dōkyō no shuitsu shisō to Bukkyō: Tokuni *Taiheikyō* o chūshin toshite" 初期道教の守一思想と佛教–とくに太平經を中心として (The thought of guarding the one in early Daoism and Buddhism: With special reference to the *Book of Great Peace*). *Taishō daigaku kiyō* 大正大學紀要 53 (1968): 61–82. Reprinted as "*Taiheikyō* no shuitsu shisō to bukkyō" 太平經の守一思想と佛教 (Buddhism and the conception of "guarding the one" in the *Taipingjing*) in *Dōkyō to Bukkyō,* vol. 3, 315–351. Tokyo: Kokusho Kankōkai, 1976.

Yoshizu Yoshihide 吉津宜英. "Hōzō-den no kenkyū" 法藏傳の研究 (The biography of Fazang). *Komazawa daigaku Bukkyō gakubu kenkyū kiyō* 駒澤大學佛教學部研究紀要 37 (1979): 168–193.

Yūki Kyōju Shōju Kinen Ronbun Shū Kankōkai 結城教授頌壽紀念論文刊行會, eds. *Bukkyō shisōshi ronshu: Yūki kyōju shōju kinen* 結城教授頌壽紀念: 佛教思想史論集 (The history of Buddhist thought: Festschrift in commemoration of Professor Yūki Reimon's sixtieth birthday). Tokyo: Daizō Shuppansha, 1964.

Yūki Reimon 結城令聞. "Shina Yuishiki gakushijō ni okeru Ryōgashi no chii" 支那唯識學史上に於ける楞伽師の地位 (The place of the Laṅka teachers in Chinese Vijñānavāda history). *Shina Bukkyō shigaku* 支那佛教史學 (Studies in Chinese Buddhist history) 1 (1937): 21–44.

Zengaku Daijiten Hensanso 禪學大辭典編纂所, eds. *Zengaku daijiten* 禪學大辭典 (Great dictionary of Zen studies). 3 vols. Tokyo: Komazawa University, 1977.

Works in Western Languages

An, Kye-Hyŏn. "Silla Buddhism and the Spirit of the Protection of the Fatherland." *Korea Journal* 17:4 (April 1977), 27–29.

Austerlitz, Robert, et al. "Report of the Workshop Conference on Korean Romanization." *Korean Studies* 4 (1980): 111–125.

Bascom, William R. "Four Functions of Folklore." In *Study of Folklore,* ed. Alan Dundes, 279–298. Englewood Cliffs, N.J.: Prentice-Hall, 1965.

Beal, Samuel. A *Catena of Buddhist Scriptures from the Chinese.* London: Trübner, 1871.

Best, Jonathan. "Buddhism, Art and the Transforming Power of Faith in Early Korea." Paper read at the Forces of Tradition in Modern Korea Symposium, May 12, 1988, University of California, Los Angeles.

Bielefeldt, Carl. "Ch'ang-lu Tsung-tse's *Tso-ch'an i* and the 'Secret' of Zen Meditation." In *Traditions of Meditation in Chinese Buddhism,* ed. Peter Gregory, 129–161.

Bielefeldt, Carl, and Lewis Lancaster. "T'an Ching (Platform Scripture)." *Philosophy East and West* 24 (1975): 197–212.

Bochenski, Joseph M. *A History of Formal Logic.* Trans. and ed. Ivo Thomas. Notre Dame, Ind.: Notre Dame University Press, 1961.

Bokenkamp, Stephen R. "Stages of Transcendence: The *Bhūmi* Concept in Taoist Scripture." In *Chinese Buddhist Apocrypha,* ed. Robert Buswell Jr., 119–147. Honolulu: University of Hawai'i Press, 1990.

Bond, George D. *The Word of the Buddha: The Tipiṭaka and Its Interpretation in Theravāda Buddhism.* Colombo: M. D. Gunasena and Co., 1982.

Brock, Karen L. "The Case of the Missing Scroll: A History and Reconstruction of *Tales of Gishō and Gangyō." Archives of Asian Art* 41 (1988): 6–31.

———. "Tales of Gishō and Gangyō: Editor, Artist, and Audience in Japanese Picture Scrolls," Ph.D. dissertation, Princeton University, 1984.

Brough, John. "Thus Have I Heard. . . ." *Bulletin of the School of Oriental and African Studies* 13 (1950): 416–426.

Broughton, Jeffrey, "Early Ch'an Schools in Tibet." In *Studies in Ch'an and Hua-yen,* ed. Robert M. Gimello and Peter N. Gregory, 1–68. Studies in East Asian Buddhism, no. 1. Honolulu: University of Hawai'i Press, 1983.

Buswell, Robert E., Jr. "The 'Aids to Penetration' *(Nirvedhabhāgīya)* According to the Vibhāṣika School." *Journal of Indian Philosophy* 25 (1997): 589–611.

———, trans. "Arouse Your Mind and Practice! Wŏnhyo's *Palsim suhaeng chang.*" In *Sourcebook of Korean Civilization,* vol. 1: *From Early Times to the Sixteenth Century,* ed. Peter H. Lee, 154–157. New York: Columbia University Press, 1993.

———. "Buddhism in Korea." In *The Encyclopedia of Religion,* ed. Mircea Eliade, vol. 2, 421–426. New York: Macmillan, 1987.

———. "Ch'an Hermeneutics: A Korean View." In *Buddhist Hermeneutics,* ed. Donald S. Lopez, Jr., 231–256. Studies in East Asian Buddhism, no. 6. Honolulu: University of Hawai'i Press, 1988.

———, ed. *Chinese Buddhist Apocrypha.* Honolulu: University of Hawai'i Press, 1990.

———. "Chinul's Systematization of Chinese Meditative Techniques in Korean Sŏn Buddhism." In *Traditions of Meditation in Chinese Buddhism,* ed. Peter N. Gregory, 199–242.

———. "The Chronology of Wŏnhyo's Life and Works: Some Preliminary Considerations." In *Wŏnhyo yŏn'gu nonch'ong: kŭ ch'ŏrhak kwa in-gan ŭi modŭn kŏt* (Wŏnhyo studies: Various aspects of his philosophy and humanism), ed. Kim Chigyŏn, 931–964. Seoul: Wŏnhyo Sasang Yŏn'guwŏn, 1987.

———, ed. *Currents and Countercurrents: Korean Influences on the East Asian Buddhist Traditions.* Honolulu: University of Hawai'i Press, 2005.

———. "Did Wŏnhyo Write Two Versions of His *Kŭmgang sammaegyŏng-ron* [Exposition of the *Book of Adamantine Absorption*]? An Issue in Korean Buddhist Textual History." *Papers of the Fifth International Conference on Korean Studies: Korean Studies, Its Tasks and Perspectives,* vol. 2, 585–601. Sŏngnam, Korea: Academy of Korean Studies, 1988.

———, editor-in-chief. *Encyclopedia of Buddhism.* 2 vols. New York: Macmillan, 2004.

———. *The Formation of Ch'an Ideology in China and Korea: The "Vajrasamādhi-Sūtra," a Buddhist Apocryphon.* Princeton Library of Asian Translations. Princeton: Princeton University Press, 1989.

———. "The Hagiographies of the Korean Monk Wŏnhyo (617–686)." In *Buddhism in Practice,* ed. Donald S. Lopez Jr., 553–562. Princeton: Princeton University Press, 1995.

———. "Icchantika." In *Encyclopedia of Buddhism,* ed. Robert E. Buswell Jr., vol. 1, 351.

———. "Imagining 'Korean Buddhism': The Invention of a National Religious Tradition." In *Nationalism and the Construction of Korean Identity,* ed. Hyung Il Pai and Timothy R. Tangherlini, 73–107. Korea Research Monograph no. 26. Berkeley: Institute of East Asian Studies, 1998.

———. *The Korean Approach to Zen: The Collected Works of Chinul.* Honolulu: University of Hawai'i Press, 1983.

———. "The Korean Origin of the *Vajrasamādhi-Sūtra:* A Case Study in Determining the Dating, Provenance, and Authorship of a Buddhist Apocryphal Scripture." Ph.D. dissertation, University of California, Berkeley, 1985.

———. "The Path to Perdition: The Wholesome Roots and Their Eradication" In *Paths to Liberation: The Mārga and Its Transformations in Buddhist Thought,* ed. Robert E. Buswell Jr. and Robert M. Gimello, 107–134. Kuroda Institute Studies in East Asian Buddhism, no. 7. Honolulu: University of Hawai'i Press, A Kuroda Institute Book, 1992.

———. "Prolegomenon to the Study of Buddhist Apocryphal Scriptures." In *Chinese Buddhist Apocrypha,* ed. Robert Buswell, 1–30. Honolulu: University of Hawai'i Press, 1990.

———. "The Proliferation of *Cittaviprayuktasaṃskāra*-s in the Vaibhāṣika School." *Journal of Indian Philosophy* 25 (1997): 451–466.

———, trans. "The Reception of Buddhism in Korea and Its Impact on Indigenous Culture." Translation of Inoue Hideo, "Chōson ni okeru Bukkyō juyō to shinkan-nen." In *Introduction of Buddhism to Korea: New Cultural Patterns,* ed.

Lewis Lancaster and C[hai]-s[hin] Yu, 29–78. Studies in Religions and Culture, vol. 3. Berkeley: Asian Humanities Press, 1989.

———, trans. "Wŏnhyo's Philosophical Thought." In *Assimilation of Buddhism in Korea: Religious Maturity and Innovation in the Silla Dynasty,* ed. Lewis R. Lancaster and C. S. Yu, 47–103. Studies in Korean Religions and Culture, vol. 4. Berkeley: Asian Humanities Press, 1991. Translation of Pak Chonghong, "Wŏnhyo ŭi chŏrhak sasang," in *Han'guk sasang sa* (History of Korean Thought), 59–88. Seoul: Ilsinsa, 1966.

Cabezón, José Ignacio. *Buddhism and Language: A Study of Indo-Tibetan Scholasticism.* Albany: State University of New York Press, 1994.

———, ed. *Scholasticism: Cross-Cultural and Comparative Perspectives.* Albany: State University of New York Press, 1998.

———. "Vasubandhu's *Vyākhyāyukti* on the Authenticity of the Mahāyāna *Sūtras.*" In *Texts in Context: Traditional Hermeneutics in South Asia,* ed. Jeffrey R. Timm, 221–243. Albany: State University of New York Press, 1992.

Campbell, Joseph. *The Hero with a Thousand Faces.* Princeton: Princeton University Press, 1949.

———. *The Masks of the Gods II: Oriental Mythology.* New York: Viking Press, 1962.

Chan Hing-ho. "Ta Sung Kao-seng chuan." In *A Sung Bibliography (Bibliographie des Sung),* ed. Etienne Balazs and Yves Hervouet, 349–350. Hong Kong: Chinese University Press, 1978.

Chappell, David W. "Early Forebodings of the Death of Buddhism." *Numen* 27:1 (1980), 122–154.

———. "Introduction to the 'T'ien-t'ai ssu-chiao-i,'" *Eastern Buddhist,* n.s. 9 (May 1976): 72–86.

———. "The Teachings of the Fourth Ch'an Patriarch Tao-hsin (580–651)." In *Early Ch'an in China and Tibet,* ed. Whalen Lai and Lewis Lancaster, 89–129.

Chappell, David W., ed., and Masao Ichishima, comp. *T'ien-t'ai Buddhism: An Outline of the Fourfold Teachings.* Tokyo: Daiichi Shobō, 1983.

Charles, R. H. *The Apocrypha and Pseudepigrapha of the Old Testament in English.* 2 vols. Oxford: Clarendon Press, 1913.

Ch'en, Kenneth K. S. *Buddhism in China: A Historical Survey.* Princeton: Princeton University Press, 1964.

Chi, R. S. Y. *Buddhist Formal Logic.* Dr. B. C. Law Trust Fund, vol. 1. London: Royal Asiatic Society of Great Britain and Ireland, 1969.

Chou Yi-liang. "Tantrism in China." *Harvard Journal of Asiatic Studies* 8 (1945): 241–332.

Chun Shin-yong (Ch'ŏn Sin'yŏng), ed. *Korean Folk Tales.* Korean Culture Series, no. 7. Seoul: Si-sa-yong-o-sa Publishers, 1982.

Cleary, J. C., trans. *Zen Dawn: Early Zen Texts from Tun Huang.* Boston: Shambhala, 1986.

Cohen, Alvin P., ed. *Selected Works of Peter A. Boodberg.* Berkeley: University of California Press, 1979.

Collcutt, Martin. "The Early Ch'an Monastic Rule: *Ch'ing kuei* and the Shaping of Ch'an Community Life." In *Early Ch'an in China and Tibet,* ed. Whalen Lai and Lewis Lancaster, 165–184.

Collins, Steven. *Selfless Persons: Imagery and Thought in Theravāda Buddhism.* Cambridge: Cambridge University Press, 1982.

Combaz, Gisbert. "Masques et dragons en Asie." *Mélanges chinois et bouddhiques* 7 (1945): 1–328.

Conze, Edward. *Buddhism: Its Essence and Development.* New York: Harper and Row, Harper Torchbooks, 1959.

———. *Buddhist Thought in India: Three Phases of Buddhist philosophy.* London: George Allen and Unwin, 1962. Reprint, Ann Arbor: University of Michigan Press, 1967.

———, trans. *The Perfection of Wisdom in Eight Thousand Lines and Its Verse Summary.* Bolinas, Calif.: Four Seasons Foundation, 1975.

Conze, Edward, et al., eds. *Buddhist Texts through the Ages.* New York: Harper and Row, 1964.

Cox, Collett. *Disputed Dharmas: Early Buddhist Theories of Existence, an Annotated Translation of the Section on Factors Dissociated from Thought from Saṅghabhadra's "Nyāyānusāra."* Studia Philological Buddhica Monograph Series, 11. Tokyo: International Institute for Buddhist Studies, 1995.

Dalia, Albert A. "The 'Political Career' of the Buddhist Historian Tsan-ning." In *Buddhist and Taoist Practice in Medieval Chinese Society: Buddhist and Taoist Studies II,* ed. David W. Chappell, 146–180. Asian Studies at Hawaii, no. 34. Honolulu: University of Hawai'i Press, 1987.

Davidson, Ronald M. "An Introduction to the Standards of Authenticity in Indian Buddhism." In *Chinese Buddhist Apocrypha,* ed. Robert E. Buswell Jr., 291–325. Honolulu: University of Hawai'i Press, 1990.

Demiéville, Paul. *Le concile de Lhasa: Une controverse sur le quiétisme entre bouddhistes de l'Inde et de la Chine au VIIIe siècle de l'ère chrétienne.* Bibliothèque de l'Institut des hautes études chinoise, vol. 7. Paris: Impr. Nationale de France, 1952.

Demiéville, Paul, Hubert Durt, and Anna Siedel, eds. *Répertoire du canon bouddhique Sino-Japonais.* Revised ed. Tokyo and Paris: l'Académie des Inscriptions et Belles-lettres, Institut de France, 1978.

Donner, Neal. "Sudden and Gradual Intimately Conjoined: Chih-i's T'ien-t'ai View." In *Sudden and Gradual: Approaches to Enlightenment in Chinese Thought,* ed. Peter N. Gregory, 201–226.

Dundes, Alan, ed. *The Study of Folklore.* Englewood Cliffs, N.J.: Prentice-Hall, 1965.

Durt, Hubert. "La biographie du Moine Coréen Ui-sang d'après le Song Kao Seng Tchouan." In *Kim Chawŏn paksa hoegap kinyŏm nonch'ong* (Essays presented in commemoration of Dr. Kim Chaewŏn's sixtieth birthday), 411–422. Seoul, 1969.

Eberhard, Wolfram, ed. *Folktales of China.* Chicago: University of Chicago Press, 1965.

Edgerton, Franklin. *Buddhist Hybrid Sanskrit Dictionary.* New Haven: Yale University Press, 1953.

Elwin, Verrier. *Myths of Middle India.* Specimens of the Oral Literature of Middle India. Oxford: Oxford University Press, 1949.

Emeneau, Murray B. *Koṭa Texts: Part Three.* University of California Publications in Linguistics, vol. 3. Berkeley: University of California Press, 1946.

Epstein, Ronald. "The *Śūraṅgama-sūtra* with Tripiṭaka Master Hsüan-hua's *Commentary and Elementary Explanation of Its General Meaning:* A Preliminary Study and Partial Translation." Ph.D. dissertation, University of California, Berkeley, 1975.

Faure, Bernard. "Bodhidharma as Textual and Religious Paradigm." *History of Religions* 25 (1986): 187–198.

———. "The Concept of One-Practice Samādhi in Early Ch'an." In *Traditions of Meditation in Chinese Buddhism,* ed. Peter Gregory, 99–128.

———, trans. *Le Traité de Bodhidharma.* Paris: Le Mail, 1986.

———. "La volonté d'orthodoxie: Généalogie et doctrine du bouddhisme Ch'an de l'École du Nord—d'aprés l'une de ses chroniques, le *Leng-chia shih-tzu chi* (début du 8è siècle)." Ph.D. dissertation, University of Paris, 1984.

Forte, Antonino. *Political Propaganda and Ideology in China at the End of the Seventh Century: Inquiry into the Nature, Authors and Function of the Tunhuang Document S. 6502 Followed by an Annotated Translation.* 2 vols. Naples: Istituto Universitario Orientale, 1976.

Foulk, Theodore Griffith. "The 'Ch'an School' and Its Place in the Buddhist Monastic Tradition." Ph.D. dissertation, University of Michigan, Ann Arbor, 1987.

Frauwallner, Eric. "Amalavijñānam und Ālayavijñānam." *Beitrage zur Indischen Pilologie und Alterumskunde: Festschrift W. Schubring,* 148–159. Hamburg: Cram, 1951.

Fujieda, Akira. "The Tun-huang Manuscripts." In *Essays on the Sources for Chinese History,* ed. Donald D. Leslie, Colin Mackerras, and Wang Gungwu, 120–128. 1973. Reprint, Columbia: University of South Carolina Press, 1975.

Gardner, Daniel K. "Confucian Commentary and Chinese Intellectual History." *Journal of Asian Studies* 57:2 (May 1998), 397–422.

Giles, Lionel, ed. *A Descriptive Catalogue of the Chinese Manuscripts from Tunhuang in the British Museum.* London: British Museum, 1957.

Gimello, Robert M. "Apophatic and Kataphatic Discourse in Mahāyāna: A Chinese View." *Philosophy East and West* 26 (1976): 117–136.

———. "Chih-yen (602–668) and the Foundation of Hua-yen Buddhism." Ph.D. dissertation, Columbia University, 1976.

———. "Random Reflections on the 'Sinicization' of Buddhism." *Bulletin of the Society for the Study of Chinese Religions* 5 (1978): 52–89.

Gómez, Luis O. "Buddhist Literature: Exegesis and Hermeneutics." In *Encyclopedia of Religion,* ed. Mircea Eliade, vol. 2, 529–540. New York: Macmillan, 1987.

———. "Indian Materials on the Doctrine of Sudden Enlightenment." In *Early Ch'an in China and Tibet,* ed. Whalen Lai and Lewis Lancaster, 393–434.

———. "Proto-Mādhyamika in the Pāli Canon." *Philosophy East and West* 26 (1976): 137–165.

———. "Purifying Gold: The Metaphor of Effort and Intuition in Buddhist Thought." In *Sudden and Gradual: Approaches to Enlightenment in Chinese Thought,* ed. Peter N. Gregory, 67–165.

Grayson, James Huntly. *Early Buddhism and Christianity in Korea: A Study in the Implantation of Religion.* Studies in the History of Religions, no. 47. Leiden: E. J. Brill, 1985.

Gregory, Peter N. "The Problem of Theodicy in the *Awakening of Faith.*" *Religion* 22 (1986): 63–78.

———, ed. *Sudden and Gradual: Approaches to Enlightenment in Chinese Thought.* Studies in East Asian Buddhism, no. 5. Honolulu: University of Hawai'i Press, 1987.

———. "Sudden Enlightenment Followed by Gradual Cultivation: Tsung-mi's Analysis of Mind." In *Sudden and Gradual: Approaches to Enlightenment in Chinese Thought,* ed. Peter Gregory, 279–320.

———, ed. *Traditions of Meditation in Chinese Buddhism.* Studies in East Asian Buddhism, no. 4. Honolulu: University of Hawai'i Press, 1986.

———. "Tsung-mi's Synthetic Vision." Photocopied manuscript, n.d.

Grosnick, William. "*Cittaprakṛti* and *Ayoniśomanaskāra* in the *Ratnagotravibhāga:* A Precedent for the *Hsin-Nien* Distinction of *The Awakening of Faith." Journal of the International Assoication of Buddhist Studies* 6:2 (1983), 35–47.

———. "Nonorigination and *Nirvāṇa* in the Early *Tathāgatagarbha* Literature." *Journal of the International Association of Buddhist Studies* 4:2 (1981), 33–43.

Guenther, Herbert B. *Philosophy and Psychology in the Abhidharma.* Delhi: Motilal Banarsidass, 1957.

Ha, Tae-hung, and Grafton K. Mintz, trans. *Samguk Yusa: Legends and History of the Three Kingdoms of Ancient Korea.* Seoul: Yonsei University Press, 1972.

Hadas, Moses, and Morton Smith. *Heroes and Gods: Spiritual Biographies in Antiquity.* 1965. Reprint, Freeport, N.Y.: Books for Libraries Press, 1970.

Hakeda, Yoshito S., trans. *The Awakening of Faith, Attributed to Aśvaghosha.* New York: Columbia University Press, 1967.

Henderson, John B. *Scripture, Canon, and Commentary: A Comparison of Confucian and Western Exegesis.* Princeton: Princeton University Press, 1991.

Hong Jung-Shik (Hong Chŏngsik). "The Thought and Life of Wŏnhyo." In *Buddhist Culture in Korea,* ed. Chun Shin-yong, 15–30 (Korean version, pp. 163–181). Korean Culture Series, vol. 3. Seoul: International Cultural Foundation, 1974.

Hurvitz, Leon. "Chih-i (538–597): An Introduction to the Life and Ideas of a Chinese Buddhist Monk." *Mélanges chinois et bouddhiques* 12 (1962): 1–372.

———, trans. *Scripture of the Lotus Blossom of the Fine Dharma (The Lotus Sūtra).* New York: Columbia University Press, 1976.

In Kwŏn-hwan. "Buddhist Preachings and Their Korean Acculturation." *Korea Journal* 12:10 (October 1972), 18–27.

Inaba, Shōju. "On Chos-grub's Translation of the *Chieh-shen-mi-ching-shu.*" In *Buddhist Thought and Asian Civilization: Essays in Honor of Herbert V. Guenther on his Sixtieth Birthday,* ed. Leslie S. Kawamura and Keith Scott, 105–113. Emeryville, Calif.: Dharma Publishing, 1977.

Jackson, Roger. "Terms of Sanskrit and Pāli Origin Acceptable as English Words." *Journal of the International Association of Buddhist Studies* 5 (1982): 141–142.

Jaini, Padmanabh S. "The Development of the Theory of the *Viprayukta-Saṁskāras.*" *Bulletin of the School of Oriental and African Studies* 22 (1959): 531–547.

———. "The Vaibhāṣika Theory of Words and Meanings." *Bulletin of the School of Oriental and African Studies* 22 (1959): 95–107.

Jan, Yün-hua. "Buddhist Historiography in Sung China." *Zeitschrift der deutschen morgenländischen Gesellschaft* 114 (1964): 360–381.

———. "Hui Chiao and His Works, a Reassessment." *Indo-Asian Culture* 12 (1964): 177-190.

———. "Tsung-mi: His Analysis of Ch'an Buddhism." *T'oung Pao* 58 (1972): 1–54.

Jansen, Wm. Hugh. "The Esoteric-Exoteric Factor in Folklore." In *Study of Folklore,* ed. Alan Dundes, 43–278.

Jorgensen, John A. "The Earliest Text of Ch'an Buddhism: The *Long Scroll.*" M.A. thesis, Australian National University, 1979.

Keel, S. (Hee-Sung). "Buddhism and Political Power in Korean History." *Journal of the International Association of Buddhist Studies* 1 (1978): 9–24.

King, Sallie B. *Buddha Nature.* Albany: State University of New York Press, 1991.

Kluckhohn, Clyde. "Recurrent Themes in Myths and Mythmaking." In *Study of Folklore,* ed. Alan Dundes, 158–168.

Koh, Ik-Jin (Ko Ikchin). "Wŏnhyo's Hua-yen thought." *Korea Journal* 23:8 (August 1983), 30–33.

Koseki, Aaron L. "Prajñāpāramitā and the Buddhahood of the Non-Sentient World: The San-lun Assimilation of Buddha-Nature and Middle Path Doctrine." *Journal of the International Association of Buddhist Studies* 3:1 (1980), 16–33.

La Vallée Poussin, Louis, trans. *Abhidharmakośabhāṣyam.* English translation by Leo M. Pruden. 4 vols. Berkeley: Asian Humanities Press, 1988–1990.

Lai, Whalen. "The Pure and the Impure: The Mencian Problematik in Chinese Buddhism." In *Early Ch'an in China and Tibet,* ed. Whalen Lai and Lewis Lancaster, 299–326.

———. "T'an-ch'ien and the Early Ch'an Tradition: Translation and Analysis of the Essay 'Wang-shih-fei lun.'" In *Early Ch'an in Chin and Tibet,* ed. Whalen Lai and Lewis Lancaster, 65–87.

———. "Tao-sheng's Theory of Sudden Enlightenment Re-examined." In *Sudden and Gradual: Approaches to Enlightenment in Chinese Thought,* ed. Peter N. Gregory, 169–200.

Lai, Whalen W., and Lewis R. Lancaster, eds. *Early Ch'an in China and Tibet.* Berkeley Buddhist Studies Series, vol. 5. Berkeley: Institute of East Asian Studies, 1983.

Lancaster, Lewis R. "Buddhist Apocryphal Words." Paper delivered at panel on Chinese Buddhist Apocrypha, American Academy of Religion annual meeting, November 24, 1986.

———. Review of *Repertorie du Canon Bouddhique Sino-Japonais,* edited by Paul Demiéville, Hubert Durt, and Anna Seidel. *Journal of the International Association of Buddhist Studies* 5 (1982): 128–131.

Lancaster, Lewis R., and Sung Bae Park, eds. *The Korean Buddhist Canon: A Descriptive Catalogue.* Berkeley: University of California Press, 1979.

Lau, D. C., trans. *Lao Tzu Tao Te Ching.* New York: Penguin Books, 1963.

Ledyard, Gari. "Yin and Yang in the China-Manchuria-Korea Triangle." In *China among Equals,* ed. Morris Rossabi, 313–353.

Lee, Ki-Baik. *A New History of Korea.* Trans. Edward W. Wagner, with Edward J. Shultz. Cambridge: Harvard University Press, 1984.

Lee, Leo. *Le maître Wŏn-hyo de Sil-la du VIIè siècle: Sa vie, ses écrits, son apostolat.* Seoul: Librairie catholique, 1986.

Lee, Peter H. *Anthology of Korean Literature.* Honolulu: University Press of Hawai'i, 1981.

———. "Fa-tsang and Ŭisang." *Journal of the American Oriental Society* 82 (1962): 56–62.

———, trans. *Lives of Eminent Korean Monks: The Haedong Kosŭng Chŏn.* Harvard-Yenching Institute Studies, no. 25. Cambridge: Harvard University Press, 1969.

———, trans. *Songs of Flying Dragons: A Critical Reading.* Cambridge: Harvard University Press, 1975.

———, ed. *Sourcebook of Korean Civilization,* vol. 1: *From Early Times to the Sixteenth Century.* New York: Columbia University Press, 1993.

Legge, James, trans. *The Chinese Classics.* 1935. Reprint edition, Taipei: n.p., 1976.

Leverrier, R. P. Roger. "Buddhism and Ancestral Religious Beliefs in Korea." *Korea Journal* 12:5 (1972), 37–42.

———. "Étude sur les rites bouddhiques a l'époque du royaume do Koryŏ: Le rôle du bouddhisme et de la prière pour la protection du royaume." *Revue de Corée* 4:3 (1972), 61–72.

Liebenthal, Walter. "A Biography of Tao-sheng." *Monumenta Nipponica* 11 (1955).

———, trans. *Chao Lun: The Treatises of Seng-chao.* Hong Kong: Hong Kong University Press, 1968.

———. "New Light on the Mahāyāna Śraddhotpāda Śāstra." *T'oung Pao* 44 (1958): 155–216.

———. "Notes on the 'Vajrasamādhi.'" *T'oung Pao* 46 (1956): 347–386.

Liu, Ming-wood. "The *P'an-chiao* System of the Hua-yen School in Chinese Buddhism." *T'oung Pao* 67 (1981): 10–47.

Makransky, John J. *Buddhahood Embodied: Sources of Controversy in India and Tibet.* Albany: State University of New York Press, 1997.

Maspero, Henri. *Taoism and Chinese Religion.* Trans. Frank A. Kierman Jr. Amherst: University of Massachusetts Press, 1981.

Mayer, Alexander L. "Commentarial Literature," in Robert E. Buswell Jr., editor-in-chief, *Encyclopedia of Buddhism,* vol. 1, 166–169. New York: Macmillan, 2004.

———. "Das *Vajracchedikā-sūtra* und die chinesische Auslegung der prajñā: Ein Beitrag zur Expositorik, Exegese under Hermeneutik im sino-buddhistischen Sūtra-Kommentar. Habilitation-Schrift, Heidelberg University, 1999.

McClung, David H. "The Founding of the Royal Dragon Monastery: Translated, with Annotations, from Iryŏn's *Samguk Yusa.*" *Transactions of the Royal Asiatic Society, Korea Branch* 53 (1978): 69–80.

McGovern, William Montgomery. *A Manual of Buddhist Philosophy.* New York: E. P. Dutton, 1923.

McRae, John R. *The Northern School and the Formation of Early Ch'an Buddhism,* Studies in East Asian Buddhism, no. 3. Honolulu: University of Hawai'i Press, 1986.

———. "The Ox-Head School of Chinese Ch'an Buddhism: From Early Ch'an to the Golden Age." In *Studies in Ch'an and Hua-yen,* ed. Robert M. Gimello and Peter N. Gregory, 169–252. Studies in East Asian Buddhism, no. 1. Honolulu: University of Hawai'i Press, 1983.

Minn Young-gyu (Min Yŏnggyu). "Le bouddhisme Zen de Silla et de Koryŏ: D'après la relation du moine Il-yŏn." *Revue de Corée* 6:2 (1974), 47–59.

Miyakawa Hisayuki. "Local Cults around Mount Lu at the Time of Sun'en's Rebellion." In *Facets of Taoism: Essays in Chinese Religion,* ed. Holmes Welch and Anna Seidel, 83–101. New Haven: Yale University Press, 1979.

Mizuno, Kōgen. *Buddhist Sutras: Origin, Development, Transmission.* Tokyo: Kōsei Publishing Co., 1982.

———. "On the *Pseudo-Fa-kiu-king.*" *IBK* 9:1 (1961), 402–395 *[sic].*

Mundkur, Balaji. *The Cult of the Serpent: An Interdisciplinary Survey of Its Manifestations and Origins.* Albany: State University of New York Press, 1983.

Murti, M. S. Narayana. *Sanskrit Compounds: A Philosophical Study.* Varanasi: Chowkhamba, 1973.

Ñāṇananada, Bhikkhu. *Concept and Reality in Early Buddhist Thought: An Essay on "Papañca" and "Papañca-Saññā-Saṅkhā."* Kandy, Sri Lanka: Buddhist Publication Society, 1971.

———. *Ideal Solitude: An Exposition of the Bhaddekaratta Sutta.* The Wheel Publication, no. 188 Kandy, Sri Lanka: Buddhist Publication Society, 1973.

———. *The Magic of the Mind: An Exposition of the Kalākārāma Sutta.* Kandy, Sri Lanka: Buddhist Publication Society, 1974.

Nattier, Jan. *Once upon a Future Time: Studies in a Buddhist Prophecy of Decline.* Nanzan Studies in Asian Religions, no. 1. Berkeley: Asian Humanities Press, 1991.

Norman, K. R. *A Philological Approach to Buddhism.* The Buddhist Forum, vol. 5. London: School of Oriental and African Studies, University of London, 1997.

Obermiller, E. *Analysis of the Abhisamayālaṃkāra.* Calcutta Oriental Series, no. 27. Calcutta: Luzac and Co., 1933.

Ōchō, Enichi. "The Beginnings of Tenet Classification in China." *The Eastern Buddhist,* n.s. 14:2 (1981), 71–94.

Olrik, Axel. "Epic Laws of Folk Narrative." In *Study of Folklore,* ed. Alan Dundes, 129–141.

Orzech, Charles D. *Politics and Transcendent Wisdom: The "Scripture for Humane Kings" in the Creation of Chinese Buddhism.* University Park: Pennsylvania State University Press, 1998.

Pak, Chong-hong. "Wŏnhyo's Philosophical Thought." Trans. Robert E. Buswell Jr. In *Assimilation of Buddhism in Korea: Religious Maturity and Innovation in the Silla Dynasty,* ed. Lewis R. Lancaster and C. S. Yu, 47–103. Studies in Korean Religions and Culture, vol. 4. Berkeley: Asian Humanities Press, 1991.

Park, Sung Bae (Pak Sŏngbae). "A Comparative Study of Wŏnhyo and Fa-tsang on the Ta-Ch'eng Ch'i-Hsin Lun." In *Cheil hoe Han'gukhak Kukche haksurhoe ŭi nonmunjip (Papers of the First International Conference on Korean Studies),* 579–597. Sŏngnam, Korea: Academy of Korean Studies, 1979.

———. "On Wŏnhyo's Enlightenment." *IBK* 29:1 (1980), 470–467 *[sic].*

———. "Silla Buddhist Spirituality." In *Buddhist Spirituality: Later China, Korea, Japan and the Modern World.* World Spirituality, ed. Takeuchi Yoshinori et al., 57–78. Encyclopedic History of the Religious Quest, vol. 9. New York: Crossroad Publishing Company, A Herder and Herder Book, 1999.

———. "Wŏnhyo's Commentaries on the *Awakening of Faith in Mahāyāna.*" Ph.D. dissertation, University of California, Berkeley, 1979.

Plassen, Jörg. "Another Inquiry into the Commentarial Structure of Wŏnhyo's Works, Focussing on *Kŭmgang sammaegyŏng non.*" In *Proceedings of the Twenty-First Conference of the Association for Korean Studies in Europe,* ed. Antonetta Bruno and Federica Baglioni, 270–275. Frascati: AKSE, 2003.

———. "Denial and Affirmation in Wŏnhyo's Exegesis." In *History, Language, and Culture in Korea: Proceedings of the Twentieth Conference of the Association of Korean Studies in Europe,* ed. Youngsook Pak and Jaehoon Yeon, 156–168. London: Saffron, 2001.

———. "Die Spuren der Abhandlung (Lun-chi): Exegese und Übung im San-lun des sechsten Jahrhunderts." Ph.D dissertation, University of Hamburg, 2002.

Paul, Diana Y. *Philosophy of Mind in Sixth-Century China: Paramārtha's "Evolution of Consciousness."* Stanford: Stanford University Press, 1984.

Pradhan, Prahlad, ed. *Abhidharmakośabhāṣyam of Vasubandhu.* Patna: K. P. Jayaswal Research Institute, 1975.

Raglan, Lord. *The Hero: A Study in Tradition, Myth, and Drama.* Westport, Conn.: Greenwood Press, 1956.

Reischauer, Edwin O. *Ennin's Travels in T'ang China.* New York: Ronald Press, 1955.

Reynolds, Frank E., and Donald Capps, eds. *The Biographical Process: Studies in the History and Psychology of Religion.* Religion and Reason, 11. The Hague: Mouton, 1976.

Rhi Ki-yong (Yi Kiyŏng). "Wŏnhyo and His Thought." *Korea Journal* 11:1 (Jan. 1971), 4-9, 14.

Robinet, Isabelle. *Méditation taoïste.* Paris: Dervy livres, 1979.

Rogers, Michael C. "*P'yŏnnyŏn T'ongnok:* The Foundation Legend of the Koryŏ State." *Korean Studies* (University of Washington) 4 (1982–1983): 3–72.

Rossabi, Morris, ed. *China among Equals: The Middle Kingdom and its Neighbors, Tenth to Fourteenth Centuries.* Berkeley and Los Angeles: University of California Press, 1983.

Ruegg, David Seyfort. "On the Knowability and Expressibility of Absolute Reality in Buddhism." *IBK* 20 (1971): 495–489 *[sic].*

———. *La théorie du Tathāgatagarbha et du Gotra: Études sur la sotériologie et la gnoséologie du Bouddhisme.* Publications de l'École Française d'Extrême-Orient, vol. 70. Paris, 1969.

Rump, Ariane, and Wing-tsit Chan, trans. *Commentary on the Lao-Tzu by Wang Pi.* Monograph of the Society for Asian and Comparative Philosophy, no. 6. Honolulu: University Press of Hawai'i, 1979.

Rutt, Richard. "The Flower Boys of Silla (Hwarang): Notes on the Sources." *Transactions of the Korea Branch of the Royal Asiatic Society* 38 (1961): 1–66.

Schafer, Edward. "Combined Supplements to *Mathews.*" Mimeographed. University of California, Berkeley, Department of Oriental Languages, n.d.

Schopen, Gregory. "Filial Piety and the Monk in the Practice of Indian Buddhism: A Question of 'Sinicization' Viewed from the Other Side." *T'oung Pao* 70 (1984): 110–126.

Shih, Robert. *Biographies des moines éminents (Kao seng tchouan) de Houei-kiao* (The *Biographies of eminent monks* by Hui-chiao). Bibliothèque de Musëon, vol. 54. Louvain: Institut Orientaliste, 1968.

Shim Jae-ryong, "On the General Characteristics of Korean Buddhism: Is Korean Buddhism Syncretic?" *Seoul Journal of Korean Studies* 2 (1989): 147–157.

Sørensen, Henrik H. "Ennin's Account of a Korean Buddhist Monastery, 839–840 A.D." *Acta Orientalia* 47 (1986): 141–155.

———. "The History and Doctrines of Early Korean Sŏn Buddhism." Ph.D. dissertation, University of Copenhagen, 1987.

Staal, Johan F. "Room at the Top in Sanskrit: Ancient and Modern Descriptions of Nominal Composition." *Indo-Iranian Journal* 9 (1966): 165–198.

Stcherbatsky. F[edor] I[ppolitovich]. *Buddhist Logic.* 2 vols. New York: Dover, 1962.

Stone, Jacqueline I. *Original Enlightenment and the Transformation of Medieval Japanese Buddhism.* Kuroda Institute Studies in East Asian Buddhism, no. 12. Honolulu: University of Hawai'i Press, A Kuroda Institute Book, 1999.

Strickmann, Michel. "On the Alchemy of T'ao Hung-ching." In *Facets of Taoism: Essays in Chinese Religion,* ed. Holmes Welch and Anna Seidel, 123–192. New Haven: Yale University Press, 1979.

Suzuki, Daisetz Tcitaro. *Essays in Zen Buddhism.* Series 1. London: Routledge and Kegan Paul, 1970.

———, trans. *The Laṅkāvatāra Sūtra.* 1932. Reprint, Boulder: Prajñā Press, 1978.

———. *Studies in the Laṅkāvatāra Sūtra.* 1932. Reprint, Boulder: Prajñā Press, 1978.

Swanson, Paul L. *Foundations of T'ien-t'ai Philosophy: The Flowering of the Two Truths Theory in Chinese Buddhism.* Berkeley: Asian Humanities Press, 1989.

Tachikawa, Musashi. "A Sixth-Century Manual of Indian Logic (A Translation of the *Nyāyapraveśa*)." *Journal of Indian Philosophy* 1 (1971): 111–145.

Takasaki, Jikidō. *A Study on the Ratnagotravibhāga (Uttaratantra): Being a Treatise on the Tathāgatagarbha Theory of Mahāyāna Buddhism.* Serie Orientale Roma, 33. Rome: Istituto Italiano per il Media ed Estremo Oriente, 1966.

Tambiah, Stanley Jeyraja. *The Buddhist Saints of the Forest and the Cult of Amulets: A Study in Charisma, Hagiography, Sectarianism, and Millennial Buddhism.* Cambridge: Cambridge University Press, 1984.

Tamura, Enchō. "Japan and the Eastward Permeation of Buddhism." *Acta Asiatica* 47 (1985): 1–30.

Thompson, Stith, and Jonas Balys. *Oral Tales of India.* Bloomington: Indiana University Press, 1958.

Thurman, Robert A. F., trans. *The Holy Teaching of Vimalakīrti: A Mahāyāna Scripture.* University Park: Pennsylvania State University Press, 1976.

Tokiwa, Gishin, trans. *A Dialogue on the Contemplation-Extinguished: A Translation Based on Professor Seizan Yanagida's Modern Japanese Translation and Consultations with Professor Yoshitaka Iriya.* Kyoto: Institute for Zen Studies, 1973.

Tokuno, Kyoko. "The Evaluation of Indigenous Scriptures in Chinese Buddhist Bibliographical Catalogues." In *Chinese Buddhist Apocrypha,* ed. Robert E. Buswell Jr., 31–74. Honolulu: University of Hawai'i Press, 1990.

Tucci, Giuseppe. *Minor Buddhist Texts.* Part 1. Rome: Istituto Italiano per il Medio ed Estremo Oriente, 1956.

Twitchett, Denis. "Problems of Chinese Biography." In *Confucian Personalities,* ed. Arthur F. Wright and Denis Twitchett, 24–39.

Ueda, Yoshifumi. "Two Main Streams of Thought in Yogācāra Philosophy." *Philosophy East and West* 17 (1967): 155–165.

Visser, M. W. de. *The Dragon in China and Japan.* Amsterdam: Johannese Müller, 1913.

Wagner, Rudolf G. *The Craft of a Chinese Commentator: Wang Bi on the "Laozi."* Albany: State University of New York Press, 2000.

Watson, Burton, trans. *The Complete Works of Chuang-tzu.* New York: Columbia University Press, 1968.

Wayman, Alex. "Notes on the Three Myrobalans." *Phi Theta Annual* 5 (1954–1955): 63–77.

Wayman, Alex, and Hideko Wayman. *The Lion's Roar of Queen Srīmālā.* New York: Columbia University Press, 1974.

Wei, Tat, trans. *Ch'eng Wei-Shih Lun: The Doctrine of Mere-Consciousness.* Hong Kong: Ch'eng Wei-shih Lun Publication Committee, 1973.

Weinstein, Stanley. "A Biographical Study of Tz'u-en." *Monumenta Nipponica* 15 (1959): 119–149.

———. "Chinese Buddhism." In *The Encyclopedia of Religion,* ed. Mircea Eliade, vol. 2, 482–487. New York: Macmillan, 1987.

———. "The Concept of Ālayavijñāna in Pre-T'ang Chinese Buddhism." In *Bukkyō shisōshi ronshū* (Essays on the history of Buddhist thought), ed. Yuki Kyōju Kenkyūkai, 33–50. Tokyo: Daizō Shuppansha, 1964.

———. "Imperial Patronage in the Formation of T'ang Buddhism." In *Perspectives on the T'ang,* ed. Arthur F. Wright and Denis Twitchett, 265–306. New Haven: Yale University Press, 1973.

Werner, E. T. C. *Myths and Legends of China.* New York: Farrar and Rinehart, 1936.

Woodward, F. L., trans. *The Minor Anthologies of the Pali Canon.* London: Oxford University Press, 1948.

Worthy, Edmund H., Jr. "Diplomacy for Survival: Domestic and Foreign Relations of Wu Yüeh, 907-978." In *China among Equals,* ed. Morris Rossabi, 17-44.

Wright, Arthur F. "Biography and Hagiography: Hui-chiao's *Lives of Eminent Monks.*" In *Silver Jubilee Volume of the Zinbun-kagaku-kekyusyo, Kyoto University,* 383-432. Kyoto: Kyoto University Press, 1954.

———. "Values, Roles, and Personalities." In *Confucian Personalities,* ed. Arthur F. Wright and Denis Twitchett, 3-23.

Wright, Arthur F., and Denis Twitchett, eds. *Confucian Personalities.* Stanford: Stanford University Press, 1962.

Yampolsky, Philip. "New Japanese Studies in Early Ch'an History." In *Early Ch'an in China and Tibet,* ed. Whalen Lai and Lewis Lancaster, 1-11.

———, trans. *The Platform Sūtra of the Sixth Patriarch.* New York: Columbia University Press, 1967.

Yanagida Seizan. "The *Li-Tai Fa-Pao Chi* and the Ch'an Doctrine of Sudden Awakening." Trans. Carl Bielefeldt. In *Early Ch'an in China and Tibet,* ed. Whalen Lai and Lewis Lancaster, 13-49.

Yeyama, Daishun. "The Study of Tibetan Ch'an Manuscripts Recovered from Tunhuang: A Review of the Field and Its Prospects." Trans. Kenneth W. Eastman and Kyoko Tokuno. In *Early Ch'an in China and Tibet,* ed. Whalen W. Lai and Lewis R. Lancaster, 327-349.

Zimmer, Heinrich. *Myths and Symbols in Indian Art and Civilization.* Ed. Joseph Campbell. Princeton: Princeton University Press, 1946.

Zŏng, In-sŏb (Chŏng Insŏp). *Folk Tales from Korea.* 3rd ed. Elizabeth, N. J.: Hollym International, 1982.

Zürcher, Erik. *The Buddhist Conquest of China: The Spread and Adaptation of Buddhism in Early Medieval China.* 2 vols. Leiden: E. J. Brill, 1959.

Index

INTERNATIONAL ASSOCIATION FOR WŎNHYO STUDIES'
COLLECTED WORKS OF WŎNHYO, VOLUME 1

Cultivating Original Enlightenment

Wŏnhyo's Exposition of the *Vajrasamādhi-Sūtra*

(Kŭmgang Sammaegyŏng Non)

Translated with an Introduction by Robert E. Buswell Jr.

Wŏnhyo (617–686) is the dominant figure in the history of Korean Buddhism and one of the two or three most influential thinkers in the Korean philosophical tradition more broadly. Koreans know Wŏnhyo in his various roles as Buddhist mystic, miracle worker, social iconoclast, religious proselytist, and cultural hero. Above all else, Wŏnhyo was an innovative thinker and prolific writer, whose works cover the gamut of Indian and Sinitic Buddhist materials. The some one hundred treatises and commentaries attributed to Wŏnhyo, twenty-three of which are extant today, find no rivals among his fellow Korean exegetes. Wŏnhyo was comfortable with all of the major theoretical paradigms prominent in Buddhism of his day and eventually came to champion a highly synthetic approach to the religion that has come to be called *t'ongpulgyo,* or the Buddhism of Total Interpenetration, an approach that left an indelible imprint on the subsequent course of Korean and East Asian Buddhism. Indeed, it is no exaggeration to say that it was Wŏnhyo who created the Korean tradition of Buddhism. His importance is not limited to the peninsula, however. His writings were widely read in China and Japan as well, and his influence on the overall development of East Asian Mahāyāna thought is significant, particularly in relation to the Huayan, Chan, and Pure Land schools. The volumes in this series will offer full translations of all of Wŏnhyo's extant works, with complete annotation, and extensive introductions framing Wŏnhyo's insights and contributions in the broader context of East Asian Buddhism.

In this first volume in the series, *Cultivating Original Enlightenment,* Robert E. Buswell Jr. translates Wŏnhyo's longest and probably culminating work, the *Exposition of the Vajrasamādhi-Sūtra (Kŭmgang sammaegyŏng non).* Wŏnhyo here brings to bear all the tools acquired throughout a lifetime of scholarship and meditation to the explication of a scripture that has a startling, even unique, connection to the Korean Buddhist tradition. In his treatise, Wŏnhyo examines the crucial question of how enlightenment can be turned from a tantalizing prospect into a palpable reality that manifests itself in all activities. East Asian Buddhism is founded on the assurance that the prospect of enlightenment is something innate to the mind itself and inherently accessible to all living creatures. This doctrine of "original enlightenment," along with its related teaching of the "womb (or embryo) of buddhahood," is foundational to the Korean Buddhist tradition. Given, however, the delusion we persistently face in ourselves and the evil we see surrounding us every day, it is obvious that the fact of *being* enlightened does not mean that we have necessarily learned how to *act* enlightened. In Wŏnhyo's presentation, the notion of original enlightenment is transformed from an abstract philosophical concept into a practical tool of meditative training. Wŏnhyo's *Exposition* provides a ringing endorsement of the prospect that all human beings have to recover the enlightenment that is said to be innate in the mind and to make it a tangible force in all of our activities.

Robert E. Buswell Jr. is professor and former chair of the department of Asian Languages and Cultures at the University of California, Los Angeles (UCLA), and founding director of UCLA's Center for Buddhist Studies and Center for Korean Studies. He is the author or editor of eleven books in Buddhist studies and Korean religions, including *Currents and Countercurrents: Korean Influences on the Buddhist Traditions of East Asia* (2005), *The Encyclopedia of Buddhism* (2004), and *Religions of Korea in Practice* (2007).

Books of Related Interest

Yogācāra Buddhism and Modern Psychology

TAO JIANG

"Are there Buddhist conceptions of the unconscious? If so, are they more Freudian, Jungian, or something else? If not, can Buddhist conceptions be reconciled with the Freudian, Jungian, or other models?" — These are some of the questions that have motivated modern scholarship to approach *ālayavijñāna*, the storehouse consciousness, formulated in Yogācāra Buddhism as a subliminal reservoir of tendencies, habits, and future possibilities.

Tao Jiang argues convincingly that such questions are inherently problematic because they frame their interpretations of the Buddhist notion largely in terms of responses to modern psychology. The book puts forth a fascinating, erudite, and carefully argued presentation of the subliminal mind.

From Vasubandhu to Caitanya

Studies in Indian Philosophy and its Textual History

Ed. by JOHANNES BRONKHORST and KARIN PREISENDANZ

The chapters in this volume are a selection of papers presented in the general Philosophy Section at the 12th World Sanskrit Conference in Helsinki, Finland. The first part of the book, Studies in Indian Philosophy, contains nine studies on individual topics and concepts in Indian philosophy from various perspectives: historical–philological, philosophical and comparative. They are *inter alia* concerned with such fundamental issues as the characteristic signs of the Self, the concept of *vijñaptimātratā* in Vasubandhu's Yogācāra, the notion of unchanging cognition in the writings of the Kashmirian author Rāmakaṇṭha, the definition of existence according to the late Buddhist philosopher Jñānaśrīmitra, and the significance of the *sādhana-catuṣṭaya* in Vedānta. In the second part of the book, two papers contribute to the study of the textual history of Indian philosophy, with a focus on the *Pātañjalayogaśāstra* and Candrānanda's commentary on the *Vaiśeṣikasūtra*.

Bodhisattvas of the Forest and the Formation of the Mahāyāna

DANIEL BOUCHER

Bodhisattvas of the Forest delves into the socioreligious milieu of the authors, editors, and propagators of the *Rāṣṭrapālaparipṛcchā-sūtra* (Question of *Rāṣṭrapāla*), a Buddhist text circulating in India during the first half of the first millennium C.E. In this meticulously researched study, Daniel Boucher first reflects upon the problems that plague historians of Mahāyāna Buddhism, whose previous efforts to comprehend the tradition have often ignored the social dynamics that motivated some of the innovations of this new literature. Following that is a careful analysis of several motifs found in the Indian text and an examination of the value of the earliest Chinese translation for charting the *sūtra's* evolution. It concludes with an annotated tranalstion of the *Rāṣṭrapālaparipṛcchā-sūtra* based on a new reading of its earliest extant Sanskrit manuscript.

The Middle Way

A Commentary on ŚĀNTARAKṢITA'S
Madhyamakalaṁkāra

MIPHAM JAMYANG NAMGYAL GYATSO

In his *Madhyamakalaṁkāra* the great Indian master, Śāntarakṣita, reveals how the path of reasoning can lead the mind to increasingly profound insight and experience, and how the process of refining our view of reality through intelligent and open-minded enquiry can bring about complete liberation within the discovery of the natural state.

Ju Mipham's illustrious commentary, highlights and explains the pithy reasoning of this classic treatise, and unfolds the expansive view of the Great Vehicle in a clear, engaging and compassionate way. Treasured dearly as "The Eyes of Ju Mipham Rinpoche," this commentary is a key element in the curriculum of many of the monastic colleges in Tibet and South Asia. Simultaneously direct and profound, it displays the hallmarks of Mipham's accomplished authorship.